**Ansell gritted his teeth as he saw what awaited them.**

Hanging by the neck from one of those trees was a single corpse. He recognised the face from so many days ago—a woman, skin weathered and limbs lean from years of hard work in the manufactories. She had been brave enough to single herself out from the rioting crowd at the Burrows and speak to the Archlegate of how their livelihoods had been destroyed. To implore him to help her people. In return she had been offered promises of a better future. Now she was dead for her trouble.

Was this some kind of message? A warning of what might happen if the Archlegate's will was defied? If so, why do it here, and not in the Burrows where this example could be stamped plain for all to witness? Perhaps this message was for Ansell alone.

"As you can see," Sanctan said, gazing up at the body, "sacrifices have been made by everyone. It pains me to see such suffering among my brood, but we must all endure. At least for a little while longer."

Ansell glanced over his shoulder. They had been followed along the path by Olstrum and Kinloth, who still struggled with that blade. To his relief, Grace was not here to see this.

He regarded Sanctan as coldly as he could manage. It wouldn't do to reveal how sickened he was by the sight before him. "I am sure you have suffered greatly too, Archlegate."

Sanctan's mask of serenity did not slip an inch. "Oh, I have indeed. But I am prepared to suffer—to do what is required of me so that the Wyrms may rise." He stepped closer. "I hope you are too."

**As R. S. Ford**

The Age of Uprising

*Engines of Empire*
*Engines of Chaos*
*Engines of War*

War of the Archons

*A Demon in Silver*
*Hangman's Gate*
*Spear of Malice*

Steelhaven

*Herald of the Storm*
*The Shattered Crown*
*Lord of Ashes*

**As Richard Cullen**

The Wolf of Kings

*Oath Bound*
*Shield Breaker*
*Winter Warrior*

Chronicles of the Black Lion

*Rebellion*
*Crusade*

# ENGINES OF WAR

## BOOK THREE OF
## THE AGE OF UPRISING

### R · S · FORD

orbitbooks.net

This book is a work of fiction. Names, characters, places, and incidents are the product of the author's imagination or are used fictitiously. Any resemblance to actual events, locales, or persons, living or dead, is coincidental.

Copyright © 2025 by R. S. Ford
Excerpt from *The Last Vigilant* copyright © 2025 by Mark A. Latham
Excerpt from *Grave Empire* copyright © 2025 by Richard Swan

Cover design by Lauren Panepinto
Cover illustration by Mike Heath | Magnus Creative
Cover copyright © 2025 by Hachette Book Group, Inc.
Map by Tim Paul
Author photograph by R. S. Ford

Hachette Book Group supports the right to free expression and the value of copyright. The purpose of copyright is to encourage writers and artists to produce the creative works that enrich our culture.

The scanning, uploading, and distribution of this book without permission is a theft of the author's intellectual property. If you would like permission to use material from the book (other than for review purposes), please contact permissions@hbgusa.com. Thank you for your support of the author's rights.

Orbit
Hachette Book Group
1290 Avenue of the Americas
New York, NY 10104
orbitbooks.net

First Edition: June 2025

Orbit is an imprint of Hachette Book Group.
The Orbit name and logo are registered trademarks of Little, Brown Book Group Limited.

The publisher is not responsible for websites (or their content) that are not owned by the publisher.

The Hachette Speakers Bureau provides a wide range of authors for speaking events. To find out more, go to hachettespeakersbureau.com or email HachetteSpeakers@hbgusa.com.

Orbit books may be purchased in bulk for business, educational, or promotional use. For information, please contact your local bookseller or the Hachette Book Group Special Markets Department at special.markets@hbgusa.com.

Library of Congress Cataloging-in-Publication Data
Names: Ford, R. S. (Richard S.), author.
Title: Engines of war / R.S. Ford.
Description: First edition. | New York, NY : Orbit, 2025. | Series: The Age of Uprising ; book 3
Identifiers: LCCN 2024059807 | ISBN 9780316629638 (trade paperback) | ISBN 9780316629621 (ebook)
Subjects: LCGFT: Fantasy fiction. | Novels.
Classification: LCC PR6106.O757 E59 2025 | DDC 823/.92—dc23/eng/20241220
LC record available at https://lccn.loc.gov/2024059807

ISBNs: 9780316629638 (trade paperback), 9780316629621 (ebook)

Printed in the United States of America

LSC-C

Printing 1, 2025

*For Steven Savile.*
*Old age and treachery will always beat youth and skill.*

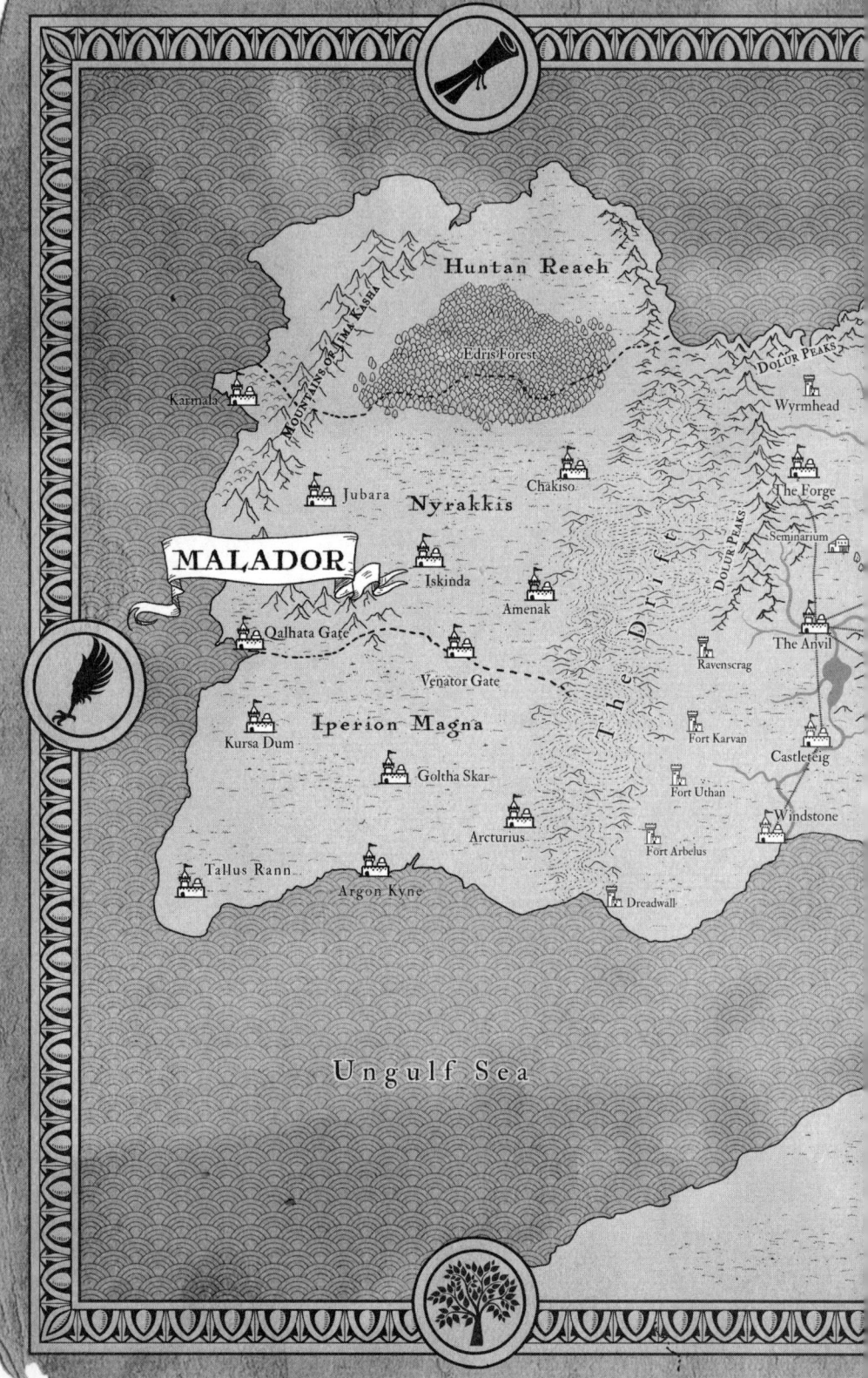

# DRAMATIS PERSONAE

**THE HAWKSPURS**

**Conall Hawkspur**—Son of Rosomon. Captain of the Talon.

**Crenn**—An artificer. (Deceased.)

**Fulren Hawkspur**—Son of Rosomon. A skilled artificer.

**Melrone Hawkspur**—Husband of Rosomon. (Deceased.)

**Rosomon Hawkspur**—Guildmaster. Mother to Conall, Fulren and Tyreta.

**Stediana Walden**—Sted. A lieutenant in the Talon.

**Tyreta Hawkspur**—Daughter of Rosomon. A webwainer.

**THE ARCHWINDS**

**Cullum Kairns**—A Titanguard.

**Dagamir**—A Titanguard.

**Ianto Fray**—Imperator of the Titanguard.

**Kassian Maine**—Former swordwright to Treon Archwind.

**Lancelin Jagdor**—The Hawkslayer. Swordwright of the Archwind Guild. (Deceased.)

**Lorens Archwind**—Eldest son of Sullivar and Oriel.

**Oriel Archwind**—Wife of Sullivar.

**Philbert Kerrick**—An artificer.

**Sullivar Archwind**—Emperor of Torwyn. (Deceased.)

**Treon Archwind**—Father of Rosomon and Sullivar. (Deceased.)

**Wyllow Archwind**—Youngest son of Sullivar and Oriel. A webwainer. (Deceased.)

## THE CORWENS

**Rearden Corwen**—Guildmaster.

**Wachelm**—A junior actuary of the Corwen Guild.

## THE IRONFALLS

**Maugar Ironfall**—Former swordwright of the Guild, now Guildmaster. Brother to Wymar.

**Wymar Ironfall**—Guildmaster. Brother to Maugar. (Deceased.)

**Xorya Ironfall**—Swordwright-in-training. Daughter of Maugar.

## THE MARRLOCKS

**Borys Marrlock**—Son of Oleksig and swordwright of the Guild.

**Donan Marrlock**—A minor member of the Guild.

**Emony Marrlock**—Youngest daughter of Oleksig.

**Oleksig Marrlock**—Guildmaster.

## THE RADWINTERS

**Jarlath Radwinter**—Guildmaster. (Deceased.)

**Mincloth Radwinter**—Wife of Jarlath.

**Thalleus Brisco**—Former swordwright of the Radwinter Guild.

# DRAMATIS PERSONAE

## THE HALLOWHILLS

**Galirena**—A senior webwainer.

**Hesse Fortuna**—Associate of Keara. A webwainer.

**Ingelram Hallowhill**—Guildmaster.

**Keara Hallowhill**—Daughter of Ingelram. A webwainer.

**Lucasta Hallowhill**—Mother to Keara. A webwainer. (Presumed deceased.)

**Rodita**—A webwainer.

**Ulger Vine**—Associate of Keara. A webwainer. (Deceased.)

**Vikmar**—A webwainer.


## THE DRACONATE MINISTRY

**Amiranda**—High Legate of Vermitrix.

**Ansell Beckenrike**—Knight Commander of the Drakes.

**Barnier**—High Legate of Saphenodon.

**Everis**—A junior knight of the Drakes.

**Falcar**—A young and handsome knight of the Drakes.

**Gylbard**—Former Archlegate. (Deceased.)

**Halinard**—High Legate of Undometh.

**Hisolda**—High Legate of Vermitrix. (Deceased.)

**Hurden**—A stern knight of the Drakes.

**Lugard**—A pious veteran of the Drakes.

**Marsilia**—High Legate of Ravenothrax.

**Olstrum Garner**—Sanctan's consul.

**Rassekin**—High Legate of Ammenodus Rex.

**Regenwulf**—A respected veteran of the Drakes.

**Sanctan Egelrath**—Archlegate.

**Willet Kinloth**—A junior legate.

## IPERION MAGNA

**Baenre Mokhtar**—Servant of Senmonthis.

**Bagdemagus**—Scion of Goltha Skar.

**Celebrai**—Scion of Kursa Dum.

**Ekediah the Betrayer**—Scion of Tallus Rann.

**Maelor Kytheris**—High Steward of the Obsidian Ward, Herald of the Tetrarchy.

**Nylia of Amenak**—Prisoner of Senmonthis and friend to Conall. (Deceased.)

**Orsokon**—Warmaven of Arcturius. (Deceased.)

**Senmonthis**—Scion of Arcturius.

## THE ARMIGERS

**Ancretta**—Frontier marshal of the Raptor Battalion.

**Draga**—Captain of the Mantid Battalion.

**Falko**—Drift marshal of the Mantid Battalion.

**Kagan Terswell**—Frontier marshal of the Griffin Battalion.

**Mermaduc**—Frontier marshal of the Tigris Battalion.

**Moraide**—Captain of the Viper Battalion.

**Rawlin**—Drift marshal of the Bloodwolf Battalion.

**Sarona**—Drift marshal of the Ursus Battalion.

**Sonnheld**—Frontier marshal of the Viper Battalion.

**Tarjan**—Drift marshal of the Corvus Battalion.

**Walgan**—Frontier marshal of the Auroch Battalion.

**Westley Tarrien**—Marshal of the Phoenix Battalion.

# DRAMATIS PERSONAE

## PEOPLE OF TORWYN

**Ashe Tyburn**—Fugitive artificer. Lover of Verlyn. (Deceased.)

**Colbert**—A staggeringly handsome trader turned rebel.

**Nicosse Merigot**—Disgraced artificer. Brother of Lysander. (Deceased.)

**Grace**—Daughter of Jessamine and Sanctan.

**Jessamine**—Lover of Sanctan. Mother to Grace. (Deceased.)

**Lena**—An iron welder turned rebel.

**Lysander Merigot**—Disgraced artificer. Brother of Nicosse.

**Maronne**—A weaver turned rebel.

**Sybilla**—Artificer and weaponsmith.

**Torfin**—A riverboatman turned rebel.

**Verlyn**—An unsanctioned webwainer. Lover of Ashe.

## ORGANISATIONS OF TORWYN

*Armiger Battalions*—*Military legions that defend Torwyn from foreign threats and protect its interests abroad. The eleven battalions are Auroch, Bloodwolf, Corvus, Griffin, Kraken, Mantid, Phoenix, Raptor, Tigris, Ursus, Viper.*

*Draconate Ministry*—*The ecclesiastic power in Torwyn, led by the Archlegate, which worships the five Great Wyrms:*

**Ammenodus Rex**—Great Wyrm of War.

**Ravenothrax the Unvanquished**—Great Wyrm of Death.

**Saphenodon**—Great Wyrm of Knowledge.

**Undometh**—Great Wyrm of Vengeance.

**Vermitrix**—Great Wyrm of Peace.

**Guilds**—*The ruling power in Torwyn. The six major Guilds are:*

**Archwind Guild**—Most powerful Guild in Torwyn, specialising in artifice. Its military arm is known as the Titanguard.

**Corwen Guild**—The nation's administrators. Its military arm is known as the Revocaters.

**Hawkspur Guild**—Controls transit. Its military arm is known as the Talon.

**Ironfall Guild**—Works the forges. Its military arm is known as the Blackshields.

**Marrlock Guild**—Mines for ore and pyrestone.

**Radwinter Guild**—Responsible for farming and lumber.

# PROLOGUE

An unholy wind whipped down from the Dolur Peaks as Gylbard stood at the summit of Wyrmhead, looking out at the vista. The cold air blew through his white-and-gold robes, but the old man had long since learned to ignore the discomfort. His joints would chide him for it later, despite his position as Archlegate—but age did not care for titles.

From the top of the fortress he could look out onto the northern extents of Torwyn from Kalur's Fist, rising from amid the mountain range in the north, to the Drift, falling away in the west. South and east were miles of flat country, crisscrossed by winding rivers that fed each of the Guildlands. Wyrmhead was at the apex providing succour, both literal and spiritual, to the whole of Torwyn.

As Gylbard looked out over the white stone parapet, Tapfoot stalked toward him along the balustrade. The cat paused when she reached him, rubbing her head against his hand. Gylbard lifted her gently from the edge, cradling her against him and hearing her purr softly into his chest.

"How many times must I tell you?" he whispered. "There is much danger here. You must be more careful."

He turned from the balcony, making his way back inside the vestibule that was perched at the summit of the great tower. Inside, Ansell was waiting for him.

The knight commander of the Drakes stood well over six feet, his dragon helm making him appear even taller. His armour was polished to a mirror sheen, surcoat bearing the symbol of the Draconate: a dragon rampant surrounded by five stars, each of a different hue. Gylbard might have been intimidated, but the Drakes were faithful servants of the Draconate Ministry, raised from childhood to serve the Archlegate and his priests.

Bowing his head, Ansell dropped to one knee as Gylbard approached.

"Archlegate," he said, his deep voice made even more resonant from within the close-faced helm. "High Legate Egelrath is here to speak with you."

"Ah yes," Gylbard replied. "Then I suppose we should get this over with. Send him in."

As Ansell left, Gylbard sat in one of the high-backed chairs beside the winnowing fire. He absently stroked Tapfoot's back, letting her gentle purring soothe him. For many months now Egelrath had been visiting Wyrmhead. He had voiced his concerns ever louder and more frequently, entreating the Archlegate to act against the constant erosion of the Ministry's powers. But what was Gylbard to do? The Guilds ran Torwyn now, their industry feeding its people and protecting its borders. The Ministry's authority was waning, and there was little any of them could do about it.

"Archlegate."

Gylbard turned to see Sanctan Egelrath kneeling, head bowed. Ansell stood beside him, towering over the priest. A wicked thought entered Gylbard's head that it would have been so easy to have Ansell rid him of this troublesome upstart, but the notion was gone as soon as it came.

"Please, Sanctan, take a seat," Gylbard said.

Egelrath rose, moving beside the fire. "If you don't mind, I will stand. The ride north has left me somewhat sore about the buttocks."

Gylbard smirked. Pain in the buttocks was more than appropriate for a man so bothersome. "Thank you, Ansell. You may leave."

"No, Archlegate," Sanctan said. "Please let him stay. There is nothing I have to say that a Knight of the Draconate may not hear."

Gylbard shrugged. "Very well. What may I do for you this time?"

Sanctan smiled. His teeth were white, jaw square, hair thick and well-groomed. It made Gylbard all the more conscious of how old he was—of his own bald pate and the white of his beard. Sanctan Egelrath was barely thirty, and already he had gained the position of High Legate. It was unheard of in the annals of the Draconate Ministry, but then, Sanctan was a testament to how far and how quickly an ambitious man could rise. He was popular among both the legates and Drakes—Gylbard had been left with little choice but to approve the man's ordainment.

"Firstly, you might allow me to stoke this fire," Sanctan said, approaching the hearth. "It's freezing in here." He grabbed a poker, hitching up the red robes that marked him as an adherent of the Great Wyrm Undometh, before he knelt by the fire and put some life back into the flames.

"I appreciate your concern, Sanctan, but I doubt you've come all this way to see after my comfort."

"Indeed not," Sanctan replied. He turned and fixed Gylbard with his usual serious visage. "I assume you have heard about the impending arrival of an emissary from Malador?"

Gylbard sighed, tousling Tapfoot's ears, trying to take comfort from the cat's purring.

"Of course."

"And?"

Gylbard fought to keep himself calm. He had to show patience. "And what, Sanctan?"

"What do you intend to do about it? Malador is a threat to the freedom of all Torwyn. Those demon worshippers want nothing less than the destruction of everything we have built. They will not stop until the kingdom is in flames and our idols consumed. And now Sullivar welcomes an emissary. It cannot stand."

"It can and it will," Gylbard replied, keeping his voice calm and even in contrast with Sanctan's ranting. "Sullivar only wants peace, as do we all. Receiving an emissary is the first step toward that guarantee. The first step after a thousand years."

"He is capitulating. We have faced a constant threat from the west. Our borders have been tested innumerable times. Malador is not our friend and never will be, no matter how many emissaries they send."

"I disagree," said Gylbard. He stared at Sanctan, as though willing him to defy the word of the Archlegate. The priest remained silent. "A treaty is exactly what we need. The emissary does not represent the whole of Malador, only Nyrakkis, a nation I believe wants peace."

"And Iperion Magna? You believe they want peace too?"

Gylbard shook his head. "One thing at a time, Sanctan. Once a treaty is signed with Nyrakkis, Iperion Magna will surely follow."

"And you believe that?"

"I have had assurances from Sullivar himself. There is no reason to doubt him."

Sanctan turned to stare into the flames that had now responded to his attentions. The flickering fire bestowed a devilish aspect to his handsome face. Tapfoot gave a low mewl, reminding Gylbard he had stopped stroking her.

"You know he has proclaimed himself 'emperor'?" Sanctan said, still staring into the fire. "His power grows while ours still dwindles."

"I have heard," Gylbard replied, his patience wearing thin.

"And that soon he will proclaim that the Guildlands are to be known as 'princedoms'? Princedoms, Gylbard. And he seated above them? What next? Are we to be renamed too? Cast out? Reduced to mere tokens?"

Gylbard rose to his feet, feeling a shooting pain in his knee, which he tried his best to ignore. He cradled Tapfoot in his arms, stroking her gently, reassuring her all the while.

"Your belief in the notion we are powerless does you no justice, Sanctan. Sullivar is not half the man his father was. Compared to Treon Archwind, Sullivar is but a boy playing a man's game. The Ministry has always been the sole ecclesial authority in Torwyn. The Guilds still pay fealty to the Draconate. Your fears are unfounded."

"By your own words Sullivar is weak. And a weak ruler is worse than any tyrant. Sullivar will lead Torwyn to ruin."

"You are fearful over nothing, Sanctan. You must calm yourself."

The heat from the fire was cloying now. Gylbard turned and made his way back onto the high terrace. Once again he looked out over the view of Torwyn, drawing some comfort from it.

Sanctan followed him out, coming to stand beside him.

"If we do not rise, if we do not retake what was once ours, all this will be gone," Sanctan said, gesturing at the beautiful sight of their homeland. "We have to show the Guilds who holds the real power in Torwyn. For far too long we have allowed them to govern unchecked."

"And what would you have me do? Order a coup? A revolt against the Guilds? Rise up and usurp their power by force?"

"If that's what it takes. Many of the Armiger Battalions serve their own interests in Karna Uzan protecting the flow of pyrestone. There has never been a better time—"

"No!" Gylbard shouted. Tapfoot squirmed in his grip, but he held on tight to her, feeling the cat dig a claw into his arm. More pain to ignore. "I've suffered enough of this impertinence. Now you go too far. Have you forgotten your scripture, Sanctan? Only when the Draconate return shall we rise again. Only when we have a sign."

"More talk of prophecy," Sanctan said. "You would wait for dragons to return to Torwyn before you act? Meanwhile the Ministry is reduced to what? A gaggle of petty preachers? We were once revered in Torwyn. We ruled these lands and protected them. The threat from Malador is real. We have to do something. We cannot wait for a sign prophesied in some crumbling old tome."

Gylbard felt his ire rising. He could barely quell it, yearning to rage at his underling, but Sanctan was young. Surely this boy could be curbed without resorting to extreme measures.

"I will forgive your heresy this time, Sanctan. One more word and I will not. The High Legates answer to me, and I will be the one to dictate the actions of the Ministry. I am still the Archlegate."

"And what use are you, old man?"

Gylbard could suppress his fury no longer. He held on tight to Tapfoot, trembling at the words of his subordinate.

"Enough," he spat through gritted teeth. "You are done, Egelrath. I will summon the High Legates. You will regret the way you have spoken to me."

"I doubt that, Gylbard."

Before he could redress Sanctan further, something hit him in the back. Tapfoot fell from his grip as he staggered forward, his hands grasping the parapet. Gylbard tried to stand, but his legs would no longer hold him up and he crumpled to the floor. He looked up to see Ansell standing there, sword unsheathed, blood on the blade.

"No," Gylbard managed to whisper.

"Yes," Sanctan replied. He was cradling Tapfoot, and the cat seemed comfortable in his grip. "Your time is at an end, old man. Mine has just begun."

"No," Gylbard said again, reaching out a trembling hand toward Tapfoot.

Sanctan looked down at the cat, content in his arms. "A treacherous creature. Once yours, and now clearly mine. Such a fickle little thing, and you were blind to it all this time. But fear not, Gylbard. The cat will be safe with me. As will Torwyn's future."

"This is not the way, Sanctan," Gylbard tried to say, but his words were lost on the wind. Sanctan had already turned away, was already relaying his orders to Ansell.

Gylbard could only watch helplessly as the chill seeped into his bones and the world darkened.

# PART ONE

# THE STEEL RESOLVES

# ANSELL

That dream again, returning night after night to haunt him in vivid colour. Ansell had rarely been a sound sleeper, but in recent weeks he had awoken before dawn plagued by night terrors, feeling more fatigued than when he laid down his head. But they were not nightmares. Memories would have been a better way to describe them. Stark visions of his past sent to taunt him.

In the haze of morning, it was impossible to distinguish between those dreams and his misdeeds, and there were so many misdeeds to choose from. The only sure thing was the one that cut the deepest... Gylbard. When Ansell had slid the blade into that old man's back, he had been convinced it was the right thing to do. The Archlegate's stubborn inaction would have doomed them all. Now, in the cold clarity of hindsight, the truth of it was plain; Sanctan had only wanted Gylbard removed from his path to power.

That frail old man had been a father to them all. The Archlegate they deserved. And now they were left with...

Ansell rose sluggishly, squinting in the stuttering light of the candle still burning on his table. His eyes focused on the book that sat beside it. The book he had studied since he was a boy. The book he had abandoned.

Was this his punishment for turning his back on the Draconate

Prophesies? To be tortured by dreams of the past? Was it the Great Wyrms who tormented him so?

Ansell smirked at the thought, feeling the tightening of flesh around his mouth where it still refused to heal. No, he was plagued by no gods. It was his own conscience that punished him, that reminded him each night of how far he had strayed from the right path. But he could see no way back now—not while he still followed Egelrath.

A knock at the door. A merciful distraction from his thoughts. Ansell stood, feeling the ache of old wounds and the tug of those only recently knitted shut. Conscious it might be Grace come to visit him at such an early hour, he tied a blanket to his waist, covering his nakedness before crossing to the door. When he opened it and saw who awaited him, Ansell found it difficult to disguise his disappointment.

"Knight Commander," said Legate Kinloth with a bow, ignoring the despondent sigh that greeted him.

"It is early," Ansell replied. "Even for you."

"Yes." Kinloth bowed again in apology, before gesturing toward Ansell's chamber. "May I?"

Ansell took a step back, allowing Kinloth to enter. The legate glanced fretfully about the room as though there might be someone waiting inside to attack him. Always the nervous one, this Kinloth. Fearful of his own inconsequential shadow. Constantly looking as though he had something to say, but lacking the courage to say it.

"What can I do for you at this unearthly hour?" asked Ansell.

Kinloth cleared his throat. "Actually, it is almost midday."

Clearly Ansell's fitful dreaming had gone on for longer than he thought. "Then what can I do for you at this late hour?"

"The Archlegate has requested your presence. He asked that I come see you were dressed and brought to him with all haste."

Ansell had foregone the privilege of a personal serf to help him dress since the day he was granted his position as knight. Curious that Sanctan would now send him Kinloth to do the deed.

"I can dress myself well enough."

Kinloth picked at his fingernails, jaw working as he tried to think of the right way to speak his next words. "When I say he asked me...I probably mean he commanded me."

As irritating as this was, it would only have been cruel to put Kinloth through any further discomfort. "Very well. See to it then, and be swift. We should not keep him waiting."

Kinloth went about the task meticulously, helping Ansell into his trews and gambeson, before buckling his plate. As he did so, Ansell could not quell the feeling of unease that nibbled at him like a rat on his neck. He had not seen Sanctan for days, not since their meeting in the tower of Ravenothrax. It was obvious he had fallen out of the Archlegate's favour, and it would not be out of character for Sanctan to reconsider the show of mercy he had offered that day. Nevertheless, it was doubtful he would have ordered Ansell fully decked in his regalia if he was planning an execution. Would he?

Kinloth finished securing the armour and offered Ansell his helmet. As Ansell cradled it in the crook of his arm, the legate took his sword from its stand, struggling somewhat with the weight of it.

"I should carry this for you, Knight Commander."

"There is no need, Kinloth," Ansell replied. "It is my burden, and mine alone."

Again the legate's jaw worked frenetically. "I am afraid the Archlegate insists. And it is an honour to be granted a sword bearer...I am led to believe."

Perhaps in times past, during the Age of Kings, sword bearers were considered fashionable among the nobility, but no Knight of the Draconate was ever parted from his weapon—not even in death. Ansell should have insisted he carry it, but these were clearly explicit instructions passed down by Sanctan himself.

That rat began to nibble at Ansell's neck with ever sharper teeth. "Very well. Lead the way."

Another bow from Kinloth, and perhaps a look of relief, before he made his way to the door. His spindly arms struggled to bear the weight of the sword, and his stub-nailed fingers fumbled at the doorhandle before he managed to open it.

As Ansell followed the legate through the vaults of the Mount he wondered where Grace might be. Normally he would visit with her, ensure her lessons were proceeding well and that she was eating enough. If he was absent for any reason she often took it upon herself to seek him out, but not today.

He tried to dismiss his worries as Kinloth led them up into the nave of the Mount. It was silent—there had been no visitors for days, the doors sealed and guarded against any interlopers. The lack of worshippers offered the place a strange serenity, though more akin to a sepulchre than a chapel. A pall of loss hung in the air, as though this ancient temple lamented the lack of its congregation come to seek solacement from the gods.

A few hooded legates lit votives or clasped their bunched amulets as they prayed. Of Ansell's fellow knights there was little sign, but then most had been sent to the four corners of Torwyn to secure the Archlegate's dominion. Little wonder the place had been sealed, with so few left to guard its sanctity.

Ansell followed Kinloth, still struggling with that heavy sword, toward the temple gardens. Through the archway he could see the trees and bushes that had once been carefully tended were now overgrown. Even the gardeners had been dismissed from their labours in recent weeks, and the evidence was plain to see.

Once across the threshold, he heard Sanctan's voice in the distance, crooning in that gentle preacher's tone. Kinloth proceeded toward it, and when Ansell saw who the Archlegate was speaking to it felt as though the rat at his neck had suddenly gripped him in rabid jaws.

"...and these flowers only blossom in the middle of autumn," Sanctan said, as he teased the bud of some plant or other. "We dry and crush the petals, and mix the powder with incense to turn the smoke blue."

Grace watched him intently, spellbound by his words. Sanctan's hand was laid gently on her shoulder as he appeared every inch the wise teacher, and she his attentive pupil. Father and daughter locked in a tender moment. Ansell was struck by how unusual it seemed. Had the Archlegate turned over a new leaf? Was he really teaching his daughter about the temple gardens out of some newly discovered paternal affection? Ansell found it hard to believe.

Before he could wonder further, his eye drifted to the edge of the garden, seeing Olstrum watching from the periphery. His expression gave nothing away as usual, though Ansell was sure his mind must have been racing. Perhaps he was even thinking about his own children. Of how he should be teaching them about blossoms and plants, and other carefree matters, when instead their lives hung in the balance.

"Ah, Ansell—so glad you could join us."

He turned at Sanctan's greeting, seeing that smiling mask and trying not to think on the monster that lurked behind it. There was no way Sanctan had forgiven his transgression so easily, and yet he welcomed him as an old friend. Ansell knew better than anyone that when Sanctan offered his hand in friendship there was all too often a poisoned blade hidden behind his back. His recent dream had reminded him of just that.

Ansell's eyes shifted to the overgrown foliage. If his executioner was lurking in wait they were well hidden. It was hardly likely Olstrum would try to kill him. The only possible danger would come from Kinloth, standing there with that sword, but the legate could hardly lift it, let alone swing it with any intent. There was nothing here he should fear, and yet still he could not shift the nagging dread.

"I am here at your command, Archlegate," Ansell said, trying to ignore Grace, resisting the urge to offer a reassuring wink. "But I am curious as to why we are meeting in this place."

Sanctan raised his arms, spreading them wide to take in the breadth of his surroundings. "I, like so many others, take comfort in this garden. When it is quiet there is nowhere else in the city I would rather be."

"Indeed," Ansell replied. "It is quieter than ever, now all its attendants have been dismissed."

For a moment he thought maybe he'd overstepped his mark, but Sanctan nodded knowingly. "Ah yes, I thought it best they be sent home. For their own safety."

For Sanctan's safety, more like. It was obvious he was growing ever more fearful of the very people he had freed from the tyranny of the Guilds. Seeing assassins in every shadow. In his crusade to break their shackles he had dismantled the very thing that kept them fed, and in the process made enemies of many.

"And so I am here, Archlegate. Kinloth informed me this was a matter of importance?"

"Indeed it is. The time is upon us, brother. We are about to strike back at the enemy as it approaches our gates. The Guilds must not be allowed to reach the Anvil. Our army will crush them before the walls of this city are within their sights, and you will march at its vanguard."

Ansell felt excitement at the prospect of finally going to war, of fighting alongside his brothers. "Where is the Guild army now?"

"Less than a hundred miles to the northeast," Sanctan replied. "I have placed you under the command of Marshal Sarona. She is particularly keen to exact her revenge after the massacre of her troopers at Oakhelm."

Ansell's fists clenched at the prospect of being subservient to one of the Armigers. "I am to be commanded by a battalion marshal? I should be the one to lead."

A knowing smile crossed Sanctan's face as he stepped away from Grace and onto the winding path that wended its way through the gardens. "Walk with me."

There was no other choice but to follow. Ansell glanced toward Grace, expecting her to at least offer him a smile, but she turned her attention back to the buds on the overgrown bush. That one dismissive gesture provoked an odd sense of loss within, but he forced himself to dismiss it as he followed the Archlegate.

Sanctan strolled through the gardens, and it became clear how sad this once vibrant place had become. With no gardeners to tend it, the foliage had run rampant—vines creeping their way up the walls, leaves left to fester on the ground. Sanctan barely seemed to notice how this once beautiful place had become degraded. It had been sacrificed as part of his crusade, one more casualty on his road to dominance, and he was oblivious to its suffering.

"I assume I do not have to remind you of the tenets laid down within the Draconate Prophesies, Ansell. I know that despite your recent...lapse, you are still a devout brother of my knighthood." He made a point of stressing the word *my*. "And I don't have to tell you the numerous passages which refer to sacrifice throughout that hallowed text. Believe me, I appreciate all you have suffered over the years. None of this could have been easy for you. But you must understand, we've all made sacrifices during the course of this struggle. And we must continue to do so until the whole of Torwyn is brought into the grace of the Great Wyrms."

Ansell was tempted to point out that he had sacrificed more than most, but that would be a dangerous game to play with a man who coveted loyalty above all things. "I understand, Archlegate."

That brought a smile to Sanctan's face. "Good," he replied, as they rounded a particularly overgrown part of the path, which led to the temple's orchard.

Ansell gritted his teeth as he saw what awaited them. Hanging by the neck from one of those trees was a single corpse. He recognised the face from so many days ago—a woman, skin weathered and limbs lean from years of hard work in the manufactories. She had been brave enough to single herself out from the rioting crowd at the Burrows and speak to the Archlegate of how their livelihoods had been destroyed. To implore him to help her people. In return she had been offered promises of a better future. Now she was dead for her trouble.

Was this some kind of message? A warning of what might happen if the Archlegate's will was defied? If so, why do it here, and not in the Burrows where this example could be stamped plain for all to witness? Perhaps this message was for Ansell alone.

"As you can see," Sanctan said, gazing up at the body, "sacrifices have been made by everyone. It pains me to see such suffering among my brood, but we must all endure. At least for a little while longer."

Ansell glanced over his shoulder. They had been followed along the path by Olstrum and Kinloth, who still struggled with that blade. To his relief, Grace was not here to see this.

He regarded Sanctan as coldly as he could manage. It wouldn't do to reveal how sickened he was by the sight before him. "I am sure you have suffered greatly too, Archlegate."

Sanctan's mask of serenity did not slip an inch. "Oh, I have indeed. But I am prepared to suffer—to do what is required of me so that the Wyrms may rise." He stepped closer. "I hope you are too."

Without waiting for an answer, he turned and left Ansell in the shadow of that dead woman. She had been brave, and this was her reward. It should have made Ansell more wary, keener than ever to leave this place behind, but instead he feared more for Grace. Despite Sanctan's seeming change of heart regarding his daughter, it was obvious he was still black as night on the inside.

Ansell turned to Legate Kinloth and held out his hand. "Give me that weapon, before you do yourself a mischief."

Kinloth looked grateful as he shuffled forward and held out the heavy blade. Ansell took it from him, dismissing him with a wave of his hand before strapping the sword to his waist. As Kinloth disappeared into the overgrown garden, Olstrum stepped closer, hands clasped in front of him as he leaned in.

"We are standing on a precipice," he said quietly.

"What does that mean?" Ansell replied, heedless of anyone listening, in no mood to be cowed by the prospect of eavesdroppers. If Sanctan had left spies behind, let them listen.

Olstrum sighed in frustration. "You are being sent to die, can't you see that? Sanctan has removed your authority and placed you under the command of one of his generals. She will use you as fodder, and it will be your end. You must live, Ansell. Remember you made me a promise you have yet to fulfil."

"I think you underestimate how difficult I am to kill, Olstrum."

"Anyone can be killed. Even you."

"So what do you suggest I do?" Ansell growled, feeling more helpless than ever. "I cannot refuse the word of the Archlegate, as you well know. And I do not need to be reminded of the debt I owe."

Olstrum wrung his hands, knuckles white. It was an affectation Ansell had seen often. At first he had thought the man merely twitchy, or stricken by bad humours. Now he knew what burden Olstrum carried, that he feared for the safety of his family, it made more sense.

Slowly, Olstrum's look of frustration turned to defeat. "It doesn't matter anyway. I don't even know where they are."

"Then you have work to do, Consul. I suggest you get to it."

"How? Where do I look? Who do I ask?"

Ansell shook his head. "You are the spymaster, not me. Find out where they are and I will keep my promise. Until then, stay away from me."

If Olstrum had more to say, he lacked the will to say it, and left Ansell alone in the garden to look up at the body of that once brave woman. He could only wonder how many other brave folk would die before all this misery was brought to an end.

Turning from the corpse, he considered making his way back through the garden to find Grace, but dismissed the idea. Perhaps she was better left alone. He had already spent so much time on that girl, and what good had it done either of them?

Olstrum was right; very soon Ansell might become fodder on the battlefield. Better that he think on winning this war, rather than becoming one more casualty.

# CONALL

The further their horses plodded eastward along the road, the safer Conall felt. Strange that he felt better for leaving the impenetrable walls of a fortress behind, but then impenetrable was only a matter of perspective. Those walls hadn't stopped Nylia from trying to murder him. Hadn't stopped that demon whispering in his ear and offering its shadow blade when he needed it most. No, the walls of Fort Karvan had been little safer for him than the wilds of the Drift.

Not that it was any safer where he was going. Right now he was riding his horse straight into the teeth of the Draconate Ministry. There was nothing to protect him behind, nothing to save him in front, so he may as well keep going and hope his salvation would present itself sooner or later.

Deep down, though, he knew there was only one answer to all his ills. The only person who could protect him in all Hyreme was his mother. Maybe if he could reach her, tell her what he'd been through, what he knew, then she would know what to do. But was that wise, or was it just selfish? He knew what Senmonthis wanted; for Conall to murder the great Lady Rosomon. They had foreseen that she would lead some crusade against the alliance of Malador's Scions, and he was the weapon sent to kill her. If he ran to hide behind his mother's skirts it would only endanger her further.

Conall had been strong enough to resist that alluring voice so far, but could he keep it at bay forever? There was no way of telling how much stronger the voice would become. He had already seen how those demons controlled Nylia and the others. It might only be a matter of time before he fell under thrall to the same creatures.

Perhaps he should just flee into the wilderness, get as far from everyone as he could, but he knew he'd never be able to do that. The prospect of being alone with only a demon in his head for company filled him with more dread than he could stomach. Then again, looking around him, he realised he was already alone.

Despite being surrounded by troopers of the Mantid Battalion he felt completely on his own. He'd seen them looking at him with suspicion. With fear maybe? But after what had happened at Fort Karvan, could he really blame them?

Captain Draga led their group from the front, but he'd spoken barely a word to Conall since the day they'd set off from the fort. It was hardly surprising after what had happened to his men. A dozen of them dead, and all because Conall had led Nylia there, but surely they couldn't know that. They couldn't blame him for what she had done.

Or maybe they could. Her corpse had been examined by their surgeon, and he'd found that red gem in her skull. Conall might not have a pyrestone jewel in his head anymore, but there was still a gaping cavity where it used to sit. It didn't take a genius to see the similarities.

At first he'd expected them to interrogate him, and weak as he was it would only have been a matter of time before he sang like a bird and told them everything they wanted to know. To Conall's relief, Draga had instead ordered that he be taken back to the Guild army immediately, and decided that he and his men would do the taking.

They hadn't been on the road for more than a day before Conall heard the troopers grumbling about a curse, not that any of them mentioned it to him outright. But then none of them talked to him at all. Not much of a surprise considering what had happened, but the silence was really starting to piss him off.

By the Lairs, he missed Sted. Missed his brother, his sister. Shit, he even missed Donan's sad little face. Just a single friend in all this might have made a big difference, but instead he was surrounded by hardy warriors who thought he was some kind of jinx, and he'd never felt more vulnerable in all his life. Well, maybe when he'd been stumbling alone through the Drift, but that had been a different situation altogether.

"Let's pick up the pace," Draga called from up ahead. "Ministry forces could be close by, and we don't want to get caught out here on the road with our pants down."

Heels were put to the flanks of horses, and they sped to a trot, veering off the road and down a sharp ravine. Their path soon brought them to an old farmstead, abandoned to the wild, and when he saw a burned-out house, Conall could only guess it was the Ministry's doing. Pigs lay dead in their pens, and in the distance a windmill sighed in the breeze as it turned redundantly. He could only wonder who might have lived here and what had happened to them.

"Bastard Archlegate," one of the troopers mumbled as he took in the scene. "Wants to crush the whole of Torwyn just so it stays in his grip."

To Conall's eye the man was right—that was exactly what Sanctan was doing. But as the other troopers nodded their agreement in solemn silence, Conall had a strange sense that maybe that was what Torwyn needed. To be swept away and rebuilt. He almost shook his head to clear such an alien thought, but instead he kept his head down and his feelings to himself.

He'd been close to his cousin Sanctan in years past, but could never have suspected the depth of his ambition. Nor what he'd do to see it realised. Those secrets had been hidden behind a winning smile, but right now Conall had his own secrets to think on. He could only hope he'd be as deft as Sanctan at keeping them concealed.

After passing what remained of that farm, they drove their horses up the other side of the ravine. At the top he could see a lake stretching away toward hills on the far horizon, and the Serpentspin River winding its way south. The twilight made those hills look beautiful, and Conall should have been glad to be home. Still, he couldn't stop the relentless feeling of unease clawing at his innards.

As they followed a path down to the shore, the encroaching night shrouding everything in grey, that sensation only worsened. A stark memory niggled at him—a voice whispering for him to reach into the shadow, the feel of his hand closing on a demon blade. By the time they reached the ferry station hunkered on the shore, Conall was gritting his teeth lest he double up and puke.

"Shite," Draga hissed as they drew up their horses. "Where's the bastard ferry? This could add days to the journey."

They sat atop their horses within the shadow of the boathouse, glaring at the empty jetty. Conall had never felt more of a burden, and it might have been gallant of him to offer to continue alone, to tell Draga and his men they had already done enough to help. Instead, he just shivered in his cloak as the horse beneath him whickered in the dark.

"Captain," one of the men said, pointing along the shore of the lake. "Looks like a rowboat."

Draga squinted through the inky twilight. "Well, we can't just sit around waiting for a ferryman who might not be coming. Jerem. Kastor. You'll wait here with the horses. Rest of you, get your rowing heads on."

With that he and his men dismounted, not one of them offering a hand as Conall struggled from his saddle. His limbs still ached as they moved in silence along the bank until they reached the rowboat. Conall half expected it to be holed or have no oars, but it was covered by a tarp, oars lying within, all ready to take them across the lake. Whoever had abandoned it here had most likely left in a hurry. Conall could only be thankful, and might even have said a prayer to one of the Wyrms, but that seemed inappropriate now. The less he think on the gods the better.

He clambered into the boat alongside the others and reached for the last oar, but Draga clamped a hand to his wrist.

"Best you sit up at the prow, lad. You'll be no use with the rowing."

That stabbed at Conall's pride, but he was happy enough to stomach it. He'd felt nothing but exhausted for days and was only too happy to silently take his place at the front of the boat. It didn't matter that Draga thought him weak—after what he'd been through in the Drift he should have been dead.

The troopers pulled their oars in unison, making fast progress across the wide expanse of lake. Twilight succumbed to night all too quickly, and the gentle swish of the oars began to lull Conall to sleep. He tried his best to stay awake, not wanting to look like the only one not pulling his weight, though he supposed it was a little late for that.

The sky was full of stars, those old familiar constellations—the five Great Wyrms depicted in their celestial glory. He'd followed those same stars as he wandered through the expanse of the Drift, wondering if he'd ever get to see them from his homeland. Now it felt as though there was something forever changed about them, like he were seeing those constellations for the first time. A veil had been ripped away. His world would never be the same, and the uncertainty of what lay ahead was almost too grim to bear.

The longer that trip across the lake took, the more unnerved he became. The last time he'd been on a boat it had taken him to the dread port of Argon Kyne. Just the memory of it made his hands tremble, and he clasped them together, blowing into them to make it appear they were just cold, and not quaking in fear.

This was not Conall Hawkspur. He could have spat in rage at how pathetic he'd become. Howled and vented at the injustice of a life lost, but that was not how he had been raised. Conall had to remind himself he was of a proud line. His father had died fighting for the honour of the Hawkspur name. He had not perished so that his eldest son and heir could quake in fear at the first sign of adversity.

Still, when they reached the opposite side of the lake, Conall could barely quell his sense of relief. No sooner had the boat slid onto eastern bank than the troopers jumped out, weapons drawn, splintbows trained at the darkness, expecting the worst. For his part, Conall almost fell on his face as he stumbled along behind them, feeling helpless as an old maid.

"Which way now?" one of the troopers asked quietly.

Draga paused on the shore, glancing northeast toward the hills, then north along the road. "We could stick to the towpath, but we might be spotted as soon as the sun comes up. May be better for us to cut across the hills. What do you think, Hawkspur?"

Conall could only envision danger in both directions. The safest way was the hills, but it would be a faster journey if they kept to the path. The old bold Conall would never have shirked the risk. Then again, he was in no mood for unnecessary peril.

"The hill trail should be the safest," he replied, not caring if it made him sound craven.

Draga nodded his agreement, before leading them off toward the slope. Conall was keenly aware it should have been him guiding the way—he was the most qualified scout after all—but he followed anyway, happy to be led along by the nose like a prize calf.

They moved up a grassy slope, and it became almost impossible to see the narrow path that wound its way through the hills. Conall slogged on for what seemed like half the night with no respite, and just as he was about to suggest they might want to make camp, Draga raised a hand, fist clenched.

Conall held his breath as the rest of the men huddled together, surrounding him in a tight unit. He squinted through the dark, seeing no sign of what had spooked Draga. All he could hear was the sound of men breathing, waiting to spring into action at the first sign of trouble. Conall carried no weapon, but he knew with dreadful certainty that was he to reach for it there would be a sword in his grip in an instant. It took all his will not to summon that vile weapon as the tension wore on.

Just as he thought he might turn tail and run, someone stepped out of the darkness in front of them, hands raised to show he was no threat. Conall recognised the uniform of the Viper Battalion—scale armour, a serpent emblazoned on the chest—but he had no idea if that was good or bad. When the trooper nodded his greeting at Draga, who offered a nod of his own before lowering his axe, Conall could barely quell his sigh of relief.

"Didn't expect to find any of the Mantid here," the Viper trooper said. "Thought you were all north at Oakhelm."

"Most of us are," Draga replied. "We've come from Fort Karvan, just making our way north to meet them."

The Viper trooper looked them over with a dubious expression.

"No offence, but you're not much in the way of reinforcements."

Draga moved aside, gesturing to Conall. "We have a Hawkspur with us. Taking him back to Lady Rosomon."

The trooper raised his eyebrows on seeing Conall's shoddy condition. "Then you'd best follow me to camp. Looks like you could all do with the rest."

Draga looked like he might argue, and perhaps his urgency to be rid of Conall had overcome his need to sleep, but instead he nodded, signalling for his men to follow the trooper further along the hill trail.

This was a welcome turn of fortune, but Conall didn't know if he felt safer or not. From Draga's reaction it was obvious the Viper Battalion were on the side of the Guilds, but he still couldn't shake that niggling feeling he was walking into yet more danger.

The camp wasn't far along the trail, hidden at the bottom of a ravine. A few makeshift hide shelters had been erected, but not a single fire lit. Sensible, considering it would have signalled their position to any Ministry forces within ten miles. Did little to stave off the cold though, hence the miserable faces that greeted their arrival.

As Conall passed by groups of troopers he could see they'd been through the mill. Half of them were wounded, the other half bruised and battered, as though they'd walked through each of the Five Lairs and paid a heavy price for it.

The trooper led them to the far end of the camp where a man sat alone, hunkered in a fur cloak that covered his bronze armour. Leaning against each knee was a masterfully worked sword, and as he looked up Conall recognised the scarred face of Marshal Sonnheld. Even in the scant light of the moon his mismatched eyes shone distinctly as they regarded Conall.

"Hawkspur," Sonnheld said, gravel voice making him sound parched. "Seems your family are ranging all over this Wyrmforsaken land. What brings you here?"

"Heading to meet my mother," Conall replied, before Draga could do it for him. "I'm surprised you have not answered her call and joined with her forces to the north."

"Your mother's is not the only fight in Torwyn. Though now Castleteig is lost our fight grows more desperate, but while the

Ministry's Armigers stand against us we will harry them to the end."

He seemed determined, despite the sorry state of his troopers. "I know my mother appreciates your efforts."

Sonnheld snorted, as though he were unconvinced. "Yes. I'm sure."

Conall would have tried to argue her case, but he doubted it would do any good. "What did you mean when you said my family is ranging across the land?"

"I met your sister at Castleteig. She was also keen to rendezvous with Lady Rosomon."

Conall had to catch his breath at the mention of Tyreta. She had been on her way to the Sundered Isles the last time he had seen her. If she'd remained there, most likely she would have stayed out of danger. Now it seemed she had willingly thrown herself into the crucible.

"Was she well?" he asked, bracing himself for the worst.

"She was when I last saw her, but that girl was determined to head into enemy territory."

"And you let her?" Conall barked before he could stop himself.

Sonnheld rose to his feet, letting the fur cloak slide from his huge shoulders, and Conall suddenly appreciated the imposing size of the man. "It's not my job to chaperone every Guild heir that crosses my path. Just like it's not my job to wetnurse you. The Viper Battalion owes the Guilds nothing. We've bled enough."

Conall could tell he had touched a nerve. Sonnheld and his men had obviously fought hard since this whole thing began and paid heavily for their loyalty to the Guilds. Besides, Conall knew all too well that if Tyreta had set her mind to something, there were few who could talk her out of it.

"I understand, Marshal. And I appreciate you telling me. So what's your plan now?"

Sonnheld gestured south across the hills. "The bulk of the Raptor and Auroch Battalions are garrisoned at the Rock. I've received intelligence that they intend to move north toward the Anvil and help defend it against the Guild alliance. They will bolster the Archlegate's forces there and make it nigh-on impossible for your mother to take the city. So, I intend to stop them."

It sounded like suicide. It also sounded like just the excuse Conall needed not to travel to his mother's side. Perhaps there was a way he could help her against the Ministry without putting her in danger from the curse Senmonthis had afflicted him with. Facing two battalions of Armiger alongside this ramshackle excuse of an army was a mad idea for sure, but not as mad as the thought of exposing his mother to the sorcery of a Scion.

"That has the makings of a sound plan, Marshal," Conall replied, though in truth it sounded like the worst plan he'd ever heard. "If it's all the same, I'd like to join you."

Sonnheld looked him up and down, unable or unwilling to hide the dubious look in his mismatched eyes. "Just what help do you think you could be, Hawkspur? You look like shit."

"Give me the chance, and I'll show you," Conall replied, trying to stand straight and proud, but failing abysmally.

"Very well," Sonnheld said, taking no time to make his decision. "If that's what you want then you're welcome to join us. I need all the men I can get, but don't think we're carrying any baggage."

"I'll pull my weight, don't worry on that score," Conall replied, this time sounding just as confident as he wanted.

He turned, ready to thank Draga and dismiss him back to Fort Karvan, but the captain was already mustering his men. It seemed in their eagerness to part company with him they were more than happy to forego the hospitality of the Viper Battalion.

"I intend to stay," Conall told him.

"Aye, I heard," Draga replied. "We'll send word to your mother where you are if that's what—"

"No," Conall said. "Best if she doesn't know I'm here. I wouldn't want to add to her problems."

Draga looked only too pleased to be rid of his own problem. "Suit yourself. Best of luck, Hawkspur. No offence, but I hope we don't cross paths again." Without another word, he and his men disappeared into the dark.

Conall could hardly blame them. They thought him cursed, and he wasn't sure if they were wrong about that, but he was Sonnheld's problem now. With any luck, if he could manage to get his head together, he'd make himself a problem for the Ministry.

# ROSOMON

Everyone had implored her to bring more men on this mad dash south. Of course, she had ignored them all. The last thing she wanted to do was spook the Hallowhills. Make it look like she was the aggressor. It might put Tyreta in even more danger. Now, with every mile further south they plodded, the more she began to regret that decision.

Kassian rode to her left. If he had any opinion on her choice of travelling companions he didn't make it vocal. To her right was Ianto. In contrast, he had expressed his objection often, and loudly, reminding her of all the ways this could end poorly. Not that she needed any reminding.

The nearer they rode toward their goal, the more unsafe Rosomon felt. Every mile closer to the Web put them in ever greater peril, but she would not be deterred. That vile woman's words haunted her with every step: *You are expected at the Web within five days. Or Tyreta might meet with an unfortunate...*

She hadn't had to finish her sentence. The implications had been obvious, and the road south had given Rosomon time to consider every way that threat might have been enacted.

"My lady."

Ianto again. Though they were annoying, she had grown accustomed to his constant warnings.

"There is no need to repeat yourself once again, Imperator."

"But I will. This could be our last chance to reconsider this folly and turn back before we reach the Web. Please, at least wait here where it might be safe and allow me and Kassian to approach the city. We are more than capable of negotiating on your behalf."

"I appreciate the offer, Ianto. I really do. And I know how much danger we're in, but whatever we might face, I know you are both more than capable of keeping me safe."

She felt the nudge of guilt just saying it. Ianto had already faced death more than once trying to protect her from assassins, rogue Armigers, and even her own nephew. Now she was leading him into yet more needless danger.

But it was not needless. She had left Tyreta to the vagaries of the Sundered Isles before. Chosen duty to her Guild over responsibility for her daughter. She would not make that mistake a second time.

Mistakes. It seemed that was all she had made in recent weeks, and yet she still lived. Still fought. Maybe Ianto was right, maybe this would be one mistake too many.

She turned to Kassian, his dark eyes fixed on the road ahead. "What about you? I suppose you agree we should turn back from this?"

A twitch of his mouth—very nearly a display of emotion. "It's not my place to question your decisions, Lady Rosomon. I'm your swordwright, not your consul. It's my place to obey."

"But I would hear your opinion anyway. I assume you have one?"

Kassian glanced across at Ianto. "The lad is right. We are walking into needless danger." Then he fixed her with a stern glare. "But you're right too. Family is all that matters. It should always come first."

It seemed an uncharacteristically insightful view, but then Rosomon understood little about Kassian's character anyway. All she'd ever known was her father's stoic swordwright. Every day revealed a new facet to him.

"Strange you would think that, Kassian. You have no family of your own."

"The Archwinds were my family. After that, the mentees under my tutelage at the Seminarium."

"And now?"

He gave the slightest of shrugs, as though he didn't know, or didn't want to admit to it. Maybe he felt she was now his responsibility, though perhaps that was a hope too far.

"What about Lancelin. Did you consider him family?"

He gazed at her again, only this time she could read nothing in those eyes of his. "You told me once never to mention his name."

She had. And in her grief and anger she had blamed Kassian in some way for all her woes. Not her proudest moment.

"That was...that was before..."

"Before you could trust me?"

Kassian had more than proven himself in the months since Lancelin had perished. "Yes. I guess so."

"Aye, Lancelin was like a son to me. I would have done anything for him. And so I appreciate why you're willing to ride into danger to save your daughter. Why you would risk everything for just the chance to see her safe."

Before she could thank him for his understanding, they trotted out of the surrounding woodland, and the road became more solid beneath them. Pulling up her horse, Rosomon focused down the hill to the city sprawling below. The Web.

Despite her role in a Guild devoted to transportation and commerce, Rosomon had never visited the city before. Now that she saw what state the place was in, she couldn't bring herself to regret it. She had been told it was a once great city now fallen to ruin, and they weren't wrong.

The Web sprawled like a canker amid the green pastures that surrounded it. The crumbling facade of its outer walls was grey and drab, the broken roofs of manses clawing up from beyond them, interspersed with broken spires. To the west she saw the main gate was open, the landship line leading right through it. Flanking it stood the imposing forms of stormhulks, like iron statues guarding the way.

"This is our last chance, Lady Rosomon." The concern in Ianto's voice sounded more pressing than ever. "Once they see us it'll be too late to reconsider."

"If this was a trap, their webwainers would have been waiting on the road for us. Keara Hallowhill wants something, and I have to know what it is. If there's any chance we can form an alliance with them I have to consider it."

Ianto shifted in his saddle uncomfortably. "After all they have done?"

"We are in no position to pick and choose our allies. The Hallowhills may be duplicitous, but that could be to our advantage. Sanctan cannot be bargained with. He will not stop until we are all consumed in his fire. With any luck, the Hallowhills have realised that."

She kicked her horse, more determined than ever to see this done, but still feeling the pull of apprehension. Despite her assurances to Ianto, Rosomon wasn't certain about any of this. Ingelram she could have dealt with. Though he was a treacherous slug, he was also a known quantity—a self-serving wart of a man, but he could still see reason. His daughter was an enigma, but Rosomon could only hope Keara Hallowhill had seen enough of the degradation wrought by the Ministry to be ready to swap her allegiance. Or in the least that she could be reasoned with, though reason was the last thing on Rosomon's mind. Tyreta's life was in danger—she had been abducted and threatened. If backed against a wall, there was nothing Rosomon wouldn't do to see her daughter safe.

As they neared the gate, she began to wonder what her father would have done. Would he have been ruthless? Pragmatic? Would he have razed this place to the ground to defend his family? Or would he have bargained with Ingelram Hallowhill—a man rumoured to have murdered his own wife—like a diplomat?

Best not think on things that might have been. They were about to enter the lair of the enemy, and Rosomon could only imagine the horrors that had taken place in this nest of snakes. She had to concentrate on the now, and keep her wits about her.

The two stormhulks reacted to their approach, hydraulics hissing as they stood to full attention, weapon mounts whining as they aimed at the approaching riders.

"Looks like they're expecting us at least," said Kassian, still sitting casually in his saddle.

In contrast, Ianto had his hand on the hilt of his sword, though what he might have done against these behemoths Rosomon had no idea. She reined her mount to a stop, sitting as tall and confident as she could manage in the face of these inhuman machines.

"I am Rosomon Hawkspur. I have come at—"

"We know who you are," came the tinny reply from within the cockpit of the closest hulk.

With that they turned, leading the way inside, the rumble of their tread making the horses skittish. Rosomon pulled on the rein before urging her horse forward and through the gate, closely followed by her bodyguards. The hooves of their steeds clopped along the worn cobbles, and on seeing the city up close she began to realise just how far Ingelram had allowed his city to fall.

The place was a ruin. Veneers crumbling, woodwork rotten, eaves hanging drab and unkempt. Ahead of them the stormhulks stomped in grim mockery of an honour guard, but there was no honour here. Only decay. Thankfully the streets were quiet, only a few of the Web's residents come to watch as they rode deeper into enemy territory. Rosomon did her best to ignore those suspicious eyes, harbouring the pent-up hatred of generations. Most likely they blamed her for how far their Guild and their city had fallen. Perhaps they were right. Perhaps that was how Sanctan had so easily persuaded the Hallowhills to join his cause.

"There's little love lost for us here," Kassian said in a low breath.

Rosomon couldn't disagree. "I imagine they blame my father for their lot."

"Let's hope this Keara has a different attitude."

"Ingelram and my father rarely saw eye to eye on anything. I'm hoping I might come to a more cordial agreement with his daughter, despite what happened the last time we met."

The memory of violence in the palace gardens was quickly expelled from her mind as the crackling voice from one of the hulks ordered them to be quiet. Ahead loomed a soot-blackened building, from the look of it a garrison. Atop the surrounding wall stood Hallowhill webwainers, their purple uniforms stark against the drab stonework. Alongside them were other sentries carrying splintbows—most likely mercenaries since the Hallowhills had no standing army of their own. Her father had forbidden it years before, but it seemed with war came yet more change.

Rosomon rode through the open gate into a courtyard. Pennants hung limp from their stanchions, their spider symbols marking this place as the Hallowhill academy. Here, webwainers came from across Torwyn to learn how to manage and control their gift, and eventually be sanctioned by the Guilds. Years earlier, Rosomon had considered there might be some advantage to having Tyreta learn here, but it had been a fleeting notion. Fulren had trained in the auspice of the Archwinds, but that had been under his uncle's watch. She would never have allowed her daughter to be trained by another Guild, or at least not one as lowly as the Hallowhills.

Webwainers gazed down from every window and parapet, eyes smouldering with disdain. If they intended to intimidate her, they were wasting their time.

"No love lost here either," Kassian said.

He looked slightly less self-assured as the stormhulks ground to a halt in front of them. Ianto had nothing to say, his eyes scanning for danger, and seeing it everywhere he looked.

"It's not love I've come for," Rosomon replied as she climbed down from her horse.

No sooner had they dismounted than a figure she recognised strutted from within the academy building and down the stairs to the courtyard. Those dark glasses were fixed to her face, black hair unruffled despite the slight breeze. She made her way across the courtyard as though stalking prey rather than greeting guests. Rosomon felt her grip tighten on the horse's reins, trying her best to control her lingering anger.

"Lady Rosomon," the woman said, with the trace of a smile it would have been so satisfying to slap off her face. "How good of you to join us."

"Where is my daughter?" No point in wasting time with pleasantries.

"All in good time. First, the Guildmaster would like to speak with you." She gestured toward the building.

"I'll go nowhere until I know Tyreta is unharmed."

The smile wavered. "Then I suppose we are at a slight impasse. Because you need to come with me. And you need to come alone."

Rosomon had to pick her fights. This one she didn't think she could win—and it was no use arguing with the monkey, when the organ grinder was nowhere to be seen. She turned to her companions, already seeing how concerned they looked.

"Wait for me here," she said, handing her reins to Ianto.

He did not take them, instead shaking his head. "I don't think—"

"They wouldn't have made us travel all this way if they were just going to hand me over to Sanctan."

"This is unwise."

Kassian stepped closer, taking her reins. "You're right, son. But she won't be dissuaded."

"It's good you both know that," she replied.

Kassian almost grinned, but thought better of it. "There's no doubting whose daughter you are."

"Really?"

"Without question. Treon would have done exactly the same. He would have thrown himself to wolves to see you freed."

Was that just bluster? Her father had wedded her to a lascivious drunkard to cement the power of the Guilds, but then how could he have known what a brute Melrone would turn out to be? Had he been alive to see what had become of that man, what he did to her at the end, it might have been Treon who fought that duel instead of Lancelin.

She turned back to the tall, striking witch. "Lead the way."

With a mocking bow, the woman turned, and together they made their way toward that daunting building.

# TYRETA

She had been trapped in a red haze for days now. How many she couldn't count. All she could recall was riding that storm of sensations—soaring on an exquisite breeze before plunging down and down to hit the rocky ground before the cycle started anew. It had been a while since they'd forced that red drop into her eye, though, and now she was back to earth with stomach-churning clarity. With it, unwelcome memories had come knocking.

They'd killed Cat. Not right in front of her, but she'd felt it through the murk of her drug haze. From a distant chamber she'd heard the panther howl its last and felt each cut as though it were her own flesh being flensed. Every hack and slice of the knife as she was butchered slowly. Through Cat's eyes she'd seen that woman with her black eyeglasses, her wicked smile, the pleasure she took from what she inflicted. Tyreta had screamed long and loud—feeling that pain, that terror. Shared every gasp until the breath from her lungs finally ebbed away.

She had died that day. Her insides eaten away by the loss, to be replaced with hate. If not for the red drop keeping her sedated she might have railed and screamed and battered her head against the ground till her skull split. Instead she had been consumed by the agony and ecstasy of that potent narcotic. But now...now she was back. Feeding on the nausea it left behind. Letting the stink of the room wash over her, focusing on the dank surrounding, trying to anchor herself in the real.

She was chained to the floor, her hands held fast in immovable steel gauntlets lest she claw the eyes from her captors. Every day she had been given food and water. Made to do her daily waste in a bucket. The ignominy of it had not registered at the time, but as she regained her faculties it only made the rage burn hotter.

In the silence of the room she did her best to press with her powers. So far, the red drop had made that impossible, but now her head was clearing. Had they decided to wean her off it for some reason? That would be their mistake. Maybe they'd come back to dose her again soon. There might not be much time left. She had to pull herself together and make the most of this brief clarity.

Daylight filtered into the cell from a barred window high on the wall. She focused through those bars, pressing her senses along the web, but it was still blurred and incoherent. The remnants of the red drop made everything hazy and she couldn't latch on to the power with any lucidity. She had to find a way, had to grip tight to something that might set her free. Anything would have done. Any small sign that she was still—

A flutter of wings, heralding a tiny bird that landed on the windowsill. It was green, a little red plume flicking on its head as it took in the cell. Tyreta smiled at the little creature, come to greet the prisoner. A small hope indeed, but maybe it was her only chance.

She gritted her teeth, focusing on the bird, desperate to send her consciousness soaring along the web to meld with that of the bird. With the latent effects of the red drop still in her system her mind was spinning, and it was all she could do to focus her vision.

A growl deep in her throat and she bit her tongue hard, hoping the pain would clarify her thoughts. Her jaws clamped down, teeth biting deep until she tasted blood in her mouth, but it did the trick. The sudden pain focused her on the little animal, that coppery taste fuelling her senses as she communed with the green bird and became one with it.

A sensation of freedom flooded her—a feeling she hadn't felt for what seemed an age. She almost cried out at the joy of it, but she had to stay focused, had to use this creature to at least view her surroundings. Maybe if she could see through its eyes it would reveal some way to escape.

As she knelt there, she began to get the growing sense the bird understood her. Sharing her need for escape. For freedom. To be unshackled so she could soar away on feathered wings. A smile crossed Tyreta's lips, but before she could command the bird to aid her, the latch to the cell door snapped back with a solid *click*.

Her concentration broken, the bird immediately gave flight, fluttering out into the bright day. Again her teeth gnashed, and she spat blood in fury, quelling the urge to scream. She would have sobbed her frustration, but the welling hate inside wouldn't allow it.

The cell door swung wide with a creak of hinges, and a familiar face appeared. He was thick about the neck and gut, his green tunic straining to hold his fleshy girth at bay. Despite the fat he bore about the middle, his bare arms were muscular, and covered in tattoos too faded to be recognisable.

Her gaoler walked to stand before her, leering down. Enjoying himself as he always did. A familiar rage began to build. How she would have loved to claw that grin from his face, but it was impossible, chained as she was. There was no use raging—it would only have made her look weak, and most likely widened that shit-eating grin on his face.

Behind him entered a woman—slimmer, more serious, but wearing the same green tunic marking them as mercenaries of the Hallowhills. She knew what this was. Another dose. Just enough to keep her compliant, but not so much as to put her in a stupor.

He reached into the pocket on the breast of his tunic and took out the vial. With surprising deftness for a man with fingers thick as ship's rigging, he unscrewed the stopper.

"Don't think you'll be in here much longer," he drawled, tapping the dropper against the lip of the vial so there was just enough liquid on it. "So this is just a little dewdrop to keep you quiet for a bit."

Her eyes scanned the room for anything she might use against them, but as usual there was nothing. These mercenaries were careful, neither carried any pyrestone. Nothing but a splintbow and a couple of shithouse grins.

The mercenary knelt down beside her. "You've gone quiet. Normally I get a little abuse when I come see you. No curse words for me? No insults, milady?" He waited, as though expecting her to speak. When she had nothing to say he shrugged at the woman, who kept her eyes locked on Tyreta. "Nice that she's calmed down. Almost like she's learned her lesson. All compliant like."

As he raised the stopper, she worked her mouth so there was a nice juicy gob of blood on her tongue, before spitting it right in his face.

He staggered back, almost dropping the vial as he wiped the bloody phlegm from his face. "You fucking cow."

She tried to pull away as he grabbed her hair, but wasn't quick enough. Chained to the floor as she was, she could barely move.

He raised the dropper, dragging her head back. "Maybe this time I'll put too much in your damned eye. Maybe you'll have an accident. Overdose. Go mad and writhe till your neck breaks. I've seen it happen before."

Tyreta tried to close her eye, but the other mercenary stepped forward, thumb pressing her eyelid back as the red drop went in. She snarled as her vision reddened, and the two mercenaries took a step back to view their handiwork.

Their faces began to morph and writhe as the red drop took immediate effect. Her stomach heaved with sudden elation, and she did her best to fight back, trying to keep control, but it was no use. Desperate as she was, Tyreta was powerless against the dose, feeling herself begin to soar, the world around her turning hazy, blending in a medley of colour.

The daylight lancing in through that high window began to brighten, becoming almost blinding, and something fluttered in her periphery. Tyreta concentrated, focusing, forcing that light to coalesce until she could make out that little bird sitting on the sill again. It had returned, but for what? To watch her humiliation? That seemed cruel for such a little...

No, it held something in its beak. A tiny gift, winking in the sunlight.

As the bird dropped the stone on the sill, Tyreta heard the mercenaries laugh. With the red drop coursing through her system, it sounded like a deafening roar.

"Look at her," the man said, leaning close, his broad features swelling, giving him a bulbous aspect. "Like a baby that's sucked too much milk from her mother's tit."

The words were a drawl, but Tyreta ignored them, focusing on the sill. Focusing on the lifeline that little bird had brought her. Had it understood her need for freedom? Was it trying to help?

No matter. Intentional or not, it had offered her a chance.

As the bird took wing and flew from the windowsill, she focused on the stone. She couldn't quite see it, but she could feel its power through an indistinct thread of the web. A yellow pyrestone, burning with untapped energy. Energy she could use.

"You need to stop baiting her," the woman said, her lips moving but her words not quite syncing in time with them. "We're paid to do what we're told. I think you're enjoying this a bit too much."

The grin spread on that big face of his. "No reason we can't have fun while we're getting paid."

Tyreta ignored them. All her will was trained on the windowsill as she began to fuel the pyrestone with power. She strengthened her connection along the web, and a staccato tapping reverberated from the window as the pyrestone began to agitate, dancing to Tyreta's tune.

"What the fuck is that noise?"

The mercenary stood, turning to see what was tap-tap-tapping at the window.

Tyreta snarled as she fuelled the pyrestone with all the power she could muster. It flared with light, streaking across the room, burning with blinding energy as it blasted through the mercenary's skull and bounced off the wall opposite.

The woman raised her splintbow, cursing as her friend fell, his dead eyes staring, the tiny entrance wound still steaming where the pyrestone had smashed through his forehead.

"What in the Lairs?" she screamed, aiming her splintbow toward the window, toward Tyreta, toward the door, but there was no target to be found.

The pyrestone sat on the ground, flaring and spitting with energy. The woman aimed her splintbow at it, glaring as though it had a life of its own. Tyreta gritted her teeth again, energising the stone, elevating it from the ground, where it hovered in midair, burning bright.

"What are you—?"

She realised all too late what was happening, pointing her splintbow at Tyreta once more, but far too late. Tyreta squeezed her eyes shut as she fuelled the stone with all her might, detonating it right in the woman's face.

The noise was deafening, light flaring even though she had her eyes tight shut. When she opened them again, there were two corpses on the ground, and she forced herself not to look at the blackened ruin of the woman's face. Instead she focused on the man's corpse.

A bunch of keys were attached to his belt. Tyreta pulled tight on the chain binding her to the ground, stretching as far as she could, teeth gnashing as she tried to clench the keys between them. The iron ring tasted bitter as she managed to bite down on it and wrench the keys free of his belt.

Sudden elation made her head spin, and she shook it. She had to stay awake, stay focused. If someone came and found these bodies there'd be no telling what might happen to her.

There were only two keys on the ring—one for the door, one for the manacles at her wrists. With some difficulty she managed to feed the right key into the lock, her teeth grinding as she twisted her head. The click of the lock releasing resounded in her head, and she sighed in relief as the metal gauntlets fell away.

Tyreta staggered to her feet, legs aching from too long kneeling on that filthy floor. There was no time to regard the corpses she had made, all that mattered was getting out of here, but as she staggered toward the door her desire to escape quickly vanished. The red haze that assailed her turned to a crimson rage. Memories of Cat, of her humiliation. Of that fucker Keara. She had ordered all this—she was ultimately responsible. And even now she would be trying to manipulate Tyreta's mother. Trying to manipulate this war for her own gain.

It could not be allowed to happen.

The claws began to extend from her fingers as she staggered out into the corridor. Immediately she was met by the diminutive figure of a man, leather jack and skullcap marking him as a Hallowhill artificer. He held something in his hand—a weapon?

Tyreta felt the latent power of the pyrestone within it. She had no idea what it was for, but her instinct to survive took over. She fuelled the device, overloading the stone in an instant, and the artificer cried out in panic as it exploded in his hand. Gripping his wrist, he fell to his knees.

She loomed over him, resisting the urge to claw out his throat. Surely she should have run—fled this place and not looked back—but instead she leaned closer, teeth clenched, the taste of blood and slaver filling her mouth.

"Where is she?"

The man stared back, terrified. "I...I don't know who you mean."

"Keara fucking Hallowhill. Tell me where she is."

"The main hall," he replied in a high-pitched squeal. "Don't... don't kill me, I'm just..."

She was already moving, leaving that artificer behind, gripping the blackened mess of his hand. The corridor was spinning as she made her way along it, and again she had to shake her head to stay focused, the red rage building. She had to stay in control. Not let it take over...

A door at the end of the passage led down a short flight of stairs, and she almost tumbled down them. Voices, close but indistinct, and she lurched into the shadow of a wide column. Two webwainers walked past, no idea she was even there, and it took all her will not to leap forward and rip out their throats.

When they had gone she staggered on, claws pressing into her palms, drawing blood, the pain forcing her to stay lucid. With every step her vision began to narrow. Memories flooding back to her in harsh flashes. Violence. That torment as Cat had been torn from her, their connection waning until it was cut off completely with one final flash of a blade.

Tyreta sniffed. She could smell something on the air, at first faint, but growing stronger. Keara was here, and she was close.

The long hallway led to an arch, and from beyond it echoed the heavy tamp of a hammer. Glaring through that arch she saw a manufactory of sorts, long tables and heavy machinery, all abandoned but for one artificer busy with his work.

As deftly as she could she crept forward, gripping the shadows, letting her instincts take over as she continued to fight the effects of the red drop. She prowled closer to the hapless artificer as he tapped and whacked with his hammer, the latent energy of the pyrestone buzzing in her ears, the pressure of it threatening to make them pop.

When she was close enough she struck, leaping on the little man and his worthless machine. The hammer fell from his hand, clattering on the ground as she clamped a clawed hand over his mouth to stop him crying out. Her other hand was raised, ready to lash forward and rip out his throat, but she stopped when she looked into his eyes, glaring at her in terror.

This was not her. She was not some wild beast. Was it the red drop making her act this way or...something worse?

Was it the nightstone that had become a part of her in the Sundered Isles? Is that what had turned her into a monster?

Suddenly all thoughts of murderous vengeance fled. She was no assassin. She was Tyreta Hawkspur. Heir to a proud Guild and daughter to a Guildmaster. And the sooner she could get out of here and return to her mother's side the better.

Slowly she took her hand from the man's mouth, pressing a single finger to her lips. "How do I get out of here?"

Still staring at her in horror, the artificer raised a trembling hand and pointed toward a door at the far end of the manufactory. With a nod, she stepped back, hearing the man sigh in relief. Before she could make her way toward the door he said, "Wait."

She turned back, seeing him trembling in fear. "What?"

"Your mother."

Tyreta frowned. "What about her?"

"Lady Rosomon. She is here."

"Now? What is she doing here?"

"She's come to meet with the Guildmaster, Keara. To bargain for your life."

All the rage she had forced down suddenly bubbled to the fore. Keara Hallowhill had forced her mother into this. Brought her here to prostrate herself, and used Tyreta to do it. The hate she had been so desperate to quell, the beast she had kept at bay, began to well up once more. And this time it could not be chained.

"Where?" she growled.

With his hand still trembling, the artificer pointed to an open archway.

Tyreta didn't even think to threaten him into silence. With the red drop numbing her head, she stalked across the room, determined to show that Hallowhill bitch the folly of her ways.

# KEARA

Sybilla sat smiling from across the table. She looked relaxed enough, but then that was the way with artisans like this. Settle on a price, do the work, renegotiate the price. All this theatre made Keara uncomfortable, but then she supposed it was how these merchants and tinkers always worked.

"So...you have the money?" Sybilla asked.

Of course she had the damned money, but should she haggle? Maybe once she'd seen the goods.

"You first," Keara replied.

Sybilla gently raised the box she'd been resting on her lap and placed it on the table, spreading her hands as though she'd just conjured it in a magic show. Reverently she opened the clasp and raised the lid. Keara had to admit, what lay inside was worth the showmanship.

Two daggers. So similar to the ones she'd lost in her father's manse, but at the same time so different. These looked far from antiques, masterfully crafted, and easily worth every penny she'd been asked to pay.

The steel was herringbone pattern. Handles wrought from stag antlers. It was craftsmanship of the finest sort, and exactly why she'd had an outsider craft them. None of her own artificers could have produced something so beautiful—they had neither the skill nor the creativity.

"That's good work," she breathed, trying to sound less impressed than she was.

Sybilla's smile grew wider. "I'm glad you think so. Because the final price is a little more than we first agreed."

There it was—just the words she'd been expecting, but then Keara always knew when she was being played. And despite the fine work laid before her, she was no pushover. "How so?"

"To get the relevant strength I had to craft a specific alloy, so these particular weapons will be sharper and stronger than Novik steel, but light as ashwood. Each of the conversion chambers is also of a bespoke design, which requires smaller pyrestones for the same power and durability as larger models of Archwind design. I'm sure you agree, they're worth a little extra."

Keara reached forward, running her finger along the hilt of one dagger. The Hallowhill spider had been engraved on each pommel, and they looked far superior to the ones she had lost. She had to admit, she always appreciated it when someone exceeded her expectations. It was so rare to find people like that nowadays.

"Usually I'd say the price is the price, but you know what; reward where it's due."

She pulled a folded square of parchment from her tunic and slid it across the table.

Sybilla frowned at it. "What's this?"

"A letter of Guild credit. Signed by the Guildmaster of the Hallowhills."

The frown was gone from Sybilla's brow quickly, replaced by a half smile. "Very generous. And yet, nothing says credit quite like gold."

Keara sighed. It was worth a try, she supposed.

"Fair enough." She opened the drawer in the desk she sat behind, taking out roll after roll of gold coins, each one encased in thick paper. There were twelve in all—they'd agreed on ten. As she slid them across the desk, Sybilla deposited the rolls into the same satchel she had delivered the wooden box in.

"It was so nice doing business with you," she said as she stood, and gestured to the finely wrought daggers. "Keep the box."

Keara watched her leave, still not sure if she liked her style or hated her for her arrogance. More likely the first one.

No sooner had the door closed than in breezed Hesse, heels clicking on the polished floor, mouth a hair's breadth between sneer and leer. But then she'd always known how to make an entrance.

"Well?" Keara asked.

"Her ladyship is comfortable for now. But that old whore won't wait forever."

Comfortable. That could have meant anything from sitting patiently to seething in rage. Keara stood, taking one more look at those masterfully worked knives before plucking them from the box. Sybilla had also provided a knife belt, which Keara strapped to her waist and secured at the thighs. The blades sat comfortably at her hips. It almost felt as though she was whole again. As she made her way to the door, she caressed the pyrestones fitted into those weapons. They reacted to her touch with a hum, a contented purr like a faithful old tomcat.

"We'd best not keep her waiting any longer."

"What's the plan?" Hesse asked as they left the room and made their way along a corridor lit by pyrestone lamps.

"The plan is to get back what we've lost. And Lady Rosomon will be only too happy to hand it over in return for her daughter."

Hesse peered down at her. "You do remember burning down your own manse? Maybe you should start by doing less damage to yourself. Then we wouldn't need the Hawkspurs or the other Guilds."

Something she didn't need reminding of, but it had seemed necessary at the time.

"Don't talk to me about damage. You were the one who killed that panther, when I told you to just cut off its tail. We could have used it as more leverage."

"You told me to send a message." If Keara had been expecting Hesse to show how guilty she felt, it wasn't working. "That's what I did. That's my job—to do the things you don't have the stomach for."

A sudden flash of anger, the pyrestones humming at her hips in reaction to her sudden emotion. Keara was Guildmaster now—she shouldn't have had to suffer being spoken to like that. But then Hesse had always been given special dispensation. That little extra leniency to speak her mind.

"You don't think I have the stomach for this?"

Silence at first. Doubt? "It's just..."

"What?

"We made a shit bargain with Sanctan. Now you're about to do the same with Hawkspur. Are we just going from bad to worse?"

Keara gritted her teeth, quelling the urge to tell Hesse where to go, despite the fact she was only confirming her own fears. Damn it, Hesse was starting to sound like her father. Always questioning. Always second-guessing.

"This gamble will be different. This time we've loaded the dice."

"Sure. I've heard that before. But loaded dice are all well and good...when they can't kill you. And everyone around you."

"All right, that's enough of the frigging pep talk."

They'd reached the doors to the meeting room where two mercenaries stood guard. Keara wasn't happy having these sell-swords and their ilk lurking all over the Web, but they were a necessary evil. As powerful as her webwainers were, they were few in number. Having a bunch of grim-looking bastards armed to the teeth hanging around was a good way to show your strength—even if they were only loyal because of the gold you were paying.

The mercenaries opened the doors, revealing an opulent dining room. A fire burned in the hearth, a long oak table in the centre, surrounded by satin-covered chairs, but Rosomon wasn't sitting in any of them. Instead she was not too far from the fire, not too close, standing tall like she'd been waiting there all this time for those doors to open.

Keara wasn't sure what to expect. Maybe a furious rant? Maybe cold hard pragmatism? Or maybe just silence, as Lady Rosomon watched them enter and those doors were closed behind.

She was emotionless. Keara could only imagine the will it took to keep all that rage locked inside. It made her uneasy, like she was talking to her father all over again.

"Thank you for coming," Keara said.

She had seen Lady Rosomon only twice before. The first time in the Guildhall where Rosomon had been in control, though Sanctan had managed to swerve her enquiry into his subterfuge. The second time had been in the palace gardens, where she had been anything but in control. Now...now she looked like she owned this room and everyone in it, despite the fact she was alone and surrounded by enemies.

"I didn't really have a choice, did I."

"No, I guess you—"

"Where is my daughter?"

Keara had expected to be leading the conversation, but now it was slipping out of her grasp. "She's...quite safe. Not particularly comfortable, but safe."

That last quip had sounded sharp in her head, but on speaking it she realised how stupid it was. Rosomon glared back, those eyes more steel than blue. Keara was in her own city, surrounded by her own people, but under that gaze she felt more vulnerable than ever.

"I want to see her. Now."

Keara swallowed, her trepidation going down with it. Damn, she had to get in control of this.

"Please, sit. We have some things to talk over first."

"You mean things like an alliance." It wasn't a question. Rosomon knew exactly why she was here. "We'll discuss nothing until I have seen Tyreta with my own eyes."

Keara was aware of Hesse making her way over to a cabinet. She slowly opened it, taking out a decanter full of brandy and three glasses. What must she have been thinking? That she was following a weakling? Someone who didn't have the strength or will to get things done? Someone who was even now failing at negotiations on her own territory.

"I'm afraid we will." It came out too fast. Too desperate. "This is the Web. You're not at the Anvil or Wyke anymore. I rule here."

Rosomon's jaw worked as she ground her teeth. "No, I am not in Wyke. That city is no more. You saw to that."

She had heard of the horrors. The number of dead. The ruthless way Sanctan had stamped his intentions and drowned thousands in his attempt to defeat Rosomon.

"What happened in Wyke had nothing to do with me. It was an atrocity. Rosomon, there has already been too much death. Too much suffering. We need to think about the future of our nation. About the new order we could build. Please, let's just cool our engines, sit down and we can discuss this calmly."

Hesse had poured the drinks now, and made her way over to hand one to Rosomon.

"Brandy?" Hesse asked in that crooning voice of hers.

Without taking her eyes off Keara, Rosomon slapped the glass from Hesse's hand. It smashed on the stone floor, making her feelings all too clear.

Keara let out a cleansing breath. "I was hoping we could be more civilised about this."

"That time has passed," Rosomon replied, those eyes of hers still tearing into Keara. "It ended when you helped Sanctan rip apart our country. Everything we built torn down. And for what? So you could claw back a little bit of power? You will return Tyreta to me now. If you don't, I'll burn the Web just as soon as I've destroyed the Anvil and ripped the heart out of the Ministry."

No. This had to be some kind of bluff. But it was so convincing. As though she could have smashed the walls of the Anvil with that glare alone.

"You need me. There's no way you'll take the Anvil without the help of the Hallowhills."

For the first time there was a little doubt behind Rosomon's steely gaze. She took a step forward, pulling one of the chairs out from under that long table and sitting herself in it.

"So what do you propose?"

Now they were getting somewhere. Keara moved forward, taking the chair opposite as Hesse placed a brandy glass in front of her, taking a swig from the one she held in her hand.

"I propose this—we crush the Anvil together. Burn down the Ministry's base and return the Guilds to their rightful position. In return, you will grant the Hallowhill Guild its own charter." As though they'd practised it, Hesse laid down a sheaf of parchment—official documentation marked with the seals of Hallowhill and Hawkspur. Keara slid it toward Rosomon. "I don't expect you to read it all now. But as you'll see, it's a contract of mutual accord. We can discuss the specifics when you're ready, but as soon as you sign I'll hand Tyreta over."

Rosomon glanced at it but didn't bother to touch the intricately detailed document. Suddenly she didn't seem so desperate for her daughter to be released. "Why don't you give me the gist?"

Keara chose her moment to pick up the brandy glass and take a drink, before carefully placing it back on the table. "It's a treaty of assurance that once this is all over, the Hallowhills will have a seat in the Guildhall, and a say in all future decisions concerning Torwyn. The Guilds will be reformed under a single banner, controlled by you. The Hallowhills will take governorship of the Anvil and control the administrative function of the nation."

Rosomon raised an eyebrow, but it was only to be expected. It was an audacious proposal, but Keara was determined to aim high. "You will control the Anvil? Our nation's capital."

"I will."

Now a smile—and a wry one. "So you will effectively become empress, and the Guilds your vassals."

Keara resisted taking another drink to help gird herself. "I suppose that's one way of looking at it."

"How could you ever think I would agree to this?"

Keara leaned forward. "Because if you don't you'll have no webwainers. Without us you won't even make it to the Anvil. Sanctan will crush you, consolidate his control over the country, and then we're all finished."

"Possible," Rosomon said, though she seemed unmoved by the prospect. "But have you thought about what happens to you if I refuse? If I take my chances? If I win?"

Keara gripped the brandy glass so tight she thought for a moment it might break. Rosomon was a tough bitch—she'd proved that at Oakhelm. This was all to be expected, but Keara could act tough herself.

"Of course I've considered it. I've also considered that there's no way you'll abandon your daughter. No way you'd want her to meet the same fate as that panther of hers."

A flicker of doubt in Rosomon's eyes. Then it was gone.

"You don't have it in you."

Keara let go of the brandy glass before she shattered it in her grasp. Damn this woman. Damn her stubbornness. Did she want them all to die at the hands of a mad priest?

"Don't push me, Hawkspur. I'm warning you—"

"Warning me of what?"

Keara fell silent. Embarrassed. Afraid. It only served to make her guts boil with anger. Damn this woman. "You have no idea what I'm capable of."

"I know exactly what you're capable of. And I know your limits. Do you think because you murdered your father it makes you ruthless? One old man. It will take more than that to seize power in a time of war. You are no threat to me, and neither is your Guild. You're no one. You and your people are lost. Once this is all over, no matter who wins, you'll be hunted down and slaughtered. I'm the only chance you've got, so give me my daughter and perhaps I'll allow you to negotiate for your life."

Keara slammed her hand down on the contract, chair scraping back as she shot to her feet. "These are the terms. I won't negotiate with—"

Someone shouted just beyond the double doors. It was impossible to make out the words, but the panic in that yell was unmistakable. Violence followed—the clap of a splintbow, the sound of something hitting a wall or the floor, then a snarl of rage.

Keara moved back from the long table, standing a little closer to Hesse, for all the good it might do her. She glared at the locked doors, hands teasing the knives at her side, just as they burst inward. One of her mercenaries slid along the floor, coming to rest a few yards inside the room. Blood pooled beneath his corpse, green tunic rent and torn as though he'd been mauled by an animal.

Tyreta prowled into the dining hall. Keara froze, suddenly forgetting those knives at her side as she saw what the Hawkspur girl had become. She'd seen her enraged before, seen the animal in her eyes, the claws that could rip and tear so easily, but now... now she looked every inch a beast as she scanned the room for prey. If she recognised her mother it did little to stifle the fury in her eyes, before they fell on Keara—the target of her hunt.

Keara moved—she had to—there was only death here. She had fought this animal before, and it had not ended well. The scar on her cheek was testament to that.

She leapt across the table, drawing one of her newly crafted blades, grabbing Rosomon and holding it to her throat. Hesse staggered back against the wall, long legs stumbling like a newborn foal as she plucked a splintbow from a nearby rack of weapons, wrenching back the stock to load a bolt in the breech.

"That's far enough," Keara snarled, too high-pitched, too panicked, but that didn't seem to matter right now. "I'll kill her. I mean it, your mother will die."

Tyreta stopped. There was blood on her lips. Yet more dripping from those wicked claws. Her eyes were no longer human as they glared across the room, and she looked like she barely understood, barely remembered anything but how to kill.

"What have you done to her?" Rosomon hissed.

Keara shook her head. "You think I did this?"

Hesse took a step forward from the edge of the room. Splintbow aimed at Tyreta. "I have the bitch. Just say the word."

"No!" Rosomon bellowed. "Don't hurt her."

Tyreta crouched, every muscle tensed, ready to strike as her eyes darted from one of them to the next, as though deciding who to rip apart first.

"Just give the order," Hesse whispered, calmly—the only one of them still in control.

Keara didn't know what to do. She had thought this would be easy. She'd already talked about loading all the dice, but now the table had been overturned and those dice didn't matter anymore. This whole thing was out of control.

Rosomon turned her head, despite the blade at her throat. "Hurt my daughter and there's no deal. No amount of bargaining will save you. There's no way you'll get out of this alive."

Tyreta raised her hand, pointing a clawed finger at Hesse. "Her," she breathed, a low growl more inhuman than anything Keara had ever heard. "She killed Cat. Tortured her, and I felt everything."

There were tears in those feral eyes. Inconsolable grief in that beast's voice.

"I've got her," Hesse repeated. "I can end this, just say it."

"Don't you dare," Rosomon snarled.

This was all slipping away. All Keara's well-laid plans. All she had suffered and forfeited to pull herself out of the mire. She had betrayed Sanctan, murdered her father, and now it was all going to shit. Damn Tyreta and damn the Hawkspurs to the Lairs. She needed them, there was no doubt about that. Without Rosomon this whole thing was over. And without Tyreta alive, her mother would never help her.

"Fuck this," Hesse said, raising the splintbow to sight down the barrel. She was going to shoot.

Keara shoved Rosomon aside, already drawing back the knife in her hand—the one with blue pyrestone. A flash of light filled her vision as she flung it toward Hesse, and it flared as she powered it with sparking energy. The blade soared, a flaring contrail in its wake, crossing the room with blinding speed to embed itself in Hesse's throat.

Silence as the light of that pyrestone sputtered out. Then a choking sound as Hesse fell to her knees, not enough time to even pull the trigger of her splintbow. It fell from her hands, clattering on the ground, and she just had time to paw at the blade in her neck before collapsing forward, face slamming against the stone floor.

No. This wasn't supposed to happen.

Keara ignored Rosomon, ignored the monster Tyreta had become, as she moved a little closer to her last friend in the world. A friend she had just murdered.

In the dim pyrestone light she saw that the dark glasses on Hesse's face were askew, one of the black lenses cracked. Her eyes were still open, eyes Keara had seen so rarely. It looked like they were glaring right at her. Accusing her. Damning her.

A roar, deafening in her ear. By the time she'd dragged her gaze from Hesse's corpse, Tyreta was on her, hands about her throat, powerful arms raising her into the air before slamming her onto the table.

All the air was knocked from her lungs, all thought of going for the one dagger still at her hip abandoned as she raised her hands, shielding her face before Tyreta raised a bloody claw.

"No!"

Rosomon rushed forward, stopping mere feet away, but her call for mercy was enough to stay that clawed hand. Tyreta held tight to Keara's throat, pressing her down on that table, blood still dripping from the corner of her mouth as her eyes bored into her victim with unbridled hate.

"Tyreta, don't do this."

At her mother's gentle words, Tyreta dragged her eyes from Keara, regarding Rosomon with little recognition.

"Don't do this." Rosomon's voice was soothing, but there was still an air of authority behind it. "This is not you. It's not who you are."

A lone tear beaded from Tyreta's eye, tracking its way down her cheek. For a moment the feral aspect faded from her face, her eyes bloodshot. Then she looked back at Keara, teeth still bared, hand still raised and ready to strike.

"Like it or not, we need her," Rosomon said. "And she'll be compliant. Work with us to defeat our enemies. Isn't that right?"

The hand gripping Keara's throat loosened ever so slightly, allowing her to speak. She would have chosen her words carefully, but right now there was only desperation talking.

"Yes, she's telling the truth, Tyreta. We need each other. I'll help you. Together we can defeat Sanctan, and put all this right. You'll have every webwainer in Torwyn on your side."

With those words, Tyreta let out a long breath of resignation. Or was it just exhaustion? Either way, she took a step back, shoulders sagging.

Now it was Rosomon's turn to glare down at Keara. "So we have a deal?"

Keara nodded. Maybe not what she had in mind, but at least she'd get to live. "Yes. Whatever you want."

Rosomon stepped back and Tyreta collapsed in her mother's arms. Keara tried to swallow down her envy. Despite what these women had been through, at least they had each other. The last woman Keara trusted was lying dead on the floor with a knife in her neck.

She was alive at least, and that would have to do... for now.

# ANSELL

He watched from the door. Grace had no idea he was there as she swung her legs on a chair too big for her body, scrawling upon the parchment at her table with a stylus. Legate Kinloth sat close, offering close instruction on her letters.

Willet. That was his name. He had asked her to call him by his first name, and Ansell supposed that Legate Kinloth was far too officious a title for a little girl. It was a nice gesture, an insignificant breach of protocol to make her more comfortable. The young legate was obviously thoughtful and attentive. Caring even. She would need such a man to watch over her, especially now.

"Would you give us a moment, Legate Kinloth?" Ansell said, entering the room.

Willet turned, startled. "Yes... Knight Commander."

He rose quickly and left them alone in the airy chamber. Grace did not even look up from the table as he drew closer to her. Over her shoulder he could see the letters she had scrawled. They were accurate enough, though her penmanship left much to be desired.

"You are learning quickly, Grace. Usually I see you drawing some picture or other."

Still she didn't look up. "The Archlegate says pictures are an affectatious distraction. Only the idols of the Wyrms should be displayed in plain view for all to..."

She stopped, clearly having forgotten Sanctan's exact words.

"That's a lot for you to remember, Grace. But...perhaps the Archlegate is right."

It seemed the appropriate thing to say, but now he was stuck for more words, unsure of how to tell her why he had come to visit. There was none other than the direct way.

"I have to go away for a while."

Grace nodded, still not turning to regard him. "Yes. You have your duties to perform."

He could sense no emotion in her reply. If it grieved her that he was leaving, she did not show it. But then how could she have understood the danger he was about to ride into?

"I don't know when I'll be able to return. Or if I will at all."

He wasn't sure if she even needed to know that last part. It seemed a cruel thing to tell a child, but again, if she felt any sense of loss she did not show it.

"I am sorry, Grace."

Before he could turn to leave, she slammed down the stylus. When she turned to face him he could see there were tears in her eyes, threatening to pour down her pale cheeks.

"You made a promise." Her voice almost faltered, but her anger won through.

"I know. And if I return I will keep that promise. We will still go away, you and I. To see the mountains and the sea."

"When?"

There was a question. "I cannot say."

"It doesn't matter anyway." She was angry now, but still managing to quell an infantile tantrum. Still acting brave, when she should not have to. "The Archlegate says adventures are for children. It is better for me to think on more mature matters. Not the fanciful daydreams of an infant."

She was parroting more of Sanctan's puerile maxims. Had she taken them to heart? Was Sanctan even now stripping away Grace's innocence, just as he had robbed the girl of her mother.

Ansell moved closer. "I do have to go. But I will return, Grace."

Another lie slipping so easily from his lips. In truth he had no idea if he would survive this. No idea what he faced on the road north. What devastation the Guilds might bring with them from Oakhelm.

"I understand," she replied quietly.

Did she? For all her maturity it was doubtful she could comprehend the horrors of this war.

"You understand I have a duty. It must come before all else."

But did it?

Ansell had already abandoned that duty and disobeyed his master to save this very child. Yet the memory of that was already fading. Now he was back in the fold of the Ministry, and serving Sanctan's will was once again his only priority.

"We all have a duty," Grace said, sounding more like an adult than ever. "The Archlegate says—"

He knelt beside her, taking her arms, forcing her to look at him. "You have to listen to me, Grace. Do not believe everything you are told by the Archlegate. He is not always as wise as he may seem. Rather, look into your own heart. It will tell you what is right, and show you the path you should take. Always. Will you do that? For me?"

She nodded, but couldn't manage to speak her answer. In that moment Ansell felt almost bereft. This little girl should not have to consider such things. Such a burden was not hers to carry. But if she was to stay safe without him, consider it she must.

He stood. "I must go now."

"Goodbye," she managed to say, before turning back to the table and the parchment of letters.

Ansell stood rooted for a moment. Unable to move. Unable to leave her here for the Wyrms knew what. He should have taken her up in his arms and fled. Should have cut down anyone who stood in their way and never looked back.

He turned, walking out into the corridor, feeling the knot tighten in his stomach. Before he had taken two paces, he heard the scrape of a chair, followed by feet padding along the tiled floor.

Grace rushed from the room, and Ansell barely had time to kneel before she flung her arms around him. He felt her tremble as he hugged her close and it almost broke him, almost made him forget those old vows he had spoken when he had abandoned Stone and taken the name the Ministry gave him.

Before he could think to speak, to offer some words that might take away her sadness, she let him go and scurried back into the room. Ansell stood, gritting his teeth, trying hard to shake off this feeling. A feeling he barely understood.

Willet still waited in the corridor, his eyes trained on the ground. Was he embarrassed at spying on such an intimate moment? Shocked to see one of the Draconate's holy warriors engaged in an act of tenderness? No matter.

"Will you watch over her while I am away, Legate Kinloth?"

Willet looked up, with an expression of surprise. Then he nodded. "I will."

It was enough. It would have to be.

Ansell left before his yearning to see Grace safe took over his need to perform his duties. He shook his head as he made his way down through the Mount, desperate to clear it of any thought other than the task at hand. If he was to go to war, that had to be his only focus.

Out in the courtyard, Falcar was already securing the harness of their horses, and strapping their meagre supplies to the saddle. A bedroll each, and some scant rations. Hopefully when they reached the Armigers to the north they would be appropriately accommodated.

Before he could help Falcar, Regenwulf approached him. The stout knight looked almost proud of them—like a father come to see his sons off to war.

"A dangerous road lies ahead," he said, as though it even needed saying.

"It does," Ansell replied.

"This could be the turning point in our fight. I envy you, brother. You will be there when we seize our victory. You will witness history as it is made."

If only Regenwulf could have known the doubt that clouded Ansell's mind. The doubt he had harboured for so long. That deep in Ansell's heart he had no yearning for victory. Only peace.

Regenwulf placed a hand on his shoulder. An odd gesture of intimacy. "Are you ready?"

A curious question. Did he suspect Ansell's reservations? "Of course. I am ready to do battle with the enemies of the Ministry, as always."

"This challenge may be the hardest you have yet faced."

Another curious comment. They all knew what lay ahead. What exactly was Regenwulf fishing for?

"I realise that."

Regenwulf regarded him intently. "I hope so."

Ansell knew he should have held his peace, but there was something behind Regenwulf's eyes. Some suspicion, perhaps? Ansell had disobeyed the Archlegate when rescuing Grace from the Burrows. Did his brother now also doubt Ansell's commitment to their cause?

"If you have something to say, brother, then say it."

Regenwulf's glare only grew more intent. "It is no secret you have your doubts, Ansell. About who we serve. About why. If you are to survive this, you need to—"

"I serve the Ministry. Now and always." He spoke the lie with such venom he almost convinced himself it was truth.

"Yes. You have made that clear with your words. Only—"

"Only nothing. Do not question my loyalty, Regenwulf. I know what is at stake."

In the face of Ansell's anger, any other man might have backed down, but not Regenwulf.

"Make sure you do. Prove it. In your deeds as well as your words. If you harbour any doubts, any at all, it will be the death of you."

And he was right about it all. He saw into Ansell's heart better than anyone, and, in his own way, this was perhaps Regenwulf's way of keeping him alive. As he always had done, since that first day he'd rescued Ansell in the Riveryard. Since he'd been no one but a boy named Stone.

"If one thing is certain, brother, it is that I have never shied away from battle."

A knowing smile crept up one side of Regenwulf's moustachioed mouth. "Aye. I know that all right." He glanced back toward the leering monument of the Mount. "I suppose you would have me look after that child for you, until your return."

So that was it. He saw Grace as Ansell's weakness. And maybe he was right. "I have already seen to her safety."

Regenwulf gripped Ansell's shoulder tightly. "I'll do it anyway. And we will be here, waiting on your victorious return."

Ansell should have accepted that. Should have done as Regenwulf said and forgotten about the Anvil until he was riding back to it, but he felt obliged to return the favour.

"And you, brother, should be mindful of what dangers lurk here. It is more than just the Guilds that threaten us."

If Regenwulf regarded the warning as a slight on the Archlegate he made no mention, responding instead with an easy shrug. "We are men of faith. Me more than most. The Wyrms will guide and protect me as always."

Ansell should have said more. Should have accused Sanctan directly and tried to persuade his brother of the man's iniquity. Told him that faith would not save him. That it might even betray him as it had Gylbard.

The words would not come, and all he managed instead was, "Goodbye, brother."

When he turned back to the horses, Falcar was already seated in his saddle. A squire held the reins to Ansell's horse, offering them with a bowed head as he approached. He mounted, taking a breath as he prepared for the long ride ahead.

"What was that all about?" Falcar asked.

Ansell resisted the temptation to look back one last time. "Our brother Regenwulf will miss us, is all."

Falcar considered that for a moment before barking a laugh. "I am sure. Like a bird whose hatchlings have just flown the nest."

Ansell kicked his horse, suddenly glad of Falcar's easy manner, if only for a moment. They trotted through the archway that led north from the Mount. The gates at the end of that tunnel were open, but before they reached the main road of the Anvil, Ansell spied someone standing to the side of the arch, half hidden in shadow.

Olstrum watched as they rode past, offering the faintest of nods. Ansell gave no response, wondering if it was an offer of good luck, or merely a reminder of what Ansell owed. Either way it meant little. He had indeed made an oath to Olstrum and intended to keep it, but there was nothing he could do about it now. First, he had a war to win.

Corvus troopers awaited them on the main road through the city, and as the two knights left the Mount they joined a union of Ministry and Armiger marching north to face the might of the Guilds. There was no bunting-strewn parade as they headed off to face the enemy. In fact it appeared the inhabitants of the Anvil cared little for the army making its way through their streets. Did they even know where they were going? That the Guilds were on their way, prepared to set this city aflame if it meant rooting out the very Ministry who had offered them salvation?

"We should have a crowd to cheer us on," Falcar said, putting Ansell's thoughts into words.

"Cheer us on to what?"

Falcar frowned. "On to victory against our enemies. What else?"

Enemies. Was that what the Guilds were? Certainly they stood in opposition to the Ministry, but it was doubtful the people of the Anvil saw it that way.

"Do you think the Guilds are the enemy of these people?" Ansell gestured along the sparsely occupied street.

Falcar shook his head in dismay. "Don't you?"

In truth he had no idea. Certainly the Guilds had held their people in bondage, and it was the Ministry's mission to see them released. But he also couldn't dismiss the memory of that woman hanging in the Mount gardens. Was that what saviours did? Hang any dissenters without trial?

"I cannot say," Ansell replied. "All I know is, I don't need a cheering crowd. Only the favour of the Great Wyrms."

He was sure that would be what Falcar wanted to hear, and was pleased when his brother knight nodded in response.

"You are right. And under their keen eye we cannot possibly fail in our crusade north."

"I would not be so complacent. Even with the favour of Ammenodus Rex, all servants of the Wyrms fall in time."

Falcar nodded his acknowledgment. "Indeed. But what a glorious end. To fall in service to the Draconate. Could there be any better way to die?" He sounded almost gleeful at the prospect.

"There is no glory in death, brother. No matter the cause."

Silence. Had Ansell gone too far, and so soon after almost revealing his feelings to Regenwulf?

"Are you all right, brother?" Falcar asked.

For a moment he considered opening up to Falcar. Instead he raised a hand to scratch his perpetually itching face, before thinking better of it. "I...of course. It is just better that we remember that despite the favour of the Wyrms, every man still controls his own fate. Faith can only deliver us so much strength in return."

Falcar nodded, but there was still a frown atop his handsome brow. He didn't speak again, and Ansell felt some relief that the conversation was over. When they finally marched from the city and onto the road north, the road that took them to war, that relief was consumed by trepidation once more.

# FULREN

Voices roiled in his head, babbling a discordant clangour of indiscernible words. Not just whispers but bellows, and he was lost in the darkness, consumed by it. He had been abandoned here in the black with nothing but a cacophony that threatened to crack his brittle skull.

*Blank them out.*

Those words were an order, cutting through the dirge.

*Make them silent, Fulren.*

"I can't," he wailed. "It's too loud. They're too strong."

*Drown them out, boy. You are their master. You are in command.*

His teeth gnashed, sweat beading on his brow, cold against his clammy skin. Those voices were so thunderous his ears were ringing, and strain as he might Fulren could not push them down, could not stymie the roar.

"I can't," he snarled. "I can't do it, damn you."

A scream from his lungs, a last desperate yell of pain and frustration that only stirred those voices to greater volume.

Firm hands grasped his shoulders, shaking him so hard his teeth rattled in his head.

*No. Be silent. Not a word from you, that will not stop the noise. Use your power. Your will. Become its master.*

Fulren issued a noise from his throat—a whimper so pathetic he felt ashamed. No matter how he tried he could not quell the fear. Emotions roiled—all the pain he had suffered, the sadness and grief at what he had lost. The anger and fear at what he faced.

*Don't get angry. That will not help you now.*

"I'm not strong enough. I'm nothing but a shell. A shade of what—"

*You are far stronger than you could ever imagine. Born of a line of kings. You are a Hawkspur, boy. What you face is nothing more than desperate gods; spirits long banished and forgotten. They beseech your attention because they are the weak ones. Dismiss them.*

He took a breath, surprised at how much it cleansed his lungs, and in turn his mind. In front of him he saw that outline, now so familiar. Lysander drew himself up to full height, the crimson vortex of light that formed his silhouette growing beyond all human proportion, the demon inside him reacting to his will.

*Obey me.*

Fear of the being in front of him began to overcome the terror inspired by those myriad voices. It was all Fulren could do to hold on to his faculties, his sanity stretching so thin it might break like a frayed thread. He was drowning in this darkness, but something inside would not give in. Would not allow that last link to reality to snap.

Focus—cold and grim—and he could suddenly hear every voice. No longer were they discordant. Now they were distinct. Each one clamouring for his attention.

"Be silent."

His voice was steady, in control. In response, those voices quieted just a touch, but with that also came clarity. Around him he began to see once more, the grey extent of the cavern coalescing. The outlines of the workshop more distinct with every passing moment.

*Yes. That's the way.*

His body shook at the effort, sweat running in rivulets, but the more he exerted himself the quieter the noise became. Breath came in panting gasps, his head spinning. The notion of power began to grow. Of mastering these beings who only wanted to do him ill. Who wanted to control him and make of him a slave.

"Be silent."

The words were in his head, but they boomed like the clash of a drum.

Too much.

Too far.

In that instant he had lost. Blackness returned.

The voices laughed in a deafening crescendo. Telling him he was weak. That he would be theirs in time.

Fulren began to fall, to slip from the real, dragged down and down further toward an infinite pool of despair. He should have fought. Should have railed against his inevitable doom, but he knew to resist was folly.

Better to let them take him... but no...

He tried to reach out, but he had only one arm left. Not enough to save him.

He could have run but there were no legs to carry him.

But if he gave in... let them win... succumb to their promises... they might make him whole again...

*Resist, boy. Do not surrender.*

"I can't."

But perhaps he could. Perhaps Lysander was right.

Even as he considered that notion, those laughing voices promised more. To make him more. To make him a god, if only he ignored the urgings of this worthless mortal. To slough off his earthly shackles.

Were they right?

Something grabbed him, but not within the corporeal confines of the workshop. This was in his mind, first one hand, then another. Grasping his soul, dragging him deeper into an ocean of darkness. Taking him beyond this plane and away to... where? A better place? Or to face his unearthly doom? Right now, it didn't seem to matter...

Red light, brighter than anything he had ever seen. Brighter than a sun—crimson in his vision, and Fulren could not close his eyes against it.

A demonic form, wings spread—a bright red angel of doom come to sweep those shadows away.

Fulren felt their disembodied hands release him, and with it he was suddenly left with no purchase. He fell, faster and farther than he could have thought possible, consumed by the void—that red demon disappearing into the distance...

Fulren hit the ground. He hissed at the sudden pain in his shoulder. Everything had stopped—the noise, the darkness. Breath came to him, cloying and fetid, but he sucked it in anyway, filling his lungs with it.

"I told you it wouldn't work." He almost sobbed at the familiar sound of Verlyn's voice. "You're pushing him too damn hard and too bloody fast."

He could see her outline as she crouched over his prone form. He had fallen from the chair, but it wasn't the first time. His shirt was drenched with sweat, but the cold of the floor offered relief as he rested on it.

With some effort, Verlyn helped him up and back into the chair. Surrounding him was the workshop again, the distant pyrestone lights casting everything in grey.

"I'm not pushing him hard enough," Lysander said. He was close, but as usual Fulren could not see exactly where. "If he doesn't overcome this weakness, he'll be no use to you in the fight to come. No use to anyone."

"You're driving him too close to the edge," she said. "You could kill him."

"I wasn't the one who brought him here. That's on you. If you want my help, we have to do it my way."

"All right, that's enough, both of you," Fulren gasped, when he'd filled his lungs enough to speak. "I'm not doing this for anyone else. I'm doing this for me. And Lysander's right—if I'm going to be any use I need to beat this."

He heard Verlyn let out a frustrated sigh. "I understand. More than you know, but this is too dangerous. You have no idea what powers you're messing with. What you might conjure."

"Maybe. But it could also be dangerous to do nothing. If I can't control the necroglyph, bend it to my will, then eventually it might control me. Then who knows what I'll be condemned to."

"Is that true?" Verlyn asked.

Lysander was close, Fulren could sense him even if he couldn't see him. "Perhaps. The necroglyph is designed to tear down the barrier to a world even I know little about. There are things dwelling there that can look through, see into our world and manipulate it. Sometimes they will offer gifts, but their intentions are always malevolent, unless they can be controlled. Whether Fulren likes it or not, his necroglyph has opened a window to his soul. Something is watching, waiting. If he cannot master it soon, then *it* will become the master. And he the slave."

"Great," Verlyn snapped. "That's just bloody great."

Fulren shook his head, still trying to shake the memory of what he had so recently experienced. "There's no other way. I need that power. I need to become the master."

"Even if it kills you?"

He tightened his grip on the arm of the chair with the one hand he had left. "Look at me. I'm dead already."

"No. That's not true, Fulren. You're a survivor. You've already proven that."

"Surviving isn't enough. This is no life. And if Lysander speaks the truth, then I'll lose my mind as well as my body if I don't learn how to control this curse."

But was it a curse? Or a gift? It was obvious it was both, but if he learned to control it, then he would at least become the master of his own destiny.

"The decision is made then," Lysander said. "The only question is whether Fulren's strong enough to succeed."

"I am." Fulren did not hesitate in answering, but there was still that little morsel of doubt lurking at the back of his mind. That one tiny seed that might grow to failure in the end.

Lysander moved nearer, and Fulren could feel his breath close to his ear. "You have to believe that, boy. If you have any qualms you will fail. Harness those words. Turn them into purpose. Dominate. Conquer."

"I will." Fulren did his best to sound determined.

Verlyn placed a reassuring hand on his shoulder once more. "All right then. But now he needs to rest. We'll dominate later."

Fulren moved her hand away. He was done with being mothered. "I don't have time for rest. We have to do this now."

Silence. He could vaguely see Verlyn gazing toward Lysander, the red motes of her silhouette moving with sullen speed.

"Then let's begin again," Lysander said.

Verlyn moved away as Fulren settled back into the chair. He closed his eyes for all the good it might do him—just a reflex action to help him concentrate on the necroglyph at his neck. It gave off a dull warmth and he began to focus on it—fuelling it as far as he could, feeling that heat turn to an itch, and then begin to burn.

The light around him extinguished, quicker than ever before this time. Was he starting to control it? No matter, those voices were returning—endless chatter in a sea of black. Instantly his teeth began to grind, his anger and pain and grief rising to the fore.

Before he could even think how he might defeat the myriad mouths at his ear there was a flash of crimson. Lysander's demonic form grew unspeakably large, a vast behemoth in the void, those red wings spread wide.

*Control it.*

That voice boomed, drowning out the ocean of noise that surrounded him. But even as Fulren forced his mind to seize control, he was falling.

*I said master it, boy,* that vast demon demanded.

All his will, all his strength, was funnelled into that one act, and he harnessed every painful memory, every grain of hurt he had suffered. His old malice toward Jagdor. The sacrifice he made at the Bridge of Saints. Ghobeq stealing his eyes in his moment of victory. And with those memories, a feeling of dominance began to surge. A sense of supremacy rising to the fore, as the voices wailed at his unexpected mastery of them.

*That's it, boy. Use those memories. Use them to—*

Fulren was torn away into the darkness on a hot gale.

Lysander's demonic form shrank to nothing, but so did those yammering voices.

He was pulled through a tunnel of black, whipped by the burning wind until...

\* \* \*

He stood on a blasted plain. The ground beneath his feet was cracked and parched, desiccated trees dotting the landscape. He raised his left hand—the one he had lost. Looking down he saw legs, and felt dry earth beneath bare toes, remembering how much he had missed them.

The caw of a bird pulled him from the reverie of his restored body.

A single crow sat on the parched branch of the nearest tree. It was the only other thing alive in this alien place, watching him intently, head flitting, feathers ruffling, but all the while its eyes were focused on him.

The silence was so pure. So cleansing. Fulren felt as though he could have let it wash over him forever.

*What do you want?*

A voice so close—one he didn't recognise. He turned, but there was no one there. Just him and the crow, and nothing else for miles around.

*I am here.*

Fulren turned to see the crow glaring at him, no longer agitated on that dried-out branch. "What are you? What do you—?"

*I asked first.*

It seemed a reasonable enough question, and from such an innocuous creature, but deep down he knew this was no crow. This was the thing that had plagued him. Stalked him from the shadowy recesses of his mind. Watched him suffer. The being that peered through the window opened by his necroglyph.

Still, he could not resist telling it the truth. "I need to be whole again. I need to fight."

He spoke the words before thinking on their implication. Would he enter some fell bargain with this demon by revealing his innermost yearning?

*I can give you that. You know I can.*

Of course it could, but what might it want in return? This was a covenant, pure and simple. He could have his heart's desire, and all he had to do was say yes. It had teased him with such promises before. Why shouldn't he accept now?

But Lysander had told him he must become the master here. The conqueror. If he succumbed to this offer, he was damned. Fulren didn't know much about this place or its sorcery, but he knew that much.

"No. I will make no deal with you. I will never become your slave."

*But you will*, said the crow.

Doubt began to cloud his thoughts. Any notion he'd harboured that he could be the master here began to fade.

Should he just give in? Take what was offered...?

No. He was Fulren Hawkspur. He had survived where all others might have perished. He had cheated death with nothing but his stubborn will. There could be no doubt in his mind. Not here. Not at the end. He had to be in control, not a puppet for some lurking horror.

"I am not yours. You have it all wrong. You are the one who will obey. You are mine to—"

The crow laughed and it was deafening, echoing across the flat dry land like a hurricane.

*Of course you are mine*, it said, voice dripping with disdain. *Foolish child. This is my temple, Fulren Hawkspur. My lair. There are things here far beyond your ken. Your attempt to taunt me is stupid, but I will forget your lack of respect. Instead, I make you the offer one more time. I can give you everything you desire. All you need do is—*

"Enough," Fulren snarled, channelling all his hate and fury toward that crow.

It silenced the creature, but only for a moment. *You dare bark at me, mortal.*

With its words, Fulren could hear the quiet whisperings of those voices in the distance, taunting him from afar. They threatened to bubble up, to deafen him again with their entreaties, but that held no fear for him now. He was no longer afraid. No longer burdened by doubt. No longer troubled by the unknown. Now he knew. This thing before him was less than a crow. Just a shade of... what had Lysander called it? A desperate god?

"I dare. I am the son of a warrior. The greatest to ever lay hands on a blade. I carry the blood of kings in my veins."

Again the crow laughed, but this time quieter than before. *King? Kings are nothing here. This place is—*

"Silence!"

Fulren bellowed his command. This time when the crow stopped its prating so too did the whispering voices it had conjured to torment him. He took a step toward the tiny creature, and in response its wings fluttered in trepidation, but it did not take flight.

"I am not yours. I never was. It is you who will serve. I will bend you to my will. Take your power. Use it as I see fit."

In response, the crow's eyes burned, glaring back at him in defiance, refusing to be cowed, even in the face of such superior will...

Fulren gasped, as his shadowy vision focused on the cave's interior.

Verlyn was close, the red motes of her face outlined against the dark, but she was not alone. Lysander looked down at Fulren, and for the first time his human form was so clear—no longer the crimson demon he could conjure at will. Just a man.

"Well?" he asked. "What happened?"

Fulren sank into the chair, his bunched muscles relaxing. "I think...I think I did it."

A smile crossed Lysander's face. "Show me."

Fulren swallowed down the spit that had pooled in his mouth. With little effort he began to fuel the necroglyph, feeling that familiar burning sensation, only this time instead of pain it was feeding him. Where before there had been whispers along with the promise of sorcerous energy, now there was nothing but silence. Nothing but the certainty that he was in control.

And in the dark of his vision he saw something in the corner of his eye. Dark wings, misty and ephemeral, began to sprout from his back where the necroglyph marred his flesh. The huge black wings of a crow, sprouting forth, surrounding him in night-dark blackness.

"Good enough?" he asked.

Lysander nodded. "A good enough start. But now the real work begins."

He moved toward a rack nearby, motioning for the others to follow. Verlyn pushed the chair closer, and Fulren could already make out the rack was covered by a velvet sheet. What lay beneath crackled with untapped energy.

Pyrestones.

With one hand, Lysander tore the sheet aside. Upon the rack was affixed a mannequin, arm and legs missing. In their place were hydraulic limbs, the metal winking in Fulren's greying vision...his glyphsight. Each was adorned with pyrestones, intricately studded into the steel. But that was not all. Alongside it was a domed greathelm, features blank upon the face. And there the final gift—a blade of such intricate design it almost took Fulren's breath away. Almost.

"Yes," he managed to whisper. "Time to get to work."

# ROSOMON

She glanced toward Tyreta as they rode, something she'd done a hundred times since they'd left the Web. Her daughter looked exhausted, but then that was hardly surprising after all she had been through. Tyreta just kept her eyes fixed on the surrounding woodland. How Rosomon yearned to gather her girl up in her arms and tell her everything would be all right, but she didn't know if that would have been a lie.

She had struck a dark bargain with Keara Hallowhill. A gamble that, should it pay off, might well seal her victory. If it didn't... well, they might all be doomed.

Rosomon turned her attention to the men riding with them. Kassian was his usual brooding self, and Ianto had chosen to remain silent on the long ride north. He had not even attempted to castigate her for leaving them behind at the Web and needlessly endangering herself. Despite that, there was something on his mind, for sure.

"Go on then," she said. "What is it?"

"My lady?" he replied, feigning ignorance, and failing at it. That in itself was reassuring. Ianto's lack of guile meant she could trust him above all others.

"What is wrong, Imperator? You have something to say, so say it."

He opened his mouth to protest his innocence once more but

thought better of it. A frown and a grimace as he picked his words carefully.

"I am just unsure it was wise to strike a bargain with the webwainers. They cannot be trusted. They have already betrayed one ally, and now..."

He didn't need to go on. They both knew the implications.

"I understand your concerns and believe me I feel them too. But without the Hallowhills we have little chance of defeating the Ministry and their allies. There really was no choice to make."

Not entirely true, but she had made a choice anyway. Seen her opportunity and taken it. Besides, she had seen the expression on Keara's face when it looked like their bargain might crumble. She wanted this alliance—and she needed it to work just as much as Rosomon did.

"I just hope the deal is worth the price we will have to pay," Ianto grumbled.

Glancing toward Tyreta, Rosomon knew it was. It had spared her daughter, and with a little luck might liberate the nation from Sanctan's hold.

"For now, we have the Hallowhills. That's more than we had a week ago. And if they betray us, then—"

A rustle of leaves among the surrounding woods. Kassian's blade rang from its scabbard, and Ianto kicked his horse closer to Rosomon. She barely had time to think on the danger before two riders trotted from the woodland and she recognised the green of their Talon uniforms.

"Thank the Guilds we have found you," said one of the scouts. Her face was filthy, riding leathers scuffed and mud-strewn.

"You have news?" Rosomon asked, expecting the worst.

"Our scouts have ranged west toward the Anvil and reported movement. The Corvus and Griffin Battalions have mobilised east to block our advance."

"Mobilised where?"

"A small town at a crossing on the River Mordant, my lady."

Kassian cricked his neck in annoyance, as though he had expected the move. "That's trouble."

Rosomon tried her best to ignore the prospect of another battle before they reached their goal. "Inform Guildmaster Oleksig we are on the way. And that we will be joined by the Hallowhills. How far is the Guild camp?"

The scout couldn't hide her look of surprise. "Another day north."

"Very good. We will make camp here. Tell Oleksig we will arrive tomorrow."

With an obedient nod, the scouts made their way back along the trail, before striking into the woods. Ianto had already dismounted, helping Tyreta down from her horse. She looked groggy, her eyes bloodshot from the red drop she had been forced to endure, but there was something else different about her, more sinister than mere grogginess.

Rosomon had witnessed the animal her daughter had become, seen how wild she was, with those claws and eyes. It had frightened her, but she had pushed that down, and her concern for Tyreta had made her dismiss the idea that her daughter was possessed of some feral sorcery. Now, as Rosomon watched Ianto guide her from the road, she began to wonder how much Tyreta had been consumed by that power, and how much of the old Tyreta remained.

They led their horses from the trail until they found a clearing. Kassian built a fire, and the four of them gathered around it as night fell. Tyreta gripped tight to the blanket around her shoulders, eyes lit up by the flames. Perhaps Rosomon should have let her be, and allowed her time to recover, but she could not fight that maternal urge. Carefully she took some bread and meat from their bag of rations and offered them to Tyreta.

"You need to eat," she whispered. "Get your strength back."

Tyreta shook her head. "I'm not hungry."

"Nonsense." Rosomon held out the bread. "There's hardly a pick on your bones."

In truth, the muscles along her daughter's arms and shoulders were even more defined than when she'd returned from the Sundered Isles.

Tyreta regarded Rosomon closely. Her face hung slack, but her eyes held their intensity. "Stop fussing, Mother."

"It's my job," Rosomon replied, vainly trying to make light.

She thought Tyreta might lose her temper, jump to her feet and rage, but instead she took the bread that was offered along with the dried meat.

"So we're in bed with the Hallowhills now?" Tyreta asked, tearing a piece of meat off with her teeth.

Yesterday Rosomon would have thought that a horrific idea, but how quickly things changed in war. "Yes. We need them."

Tyreta stared deeper into those flickering flames. "You should have let me kill her. Keara."

"I'll admit, I was in two minds whether to stop you, but I didn't have a choice. I have to pick the most expedient path, and right now this is it. Don't worry though. You might get your chance eventually."

Rosomon thought back to the conversations she'd had with her daughter in the past. Mostly they'd been about duty and deportment. Now they were about who should live and die. They would never have spoken so casually about these things before, but now they had both taken lives. Rosomon more than most.

She looked into those flames, wondering what Tyreta could see in them. "We might have more people to kill before Keara. Sanctan for one. That bastard Olstrum."

"Maybe not Olstrum," Tyreta replied, taking a drink of water.

"What do you mean?"

She shrugged. "Back in Castleteig, before Keara took me, I got the impression he was trying to free me. Just so he could get in your good books."

Rosomon almost laughed at the notion. "Whatever Olstrum wants, he wants it for his own ends. Much like Keara. Neither of them is to be trusted."

Tyreta gave a sudden shiver, pulling the blanket tighter about her. Rosomon resisted the urge to put an arm around her. Or was she afraid to?

"I can't get it out of my head," Tyreta whispered. "What they did to Cat. It was like I could feel it. Like I was suffering every cut of the knife right along with her."

"Use it," Rosomon replied. "It hurts so use it. Endure this pain, and let it fuel you. It will help you when we finally face our enemies, because we can show them no mercy. There will be time enough to grieve when this is over."

She gritted her teeth, placing a hand on Tyreta's, who gripped it back. It had been so long since she had held her daughter's hand, it almost brought her to tears. Tyreta might have been a woman grown, a warrior even, but there was still something of that gentle, headstrong little girl in there.

"And I thought I'd changed," Tyreta whispered.

Rosomon had never considered how different she was from when this all started. It was true though. She had been forged anew, and didn't really know if she liked what she had become.

"So what now?" Tyreta asked. "For me I mean. Are you going to make me sit in the supply train for the rest of this, now that I've failed my mission?"

"If that's what you want," Rosomon replied, half hoping it was. "You could go back to Wyke, if need be. There is plenty there to—"

"No. That's not what I want. I need to fight. I know I haven't done a great job so far. I know I've let you down but—"

"Nonsense." Rosomon squeezed Tyreta's hand, turning her head so they were facing one another. "You took on an impossible task. No one could have achieved what you did—not even my best swordwright. I could not have asked for more from you."

"So . . . what now?"

Rosomon smiled at Tyreta's naivety. Not so much the wild beast after all. "So, I've been asking you to rise to your responsibilities for longer than I can remember. What better time than now. We have a war to win, and I'll need you to help me do it."

Tyreta looked confused, as though not quite believing her mother's words. "Are you serious? There'll be danger ahead. You know we might—"

"There's danger ahead for all of us. We have to face it. We have to destroy it. It's that or there will be no Guild for you to inherit."

Tyreta's eyes shone in the firelight, and not for the first time Rosomon saw that animal aspect. "I . . . don't know what to say."

"You don't have to say anything." She tried on a smile, but it just didn't seem to fit anymore. "But I do need you to tell me what's going on. Inside you. Something happened in the Sundered Isles and I need to know what it was. What did they do to you?"

Tyreta shook her head. "I was... given something. From Father's nightstone. It's a gift, but... sometimes I can't control it. I can see everything. Feel everything. It's like I've been awakened to a new world, and I'm not sure what my place is in it."

Rosomon hardly understood, but it was obvious her daughter was suffering with it. "We've all gone through changes. Things that have been forced upon us."

"It's not like that. It's this place... it doesn't feel like home anymore. It's like I don't belong."

Those words resonated in Rosomon's head. She too felt like a different woman. "I know what you mean."

"Do you?" Tyreta sounded annoyed at Rosomon's attempt at sympathy. "I can hear your heart beating, Mother. And this food fills my belly but I'm still hungry. It feels like I'll never be full again."

Tyreta's eyes shone brighter, more intense, her pupils narrowing to slits. It filled Rosomon with dread, but she still held tight to her daughter's hand.

"When this is all over, we will deal with the changes we've had to endure. I'll make this right. I'll put things back the way they were."

Tyreta gritted her teeth, quelling whatever was welling up deep within. "Nothing will ever be the same."

Again, Rosomon wanted to put her arms around her daughter. Hold her close, tell her this was just a fleeting moment and they would get through it together. Instead she had to satisfy herself with holding Tyreta's hand. There had always been a rift between them—and Rosomon knew that was as much her fault as anyone's. She had always wanted to protect Tyreta, and would have done anything to keep her safe, but now it appeared the last thing her daughter needed was protection. More likely it was the world that needed protecting from Tyreta.

Rosomon let go of her hand, standing and flattening her skirts. "Get some rest, we have a hard ride ahead. Tomorrow is a new day, and maybe things will be clearer then."

Tyreta looked up at her—her eyes doleful and innocent, the way Rosomon had always remembered. "Yeah, maybe."

With a nod, Rosomon made her way to her bedroll and settled for the night. As she drifted toward sleep, she saw Tyreta was still staring into those flames. This time they were lit yellow, like a panther on the hunt. An animal searching for prey.

# ANSELL

Two days of riding, and they eventually reached their goal. The sun was dropping behind the distant hills as they plodded through the busy encampment. Pennants fluttered in the breeze, marking the griffin, bear and crow, but no dragons of the Ministry flew proudly alongside. It seemed Ansell and Falcar would be the only ones to represent the Archlegate in the battle to come.

"We need to find a place to pitch a tent," Falcar said, drawing back his reins. "And more importantly, get some food."

Before Ansell could tell him what a good idea that was, an adjutant made his way toward them with purpose. He wore the dark armour of an Ursus trooper, green flashes on his arm denoting his rank, bear pelt across his shoulders.

"Ansell Beckenrike?"

"I am the knight commander," Ansell replied.

"Marshal Sarona wishes to see you." He pointed over his shoulder toward a dilapidated building on the edge of the camp, flying the flags of all three Armigers.

"Now?"

The adjutant shrugged. "That's what she said. We've been waiting—"

"You'll wait as long as we say," Falcar snapped.

The adjutant looked as though he might argue, but thought better of it. "Suit yourselves. I'll tell her you've arrived, and you'll be along... whenever you say." He turned, marching off across the camp with an imperious gait that made him look more waddling duck than officer.

"Is this what we're in for?" Falcar growled. "To be ordered around by lackeys? Undometh's teeth, how far we have fallen."

Ansell let out a long breath, feeling as frustrated as his brother. "I don't like this any more than you do, but the Archlegate has sent us to do his bidding and we must obey. There's no harm in finding out what the plan is."

He dismounted and handed his reins to Falcar. Ansell's backside was sore from the ride, but a few strides and the numbness receded. Guards had been posted outside the old wreck of a building, but they did not bar his way as he moved toward the entrance. Clearly they'd been told to expect the hulking knight with a scarred face.

Inside, the ruin had no roof to speak of, its walls thick with vines, choking it to death. At the centre of the structure stood a table, and Sarona was glaring at it, fists clenched as she regarded the yellowing maps laid out before her.

Leaning against one rotting brick wall was Kagan Terswell—marshal of the Griffin Battalion. He looked just like a patron in a backstreet inn, standing without a care, tankard in his hand.

Sarona glanced up as Ansell entered. Kagan barely even acknowledged him.

"You're here," Sarona said admonishingly. "We expected you yesterday."

Not quite the mutually respectful start Ansell had been hoping for. "I am here now, Marshal. Ready to perform the Archlegate's bidding. I assume you have formulated a plan of attack?" He gestured to the poorly drawn maps Sarona was staring at with frustration.

Terswell smirked, almost spilling his drink. "Yes and no, Drake. We were just disagreeing on the details before you arrived."

Sarona prodded the map with a slender finger. Ansell glanced down at the depiction of the terrain, seeing that the road from their current position ran northeast, following the landship line and crossing a river. There was a town drawn at the crossing.

"Our scouts tell us the Guilds are on the march along this main road which follows the landship route. They will cross the bridge here and be funnelled into the town of Alumford." She gestured to the poorly drawn houses on the map. "I've suggested we wait in ambush in this urban area. Lots of disused mills. Plenty of cover from both sides. But Marshal Kagan disagrees."

Terswell shrugged his broad shoulders. "I think we should blow the bridge, just as the Guild forces are crossing it."

Ansell had heard the Griffin Battalion were fond of such strategies. "You mean obliterate it as you did at the Forge?"

A smile crept up Terswell's face. "Of course."

"Surely the Guilds will not fall for that a second time."

A brief shadow of doubt crossed the marshal's brow. "How do you know that?"

"Because *I* would not fall for it twice. I would cross at the ford further north of the town." Ansell gestured to its position on the map. "It is less exposed and any potential ambush would be spotted a mile away. We should concentrate our defences there."

"No," said Sarona. "That would take the entire Guild army miles out of its way. They won't waste time on that. They'll take the most direct route to the Anvil which is right through Alumford. Besides, I've already begun to install artillery at the crossroads."

"And the Guilds will already know it."

Sarona shook her head. "My scouts have seen no sign of enemy spotters."

"But they will have seen sign of you. Rosomon Hawkspur controls the Talon. They will be watching your every move."

Marshal Sarona pressed her fist into the table once again. "So what do we do?"

"Carry on doing what you're doing. Make them think that is your plan, but position the bulk of your army in the woodland here." Ansell stepped forward and pressed his own finger to the map."

"No. I won't split my forces. If the Guilds march with their entire host, I won't have enough troopers to defend the town."

"If you don't you'll—"

"I've already lost too many." It was a growl from the bottom of Sarona's throat. Ansell could sense her rage, visceral and barely held in check. "That fucking bitch drowned my people at Oakhelm."

"Just as you drowned Wyke," Ansell replied. "Both clinical moves to provoke the enemy, and you are falling for it. You should not let your desire for revenge cloud your judgement."

Sarona shook her head, as though clearing the fog of hate from her mind. "Wherever they cross they will eventually have to pass the town. I will be waiting at the crossroads. The bridge will stand."

Sarona's forces would be sitting in wait for the Guilds to fall on them. Alumford was accessible from four directions, ripe for a counter-ambush.

"I could take a small mobile force and wait within the woodland. Then, no matter which direction they advance from we could strike to their rear as you strike from the front."

"No," Sarona said, her mulishness making Ansell clench his fists in frustration. "We wait at the crossroads. All of us. I won't split my forces and risk them being picked off. If we fortify the town we can adjust our defensive structure no matter which direction they come from." She pressed her finger to the map again at the southern side of the bridge. "You will be waiting here with the Griffin Battalion. Visible from across the bridge to draw them toward your position."

There was a clatter as Marshal Terswell flung his cup across the room. "Like sacrificial lambs?"

"What's the matter. No stomach for a real fight? Is that why you're so desperate to sabotage that bridge?" The two marshals stared at one another for a moment, before Terswell lowered his gaze. "The Guilds won't even reach your position before we attack their flank with artillery. So don't worry, Marshal. You'll be fine."

Ansell stared at the map. There were so many ways this could go wrong. Sarona was relying on the Guilds marching straight into their trap, and it seemed her mind was made. But what could he do? He had no authority here.

"Very well, Marshal Sarona. I will prepare."

"You do that," she said without looking up.

Terswell stared at the ground like a boy who'd lost his favourite toy, but he had no more to say. It was obvious he was as much a subordinate as Ansell, and his opinion mattered for nothing.

Outside, Ansell breathed in a deep lungful of the night air, taking some comfort from the smell of campfire smoke. At least he would get to spend some time in the warm before he was thrown to the wolves in a few days.

When he eventually found Falcar at the edge of the camp, night had fallen and a fire roared in wait for him. Their horses were being tended by one of the Armiger farriers and their tents had already been erected. It was a blessed relief as he sat by the fire, and Falcar handed him a bowl of hot, watery stew.

"Well?" Falcar asked. "What did you find out?"

Ansell tasted the stew. It was tepid but spicy; far from the worst thing he'd eaten on a campaign like this. "I learned that we are little more than bait."

Falcar considered his words as he took his sword and drew it, before proceeding to oil the blade with a rag. "The Wyrms protect, brother."

Did they? Ansell was beginning to wonder, since they had done such a poor job up to now. He finished his stew in quick order, sipping the dregs from the bowl, all the while thinking about the injustice of all this. And not just for him. Watching Falcar oil his sword, preparing for war, he could no longer quell his feeling of guilt.

"I am sorry, brother," he said.

Falcar stopped what he was doing and turned to regard Ansell with confusion. "For what?"

Ansell sighed. He should have held his peace, but he could not help but unburden himself. "I feel you have been condemned along with me in this. I was sent here as punishment for my transgressions. The Archlegate has seen fit for me to pay a penance. And here you are, paying it right alongside me."

Falcar shrugged casually and smiled that familiar easy smile. "We are brothers, Ansell. We always have been, and will be unto death. I would stand beside you in the face of any danger." Then his smile fell from his face, his eyes growing more serious than Ansell had ever seen. "Besides, we are all forced to perform tasks that we might question... but obedience is our duty."

"It is. But sometimes..." He stopped short of saying his true feelings. Of confessing his need to be free of the burden of his rank and title.

Falcar reached across and slapped a hand to Ansell's shoulder. "I know. This whole thing is unconscionable. It is an insult that we should be made to tolerate it."

"You think so?" Ansell had never expected to hear such words from one of his brothers. He had always thought himself alone in his questioning of the Archlegate's will, and it offered hope that it was not just he who had doubts.

"Of course. We are being forced into a role to which we are wholly unsuited. We should be in charge. Not following these mercenaries like temple serfs." He looked at Ansell and fell silent, seemingly embarrassed at his sudden outburst. "My apologies, brother. I should not speak out of turn. The Archlegate clearly has a plan, and we should not question it."

"Do not apologise." For a fleeting moment Ansell thought that perhaps he might have a kindred spirit in Falcar. A brother who might share his own reservations. "If it makes you feel better, I too harbour my own doubts. I have been tasked with things in the past that have never sat right in here." He tapped a hand to his chest.

Falcar opened his mouth to speak, perhaps a confession, but thought better on it.

"What?" Ansell asked, curious to know what his brother might say.

Falcar shook his head. "It's nothing. I should not share my fears. Least of all with you."

Ansell should have let the matter lie, but he knew Falcar was on the brink of a confession. One that might settle matters in Ansell's own mind. "You can tell me. I don't think anyone would understand better than I."

Falcar let out a long sullen sigh. "It's just that I... have held doubts for the longest time now. Questioned my purpose. The things I have been forced to do. When we killed that witch at the library.

Wounded that boy. I know it is heresy to doubt our actions or the man who set us to them, but..."

"It is only natural you would question what we have been forced to do. It goes against every tenet we are bound to. The Knights of the Draconate are bred to protect the people of Torwyn, in body and soul. I too have been ordered to perform duties I did not relish. They haunt me still."

Falcar nodded his understanding. "They must, I am sure. Our part in the death of Sullivar was... unfortunate. Even though he was a tyrant I would rather he had seen the light of the Wyrms than..."

Falcar stopped, as though the memory of that day was too painful to recall. All Ansell could think was how little a tyrant Sullivar had been. He was certainly no more wicked than Sanctan.

Falcar looked at him again. "It is just... the sins I have committed in the name of the Draconate go beyond that. Something I was forced..."

Again he fell silent, too pained by his memories to share them.

"Tell me," Ansell asked.

Falcar stared into the fire, all his mirth fled. He looked as grim as Hurden, as steely as Regenwulf.

"I was tasked with seeing a family taken from the Anvil. I led a group of Revocaters in the deed. Took a mother and her child from their home, and forced them from the city. I had no idea who they were, but I was ordered to dress as any other civilian to do the task. Like some common pirate plucking innocents from the coast to sell as slaves."

Ansell felt a sudden tingle along his spine. Could his brother be speaking of Olstrum's family? "Where did you take them?"

"That's the thing—it wasn't too far from here. There's a farm fifteen, twenty miles north. Gravedell, I think it was called. We handed that family over to mercenaries who waited there. I just... I can't get the image of that woman and her children out of my head. They made no fuss about any of it, as though they were resigned to their fate. When I returned I didn't even ask what they had done— but what could they have done? It was obvious they were just pawns in some game. And I was made a pawn right alongside them."

Ansell had also played his part in this game. And he too was a pawn in it—easy enough to sacrifice so the king might survive. "Better not to think on it now."

"Easier said than done." The smile was back on Falcar's face, but it was hollow. "Do you think the Wyrms will forgive us for such dark deeds? If those deeds are performed in their name, surely we are absolved of any sin?"

"The innocent shall be spared from iniquities, brother. You know that as well as I."

Even as he parroted the words, Ansell could taste how sour they were. He knew they would both be punished in the Lairs forever for what they had done. But perhaps, now that he had an inkling of where Olstrum's family were, he could assuage his guilt a little by satisfying the oath he had made to save them. If he lived long enough.

More likely he would soon be dead...just as Sanctan had planned.

# TYRETA

They rode into camp just as the sun had crested the distant treetops, greeted by a sight she never thought she'd witness. When she'd left her mother to find Merigot, the Guild army had been nothing but a bunch of sorry civilians and a few Titanguard. Now it looked more than a force to be reckoned with.

The camp sprawled as far as she could see in either direction, pennants flying for the Bloodwolf and Mantid, Ironfall and Marrlock. Guild miners polished their instruments, playing the odd refrain to one another. Armiger troopers stood vigilantly, along with Blackshields and the Talon. Lady Rosomon was greeted with deference—a bow here or a nod of respect there. Tyreta was even met with her own shouts of welcome and the odd wave from people she'd never seen before.

When they reached the centre of the encampment, they were welcomed by squires only too happy to take their horses, and after dismounting Tyreta recognised the tall figure of Oleksig Marrlock making his way to meet them.

"Good to see you alive, Hawkspur," he said, gripping a pipe in one corner of this mouth.

Tyreta thought he must be addressing her mother, but when Marrlock grabbed her and squeezed her in a tight embrace she almost laughed at the shock of it. She had never met the Guildmaster of Marrlock before, but it seemed all former propriety had been abandoned.

Maugar she did recognise as he stomped closer, nodding his greeting. There was also a woman with him, dark hair shaved close to her temples, sword slung at her hip. His daughter, Xorya, no doubt.

"Glad you're with us," she said to Tyreta.

"Yes," Maugar grunted. "Looks like your gamble paid off, Ros. But we were told the Hallowhills would be here."

"They will be, soon enough."

Maugar ran a hand through his beard. "I hope you know what you're doing."

Lady Rosomon didn't answer, and Tyreta could sense the unease. Everyone was watching them now, dozens focused solely on her, and all she wanted to do was flee in the face of that attention. Just as she thought she might run, an Armiger officer of the Bloodwolf made his way toward them before offering a curt bow to her mother.

"Marshal Rawlin," Rosomon said. "I trust all is in hand?"

"It is, my lady, but there is much to discuss. The Talon have scouted west, and report Ministry forces entrenched at Alumford. We will have to use the crossroads there if we're going to reach the Anvil before it is relieved by Armiger forces from the south. It looks like a battle is unavoidable."

"Very well. Is everyone assembled?"

"They are," he replied, turning on his heel to lead the way.

As the group followed Rawlin, Tyreta was unsure of what to do until her mother turned, giving one of those almost imperceptible nods. One of those *come along* gestures she was so used to. With no other choice, Tyreta joined the group, bewildered at the speed things were moving. When she had left, the situation had appeared almost hopeless. Now they were an army, ready to go to war.

Rawlin marched them toward a lonely cottage sitting in the shadow of the tree line. They filed past the ominous figures of Thalleus Brisco and Borys Marrlock standing at the entrance, and crowded into what had once been a cosy sitting room. Now it had been cleared, and turned into a war room, complete with a table whose surface had been carved with a map of the surrounding land.

Marshal Rawlin stood next to the table, before unsheathing the dagger at his belt. He stabbed it into the wood, slicing a gash right across it. "Our road toward the Anvil." Then he gouged another line across the first. "The River Mordant." He stabbed his finger at where the lines crossed. "The Griffin Battalion, and what remains of the Ursus, wait for us at the crossroads here. The only place to make the crossing is this bridge at Alumford."

Maugar leaned his bulk over the table. "It'll be rigged with explosives by now. Whoever crosses that bridge will be blown to shit."

Rawlin shook his head. "No. The Talon have already checked the stanchions under cover of darkness. There are no charges."

"Almost as though they want us to advance along that route," Rosomon said. "And if we do, we'll no doubt be walking into an ambush. We could divert our advance to the north but that will add days to the journey."

The gathered crowd around the table pondered the issue, before Rawlin tapped his finger at the crudely drawn map north of the crossroads. "Even if we do move north, chances are they'll have a force waiting there too. Most likely in the woodland south of the ford."

"Then there's no advantage to extending our route north," Rosomon replied. "And moving south takes us closer to the Phoenix and Tigris Battalions making their way to the Anvil. We cross at Alumford. There's no other way."

Oleksig took his pipe from his mouth, blowing pungent smoke across the room. "They'll be ready for us. We'll be walking right into their trap."

"So we need a diversion," Rosomon replied. "Something to—"

She stopped as someone yelled outside. Tyreta could hear a commotion through the open door, and two Armiger troopers rushed by the little window. Rosomon was the first to react, making her way outside, and Tyreta followed closely, ready for trouble. People were hurrying toward the east, and the sound of startled voices pealed across the encampment.

In the distance, the lumbering form of a stormhulk made its way toward them. Then another, the sound of them growing more distinct—their hydraulics humming in time to the echoing stamp of their legs as they churned up the road.

Tyreta followed her mother as she made her way to greet them, and they pushed past the gathered troopers watching nervously, weapons trained on the new arrivals. As she reached the front of the crowd, she recognised Keara walking at the head of her armoured column, untroubled by the score of splintbows pointed at her.

The pit of Tyreta's stomach grew hot, saliva pooling at the corners of her mouth, and she gripped her fists tights lest those claws burst from her fingertips. The arrogance of this woman—just strolling into camp like she was a conquering hero come to save the day.

Keara stopped, holding up a clenched fist, and behind her the striding stormhulks came to a standstill. Then she regarded Lady Rosomon with a sardonic smile. "Am I on time?"

"You are," Rosomon replied, sounding in no mood for theatrics as she turned and led Keara back toward the little house at the edge of the wood.

All the while Tyreta resisted the urge to look Keara in the eye, unsure of what she might do if that woman offered her even the slightest provocation. Once back inside, the tension was almost palpable when Keara showed her face. Not too long ago, everyone here had been fighting the Hallowhills. Now they were planning their next advance right alongside them.

Rosomon regarded everyone in turn, making sure she had their attention. "Now the Hallowhills are here we have an opportunity to turn the Ministry's ambush against them. They have no idea whose side the Hallowhills are on, so Keara's forces will make their way along the river, crossing the shallows at Bullcross and approaching Alumford from the south. We will advance toward the bridge. When all attention is on us, the Hallowhills will attack the Ministry forces from the rear, giving us an opportunity to cross and take them head-on."

"Agreed," Keara said, as though she had any say in this at all.

The rest of them grumbled their assent. It was obvious none of them were happy with having to fight alongside the Hallowhills, but this was an opportunity they could not pass up. Tyreta wiped her mouth, managing to quell her disgust at being forced to stand near Keara, to fight beside her.

As she looked at that crudely carved map, she could almost see the battle unfold before her. But even if they won it would not be enough. It seemed her mother was taking each obstacle as it came, but Tyreta couldn't shake the feeling that even if they beat the Ministry at Alumford, Sanctan would still be a step ahead of them by the time they reached the Anvil.

"It's all well and good winning this battle, but what then?" she asked, conscious that all eyes had turned toward her. "I mean...if we win at the river, we still have to take the Anvil. Do we have a plan for that?"

Her mother regarded her with a strangely satisfied look. "A good question. And one we should discuss in private." She turned to the others. "If there is nothing else, I suggest you all make your preparations. We march toward Alumford tomorrow."

There were no other questions, as some of them bowed, while others, like Maugar and Rawlin, merely turned and left the little cottage. As Keara made her way toward the door Rosomon said, "Not you."

Keara turned, smug smile wavering, hand pressed to her chest in mock surprise. "You want to talk to me? In private? What an honour."

The three of them were alone now, and Tyreta's fists bunched tight as she fought to stay calm. As her mother regarded her, it was all she could do not to launch herself at Keara.

"On the way back here, you suggested Olstrum wanted an alliance," Lady Rosomon said. "That he could be persuaded to our cause. How do you know this?"

Tyreta managed to drag her eyes away from Keara. "He asked that I do him a favour. Said he wanted me to send his sincerest regards. I guess he had planned that I be returned to you. And I would have been, if this one hadn't got in the way."

"Look." Keara raised her hands in mock surrender. "Mistakes were made, but we're all friends now. And if we're talking about Olstrum, I think I can shed some light on that. He regrets his position. Wants the Guilds to win. He only did as Sanctan demanded because his family would have been in danger if he'd refused. He could be a good ally to have on our side; there's not much goes on within the Anvil he doesn't know about. If you want, I'm sure I could give him a little nudge, persuade him that the Guilds are the best option."

Tyreta almost spat her reply. "Didn't you betray him the last time you saw him? Wasn't your deal for me to be handed to my mother? You seriously think he'll trust you now?"

Keara frowned as though it were a stupid question. "Olstrum knows the game. He won't hold a grudge, and I'm sure he'll see sense in joining us. Doesn't matter who tells him."

"Do you really think he can be persuaded?" Rosomon asked. "And even if he could, what use would he be?"

Keara grinned wider. It was a wicked smile full of white teeth that Tyreta would have been only too happy to smash. "Olstrum can open the door to every bastion in the Anvil. He could give us a route straight to Sanctan. Could help end this with one turn of a key."

Rosomon looked at Keara gravely. "And you could find him if you got inside the city?"

"I could put out a discreet word. I know enough of his contacts."

Tyreta had heard enough. "Mother, you must be mad. You seriously think we can trust her with something as important as this?"

Keara turned to her, those bright eyes darkening. "You keep doubting me, girl, you'd better be ready to get those claws out again."

Her hand drifted to the dagger at her side. In response, Tyreta felt the nails begin to extend from her fingers.

"Enough of this," Rosomon snapped. "Hallowhill, you need to get inside the Anvil. Find Olstrum. Parley with him."

Keara shook her head. "No. I need to lead the attack at Alumford. My people are relying on me to fight alongside them. Olstrum will have to wait."

Rosomon shook her head. "Your webwainers are more than capable of launching the attack without you mothering them. You won't be missed."

Keara considered her words for a moment, opening her mouth to argue, before reconsidering. "All right then. My people won't like it, but I guess you're in charge."

"Glad you've finally realised it. You can use the distraction of the battle to slip past the Ministry forces. Getting into the Anvil without being seen will be a little trickier."

As they mused on it, Tyreta found herself unable to keep her mouth shut again. "Mother, you can't possibly trust her with this."

"I don't," Rosomon replied. "But we have a common goal. Keara will do what's best for us all—won't you?"

Keara's face was a picture of insincere innocence. "Of course."

"Mother, she'll betray us the first chance she gets."

"No. Keara needs us as much as we need her. If Sanctan wins we're all doomed. Agreed?"

Keara shrugged as though the answer were obvious. "Of course, agreed."

"Not agreed," Tyreta snapped. "Not agreed at all. I don't trust her as far as I can sling her uphill. I'm going with her to the Anvil. She's not leaving my sight."

Silence, as Tyreta waited for her mother to disagree. To tell her it was too dangerous. To chide her stupidity.

"All right," her mother said, eventually. "That's probably a good idea."

"It is?" she said, not quite believing it. Despite her mother's talk of fighting back together, she hadn't expected her to agree so easily.

"You are the only one I can trust with this."

Keara took a step forward, almost planting herself in between them. "Wait a minute—I don't need someone to hold my hand. I can do this without—"

"We need Olstrum's help." Rosomon cut her off at the quick. "This is the best way. He knows the both of you. He is more likely to trust us to do the right thing if he knows the alliance between Hawkspur and Hallowhill is a strong one. So you both go."

There was nothing Keara could argue with, and she glanced toward Tyreta. "I suppose you'll have to put off killing me for later."

Almost like Keara had read her thoughts on the matter. "Yeah, maybe I will."

"Thanks," Keara replied, not looking worried in the slightest.

"This is not a joke," said Rosomon, done with their bickering and fixing her gaze on Keara. "If anything happens to my daughter, I'll hold you responsible. Any arrangement we might have made will be moot."

The perpetual wry grin on Keara's face wavered for a moment. "I'll make sure she's well looked after. Not a scratch, trust me."

Before Tyreta could protest that she didn't need coddling, her mother said, "Then you'd both better get some rest. Who knows if there'll be another chance before you get to the Anvil."

Keara bowed extravagantly before strutting from the little cottage. Tyreta followed her out, watching her make her way toward the Hallowhill encampment. That urge to kill was still there, lurking in the back of her mind, but at least she could control it now. Hopefully she'd be able to keep it that way... at least until they found Olstrum.

# FULREN

The metal legs were connected by a leather sleeve, buckled about the waist and thigh—an ingenious piece of design much more comfortable than the rig Ashe had created for him. Their pneumatics responded to the merest shift of his weight or flexing of a leg muscle, reacting intuitively as he moved. Each stanchion was articulated like the hind leg of a beast, and he walked with plantigrade locomotion, granting him stability and balance. But he could also extend his gait to digitigrade or even unguligrade, elevating his height to seven feet and allowing him to move at speeds he never thought possible, with a grace and dexterity he had thought lost forever.

Today, though, Fulren was concentrating on an altogether different piece of his missing puzzle. He sat on a bench, stripped to the waist in the cold of the cavern. Lysander was silent as he strapped the metal prosthetic to the stump of his left arm, tightening the drawstring of the leather sleeve that fitted across his shoulders, buckling the straps that secured it across his chest and neck.

"Remember what we talked about?" Lysander asked in his deep voice.

"I remember," Fulren replied, already feeling the necroglyph agitate, sensing the pyrestones set in the metal alloy of the arm respond to his will. He flexed his fingers, hearing the hiss of hydraulics and the sigh of those well-oiled joints.

Against the grey murk of his vision, the pyrestones in the arm shone brightly, illuminating the darkness around them. When he glanced down at his body it almost looked like he was whole again.

"Now it's time for this," Lysander said.

He stood some feet away, but Fulren could see him outlined against the dim grey of the workshop. In his arms he carried a huge hunk of metal, a sword the likes of which Fulren had never seen, inlaid with pyrestones from pommel to tip. It looked huge and unwieldy, but Lysander held it out with reverent pride.

Fulren stood, swallowing down his apprehension as he reached for it. When Lysander placed the grip in his palm, Fulren tested the full weight, feeling how unwieldy it was. The four feet of thickset blade reminded him of the one he had crafted in Nyrakkis, only this weapon was much less crude. Lysander was indeed a true craftsman, but it didn't take away from the fact that the sword was almost too heavy to lift. Nevertheless, Fulren knew this was no simple hunk of steel.

He channelled the power of his necroglyph into that blade, just as he had done with his legs and arm to bring them to life. Immediately the pyrestones glowed in response, the blade feeling instantly lighter in his hand.

"Go on, boy," Lysander said with relish. "Swing away."

Fulren almost smiled as he did as instructed, swinging the weapon in an arc, feeling the power behind it. Against the grey of his glyph-sight, the pyrestones left a multicoloured contrail, humming their delight as they fuelled the sword...or did they thirst? Did this weapon yearn for combat as much as Fulren did?

He noticed Lysander was already holding out the domed helm—the last piece of the puzzle. With his alloy arm, Fulren took the gift and placed it over his head. The world coalesced in an instant, switching from dull grey, to bright startling light, to vivid colour.

Lysander was standing before him; tall, shaven-headed, face an emotionless slab. He could have been a statue, sculpted like a saint—broad-shouldered and square-jawed.

"You look like a crow," the artificer said.

Fulren glanced down at his body, armoured in all its artifice. Then he remembered that vision he'd had—that crow watching him from its rotting tree. Did Lysander know something he wasn't saying?

"We should fight," Lysander announced, before Fulren could question him further.

"We should what?"

He would have refused, said he wasn't ready, but Lysander had already taken up his own weapon—an ornate broadsword, long in the grip, embellished with its own intricate web of pyrestones.

The artificer moved with such sudden speed, Fulren had to rely on his instinct to bring his blade up to parry. Their swords clashed, pyrestone energy spitting in fury as Fulren almost toppled over.

He tried to retreat across the wide expanse of the workshop, but Lysander pressed him, swinging again, the only sound the hum of pyrestones in his blade. Fulren darted back again, gathering his wits enough to jab back at Lysander, but the man was too fast, sword easily batting aside the flailing attack.

"Stop," Fulren said, still bewildered by the unexpected violence.

Lysander's face retained its grim mask. He offered no reply, and no clemency. Through the visor of his helm, Fulren watched as the silhouette of the crimson demon began to manifest behind Lysander. The shadow of his soul. An aspect of his fury, perhaps?

Did he truly mean Fulren harm? Surely he would not have armoured him so effectively if he only meant to kill him.

Whatever Lysander's motive, the conjuration of that red demon provoked a visceral response, and Fulren felt the necroglyph at his back begin to tingle. It filled him with animus, boiling his blood. He could barely control the sudden spark of hate and malice, and in the distance he heard a voice he recognised. A whisper he had tried so hard to suppress.

Fulren growled deep within his throat, his vision narrowing to focus on his one enemy. The newly forged sword sparked, mirroring his rage as he charged, pistons hissing in his legs as the blade lanced forward with unnatural speed. In his periphery he could see dark wings flutter—a flock of birds dull against the black, come to witness his victory.

Saliva filled his mouth as Lysander was forced back, holding his blade in both hands as he parried again and again. The artificer was hard pressed. Now it was his turn to be put on the back foot.

"All right, boy," he said.

The panic in his voice only served to spur Fulren to greater effort, and the pyrestones in his weapon spat and fizzled in response to his vigour.

"That's enough, Fulren," Lysander barked, panicking as he desperately swung his sword in a defensive arc, its power waning compared to the one in Fulren's hand that only seemed to grow stronger.

At the edge of his vision that flock of birds had become a storm. Dark wings fluttering, their fury rising to a crescendo that matched his own. Fulren spat, screaming from the bottom of his lungs as he swung one last time, shattering Lysander's weapon, its pyrestones exploding in a cavalcade of light.

The artificer fell back, landing heavily, but Fulren was not done. He planted his steel legs, looming over his defeated enemy, the sword in his hand singing as he raised it high. Lysander held up a hand—one last pathetic gesture, as he prepared to meet his doom...

Wasteland. So familiar, and yet so alien all at once. Fulren was gasping—tiny shallow breaths as his heart thrummed, every hair standing on end. When he looked down his hands were trembling. Knees shaking. Those limbs so human—the limbs he knew he had lost, returned to him once more.

With a deep cleansing breath, Fulren allowed himself to relax, closing his eyes, letting the calm wash over him.

*Back again.*

When he opened his eyes he saw the crow sitting in its tree once more.

*Just can't stay away, can you. It's almost as though you need me.*

This time when he looked upon that bird he felt no fear. No apprehension. This place might have been a window into another realm, but Fulren now knew that he was the master here.

As though reading his thoughts, the crow fluttered and squawked.

*You are insignificant. A worm on a hook, boy. Accept it.*

A seed of doubt crept in. Was the creature right? Was all his new-found confidence merely an affectation? He looked down once more, seeing that his legs had faded in the wan light. He held up his hand—realising it was not his hand at all, but just an incorporeal illusion. It faded in and out of existence just like his legs.

"If I give in, if I tell you what you want to hear, can you truly make me whole again?"

The crow bobbed up and down on its branch. *Yes. Yes we can. All you have to do is give yourself over to it. Accept your fate, boy. Let us in.*

Not for the first time, Fulren felt himself succumbing to the temptation. He could be whole again. Run with his own legs. See with his own eyes. All he had to do was let this demon take his soul.

No. That would never stand. He was Fulren Hawkspur. Born of a line of kings. He would be no demon's slave.

*Then what will you do instead?*

He had spoken no words, but still that crow could read him. It knew it had lost, and now it was panicking. Desperate. And as Fulren moved closer, he could sense the bird knew this was the end.

*You will forever be a shell*, it said as he took a step toward it. *Forever be a shadow of what you were. Nothing but a—*

Fulren snatched the crow from its branch with his right hand. There was no emotion as he raised it to his mouth. No sense of victory as he bit down on its head, tearing it off at the neck. Blood exploded in his mouth, running across his lips and down his chin. As he crunched on the crow's skull, he felt it drip into his chest, anointing him.

Around him, the wasteland darkened. Everything turning to shadow. The illusion shattered by his single act of defiance.

The wind howled...

Lysander still lay on the ground. His eyes displayed no emotion, but the sight of him, the realisation of what he had almost done, froze Fulren where he stood. Slowly, he lowered his sword, the energy coursing through its pyrestones waning and sputtering to nothing.

He reached out his alloy arm, and Lysander grasped the steel claw of a hand. As Fulren pulled the artificer to his feet, an uncharacteristic grin spread across Lysander's face.

"You did that on purpose?" Fulren asked.

"It worked, didn't it? Although I didn't expect you to harness that power quite so violently."

"You took too much of a risk." Fulren took the helm from his head, drawing in a deep breath of the musty air. "I could have killed you. But... yes, it worked. I no longer hear any voices."

"Then you showed it who is the master. And my work is all but done."

Fulren made his way to a bench nearby, sheathing his sword, a little relieved to be putting it away. The power it held, the energy he could imbue it with, was frightening. But he was in control now. Surely there should be nothing more for him to fear.

Lysander led him from the workshop and back into his little cave of a house. Fulren followed, footsteps clanking softly as he walked on metal legs. Verlyn was waiting for them, and from the red motes agitating throughout her body he could read her unease. Was she shocked at how well he moved? Or was it something else?

"Well?" she asked, not taking her eyes off Fulren. "Is he ready?"

Lysander was at the kitchen table, pouring water from a pitcher. Fulren could see him clearly—even without his helm the world now carried greater clarity. The old man sitting in the corner of the room was more distinct, watching from within his stupor, although his eyes were focused on Fulren, like they were seeing him for the first time.

"Maybe," Lysander said. "Maybe not, but it won't be long before he can leave here, Verlyn. You'll have your weapon, don't worry on that score."

Verlyn didn't look too convinced. "I don't know. This is all happening so fast."

As she spoke, Fulren found his attention drawn to the old man in his armchair. Drool was pooling in one corner of his mouth, but those eyes were glaring at him with such clarity. As Fulren watched, a pall of darkness began to coalesce around him, growing within him. A shadow that only deepened, and all the while those eyes stared.

Was there something he wanted to communicate? Some portent this infirm old man had to impart?

"I've told you before," Verlyn said to Lysander. "This isn't just about me or you. It's as much up to Fulren."

Their conversation was fading into the background. Fulren couldn't take his eyes away from the old man, who in turn was staring intently back at him, eyes full of clarity. Without thinking, Fulren took a step toward him, unable to hold himself back.

"Then maybe we should let the boy decide." As Lysander spoke the words, Fulren reached out with this right hand. He was inextricably drawn, unable to hold himself back as he grasped the old man's palsied hand.

"No!" Lysander yelled.

All too late.

Fulren's teeth clamped together as he was assailed by visions not his own...

*He could see for miles as he stood atop a flat mountain. The peaks surrounding him were snowcapped, the sky stained ink-grey. There was fear, but also exhilaration.*

*Surrounding him were others—the nine?—his acolytes in this. Their zeal was palpable.*

*A roar from across the mountains, five dark shapes soaring ever nearer. Those ancient wyrms arisen to stop them... but they could not stop them.*

*The world erupted in a cataclysm of magic. Breath of both fire and ice. The Sundering, as it would be known.*

*The destruction of Hyreme before its rebirth.*

*His mind torn asunder. Darkness. Betrayal...*

Fulren staggered back, wrenching his hand away from the grip of that old man.

As he grasped his wrist in a metal claw he stumbled, knocking over the table and falling backwards. On his backside he could not take his eyes from that enfeebled figure in the corner of the room. But then, he knew now this was no ordinary man. Not by any means.

"I saw through his eyes," Fulren spat. "I saw... who is he?"

Verlyn was kneeling by his side, but Lysander stood back, looking as though he had been judged and found guilty.

"You know who he is, boy."

"Say it," Fulren gasped, almost unable to believe what was happening. "Say his name."

"I told you, Fulren. You already know it." Lysander's voice was raised, as though the knowledge of his guilt made him angry. "He is a mage from a time before—"

"He not just a mage. He is *the* mage. The Archmage himself."

"What are you both talking about?" Verlyn asked. "What's going on?"

"That old man." Fulren pointed an accusing finger. "That's Cornelium Obek."

Verlyn shook her head. "What are you talking about? That's... that's impossible. He died a thousand years ago."

Lysander crossed the room to stand by the old man, whose eyes had now lost their focus. "Does he look dead? The boy is right. This is Obek—an ancient mage one thousand years old. Now nothing but a shell. His reward for the powers he conjured and harnessed. He was once the most powerful sorcerer in Hyreme." The old man murmured, hand shaking, drool now dangling from his mouth and running down his chin. "But as you can see—even the strongest of us cannot cheat time. None of us are immune to its ravages."

Verlyn stared at the old man. "Where did you find him?"

Lysander knelt beside Obek, placing a hand on the old man's twitching arm. "Among the ruins of the Drift. How I found him is a longer story."

"But why bring him here?"

A grin crept up one side of that usually grim face. "He is just a keepsake. An antique from a time long forgotten."

"Forgotten?" Fulren said, climbing to his metal feet, trembling with the shock of all this. "Who could forget the horrors he brought to the world? Even neophyte scholars are well versed in what he did. This is the most dangerous man in all Hyreme."

Lysander shook his head, regarding Obek with sorrow. "Not anymore."

Verlyn took a threatening step toward him. "This is madness, Lysander. You endanger us all just by having him here."

The red motes in her flared angrily, and Fulren took her arm to hold her back. "Not our problem anymore. It's time. We should leave now."

She turned to look at him, and he sensed the apprehension in her.

"The boy is right, Verlyn," Lysander said. "And there is nothing more for him to learn from me."

Verlyn looked back at Obek, and the fear in her was palpable. "I'll get the horses ready. And I won't be setting foot in this house again."

Lysander nodded his goodbye as she made her way outside, unable to take her eyes from the old man in the corner. Fulren stood, drinking in the silence as he regarded Obek in his chair. Could it really be him? An ancient mage weakened by the centuries?

Before he could think further on it, Lysander pressed the blank-faced helm into his hand.

"Good luck."

Fulren nodded, patting the sword sheathed at his shoulder. "Thank you. I don't know how to repay you for the gifts you have given me."

"Win your war, boy. That should be gift enough."

"I...I doubt I'll see you again."

"Never say never, Hawkspur. Who knows—we might cross paths in the future. When we are different men."

Fulren nodded his understanding, though as he made his way outside he realised he didn't really understand at all. He had already become much different. Barely recognisable from the boy who'd been stolen from his homeland and punished for a crime that was not his own.

He dismissed the thought as he made his way to where Verlyn had almost finished harnessing the horses. As he waited for her he noticed a crow watching him from a tree nearby. No sooner had he turned its way than it fluttered off into the dark.

"Are you ready?" Verlyn asked, climbing up onto the wagon.

Fulren climbed up into the seat beside her. As she whipped the reins, he had no idea if he was ready or not, but it was too late to wonder now.

# KEARA

They moved southwest toward the river, webwainers pushing their stormhulks to the limit, crossing the rough ground and smashing through the brush as fast and hard as they could. The river crossing at Bullcross was difficult with no bridge, but their engines waded across with little fuss, and eventually made it to the road that would take them north to Alumford.

All the while, Keara couldn't help but feel like a stranger among these wainers. She was Guildmaster of the Hallowhills, but everyone seemed to be giving her a wide berth. Some wider than others.

She had seen Tyreta among the crowd, sometimes moving with the column of stormhulks and webwainers, sometimes hidden for miles before appearing like a ghost from the brush. Keara's people were wary of her, if not outright hostile, though none of them had complained... yet. Nevertheless, she couldn't shake the feeling that both she and Tyreta were outsiders here.

A few miles south of Alumford and night was starting to crawl its way across the overcast sky. Keara found Galirena, one of her senior webwainers, and ordered her to make camp. Though the woman nodded her agreement, there was no conversation, no respect, before she hailed the stormhulks and told them they would stop here for the night.

Keara watched as those stormhulks lumbered from the road and the webwainers followed. Once in the clearing they began to split off into their little groups—wainers who had been close since the academy, their friendships formed, all flocking together to share their rations and talk about the old times.

The encampment was erected quickly, and Hallowhill artificers set about their daily maintenance of the stormhulks, and the few pyrestone weapons they'd brought. She thought maybe she should check how they were progressing, make herself visible among her people, accessible even, but they showed little interest in Keara as she walked among them.

At the edge of the clearing the quartermaster was busy marshalling his undercooks, as they lit fires and prepped what fresh food they'd brought for the pot. No one even bothered to catch her eye. So many men and women in the purple of Hallowhill and not one of them showing an ounce of regard for their Guildmaster.

As she reached the far edge of the camp she heard voices from beyond the flap of an awning. There was something conspiratorial about that conversation, those hushed voices prompting Keara to keep to the shadows as she moved closer to listen.

"But we're heading into even more danger. And for what?" A woman's voice. Mature. Grizzled even.

"We are Hallowhills. That's what we do." This one was younger but bore more authority than the first.

"And for what, eh? What do we do it for? What's the gain? Just to change sides again? One minute we're fighting for the Ministry and freedom from the Guilds. The next we're fighting for that whore Rosomon Hawkspur."

"Those are our orders," the younger of them insisted. "We follow our Guildmaster."

"Really? We were following him not too long ago and then he ended up dead. And under pretty dubious fucking circumstances."

"He was an old man. It was—"

"Convenient, is what it was," the woman said in her gravelly voice. "His house just burning down like that, with him sat in the middle of it."

"Convenient or not—Keara is our Guildmaster now."

"And we should just follow her blindly? Anyone who gets close to her ends up dead. Her father. Ulger Vine. And now Hesse gone missing. Rumour is Keara killed her when she complained about us changing sides."

"You need to keep your mouth shut. That kind of talk could get you—"

"Killed? Well... looks like there's a lot of that going around."

Keara could barely hold herself back from wrenching the awning aside and telling them yes, she was in charge now and should be obeyed, but... wasn't there some truth to what they were saying? In fact, wasn't the truth much worse?

"I'm almost done with taking this shit," the older woman continued. "We've been through the meat grinder more than once and I'm just about at my limit. Now this—walk into a battle and slaughter the very people we've been fighting beside for almost a year. It makes no damned sense."

"The sense is it could be the first step toward ending the war. Keara knows what she's doing. Sanctan would have been the end of us all. This is the only way for the Hallowhills to survive."

"Yeah. Maybe."

"There's no *maybe* about it. Now, let's go eat. I'm starved, and who knows when we might get another chance to fill our bellies after tomorrow."

Keara slid further into the shadows as she heard the women moving. She watched as they stepped out from beneath the canvas and made their way toward the campfires and the smell of the cookpots. All the while she felt a growing sense of shame at the notion that, despite their harsh words, they were right about her.

Perhaps the position of Guildmaster had not been hers to take after all. At the time she had thought it necessary, that by making the ultimate sacrifice and removing her useless father from his seat, she would be a worthy successor. But maybe she'd not deserved the honour after all—and it looked like her followers knew it. To make matters worse, she wouldn't even be marching into battle alongside them. She intended to sneak off with Hawkspur on a mission of her own.

Would the right thing have been to ignore the Hawkspurs and

just fight anyway? Abandon this mission and prove herself to her people first?

"Why are you skulking in the dark?"

Keara started, turning with a gasp, hands on her daggers, manifesting the web around her in stark colour. When she saw Tyreta's shining eyes peering at her from the woods, she cursed under her breath.

"I could say the same thing about you, Hawkspur."

Tyreta moved into the light, stalking like an animal on the hunt, which did nothing for Keara's nerves. "Skulking is all I've got. I don't really fit in around here. But from the sound of it, I'm not the only one."

Had she heard those webwainers talking? "Don't underestimate the loyalty of my people. They will do as I ask, when they have to."

"Will they? From what I just heard, Sanctan's is not the only revolt in Torwyn."

"They're just scared, that's all," Keara replied, hoping that was true. Hoping she hadn't lost control of her own followers. "They fell under Sanctan's spell, like so many others, but everything has changed now. It's only natural they'd have their doubts."

"Everything has changed?" Tyreta took a step closer, and it was all Keara could do not to take a step back. "Not for me it hasn't. I was always on the right side. Not everyone was drawn in by the Archlegate's lies."

"Then I guess it was easy for you." Now it was Keara's turn to take a step forward. "With your high and mighty sense of duty. With your family being at the top of the heap. You had more to lose than most. Than anyone. What did I have? Nothing—your grandfather made sure of that when he cast the Hallowhills down. You had everything given to you, Hawkspur. You've never had to fight like I have."

She expected Tyreta to lash back with a barb of her own, but instead the words seemed to calm her. "You're wrong about that. I've been fighting all my life. For acceptance. To live up to an ideal that was always forced upon me."

"Horseshit! Lady Rosomon would have brought down mountains to make sure you and your Guild stayed on top."

Tyreta shook her head. "You don't know anything. You don't know what I've been through. How I've had to change."

"We've all had to change," Keara snapped, thinking about the friends she'd lost, the sacrifices she'd made. "Some more than others."

Tyreta took another step away from the shadows and into the light. Her eyes still shone, and the scars and markings on her flesh stood out starkly, enhancing that feral aspect that so unnerved Keara. "Look at me. You think I'm the same person I was before all this began?"

Keara raised a hand to the three track marks on her cheek. "We've all got our battle scars, Hawkspur. I'm not talking about those. I mean what's inside. What we've had to deal with. What we've had to do. You haven't given up a damn thing."

Was that doubt on Tyreta's face? Keara knew only too well that hard truths would do that to you.

"I've had to become someone different," Tyreta said, her voice almost a whisper. "All because of what you did. You're not the only one who will never be the same."

"I did what I did out of necessity. You expect me to feel sorry for you? For what you've suffered? The Hallowhills were treated like scum. Tools for their betters to use. I will not settle for that. Do you think your mother would?"

"My mother would have done her duty. Done what's right for her family. For her Guild. But she would never have burned down Torwyn just so she could rise above the flames."

Keara had to quell a bark of laughter at that notion. "I don't think you know your mother at all."

"Better than you know yours," Tyreta shot back. Cutting, and she knew it. Keara could see the immediate regret on her face.

"You're right about that. But I do remember the last time I saw her. I remember the smile on her face. I remember how it made me feel. Before she..." Was murdered? Ran away? "...disappeared. At least I knew what I meant to her. I'll always remember that look. When was the last time your mother smiled at you?"

All the guilt had drained from Tyreta now and she just stared. There was an animal behind those eyes, but Keara didn't fear it anymore.

"What's the matter," Keara asked, leaning closer. "Cat got your tongue?"

She realised her mistake immediately, as Tyreta's gaze intensified. Damn her smart fucking mouth.

Despite her stupid remark, Tyreta's claws didn't spring forth. "Don't you have an inspirational speech to make? You know—before you send all those loyal followers into a battle you'll be running away from?"

Before Keara could even think of something clever to say, Tyreta turned, shrinking back into the darkness of the woods like a ghost. Damn but she was right. Keara did have to talk to her people—and explain why she was sending them into a fight without her.

By the Wyrms, she missed her friends. Missed Ulger's shining bald head and toothy grin. Missed that bitch Hesse. Even more, she missed the red drop, but now more than ever she needed her faculties unmuddied by that exquisite high. She only had herself to rely on.

Keara walked toward the centre of the encampment, fists bunched, jaw set, trying for all her might to instil some confidence, some flash of inspiration. Everyone ignored her as they chatted idly in their groups. There was a subdued hush about the place. Best see what she could do about that.

"Everyone," she called. "I need your attention."

A few of them glanced toward her, some even stopping their conversations, before quickly turning their heads away. Her nerve almost gave out at their lack of respect, but this had to be done if she had any chance of seizing her authority as Guildmaster.

"I said fucking attention, people." It was almost a scream. Almost going too far and losing control.

They went silent, just for a moment, and she thought that had done the trick. No such luck, as one by one they turned back to each another, talking even louder this time. Nothing like making a point, she supposed.

Time to make a point of her own.

Two stormhulks stood on the edge of the woodland being checked over by a group of Hallowhill artificers. Keara let her simmering anger dance along the strands of the web, fuelling the pyrestones in those engines. The infernus cannon on one stormhulk blossomed into life, sending fire roaring overhead.

Artificers shouted in alarm, one of them falling from his perch atop one of the vast machines. A gaggle of webwainers scattered from the heat of the flames. The camp fell silent. All eyes turned to her.

"Do I have your attention now?" She glared, waiting to be defied. No one dared, but she could still register the contempt in every eye that fell on her. It was doubtful shooting fire at them would earn any friends—but then it was better to be regarded with fear than disrespect.

"Tomorrow the Hallowhills march to battle," she said to those scornful faces. "This will be the first step we take, out from the shadow of the Ministry. And I know what you're thinking—that we've already fought and bled for them. That we agreed an alliance that has now been broken. But we were conned. Duped by Sanctan Egelrath's lies."

"You mean *you* were," said an anonymous voice.

Her jaw clamped tight as she scanned the crowd to see who had spoken, but what did it matter who? It was obvious they all thought the same.

"Yes, I was. And so was my father, the man you all followed just as blindly as I followed Sanctan. He was wrong about all this, but now he's dead. So you have a new Guildmaster—one who can see things clearly for the first time in decades. One willing to drag this Guild from the mire, and with your help I can make it happen. Once the Ministry is destroyed we'll rebuild. Regain our position of respect."

Those last few words stirred some of them to rise from their seats. Was this courage? Was it hope? Was this how it felt to inspire?

"Tomorrow, I know you will all fight with venom. For your Guild. For your future. You will show everyone what the Hallowhills are capable of."

A couple of them shouted their assent, while others nodded their heads. For a moment Keara thought she might just have won them over, until a woman in a shabby purple tunic stepped to the fore.

"What do you mean, 'I know *you* will all fight'? Are you not fighting with us?"

Shit.

Keara glared at the woman, desperate to remember her name. Damn it, she had to show she was one of them if she was going to deliver the news that she wouldn't be joining them in battle.

"I'm glad you asked...Roderica."

"It's Rodita," the woman replied.

Shit, shit, shit...

"Rodita, of course. And I want to march with you. I really do. But I have another mission. A task at the Anvil that will make tomorrow's battle matter. And I can't put any of you at risk by joining me. It's just too—"

"Dangerous?" asked a man to her left. "You won't risk any of our lives on this dangerous mission, but you'll let us march onto a battlefield?"

Damn it, what was his name? "Volkmar, is it?"

His brow creased in contempt. "Vikmar."

"Yes, I knew that, Vikmar. Look, I would do anything to join you, but this is something I must do if we are to triumph over the Ministry and regain our rightful position. But trust me, while you are fighting the Ministry on the field, I will be bringing them down from within."

Vikmar, or whatever his damned name was, looked unconvinced. There was grumbling discontent, but what had she expected? A cheer?

Perhaps a cheer was what she deserved. She'd already sacrificed her father, her friends. Now she stood before her own Guild and they were treating her like some spoiled brat.

"Fine. Fucking walk away then." That stirred them, but she couldn't tell if it was good or bad. Whichever it was she hadn't much choice. Reasoning had got her nowhere. Now it was time to provoke them. "Take your stormhulks. Take whatever pyrestone weapons the Hallowhills have provided you with, and march back to the Anvil. Prostrate yourselves at the feet of the Archlegate. See what he will do for you. I imagine there will be promises made. Guarantees. Perhaps even contracts signed. But once this is all over, he will destroy you. Is that what you want? Is it?"

More silence. Considering her bluff, no doubt. Time to double down.

"Anyone?" she continued. "You can walk away anytime you want. I won't stop you. Or... you can fight for that." Keara jabbed a finger toward the spider pennants that hung limp over the camp. "Fight for the Hallowhills one last time, because if you don't, that flag will be erased from history. You'll never see it fly again. All you will see are dragons, and you'll soon learn to fear them. Your gifts will no longer matter, because with artifice gone you won't be able to use them. At best you'll be cast down with the peasants. You'll be nothing. Ordinary. Condemned to a life of drudgery and toil. At worst you'll be sanctioned. Hunted down. Persecuted. Caged or executed just for who you are. The only way for us to be free is if we fight. And don't think you're fighting for me. You're not doing this for Guild or Guildmaster. You're fighting for yourselves. For your lives."

She was almost out of breath as she stood there in the silence. There was no great cheer of assent, but then she had no idea what to expect. She'd been making all this up on the hoof.

A few mumbled conversations among the crowd, her words clearly having some effect. Rodita and Vikmar were toward the front, gazing at one another, something silent and complicit passing between them.

Then Rodita took a step forward. "I am with you."

Vikmar offered a nod of agreement. "And I am with you."

It spread through the gathered crowd. Webwainers stepping out into the light, the mood of that crowd slowly transforming. Was it pride? Hope?

"For the Guildmaster!" someone cried.

It was followed by a cheer.

Keara wanted to smile. Maybe even break down in tears, but she kept a stoic set to her jaw at the rising noise. At her people finally acknowledging her as their leader. Her pride began to swell... until her gaze fell on the trees at the edge of the camp.

Tyreta was watching from the shadows, those yellow eyes regarding her with animal clarity. Was that respect? Not likely, but at least it wasn't contempt. Ambivalence maybe?

Keara supposed she'd just have to settle for it.

# CONALL

An old quarry, reeking of rust and oil. Even before the Ministry tore this country apart it must have looked like a dump. Now this abandoned place just looked sad. What better location for them to make camp.

The Viper Battalion had moved quickly, and Conall had struggled to keep up with them at times, but he was getting stronger every day. Perhaps too strong, but he did his best to ignore that. Did his best to forget what dark powers might be helping him recover so quickly, despite the lack of food and shelter on their journey eastward.

He'd received no special treatment, that was for certain. No one had shown any deference, and despite him being a totem of the Guild resistance, the Armiger troopers all but ignored him. Marshal Sonnheld had not so much as spoken a word to him on their travels, but what could he expect? These soldiers had been fighting for weeks—they were hardly going to fluff his pillow and tuck him in at night, Guild heir or not.

As he rubbed sand and vinegar into the sword he'd been given, trying to remove the last vestiges of rust that tainted the blade, an adjutant made her way toward him with purpose. Something was up.

She jabbed a thumb over one shoulder. "New arrivals in camp.

One of them claims they're Hawkspur. Sonnheld says you'd best go make sure they're genuine."

Conall stood, sheathing his sword. As he walked in the direction the adjutant had gestured he could see troopers surrounding someone at the edge of the quarry. They were seated, just out of sight, but as he made his way closer he heard an all too familiar sound.

"I'm with the fucking Talon."

Sted's voice. Unmistakable, and so damned welcome.

Before the troopers could question her further, Conall pushed his way through. Sted looked up at him with sudden shock, before a rare smile beamed from her face, revealing those disgusting, red-stained teeth he'd missed so much.

He grabbed her before she could stand, pulling her to her feet, squeezing her tight. When he released her, she looked uncomfortable with such a rare display of affection, but didn't protest.

"Captain?" she grunted.

He could tell she couldn't believe it. That she wanted to tell him how much she'd missed him. How she had mourned. Perhaps even shed a tear. Instead, she just stared.

"Lieutenant," he replied, unable to keep the grin off his face. "It's good to see you."

More staring. Was that a glistening in her eye? Conall resisted the urge to point it out—he'd have as likely got a punch in the gut as a welcome embrace for his trouble if he had.

To her right, the second newcomer rose to his feet—Donan, looking awkward as ever. Conall drank in the sight of him for a moment, before realising one of his legs was crafted from artifice. The memory of what happened on that ship flooded back, and he was suddenly struck with the urge to apologise.

"Donan, you're..."

"In one piece." Donan beamed. "More or less."

"What are you both doing here?" On seeing Conall greet the pair like old friends, the troopers on guard stepped away, leaving them to their reunion.

Sted regarded him with a look akin to embarrassment. "We were on our way north. Had to take a bit of a detour due to the Ministry fuckers roaming everywhere. Then we, er..."

"Got lost," Donan finished. "My fault really. I thought I knew a shortcut."

Conall could barely quell a laugh. "Don't take the blame." He slapped Donan on the shoulder. "You're not the scout."

Sted looked annoyed with the accusation. "Hang on a min—"

"Doesn't bloody matter anyway," Conall said, resisting the urge to grab them both and hug them once again. "You're both here now."

"And so are you," Sted replied. "When you should be at the bottom of the ocean. What happened? Where did you wash up? And when did you lose that?" She jabbed a finger toward the patch that covered his missing eye. Diplomatic as ever.

"It's..." How to say it? How to explain any of what he had been through? There was no way Sted would understand, and as much as he wanted to tell her, he just couldn't find the words. "...a long story. I was picked up by pirates. Taken to the Magna. Escaped. That's about the long and short of it."

"Escaped?" Sted replied. "It sounds like you're skipping a lot here, Con."

"And one day I might fill in all the blanks. Needless to say, the Drift is a shithole, and I don't recommend going there."

"You crossed the fucking Drift?" Her mouth hung open in disbelief, and he could well understand her scepticism.

"And it was tough. But look, we're all together now. Let's not pick over the past. Let's work out how we're going to beat the Ministry and get everything back to the way it was."

"Yeah, about that." Sted scratched at something behind her ear, reluctant to speak. "We met your sister. Travelled with her."

"Tyreta?"

"That's your fucking sister, yes. Your mother sent us on a mission. Long story but...things went south. We ended up in Castleteig, managed to escape, but she went back for..."

"For her pet," Donan interjected.

This was getting more confusing by the second. "Her what?"

"That doesn't matter," said Sted. "All we know is she went back, while we went north. There's a chance she could still be there."

"In Castleteig? You're sure?" The thought of having to rescue his sister on top of everything else only added to his woes.

Sted shrugged. "We don't know. But she said we should rendezvous with your mother in the north. That she'd meet us there."

Conall rubbed at his stubbly chin as he mulled over what to do. The last thing he wanted right now was meet up with his mother. That voice in his head had remained quiet, but that was no guarantee it was gone for good. Worse still, breaking into Castleteig, a city occupied by the enemy, to rescue Tyreta, who might not even be there?

Damn it, when would he get an easy decision?

Before he could begin to work out what to do, riders came galloping into the quarry, hooves splashing through those oily puddles. One wore the green fatigues of a Talon scout, while the other was a lightly armoured Armiger trooper, who immediately shouted for the marshal.

Conall's eye was drawn across the flat bed of the quarry as Marshal Sonnheld responded to the call. He strode out in his ornate armour, hands resting on his twin swords. For now, Conall supposed he would have to forget his sister's woes. It sounded as though they had trouble of their own.

"What to report?" Sonnheld demanded.

Conall moved closer, keen to hear the news as the Talon scout dismounted.

"We were ranging to the southeast. Met up with refugees from the Rock and they gave us grave news, Marshal. The Raptor and Auroch have already mobilised. They're only two days' march from here."

Sonnheld scratched at the scar on his face as he considered the news. He had been hoping to face them further south and harry their progress. Now it seemed those plans were ruined.

"What do we do?" Conall asked. "Warn my mother?"

Sonnheld shook his head. "I'm not sure what good that would do."

"There must be something." Conall would have liked to sound less desperate, but this was a pretty desperate situation. Two more Armiger Battalions to defend the Anvil and his mother's forces were as good as done for. "They cannot be allowed to reach the Anvil, Marshal. The Guilds are relying on us to stop them."

To Conall's surprise, Sonnheld nodded his agreement. "You're right, Hawkspur. The only question is how." He turned, signalling to the adjutant Conall had spoken to earlier. "Bring me the cartographer."

In short order, a little man bustled from a tent. He cradled several scrolls and sheaves of parchment as he scuttled toward them.

"Show me everything between our position here and the Rock," Sonnheld demanded.

The little man nodded, his spectacles sliding down his nose as he did so. "I have just the thing."

Dropping most of the parchments, he took a scroll and unfurled it. Conall could see it displayed the settlements between the hills south of the Anvil and the plains north of the Rock in surprising detail.

Sonnheld leaned in close, examining the map before pointing a gauntleted finger in its centre. "Here. The most direct route from the Rock to the Anvil passes through this valley, creating a choke point. If we reach the valley mouth to the north before they do, we can establish a defensible barricade and keep them pinned in place for days. They will never reach the Anvil in time to stop the Guild's advance." A smile crossed his grim face. "Few of us will survive, but it will make a glorious final engagement for the battalion."

Conall could see the sense in the plan—it would indeed halt the enemy advance. However, he didn't like the notion of a *glorious final engagement*. That sounded pretty much like suicide.

"What about these?" he said, pointing to what looked like buildings sketched onto the side of the valley. "What are they?"

The cartographer peered over his spectacles. "They're processing factories I believe."

"Processing what?"

The cartographer shook his head.

Donan cleared his throat. "Erm...I believe those are infernium refinement plants."

All eyes fell on him and he squirmed under the attention. Conall tried to suppress a smile. "Then maybe a final engagement isn't necessary. If we blow the plant to the south of the valley it will collapse the entrance. The Armigers have no chance to go through it. Going around those hills will add days to their advance."

"No," Sonnheld replied, tapping his finger against the parchment again. "There is another route here. Taking out the mouth of the valley will only delay them a day at most."

Conall ground his teeth, feeling the frustration of it. Or was it the fear of being forced to fight to the death in some anonymous valley? "Then we blow both." He gestured to the second plant at the north side of the canyon. "Pin them in the valley between the two."

Sonnheld peered closer. His zeal at making a heroic last stand appeared to fade. "Yes. Maybe that might work, Hawkspur. But I'm not sure we have enough munitions to blow both depots."

Now it was Donan's turn to peer closely at the map. This time he was oblivious to the attention from everyone, the pneumatics in his leg gently sighing while he pondered.

"There." His finger made a little circle on the map not far from their current position. "That's a Marrlock supply dump, pretty much right in our path to the valley. Unless it's been looted, it should have plenty of spare explosives. All we need to do is walk right in and pick up what we need."

This was all falling into place...a little too easily. Conall knew it couldn't last. From the silence that surrounded him, he was pretty sure no one else could believe it either.

"Very well," Sonnheld said eventually. "We can have our scouts pick up the munitions on the way, but that doesn't solve the problem of who will climb up there and plant them. Those charges have to be laid with precision, and primers timed to the second. We have no artificers to help us do that."

"Donan can do it," Conall said, without even thinking to ask his opinion.

His metal leg breathed a sigh of air as he took a step back. "I can what?"

"You must know how to set those detonators. When I found you in the Karna you were in charge of an entire mining outpost. Didn't you use munitions there?"

"Well...yes."

Conall clapped Donan on the shoulder, almost toppling him over. "Then it's settled. We'll do it."

"Fuuuck," Sted breathed.

Conall turned to her, feigning a frown of confusion. "What's the matter with you?"

Her mouth twisted in a sneer. "What's the matter with me? You and Donan heading into danger? That means I'll be heading into danger too, I expect?"

"No," Conall replied, doing his best to look innocent. "I didn't want to speak for you, Sted. You don't have to come if you don't want to."

There it was; the easiest way to get her to do something she didn't want. He could see the range of emotions on her face; the relief, the indignation, the annoyance.

"Like fuck you'll leave me behind...I mean, like fuck, Captain. I'm with you every step."

He patted her arm in thanks. "Well volunteered, Lieutenant."

"Settled then," said Sonnheld. "We break camp immediately. It's a long road south and if we're to beat those Armigers we need to get moving. Hawkspur, I suggest you make sure your team is prepared."

Conall nodded his acknowledgment before Sonnheld turned and began to bark orders. The troopers hustled at his word, breaking down the camp, as the cartographer scrambled to pick up his fallen maps.

"Shit," Donan whispered, as though only just realising what he'd let himself in for. "We're dead."

Sted leaned an elbow on his shoulder. "It's nothing, Marrlock. We've been in worse scrapes than this and come out in one piece."

Donan regarded her wryly, before gesturing to his metal leg.

"Don't worry," Conall said. "This will be a breeze. We'll be in and out before the Armigers even know we're there, and miles away by the time they realise what's going on. By then they'll be stuck in that valley."

Donan looked unconvinced. "Yeah...miles away. Easy as that."

"That's the spirit." He clapped Donan on the arm before turning to collect his gear. There was no way he wanted his friends to see any doubt. Conall was more than aware it was never going to be that easy.

# ANSELL

They had erected a barricade of sorts just yards from the southern side of the bridge. Despite the stalwart defence, Ansell still felt exposed, even with Falcar at his side, even with the troopers of the Griffin Battalion crowded about them. They were only a small force—a sacrificial goat upon which the Guilds would fall before Marshal Sarona launched her ambush. And not long now.

Across the river he could see the Guild pennants flying—the fire of Ironfall, the winged talon of Hawkspur, the crossed hammers of Marrlock. Around him those battalion troopers were breathing heavier, frantically checking their weapons, licking moist lips, peering over the barricade with frightened eyes. It was always the same—the urge to run, the urge to vomit, only held in check by the shame of cowardice. But Ansell had long ago learned to quell those emotions. For him, there was only the anticipation of righteous fury.

But this time he felt different. This time he was plagued by an alien emotion he could not identify. No longer was he cloaked in the might of the Wyrms. Now he felt vulnerable, and no matter how he tried to shirk that feeling it only grew stronger the closer the Guilds marched.

He drew his sword, hoping it would help gird him. Cloak him. Armour him. Falcar did the same, which offered some reassurance, but still he could not take his eyes from the approaching army. Could not help but think this might well be his final day.

It appeared as though the enemy might rush the bridge as Sarona had predicted. Maybe it would have been better if they had planted charges beneath the bridge supports after all, and drawn them into—

"Peaceful, isn't it, brother?"

Ansell turned his head to see Falcar standing proud. Behind his helm those big brown eyes of his looked almost spellbound as he took in the scenery. A bird chirruped in the woods to the north. The river tinkled its tune as it flowed past. Only the distant tramping feet of their enemy spoiled the serenity.

"Strange," Falcar continued. "But I have always enjoyed these calm moments before battle. So much clarity."

There was no answer Ansell could give. He had always hated the calm. Hated the wait. But they did not have to wait any longer.

As he looked back across that bridge they appeared. Among those Guild pennants flew Armiger banners—the Bloodwolf and Mantid. The army of the Guilds marched relentlessly, approaching that bridge with inexorable tread. Yes, Sarona had been right after all. They would simply charge head-on and fall right into their trap.

Ansell glanced south, seeing the mess of wooden buildings and the tangle of streets amid them. The marshal of the Ursus would be somewhere within that labyrinth, watching her enemy approach. For a moment, Ansell considered how pleased she would be that her plan was coming to fruition, but just as he thought the Guilds might begin their charge, their tramping march came to a stop at the opposite side of the bridge.

"What are they doing?" Falcar breathed.

Ansell had no answer. He merely stood gripping sword and shield, waiting as he had been ordered. Nothing about this seemed right. Just the day before, one of the Ursus troopers who had escaped the battle at Oakhelm had told him of the Marrlock minstrels. How they would play their instruments proudly to herald the Guild armies. How it made such an inspiring racket. Now they were silent, waiting for…

He looked to the north. The woodland was still for now, but Ansell had warned Sarona of how vulnerable they would be to attack from there. She had offered some compromise and sent scouts to patrol the area, but so far nothing. Not a bird stirred in the trees.

He looked south, just beyond the boundary of Alumford where the land rose to hills. Hidden behind the brow waited Hallowhill stormhulks. As soon as the Guilds crossed the bridge they would advance and unleash a tempest, but first Ansell and these few Armigers would have to weather a storm all their own. But the Guilds were content to wait, for now.

Movement behind. Ansell turned to see Marshal Terswell pushing his way through the waiting ranks of Griffin troopers. He looked imperious in his armour, but his face was marred with concern.

"What in the Lairs is going on?" he asked. "Why are they just standing there?"

Again Ansell had no answer to give. Maybe they did suspect an ambush. Perhaps they believed the bridge had indeed been rigged with explosives, but then why would they have taken this approach, just to stand and wait?

"Do they want to parley?" Terswell asked.

Ansell shook his head. "There is no sign of a herald. No flag of peace. They are waiting to attack, but something is holding them back."

Terswell slammed his gauntleted palm against the pommel of his sword in frustration. "Then maybe they need a little provocation." He turned to one of his men. "Get me a sharpshooter. A little ranged fire should stir them into action."

The trooper looked embarrassed. "I am sorry, Marshal. We have no longbarrels. Marshal Sarona demanded all sharpshooters be positioned in the town."

As Terswell began to curse through gritted teeth, Ansell's attention was drawn back to the woodland. A flock of crows took to sudden flight, flapping into the sky as they cawed their contempt. He grabbed Terswell by the ornate pauldron of his armour, spinning him to face northward.

"There. Did you see? You must send a unit to check the woods."

Terswell's brow creased in confusion. "What are you talking about? We already have scouts deployed to—"

There was a hiss, the air heating up close to his face as he heard a whipcrack noise echo from the north. Then a sound of metal being punctured and one of the troopers fell forward at the barricade. It heralded a fusillade, bows snapping from the north, the sharp report of longbarrel fire. Splintbolts and superheated shot peppered the line of defenders, penetrating armour and sandbags.

Ansell ducked on instinct, hearing something ring close by as his armour was struck by a ricochet. Another man in front of him fell silently, his body riven with holes.

"Take cover!" Terswell screamed. "Return fire!"

Most of their defences were concentrated toward the bridge, the barricade vulnerable from the woodland, but Terswell's troopers did their best to adjust their line. Ansell hefted his shield, the fleeting thought that Sarona had made a grave mistake flitting through his mind before he dismissed it. Now was not the time for admonishment, now was the time to survive. A splintbolt struck his shield as though to labour the point.

"The woods," Terswell growled. "Form ranks and advance on those trees."

The enemy had still not made themselves visible, but volley after volley soared at them from the woodland. There was no way to know what awaited them within those dark confines.

"No!" Ansell bellowed. "Hold position!"

Terswell turned on him, his face reddening. "I'm in charge here, Drake. These are my troopers. They follow my orders."

Ansell gestured over the barricade toward the bridge. "If we break cover, the barricade will be left undefended. Look! The Guilds wait just across the river. We cannot abandon our position."

The anger faded from Terswell's face as he regarded that army standing in wait. He opened his mouth to speak, but couldn't find the words. He looked north, from where yet more missiles rained before pattering down around them.

"What do we do?" he said to no one.

In the distance there was a sudden noise. Ansell turned to the south. The stormhulks had crested the rise, advancing relentlessly, and he could feel the tremor as their steel feet chewed up the ground.

"Oh, thank the Wyrms," Terswell breathed.

As they reached the first of the wooden dwellings, the stormhulks came to a stop. There was a pause, those machines standing like iron statues, as though they were silently communicating with one another.

Then the carnage began.

Fire burst from the arm of one engine, setting the roof of a house aflame. On the shoulder mount of another, the barrel of some infernal weapon revolved, letting out a terrifying roar before it spat molten shot through solid stone.

Screams of alarm echoed from within the houses as the Ursus Battalion came under a deluge of artillery. The score or more of stormhulks began to tramp through the maze of streets, destroying all in their path. Those Ursus troopers who broke from cover were mercilessly cut down by a hail of fire.

"What?" Terswell yelled. "What is happening?"

Betrayal. That's what was happening, but Ansell had no time to point that out as he ducked more missiles from the woods, his shield raised high.

Back over the river, the Guilds recommenced their advance, the Blackshields at their fore marching across the bridge with relentless stride. Sarona's trap had been turned against her, and it would be Ansell and these few Armiger troopers who were caught in its jaws.

Falcar stood firm at Ansell's side, but all around them panic was beginning to overwhelm the Griffin Battalion troopers. Some hunkered behind the barricade, their weapons forgotten as they suffered the tirade striking their position from the woods. Others hid behind their shields, doing their best to return fire, but they were shooting at ghosts hidden behind those trees.

Marshal Terswell grabbed hold of his adjutant. "Holding this position is hopeless. Sound the retrea—"

There was a dull clank of metal as his helm was punctured by longbarrel shot. Blood spattered the face of the adjutant, and he stared in horror as Terswell fell to his knees, a crimson stream running from beneath the brim of his helm to cover his face.

On seeing their leader fall, a couple of troopers lost courage, breaking cover and fleeing back along the road. As soon as they emerged from behind the barricade they were cut down, bodies riddled with missiles as they fell.

"Steel yourselves!" Ansell bellowed, before any more tried to abandon their position. "Form ranks on the northern barricade! Return fire in volleys!"

His voice was raised above the din, the authority it bore doing enough to instil some courage in the foundering ranks of the Griffin troopers. They obeyed, a score of them rushing to man the sandbags at the northern barricade, as one of their sergeants ordered them to load splintbows.

Hoping that was enough to see their flank defended, Ansell turned his attention back to the bridge.

"What do we do, brother?" Falcar asked. There was no fear in his voice. Only zeal. "We cannot hope to prevail with just the two of us."

Falcar was right, his point driven home as to the south another of the houses was assaulted by a stormhulk cannon and exploded in wooden shards. There would be no help from Sarona and the Ursus. No help from anyone, now the Hallowhills had shown their true colours.

"Rally to me, Armigers!" he cried. The troopers behind him looked up, some in disbelief, some in fear. "The Guilds march upon us, but we will not be bowed. They cannot be allowed to cross that bridge. We are the last line of defence—the gnashing tooth of the Wyrms—and we must stand."

He raised himself to full height as the missiles whipped past him. One of the sergeants, roused by such a brave display, stood up beside him.

"For the marshal!" he shouted.

His cry was joined by several others, and within a moment there was a phalanx of troopers at Ansell's shoulder, shields gripped tight and swords drawn. As the splintbowmen of the battalion returned fire toward the woods, and the Hallowhills and Ursus fought to the south, Ansell struck out from behind the barricade.

He and Falcar marched at the vanguard, eyes focused on the

approaching enemy. Behind them came the Griffin troopers, shields braced as they advanced toward the approaching Blackshields. When they were within a dozen yards of the bridge, they were met with a volley of splintbow fire. It arced its way over the helms of the approaching warriors, and Ansell barely had time to shout "*Shields!*" before they were struck by the deluge. He felt the thud of bolts from behind his own shield, heard the scream of a trooper hit by a missile, but still they marched.

They were almost at the mouth of the bridge, the Blackshields having made their way to its midpoint. Behind that phalanx of black armour Ansell could see the pennants flying—affirming the might of the Guilds as they tramped relentlessly, the sound of their iron-shod feet clanking across the wood of the bridge. Among those pennants was one Ansell had never seen before—the winged talon of Hawkspur set upon the cog of Archwind. Two Guilds united. A union that he was determined to break.

He gave no call to charge, instead raising his sword high and increasing his stride. Then he was racing at the enemy, Falcar at his side with a cry of "*For the Wyrms!*" bellowing from the bottom of his lungs.

Those blackened shields braced together the moment before he fell upon them, his sword hacking down, smashing against the wall of steel. The enemy advance halted as Ansell, Falcar and the few brave Griffin troopers took their fight to the Guilds.

Violence erupted. Men grunting in rage. A spear shaft lanced forward only to be turned by the steel of Ansell's pauldron. An axe crashed through the shields, ricocheting off his helm, instilling urgency, pain, fury. His arm rose, hacking down at the enemy, smashing into the wall of metal and sending motes of soot billowing into the air. He struck again, the Blackshield in front stumbling back a step before the gap in the shield wall was swiftly plugged.

Alongside him, the Griffin Battalion attacked with a fury, flinging themselves at the enemy with abandon. Falcar roared, his good humour replaced by righteous fury. In the face of their assault the Blackshields were halted, an immovable object sent back apace by the unstoppable force of the Ministry onslaught.

A cry of pain and terror to Ansell's left, and a Griffin trooper fell. Another stepped forward to fill the breach, but a rising hiss and blossoming heat heralded the front of his helm exploding in a shower of crimson.

The blast of a horn rose above the din of battle. In response, the Blackshields withdrew a few paces in a single disciplined row.

"Hold!" Ansell bellowed as a gap formed between him and the enemy.

The urge to charge forward was overwhelming, but Ansell sensed danger, pausing for a moment to catch a breath and consider the next move. He realised his mistake all too late.

From beyond the Guild front line came an ominous thud, hollow and resonant. Ansell barely had chance to scream his warning before the first of the mortar shells struck among their ranks. The blast was deafening, and Ansell ducked as men behind him were flung into the air, along with searing debris. Another dull thud, and he saw more ordnance land right by Falcar. The device did not detonate immediately, but Ansell could see the pyrestone winking on its metal carapace, burning intensely, ready to explode.

He bolted, dropping his shield, grabbing Falcar, and the pair fell to the ground just as the explosive detonated. Ansell was flung through the air, slamming into the bridge bulwark and coming to rest among the twisted metal.

Silence.

Ansell struggled to breathe, forcing air into his lungs, feeling trapped within his armour. His focus slowly returned as he clawed his way to his feet, seeing his blade where it lay a yard or so from his feet, and stooping to reclaim it.

A groan, and he saw Falcar lying amid the rubble. Stumbling forward, he grasped his brother's arm and hauled him up. Falcar snarled in pain, tottering on his leg, armour blackened and dented.

"Can you fight?" Ansell asked, his senses fast returning.

Falcar's teeth were gritted, his desire to stand and defend the bridge warring with his injuries. Blood poured from his nose, and his helm was lost, his eyes unable to focus.

Ansell turned to those men of the Griffin Battalion still standing. "Get him to safety. And fall back to the other side of the bridge."

The troopers obeyed, taking hold of Falcar and bearing him back across the bridge. Other troopers were already rising as the dust settled, and stumbling back the way they had come. The bridge was lost, but before Ansell could consider retreat he heard the relentless tramp of feet as the Guilds began to advance once again.

They were coming, but he could not flee. He had been sent here to fight and, if necessary, die. It was his duty to serve. To make amends for all his many wrongs. An opportunity Ansell could not spurn.

Those marching feet drew closer, and he struggled toward them through the thick pall covering the bridge. Gripping his sword in both hands, he braced himself for what was coming, for those Blackshields to surround him and he to fight like a lion among wolves.

Instead, a single warrior strode from the dust cloud. Her eyes were focused, jaw set as she locked him in her gaze. Ansell set his feet, swinging his sword, but she was too fast, ducking his blade and striking his breastplate with her own slender weapon. It did not breach the metal of his armour, but the strength of it still sent him staggering.

Undaunted, he swung again, and she ducked her helmed head, countering with an upward swipe he was at pains to lurch away from.

She was fast. Skilled. He had faced such warriors before, but she could be no swordwright. She was too young, surely.

Ansell dismissed the notion. Those tramping steel-shod feet were drawing closer, and he could already see black helms through the dust. He had to defeat this foe before they overwhelmed him with sheer numbers.

She lunged again and he batted the thrust aside with a gauntleted hand, countering with strike of his own. The sword rang off her pauldron, and she staggered back, snarling her response. Ansell pressed his attack, raising his sword in both hands, but she barged into him with a shoulder, hard enough to send him off balance. His boot slipped on the debris underfoot and he was knocked off the bridge, but in a last-ditch effort he managed to grab her, dragging her with him over the edge.

They were both consumed by the river. Ansell flailed in panic for a moment, before realising they had landed in the shallows. He gasped as he stood squinting through the smoke that had drifted down from the bridge. No time to get his bearings, as that woman's slender sword struck at him again, clashing against his vambrace and sending a jolt up his arm.

Her eyes bored into his as she attacked relentlessly, but waist-deep in the river she was slower than on solid ground. Ansell countered and she was at pains to parry, grunting as their swords rang. Another mighty stroke of his blade and the weapon was knocked from her grip, to disappear beneath the surface of the river.

Ansell's hand shot forward on instinct and he grasped her throat. She still fought him, struggling like an eel in his grip, but she would never be strong enough. As she vainly snatched at his face, he plunged her head beneath the surface, feeling her strain against him, but it was futile. Her hands battered against his arm, grasping at the gauntleted hand about her throat, but she could not release his grip an inch.

Her face was visible beneath the surface, contorting from anger to panic as she realised there was nothing she could do to stop him. Those eyes still bored into him, but they no longer held such fury, and for a moment, as he stood in the water with the sound of violence echoing from atop that bridge, he no longer saw a warrior woman.

This was a girl he was drowning. Someone's daughter. Just a child fallen far from the sight of the Wyrms. She did not deserve to drown at Ansell's hand. That was a fate reserved for only the most heinous of sinners, not a soul so young.

Ansell released his hold, wading back a step as she burst from beneath the surface, coughing and hacking up water. He suddenly felt weariness gripping him, as he fought to stay on his feet in that river.

A snarl from the dark smog brought him back to sharp focus. An armoured bear of a warrior burst from the mist, sword raised, and Ansell only just managed to parry.

As they regarded one another, Ansell recognised the grim bearded face that peered from beneath a dark helm. Maugar, swordwright of the Ironfalls, had come to challenge him with all the wrath of the Guilds. Ansell could not refuse it.

They traded blows back and forth, Ansell doing his best to weather the storm of steel Maugar unleashed, but his strength was waning with every laboured step. Ducking a wayward swing, he retreated toward the bank, feeling his strength ebb, growing more desperate as he waded into the shallows, feet sucked down by the boggy ground.

Ankle deep in the slop he found it all but impossible to manoeuvre, where Maugar trod with purpose, swinging his blade in relentless arcs. Ansell grunted as he parried each one, but he could not last forever against such rage. But neither could he give in.

Maugar growled again, hacking down. Ansell did his best to catch the blow, but the blade still struck his shoulder, driving him back into the mud. A kick from Maugar and he was laid on his back. He had never stood a chance. The swordwright had merely been toying with him all the while, but still he would not yield.

He foundered in the muck, seeing his sword only feet away. With a heavy fist he dug into the mud, dragging himself closer. His other reached out, nearly grasping the hilt, but before he could touch it Maugar kicked the sword further along the shore.

Ansell's breathing was fevered. The sounds of battle on the bridge had begun to grow quiet, and a glance over his shoulder confirmed that the violence had all but ended. From the bridge they were being watched—all eyes focused on his execution. There was no one to save him now. Across the open ground, he could see the town of Alumford burning.

A boot slammed down his head, pushing his face further into the riverbank. Ansell struggled to breathe as he was drowned in the dirt, but he was too exhausted to resist, tasting the mud as it filled his mouth and nose. He flailed helplessly, desperate to defy these heretics, but all the strength had left him.

The Wyrms had abandoned him to his fate. Whatever that may be.

# ROSOMON

She walked among the wounded. It had become a familiar ritual, but one Rosomon knew she had to endure. She had to witness every consequence of her actions, and those of her enemies. Had to see what misery this war wrought so that when it was over she could be sure that Torwyn would never suffer like it again.

Her only solace was that, despite the sorrow and sacrifice, they had been victorious. One more triumph. One more step and they were almost there. Almost at the great white gates of the Anvil.

The sudden thought of that city only served to remind Rosomon that her daughter was heading toward its walls. She could even now be walking into certain peril, and it was Rosomon who had allowed her to go. Allowed her to run straight into the mouth of the dragon. Yet again, she had to remind herself that Tyreta was a woman grown. Strong. Capable. Dangerous even. It still did little to assuage Rosomon's fears. Tyreta was all she had left. The only thing precious to her.

She shook her head, trying to dismiss the thought. It was self-indulgent. Unbecoming. Especially when there were so many around her who had sacrificed just as much, if not more, to secure their victory in this war.

Rosomon turned her attention to her surroundings. Before it

became a graveyard, Alumford had been home to a huge dye factory, the River Mordant given its name from the myriad colours it bore from the manufactory run-off. The only colour that ran along it now was red.

Scouts of the Talon hunkered on the riverbank, gathering water, some of them binding wounds. As she walked by, they bowed their heads in respect, and she offered them each a nod in return.

A little further on she saw rows of corpses, neatly laid side by side. Each was covered by a cloak or a sheet, hiding their faces from view, and once again Rosomon was reminded of how little dignity awaited any of them in death.

Not much further on, a mix of Armiger, Blackshield and miner were digging up the earth in which to inter the bodies. It made her wonder how many more pits they would have to dig before all this was over.

A tinkle of laughter rose above the sound of the river. Rosomon saw a group in the distance, purple-clad and seemingly unaffected by the aftermath. At the edge of the nearby wood glinted metal carapaces, a score of stormhulks standing boldly against the tree line. How different they looked now to the relentless titans that set the town afire a few short hours earlier. At their feet lounged the Hallowhill webwainers, talking casually, oblivious to everyone else's mournful reflection.

Rosomon had certainly taken a risk allying herself with them, but recent events proved it had paid off. The full consequences of striking such a bargain would only become evident when all this was finished. For now, she had other troubles to lament on.

As she saw Ianto marching toward her from the derelict town, Rosomon braced herself for the news he would bring. She knew what he was about to say—the report which it was his burden to relay after every battle they fought.

"Casualties were relatively light, my lady," he announced after a stiff bow. "The remainder of the Griffin Battalion troops have fled west. Marshal Terswell's body has been identified among the dead. The Ursus have suffered heavy losses thanks to the Hallowhills."

"And Marshal Sarona?" Rosomon half hoped there would also be news of her corpse. No one deserved to die more than she did after what the Ursus had done to Wyke.

"Survived. She is being held close by." Ianto paused for a moment. "And she demands to know what her fate might be."

"She demands?" said Rosomon, quelling her sudden fury. That woman had been responsible for the death of thousands; she was in no position to make demands. "Perhaps I should tell her myself."

Ianto led Rosomon further into the town, past the wrecked buildings, their burned carcasses leaving a bitter tang in the air. This had been a hive of activity once, much like Wyke. Now it was little more than ash. Rosomon wondered what had happened to the workers who used to live here. She could only hope they had managed to escape before the Ministry fell upon them.

A single wood-built dwelling stood intact, seemingly untouched by the inferno that had consumed the rest of Alumford. Two Titanguard stood vigil outside it, and Rosomon found herself fingering the hilt of the Hawkspur blade at her side as she drew closer. The door opened, and Kassian stepped out into the light. His head was bandaged, another wound to add to his tally, but it didn't seem to bother him.

"She's been asking for you," he said.

"So I hear," Rosomon replied. "Asking? Or demanding?"

Kassian shrugged. "Where the Armigers are concerned, there's little difference."

Rosomon followed the swordwright inside, where two more Titanguard stood waiting. Between them, tied to a chair, sat the woman she had hoped to meet for some time. Sarona struck a surprisingly insignificant figure, and the huge guards watching over her suddenly seemed a little excessive. Nevertheless, she looked up defiantly, but there was no hiding her shame. How it must have stung, this defeat. To be lashed to a chair awaiting her fate. There was dirt and blood caked about her narrow face, and she had been stripped of her armour. All she looked now was beaten.

"Rosomon Hawkspur," she said, affecting a wry smile. "It's good to see you. Although I'll admit, I'd have preferred it under different circumstances."

Rosomon gripped tight to the pommel of the sword at her waist. "You mean if I was the one tied to a chair? Or consumed by the sea?"

Sarona winced at that one. "Not my idea. Believe me."

"That was Sanctan, I assume?"

"I did my best to dissuade him. I knew it was a step too far but... well, you know how he is better than anyone."

Rosomon grasped the sword hilt so tight the leather around the grip offered a gentle creak. "Yes, I'm sure you were the voice of reason. I'm sure you struggled with it, just before your battalion murdered thousands."

"This is a war, Rosomon. People die."

She didn't need reminding of that. Of the graves dug. The loved ones lost. "Soldiers die. Civilians are murdered."

"Is that what you tell yourself to justify what happened to my troopers?" Sarona snarled.

Rosomon resisted rising to the bait. "Of course there's a difference. It's sad that you can't see it."

Sarona swallowed her ire, reclining in her chair as though resigned to her fate now. "So what next? Are you going to do what you did in Oakhelm? Your Titanguard going to drag me to the river and hold me under?"

It was a tempting notion. One Rosomon had pictured every day since Wyke, but she had already taken her vengeance for that. Now was the time for a cooler head.

"When I win this war, you will face the consequences of your crimes. You, along with your fellow conspirators, will be tried under the laws of Torwyn."

"When you win this war?" The wry smile was back on Sarona's lips. "That's confident. I like it."

"Trust me, you won't."

Sarona laughed defiantly, and it was all Rosomon could do not to draw that sword and use it.

When the laughing was done, Sarona regarded Rosomon through narrowed eyes. "You know, I saw you in the flesh once before. We were even introduced, but you don't remember that, do you?"

Rosomon couldn't, no matter how much she tried to think back.

Surely she would have remembered such a striking woman, but she had no recollection.

"No, I didn't think you would," Sarona continued. "It was years ago, but you were still so fucking haughty, even then. So confident. Sister to the emperor. Guildmaster. You didn't even offer me a second look." She leaned forward in her chair. "But you're looking now."

Rosomon swallowed down all her hate, doing her best not to shake with fury. She should have spat in this woman's face. Damned her for her petty vendetta. Instead she turned and left the confines of the house.

Once outside, she took a deep breath of the smoky air, feeling filthy after just being in that woman's presence. All she wanted was a hot bath to wash away the stench of this place, but that was a distant dream. Any thought of cleaning away the stink of Alumford faded when she saw riders approaching from across the bridge.

Kassian joined her as she made her way toward the approaching horses. As they trotted over the bridge she recognised the banners of the Mantid Battalion. Marshal Falko rode proudly at their head, and alongside him was the much smaller form of Emony Marrlock.

They reined in their steeds, and Emony dismounted, unable to hide the smile on her face as she approached Rosomon. Falko climbed down beside her, blond hair cut square across his scalp, face stern in comparison to Emony's beaming grin.

"Marshal Falko," Rosomon said in greeting. "This is unexpected."

"Lady Rosomon." He bowed courteously. "Apologies for my tardiness. I am sorry to have missed the battle, and I am sorry to have abandoned Wyke in favour of joining your advance on the Anvil. Rest assured I have left enough men behind to see it defended, but the fight is here. My battalion deserves to be at the vanguard when the final blow is struck against the Archlegate."

"I understand, Marshal." Not that there was anything she could have done to stop him had she even wanted to. "And I am grateful for your support. Our next push will see us reach the capital, and your troopers are more than welcome."

"What the bloody bollocks are you doing here?"

Rosomon turned at the bellow close behind her, seeing Oleksig striding toward them. Emony stepped toward her father, looking not a little embarrassed at his overbearing welcome.

"Father, I—"

"Never mind that—I told you to stay in Wyke. It's too dangerous—"

"I am a Guild heir," she interrupted, standing her ground as best she could. "I have come to fight alongside the rest of you. I can't be protected from this."

"There's no need for you—"

"There's every need."

Her chin was raised in defiance, and for a moment Rosomon saw just how similar she was to Tyreta. And what a good match she would have been for Fulren, had things turned out differently.

Rosomon stepped forward, laying a calming hand on Oleksig's shoulder. "Emony is right. You cannot protect her forever."

He opened his mouth to disagree but stopped. Despite his stubbornness, he was clearly in no mood to argue with Rosomon, especially when she had allowed her own children to take such risks. If Emony was to inherit any of his Guild responsibilities, she would have to make a stand with the rest of them.

Before any more could be said, there was a shout of warning from the west of the town. Two riders approached, Talon scouts, and between them stumbled a bound prisoner, desperate to keep up with the trotting horses lest he be dragged along behind.

"Lady Rosomon," one of the scouts said as they drew up their steeds. "We found this one lurking in the woods nearby. Says he was lost. Looks like a Corwen agent, by the way he's dressed."

Rosomon could see he did indeed bear the yellow garb of a Corwen actuary, but he clearly wasn't much of a spy. The sallow youth looked forlorn, for a moment reminding her of young Wachelm. She could only wonder what had happened to that poor boy in all this strife.

"Doesn't look like a spy to me," she said. "He wouldn't be dressed so obviously if he were."

The boy shook his head vigorously. "I'm no spy, my lady. Just a messenger."

"A messenger? Why would they have sent an actuary with a message?"

"I wish I knew," said the boy forlornly. "I've been lost in the woods since yesterday. I just do the bookkeeping, my lady. I was one of your administrators at the Anvil."

For the life of her she couldn't remember the face, just like she'd forgotten all about meeting Sarona however many years ago.

"So what's your message? Has Rearden Corwen seen the error of his ways? Does he wish to strike a bargain?"

"No," replied the boy. "My message comes directly from the Archlegate."

Rosomon took in a cleansing breath, but it did little to steady her anger. "And what does he want?"

The boy tottered on one foot as he removed his shoe. From inside it he took a piece of folded parchment. Kassian stepped forward and plucked it from the boy's bound hands before offering it to Rosomon.

She glanced at the waxed dragon seal for a moment before snapping it in two. Unfolding the paper, she recognised Sanctan's handwriting from the missives she had seen during her time in the Corwen administrative bureau.

"He wants to talk," she told the rest of them. "On neutral ground."

Oleksig reacted with a guffaw. "The insane priest wants to parley? Does he think we're as mad as he is?"

Rosomon crumpled the paper in her fist. "*I* want to talk."

That silenced Oleksig, who glanced at the others, wondering if he'd heard right.

Kassian let out a sigh. "How many times will you just walk into danger, Lady Rosomon? You certainly don't make things easy for your swordwright."

She offered him a shrug. "It will be on neutral ground. I'll be quite safe. Besides, it's just a casual chat with my nephew. What danger could I possibly be in?"

# KEARA

They rode south with all speed until they hit the banks of the Whitespin, then followed it upriver toward the Anvil. The hills hid their approach from prying eyes—any Ministry scouts hoping to catch them unawares. Not that Keara was worried about anyone sneaking up on them. She was pretty sure her travelling companion would sniff them out long before they got close.

As she regarded Tyreta atop her steed, she could sense the danger, the feral aspect to her. They'd ridden together for miles now, but still Keara couldn't shake that feeling of unease. Worse still was her curiosity nagging at her all the while. Only a matter of time before it won out over her sense of self-preservation.

"So what happened to you?"

No reply at first. Just the silence they'd shared for so many miles already.

"What do you mean?" Tyreta replied, without turning around.

"I mean why are you like that? The eyes. The claws. The weird markings. All of it. A curse or something? What is it?"

"None of your bloody business is what it is."

Keara sucked in a deep breath, ignoring the disrespect. She supposed if anyone deserved to give her a hard time it was Hawkspur.

"Look, this journey has been piss boring enough already. I'm just trying to pass the time."

Tyreta looked at her, brow creased in annoyance. "We're not on a casual jaunt, Hallowhill. This isn't supposed to be fun."

"No, I suppose you're right."

More silence as their horses clopped along the riverbank. But there was only so much silence Keara could take.

"You can trust me, you know. I realise now how wrong I was to—"

"Kill my friend? To murder my—"

"And I'm sorry for that. I already told you. It was nothing personal."

And it wasn't. If it had been, she might have felt some guilt when she'd killed that old man back in Castleteig. She hadn't felt a thing, unlike when she'd stuck her knife in Hesse's throat. That one had stung quite a bit.

"I doubt anything gets personal where you're concerned. I doubt the people you've killed mean anything. You'd sit there pulling the wings off flies if it kept you amused long enough."

"I'm not a monster."

She answered that too quickly, suggesting it had got to her. Then again, Hawkspur was probably right. All the evidence suggested she *was* a monster, old Ingelram's burned-up corpse was proof enough of that.

"Look," Keara said, "we've both done things that go against our better nature. Both made mistakes."

"You've got that right."

At last, some common ground. "Exactly, but now we have to work together or we're both lost. Your mother was right."

A sour look crossed Tyreta's face. "Don't I know it. Everyone is so quick to remind me of that fact."

"Families, eh. Can't live with them. Can't..."

Kill them? Keara had proved that wasn't true, and the memory of her father's screams would serve as a constant reminder.

"You should count yourself lucky," Keara continued, desperate to dispel that memory. "At least you still have a mother. One who loves and supports you. I lost mine years ago."

"Lost? I heard she ran away in the middle of the night. As far from you and your father as she could get. I haven't known you that long, but I can hardly blame her."

Keara felt the sting in that one, but what could she expect? "That hurts, Hawkspur. Especially since it's most likely a lie."

"Oh?"

"Oh yes. Chances are it was my father that had her killed."

A nonchalant shrug from Tyreta. "And you killed him. So I suppose now you're even."

It might have looked that way, but it didn't feel like she'd settled any scores. All she felt was alone. Head of a Guild that held her in nothing but contempt, desperate to salvage some glimmer of hope from this whole mess she'd helped create. Travelling beside her mortal enemy to betray the very man she'd followed into this Wyrm's lair.

"Getting even isn't the point. It never was. And it shouldn't be now. We've had our differences, hurt one another, but we have to get past that. We're allies now."

Keara surprised herself at how reasonable she sounded. Tyreta didn't seem to share her opinion, though, barely hiding the sneer on her face.

"But we're not friends. Make sure you remember that. Just keep your mouth shut and do as I say. Maybe that way we'll get out of this in one piece."

Keara bit her lip, curbing the insult she wanted to spit. She'd been disrespected for sure, but for Hawkspur to think she was somehow in charge... that would never stand.

"Listen, your mother might have been the one to send us on this mission, but I'll be damned if you—"

Tyreta held up her hand, reining her horse to a standstill. Keara did likewise, squinting down the road, trying her best to see in the waning light.

"What is it?"

Tyreta peered along the road. "We're here."

She kicked her horse further along the winding towpath and Keara followed, still unable to see a thing through the murky twilight. It wasn't until they rode up a steep incline that she spied the city, stark against the darkening horizon.

She was struck by how normal it looked. But for the lack of lights winking amid the rising spires, the place looked as it always had, as though it had no idea what was on its way, ready to change down its walls.

"So what's the plan?" Keara asked. "Ride up to those gates and bluff our way in?"

Tyreta shook her head. "Not likely. They'll be looking for me for sure. And by now, they'll have an inkling that you've betrayed them. Ride up to that gate and we'll be lucky to make it within a hundred yards."

"That's still not a plan, though, is it, Hawkspur. So what are we supposed to do? Fly over the wall?"

Tyreta gazed up toward the faint outline of the moon in the grey sky. "It'll be night soon. We'll head to the southern river gate and swim right through."

"We'll fucking what?"

Now Tyreta was smiling, gazing at Keara as though she were prey. "What's wrong? Can't swim?"

"I swim just fine, but generally I choose not to. Especially against the current of a fast-flowing river in the pitch dark."

"Well, right now our options are slim, so it's that or climb the wall. Take your pick."

Before Keara could argue further, Tyreta kicked her horse along the towpath. All Keara could do was follow, eyes on the murky waters as they flowed by. The river was mercifully bereft of traffic, which was one good thing, and the surface wasn't quite so slick with sludge from the manufactories as usual. Maybe it wouldn't be so bad after all.

By the time they drew within sight of the Anvil's southern gate, night had fallen. They both dismounted, leading their steeds into a thick spinney by the riverside. Tyreta removed saddle and bridle from her horse and slapped its rump, setting it free. As much as it pained her to lose her ride out of here if things went bad, Keara saw the sense in doing the same. She had no idea how long they might be in the city, and the horses would be no use to anyone if they starved.

When she was done, Tyreta led her the rest of the way through the dark. At times it was impossible to see, but Keara managed to keep up, stumbling every now and again, resisting the urge to curse, until they could finally see the southern river gate.

Of course, the portcullis was down, cutting off their only means of entry. So much for swimming.

"What do we do now?" She tried to whisper, but it came out as more of a hiss.

Tyreta held up a hand for her to be quiet. "Wait here. I'll open the gate, then you can swim through."

Keara shook her head. "How are you—?"

Tyreta had already vanished into the darkness.

Left alone with nothing but the rushing sound of the river, Keara resisted the urge to curse. It didn't take long for the dark to seem a little more imposing. The cold to be that much more chill. The longer she waited, the more she began to think Hawkspur had left her behind altogether. There was no sound from beyond the wall. No signal that Tyreta had even managed to make it inside.

A dull click broke the silence. Then another, as a windlass began to turn and the portcullis slowly rose in front of her. Maybe Hawkspur was good for something after all.

Reluctantly, Keara made her way down the bank of the river, pausing for a moment before she stepped in up to her knees. The cold of the water was shocking, but she forged ahead. There was no turning back now, and no way she'd balk at this and give Tyreta an excuse to call her a coward.

As she waded in to chest height, the freezing river almost stole her breath away. Taking a gulp of air, she kicked off, powering herself toward the open river gate. She wasn't prepared for the strength of the current or how cold those waters would be. It nearly dragged the breath from her lungs as it tried to suck her to the bottom of the riverbed.

She began to panic. Her long, lean strokes turning to a pawing, thrashing frenzy. Swimming against the flow of the river became a battle, and her head sank beneath the surface before she kicked her way back up.

It was pitch black, freezing cold, but still she fought, taking another gasp of air as she saw she had reached the threshold of the river gate. The portcullis hung above her, just out of reach. Not close enough, but too far to turn back. She had to carry on or she would be consumed by that damned river.

Her clothes were weighing her down. Too late to do anything about that now other than kick off her boots, but the effort of that might be the end of her. Should have thought about that earlier. The daggers at her waist seemed to weigh a ton, and as her head went under again she resisted the temptation to strip them from their scabbards and let them sink to the bottom of the river.

A stone jetty was just in sight, but still beyond reach. She kicked out, forcing herself to stay in control, to not panic. The river had all but leached every ounce of energy she had, but one last effort and she'd make it. Another gasp, another stretch of her arm, but her fingertips just missed the stone. The river took its chance, grasping her in a covetous grip, pulling her down, down...

Iron fingers snatched her wrist. Before the river could claim its victim, Keara was dragged free of its cloying arms and dumped unceremoniously onto the stone jetty.

She shivered, trying her best not to retch up the bitter waters. Her lungs heaved and she spat a string of bile, before managing to fill her lungs with air. Tyreta was standing over her, emotionless yellow eyes regarding her from the dark.

Keara shivered again, before rising to her knees, sopping wet at the side of the river. "Thanks, I guess. Don't suppose you brought a towel?"

"What does it look like?"

"So what? Am I supposed to walk these streets half drowned and sodden?"

"Stop whining and deal with it."

If Keara had been looking for sympathy, she was clearly in the wrong place. "Some fucking plan this was."

Tyreta grabbed hold of Keara's arm and pulled her to her feet. "The plan was you'd lead me to Olstrum. So how do we find him?"

Keara stripped off her wet tunic with some difficulty, and did her best to wring it out. "I know a man who will be able to find him. I think he lives just north of the Burrows."

"You think? That's a great start. Do you at least know his name?"

Keara squeezed as much river water as she could from her soaked hair. "I can't remember. We weren't exactly on first-name terms."

She could see Tyreta's jaw working in frustration. "That's just great. So how are we supposed to find him?"

"Calm yourself, Hawkspur. You think I'd lead us into this dragon's lair without some idea where I could find our man? He's a construction foreman for the city. We worked together to rebuild Archwind Palace after your Guilds tried to raze it to the ground. Every day he and his men would meet at one of the lower street taverns. It's called *The Gallows* or something. If we find it, we find him, though I'm going to look a little conspicuous turning up wetter than an otter's pocket."

Tyreta's look of concern never left her face as she unclipped the cloak from her shoulders and thrust it toward Keara. "Here."

"Oh, thank you. This will make all the difference."

Keara donned the cloak before leading the way up from the river, doing her best to ignore the squelching sound her boots made and the way her clothes clung to her like glue.

It was night, but they still had to be cautious. Luckily, before Keara had a chance to stumble into the path of a Revocater patrol or a group of marching Armiger troopers, Tyreta was there to stop her, leading them into the shadows until the threat had passed by.

Keara already had her suspicions that Tyreta could see in the dark, but the way she anticipated every danger was starting to get unnerving. Still, by the time they reached the northern end of the Burrows she couldn't help but feel grateful they'd got so far through their enemy's territory without being challenged.

"There it is," Keara whispered, gesturing across the street to the tavern that squatted on the corner. It was a seedy-looking place, even from the outside, a limp sign hanging above the door on rusted iron hinges with the words *The Noose* scrawled across it. A worn rope hung from it, but with no actual noose on the end.

"Seems very welcoming," Tyreta said, before leading them across the road.

Keara ignored the sarcasm as they approached. The windows to the tavern were boarded, and they could see no light from within. Listening at the door, she could hear muffled voices.

"All right, let me do the—"

"Talking?" Tyreta said. "Yeah, I get it. Not much I can do to stop you anyway."

The jibes were starting to grate on her, but Keara ignored it yet again and pushed the door open, leading them inside. The interior was pretty much what she'd expected—candlelit tables, muted conversation, that noxious blend of pipeweed and liquor that she'd never really liked.

A quick scan of the room and she was relieved to see the very man she had come for. The foreman sat at a table close to the long wooden bar, playing cards with a group of labourers she thought she recognised. If anyone would know how to find Olstrum it would be him. During the reconstruction of the palace, they'd both reported to the consul, and there was every chance this old curmudgeon still did.

She walked across the room as casually as she could manage with the wet clothes still clinging to her, but at least her boots had stopped squeaking. Tyreta was right by her side as she sat herself at a table close to the card players.

A boy approached them from a back room, his face showing how little he wanted to be there. Keara could only feel for him—she didn't want to be here either.

"What's your poison?" the boy asked with little enthusiasm.

The musty smell that hung about the place was starting to irritate Keara's nose. "Where do you get your wines from?"

The boy's brow furrowed in confusion, before he turned and gestured toward the bar. "I get them from that rack over there."

She tried to quell her sigh of frustration. "I mean, what kind have you got?"

That frown deepened on his perplexed forehead. "We've got red...or white."

"Red then," Keara replied, gesturing to Tyreta.

She shrugged at the boy. "I'll just have water."

This time that frown turned to a pained wince. "You'd be better off with wine." He leaned closer and whispered, "It's cleaner."

"Two red wines then," Tyreta replied.

"All right," the boy said. "But I'll be honest, it'll taste like shit either way."

"Thanks," said Tyreta. "We're not interested in the vintage."

"No, we're not." Keara rose to her feet, keen to get on with the job at hand.

Tyreta looked surprised at her sudden burst of enthusiasm. "Where are you—?"

Keara ignored her, striding across the room with as much confidence as she could, fixing a nonchalant grin to her face, despite how uncomfortable she felt in soaking wet clothes. There was a noisy scrape as she pulled one of the empty chairs back at the card table and sat herself down.

"Hello…" Damn it, she should have learned what at least one of these men was called when she had the chance. Hadn't seemed important at the time and too late now.

The foreman looked up from his cards. "Hallowhill?"

"You remember me. I'm flattered."

His look of surprise changed to annoyance. "What the fuck are you doing in here? Never mind that—what the fuck are you doing in the Anvil? Word is the Hallowhills have changed sides. Not that I'm surprised." He looked her up and down. "And why are you so wet?"

Keara raised her hands as though weighing something between them. "Ministry. Guilds. In the end aren't we all just citizens of Torwyn at heart?"

The foreman glanced at his labourers, as though one of them might have the answer, before looking back at her. "No."

Yeah, he was probably right about that. "Look, I'm not here to talk shit. I need to speak with Olstrum. You can get a message to him, I assume? You're one of his, right?"

He worked his mouth for a moment, suddenly on the spot. "I mean…I…"

"Olstrum has a dirty finger in every pie in this city, and whispers in every ear. Yours included. I need you to get word to him. Discreetly."

"I guess…I could. If properly motivated."

"Trust me, it'll be worth your while. When all this is over and done, you'll be on the winning side. And the Guilds will pay you better than whatever Sanctan's offering."

Again, the foreman looked around at his fellow card players. None of them had anything to say, but Keara could see they didn't think the idea was a bad one.

He looked back at her and nodded. "All right. You have yourself a deal. But you've got to get out of here. Rearden's boys have eyes and ears everywhere, and if you're spotted the game is fucked."

"Let's go then," she replied, standing up and gesturing for Tyreta to follow them.

As the foreman led them toward the door, the boy came toward them with two glasses of deep red, balanced precariously on a tray. Seeing she was leaving he looked forlorn that he'd made the effort in vain.

"You drink them," Keara said with a wink, before flicking a coin onto his tray.

The foreman was already at the door, leading them out into the night. Keara and Tyreta followed as he quickly walked along the street and ducked down an alleyway. As they continued down the lightless passage, Tyreta leaned in close.

"Don't you think this is a little too easy? How do you know we can trust him?"

Keara was starting to think the same thing. "What should we do instead? Wander the streets shouting for Olstrum at the top of our voices? We don't have much choice but to trust him. Besides, these workers are artless. They appreciate candour and know a good deal when they hear it. When you've spent as much time with the common man as I have, you get to learn their language."

"You speak the language of the common man, do you?"

Keara shrugged as though it were obvious. "Just trust me, Hawkspur. I've got us this far, haven't I?"

The foreman had stopped up ahead, and fumbled a key from his pocket. "In here," he said, unlocking a heavy iron door and leading them inside.

It was dark beyond that door, but when a pyrestone light winked on above them, Keara could see the room was iron banded like a cell. The foreman was already heading through another door in front of them, but before Keara could reach it he slammed it shut behind him. She spun in time to see the door they'd come through close with an even more resounding clang.

"Fuck," she spat.

She rushed to the door he'd escaped through, but there was no handle. A shove with her shoulder and it was obvious they were trapped. Likewise, Tyreta pushed at the door they'd come in, but that wasn't budging either.

Slowly Tyreta turned, with a *told you so* look on her face that was the last thing Keara needed. "Yeah. You really spoke his language."

Keara punched the metal door in frustration. "That duplicitous bastard. Why would he do this? How could I be so stupid?"

"Maybe he just thinks you're a patronising arsehole. Maybe you're not as good at reading people as you think. Maybe you're a privileged little princess who thinks everyone looks up to you, when really they think you're a stuck-up prig."

"And you're not? You followed me here, remember."

Tyreta took a step forward, those animal eyes glaring. "Only because I thought maybe you knew what you were doing. All you've proven is what a moron you are. You've just handed us both to Sanctan on a plate."

"Didn't see you coming up with a better idea." Keara's hands moved closer to the knives at her hips. Her palms tingled as the energy in their pyrestones began to agitate.

Tyreta was gritting her teeth, the dark claws slowly extending from her fingertips.

It had always been bound to come to this. "Make your fucking move, Hawkspur."

"Don't think I won't, Hallowhill."

A resounding click behind her, as a bolt was slid back. Keara glanced over her shoulder as the metal door opened with a creak. She expected to see the foreman, accompanied by a bunch of Revocaters, but instead it was a familiar face, wearing a familiar smug smile.

"What a lovely surprise," Olstrum said. "And how nice to see you both getting along so well."

# TYRETA

She hadn't meant to lose control, but lately she was finding it more difficult than ever to quell the feral urges. It might have felt good to put Keara in her place, but killing her would have been a step too far. Right now, anyway. When all this was over, if they both still lived, there'd be a score to settle, but seeing Olstrum made her remember this was far from over.

Tyreta allowed herself to calm down as he entered the chamber. She could sense Keara relaxing too—her hands moving from those daggers, unfettering her attachment to the web.

"What the fuck is going on here?" Keara snapped, Olstrum now the target for her frustration.

He raised his hands defensively. "You wanted to find me? Well, here I am."

"Yes... but... I meant—"

"Under different circumstances?" He grinned. As usual it didn't quite reach his tired eyes. "Come now, you didn't expect this meeting to be on any other terms than mine? Especially after you stabbed me in the back last time. But now we're all friends again, shall we perhaps continue this somewhere more comfortable?"

He beckoned them through the door. Tyreta let Keara go ahead, not quite trusting that she'd calmed down completely, and beyond the dingy chamber was a well-lit hall that twisted down beneath street level. They passed several bolted doors, corridors branching off every now and again—a labyrinth that seemed to suit Olstrum's purposes down to the ground.

Eventually they arrived at a nondescript door and Olstrum led them through into a huge chamber dripping with opulence, more a cosy homestead than a hidden lair. Armchairs lined the room, bookshelves reached to the ceiling, and a table with a decanter and crystal glasses stood in one corner beneath painted forgeries of old masters... or perhaps they weren't forgeries at all.

"Make yourselves at home." Olstrum gestured toward a cushioned sofa that rested by an archway. Tyreta could see it led through to a bedchamber with a huge iron-framed bed. Keara flung herself onto the sofa, exhausted, but Tyreta remained on her feet, still on edge. She'd never trusted Olstrum and wasn't about to start now, just because he'd invited them into his secret lair.

"How did you find us so quickly?"

He shrugged as though it was only a trifle. "You're stealthy, Tyreta, but nothing goes on within the walls of the Anvil I don't know about."

One of the bookshelves swung open, making the women flinch. A small, nervous-looking man entered, handing a bundle to Olstrum.

"Thank you, that will be all," he said, and the man quickly returned the way he'd come. Olstrum offered the bundle to Keara. "I took the liberty of sending for a towel and dry clothes. No need to be shy." She took them begrudgingly and began to strip off her damp outfit. "So why are you both here?"

"I finally got to give my mother your regards," Tyreta replied. "She assumed you were willing to help us, and sent us here to find you. Have we wasted our time?"

"No, you have not." He offered Keara a sour glance. "I was hoping to offer my help much sooner, but someone had other ideas."

Keara stopped rubbing at her long curls with the towel. "You mean me, right?"

"I thought we'd come to an accord, Hallowhill. Especially since I was the one who saved you from execution for murdering a High Legate."

"Look, I saw an opportunity and I took it. Don't tell me you wouldn't have done the same in my position."

Olstrum shrugged. "A fair assessment, I suppose."

Keara picked up the flowery blouse he'd given her, looking forlornly at the ruffled sleeves. "Is this change of clothes your way of punishing me?"

"What's done is done," Tyreta said, little interested in Olstrum's choice of fashion. "We need to move forward, and quickly. Can you get us access to Sanctan? Get us close enough to end this?"

Olstrum rubbed at his grey beard. "That could be tricky. He is guarded by Drakes night and day. I don't think I have to tell you how difficult that makes it to kill him. As gifted as you both are, I doubt even you're a match for a dozen armoured knights."

After what she'd been through at Castleteig against just two Knights of the Draconate, Tyreta was inclined to agree. "Then what about resistance fighters? There must be someone within the city still loyal to the Guilds. Still willing to fight."

He nodded. "Yes, that'll be less tricky. It might not seem it, but below the surface this city is roiling. There are hundreds, maybe thousands just waiting for their moment to rise up against the Ministry."

At last, the first sign of hope. "So when my mother arrives at the gates she'll have support from within?"

"She will. But right now they're too afraid to raise their heads. A revolt won't happen unless they're sure the Guilds can protect them. Sanctan has them cowed, afraid to even speak a word of dissent, and I don't blame them."

"My mother is coming. It won't be long, and then the Guilds will attack in earnest. And if we can spark an uprising from within the Anvil at the same time there's no way the Ministry will be able to stop her."

Olstrum listened intently before offering the faintest of nods. "That does sound like a plan. There's only one question I need answering... what's in it for me?"

Keara snorted a laugh. "There it is, but what could we have expected from you, Garner? Tell you what—how about you help us out and we'll forget the fact you betrayed the emperor and let Sanctan burn half the country down?"

Olstrum met her curt suggestion with steel in his eyes. "That's not enough."

Tyreta could see he was dead serious. "What then? Money? Land? Power? If you help us win this, you know it's all yours for the taking."

He looked at Keara, and for a moment it was as though they had a silent understanding. "She knows what I want."

"She does?" Tyreta asked. "Then does one of you want to let me in on it, or do I have to guess?"

Keara fixed her with a knowing grin. "Your ever benevolent cousin took Olstrum's family. I'm guessing his price is their safe return."

From Olstrum's silence, Tyreta knew that was exactly what he wanted. "Then we'll do it. We can rescue them, right? My mother has more than enough—"

"Just one problem," Keara said. "We have no idea where he's keeping them."

"Ah. Yeah, I suppose that's...an issue."

Olstrum moved a step toward the table and its decanter of wine, looking almost longingly at it before changing his mind. "I have used every contact, dispatched every agent at my disposal. Even I can't discover their location. Only Sanctan knows their whereabouts."

"But if you help us defeat the Ministry, capture Sanctan, we can find them. We'll force him to tell us."

Olstrum found that one amusing. "They'll be dead before you can clap Sanctan in irons. His spite knows no bounds."

Tyreta did her best to quell the frustration. "So what are we supposed to do?"

"That's your problem, Hawkspur. But know this—if you don't find them, and see them safe, you'll get no help from me."

She wanted to grab him and shake him. To explain that this was bigger than any of them, that they had all made sacrifices and it was his selfishness that had got them into this in the first place. But she could see from the determined set to his jaw he would not be moved.

"Fine. Then I'll return to my mother. Tell her your demands.

She'll know what to do. She has the Talon. If anyone can find your family it's them."

"That's a great idea." Keara was vainly trying to flatten the pleats in the unflattering skirt she had donned. "And I'll stay here. Olstrum can introduce me to this resistance movement. I can—"

"No," Olstrum said. "I can't trust you, Hallowhill. You've already betrayed me once. It won't happen again."

Keara glanced helplessly at Tyreta, then back to Olstrum. "Don't you think we're a little past that now?"

"No. I don't trust you as far as I can throw a boulder. And look at me." He held out his slender arms to show that boulder throwing was definitely not in his wheelhouse. "You go back to Rosomon. Tyreta stays. Besides, might be better if you're the one looking for my family. Your methods are probably better suited to it. Do whatever it takes. Kill whoever you have to. But make sure they're safe."

Keara shook her head. "I need to be here. I'm the one who should spearhead the revolt against—"

"No." It was a word spoken with such finality that even Keara couldn't argue with it.

She raised her hands forlornly. "I've only just arrived. I almost died swimming that river and you expect me to—"

"Your way out will be dryer. Trust me. And when you get back to the Guild encampment, I suggest you start by asking your prisoners what they know. Sanctan will have loyal followers among them. Maybe one of them heard something."

"Thanks for the tip. So if I do manage to make it back in one piece, and do manage to find their location, and do manage to rescue them, how do you expect me to let you know about it?"

"A signal might do the trick."

"A signal like what?" Keara asked, not even trying to hide her exasperation.

Olstrum considered it for a moment, before a slight smile crossed his lips. "When my wife and I were first courting it was midwinter. One night I gifted her a scarf, it was all I could afford at the time. She kept it all these years. When I see a flare from the east that's the same colour as that scarf, I will know she's safe."

Keara looked distinctly unimpressed by Olstrum's uncharacteristic openness. "How romantic."

He picked up a tiny bell that sat beside the decanter and rang it. "Actually... it was."

That bookshelf slid open once again, and the silent servant appeared. Olstrum gestured toward the diminutive man. "Go. You'll be seen safely beyond the boundary of the city."

"Now?" Keara asked.

"The longer you remain here, the more time you waste, Hallowhill. Safe travels."

"I swam a river to get here. I almost drowned."

Olstrum had nothing more to say and Keara gritted her teeth, offering neither of them so much as a second glance as she followed the tiny man through the secret door, and the bookshelf closed again.

They were alone. Tyreta began to feel slightly awkward, and thought maybe sitting down might help. Once she had eased herself into one of the comfortable chairs she realised how much it didn't.

"So, how is your mother?" Olstrum asked.

"How do you think she is? The nation she is charged to protect is burning down around her, and she faces the might of an entire religion."

"Yes. I'm sure that's troubling. But I meant, how is she in regard to me?"

She should have realised that was what he meant. "I'll be honest, I don't think you're at the forefront of her mind right now."

"Of course. I imagine she has more important things to think on." He looked at her as though seeing her for the first time. "It does surprise me that she let you come here, though. I would have thought Lady Rosomon would be much more protective, considering what happened the last time she let you out of her sight."

"I'm my own woman now, Olstrum. I make my own decisions. Besides, we've all had to stand and be counted."

He nodded his agreement, but there was a shadow that crossed his eyes. "Yes. Yes we have."

"If you're worried about what she'll do to you once this is all over, then don't be. She has changed, for sure, but she's still a fair woman. Despite all she's lost, and your part in that, I'm sure if you help us win this your past... mistakes will be forgiven."

Olstrum still looked no nearer to being convinced. "You have to understand, I had no choice."

The sound of him trying to justify his actions, ones that had seen so many perish, made Tyreta grip tight to the arms of that chair. "Yes you did. You had a chance to stop this from happening, you just didn't take it. You could have gone to my mother. My uncle. You could have told them what Sanctan was planning before he had a chance to—"

"And my wife, my children, would be dead right now."

"Instead of the thousands who've died in their place." As much as she felt sympathy for his plight, she still couldn't forgive him for the things she'd seen. The things she'd lost.

If those words stung him in any way, he didn't show it. "One day, if you ever have children of your own, you'll understand why I did what I did. You'll have that same feeling toward them. That same certainty of purpose every parent shares. You'd happily see the whole world drown so they could have just one more day safe on dry land."

Tyreta didn't think she would ever understand, but then she had never seen Olstrum so impassioned before. It made her squirm a little in that chair. Probably best to change the subject. "So what do you expect me to do here while we wait for your signal?"

He grinned an empty grin. "I may not trust Hallowhill with meeting the resistance movement, but you... I think it might benefit them to know the Hawkspurs are on their side."

"When?"

"Don't be so eager. I'll gather the key leaders and arrange a meeting. First, I suggest you get some rest."

He gestured toward the bed in the other room. As much as she was keen to stoke the flames within the Anvil, it did look inviting. Maybe those flames could wait, at least for another night.

# FULREN

A moonless night along a twilight road, but even without his helm he could see distant lights on the eastern horizon. The faint tang of cinders hung on the air. A battlefield some days old, the ghost of it still haunting their path.

"Can you tell where we are?" he asked.

Verlyn didn't answer right away, as though working out their rough location. "Passing Castleteig, I reckon. It must be just beyond the hills over there. From that smell the whole place must be burning. Best we keep going through the night."

He yearned to get nearer, to see what was happening. To help if he could. But Verlyn was right. They had to keep going. Find his mother. She would know what to do.

Besides, he had no idea what he was capable of yet. He remembered that rush as he'd used his new gift. The one Lysander had helped him tap into. It had been a strange kind of reverie, limitless power to be harnessed, but he had to be cautious. There was still no telling what might happen were he to channel that sorcery again. He might be a danger to everyone around him. To himself. Probably best he keep that power buried until there was no other choice than to call upon it.

The memory of that crow came back to him as they rumbled

along the road. He had quelled its voice, silenced it forever, but now there was something else within him, roiling just beneath the surface. It should have been frightening. Instead Fulren couldn't wait to see it unleashed.

He was stronger, for sure. More than ever, despite the loss of his limbs. If only he could learn to control the artifice that was almost as much a part of him as his real arm. But those legs and that arm still felt odd. He was still a little clumsy, a little slow, but maybe with practice he would learn to master them.

A distant caw. He turned toward it, sensing a bird in a tree nearby. Verlyn didn't react to it, just another crow on the branches watching them pass by. Fulren had seen its like a hundred times on their path, though. Too many times to be normal. Were the crows drawn to him? Was this some legacy of the power he had defeated in his visions? Certainly they seemed to stand in vigil wherever he went, when all the other creatures that lurked in the undergrowth hid from his passing.

The air gradually cleared as they left the blasted city of Castleteig in their wake, but they hadn't left it too far behind before Fulren saw a faint flickering of yellow light just off the road ahead.

"Is that a camp?" he asked.

"Looks like it," Verlyn replied. "They're not doing anything to hide themselves, so probably not military. Refugees most likely."

He could hear the faint sound of voices drifting on the breeze. "Should we stop here? Might be safer for us among a group of people."

He could see her faint red outline looking him up and down. "Your call, I guess. But I'm not sure how they'll react when they get a look at you."

Fulren pulled his cloak tighter around him, suddenly more aware than ever of what he had become. How he might be regarded by folk already fearing for their lives.

"Maybe we'll stop nearby. No need to spook anyone. I just think it'll be better than setting up camp in the middle of nowhere. We'll be less conspicuous in a crowd."

Verlyn tugged on the reins, driving the horses off the road. They followed a path through the trees and he could see more fires ahead. There must have been at least a hundred people sheltering beneath the canopy, whispering to one another. Lamenting their loss.

"All right," Verlyn said, drawing the horses to a stop. "Let's just mind our business. Remember, we're refugees. We need to act like any other ordinary travellers. Think you can manage that?"

"I'll do my best." He climbed down from the cart, the slightest whisper as his hydraulic limbs eased him to the ground, reminding him that he was anything but normal.

As Verlyn unhitched the horses, he hunkered at the edge of the trees, listening to the hushed conversations from the distant camp. He couldn't make anything out but whispers, but they carried with them a sense of the forlorn. A sadness on the breeze as it drifted through the woods.

From that unquiet dark, someone approached. Just a hazy grey figure against the black, but he was definitely heading their way.

"Someone's coming," Verlyn said. Fulren continued to crouch within his cloak as the figure reached them.

"Welcome." A man's voice. Mature. Nervous. "Where have you both come in from?"

"From the southeast," Verlyn lied. "Me and my nephew."

A pause as the man regarded Fulren crouching there. If he had any thoughts on the blind man hunkering in his cloak he didn't say it.

"From the Rock?" he asked. "Yes, we heard what happened. It was a crime what they did to that place." Fulren had no idea what he was talking about, but he could well imagine what the Ministry might have done to any city that resisted their dominance. "Where are you headed?"

"Where are any of us headed?" Verlyn replied. "We're just trying to stay out of trouble. And ahead of the Armigers."

"Then I'm afraid you'll need to be moving on at first light, along with the rest of us. Rumour has it the Auroch and Raptor Battalions are moving this way from the east. They're most likely going to meet up with the rest of the Ministry forces to the north and take on the Guilds."

"We only intend to stay here the night. We'll be moving on in the morning."

"Wise," he replied. "But there's a warm fire just through the trees, and food if you're interested. We have enough to share."

"I don't think—"

"Please. You and your nephew must have been through a lot. We're all just trying to ride out the same storm here. You're proud, I get that, but don't suffer because of it when there's no need."

Verlyn thought on it. "All right. No harm in that, I guess."

"Good. My name is Rufus. Please, follow me," he said, before moving back toward the encampment.

Verlyn sighed. "Looks like we're getting to know these people after all."

Fulren stood. "It's all right. Would be good to just sit and listen to some ordinary people for a while. I can't remember the last time I did that."

Verlyn offered her arm, and he took it as they followed the man through the trees. Better they think he was blind, it might stop them asking too many awkward questions.

In a clearing beyond the woodland he could see so many bodies, hear so many hushed voices. Verlyn led him to the nearest fire, and he suddenly appreciated the warmth as he knelt down, careful to make sure his metal limbs were hidden within the cloak that was pulled tight around him. There were others around that fire, he could sense them in the dark, but no one spoke.

"Make yourselves comfortable," Rufus said. "You'll be safe here."

They were both brought food as promised. Fulren surprised himself at how quickly he consumed the meat stew, but then he'd been ravenous for days. Even when he was done, he still felt hunger clawing at his innards, but didn't think it right to ask for more. There were so many people here. So much misery. His needs seemed inconsequential by comparison.

"Where have you all come from?" Verlyn asked, when they'd finished eating.

"When the Armigers came to Castleteig, most of us ran," Rufus said. "We formed a camp just east of the city. Maybe a couple thousand of us. When the fighting started in earnest we thought it best to move on, and split up into smaller groups, trying to avoid the patrols. Mostly they leave us be, but we've heard stories. There's a town not too far north been taken over by one of the Armigers and we heard rumours about it. Dark stories. Don't know if they're true or not, but we thought it best to avoid any troopers now, so we keep moving."

"Who holds Castleteig?" Fulren asked.

"Phoenix and Tigris hold it for the Ministry. They fought the Viper Battalion for weeks back and forth across the river. But there was no way the Viper could last forever. By all accounts they withdrew from the city last month."

"And where are they now?" he asked, hoping they were close. Maybe if they could find what remained of a battalion loyal to the Guilds it might make their journey north easier.

"No one knows," Rufus replied. "They disappeared into the hills. Left us and the city behind. Abandoned us just like the Guilds."

"The Guilds haven't abandoned you," Fulren replied, feeling suddenly defensive. "They'll put things right. Lady Rosomon won't give up until things are back the way they were."

"You think?" he said, sounding unconvinced. "It's the Guilds got us into this."

"The Ministry did this. They were the ones who murdered Sullivar. Who burned everything—"

"Does it matter?" Rufus said. Fulren could feel the rising anger in his voice. See his silhouette suddenly agitate with red. "Ministry, Guilds, who cares. Fact is they're the ones at war and everyone else is suffering for it."

"Of course it matters. We've been—"

He felt a calming hand on his arm. Verlyn, letting him know he was talking too much, letting his emotions take control.

"Who are you?" Rufus asked. "Some Guild lackey?"

Fulren tried to calm himself. "No. I'm no one."

Silence for a moment, and he wondered if Rufus would accept that.

"I'm sorry, son," he said eventually. "It's just...I've lost everything. We all have. I didn't mean to take it out on you."

"There's no need for you to be sorry," Fulren replied. And there wasn't. Rufus had been caught up in this war between Ministry and Guild, and had clearly picked neither side. Still, he suffered for it just the same.

All these refugees had their own people to care for, whether it was family or friends. What did it matter to them who won this war? They were ordinary folk, and to them there was no advantage to either victor in this conflict. It was up to the Guilds to persuade them they were worthy of support, and it was clear they had done a poor job until now.

The Guilds had failed these people, that was the truth of it. A gap had been left for the Ministry to fill. The good the Guilds were supposed to do had obviously not been as far-reaching as Fulren always thought. They had failed in their duties, and he could only feel responsible for that.

"Mind if I join you?"

Fulren turned his head at the voice, hearing someone approach their fire.

"Please do," said Rufus, and a man crouched down by the flames. "Where are you from, friend?"

The man finished chewing on something, then took a drink to clear his throat. "Just came down from the north. Thought things would be quieter down this way, but I guess not."

Fulren felt his excitement grow. "What word from the north?"

"Not so great," he replied. "There was a battle at the River Mordant. Guilds met the Ministry on their way to the Anvil."

Fulren gripped his cloak tighter about him, trying his best not to seem too invested in what the man was saying. "And they won? The Hawkspurs?"

"They did. But then Lady Rosomon has cut a swath all the way from the coast. Not that you can blame her after what happened to Wyke. She took Oakhelm then—"

"What happened to Wyke?" Fulren asked, failing to hide the desperation in his voice.

"I thought everyone knew. There was a flood. Took the whole city. Ursus Battalion blew the dam and drowned the place. They say Lancelin Jagdor was killed, but Lady Rosomon and the rest of the Guilds managed to—"

"Lancelin Jagdor is dead?"

"Yes. And thousands beside. It was a massacre, but those Ministry fuckers don't care how many of us die as long as they cling on to power."

Fulren suddenly felt sick. He could hear a sudden low buzzing noise, as though a pyrestone were about to burst in its conversion chamber. The necroglyph at the nape of his neck began to stir, heat coursing along his spine. He didn't want to believe it, that thousands had been murdered, but there was no reason for this man to lie. Wyke was gone. So many souls. And Jagdor along with them.

He felt Verlyn place a hand on his shoulder as she leaned in. "It's all right, Fulren."

The pulse of the necroglyph intensified, burning, emulating the red rage building up within him. "No, it's not all right."

"You have to stay calm," she said.

Those limbs of steel had never felt more alien. As though they had a life of their own, now fuelled by his frustration, they began to articulate. His left hand curled into a fist. Hydraulics hissing as he rose to his feet.

He could hear gasps of alarm and a sudden shriek as he raised himself to full height. His limbs reflected the firelight as he was revealed to the gathered refugees; a beast of metal and flesh. A woman screamed into the night, but Fulren did not care, did not balk at the fear he inspired.

It only fed him.

"What is that?" he heard Rufus scream. "What in the Lairs are you?"

Fulren strode toward him, leering down, spitting through his gritted teeth. "The Lairs? The fucking Lairs? You think that's what waits for you? You still believe in your dragon gods after all the Ministry has done to you?"

"Fulren." Verlyn's call cut through the panicked yells as she tried to quell his fury, but it did no good.

He tore the cloak from around his shoulders, showing them what he was, what he had become. Fear fast spread through the camp as people began to flee—he could see them silhouetted against those fires, running for their lives. It should have given him pause, made him stop this madness before it went too far, but instead Fulren stalked further into the camp.

In the light of the flames he saw one man brave enough to grasp a burning brand and bar his way. Defending his family, perhaps? It didn't matter.

Fulren planted his feet, their steel talons gripping the ground. "Strike if you dare."

The brand fell from the man's fingertips. He staggered back, before turning and racing into the night. Fulren fought the urge to pursue him, to run him down. Instead, he walked deeper into the camp, searching for the next pathetic cur with enough courage to stand in his way. Hoping he would have the chance to vent his ire.

He only heard a whimper.

Fulren turned. Scant yards away he saw the outline of someone crouching, could hear her sobs. Peering through the dark he discerned a woman holding a child close, too fearful to flee. In response, the necroglyph burned more intensely than ever, urging him on...

No. It did not control him. He had already proven his will was stronger.

In that instant his body felt less invigorated, his metal limbs becoming more cumbersome. Fulren staggered away from the cowering woman, realising what he had done. All those people, filled with terror, running from his path like frightened animals. He had allowed his anger to best him. Allowed the demon within to take control.

In a tree close by he heard the squawk of a crow...

"Fulren." He turned at Verlyn's voice, seeing her scarlet outline roiling with as much panic as those refugees. "We have to go. Now."

With a whine of hydraulics, he lowered himself on those metal legs. The false arm at his shoulder felt heavier than ever, and he was tired. So very tired.

"Yes...let's go."

She led the way back toward their wagon. When they reached

the horses, she swiftly hitched them before turning to face him once more. "We can't be around people. It's too dangerous. We've got to get you to your mother."

Fulren shook his head, trying to clear the lingering rage. "What do you think she can do?"

"I don't know, maybe help you? Maybe point you at the real enemy and let you loose? It's got to be better than wandering the wilds frightening ordinary folk."

"I don't need her to point me at the enemy," he said.

"What do you mean?"

Fulren thought back to what Rufus had told them. "There's a town north of here, remember? An Armiger Battalion has taken it over."

"Whatever you're thinking, don't. We have to get north. We don't have time to—"

"Yes we do," he said, feeling that familiar tingle at his neck. "I need to know exactly what I'm capable of."

At first she didn't reply, considering his words as the horses snorted in the dark. "Then I guess I can't do anything to stop you."

And she was right.

# CONALL

It was a vast complex perched upon the summit of the valley wall. Within its huge steel-lined walls, thirty-foot silos surrounded a gaping hole in the ground. Pump jacks and piping and all manner of artifice delved into the borehole, used to churn up the raw infernium that lay within. Conall had no idea how any of this still worked, but he guessed it didn't matter now they were about to blow the entire thing.

Despite how valuable this place was to the Guilds, how crucial it was for the powering of artifice, it had to be destroyed. The Auroch and Raptor Battalions were even now moving their way north. He had to stop them linking up with the other Ministry forces at the Anvil. Had to give his mother a fighting chance.

Sonnheld had put him in charge, and he was determined not to mess this up. Unfortunately, now he was here, he realised he had no idea what he was doing.

Luckily, Donan did.

Conall had never seen him so animated as he bossed those Viper troopers, instructing them with all the authority of an Armiger marshal. He knew exactly where the charges needed to be fitted to be most effective, explaining to anyone who would listen how the subsequent explosion would affect the geological integrity of the valley wall. It was doubtful any of them had a clue what he was babbling about, but he certainly talked a convincing game.

It was good to see him enjoying his role. Good to see him walking with confidence on that hydraulic leg. Good to see him smile. Sted, however, looked far from happy. But what else had he expected?

"Something you want to tell me?" Conall asked, as she watched the proceedings with her trademark scowl.

She didn't even look at him. "Certainly not, Captain. I am performing my duties as ordered. No complaints from me."

"Are you sure? Only I'm sensing a little tension."

She sucked a long breath of air through her nose. "Compliance is my middle name, Captain. I mean, I'll stink of oil for a week, and there's every chance I'll get blown to shit before this is over, but I am here to serve."

Conall did his best not to grin. Of everything he had missed about being home, Sted's bad attitude was among the most cherished.

"All right," Donan called, his voice echoing through the colossal structure. "That should do it."

Conall nodded to Moraide, signalling that they were finished here. She barked at her men to move out, and Conall was impressed at how obediently they responded to her orders. Seeing Sted with that permanent scowl made him suddenly yearn for obedient troopers of his own. Then again, he guessed you got exactly the kind of soldiers you deserved.

As a single unit they hurried from the facility, out into the bright sunlight. The ground was rocky, but they picked their way along the ridge with all haste, putting as much distance between them and the explosives as they could. Conall chanced a look over the edge, seeing a long drop to the valley floor. East, along the top of the valley, was the second infernium facility in the distance. They hadn't progressed more than a hundred yards before Conall saw a sight that made him stop in his tracks.

"Shit," Sted hissed. "I knew this was going too well."

They were more than a mile away along that valley floor—Armiger troopers marching like an advancing horde. The dull tan armour of the Auroch Battalion was just discernible, pennants flying proudly, weapons glinting as they tramped along the wide road that cut through the gorge. Even from this distance Conall could see they had come in force—thousands of them, and the Raptors would not be far behind.

"That's sooner than we thought," Donan breathed, staring ahead fearfully.

"Then we'd best get a move on," Conall replied, signalling for them to keep going.

The group ducked down as they moved, keeping their heads below the ridgeline. If they were spotted the whole game would be up. Those troopers might be at the bottom of the valley, but this job would be a lot more difficult if they started lobbing mortar shells while Conall and his team tried to plant volatile explosives.

The second facility loomed up ahead, and Conall had to resist the urge to burst into a sprint to reach its huge doors. They were all panting heavily by the time they eventually made it, and silently Conall gave the signal for Moraide and her troopers to enter the place. The doors slid open on rusted hinges, creaking so loud Conall had to grit his teeth. When they were wide enough, he squeezed through and immediately noticed how this place didn't stink like the first building. As his eyes adjusted to the gloom he saw there were no tanks of infernium, nor a vast gaping hole in the centre of the structure.

"What's going on, here? Where are the silos?"

Donan looked around nonplussed. "I don't...oh dear."

He gazed through the huge open window that shed light on the interior. Conall moved closer, gazing out to a bridge that spanned the valley. On the other side was another metal structure.

"This isn't good news is it, Donan?"

He winced. "Well, it must have skipped my mind." He pointed across the metal bridge. "But the infernium refinery is on that side of the ravine. This is just a storehouse."

"Of course it fucking is," Sted snarled.

"All right." Conall tried to stay calm, desperate not to panic. "We just have to get across, plant the charges, and get back without being spotted. Easy as that."

"Easy as that," Sted repeated, fury in her eyes.

"You heard the man," Moraide said. "Let's move."

At her order, the Viper troopers turned toward the door, but Conall held up his hand to stop them. "No, wait. The fewer of us cross that bridge, the less chance we'll be spotted. We'll go." He gestured to Donan and Sted. "Just the three of us."

Moraide shook her head. "Captain, I have my orders. Marshal Sonnheld told me—"

"Marshal Sonnheld isn't in charge here. I am. You have your troopers to think of. If we all go tramping across that bridge we'll be spotted before we've made it halfway. Trust me on this. I know what I'm doing."

He didn't have any idea what he was doing, but luckily Moraide looked like she saw the sense anyway. "All right, Captain. We'll be waiting here for you when you get back. Don't take too long."

She turned to her troopers and gestured for them to move out. Conall watched as they made their way outside in perfect order, wondering if he'd made a mistake. Too late to lament now.

"And then there were three," Sted said.

"I'm not happy about this either," Conall replied, leading them toward the bridge, hearing the distant tramp of feet echoing up from within the valley. It was enough to make his stomach lurch.

They reached the lip of the ravine, and Conall crouched down. The relentless armoured might of the Armigers had almost marched to within the shadow of the bridge. They were a hundred feet below, but unless they looked directly up they wouldn't spot anyone crossing... with a little luck.

"How far to the other side, do you reckon?" he whispered, gazing across the metal structure.

Donan squinted. "Maybe two hundred yards."

"We can make that without being seen... right?"

"Sure," Donan replied enthusiastically.

Sted had nothing to add, but from the look on her face she was far from convinced.

"All right then. Let's get this over with."

He kept his head down, stepping out onto the bridge. It was

solidly built, not a creak or groan as he placed his foot on it, but the steel slats that crisscrossed its base were wide enough to see through. Below those Armigers marched on, and with every step he willed them not to look up.

Behind him he could hear Sted cursing through gritted teeth. A glance back over his shoulder and he was relieved that Donan was with them, picking his way carefully across the bridge, that metal leg of his barely making a sound.

Halfway across and it was all he could do to stop himself sprinting the rest of the way, but that would surely give the game away. He just had to keep moving, just had to hope they weren't spotted, that the facility at the other side was filled with enough infernium to make this risk worthwhile.

As he stepped onto solid ground at the other side he almost gasped in relief. Sted was right behind him, brow beading with sweat and creased in concentration. Donan brought up the rear. They didn't speak as Donan led them toward the facility and took hold of the handle that would slide one of the doors open.

"Please, please, please," he whispered as he gently pulled open the huge door, revealing a dark interior.

Conall peered in, his eyes adjusting to the gloom, but before he could see whether the silos of infernium were inside he smelled that oil tang on the air. Stepping inside, a smile spread across his face as he saw a dozen huge storage tanks lining the walls.

"Let's get to it," he said, in no mood to hang around.

Donan was only too eager to do as he was told, locating the most strategic spots where their explosives would do the most damage and laying the charges.

"We don't have long before the last of those troopers marches into the gorge," Conall said. "Best we set these charges on a short fuse."

Donan nodded, tinkering with the mechanical timer.

"Let's just hope there's no more fucking surprises," Sted griped.

Donan fiddled with the setting on the device. "I think it would surprise us all if you could utter a sentence that wasn't laden with profanity."

Conall had to suppress a grin. "Whoa, Donan. Is that you finally growing a pair of balls?"

Sted didn't look nearly as impressed. "Looks like it. Though if you want to keep them, Marrlock, you'd best watch who you're talking to."

"All right," Conall said, moving to the door. "If we've all quite finished, can we get out of here now?"

Donan nodded, placing the timer down and stepping away gingerly. Conall led them back out, hearing the echoing crunch as thousands of feet marched below. He reached the edge of the bridge, crouching down to see the last of the Armiger troopers making their way into the steep valley.

All they had to do was make it back across, not get spotted, and not get blown to bits by the charges they'd just planted. Easy.

He took a first step. The way back across that bridge looked a lot further than it had on the way here. Conall tried to put that from his mind, concentrating on one foot in front of the other. Sted and Donan were close behind. One of them was breathing pretty heavily, but he didn't bother looking back to find out who.

Halfway, and he let out the breath he'd been holding. They were almost there. They were gonna make it.

Sparks flew as something struck the corrugated bulwark next to his head. Shouts of alarm bellowed from below. Auroch troopers were pointing at them—a sharpshooter raising his longbarrel.

"Move!" Conall yelled, rushing across the bridge as fast as he could.

The others followed, all thoughts of stealth abandoned as their heavy tread shook the bridge. Donan's voice pealed out behind as he shouted "Fuck, fuck, fuck" repeatedly. So much for his aversion to potty mouths.

A snap of volley fire from below and the bridge came alive with the sound of ricocheting shot. Splintbows clapped, but the range was too far for their bolts to be much of a worry. Nevertheless, Conall threw himself to the floor as a projectile whizzed past his head.

Looking up, he saw Moraide was at the far side of the bridge—maybe forty feet away. She was yelling at her troopers above the din, their splintbows unleashing bolt after bolt onto the Auroch Battalion beneath them.

Another loud snap, as superheated shot smashed a hole in the corrugated bridge not three feet from Conall.

"How short was that fuse, Donan?" he yelled above the noise.

"Pretty short!" wailed the reply.

Sted rose to a crouch behind him, stealing enough time to shoot a few bolts from her splintbow, but in response a missile lanced by, slicing a divot in her arm. She cursed, falling back as the weapon slipped from her grip.

Conall reached forward to grasp the fallen splintbow, but as he did so there was a faint voice in his head, urging him to run. To flee as fast as he could and abandon his friends.

Was it the demon inside him, or just the sudden urge to survive? Self-preservation quashing all sense of loyalty?

"Go," he snarled, aiming down on the firing Auroch troopers and squeezing the trigger. "Get moving."

Donan grabbed hold of Sted, doing his best to haul her across the bridge as more shot zoomed by them, blasting into the corrugated bridge and punching through metal.

As Conall aimed again, there was a deafening explosion.

He was thrown to the floor, the bridge rumbling beneath him, its tremor rattling his teeth. Opening his eyes, he saw that the complex had collapsed into a smoking heap, dust billowing into the air, covering everything. The splintbow had fallen from his grip and he scrambled to pick it up, knees shaking as he stood. He squinted through the cloud, seeing that Sted and Donan had reached the safety of the other side.

Conall sprinted after them, but half a dozen steps and he could feel the bridge giving beneath him. Steel girders groaned, the platform lurching under his feet, then listing forward. Still he ran, twenty yards to go, fifteen. He abandoned the splintbow, desperate not to panic, as the bridge began to collapse. With five yards to go, he leapt.

The bridge fell away beneath him.

He hit the wall of the ravine, managing to grab on to a spike of jagged metal. It was a struggle to gasp in air as he hung there, his moist grip loosening by the second. Stupid to look down, but he couldn't stop himself, seeing certain death staring back through the choking dust cloud.

The metal he was holding on to began to bend under his weight, his fingers slipping, the ground beckoning...

A hand grabbed his wrist. Donan's face stared down, eyes wide in desperation. Sted leaned down too, snatching Conall's outstretched hand.

He kicked his legs, boots scraping at the wall of the ravine as they dragged him up and hauled him onto firm ground. Conall gulped in the dusty air, relieved he hadn't soiled himself.

"You cut that one close, Hawkspur," Moraide said, standing beside her troopers.

"Yeah, you could say—" He didn't have a chance to finish before something shot past his ear.

More missiles soared past, and they were ducking again, stumbling away from the cliff edge. As they made their way across the sloping ground and down the other side of the valley, the charges finally exploded at the first facility.

Conall watched in awe as it blew, shooting fiery blasts of infernium a hundred feet in the air and lighting up the sky like a festival day. Damn it was impressive.

After they'd clapped one another on the back for a job well done, they increased their pace, only too eager to get back to safety. They left the blazing fires and the collapsed valley behind, moving along the arid ground that soon gave way to rocky hills. Another hour and they were almost back at their encampment.

Sonnheld was watching from the edge of woodland through a monocular, and when they reached him Conall was surprised to see he wore an uncharacteristic smirk across his stony features.

"Well done, Captain," he said as they stumbled by exhausted.

Conall couldn't hide a smile of his own. But then he'd been the architect of this, and it was nice his worth had finally been recognised.

"Thank you, Marshal," Moraide replied.

Or perhaps not.

"You've earned a rest. Take your troopers back to camp. There's food and drink waiting for you."

Moraide nodded her appreciation. "Just to say, Marshal—Captain Hawkspur acquitted himself with courage. We couldn't have done this without him."

Sonnheld regarded Conall with barely concealed scepticism. "Really? Not such a burden after all. That will be all, Captain."

Moraide left, Donan, Sted and her men following, but before Conall could join them and bask in the glory, Sonnheld raised a hand for him to wait.

"Looks like I may have been wrong about you, Hawkspur."

Yet more high praise. How would he cope? "Most people are, Marshal. One way or another." Or were they? Maybe everyone was right, and he just didn't want to accept it.

"I guess we'll find out soon enough. We still have the other battalions to take care of."

Conall felt a keen ache in his legs, but he still had to know. "In what respect?"

"The Phoenix and Tigris Battalions are making their way north to the Anvil as we speak. If we can hamper their progress it only helps the Guilds."

"Then I'm with you, Marshal." It seemed the right thing to say under the circumstances.

Sonnheld placed a meaty hand on Conall's shoulder. "Good to hear it. Get some rest. You deserve it."

Was that actual praise? Conall couldn't quite believe it as he nodded his acknowledgment and made his way through the trees to their hidden camp. He expected there to be laughing, toasting the success of their mission, but the troopers sat in silence. Not that he could blame them—it had been a tough day.

By the time he found Sted and Donan by their fire his enthusiasm for celebration had waned to almost nothing. Sted was drinking brandy she'd found at an abandoned trade post, but he felt in no mood to join her. As for Donan, he sat in sullen silence as usual.

"Good job you were there to stop me falling," he said as he sat and gestured to Donan's leg. "Looks like we're even."

Donan looked down at the artifice and nodded. "I guess we are."

"You did well. You're brave, Donan, and I'm glad you're with me."

Sted held up her hands forlornly. "So nobody thinks I'm brave too?"

Conall almost laughed. Almost. "Just pass the bloody brandy."

# ROSOMON

Wind swept over the brow of the hill and down across the plain. The grass danced, swaying back and forth as though beckoning her right to the gates of the Anvil beyond, but this was as far as they would go for now.

When she had pictured coming here with an army at her back, Rosomon had anticipated a triumphant welcome. The citizenry cheering the arrival of the Guilds and railing against their oppressors. Now, as she looked at those stark white walls, the wind the only sound, she realised what a mountain there was still to climb.

The Anvil had once been welcoming. Familiar. Now it held nothing but foreboding. Looking toward Oleksig, she could see he shared her concerns, that generous forehead creased as he gazed down on the city walls, pipe clamped between his teeth.

"I'd forgotten how unassailable it looked," he said. "There's no way we can launch an assault and hope to prevail."

"But we will," Rosomon replied.

She understood his reservations, but there was nothing she would allow to stop her. Rosomon had not endured so much to give in here.

"Even if we breach those walls, fight through Sanctan's army, will its people accept us. Accept our victory?"

"I don't believe Sanctan has them under his spell. Just his heel.

But if you're worried about the Anvil's populace coming to our side, rest assured I have that in hand." Or at least she hoped her daughter did. "Let's just deal with one thing at a time."

Her gaze shifted to Kassian and Ianto looking on, assessing those stout defences, formulating plans. They had nothing to share yet, and she could only hope they'd think of something before their time ran out and the Armigers loyal to the Ministry arrived to relieve the siege.

There was sudden movement at the city wall. The great eastern gate began to open, revealing a landship carriage just beyond the threshold, waiting to proceed along the line.

"What's this?" Oleksig murmured as he took the pipe from his mouth.

The landship's engine began to rumble before pushing its single carriage along the line. Its keening howl rose above the noise of the wind as it moved slowly toward the foot of the hill. The engine never increased its speed, just cruised along at little more than walking pace, before it eventually came to a stop not five hundred yards from the city gate.

As they watched, two Drakes debarked from the carriage, moving to the rear and uncoupling the engine. It rumbled again, before making its way back toward the city and leaving the carriage alone amid the swaying grass.

"Looks like that's Sanctan's invitation," Oleksig said.

"Then we'd best not keep him waiting," Rosomon replied, regarding Oleksig as he took a long draw on his pipe. "Are you coming?"

He winced. "I mean... he's your nephew."

"More's the pity," she said, understanding his reluctance. There had been so many traps laid in their path already. Pitfalls she had blindly walked into, and here she was, ready to do it all again.

"I'll go," rumbled Maugar's deep voice. "I don't mind taking another Drake scalp for the collection."

"No scalps, Maugar," she replied, relieved that at least one of them was willing to join her. "We need to tread gently. This is just a conversation after all."

"Like the one you had with Lorens at Oakhelm?" Kassian said.

"Conversation didn't solve anything there. And with respect, putting yourself in needless danger is becoming a habit."

He wasn't wrong. "There's no danger here, Kassian. I'm just meeting up with another one of my wayward nephews. What could there possibly be to fear?"

She kicked the horse beneath her, and it moved ahead of the row that watched from the brow of the hill. For a moment she wondered if anyone else might join her and Maugar, but it was a fleeting thought as Kassian and Ianto immediately urged their steeds to ride by her side. Oleksig remained, but she could hardly blame him. Were this a trap, and the worst happened, someone would still need to lead their army.

They rode down the slope and onto the flat plain. As they drew nearer to the lone carriage she couldn't take her eyes off those Drakes standing in wait for her like statues. When they rode to within ten feet, she pulled up her horse. The door to the carriage yawned wide, as if welcoming her into the abyss.

Her eyes were still on those Drakes. "Where is—?"

"The Archlegate will see you now," one of them interrupted, gesturing to the open carriage.

Maugar began to dismount. "I'll go and check."

Neither of the Drakes made a move to stop him as he approached and climbed up into the carriage. Then one followed him inside as the other continued to watch them all from behind his dragon helm. Maugar soon reappeared, followed by that Drake, and offered Rosomon a nod of reassurance.

She dismounted, as did Kassian and Ianto. With a curt gesture for them to wait outside, she stepped up into the carriage with Maugar. It looked huge, all the seats having been removed but one—a throne of sorts set at the far end. Sanctan sat upon it, a single Drake by his side.

There was an imperious look to him. A confidence. He sat adorned in all the finery of his office... too much finery if truth were told. A bejewelled ring on every finger, gold chain about his neck, a robe of comfortable silk. This was no humble and pious priest. This was a conqueror flaunting the spoils of war.

"Leave us," said her nephew as soon as she appeared.

Rosomon waited as the Drake marched past, heavy boots resounding through the empty carriage. Maugar still stood in the doorway, hand on his sword, ready to kill Sanctan should she order it.

"I'll be fine," she told him.

Maugar offered Sanctan one last baleful look before stepping down from the carriage. Finally they were alone.

Rosomon stepped closer to her nephew to better see his face. To look upon the man who had torn their nation apart.

Sanctan shivered in a mocking expression of fear. "All these fearsome warriors—so imposing. All that potential for violence just dangling in the air."

Rosomon had no answer to that. She couldn't take her eyes off this man, this monster, as she tried to remember the boy he had been. Wondering if there was any part of him left that could see reason.

"Will you take some refreshment, Aunt Rosomon?" he asked, gesturing to the table close by with its decanter and glasses.

"Why am I here, Sanctan?"

He looked surprised at her question. "I was hoping we could avoid further bloodshed."

A flash of rage that she managed to extinguish as soon as it sparked. "You should have thought about avoiding bloodshed before you murdered your emperor and drowned my city."

Regret fell over his features, an affectation no doubt. "We have all suffered loss during this war. Had Sullivar accepted the terms I offered, this whole thing would have been much less painful. Had you accepted the new order we could have avoided all this, Aunt Rosomon."

"You still speak as though we're family."

"Oh, but we are still family. Though I'll admit, those old ties of kinship have been strained of late."

Another spark of anger, this time harder to control. "You were the one who spat on any sense of familial loyalty. You did this."

Sanctan looked dubious. "I'm not sure I'm the only one who has abandoned notions of family. I saw what you did to your nephew, Lorens. I'll admit, I didn't think you had it in you."

"You pushed me to this, Sanctan. You're the one responsible, no one else."

"Am I? Because I've also heard how far you're willing to go. It wasn't me who murdered Jarlath. Wasn't me who exacted righteous vengeance on the Ursus Battalion. You really have become a ruthless, uncompromising warlord."

"Then you know you won't win this. Surrender to me, Sanctan. I have the Hallowhills now. The balance has shifted."

He looked undaunted, if not amused. "The Hallowhills have long since served their purpose. They are obsolete. I have the Anvil, and most of the Armigers. So no, Aunt Rosomon, I don't think I will offer my surrender. But I am happy to accept yours."

"I have fought my way here, across hundreds of miles. Nothing will stop me but an end to your tyranny."

"The Anvil is impregnable. I have its people at my back. My faithful brood. I have more troops than you, and more are on the way. If you were to launch a protracted siege and breach the walls, you would face the outrage and fury of the very people you've come to liberate. Even if you win, you'll be destroyed."

Rosomon had certainly feared that from the beginning, but surely he was wrong. Not all of them could be so blind to the Ministry's deceits. At the Cogwheel, when her brother had been cut down, the people of Torwyn had vented their anger at that injustice. Surely that was a sign that they still supported the Guilds.

But even if he was right, there was no way she could give up now. Not after all the Guilds had suffered. Leaving the Anvil and Torwyn to the whims of this monster was no longer an option. She would not allow him to destroy everything her father had built.

"I will never kneel to you, Sanctan. None of us will."

He looked hurt by the very suggestion. "No one is asking you to do anything so humiliating. I was always willing to work alongside you and your fellow Guildmasters. Jarlath should have conveyed that message, but then you took his head before he had the chance. Lorens told me he did not die well. Suffered the most brutal violence at the hands of your swordwrights, and for what? I only want peace. I want us all to live together in harmony beneath the sight of the Great Wyrms."

"You want power, Sanctan. You hunger for it. You're a tyrant, no better than the Scions of the Magna."

A nerve touched as he squirmed slightly in that pathetic chair, before fixing her with a stern look. "Oh, I am so much better than those godless sorcerers. I need no magic to keep a grip on this country. Torwyn sits in my palm, and the only sorcery I have used is the word of my faith."

Rosomon took a step forward. That spark of anger flared inside her again, and for the final time she managed to wrest control of it lest she spit in his face. "Torwyn is in your fist, boy. But I will pry it free if I have to break every finger on your delicate hand."

He gazed back at her, and she could read every emotion his eyes—anger, fear, humiliation. Finally, he settled on that smug mask as always.

"Careful, Aunt Rosomon. Only a few feet away our guardians are spoiling for a fight. That temper of yours might well be the death of us all."

"What is it you want, Sanctan?" she asked, her patience for his prating growing thin. "I don't mean from me; I mean for this nation. Why did you do this? I have to believe all this death and suffering wasn't just because of a madman's thirst for power."

Sanctan averted his gaze toward the window, something suddenly wistful in his eyes, as though he could see for miles across that flat green field. "This nation lost its way. I am merely her guide. Her shepherd. Tasked with setting the flock back on the right path."

"That's horseshit, and you know it."

"Do I?" he snapped, glaring right at her. "The Guilds are corrupted to their marrow. You know it. You've seen it. A canker twisting beneath the flesh of Torwyn, spreading its avarice and ruin. They must be stopped."

"And replaced with what? Fervour? Zealotry? With you as the unchallenged sovereign? Sullivar may have had his faults, but everything he did, he did for his people. He ruled for them, not lorded over them."

Sanctan gripped the arms of his chair, knuckles white. "His god was commerce. His priests were merchants."

"And they kept his people fed. Raised them from muck."

"Not everyone. Many still wallowed in the dirt, while some of you rose higher than the gods themselves. I would see us all raised in the light of the—"

"Enough about your damned Wyrms. I have heard about as much as I can take. It was stupid of me to come here."

Sanctan settled into his chair, a trace of smugness to his smile, as though satisfied that she had almost lost control. "It was only stupid if you refuse to surrender."

She took a step back. "You knew that would never happen."

His smug mask spread into a grin. "And so did you. Yet you still came to meet me."

"Perhaps I just wanted to see you one last time before this all ends. To look on the creature you've become, and see if there's any trace of the boy I knew left inside."

He reclined further into his seat, grin spreading as he opened his arms to her. "And what's the verdict? What do you see?"

There was no answer to give but an honest one.

"Just a little man. Who I have to kill."

If she'd hoped to stoke his ire, it didn't work, and the grin on his face only grew wider.

"Goodbye, Aunt Rosomon. I'm sure we'll see one another again soon."

She turned as the sound of his laugh resounded through the carriage. The welcome chill of the wind hit her once she stepped down onto the swaying grass. All five of the warriors outside stood with their hands on their swords, though none of them dared move.

"Come," Rosomon ordered, as she made toward her horse.

One by one they followed her, mounting their steeds before she tugged the reins and urged her horse back up the slope. From the city behind, she heard the engine growl as it slowly moved toward the carriage. She made a point of not offering even a glance back toward her nephew.

Oleksig stood waiting at the brow of the hill, swordwrights by his side, army at his back.

"How did that go?" he asked, as she slipped down from her horse.

"As well as I expected," she replied, only now turning to look back as the carriage was pulled through the city gate by the engine.

"He's not about to surrender anytime soon then?" Oleksig took a long draw of his pipe, as the gates to the Anvil slammed shut.

No, her nephew was not about to surrender, but then Rosomon hadn't really wanted him to. This way, she would have to offer him no mercy. Now she could destroy him.

# KEARA

The Guild camp was perched atop the hill, leering down on the city like some hungry wolf, unsure if it could take down its prey. It would have to attack soon, lest its prey grow stronger. Right now, there was no telling who might rise the victor, and the sensible move would be to sit back and wait all this out from a safe distance. But Keara had no choice other than to stick with the side she had picked. Her bed was made, with red roses strewn all over it—thorns and all—and now she'd just have to lie down and suffer the cuts.

The guards at the perimeter of the encampment had let her in, recognising her despite the grotesque clothes she wore. For her part, she didn't recognise a single soul as she wandered amid the shoddy collection of miners and Armiger troopers, until she saw one face she knew, at least vaguely. A member of the Marrlock brood; Oleksig's daughter, Emony. They'd met once, Keara was sure of it. Talked even, at one of those insipid Guild gatherings when they'd been much younger, and the world hadn't turned to shit.

The girl was talking to a couple of miners, giving orders perhaps, but as Keara approached they stopped their conversation, and Emony's expression shifted to one of disdain. Great start.

"I need to speak with Lady Rosomon," Keara said. "You know where she is?"

"She's not here." A stern reply. Only to be expected under the circumstances.

"Do you know when she'll be back?"

"No."

Yes, definitely a bone of contention there. As much as Keara wanted to show this girl little respect, perhaps a display of charm might get better results.

"Well, thanks for the help. If you happen to see her when she arrives, would you mind letting her know I'm back? I have an important message."

"Of course." Emony forced a smile.

Keara turned before she felt the urge to slap that simpering smile to the other side of Emony's face, but the girl hadn't quite finished.

"Aren't you going to ask how the battle went at Alumford?"

Keara stopped. It hadn't even crossed her mind. For all she knew, every Hallowhill under her command could have been killed.

"You're all still here. So I'm gonna guess it went well."

Emony glared, as the two miners behind her looked on with barely masked contempt. Those common people Keara had always been such a stranger to, and thank the Wyrms for that.

She turned her back on them before they could say any more, heading deeper into the camp, looking for any sign of the Hallowhill wainers. She had taken such pains to convince them she was worthy of being their leader. Might as well at least try to prove it.

Night had fallen, and it was difficult to see in the firelight. If there were any stormhulks left in one piece they must have been hidden within the nearby woodland. As she picked her way through the camp, distant music began to strike up. Those damned miners again, their discordant drone fraying at her nerves as usual. Just as she began to panic, thinking she was the last Hallowhill left, she caught sight of a huge metal machine ahead of her.

Artificers were busy performing repairs; polishing carapaces, tinkering with machinery. It almost felt like home. Webwainers sat around their pyrestoves, and the welcome smell of cooking tickled Keara's senses. As she drew closer, she spied Galirena and a few others crouching by the flames. They saw her coming, looking none too pleased to see her, but she joined them by the fire as they rubbed warmth into their hands.

"Going to be a cold night," Keara said eventually, sick of the silence.

Galirena just offered a knowing glance, as though that were obvious. This was going to be more difficult than Keara had anticipated.

"I heard you all fought with honour at Alumford," she continued, despite hearing nothing of the sort. It seemed the right thing to say anyway.

"You heard?" said a man at the other side of the flames. Volkmar... no, Vikmar.

"Look, I know I wasn't there to fight beside you all, but as I tried to explain, there was something I had to do. If you must know, I've been to the Anvil. Helped secure our way into the city. Trust me, things will be different now I'm back. We've almost won this—so why not celebrate that, eh?"

None of them looked particularly enthused. Vikmar even went so far as to turn his back on her. Their mood for celebration was clearly sodden. The battle at the ford must have been harder than she'd realised.

"Look, I'm sorry I wasn't there. I wish I had been."

Galirena rose to her feet, fists clenched. "Do you?"

"Of course. All the Hallowhills are kin, I've never forgotten that. We're a family."

They didn't look convinced. Other webwainers at other fires had ceased their talking now and were looking toward her. Right now she wished she'd learned some inspirational speeches, rather than wasting her time on hedonism. Damn it, her father had been right all along.

"I have a long way to go before I earn your respect," she announced, hoping that they could all hear her now. "But understand this—everything I've done, I've done for the Hallowhill Guild and every webwainer in it. I've upheld our creed. Strived to put every wainer in Torwyn back in their rightful place."

Even as she spoke the lies, she couldn't get the vision of the emperor's throne from her mind. How she'd lusted for it as she walked the empty corridors of Archwind Palace. That was *her* rightful place.

No one spoke, but Galirena reached out with her power to stir the pyrestone in the stove. The flame turned bright blue, the heat increasing, embracing Keara with its warmth.

"Just give me a chance," Keara said. "Let me prove myself to you."

Vikmar stepped back into the light. "By fighting by our side? Shedding your blood with us?"

"Every last drop, if I have to," she replied with such certainty she even surprised herself.

If she was expecting cheers, cries of kinship and a pat on the back, she was sorely mistaken. Instead, someone stepped from the shadows, and every eye fell on him. Keara could hardly blame them—Kassian Maine was one scary bastard.

"She'll see you now," he said.

"Rosomon?"

He didn't answer, but then who else could he be talking about?

Keara turned back to her webwainers. "I won't be long."

"Sure," Galirena replied, as though it didn't matter if she was.

Annoyed at the awkward timing, Keara followed Kassian back through the camp, leaving her webwainers behind. What a great show of resolve and kinship—trailing after the Hawkspur swordwright like some lackey. Eventually he led her to the camp's western extent. Rosomon was there, Titanguard looming at her shoulder, the distant lights of the Anvil twinkling on the horizon.

She turned as Keara approached, looking none too happy to see her. "You're back so soon? And alone?"

"Tyreta stayed behind, and I came to pass on the good news." She smiled expectantly, but Rosomon just glared, eyes ablaze in the torchlight. "Olstrum is with us, but getting access to the Archlegate is tricky. However, with Tyreta's help they can stoke dissent within the city walls. There are rebels at Olstrum's beck and call and he has a network—"

"What does he want in return for helping us?"

Damn this woman's ability to cut through the bullshit. Keara would have to ask her how she did it one day.

"He won't help us unless we guarantee the safety of his family."

"Unless we what?"

"He wants us to find his family. I told you before—"

"Yes, he only betrayed the Guilds because Sanctan took them. So where are they?"

Keara raised her arms helplessly. "That's just the problem—"

"Nobody knows."

Damn it, would she get to finish a bloody sentence? "He suggested your Talon might be able to track them down."

"With the whole of Torwyn to search? And no war eagles? He is wildly optimistic."

"Or just desperate. But he won't move against Sanctan unless he knows they are free. He also said you could ask your prisoners."

Rosomon thought on it, shaking her head in frustration. "If Sanctan has hidden them somewhere it would be far beyond the Anvil, so Olstrum couldn't use his network to find them. He would have used Rearden Corwen's Revocaters and we have not taken any..." Realisation seemed to dawn on her. "Come with me."

As Rosomon struck out across the camp, Keara was forced to follow again like a lapdog trotting after its master. Kassian joined them, a little too close for comfort, and she kept a wary eye on him.

The prisoner stockade loomed up ahead. Rows of wooden pens with their few captives within. She could see Bloodwolf troopers standing guard, eyeing Keara suspiciously as Rosomon led her past those cages.

Men and women hunkered within but there was no way to tell which battalion they'd come from. Ursus or Griffin didn't really matter anymore when you were beaten to shit and waiting to see if you'd picked the wrong side or not. It could have been Keara in one of those cages if she'd not made the decision to change allegiance.

As they passed the wooden pens the smell of it almost made her gag. She breathed a little easier as they struck further from the prisoners toward two cages set away from the rest. She could make out hulking figures within, though couldn't quite see their faces in the dark.

Rosomon stopped at the first cage, close enough to make her presence known, but not so close that whoever was inside could make a grab at her.

"You. Drake."

The bulky form moved, rising to his feet, stooping below the roof of the cage. He was thick about the neck and shoulders, hands all beef and knuckle as they gripped the wooden bars. A stern and solemn face regarded Rosomon with surprisingly little hate in those doleful eyes.

"What is your name?" she asked.

"Why would you know my name, Lady of Hawkspur," he replied, his voice revealing as little emotion as his face.

"So that we might hold a civil conversation. Why are you so reluctant to speak your name? Frightened I'm some hedge witch who will take your soul if she knows it?"

The Drake didn't look like he'd be frightened of anything. "I am Brother Lugard."

"Well, Lugard, I wonder if I might ask a favour of you?"

He shrugged his mountainous shoulders. "You may ask what you wish. But I see no reason why I should answer."

"Because I have spared your life, Lugard. Is that not as good a reason as any?"

"I am listening."

Rosomon moved an inch closer. Even though the Drake did not move, Keara could see Kassian slowly grip the hilt of his sword, ready to draw steel at a moment's notice.

"You know of Olstrum Garner?"

Was that a flash of emotion on the Drake's face? The slightest curl of his lip? "Everyone knows that feckless magpie. Twittering in the ear of one master, then the next."

Rosomon looked impressed by his assessment. "His family was abducted on the Archlegate's orders. I would know where they were taken. Are you able to help me?"

Lugard looked as though he was genuinely trying his best to remember, before he shook his head. "I am not."

Rosomon moved even closer. Kassian's sword silently slid an inch from the scabbard.

"Sanctan means this innocent family harm, Lugard. If you know—"

"I do not lie, woman," Lugard spat. "My creed forbids it."

Kassian's blade slid another inch from the sheath, but Rosomon was already backing away. Already defeated. Before she could turn and leave this Drake to his creed, a second imposing figure loomed from the next cage.

Keara stifled a gasp as she saw the giant approach the bars. He had a face she recognised, dark blemish marring his chin and mouth as he regarded them warily. Damn, what was his name? Had she ever learned it? The knight who was Sanctan's constant shadow—a little dangerous and a little sad all at the same time.

Kassian's blade slid all the way from its scabbard as Rosomon moved toward the second Drake. For a moment, the threat of violence hung heavy in the air, despite the two prisoners being caged.

"I know where to find them," the scarred Drake said eventually.

Rosomon regarded him dubiously. "That seems a little convenient for you. But I suppose you don't lie either."

Those sad eyes looked suddenly ashamed, and Keara felt a weird sense of sympathy for his plight. This once proud warrior now kept like an exhibit in a zoo.

"I could tell you that I never lie. That like my brother, Lugard, it is forbidden by my creed to speak untruths. But no, I have lied. I have deceived. Murdered. But on this matter, I speak the truth."

Kassian visibly tensed as Rosomon moved close enough to touch the Drake through the bars. "You know where they are keeping Olstrum's family?"

"I do. And were I freed from this cage I would find and liberate them. I swore as much to Olstrum himself. To my shame it is an oath I have been unable to keep."

"Will you tell me where they are?"

The Drake shook his head. "No. But I will show you the way. I will keep my oath, or I will keep my silence."

Rosomon turned to regard Keara. "Do you believe him?"

All eyes turned to her. As the sudden focus of attention, she was at a loss to answer. "Why... why are you asking me, how do I know?"

"Deception is second nature to you, Hallowhill. You must know a lie when you hear it—a rat always knows another rat. Is he one?"

Charming, but Keara wasn't about to bite back at that. Especially not with Kassian holding a naked blade so close to her. Instead she regarded that Drake with his scarred face and those eyes all scary and doleful at the same time.

"No."

Rosomon seemed satisfied with that. "Good. Then you'll go. Both of you. Find Olstrum's wife and children, then bring them back to me."

"Wait," Keara replied, not quite believing what she was hearing. "You're trusting me to travel with this Drake? How do you know I won't just send word to Sanctan that Olstrum is a traitor? You've never trusted me before, what reason do you have now?"

Rosomon casually gestured toward Kassian, who was watching the proceedings as though willing someone to refuse his mistress. "If either of you step out of line, my swordwright will end the both of you."

Keara could see the slightest twitch at the corner of Kassian's mouth. A look of relish, perhaps.

"Yes," she replied. "I guess that is a pretty good reason."

# CONALL

They marched north at speed. Despite the hardship, Conall knew this was nothing compared to what they'd face when they reached their destination. Two whole battalions were waiting for them, armed and ready. What remained of the Viper Battalion was determined, but he doubted they could keep fighting much longer, especially against those odds. Nevertheless, Sonnheld drove them on with all the zeal of a man possessed.

But he was not the one possessed.

With every mile further north, the more doubt crept into Conall's mind. That demon voice hadn't plagued him for so long, but he knew it was still there, that soul-eating blade still lurking in the shadows. And every step closer to his mother's side, Conall felt the need to run as far from her as he could get. Who knew how long he would be able to keep his curse hidden? Perhaps even now it was starting to manifest, to show itself in other ways.

Not far from his side was Sted, face twisted in a grimace, cursing every mile they laboured through. If anyone was going to spot something wrong with him it would be her, but she'd made no mention, more preoccupied with her own misery. It looked like his secret was safe. For now.

A glance up ahead, past the ranks of the Viper troopers, and he could see Sonnheld striding ahead. He set a gruelling pace, despite the heavy armour he wore, hands permanently resting on the two swords he carried at his side. The man was a pure force of nature, respected, if not adored, by his followers. Oh to be so driven, so filled with righteous purpose, so fuelled by the power of one's will alone. When Sonnheld eventually stopped, signalling for his troopers to halt, Conall almost gasped in relief.

"We'll make camp here," he ordered, gazing out beyond the ridge they had reached.

Dusk was fast closing in, and they'd be shielded from prying eyes by the woodland to the east and hills to the west. As the Armiger troopers began to break ranks and set up camp, Conall mucked in, and he eventually settled by a fire with Sted and Donan. They sat listening to the silence until, in the far distance, there came the sound of a landship making its way between Castleteig and the Anvil. Just as its lights became visible on the horizon, winking like fireflies in the night, a Talon scout appeared from the underbrush.

Conall watched as the man delivered his report to Sonnheld. After listening intently, the marshal signalled for his adjutants, and Conall joined them, keen to hear if there was news.

"Give them your report," Sonnheld commanded.

The scout turned to the gathered officers. "I followed the landship line as far north from Castleteig as I could. The Tigris Battalion are still occupying the city, but the Phoenix have struck north along the line. The route is still intact, and they're using it to transport troopers and supplies into the Anvil. Won't be long before both battalions have reinforced the city."

Sonnheld turned his gaze north. "This gives us an opportunity. If we sabotage the line, block the Ministry's supply of reinforcements and materiel, it will offer the Guilds more time. We've done it once. We can do it again." He turned back to them, focusing on Conall. "What say you, Hawkspur?"

Of all the officers present, Conall thought he'd be the last one Sonnheld might ask for an opinion. "Yes, we can. But sabotaging the line alone will be easy enough for them to repair. It might only stall them for a day, maybe two, then the tracks will be operational again. The risk of that far outweighs the gain."

He could tell it wasn't what Sonnheld wanted to hear, but he had to give his honest assessment.

"So? What's the solution?"

All eyes were on him now. He'd given them a problem, and Sonnheld wouldn't be satisfied until he'd at least tried to offer an answer.

"There's a depot halfway between the cities. An old Hawkspur aerie overlooks the line. Bring that down and it'll take them a week to pick through the wreckage and reestablish the line."

Where he'd dragged that little nugget from, Conall had no idea, but he was relieved when Sonnheld nodded his approval.

"Good. Then let's do it."

The scout who had brought his report shook his head. "Only one problem, Marshal. The Phoenix Battalion are billeted at the depot Captain Hawkspur is talking about, monitoring all supplies that pass along the route."

"How many troopers?" Sonnheld asked.

"Upwards of five hundred, as far as I could tell."

Sonnheld worked his jaw as he thought on the problem. He commanded barely two hundred men. A frontal assault would be crippling for them.

"How well dug in are they?"

"They certainly look like they anticipate an attack. The perimeter is cordoned. Regular patrols."

Sonnheld's look of concern deepened, but there had to be a way. Conall could only think of one.

"Create a diversion," he suggested, before anyone else had the chance to speak. "A night assault from the south. I can lead a small unit from the north and infiltrate the depot. Attack by night and they won't know our numbers. They'll concentrate their entire garrison on the southern defences to repel your ambush, and leave the way free for us to slip in. We can plant charges at the base of the aerie, and be gone before they even know we were there. The explosion will be your signal to retreat. Mission accomplished."

"As simple as that?" Sonnheld raised a sceptical eyebrow.

"Sometimes the best plans are, Marshal."

Sonnheld nodded, almost imperceptibly, but the rare grin that crossed his face was unmistakable.

"Very well. Let's make it happen." He turned to the scout. "I want a detailed layout of the depot, patrol routes and defensive positions. Hawkspur, I suggest you go and brief your unit. We head out tomorrow morning and attack at sundown."

The officers nodded their assent, leaving Sonnheld to gaze back across the dark northern expanse. As he made his way through the camp, Conall couldn't help but feel a little pleased with himself. He was starting to prove himself indispensable. Maybe even a Guildmaster in the making. Now all he had to do was live long enough to see it happen.

Sted and Donan were waiting by the fire when he returned. When Sted saw the look on his face her shoulders sagged.

"You've done it again, haven't you?"

"What?" Conall asked innocently.

"You've decided to race right into mortal danger, and take us with you."

He leaned in closer. "Would you have it any other way?"

Donan offered a toothy smile from the other side of the fire. "I wouldn't."

"Oh right," Sted replied. "All of a sudden Marrlock's a bloody adventurer. You've come a long way since we found you in the desert, hiding in your own shit."

Donan shrugged. "Some of us are capable of change, Sted."

She plucked a stick of redstalk from her top pocket. "Change is overrated. And rarely permanent."

As Conall watched her chew that stalk, he absently raised a hand to the patch over his eye. She was wrong about that—some things were permanent. But as he thought about what might be still be lurking in the shadows, watching, waiting to spring forth, he could only hope that there were some things that weren't.

# FULREN

They had spoken barely a word, but Fulren could still tell Verlyn was apprehensive. With every mile their cart trundled, those red motes swimming about her dark form intensified. He knew he was the cause, that what he'd done at that refugee camp had terrified her, but there was no way to reassure her he had it under control. Fact was, he couldn't control it.

Something had almost been unleashed, something he thought he had managed to chain, but the monster inside him could never really be shackled. He knew that now. Perhaps the only way he could defeat it was to let it out. Allow it to run rampant. It might destroy him, but better to find out now, and not when he was reunited with his mother. Not when she might be relying on him to help her in the battles to come.

The sound of a landship hummed in the distance as their wagon rumbled along a road that clung to the side of a steep incline. Before he could begin to wonder where it was going, they crested the hill and Fulren could sense activity in the valley below.

"The settlement they told us about," Verlyn confirmed.

"Are the Armigers there?" he asked, struggling to make out any figures through the murk of his glyphsight.

"Hard to tell. But maybe it's better if we don't find out. Let's just—"

He grabbed the reins and gently eased them back, bringing the horses to a stop.

"Might as well talk to myself," Verlyn breathed in frustration, as he grabbed his helm and climbed down from the wagon.

Fulren made his way to the edge of the road, the world coalescing in vibrant colour when he placed the helm on his head. The settlement was hunkered on the edge of a stream, mill turning gently. It looked quiet enough, until he spied armed men making their way between a row of stone-built houses.

He focused, vision becoming sharper, that familiar tingle in his spine as he pressed with heightened senses. They were troopers of the Tigris Battalion, splintbows held casually, no helms on their heads. Not expecting trouble. As he scanned the settlement he saw more of them, some standing idly by as the townsfolk gave them a wide berth, others laughing, joking, cajoling.

It felt like they were taunting him. Goading him to charge down the slope and engage them.

A caw close by made him start. He turned to see a tree not far off the road, a crow among the boughs looking back at him. Giving its approval.

Fulren made his way back to the wagon.

"Well?" Verlyn asked. "What can you see?"

He gripped the side of the wagon, trying to calm himself. "It's crawling with Armigers."

"I see. Well, just for the record, I still think it's best we keep going."

Verlyn was right, it was best, but Fulren didn't climb back into his seat. Instead he reached into the back of the wagon and took the sword that lay folded in its canvas.

"You don't have to do this," she said as he unwrapped the cover, feeling the comfort of the grip in his hand.

"I have to do something," he replied.

"What does that mean?" She sounded panicked. "If we just carry on this road no one would even know we were here. You can't be thinking you can take on a whole—"

"You were the one who wanted me to become your weapon, Verlyn. You took me to Lysander knowing what he would do."

"But... but this... this is suicide. This is not what I wanted."

"Isn't it? I thought you wanted revenge. I thought you wanted them to die for what they did to Ashe. For what they took from you. If this isn't what you intended, then what was it?"

"I wanted to get you back to your mother. So you could help her win this war. Attacking an occupied village on your own isn't going to help anyone. You'll just get yourself killed. You don't know what's waiting for you down there."

"And they don't know what's coming."

He turned, suddenly moving with more ease, that sword instilling a strange kind of vigour.

"You don't know what you're capable of yet, Fulren. Or what's really inside you. What might escape if you provoke it enough."

He stopped.

She was right, he didn't know. He could be unleashing something beyond his power to control, but until he tested his limits he'd never know. At least not until it was too late.

"If I'm not back by sunrise, don't wait for me."

He made his way down the ridge, surprised at how adept he had become on his artificial legs. They were an extension of him now as he picked his way across the rocky surface. All the while he felt apprehension growing, seeding his mind with doubt.

At the bottom of the slope he stopped, focusing through the dusk as the shadow of night closed its wings around everything. He knew he shouldn't have any doubt, but he simply couldn't shake the feeling that this was wrong. That even if he survived this encounter, he would be irrevocably changed by the violence of it. Anointed in blood by what he was about to do.

Pushing down the apprehension, he forced himself onward. The only thing that emboldened him was the increasing surety with which he moved. Where his flesh pressed against the artifice at knee and elbow he felt an increasing tingle. It became difficult to tell where his body ended and the artifice began, a strange sensation he did his best to ignore.

By the time he reached the edge of the settlement, night had all but closed in. Fulren pulled his cloak tight about him, hiding the pyrestone blade within its folds as he scanned his surroundings.

A lone sentry patrolled the edge of the town, and Fulren's vision narrowed, the trooper's silhouette sharpening with pinpoint clarity. The urge to strike was difficult to quell, but Fulren held himself back. He had killed before, back at Verlyn's farm, but then it had been justified. Was this the same, or was it just murder?

Fighting back the doubt, he crept closer. As he stalked his prey, the hydraulics in his lower limbs were silent, and he felt more shadow than man. Before the sentry even knew he was there, Fulren loomed from the dark, grasping his chin with a steel arm and wrenching it back. The speed and power was frightening as the trooper's neck cracked and he fell to the ground.

The corpse lay motionless. Fulren crouched over it for some moments, observing his kill. He had anticipated some guilt this time, some remorse at what he was forced to do, but there was nothing. Not even a sense of victory.

A distant caw from atop the hill, and Fulren was moving once again.

Laughter pealed out from within the settlement. Raucous voices. Fulren delved deeper, searching out the source of that mirth, determined to give the crows their due. Surrounding him were closely built houses, their windows boarded, no sign of life but the noise from deeper within the town.

Inside those tiny stone houses he could sense the townsfolk hunkering in their little chambers, fearful of what might happen should they step outside. If they were aware of the phantom that stalked their streets they would be more terrified still. Or perhaps they would be thankful for the dark creature that had come to exact their vengeance.

No matter, Fulren was not here for them. He was here for his own ends—to prove himself worthy of facing their enemy in the north. To strike a first blow, and be damned for it, or demonstrate he was the master of his destiny.

He passed a tall building that loomed on the eastern edge of the town, most likely a mill or processing plant. Through its thin wooden walls he could sense the abandoned artifice, its pyrestones having long since been pilfered. It would once have been the throbbing heart of this place, but was now rendered obsolete by the cruelty of the Ministry... and the betrayal of these Armigers.

Reaching the tavern at the centre of the town, he knew beyond doubt he was on the right path. Noises echoed within, howls of laughter, muffled voices filled with delight and disdain and arrogance. Here were the conquerors revelling in their victory. His test began now.

Staring at that door, Fulren felt the sword begin to hum in his hand. Pyrestones reacting to his need for blood. Thirsting, just as he thirsted.

He reached out his steel hand and pushed the door open, to be hit by a wall of noise. The cloak was still pulled tight around him as he walked in, his legs and blade hidden beneath it. At first the laughter continued, every table occupied by troopers of the Tigris. Though they were all in repose, they had seen fit to keep their weapons close, and Fulren spied carbines and splintbows lying beside jugs of ale and bottles of wine. There was even the dull glow of pyrestone energy emanating from one corner, where a longbarrel leaned against the wall.

As he took it all in, he was aware of the noise dying down. All eyes were gradually drawn to him as he stood, cloaked and helmed in the doorway.

"What the fuck do you want?" came a growl from the crowd. "You've all been told to stay in your homes."

"What's he got on his head?" whispered another voice.

"Bastard's armed," was the final cry, as one of them spotted the blade beneath Fulren's cloak.

Chairs scraped, hands reaching for weapons. The whole of the tavern looked to be moving at once, but not fast enough as Fulren let the cloak drop from his shoulders. Minuscule movements of his thighs activated the articulation of his steel legs and he rose past seven feet, eight, helm almost brushing the roofbeams.

"What the fuck is that?" screeched a voice among the mob.

One of them, keener than the rest and undaunted by the beast in their midst, ran forward. He had an axe in hand, wide at the blade and thick in the haft.

Fulren's sword issued a static hum, energy jolting up his arm as he activated the pyrestones on instinct. His cut was swift, leaving a contrail of lightning as it sliced through the axeman. The body fell, flesh cauterised, ribs smoking as they were exposed to the room.

Someone bellowed.

The tavern erupted in a mix of anger and panic, a heady blend that only fuelled Fulren's hunger.

A carbine blast shook the room, but the projectile missed by an inch, taking a chunk out of the wall. Despite the frenzy around him, Fulren's focus began to slow. Every face became distinct, some screaming in rage, others shouting in alarm. Through the din he heard the clack of a splintbow being primed, his eyes scanning the tavern in a split second before focusing on the weapon being aimed from yards away. The volley was unleashed, and his metal arm rose on instinct, deflecting the first bolt as he twisted away from the rest.

The pyrestone blade sang in his grip, slicing forward to impale the chest of another Tigris trooper come too close. Before the man had even fallen, Fulren saw another of them racing for the open door, and his sword struck again, hacking him from shoulder to spine.

Someone aimed an axe at his helmed head but Fulren responded deftly, his blade singing as it parried. Before he could counter and cut the axeman down, a sword smashed against his metal arm, sending a shudder through his shoulder.

Another blow, this one against his helm, fuzzing his vision for a moment and leaving his senses ringing. Light flashed before his eyes, and he was suddenly unsteady on those metal legs. He stumbled away from the flurry of violence as another trooper bowled into him, knocking him off balance.

Fulren smashed into the tavern bar, feeling its edge crack his rib. He growled, an inhuman noise that came from deep within his throat, but he was assailed by half a dozen troopers before he could scramble to his feet.

Swords clanged against his limbs and axes smashed his helm as he desperately fended off blow after blow.

Anger, cold and stark, flooded his body.

The memory of a crow in its petrified tree flashing before his vision.

The taste of blood on his lips.

Pain, both sharp and dull, assailed his body.

The edge of a blade caught his shoulder, another his thigh.

It was like fuel, red and hot, feeding his limbs, his bones. Stoking the demon furnace.

He would have yelled, but his teeth were clamped too tight, throat constricted by the fury. In the stumps of his legs and arm, he felt a writhing in his flesh. At first subtle, but quickly rising in intensity until it was searing.

And the necroglyph at his back raged a song of sorcery.

Flesh began to creep, bone cracking as sinew and cartilage melded with steel and artifice. Fulren writhed as his upper arm began to bond with the clawed limb, his thighs burning with fire as the stumps of his legs married the steel beneath him.

It was agony and rapture at once. An exquisite pyre of pain that fed him to his core, until his throat was no longer constricted. Now from within his helm came an unearthly roar, as the demon Fulren had become rose to its feet.

Any awkwardness in his gait was gone. His limbs were a union of flesh and steel now, and he articulated his legs, raising himself to full height. He flexed his claw, feeling it tingle. Fulren was whole once more, towering above his foes, who could only gawp in dismay. He took in the room again, vision razor sharp in its clarity.

The Tigris troopers were watching with awe, but they would not watch forever. He could offer them no quarter.

In his hand the pyrestone blade belched flame as it ignited, then sparked as its blue and yellow stones burst to life. Fulren lurched forward, his steel helm smashing into the head of the nearest trooper, before his sword lashed out, severing the leg of another.

More screaming, but he was done listening to the dirge as he strode among them, foot snatching out to grip a head and smash it into the floorboards. His blade roared again, leaving a trail of sparking light as it hacked more flesh to the bone.

A sword lanced at him, but his claw was faster, catching the blade and bending the steel. He wrenched the weapon from its owner's grip and flung it aside, ready to deal the killer blow, but they were running now, fleeing before him, struggling to squeeze through the doors to safety, such was their terror.

Fulren pursued them, unwilling to offer mercy. On the ground before him lay a wounded man gripping his leg, vainly trying to stem the gaping slash in his thigh. Fulren leered down, and the urge to kill only grew. All he felt was the need to slaughter. An inhuman sensation. One that should have been alien to him, but now it felt like the most natural thing in the world.

No. He could not let it control him. Could not let the demon win. Fulren Hawkspur was still a man, still in command, and now he had to prove it.

His legs retracted with a soft purr, as the sword in his hand ceased spitting its fire and lightning. The room was empty now but for a few wounded, groaning in the shadows. Fulren grabbed his cloak, stepping out into the chill of night, expecting more Tigris troopers to be waiting, but they had all fled.

He threw the cloak about his shoulders, hunkering down, rushing into the welcome dark to become a phantom once more. His path through the town was swift, not so much as a stray dog to bar his way, and he finally made his way from the confines of the streets and up the valley side.

When he reached the top of the rise, he could see the tree in whose branches that lone crow had sat, cawing its farewell before he left. Only now there was not a single crow but a host, filling the boughs with black feathers.

Fulren stared at them a moment, taking in their silence. Then he looked back to the town he had just left his deathly mark upon.

"Go," he whispered.

The tree erupted with the sound of a thousand dark wings. They flocked together, heralding their flight with a symphony of cries before soaring toward the town. He watched as they approached like a dark shadow, wheeling in the air around those rooftops, screeching Fulren's victory for all to hear. In turn, he heard shouts of alarm from amid the settlement. Death had come this night, and now his heralds sang a mocking song to any fortunate enough to survive.

As he walked back toward the waiting wagon, he gradually felt the weight of his exertions creep up on him. A wound in his thigh, his arm, bruises on his ribs. Fulren wrenched off the helmet, taking in a gulp of air as Verlyn came to greet him.

"Are you satisfied?" she asked, seemingly unconcerned that he might be wounded.

He had no idea if he was satisfied or not. His mind was still reeling. That feeling of power only slowly ebbing away.

"Would it help if I was?" he answered, placing the helm and sword back in the wagon.

"You have to be less impetuous, Fulren. That was needless and stupid."

"No." He turned to face her, seeing those red motes in a flurry. "Now I know exactly what I'm capable of."

"What do you mean?"

He reached across his chest, unclasping the buckle that held his artificial arm to his shoulder. The strap fell away, but the metal arm, now as much a part of him as the one of flesh, remained.

"Look," he said, reaching to her.

Verlyn took a step forward and touched his upper arm, pressing the flesh down to the steel that had cauterised with it.

"What is this? What have you done?"

"I've accepted it. Become one with it."

Verlyn shook her head, taking a step away. "You have no idea what you're messing with. This is Maladoran sorcery, Fulren. It could doom you. Doom us both."

"Do I need to remind you again whose idea it was to take me to Lysander? This is as much your doing as mine."

"Yes...but—"

"But what? Is this not what you wanted? Because if you have any doubts, it's too late to turn back now. You wanted a weapon, Verlyn. Well, here it is."

As he spoke, both of the horses grew agitated, as though his presence unnerved them. "You'd best get some rest," he said, turning toward the back of the wagon, all but spent. "I doubt there'll be any patrols to bother us now."

Without a word she moved away from him to see to the horses. He sat himself on the back of the wagon, too fatigued to even try to bandage his wounds. As his body cooled in the night, he heard the fluttering of a thousand wings.

The crows returned, flocking above him for a moment before they disappeared into the night. But he knew they would return.

# TYRETA

It was a nice room, there was no doubting that. Clean, homely even. Smelled good. Someone had also focused reverent care on the decor—polished oak with pretty patterns on the soft furnishings.

After two days though, she was sick of the bloody sight of it.

Tyreta had been sitting on her hands waiting for Olstrum to give her some clue as to who she'd be meeting, but so far nothing. If there was indeed a resistance movement within the Anvil, none of them had deigned to show their faces.

Tyreta might have thought herself a prisoner, but she could leave at any time. The safe house was in a quiet corner of the Artificers' District. No lock on the door. That strange little man she'd seen in Olstrum's underground lair came every now and again with food and fresh clothes. Still hadn't said anything though, despite her questions, but Tyreta had a feeling he didn't know anything anyway.

A muffled voice from below and Tyreta crossed the room to the balcony. From it, she could see out across the narrow streets and watch people going about their business. She'd tried to avoid that despite the boredom, keen not to be seen by anyone. Instead she would often just listen to those quiet voices. On the surface they sounded normal, but she'd sensed a disquiet under the surface. A sense of impending dread. Afraid of what the Ministry might do to them if they said the wrong thing... or what slaughter her mother might bring when the Guilds finally attacked.

A knock at the door and Tyreta started. No one had knocked before. Not even that quiet little man. Nevertheless she stole away from the balcony, creeping to the door. Listening. Hearing nothing.

"Who is it?" she asked, feigning a deep voice and instantly regretting it.

"I'm who you've been waiting for." A man she'd never heard before. But could she trust he'd been sent by Olstrum? Only one way to find out.

Gritting her teeth in frustration, she twisted the key in the lock and wrenched the door open a little, ready to fight if he'd come to do her harm. A handsome face smiled back. One that immediately put her off guard.

"Can I come in?" he asked, still beaming.

He was a little older than Tyreta, square-jawed with a smattering of stubble that made his youthful features look just a touch rugged. Broad shoulders, shirt showing a bit of chest but not too much... and damn it she had to concentrate.

"Who are you?"

"Olstrum sent me." His smile showed perfect white teeth.

"That doesn't answer my question. I asked who you are."

"Now isn't really the time or place for names, but I assure you, you're in no danger from me."

"I assure you, I know that already."

She stepped back, opening the door wider to let him in. Even as this stranger walked inside she could sense no threat from him. He looked relaxed enough, as though he knew he could trust her.

"Apologies you've been kept waiting so long. I trust you've been comfortable?"

"Yes. Comfortable and bored. Olstrum told me he was arranging a meeting with some people who might offer help to the Guilds. So far all I've seen are these four walls."

"Then your wait is over. I'm here to escort you, but we'll be moving fast. I hope you can keep up."

"I think I can manage."

He smiled, as though he already knew that. Then he plucked a yellow scarf from a hook beside the door. "You should cover your head with this."

"Wouldn't a cloak be a more appropriate disguise?"

He glanced out of the window, squinting a little in the bright sunshine. "It's not raining. Why would anyone be wearing a cloak in this weather? That would just advertise to anyone who cared to look that you were up to no good."

That was surprisingly clever of him. Handsome and smart.

She reached out and took the scarf from him, placing it over her head to disguise her hair and face from prying eyes. He opened the door and led her outside, down the stairs from the first floor and out onto the street.

It felt strange to be walking through the Anvil in broad daylight, just like old times. As she followed him she felt nervous at first, wary of anyone who might point and scream her name, but no one did. Everyone was minding their business, as intent on ignoring her as they were on being ignored.

The further south through the city they went, the more tense it grew. People weren't gathering in crowds anymore, as though unwilling to be seen with one another. Fearful of what might happen should they be seen talking to their neighbours and friends.

Before the man could lead her down a narrow stairwell from the main thoroughfare, Tyreta spotted something she had never seen before. Armed soldiers marching in a pair wearing the checked uniform of Revocaters, but instead of red and yellow their livery was grey and black.

"Who are they?" she asked, grasping his arm and stopping him before he could disappear into the alleyway.

"The Ministry's civilian militia," he replied, keeping his voice low. "A new addition, meant to keep everyone in the city honest. Brother against brother, sister against sister, that kind of thing. This is the age we live in now."

Tyreta could see how the two men watched the streets but were in turn watched warily by every passerby. She could only imagine what it must have taken for them to do the Ministry's bidding so willingly. Desperation? Zeal?

"Unfortunately we do," she replied. "For now."

Before the militia could approach any closer, she followed her handsome companion down the stairs and into the Burrows. There were no militia here, and they didn't have to travel far before he ushered her down toward the basement building of a three-storey tenement. After checking to see no one was watching, he produced a key, unlocked the door and led her inside.

It was dark within, made even darker as he closed the door behind her. Immediately her eyes adjusted to the gloom and she sensed it was not just them and the rats in here. When a match hissed and an oil lamp was lit, she saw exactly who had been waiting for them.

Two women and two men were illuminated in the flickering light of the torch. One of the men was clearly little older than a boy, the spectacles that adorned his face held together with a piece of string.

"So this is who we've been waiting for?" said one of the women, tall, solid arms, most likely a manufactory worker if Tyreta had to guess.

The man who had brought her here gestured as though she were onstage and this her audience. "This is indeed Tyreta Hawkspur."

A burly man leered at her out of the darkness, one ear cauliflower twisted. "Our illustrious leader." He grinned before bowing sarcastically.

"She's not my fucking leader," the big woman replied, not taking her eyes off Tyreta.

"All right, that's enough." The second woman stepped forward. Her eyes stared keenly from above prominent cheekbones, limbs willowy, skin weathered. "We're grateful you've come. Olstrum told us you're willing to help."

"I am," Tyreta replied. "If there's anything we can do from inside the city to drum up dissent and make trouble for the Ministry, it will only aid my mother."

"The great Lady Rosomon," said the big woman, doing little to mask her disdain.

The lithe woman turned her piercing eyes toward the burly one. "I said that's enough. We're all on the same side here."

A sneer on the big woman's face. "Now the Guilds need our help we are."

It didn't take a genius to work out she had an axe to grind, but Tyreta could hardly blame her. She'd seen firsthand in New Flaym what the Guilds were capable of. What they'd do and who they'd bury to get their way. Despite being established for the good of Torwyn and all its people, the Guilds helped themselves first and foremost, and had little time for anyone who was crushed in the process.

"Like it or not, we have to work together," Tyreta said, hoping she sounded inspiring rather than desperate. "When my mother launches her attack on the city we have to be ready. If we strike from within then we have a chance to bring the Ministry down quickly. We can't just sit and do nothing." She looked at the smaller woman, hoping she was the one with the authority here. "How many people do you have?"

The woman glanced doubtfully toward that handsome man who'd brought Tyreta here. He stepped forward into the glow of the torch.

"We're not entirely sure."

Tyreta tried not to let her frustration get the better of her. "Not sure because . . . ?"

"Because people are scared," the woman replied. "There are plenty who want to fight back and overthrow the Archlegate, but they're afraid of what the Ministry will do if they rise up and lose. Folk are already going missing . . . those with the biggest mouths at least. Dissent of any kind is not tolerated, the slightest infraction stamped on. Rise up in full revolt and who knows what the consequences will be."

Not exactly the start Tyreta had been expecting. She had hoped to meet a group of determined rebels, but these were more like frightened children.

"Someone must have an idea. Some kind of plan. Has Olstrum—"

"Olstrum hasn't told us shit," the burly woman snapped. "Just keeps telling us to stay ready."

"Ready for what?"

She shrugged her broad shoulder. "He doesn't tell us that either."

Tyreta sighed as subtly as she could manage. These most definitely weren't the counter-revolutionaries she was looking for. But perhaps they could be, if properly motivated.

"Balls to Olstrum then. If he's going to keep everyone in the dark we'll just have to make our own plans." She could see by their quizzical looks they were none too convinced. "What's the matter? Don't you think you're capable of fighting back? Or brave enough?"

That stoked a fire in the smaller woman and she took a step forward. "Don't doubt our commitment. You haven't proved yourself to us yet. We've been living under the fist of the Ministry longer than you have, so don't think to judge us."

"That's just it—I don't know anything about you. And from what I can see, you're just a bunch of scared rebels hiding in a cellar."

"We're risking—"

"Everything? You think you're the only ones? What do you think the Ministry will do if I'm found within the city walls? At best I'll be used as bait. At worst I'll be hung from the front gate as a warning. At least you know who I am. You haven't even told me your names."

"We don't have to tell you shit," the big woman spat. "You're not in charge anymore."

"No. But at least I'm still taking a stand. Still willing to risk my life to end this madness. If we do nothing, the Ministry wins. We can't just hide away in a cellar like rats."

"Fuck you," the woman growled, veins almost popping on her neck.

"Wachelm," the young man said, immediately dispelling the sense of impending violence from the fusty air. All eyes turned to him and his broken eyeglasses. "My name is Wachelm," he repeated.

"Hello, Wachelm," Tyreta said, not a little relieved at the change in mood. "My name is Tyreta. It's good to meet you."

He offered her a nervous smile. "Good to meet you too. I knew your mother. I was her...assistant for a time. When I was a Corwen actuary."

"Really? That must have been..." Tyreta knew it was hard enough being Lady Rosomon's daughter. She could only imagine what her underlings must suffer. "An experience?"

"She was good to me. It was obvious she cared about this city. About Torwyn. And because of that, I will fight. I'm brave enough, don't worry on that score."

The rest of the gathering looked a little embarrassed that it had taken their diminutive bespectacled friend to be the first to step up.

"And I appreciate your support, Wachelm. But don't take this the wrong way—we'll need more than an actuary if we're going to make a difference in this war."

The slender woman stepped forward, chin raised, those keen eyes looking more determined than before. "You have more than that." She gestured to the big man and his cauliflower ear. "You have a riverboatman." Then the broad woman. "An iron welder." The handsome one. "A market trader." Then finally at herself. "A weaver. And we'll fight. All of us. Because we know what will happen if we don't." She nodded toward Wachelm. "Show her."

The young man looked reluctant, but did as she asked, pulling his shirt over his head and turning so Tyreta could see his back in the light. There were lash marks on his flesh. Telltale scars showing he'd been whipped repeatedly.

"Lord Rearden was not very happy with the help I'd been giving your mother. He decided I was to be taught the meaning of loyalty. And believe me, I learned."

Tyreta felt a swell of anger on his behalf, but it did little to reassure her. "I get it, trust me I do, but without a solid plan, and determined fighters, we'll not get far. If we're going to make a difference, we need soldiers."

They looked at one another uncertainly. For all their talk of revolution, it was obvious none of them were warriors.

"They have prisoners," Wachelm said, a sudden spark of inspiration igniting behind those broken lenses.

"I'm listening."

"Titanguard. Maybe a dozen of them, kept in cells at what used to be the old gaol—before all its occupants were sent to the *Sternhaul* off the coast."

For the first time in too long, Tyreta felt herself get excited. "Now you're talking."

Wachelm's look of enthusiasm waned a little. "It will be heavily guarded."

"Of course it will. Almost impossible to breach. Most likely very dangerous too. But what else is there for a boatman, a welder, a trader, a weaver and an actuary to do in times like these? Other than launch a prison break? Are any of you with me, or are you going to sit on your hands in this cellar and keep company with the rats?"

They looked at one another with uncertainty, as they wondered if this was too mad an idea. Before the rest of them could answer, Wachelm jutted out his chin, his cracked eyeglasses glinting in the torchlight.

"We're in."

"Good." Tyreta glanced at each of the faces looking back at her. "So maybe now's the time to introduce yourselves?"

# ANSELL

He led the way, their horses eating up the miles with little trouble. The road had been a lonely one, and they had met no patrols, nor threat of violence so far. Not that it put his mind at ease. A glance at the pair riding with him, and he was reminded yet again that he was the only one not carrying a weapon. If they did encounter trouble he would be left facing it with nothing but his bare hands and a prayer—and his prayers had counted for little in recent weeks.

Though he had an idea where Gravedell lay, he could not be certain they were heading in the right direction without a map, and he had not asked for one. Were he to reveal the location, rather than take them himself, he doubted he would have had this opportunity to honour his vow to Olstrum. Once he revealed that secret they would throw him back in his cage, and his chance to make amends would be lost. To gain some redemption from the weight of his sins.

Ansell wasn't even certain it was Olstrum's family who had been stolen away from the Anvil. If Falcar had been talking about some other innocents, this whole thing was for nothing. Or perhaps not nothing. Even if Gravedell was not where Olstrum's family were being kept, it was still someone's kin. That family still deserved to be rescued. And what a sorry mix of rescuers.

Keara rode close to him, looking of little use for anything. She fidgeted in her saddle, fumbling with the reins when not biting her nails to the nub. A webwainer turncoat who had aided Sanctan and now fought for the Guilds, if only reluctantly. There was no way Ansell could trust her. Not least because she was a sorceress, and he had more than suffered his fill of those.

Absently he touched his mouth, feeling the scarred and necrotic flesh, before putting his mutilated face to the back of his mind.

A glance to his right and there was Kassian Maine, a man he only knew by reputation. And what a reputation it was. Ansell was still a neophyte when Kassian had served as swordwright to Treon Archwind. His deadly reputation was legend, and with such a man watching over him Ansell would be afforded little chance of escape when all this was over, but he still had to consider the option. As much as he wanted to fulfil his oath to Olstrum, he also yearned to return to the Mount and see Grace safely from the city. But that would have to wait. First he had a solemn promise to keep.

As they came toward a fork in the road, Ansell slowed his horse. The pair behind him came to a halt as he stared at the spot where a signpost should have stood. North or west to Gravedell? For the life of him he could not remember which way.

"Well?" the woman asked.

He looked north, then west again. Both roads looked much the same.

"Are we going to sit here all day?" This sorceress clearly had little patience.

"I have not trodden these roads for many years. But it will not take me long to remember my bearings."

Keara's dark eyes rolled in frustration. "Great. I knew we should have brought one of the Talon with us."

All the while Kassian sat patiently atop his horse, allowing this damnable woman to gripe on. Still, a decision had to be made.

"North," Ansell announced. "I am sure it's north."

Keara kicked her horse in frustration. "Let's get moving then, we don't have all day."

Ansell nudged his steed on, aware that Kassian was following close behind. Keara was certainly an annoyance, but despite the daggers she wore at her hip, Ansell felt no threat from her. More pressing was the silent danger that brought up their rear. He had fought a swordwright before and it had not ended well. Kassian might be old, but he was also the man who had trained Jagdor. If the worst happened and Ansell was forced to fight him, he could only hope the Wyrms would show him favour, where previously they had abandoned him.

As they made quick progress along the northern trail, Ansell hoped that they would soon see the chapel. With every woodland spinney they passed through or bend they rounded, he found himself more and more disappointed to be faced by yet more road.

Night was falling when they finally reached a town shrouded in darkness. At first Ansell thought they had simply doused their pyrestone lights, that the townsfolk were seeking shelter inside against the encroaching night, but when they reached the town's perimeter the first burned-out building told a very different story.

The entire place had been razed, every building burned black, though mercifully there were no corpses to add a tale of murder to the devastation. Still, Ansell couldn't help but feel a little guilt at the sight. The ordinary citizens of Torwyn should have been delivered from such devastation, but here they had clearly faced the brunt of the war. Just as he began to wonder if it were Guild, Ministry or Armiger who had been responsible for the atrocity, he saw a message that told him all he needed to know.

*Sedition.* A single word painted on a sign in the centre of town. It was barely visible in the moonlight, but the word stood out starkly.

The Draconate had been responsible for this. On the word of his Archlegate a whole town put to the torch. For a moment he wondered what they could have done to deserve such punishment, but Ansell knew what. They had defied Sanctan Egelrath in some way, minor or major it mattered little. That was all it had taken for their homes to be consumed in the breath of the Wyrms.

"Can we get moving?" Keara said. "This place is giving me the creeps."

Ansell could understand her feelings. This town was dead, the ghosts of its former inhabitants haunting every charred corner.

As he kicked his horse forward he caught sight of Kassian watching him. Judging him. Ansell was not responsible for what happened here, but had he been ordered to raze a town as an example to others, would he not have obeyed?

No, he wouldn't. Not now that he had seen what dark lurked in the heart of the Ministry. But still he could not blame Kassian for judging him.

They were quick to leave the town behind. Not far north sat a small farmhouse on the edge of a wide flat field. It was the only sign of shelter for miles.

"Perhaps we should stop here," Ansell suggested. "It doesn't look like anyone is home."

Keara had already slid from the saddle to approach the front door. "I don't give a shit if anyone's home. I'm not sleeping out in the open tonight, it's bloody cold."

She rapped on the door with her palm. When no one answered she tried the handle. When it didn't open she kicked out with surprising strength. The door sprang inward, and she entered, shouting for anyone who might be inside.

When it was obvious the place was abandoned, Ansell and Kassian dismounted, hitching their horses outside. The farmhouse was small, but there was a welcoming hearth in the sitting room, and before Ansell could wonder if there was anything to make a fire with, Keara had drawn one of her finely crafted daggers and used her witchcraft to ignite the blade. Within moments the flames were roaring.

Ansell settled himself in an armchair, though it was almost too narrow for his bulk. Kassian unbuckled his sword belt, taking the chair opposite while Keara rubbed her hands next to the fire. Kassian fished in a sack, pulling out a wrapped bundle of provisions and tossing it to Ansell. When he offered one to Keara she shook her head.

"There must be something to drink around here," she murmured, glancing about the room but seeing no racks for wine.

As Ansell unwrapped his provisions to see bread, cheese and half an apple, Keara spotted a trapdoor set in the floor. Without a word she opened it and, by the pyrestone light emitted from one of her knives, delved down into the cellar.

Kassian sat in his comfortable chair, looking anything but as he took a bite of his own provisions, still watching Ansell intently. One hand rested on the hilt of his sword, his eyes illuminated by the firelight. It was obvious he had something to say, some slur to spit, some question perhaps. To demand Ansell try to justify himself and all the misdeeds of the Draconate.

"What do you want to say to me, swordwright?" Ansell said, when he could stand to be scrutinised no longer.

A minuscule shake of Kassian's head. "Nothing. But then, what would you tell me, Drake? What kind of insight could you offer? You're not built to think for yourself. Only obey. There's no emotion in that heart of yours. I doubt you feel anything, least of all for the people in the town we just passed. Not like normal men, anyway."

It was the most Ansell had ever heard him say. "I feel enough."

"Do you? Gained a conscience all of a sudden? Is that why you're helping us? You've lost your faith in those damned Wyrms?"

In truth, Ansell knew his faith had been lost long before now. "We all have to believe in something. Put our faith in different idols. You have your Guilds—"

"And you your dragons."

Ansell was not so sure anymore. He doubted he had faith in much at all. There was certainly no comfort to be had in his duties to the Draconate, when once it had been his only solace. Now all he had left were the oaths he had so recently sworn.

"Yes, I dedicated myself to the gods as you did your emperor. What better duty to live for?"

Kassian's eyes narrowed. "And kill for."

"We have both done our share of killing for a cause. Yet it seems I am the one to be judged for it?"

Kassian's jaw tightened. "You're the one who helped bring down an empire. And for what? To send us all back to an age of stone and wood?"

When this had begun at the summit of Wyrmhead, the future laid out for Ansell had seemed so righteous. Now, after so long fighting for a future that appeared impossible, he had no idea what was true and what was a lie.

"At least back in such an age all men were equal under the eye of the Wyrms."

Kassian sat even more upright in his chair. "All equal in their squalor. But we fought our way out of that gutter. Treon Archwind dragged us out. And his son would have continued that legacy if Sanctan hadn't murdered him."

But it was not Sanctan who had slain the emperor. It was Ansell. And for that deed he was still crushed by guilt, not just for the life he had taken, but also for the power it had gifted the Archlegate. No reason to confess that to Kassian though. There was no telling what the swordwright might do were he to learn it had been Ansell who had cut down Sullivar that day. They still had much to accomplish together before that reckoning.

"Sullivar was not meant to die."

"But he did die. And not an hour ago we saw the consequences in that wretched town. So much loss. So much death. Good people punished. Murdered. Drowned in the blink of an eye, and for what?"

Ansell could tell Kassian was trying to hold himself back. Desperate to stay in control. It was obvious too that he had a specific death in mind: Lancelin Jagdor, drowned during the deluge in the north.

"Wyke was a travesty. It should never—"

"Never have happened? Is that your answer to everything, Drake? To hold your hands up and profess your regrets? It does not atone for the crimes of your Ministry.

"I know it doesn't. And I know Jagdor was your friend."

Kassian settled back in his chair. "He was more than a friend to me. I trained him. Raised him like my own. He had no equal."

"On that we can agree. I fought him once. I know better than anyone."

Kassian looked almost amused by the notion. "You fought him and you still live? You should count yourself a fortunate man. Your Wyrms were truly watching over you that day."

Ansell had hardly thought himself lucky, remembering how fortune had little to do with his survival. "Jagdor had his chance to kill me. And yet he chose to spare my life."

Kassian's brow creased as he found the idea an unlikely one. "Why?"

A brief memory came to him; the only thing Ansell remembered with any clarity from their battle. Jagdor's words: *He is not worth your life.*

"I think...perhaps he saw that I was being used for a dark purpose."

Kassian opened his mouth to answer when there was a sudden clatter from below. Keara struggled to pull herself out of the cellar, a bottle clutched in one fist.

"Wasn't much down there, and it's pitch fucking black." She brandished the bottle with a grin. "But I think I've found us some brandy. This should liven up an otherwise dull evening."

As Kassian reclined in his seat, Ansell realised their conversation was finished. He couldn't decide whether that was a mercy or not.

Keara pulled the cork from the bottle with her teeth before spitting it across the room. She gave a deep sniff before curling her lip.

"Arseholes. It's turpentine." She slammed the bottle down on a table, and disconsolately plonked herself in the only vacant chair. "It's gonna be a long night sitting with you two miserable bastards with no grog to drink."

Silence wore on for some moments, and Ansell could only agree that her assessment was correct. She squirmed, as though it was impossible to get comfortable in the chair, before rising to her feet once more.

"Right, I'm gonna take the back room," she announced. "Try not to kill one another while I'm asleep."

She disappeared through the door to the single tiny bedchamber, shutting it behind her. Ansell and Kassian were alone once more with nothing but the sound of the crackling fire.

"Are we good, Drake?" Kassian asked quietly.

"I am no danger to you," Ansell replied.

His reassurance did nothing to alter Kassian's grim expression. "I know that. As soon as I think you are, I'll have to kill you."

The man who had trained Lancelin Jagdor sat back in his chair to make himself more comfortable, but his eyes remained locked on Ansell. It was doubtless he would be able to see through his threat, even if Ansell had weapon and armour.

"Sleep well," Kassian whispered.

Ansell doubted he would.

# CONALL

As though taking mercy on them, there was heavy cloud in the night sky. No moon or stars to give them away as Conall peered from cover toward the landship depot. Sted and Donan were at his side along with Moraide and a couple of her men. The place looked empty, but if that scout was right, it would be teeming with enemy troopers just beyond the perimeter.

"What do you think?" he whispered.

Donan squinted in the dark, assessing the way ahead before nodding. "Yeah, we can plant the charges at the base of the main station block. But to make sure they're effective, we can also rig the aerie. It should bring enough rubble down on the landship line that it'll take them days to dig through it."

Conall turned to Moraide. "You handle the main structure, we'll take the aerie."

She nodded her acknowledgment, and he turned his attention back to the depot. It was quiet for now, but soon Sonnheld and the rest of the Viper Battalion would start their attack from the south. No need to wait all night for that though. The closer they got before the assault, the sooner they'd be out of there.

Keeping his head down, he struck out from cover. The rest of them followed, picking their way across open ground toward the northern perimeter. Even with one eye, Conall could see that the way ahead was clear. His night vision was sharper than ever before, almost as though everything were covered with a silver hue, but he put the reason why to the back of his mind.

When they were within twenty yards, Conall took cover behind a stack of barrels and peered through the dark. A guard stood at the northern edge of the complex, the details of his Phoenix Battalion uniform just discernible. For a moment Conall wondered whether he'd served with this trooper at Fort Tarkis. Maybe he'd been one of the men who kicked him bloody after Tarrien had framed him for murder. Maybe he hadn't. Either way, he was the enemy now. Old loyalties stood for nothing.

A flame flared as the trooper struck a match and lit a pipe. There rose the sudden pungent stench of wortleaf as he puffed away in the dark. Before Conall could think of striking forward to grab him, a second trooper stepped out beneath the pyrestone light. The two nodded at one another in greeting.

"Want a draw?" asked the first, offering his pipe.

The second shook his head. "Nah. Want to keep my wits about me tonight."

"What for? We won. Viper Battalion are on the wind. All the action's north at the capital now, and I think we've earned a rest."

That inspired a smirk from the second trooper. "Yeah, I guess. We'd best make the most of it too. When we get to the Anvil it will make Castleteig look like a barroom brawl."

The first trooper took a long draw on his pipe, the flare of it lighting up his face before he puffed wortleaf smoke into the night air. "Guilds will never take the Anvil."

"I wouldn't be so sure. They have the Hallowhills now. And worse by all accounts."

"What do you mean?"

"Did you not hear? There was an attack on a Tigris garrison in a town over east. Some iron beast walked right into the tavern and slaughtered half a dozen troopers."

A dubious grin from the pipe smoker. "Yeah, whatever. I think we've got enough to worry about without believing scary stories."

"I'm telling you, it's true. The Guilds are making truck with sorcerers. Tapping ancient magics. Ministry has it right—they're led by heretics and demon worshippers."

The grin faded from the pipe smoker's face. "Blimey. Looks like the Archlegate had it right all along."

Before the other trooper could answer there was a clap of thunder from the south, the night sky suddenly lighting up on the other side of the terminal. It was quickly followed by shouts of alarm. The attack had begun.

The sentries glared at one another for a moment, wondering what to do as the din grew louder. Another explosion, answered by a blast from a pyrestone weapon. Mortar and cannon fire began to clap in slow measured beats. Then they were both running deeper into the terminal, leaving the way clear.

"Right," said Conall, stepping out from behind cover. "I'm guessing that's our signal."

They advanced quickly, entering the depot complex between long sheds that lined the perimeter. When they reached the end, Moraide offered Conall a nod for good luck before leading her two troopers toward the station house. He watched her disappear into the dark before darting toward the aerie, with Sted and Donan close behind.

As the sky lit up again and the sound of fighting intensified, Conall caught sight of their target. The aerie loomed over the landship line and he could see Donan was right; if they could bring it down it would take an age to clear away the debris.

Clinging to the shadows, they made their way closer. Through the dark he could see more Phoenix Battalion troopers rushing toward the battle. They wouldn't have much time before those troopers realised they were being attacked by a much inferior force. This would have to be damned quick.

Throwing caution to the wind, he dashed the final few yards across open ground to reach the bottom of the hundred-foot tower. Sted and Donan managed to keep pace, the three of them pausing at the door for a moment to catch their breath.

There could have been someone inside, but Conall knew they had no time to be cautious as he turned the handle and rushed in.

Relief washed over him as he realised the place was abandoned.

"We need to get this done quick," he said, turning to Donan.

Sted grasped her splintbow tight, guarding the door as Donan unslung the pack on his shoulder, handing a charge to Conall before taking one out for himself. Before they could place them, the sound of ordnance blasted from the south once more.

"Sounds like Sonnheld ain't holding back," Sted said.

Conall was about to answer, when there was a deafening screech from above that filled the aerie with a chilling noise.

Donan glared up the stairwell that twisted its way to the summit of the tower. "What was that?"

Conall shook his head. "It can't be. They can't have just left an eagle here. What... what should we do?"

"What the fuck are you talking about?" Sted snapped. "We don't do anything. We have a job to finish, in case you hadn't noticed."

"We can't just leave it chained up. This place is about to blow."

Her eyes narrowed in that familiar display of annoyance. "Which is why we need to get the fuck out of here."

She was right, and he knew it. He couldn't risk this mission for the fate of a dumb animal. "All right. Donan?"

He gestured toward one side of the wide chamber. "If we load the charges against the eastern wall it will bring this whole tower down right across the landship line."

"Right then—let's get to it."

As they both made their way to the corner of the building they heard the eagle screech again. Conall had never borne any particular affection for the beasts before, not like Tyreta. Even so, it was hard to just ignore the thing, wailing in fright at the sounds of battle outside. Sted was right though, they had a job to do. There was more riding on this than the life of one war eagle.

"Remember—short timer," Donan said.

Conall nodded, gently turning the dial on the charge so they'd have only a couple of minutes before the detonator primed. "All right. That's one. Are you finished, Donan?"

"Bollocks," Sted hissed, before he could reply. "There's someone coming."

All three of them froze in place.

"It's only a small force," said a muffled voice from outside. "Don't offer any real danger, but the marshal says they must be probing at us for a reason. Most likely a distraction."

"Right," said another. "Then check every building."

Sted furtively peered through the grille at the centre of the door, before hissing, "Shite. They're headed this way."

Conall had grasped his sword without even thinking, and slowly edged the blade free of the scabbard. "Donan... get on with it."

Donan nodded, turning back to the job at hand and planting another of their charges.

"They're almost here," Sted said through gritted teeth.

Conall was already moving toward the door. "I'll rush them. Keep them busy. Once Donan's finished, you two run."

"Keep them busy?" she asked. "With that thing?"

He realised the stupidity of it. If they were armed with splintbows he'd be cut down before he could get within three feet. But Sted had other ideas, priming her splintbow and wrenching the door open before could think to stop her.

"Sted, wait!"

She was already gone, through the door and out into the clangourous night.

"Oi! Fuckers!" he heard her yell, before the thwap of her splintbow cut the air.

The door swung shut behind her, but he just stood, staring at it as shouts of warning reverberated beyond. He should have wrenched it open, should have charged into the fray right alongside her, but Donan was still busying himself with those detonators and someone had to watch his back.

"Damn it, Donan, hurry the fuck up."

"Nearly there," came the reply, as he tinkered at the edge of the room.

More splintbows firing. More yells of alarm and confusion, before Donan shot to his feet. "I'm done."

Conall stepped toward the door, ready to charge out and save his friend, but someone on the other side kicked it sharply before he had the chance. A Phoenix trooper burst in, splintbow raised. He was followed by a second, a third, and Conall didn't even have time to react before they had him dead to rights.

Donan raised his hands above his head, just before one of them gestured to the blade in Conall's hand and growled, "Drop it."

Three of them. There was no way he could take him down before they riddled him with bolts. He loosened his grip on the sword, before letting it slip from his fingers.

"What you bastards up to then?" said a trooper, his chin all big and stubbly, eyes all beady and dark.

Before Conall could answer, one of the others stepped forward into the light, squinting in confusion. "Hang on...that's Conall Hawkspur."

The first one shook his head. "Don't be ridiculous, that's not...by the fucking Lairs. Marshal!"

He shouted the last word so loud Conall flinched. Nothing he could do with so many bows levelled at him, and this time when the door opened he recognised the man who entered. All of a sudden Conall began to regret not rushing headlong into a hail of splintbow fire when he had the chance.

Westley Tarrien had a serious look to his face, but when he saw Conall, standing there helpless, that expression changed. The twist of a smile. The narrowing of eyes that couldn't quite believe what they were seeing. A gift that had just landed on his lap.

"As I live and breathe," Tarrien said. "It's been a long time, Hawkspur."

Conall's gut roiled in a mix of dread and hate. "Tarrien. They've made you marshal of the Phoenix now? Just handed over the position of the man you murdered?"

Not even a glimmer of guilt behind Tarrien's eyes. "Everyone knows the truth, Hawkspur. Spit as many lies as you want; it won't get you anywhere." He turned to one of his men. "What were they doing?"

The one with the big chin stepped forward, squinting toward the edge of the room. "Looks like they're setting charges, Marshal."

"Can you defuse them?" Tarrien asked.

The man looked doubtful before shaking his head. "I don't think—"

"No matter." Tarrien fixed Donan in his hateful gaze. "You'll do the job for us, won't you, Marrlock?"

Donan gulped hard as all attention shifted to him. He glanced toward Conall, as though asking what he should do, but there were no more orders to give. Maybe it was best if Conall just told him to comply. It would have been the easiest thing, the safest. If they didn't do what Tarrien wanted they'd both be killed anyway.

But the words wouldn't come. Instead, Conall glanced toward the shadow, so close to his empty hand. He knew it was there, watching, waiting. The temptation began to creep up the nape of his neck, overwhelming all other emotion.

*Just reach out. I am here.*

"Do it now," Tarrien demanded. "Or you're dead."

One of the troopers hefted his splintbow to shoulder height, aiming toward Donan's chest. Conall could almost hear the ticking of those detonators; not long now before they blew. If they didn't disarm them, he and Donan were dead, but do as Tarrien demanded and this whole mission was shot.

*All you have to do is—*

Conall needed no further urging, reaching out his hand to the shadow.

It was waiting.

He felt the familiar handle in his palm, that slight tingle up his arm. Before he could even think how he might attack, the black blade swept from right to left, parting the nearest trooper's head from his shoulders.

It was so swift Conall barely had a chance to acknowledge the head hitting the ground before he'd stepped forward, lightning fast, tip of the blade aimed at the second trooper. The sword slid through his chest so easily, so naturally... then the blade sang.

The room was filled with a sickening howl of triumph. Conall watched with rising horror as the eyes of the man he had just impaled began to bleed, his mouth opening in a silent scream. All the while Conall was flooded with a supreme sense of power. Of might. Of victory.

The third trooper dropped his splintbow to the ground, turning, fleeing through the door to the aerie. Tarrien staggered away, stumbling at the foot of the winding stairs that rose up through the tower.

Conall felt a cold sense of pleasure on seeing the fear in Tarrien's eyes. He wanted to spit some appropriate quip, to taunt him, goad him, ask which of them was the better man now, but instead he wrenched the sword free of the dead trooper and took a step after him. There were no trite jibes here. Only slaughter.

Tarrien clattered up those stairs and Conall watched him go, savouring his enemy's fear. He had a vague idea that perhaps he'd come here for a reason, to serve a purpose, but all that was gone from his mind now. Replaced only by the need to kill.

He was stepping toward the stairs, gripping his black blade tight, when he saw Donan's face. The horror writ in those wide eyes of his was more haunting than anything Conall had ever seen. He paused, before looking down at the shadow sword in his grip, the wisps of black vapour emanating from it, the two corpses it had made.

"I can explain," Conall said, though he had no idea how. "Donan, this is not what it—"

Donan was already running, almost falling over one of the corpses before he burst out into the clangour of night. Conall should have followed him, should have fled this place before it was reduced to rubble, but the sword still pulsed in his grip. Still thirsted. And Tarrien was so very close...

*He is your enemy. It is your right to end him. Do it now.*

An explosion nearby, deafening in its clarity, dispelling all doubt and spurring him into action. Conall leapt for the stairs, taking them three at a time, round and round that twisting staircase as he all but flew to the tower's summit.

Cold air hit him as he reached the top, the wind carrying the distant sound of battle with it. Tarrien was struggling with the securing rig of the war eagle's harness, desperately fumbling with the buckle.

"Nowhere to run," Conall said. He wasn't even out of breath, hands not even shaking as the blood pounded through his veins.

Tarrien stopped what he was doing, slowly regarding Conall as though he finally accepted his fate. Then he glanced to the shadow blade still misting in his grip.

"What the fuck have you become, Hawkspur?"

Another moment of clarity as once more Conall glanced down at the sword. It felt suddenly alien in his grip, as though he were holding a viper about to strike at his wrist. "I...I don't know."

All the while he was advancing on Tarrien. Step after purposeful step, despite the doubt. His previous conviction was gone. His thirst to kill sated, yet still he closed with his enemy.

"You don't have to do this," Tarrien whispered, taking a step back but only finding the edge of the tower, and nowhere left to go.

Conall stopped. He stared into that face. The man who had set him up as a murderer. The man he had pitied and then hated in equal measure.

"I know I don't."

*But you do.*

Tarrien wrenched his sword free of its scabbard as Conall advanced. The howling blade in Conall's hand cut down, but somehow Tarrien managed to parry, the sound of clashing metal more shriek than ring. Conall struck again, but Tarrien dodged aside, countering with a stab toward his ribs, but all too slow.

A howl from the sword as it batted Tarrien's blade from his grip and sent it spinning into the night. Conall felt the sudden swell of victory, the sense of triumph conjuring a grin that almost split his lips.

"Hawkspur," Tarrien pleaded, backing to the edge of the tower. "Wait."

The thrust was mercifully swift, driving deep into Tarrien's gut and up into the rib cage. He gasped, breath cut short. The veins of his eyes haemorrhaged as he spasmed, that demon blade drinking its fill. The flesh drained of all colour, turning stark white against the dark of night, and his final death rattle was little more than a hollow sigh.

Conall staggered back as Tarrien's spent corpse collapsed to the roof of the aerie. He was shaking, now the reality of what he had done fell upon him like an avalanche.

He gasped, glaring at the black sword that was fading fast in his grip, disappearing into the ether now that it had sated its thirst for death. Conall was left alone on top of the tower.

A tower that would shortly be nothing but ruins.

The eagle screeched again, as though reminding him it was his only hope. He dashed across the rooftop, noting for the first time how scrawny a beast it was. Obviously the thing had been poorly cared for since the Hawkspur handlers had abandoned this post.

His hand fumbled with the restraining buckle, just as Tarrien's had. He tried not to think of how little time he had, just took in a breath, forced himself to concentrate. There was plenty of time… there had to be…

An explosion across the depot. The station house erupting in flame as the charges Moraide had planted did their work. Not long now and he'd be consumed in flames just like it. If only he could…

The buckle snapped open, and he let the strap fall to the ground. The beast writhed in its restraints, fighting against the remaining strap as Conall grabbed it, doing his best to wrest enough slack so he could unbuckle it. The flesh of his palm burned as he wrenched it toward him, fingers fumbling with the clasp.

Another distant boom of ordnance, and the buckle came loose. Conall gasped as he grabbed hold of the eagle's martingale, scrambling upon its back, grasping the rein before it could set to flight. Clambering into the saddle, he prepared himself for the sudden lurch as it soared into the sky.

The eagle did not move.

"Come on then!" he yelled above the din.

The eagle took a tentative step toward the edge of the tower. Leaning its head forward it peered over the side as though it had no idea what its wings were for.

"We have to go, or we're both fucking dead."

The eagle seemed to take the hint, rustling its feathers and almost bucking Conall from his saddle, before it stepped from the tower and spread its wings.

Freezing air struck his face and stole his breath. He gripped the rein tight, falling faster and faster, until the eagle's wings caught the thermals and it soared upward.

Another boom. This one so much closer, as behind him the charges at the base of the aerie blew. A wave of hot air gusted in their wake, catching beneath those huge wings and raising them higher into the air.

The eagle wheeled, showing Conall the battle below in intimate detail. Sonnheld's troopers had taken the fight to the Phoenix all right, and half the depot looked to be on fire. The tower behind him lurched, listing painfully before the structure gave up the ghost. It collapsed onto the landship line, smashing into the surrounding carriage sheds and spreading destruction all across the complex.

Conall would have shouted for joy. Instead he held tight to those reins, desperate to stop the trembling in his hands, but no matter how tight he held on, they just kept shaking.

# ROSOMON

The map was spread in front of them, the Anvil and its surroundings sketched out in meticulous detail. Her scouts had done an excellent job of charting the city and its defences, but Rosomon didn't need to examine a map to know the Anvil was all but impregnable.

Maugar tugged at his beard, shaking his head as he stared at it. "We cannot afford to wait any longer. Our scouts have reported movement to the south. More Armigers are on the way—we need to strike now while we can."

Rosomon glanced across at those expectant faces, all grimly regarding the map. Marshal Falko gave the faintest nod, and from the keen look in his eye she could tell Rawlin was in agreement with them both. Oleksig held his peace, puffing thoughtfully on that pipe of his. These were her trusted generals, their experience to be valued, but Rosomon was not ready to give the order to attack yet.

She gripped the pommel of the Hawkspur blade. The sword she could not wield with any skill, but which still offered her some comfort nonetheless. "We must hold our nerve. Wait for word from inside the city. Without help from Olstrum and his rebels, we won't have enough support to end this quickly."

Maugar pressed his fist to the table, knuckles white. "The Raptor and Auroch still approach from the Rock. The Phoenix and Tigris from Castleteig. How long do you think we've got, Rosomon?"

"We can smash the gates of the Anvil, take the city with the army we have, but without support from within we will never hold it."

Oleksig tapped the map with his pipe. "But we can only breach the gates as things stand. The stormhulks at our disposal could turn them to matchwood, but how long will the Hallowhills stay on our side? They move with the ebbing tide, and as soon as they sense it turn against us they may well change allegiance again. Surely we should strike now before they sail right back to Sanctan?"

"No," she replied, trying not to think on that very plausible notion of treachery. "We wait."

Maugar rammed his fist into the table. "For what? Every day we sit here is another day the enemy draws nearer. Our advantage ebbs away the longer we wait, while Sanctan's only grows stronger."

She stepped back, regarding them all, seeing their eagerness. They wanted an end to this, just as she did. Doubtful they saw the bigger picture though. The sacrifice that would have to be made to hold on to what they won.

"Even if we could breach the main gate to the Anvil, have the stormhulks lead the way and flood the city with our troopers, what then? What if the city is not with the Guilds after all? What if most of the populace have succumbed to Ministry lies and fight against us? Do we slaughter our own people? We have to know that we have their support. Otherwise we're only making this war last that much longer. If we know the people of the Anvil are on our side—"

"We can never know for sure, Rosomon," said Oleksig, still looking down with concern at that map. "There is no way we can take the city without collateral damage, if that's what you're hoping. At best, perhaps half the city will side with the Guilds. Otherwise, why haven't they already risen up?"

"Don't underestimate the influence of my nephew or his faith. Sanctan will have the city under tight control. He rules with fear, but if we can show the Anvil hope—"

"The only hope we need to give them is to attack," snapped

Maugar. "To smash those gates and string Sanctan from the highest steeple of the Mount."

"You'd make a martyr of him, Maugar? An immortal symbol of the Draconate? What if Oleksig is right, and he does control half the populace? What if they follow him faithfully? All that slaughter will do is prove that he was right, and the Guilds are as brutal and cruel as his lies suggest."

Maugar held his tongue, though it was obvious he was quelling another outburst. Oleksig took a draw on his pipe and stepped away from the map.

"So how long do we wait?" he asked. "We don't have much time before our hand is forced."

And he was right. Rosomon was hanging her hopes on Keara returning soon with Olstrum's family in one piece. Then she would be able to send whatever message would spur him into action. There was still so much of this she had no control over, and it was maddening. She could not show that though. Could not offer a shred of doubt that her decision was the right one.

The flap to the tent was wrenched aside, before she could answer Oleksig. A Talon scout entered, bowing his head to Rosomon. "My lady, something is approaching the camp."

The concern on his face was worrying. "Something?"

"Well...yes. In the sky."

He led her from the tent, and her generals joined her. Outside the sky was clear, and she followed the scout's gesture as he pointed toward the western horizon. It was a black dot in the distance but clearly making its way closer to their location. As they stood watching it, she began to hear an unmistakably familiar sound.

"Good gods, what is that?" Oleksig breathed.

Maugar was already shaking his grim head. "No. It can't be."

But it could. Rosomon had seen its like before, and remembered that awful sound as it brought the herald from Nyrakkis. That day had been so wondrous, and despite the noise it made on its approach, the airship had felt like a symbol of hope. Now, as it moved closer, growing ever larger like a baleful dark beetle, it only filled her with dread.

"What is that horrendous racket?" Falko said, eyes fixed on the dark ship.

The sound grew louder with every passing second, a groaning drawl from the distance. As it drew nearer the camp began to stir, panic spreading as though they were infected by some foul Maladoran sorcery.

"Marshals, ready your troopers," Rosomon ordered.

Rawlin and Falko needed no further encouragement, striking into the camp and barking orders at their adjutants. Ianto moved closer to her, the rest of the Titanguard taking up positions all around, despite the distance of that infernal ship.

She barely registered the activity around her as hundreds of troopers mobilised, the sound of the airship growing louder, a hellish shriek that scattered every bird in the sky. All the while Rosomon watched as it crossed close to the treetops before dipping down, hovering for a moment as its deafening demon engine quieted. Clawed feet gripped the earth as the ark came to land, and there it lurked, as everyone watched on in silence.

"We should move to a safe distance," Ianto urged.

Rosomon shook her head, not taking her eyes off the beastly vessel. "No. It has come for a reason. I doubt it is at the behest of the Ministry, so let's see what they want."

A hatch began to open in the ark's hull as its whining engine powered down, groaning and belching all the while. The opening yawned wide, and all around Armiger and Guild warriors gripped their weapons pensively.

Nothing appeared. There was no dazzling emissary this time, nor magnificent tattooed warriors. Just a black yawning hole in the bowels of the iron beast.

Rosomon stepped forward, determined to show no fear, no matter what manner of creature revealed itself. When she was within twenty feet, she spied movement from within and stopped, gripping the useless sword at her hip. A small woman made her way down the ramp, wearing an assured smile, as though she knew they'd been expecting her. A familiar face Rosomon couldn't place at first, but then...

No. The witch. The one who had taken Fulren away in an airship just like this one. What had she said? *Fulren is ours now, Lady of Hawkspur.* And she had said it gleefully, as though Rosomon's misery had been a delight to her.

She curbed the desire to rush forward, to draw her sword and use it, despite the fact she could barely swing the damned thing. Even when dark-armoured knights followed the woman from the ark, Rosomon still had to quell her desire to stride into their midst and wreak revenge.

The nine knights fanned out to either side of the woman. Their armour was of ebon, swords at their sides in ornately wrought scabbards, and they looked far more imposing than the spear-wielding warriors who had accompanied Assenah Neskhon. Dark knights tasked with protecting a witch with an equally dark purpose.

Despite the grim aspect of her companions, the woman approached with a wide white smile, and opened her arms in greeting. Rosomon stood as still as she could manage, trying her best to control a tremble of rage.

"Lady of Hawkspur. How good it is to see you again. I am Wenis of Jubara. I do hope you remember me."

All Rosomon's anger balled into a white-knuckled fist. As Wenis strode confidently within range Rosomon forgot all notion of consequences and punched her square on the jaw. Wenis fell back, landing on her backside.

"What are you doing here?" Rosomon spat. "I should kill you, fucking demon."

Wenis rubbed at her sore chin but looked otherwise unsurprised. "So you *do* remember me. I must admit, I'm a little flattered."

The dark knights drew their swords in unison, stepping forward as one, like they were marionettes controlled by a single puppeteer. In response, the Titanguard levelled their spears and advanced at speed.

Rosomon raised a hand for them to halt. As Wenis struggled to her feet, she did likewise, and the nine knights stopped in their tracks.

"Peace," Wenis said, working her jaw. "Let us have peace. Such violence was not entirely unjustified. I can understand why you might be upset with me."

"Upset?" Rosomon spat. "Upset? You stole my fucking son."

Wenis looked somewhat offended by the suggestion. "Stole might be stretching the facts somewhat."

"I should kill you all."

If Wenis felt threatened by the idea she didn't show it. "Perhaps. But that would just be a waste. You would be squandering the aid of a powerful ally, who might have the means to help you defeat your dragon priest."

"An ally?"

"Indeed." The annoying smile was back on her face. "Queen Meresankh is very keen for you to claim victory."

After all that had happened, the murder of her emissary, the imprisonment of Fulren, it seemed a fanciful notion. Still, Rosomon wasn't ready to kill this woman just yet. "Why? What would she have to gain?"

"There would be much to gain, for the both of you. Her previous offer of an alliance still stands, despite the... misunderstanding we had last time."

"Then you admit you know it was not Fulren who murdered your emissary."

"Of course. And we also know it was your Archlegate who did all he could to drive a wedge between our two great nations."

"So why have you waited until now? If you knew all this why not help us sooner?"

Wenis shrugged her narrow shoulders. "Perhaps we could discuss those details in private?" She glanced around at the array of weapons levelled in her direction. "And with fewer projectiles aimed at my head?"

Rosomon would have preferred to continue with those weapons right where they were, but she had to know what this was about. "Very well."

She motioned for Wenis to follow her, but Ianto barred the witch's path. "We cannot trust her."

Rosomon stopped, before looking back over her shoulder at the diminutive woman. "I doubt she's come all the way from Nyrakkis to kill me. Especially after arriving in such a conspicuous fashion. Am I right?"

Wenis bowed graciously. "As always, Lady of Hawkspur."

"Then follow me, Wenis of Jubara."

"With pleasure," Wenis replied, before turning to her imposing guardians and shooing them off with a wave of her hand.

Rosomon led her away from the grumbling ark, past rows of hostile-looking Armigers. Past the phalanx of Blackshields glaring from beneath soot-covered helms, through a crowd of fearful miners. Eventually they reached the western extent of the camp, looking down on the swirling grasses that led to the gates of the Anvil a mile distant.

They were silent for a moment at the brow of the hill, simply taking in the view as if they were two old friends.

"Such a lovely city," Wenis said, breaking the silence. "I thought as much the first time I was here."

"I don't have the patience for small talk," Rosomon replied. "Why are you here? And more to the point; what are you going to offer me?"

Wenis beamed up at her. "I offer you all the powers at my disposal to help win your war."

"Do you have another ten thousand armoured knights in that black ark of yours? Because if not, I don't see what help you could be."

"No, I only brought nine. But they are the best Nyrakkis has to offer. And there's me of course." She spread her short arms as though offering something of value.

"Forgive me if I am less than overwhelmed."

"You should not underestimate what advantage knights of the Caste may offer you. Just ask Fulren and that man Jagdor you sent to rescue him. I assume they returned to your side safely?"

Rosomon's grip tightened on the pommel of her sword. "They did. And now they are both dead."

The sickly-sweet smile on Wenis's face faded. Perhaps the first genuine expression she had offered since stepping from her airship.

"I am sorry. Truly I am."

Rosomon ignored her sympathy, doubting its sincerity. "If you are genuinely here to help me, what does your queen want in return, should I secure victory?"

"You really don't... how do you say it... beat around the bush, do you?"

"No. In recent days I've found it only serves to waste time I don't have."

"A practical approach," said Wenis, that smile now gone completely. Perhaps her remorse on hearing the news of Fulren and Lancelin was genuine after all. "Should you prove victorious, Queen Meresankh wishes only to open a dialogue once more between our countries. That is all she asks. And I am here to help you as a show of faith."

Yet another alliance with yet another enemy, but there was nothing to lose now. She had already made a bargain with the Hallowhills. What did it matter if she was helped by the demon-lovers of Nyrakkis?

"Very well. I accept your offer. Though I'm not entirely sure what you can do with one airship against an entire city."

"If we put our heads together, I'm sure we can come up with something." Wenis held out her hand. "Now, I believe your custom is to shake on an agreement."

Rosomon regarded the slender hand as though it might bite. "I have no desire to touch you. Just take my word for it that I will keep my end of the deal. Now, move that ugly airship of yours somewhere more discreet. It's unsettling my people." She turned away, leaving Wenis at the brow of the hill.

"Whatever you desire, Lady of Hawkspur," the sorceress called after her. "I am at your service."

# FULREN

His wounds had healed fast, too fast, but he tried not to think on that. As the reverie of his newfound power had waned, it was replaced by the memory of what he had done. He had conjured dark arcanist power and it should have made him balk. Instead, all he could wonder was when he would be able to unleash it again.

The memories should have brought horror with them. He had killed wantonly, and yet the notion of what he was capable of only served to excite him. Knowing he was in control of such power, but only barely. That he was dancing amid a sandstorm of his own creation.

This was not the Fulren Hawkspur of old. The calculating, careful Fulren, always doing the right thing. This was a new beast. Looking down at his legs, fused to the steel of artifice, he realised that *beast* was the right word.

Verlyn sat in silence as she drove their horses ever northward. Perhaps he should have explained his fears to her; she was a webwainer after all. But her connection with the web was nothing in comparison to the sorcery Fulren had at his disposal. He was playing an altogether different game. One shrouded in danger. One that neither of them would ever understand.

As the wagon trundled along he began to sense movement from up ahead, a mile or more distant. Pressing his senses along the road he saw a dull cascading light on the horizon. For a moment he considered harnessing those crows, who shadowed his every move, and sending them like spies to scout ahead, but they were no longer present. Perhaps the recent slaughter had sated their need for death. Fulren was sure they would return when they began to hunger once more.

"Can you see anything ahead?" he asked. The first words he'd spoken to Verlyn in a day.

"A camp," she replied. "But we're close to the Anvil now, so no surprise."

"Armigers?" Fulren suddenly yearned for the prospect of another chance to test himself.

"My bet is your mother."

He let out a long breath. In his anticipation of further violence he had forgotten about that inevitable reunion. "Maybe we should hold back then. Scout ahead first?"

"I don't see we have any choice but to—"

A rustle in the nearby undergrowth alerted them all too late. Fulren moved his hand toward his side, but remembered his helm and blade were still in the back of the wagon.

"Stop where you are," said a deep voice. Whoever spoke clearly wasn't messing around.

Fulren scanned the surrounds, but without his helm, nothing was distinct. Someone stood a few yards away, faint motes against the grey of his glyphsight. As he looked he could sense more figures in the undergrowth.

"What are you doing here?" the voice asked, a distinct edge to it.

"Just travellers," Verlyn replied. "Are you Guild or Ministry?"

"What difference does that make if you're just travellers?" the voice demanded.

"Because we're travellers who are looking for Rosomon Hawkspur."

Fulren gritted his teeth. Some kind of plan that was, just giving the game away. It would be good news or violence now. No in between.

"For what purpose?" the voice asked, the speaker becoming clearer as he took a step closer.

"None of your damned business," Verlyn answered, her patience clearly run dry. "Do you know where she is or not?"

Fulren's vision clarified, faint outlines against the grey solidifying. There were four of them, all carrying splintbows. All aimed right at them.

"Who are you?"

It was now or never. If Verlyn had decided to risk everything, there was no point letting her do it alone.

He wrenched back his hood, sitting up in the seat of the wagon so they could all see him. "Her son. Fulren Hawkspur."

One of them gasped, but Fulren couldn't tell if that was a good thing or not.

"Shit," one of them hissed. "That *is* him."

"No," said another. "He's dead."

"Does he look fucking dead?" One of them gestured back along the road. "Ride to camp. Let her know we're coming." Obediently, one of the figures rushed off into the undergrowth, before the man turned back to them. "You'd better come with us."

As the sound of hooves clattered along the road ahead of them, the scouts gestured for them to follow along the path. Verlyn flicked the reins, the wagon jolting in response.

"That was risky," Fulren whispered.

"I'm sure you would have handled it. There were only four of them."

Fulren appreciated her confidence, but he put the thought of another fight from his mind. Right now he had a harder battle to think on.

The road led them up to the summit of a hill, and the noises of a busy encampment grew louder. They trundled out of the woodland and onto a flat hilltop, where myriad campfires burned. As soon as Verlyn drove them within the perimeter the voices started to hush.

"Is that him?" he heard someone say.

"No, it can't be," came the immediate reply.

The place was gripped by tension, and he sensed all eyes were on him.

"Here's far enough," said the scout with the deep voice. "We can walk from here."

Fulren pulled his cloak tight about him as he and Verlyn climbed down. He wasn't ready to show the world what he had become. Not yet at least.

"Just you," the scout said.

Verlyn paused, before reaching into the back of the wagon and taking something out.

"Here." She pressed a walking staff into Fulren's hand.

"I don't need—"

"Yeah, you do," Verlyn said. "You're blind. Remember?"

She was right. Best to keep up the pretence and avoid any unwanted questions, at least until he was reunited with his mother.

He gripped the staff tightly as he followed the scout the rest of the way through the camp. The air of unease only grew more intense, those whispers of disbelief following him, and for a moment he missed the wheeling crows, and the strange sense of comfort they gave him. Despite being in the midst of his mother's army, it felt as though he had no friends here.

The scout stopped in front of him, opening the flap of a tent and stepping aside. As Fulren followed him in, a gust of warm air hit him from the brazier burning bright in the centre of the tent. A hulking figure stood beside it.

"They told me a man claiming to be Fulren Hawkspur was here," the big man said, his voice young but still imposing. "I didn't believe it, but…"

"Who are you?" Fulren asked.

"I am Ianto Fray, your mother's Imperator Dominus. I often used to see you at the Anvil, when Sullivar was alive. We all thought you were dead, but… it is good to have you back."

Before Fulren could answer, the flap to the tent moved again. Someone entered, and he heard a sharp intake of breath. It could only be one person.

"Hello, Mother," he said.

If he was expecting her to yell, to rush forward and embrace him, he was sorely disappointed. She just stood watching him, as though he were a stranger in her son's skin.

"You can leave us," she whispered. "Thank you, Ianto."

The imposing warrior moved past them and out of the tent, leaving them alone. More silence as his mother stood drinking him in.

"It can't be you. I watched you die on that bridge."

All of a sudden he was conscious of the reconstructed body he was concealing from her. Of how much he had changed. Perhaps she was right, he had already considered the idea that the old Fulren was dead.

"I...I didn't die, Mother. Though there were times I wished I had."

She could hold herself back no longer, taking a step forward to grab him, to hold him. Fulren stepped away, desperate to spare her the sudden knowledge of what he had become. He held out a hand for her to stop, realising it was the wrong hand far too late.

His mother flinched on seeing the steel claw. Her gasp of horror was more painful than any wound he'd suffered since that day on the Bridge of Saints.

"I'm sorry," he said, swiftly concealing the artifice beneath his cloak. "I know what this must look like. How this is a shock to you, but I can explain it all."

And yet he had no idea how. What might he say to make her understand the dark bargain he had struck? That part of his soul had been sacrificed to make himself whole again.

"Show me," his mother said.

It was not a request; it was an order. Fulren had heard his mother's commanding tone a thousand times, and never once refused to obey it. He could not do so, even now.

The walking stick slipped from his grip. Fulren unclasped the cloak at his neck and let it fall to the ground. His body was unveiled in all its inhuman glory, his legs flexing, raising him another foot as he clasped and unclasped his steel claw of a hand.

"It's...it's just artifice," he whispered, as though that might explain all this away.

"No," his mother said quietly. "It isn't, Fulren."

"I'm sorry. I wanted this to be different. I wanted to come back and you'd be happy to see me, but—"

"I was...I am...but this...Who did this to you?"

He could sense that behind her shock and horror she was growing angry. As though someone had inflicted this upon her precious son, and she would scorch the earth until she found the one responsible.

"I asked for this, Mother. It is a gift."

She moved closer to him, fighting her fear. When she touched the steel of his arm it tingled as though she had tenderly brushed his skin. He truly was as one with the artifice; a creature of steel and flesh just like in his dreams.

Before he could try to allay her fears any further, she reached up to touch his face, as though to reassure herself it was still him. "I tried not to allow myself the luxury of hope, but deep down I still waited for you to come back."

He could hear the crack in her voice, her nearness to breaking down. "You do not have to hope any longer. I am here."

His mother allowed herself a sob, before she pressed herself against him, gripping her son tight as though she might never let him go. He folded his right arm around her, feeling her weep against him as she released all the emotion she had kept gaoled inside.

"I heard about what happened in Wyke. What happened to Lancelin. I am sorry, Mother."

She took a breath to control herself, before looking up at his scarred face. "There is something you have to know. About Lancelin."

But he already knew. Deep down he had known it since their return from Nyrakkis.

"He was my father."

She gripped him tighter. "How did you...?"

"You can be persuasive, Mother. No one knows that more than I do. But to get a man to travel all the way to Malador on the small hope he might save your son? Not even you are that convincing. There had to be another reason. A deeper connection."

"I am just sorry I never told you when I had the chance. When you both could have—"

"That doesn't matter now. All that matters is us. Our family. Have you heard from Tyreta and Conall? Are they safe?"

She loosened her embrace on him and took a step back. At first she didn't speak, as though she were searching for the right words, and Fulren prepared himself for the worst.

"Tyreta returned home from New Flaym. Much changed, as you are. Now she has gone... to the Anvil."

"She's what? And you just let her go?"

"She is a woman now, Fulren. Just as you are a man. More than a man. I sent her to be my eyes and ears within the city. To stand against the Ministry from within."

"Tyreta? Our Tyreta?"

"She is stronger and more capable than you could ever have thought."

He still couldn't quite comprehend what he was hearing. "Mother, when I last saw her she was barely capable of tying her own bootlaces. If she could even be bothered to get out of bed first."

"You're not the only one who has changed. Not the only one to accept a gift."

He would have to take his mother's word for it. "And Conall? What gift has he received? Is he emperor of the Karna now?"

His mother's silence told him more than he wanted to hear. Fulren allowed her the time to gather herself, before she had to tell him what had happened to his brother.

"He... he drowned, Fulren. His ship was caught in a storm as it returned from Agavere. He died a hero."

"No." Fulren felt suddenly dizzy, his hydraulic limbs doing little to steady him. "I won't believe it. I don't."

"I am sorry, Fulren. I know how much he meant to you."

Now it was his turn to fight back the tears and quell his grief, but in doing so he only felt the well of anger grow.

"When do we launch our attack?" he asked. It was the only thing he could think to ask. The only way he could move forward from this.

"I don't know yet. We are waiting on word from Olstrum that he has prepared resistance from inside the city. He won't do that until we have assured him his family is safe from the Ministry."

"That's what we're waiting for?"

"Until we can wait no longer," his mother replied.

Before he could ask anything further, he heard the flap of the tent once more, the slightest gust of air agitating the flames in the brazier as someone entered.

"I heard that—" A woman's voice, struck dumb when they saw the creature that stood inside.

"Emony," his mother said. "I didn't—"

"Fulren?" Emony gasped.

All too late he was conscious of the cloak that had fallen at his feet. Too late to pick it up now. Too late to hide what he had become from her. Instead, he turned slightly, trying to hide his arm of steel.

"Yes, Emony, it's me."

"No," she breathed. "You're... no. What is this thing?"

His mother stepped in front of her, their outlines blurring into one. "Emony, this is Fulren. Our Fulren. You know him, there is nothing to be afraid of."

"No!" Emony wailed.

The sound of her voice almost broke his heart, and he could not resist taking a step toward her, desperate to reassure her, to comfort her.

"It's all right. I'm alive. I've come back—"

"Get away," she spat, stumbling away from the golem of flesh and steel pretending to be Fulren. "You're a..." She ran from the tent.

He fought the urge to follow her, to grab her and hold her close and make her understand it was still him. Instead he didn't move, burdened with the realisation that she was right to run. He was not the Fulren she knew, but an altogether different creature.

"It's just the shock of seeing you," his mother said. "She will get used to it. We all will."

"No. She's right." He fished on the ground until he found his cloak, and draped it around his shoulder. "She was going to say I'm a monster."

His mother moved closer as he tied the drawstring of his cloak. She gripped his arms tight—the one of steel and one of flesh.

"You are not a monster. You are Fulren Hawkspur. My son."

"Maybe I'm both," he whispered back.

Gently she released him, and he picked up the stick to complete the disguise. An ordinary blind man once more.

"Fulren..."

"I'll wait outside camp. When you have need of me, I'll be waiting."

She moved to stop him as he made to leave. "But I've only just got you back. We have so much to—"

"And we'll still have time later, Mother. When all this is over."

He left her in the tent, taking a deep gulp of night air as he stepped outside. This time as he made his way back through the camp, hood drawn close around his face, he was relieved at the lack of attention. Just an ordinary refugee caught up in a war of someone else's making, rather than a demon creeping through the night.

Verlyn was sitting atop the wagon at the edge of the woods, and Fulren flung the stick into the back of the wagon before climbing up beside her.

"So how did that go?" Verlyn asked.

"Let's just move," he replied.

"Well, she must have at least been pleased to see you."

Fulren took the reins from her. "Some of me."

He snapped the reins, and they trundled into the woods.

# CONALL

He flung the coney as high as he could, watching as the eagle snatched it from the air and gulped it down whole. The beast had been ravenous, but Conall managed to set enough snares and catch enough game to see its belly filled, for now.

It was tethered in the middle of the wood to a pole skewered in the ground. They'd managed to fit an old harness to its beak that would at least give a rider some control, and as Conall stood watching the animal ruffling its feathers all he could do was resist the urge to jump on its back and fly as far away as it would take him.

Sted hadn't returned from their mission yet, and he'd turned his attentions to the eagle to try and take his mind off it. If she'd been captured there was little he could do about it. Sonnheld wasn't about to launch a rescue mission, and Conall couldn't very well go on his own.

Or could he? For any normal man it would have been suicide, but he knew there was power in the shadows, power that could help him accomplish anything if he had a mind to try.

Conall shook his head, dismissing the alien thought. Sonnheld had pitched his camp to the north of the terminal, hidden in a deep wood, and if she'd escaped she would make her way here eventually. Better that he wait. She was bound to come back sooner or later.

No way Sted would have let those Phoenix troopers get the better of her.

The war eagle cooed, most likely still hungry after so long starving atop that aerie. Conall reached out his hand to soothe the bird, but it shied away from him, snapping in fear as though it knew what he was. That only served to remind him it wasn't the only one.

Somewhere in the Viper Battalion camp was Donan. He'd avoided Conall since their return, but that was hardly surprising after what he'd witnessed. Maybe Conall should have gone to find him, tried to explain. But what would he say?

*Hey, Donan, I was cursed in the dread city of Arcturius, and I think I might be possessed by a demon. But don't worry about it, it's all under control.*

No, best let Donan deal with it in his own way and hope he kept what he'd seen to himself. He was a friend after all. Surely he'd understand when Conall had a chance to explain... whenever that might be.

Before he could beat himself up about it anymore, one of Sonnheld's adjutants appeared at the tree line. The officer beckoned for Conall to follow, and with a last glance at the skittish eagle, he made his way from the clearing and toward the main camp.

Sonnheld was waiting at the centre of the sparse clearing, surrounded by his surviving troopers. Bright sunlight illuminated the glade, highlighting the scarred armour and wounded flesh of the men and women of the battalion. Sonnheld himself was bruised about the eye, but he still looked imposing, standing there with his hands resting on those magnificent swords.

"Gather round," he said, sounding weary for the first time. "You've all done well. Despite what we've suffered over the months, every one of you has given a good account of yourselves. We've lost friends, brothers and sisters, but we are not done yet. We have to move further north. The Guilds are gathered at the Anvil, and we've bought them some time. Now we have to join with them. The siege of the capital will be our last chance to end this tyranny. One way or the other, the final day is within sight."

If Sonnheld had been expecting a rousing cheer, he was sorely disappointed. The gathered troopers nodded their assent, but there was little enthusiasm, and Conall could well understand why. The campaign in Castleteig had all but wiped them out, and Sonnheld had pushed them beyond endurance since then. Now he was asking for one last effort. To fight till the last trooper.

"Back to your duties," Sonnheld ordered. "We leave at first light."

As they sullenly went about their business, Conall realised they would be moving northward in the morning. He had run out of time. As he watched the rest of his campmates busying themselves, he began to wonder how he might delay the inevitable. The thought of returning to his mother filled him with incomparable dread, especially after what happened in the aerie, but there was nothing he could do about it now. He would just have to face reality... and his mother.

Before he could think of some way out, he caught sight of Donan among the troopers. Conall raised a hand, trying to attract his attention, but his friend avoided his gaze. He definitely saw him, but after what he had seen Conall do, conjuring that sword and killing those men, what else could he expect but the cold shoulder? Best leave him be...

Then again, if Donan were to tell someone, anyone, who knew what might happen? Conall could be accused of being some dark sorcerer, but surely no one would believe that. He was no arcanist, no demonist, and he certainly wasn't a danger to his friends. Conall could control this, there was no way he would let it get the better of him again. He'd make Donan understand that before long. First he had to solve the pressing matter of a journey back to his mother's side.

Conall made his way toward Sonnheld. The closer he got the more he could see how weary the marshal was, how frail, despite his imposing frame and the resplendent armour he wore.

"Marshal Sonnheld." Conall stood to his best attention. "I regret to inform you I cannot go with you to the Anvil. My lieutenant is still unaccounted for after the raid, and I need to find her."

Sonnheld nodded. "I understand your concern, Hawkspur. We've all lost good people, but I can't wait for you."

"And I can't leave her behind."

"She's most likely dead, you know. Or a prisoner on her way to the gods know where."

And he was right, but Conall couldn't just leave Sted to her fate without knowing for sure. She would have done the same for him.

"Either way, I have to at least try and find her."

Was that admiration behind Sonnheld's perpetually creased brow? "Very well. It's your call, Hawkspur. I just hope you know what you're—"

A commotion behind them. Conall turned, half expecting the Phoenix Battalion to come rushing from the surrounding trees, but instead a sorry-looking scout staggered out of the underbrush. In an instant half a dozen splintbows were levelled at her, but Moraide held up her hand.

"It's all right—she's one of ours."

And she was right. Sted was unarmed, spattered with dirt, clothes torn. She looked around at the troopers as though they were idiots. "All right, calm down. Never seen a scout come stumbling out of the woods before?"

Conall could have laughed with joy at seeing his friend, but he managed to hold it in. Now he was all out of excuses. There was no way to avoid that reunion with his mother he had gone to such pains to avoid.

Sonnheld clapped him on the shoulder. "Looks like you'll be coming with us after all, Hawkspur. You truly have a saint's luck."

If only he knew.

Conall nodded respectfully, before making his way toward Sted. Despite her bedraggled state, she still had a mischievous light in her eye.

"How did you find us?" Conall asked, shaking his head in bewilderment.

She shrugged, as though it were obvious. "I'm a scout, Captain. Sometimes I think you forget that."

"But how did you get away with half the Phoenix on your tail?"

"Any chance I can sit down for a minute, before I start telling tales of valour?"

She plonked herself down on a fallen tree trunk, and Conall called for food and drink. Sted ignored the dried meat, taking the waterskin she was offered and swallowing down a glug. Then screwed her face up.

"This is water."

Conall tried his best not to laugh. Even after all she'd been through, still desperate for a real drink. Sted took a breath before she began.

"So I ran out of the aerie and opened up a volley. Couldn't see shit so don't know if I hit anyone. Couldn't reload quick enough before they started firing back, so I started running."

She stopped, tearing a strip out of the jerky she was holding. Conall waited for the rest as she chewed.

"Is that it?" he said eventually.

Sted swallowed down the meat. "Of course not. They were coming after me, wouldn't let up. One of them had a carbine, I think, noisy fucking thing when it went off, anyways. Almost blew my damned head in half, but all in a day's work, I guess. So, I just ran. I assumed you'd be okay, since I saw that tower come down behind me. And if you weren't there wasn't much I could do about it."

Another bite, washed down with some more water. Conall thought back, to the sword, to Tarrien. Seeing the life literally drained from him.

"Yes," he replied. "We did fine."

"Nice one," said Sted without bothering to finish what was in her mouth. "How was Donan? Manage to keep his head in a crisis this time and not piss his pants?"

At the mention of Donan's name, Conall glanced around to see if he was anywhere close. There was still no sign of him.

"Yeah, he did well."

"I should find him. Give him a pat on the back, or some such. This must all be a big shock for him—getting in the mix with the rest of us. He's no soldier but—"

"Might be best to give him a day or two to deal with it."

*Or maybe just not talk to him at all.*

Sted shrugged at the suggestion. "So what's our next step?"

"Sonnheld has ordered the battalion north. We're joining up with the Guilds at the Anvil."

"Good. It's about time you let your mother know you're safe."

Conall felt the hairs stand up at the back of his neck. "Yeah. You might be right."

Moraide approached them before Sted could offer him any more unwanted assurances. She had a bottle in her hand and offered it to Conall.

"The marshal wanted me to give you this. Turned up in our stores, and he felt it appropriate you should have it."

Conall nodded his thanks and took it, before Moraide made her way back into the camp. He sat down beside Sted, gripping the bottle tight. Not too long ago he would have ripped the cork out and downed half the liquor like he was dying of thirst. Now all he could do was sit and stare at it.

"The fuck is wrong with you?" Sted said eventually. "That's the longest I've ever seen you sit with a full bottle in your hand."

He shook his head, trying to clear it of all the doubts and memories. The cork came free with a dull pop, and he raised the bottle. "To a well-executed plan." He took a long draft, feeling the warmth in his throat.

Sted wrenched the bottle from his grip. "To blind dumb luck." She took her own, much longer glug.

Instantly, Conall found himself smiling—those deep-rooted worries seeming to fade just a little. Maybe Sted was right—maybe he would be able to ride his luck. But as he stared out at the shadows of the forest, remembering what was lurking in the dark, he knew his luck would run out eventually.

Sted gasped after she took another long swig. "Damned rum. Only good for sailors and sailor fuckers."

"Give it back then." Conall held out his hand.

She raised the bottle to her lips again. "Wait your turn—any port in a storm, and all that."

"Don't remind me," he replied as she took another drink.

When she'd swallowed it down, she thought for a moment before grinning. "Oh yeah. You know, you'll have to tell me all about Argon Kyne one of these days."

He was about to suggest that would never happen, when a shadow fell across them. Donan barely acknowledged Sted, and instead stared at Conall with that empty look he'd had since they got back from their mission.

"Donan," said Sted, holding up the bottle. "Come and have a drink. You've earned it from what I hear."

Donan shook his head. "I won't. Thank you."

"Suit yourself." She took another swig.

Donan regarded Conall nervously. "I need to talk to you."

It was obvious why, and as much as Conall had been trying to grab Donan's attention so he might try to explain himself, he all of a sudden felt cornered.

"Look—we don't need to—"

"Now," Donan said, never sounding so insistent.

There was no getting away from it. "All right."

Conall stood, and Donan had already turned to lead them away from the main camp. He left Sted with the bottle and followed, a sinking feeling rising as though he were being led to the gallows.

When they were far enough from camp, Donan stopped and glanced around to make sure no one was within earshot.

"We don't have to do this," Conall said, keen to be the first to speak.

"Yes we do." A whispered hiss from Donan, like he was desperate. Afraid. "I saw... I don't know what I saw, but it wasn't anything natural. Not like webwainer magic. It was Maladoran. Something you brought back with you from beyond the Drift. So you have to tell me, what happened over in the Magna?"

"I've already told you—"

"I want the truth, Conall. What really happened?"

His voice was raised. They were far enough away from camp, but someone could have been nearby. "You have to drop this, Donan. There's nothing wrong, I promise. But you just—"

"You're lying. You haven't been the same since you got back. I put it down to you being captured, maybe tortured, to what you went through crossing the Drift, but this... this is sorcery. It's evil."

Conall took a step closer to him. "You have to keep your voice down."

"There's no avoiding this. You have to tell me what it is. Tell me what they did to you."

*He must be silenced.*

"No," Conall growled, as much at Donan as that insidious whisper.

"But maybe I can help," Donan replied.

"No," he repeated. "You can't help me. No one can. Look, I'm dealing with it. I promise I—"

"Dealing with what?" Donan was staring, fighting back his fear, desperate to help his friend. "What happened over there?"

*Kill him. Reach for me.*

Conall's teeth were grinding. Pain behind his eye, as he fought the insistent urge to...

"I can't..."

Donan grabbed his arms. "You can. Tell me—I promise I'll understand."

"I said no," Conall snarled.

They were so close, staring into one another's eyes. Everything went quiet around them, not a rustle of leaves or the tweet of a bird. Then Donan looked groggy, as though he'd suddenly succumbed to sleep.

Conall looked down, seeing the handle of the knife in his hand, its blade buried deep in Donan, just below his ribs. He hadn't even reached for that shadow sword. Hadn't even had to.

"Donan?"

His friend looked suddenly hurt, betrayed. He staggered and Conall grabbed him, lowering him as gently as he could. Donan tried to speak but all he managed was a single sigh, before his head lolled back.

"You two having a sloppy kiss out here?" Sted's voice, all too loud as she came tramping through the undergrowth, that rum bottle still in hand. Then she saw them and stopped, looking down at what Conall had done. "What the fu—"

Conall looked down at his friend's corpse, hand loosening on the blade, his fingers slick with red.

"I didn't... I didn't mean to."

Sted dropped the bottle. "What have you done?"

"Sted, it's not me."

*Reach out for me. Silence her. She will betray you, as they all will.*

He rose to his feet, taking a step toward her. "Listen to me—"

Sted staggered back, her face twisted in confusion. "What the fuck is wrong with you?"

*She will betray you. Kill her.*

Conall's hand was already reaching out, probing in the shadows. The sword teased the tip of his bloody fingers...

"Sted." He snarled it, desperate, furious. "Sted, run!"

"What the fuck are you talking about?" she answered, not running at all.

"Sted..."

The rage boiled, his hand closing around the sword's grip, feeling it become one with his flesh, with his soul. Teeth gnashed as he wrenched the blade from the shadow, swinging it in a killer arc. It stopped an inch from Sted's neck.

She stared at him, then at that blade so close to killing her, as it spewed black mist. The stench of dark sorcery hung like a thunderhead in the air.

Conall turned and ran.

He sprinted through the wood, his only thought of escape. Of running as far and fast as he could, and hoping no one came after. But how far would he get before they found him? Nowhere was far enough.

A clearing up ahead, and a sight he recognised. The eagle was still tethered, and he reached it just as the first shout of alarm echoed through the trees behind. They were coming.

The eagle let off a low squawk as his black blade hacked the first tether securing it to the ground. It shied, head bobbing fearfully. More shouts from behind and Conall knew his time was up. Another a swift strike and the beast was free. Before it could set to flight, he grasped the harness, flinging himself atop its back.

One solitary screech of alarm or freedom and those wings spread. The eagle lifted off the ground, Conall gripping tight, the stench of death and sorcery bitter in his nostrils. As they rose above the trees he could hear the shouts below all too loud. But it was too late. They would never stop him now.

# KEARA

It hadn't taken long for the banality of the journey to catch up with her, and it didn't help that her travelling companions were the dullest men alive. Lack of conversation aside, this whole thing was distracting her from her real goal, and the frustration of that was beginning to grate. It felt as though she'd been sent on this mission to get her out of the way rather than help the Guild cause. In fact, the longer the journey took, the more she became convinced that getting her out of the way had been Rosomon's plan all along.

So by the time the big knight, Ansell, told them they were nearly there, pulling up his horse and climbing from the saddle, it was all Keara could do to stop herself charging ahead to rescue that family all on her own.

Kassian dismounted, and Keara jumped down from her saddle, in no mood to be left behind. The three walked up to the brow of the hill and Ansell crouched, peering down into the valley below.

A river meandered along the bottom, with a derelict building perched on the shore. When she spied the worn statue of a dragon that marked it as a chapel, half reclaimed by the surrounding undergrowth, she felt her stomach churn with anticipation.

"Is this it?" she asked. Ansell nodded, and she squinted in the sunlight. "You sure? Looks like no one has been here for years."

Kassian grabbed the shoulder of her tunic and dragged her down into a crouching position. No sooner had he done so than the rotting door to the chapel swung open and a man appeared. He stretched his back in the afternoon light, then scratched his belly before walking around the side of the building to take a piss up the wall.

"This is the place," Kassian said.

Keara still wasn't too convinced. "Maybe he's just—"

Two more men appeared, and between them they led a child who strained to carry a bucket. The men laughed at the boy's struggle as they led him to the river that flowed by. The young lad emptied the bucket's contents and cleaned it out, before being roughly guided back to the chapel.

"All right," she replied. "I guess this is it. But they don't look like Revocaters. And they're certainly not Drakes."

"Mercenaries," said Kassian. "Doubtful they even know who they're holding."

"Then if they're hired hands, maybe they can be persuaded. Or bought? We could avoid any need for a fight altogether."

Kassian shook his head, his eyes still fixed on the chapel. "We can't risk giving away the element of surprise. We should wait until dark."

"We're just going to storm in there? When we have no idea what's waiting for us?"

"We don't have time to scout the place properly. But if you'd rather just walk right in and offer them a chance to surrender first, be my guest. Most likely they have orders to kill that family at the first sign of trouble."

"You don't know that. There's every chance they'd be open to—"

"Kassian is right," Ansell said in his gruff voice. "That's why Sanctan chose mercenaries for this and not my brothers. They would never harm an innocent family, not for any reason."

Keara wasn't too sure he was right about that. From what she'd seen, those Drakes were as emotionless as any piece of artifice. The ones who'd accompanied Hisolda had been more ruthless than any mercenary she'd ever met. Nevertheless, it looked like negotiation was off the table.

"So... do we have an actual plan of attack?"

Kassian nodded toward the chapel as though the answer was obvious. "I'll enter from the front. You take the back. With luck we can find the woman and her children before they even know we're there."

"That's it? We just walk right in? What kind of fucking plan is that?"

"It is what it is."

Keara shook her head in frustration. "We should have brought more swords."

"I will need a weapon," Ansell said suddenly.

"No you won't," Kassian replied, still staring at the chapel. "You'll be waiting here until we're done. I don't want you armed. You've brought us here, and now your part is finished."

Keara waited for the hulking Drake to argue his point, but he said nothing. Instead he and Kassian just crouched there, competing for who could be the sternest, most sullen bastard.

"So just the two of us?" she said. "Against a building full of mercenaries. Great odds. Just great."

Kassian glanced at her from the corner of his eye. "Would you rather we brought this fanatic along to watch our backs?"

She regarded Ansell, weighing up the danger against the gain. "Like you say—it is what it is."

"Yes, I do. Don't worry, Hallowhill. If you know how to use those knives, and they're not just for show, then we have the upper hand... as long as you hold your nerve."

Keara's hand absently strayed to her side, fingers brushing the hilt of one knife. The last time she'd used it had been to open up her friend's throat.

"You don't have to worry about me."

"Good. It'll be nightfall in less than an hour. Then we go."

"I'm counting the minutes already," she said with a sigh, as they began to move back from the ridge that looked down onto the valley.

They made their way to a spinney of trees upon the hill that gave them a view of the chapel while concealing them from below. The wait seemed to last much more than an hour, and all the while

Kassian sat peering toward that ruin. Ansell wasn't too far away, kneeling in prayer, or perhaps just meditating, it was impossible to tell which.

Just her luck to be stuck here with these two damned machines right before she got to throw herself into mortal danger. She could have done with someone to lift her spirits. Ulger had always been so good at that, but now there was just her. Try as she might, she couldn't stop her hands fidgeting. She hadn't thought about the red drop for so long, but right now she would have given her entire estate for just one dose.

As night fell, lights winked on within the chapel, but it was still deathly quiet. Then she was sure she heard a child's voice. Could have been a wail of anguish. Or pain maybe. Whatever it was, it provoked a strange sensation inside her. An unfamiliar pang of resentment she'd never felt before. Keara had done some sketchy shit in her time, but she was no monster. Even she would never have sunk so low as to abduct a family. She was no stranger to a bit of kidnap, but that had been Tyreta Hawkspur. All bets were off there. These were innocent children.

She shook her head, trying to clear it of those unfamiliar feelings. Now wasn't the time for sympathy. If things didn't go to plan, very soon she might have to kill someone, and that required focus.

Kassian rose to his feet. "Let's go."

She stood, feeling numb inside. As she followed the swordwright toward the slope, she offered Ansell a nod. He just watched her walk by, offering not a word of encouragement. What she would have done to have a Drake watch her back right now, but Kassian was in charge. Just the two of them would have to do.

They moved down the hillside in silence and she struggled to follow the old swordwright's silhouette in the dark. He crept along with all the stealth of a much younger man, barely making a sound as they picked their way through the scrub. When they were within a few yards of the chapel he raised a hand for her to stop.

She could see candlelight flickering through a boarded window. Hear someone's muffled laugh. As they waited, she realised there was no one on patrol outside. But then, they were in the middle of nowhere. These mercenaries would have no reason to think anyone was coming for them. Maybe this would work after all.

Kassian gestured for her to go around the rear of the building, and she acknowledged him with an upraised thumb as he began to move toward the front. She crept as quietly as she could, thankful for the sound of the river flowing by, hoping it was enough to conceal her approach.

All but holding her breath, she reached the wall of the chapel, hand brushing the brickwork to steady herself as she made her way around to the back. She ducked when she reached a window, hearing the muted clink of glass within, followed by the scraping of a chair.

"Two of cups?" someone said, clearly pissed off. "That's all you had? The two of frigging cups?"

"It's not what's in your hand," came the smug reply. "It's what you do with it, dickwipe."

"I'm gonna have no coin left by the time we're done with this shitty job."

Keara forced herself on, leaving the card players to their game, hoping they'd be distracted enough so she could enter unmolested. Maybe she'd find that family and be on her way before they even knew she was gone. Best not to count any chickens yet though.

She reached a door at the rear. Gingerly she tried the handle, wincing at the squeak as it turned. When she pushed, and it wouldn't budge, she stifled a curse.

Time was running out, and she fought down the panic. There was no sound from Kassian yet, but it wouldn't be long before he made his way through the front. But then what? He hadn't even offered any kind of plan other than sneak in and surprise them. Maybe they should have decided on something a little more subtle, but it was too late to worry about plans now.

Just as the panic began to well up, she spied a door to the cellar at the base of the chapel wall. In the scant moonlight she could see it was secured with a padlock. Time to see if the weaponsmith Sybilla was all bluster, or if her weapons were as good as she made out.

· Slowly Keara drew the blade with the yellow pyrestone and

knelt beside the door. She fuelled it with her power and the stone responded immediately, glowing bright yellow then white hot. She barely had to press the burning blade to the padlock before it sliced right through the metal. When the padlock fell open, Keara allowed herself a smile—the weaponsmith hadn't been lying after all.

Gritting her teeth, she swung the cellar door wide, relieved when the hinges didn't creak, and eased herself down the rickety stairs. The cellar stank of damp, the noise of dripping doing a good job to disguise her footfalls. Holding up the pyrestone dagger, she fuelled it again, allowing the stone to glow brighter and light her way.

She was surrounded by half-empty racks covered in rotting scrolls, but on the far side of the cellar was another staircase leading up. Keara could feel the excitement build as she pressed forward. Muffled voices from above told her Kassian was yet to make his entrance, and she moved as quickly as she could, hoping to have this done with before all the Lairs broke loose.

When she took her first step onto the stairs they screeched in annoyance. Keara froze, expecting someone to come running, but all she heard was more laughter. Wincing at the noise, she pressed on, one creaky step after the other, until the handle to another door was within reach. She turned it, half expecting this one to be locked too, but it turned with ease.

Keara breathed out as she pushed the door open and stepped into an unlit corridor. To her right was the room where all the noise and light was emanating from, ahead of her another staircase leading upward. And still no sign of bloody Kassian. No matter. She was inside now, and that family had to be up those stairs.

Hand still gripping her dagger, she crossed the corridor to the base of the stairs, wondering how in the Lairs she had managed to break in unseen, wondering if her luck really was changing. She impressed herself at how deft she was being. Perhaps this would be easier than she—

A thump and a crack as the front door was kicked in, rotted hinges snapping off the frame. Chairs scraped, someone gasped as another shouted, "What the fuck?"

Keara froze as she heard a ring of metal, followed by the grunting song of violence pealing from the other room. Kassian had made his entrance.

She should have run to help, but fuck that. He could handle himself. And besides, she was so close to rescuing that family now. The stairs were right in front of her, the way out behind. She could find them and be out of here before...

Movement in the shadows of the stairwell. Long legs making their way toward her. A woman appeared—the serious, dangerous kind of woman Keara tried to avoid at all costs, but there was no chance of that now.

They looked at one another for a moment as the sound of violence intensified. Then the woman drew the rapier at her side. Keara could have tried to explain, to reason, to bargain, but from the look on that woman's face it would have been pointless.

She drew the other knife at her hip, as the woman darted forward, leaping down the last few steps, rapier flashing. Keara dodged, tapping the web on instinct, fuelling her daggers with sparking light and burning flame, but the woman's blade was equal to both.

Four feet of narrow steel clashed against her daggers, meeting each in turn, as the woman parried Keara's attack. Her speed was dazzling, and it didn't take Keara long to realise she was outmatched. Ducking a swipe of the blade, she rushed past, up the stairs, hoping that maybe that would give her an advantage, but it was all she could do to back away, almost stumbling on the steps as she retreated up to the first floor.

At the top of the stairs was a wide-open chamber, taking up the entire top level of the chapel. Two doors were set along one side of the wall—must have been where Olstrum's family was kept, but there was no time to consider that as the mercenary came at her relentlessly.

She smiled, as though she was enjoying this, but she wouldn't be smiling for long. Keara gritted her teeth, tapping the web like never before, feeling the tingle in her hands as those new-forged blades began to spark and burn...

Before she could strike, something loomed out of the dark. Suddenly she forgot the web, forgot her knives, as an axe swung at her face. All she could do was duck, staggering away as a burly thug came at her from the shadows.

Again she reacted on instinct, grunting as she lashed out with the burning knife, managing to slash at his side. He grunted, lurching back and almost dropping his axe. His tunic was on fire and he slapped at it, growling all the while as he retreated across the chamber like a wounded beast.

No time to gloat, as the woman came at her again, that rapier slashing the air in furious, measured strokes.

"Kassian!" Keara yelled desperately, but from the sounds of violence below he was a little busy himself.

A swift slash at Keara's face, just a feint before the woman extended, thrusting that rapier right into Keara's thigh. She screamed, countering with a slash of her sparking blade, but the woman was quicker, parrying deftly and knocking it from Keara's grip.

One dagger against the reach of a rapier. It hardly seemed fair, and for a moment she thought maybe she should have tried the negotiation thing earlier, but too late now.

The swordswoman pressed in, sensing her advantage. Keara did her best to parry that blade but it was no good—only a matter of time before…

She stumbled into a stack of barrels, knocking them over as she went clattering to the floor. They spilled their contents on the ground, and before she could think to rise, she was soaked with whatever they'd been holding.

Kassian was still battling below, and swords clanged with abandon, but up here the fight was over. That woman loomed over her, grin all wide and white. From the ammonia stink that suddenly filled the air, those barrels had been full of piss. Now Keara was lying in a puddle of it on the floor.

The big man had put the fire out now and he stepped forward, brow furrowed, moustache waxed and shiny in the torchlight. He and the swordswoman glanced at one another, smug in their victory, before they focused back on Keara.

"Look at you," she said. "All covered in piss. Is this how you thought you'd die?"

She was relishing it. Savouring the moment before the end. As much as Keara wanted to tell her where to go, there was no time. No smart-mouth retorts were getting her out of this, but her pyrestone knife lying on the ground offered a little glimmer of hope.

The woman stepped forward, rapier drawn back to strike. Keara lurched to her feet, reaching up to grasp the rafter above her head. At the same time she fuelled all her power through the web and into that knife, igniting its blue pyrestone with all her desperation. Her feet were barely off the ground before the light from the knife sparked, blooming, bursting to life. Sparking tendrils danced across the piss-sodden ground right at the woman's feet, before she was caught within a blinding maelstrom. A scream as her body was gripped by a sudden rictus. The stink of burning hair and flesh.

Keara cut her connection, the sparking light instantly extinguished as she let go of the rafter, feet splashing in hot piss before she leapt forward, ramming her one remaining dagger right into the woman's chest. She wasn't smiling now, face all surprised as she staggered, coughed, then collapsed to the ground, taking Keara's weapon with her.

The elation of victory was short-lived. The man yelled—furious, bereft. He was on her before she could even think to defend herself, grasping her tunic and punching her in the side of the head. She reeled, staggered, and when she opened her eyes again she was on the ground. Her head pounded along to the sound of swords ringing from below. Kassian was nowhere in sight. There was no one to help her.

She looked up at that man towering over her, eyes ablaze with hate. He glanced to the corpse of the woman, a flash of sorrow, or grief, crossing his heavy brow. She meant something to him. Keara realised there was no talking her way out of this, no more tricks to rely on as he turned back to her and raised his axe high.

A hand from the dark snatched the haft of the weapon. The man grunted as his death blow was halted, and he barely had time to turn and face this new foe before he was butted in the nose.

Keara tried to rise, tried to shuffle away as the two brutes struggled, but her energy had been sapped. She watched helplessly as the hulking form of Ansell engaged in a wrestling match with the other brute before she slumped back to the ground.

Ansell wrenched the axe from the mercenary's hand and elbowed him in the face, sending him staggering back. Keara wanted to scream for him to use the weapon, to hack the bastard apart, but instead he cast it aside and punched the mercenary with a stone-hard blow.

The man fell, and Ansell was on him. Another smash of his fist and the mercenary's head clattered against the floor. Ansell was at him, blow after solid blow, pounding that skull to jelly. Keara thought he might stop as the man went still, but he carried on, his face emotionless, arms pumping as his knuckles hammered at meat and bone.

She dragged herself up, unable to take her eyes off the brutality. Just when she thought he might relent, he struck again, until that face was nothing but a red-spattered mask.

"I think he's dead," she said, voice weak.

Ansell stopped, breathing heavily from his efforts. All was quiet now, even the violence below had ceased. Her hands were shaking, and she suddenly missed all the noise. Ansell rose to his feet, looking to where he'd thrown the axe. For a moment she thought he might go for it, might cut her down and run off into the night.

The creak of a floorboard and Kassian stepped into the torchlight, face covered in blood, sword slick and red.

"Don't think about it, Drake. You won't even get close."

Keara raised her hand. "Don't. He just saved my life. If he hadn't come..." She didn't even want to think about that.

Ansell turned his attention away from the axe, ignoring Kassian's threats. He walked to the first of the doors, pulling back the bolt and opening it up. Inside, cowering against the wall, were two children. A boy and a girl clinging to one another in fear, locked in that cell for who knew how long.

Ansell knelt, reaching out one massive hand and beckoning them forward. Slowly, the girl released her grip on the boy, taking a tentative step toward the door. Then the boy ran past her and straight into Ansell's embrace. The girl was quick to follow, and Ansell held them both for moment before gently picking them up. This warrior, this brute, who seconds ago had smashed a man's skull to pulp, holding two children in his arms as though he would protect them with his life.

Keara limped to the second door, suddenly aware of the ache in her thigh and the blood running in a river down her leg. She unbolted the door, opening it to be greeted by the desperate face of a woman.

"It's all right," Keara said, beckoning her forward into the light. "Olstrum sent us."

Her fearful expression took on a desperate note as she looked around the chamber. Seeing Ansell with her children she rushed forward, thanking him again and again as he carefully handed them to her.

Exhausted as she was, Keara found it difficult to sympathise with such a tender moment. Instead, she reached down and plucked her daggers from the ground, sliding them into the sheaths at her hips. Considering Kassian's plan had been practically no plan at all, it had worked without a hitch. Well... almost.

She dabbed at the blood running down her thigh, gritting her teeth at the increasing pain. "I don't suppose either of you thought to bring a needle and thread, because I'm kind of bleeding here."

# TYRETA

They were going to roll right into the city gaol, pick up those prisoners, and roll right out again. Just like that. It was a pretty shit plan all told, but when the alternative was to sit on her hands and wait, then a shit plan was better than no plan at all.

They trundled along in the back of the wagon, no words, just tension hanging in the air. For the tenth time she tried to get comfortable in the jacket of her stolen uniform, but no amount of tugging on sleeves and adjusting collars would ever make it fit properly. She just had to hope it would be enough to fool the gaolers. The fact that they were approaching the gaol at night might help at least, but she doubted those gaolers were blind. Luck would have to be on their side if they were even to make it past the main gates.

She glanced across at the others. At least she knew their names now, which was something to be thankful for. It didn't mean she could trust them, but they were all she had, and just like with her stolen uniform she would have to make do.

Torfin, the big riverboatman, sat opposite her. Beside him was Lena, the woman, who was almost as big as he was. Driving the wagon was handsome Colbert, the one who'd met her at Olstrum's safe house. And with him was Maronne, the weaver, who'd had so much to say for herself when Tyreta had first been introduced to this unlikely bunch of rebels.

They were all in disguise, apart from Wachelm, who sat in the back of the wagon wearing his yellow actuary robes. He looked nervous enough for all of them. Too nervous. They'd be conspicuous enough turning up to the gaol in the dead of night, but the last thing they needed was him giving them away.

"Just stick to the plan and we'll be fine," Tyreta reassured him.

He nodded. "Sure. I mean... it was my plan after all."

"And it's a solid one."

"Is it?" he said, eyes looking big and scared behind those eyeglasses of his.

She tried on a smile, hoping it would fool him. "I'll be with you every step, Wachelm. Don't worry."

It seemed to do the trick as he relaxed into his seat a little. At least one of them was reassured. Tyreta just wished she had someone she could trust watching her back and not a bunch of strangers. As the wagon trundled to a stop, she realised it was too late to worry about that now.

She pulled back the latch, opening the rear door of the wagon, and led Wachelm out into the night. Pyrestone light illuminated the gate to the courtyard, and beyond it she could just make out the foreboding gaol looming ahead.

Wachelm wasted no time, approaching the guards at the gate, their black and grey uniforms making them almost blend into the murk. They stood to attention as Wachelm advanced, clutching the forged papers in his hand.

"We're here to transfer a consignment of prisoners," he said all too quickly, thrusting his documents toward the guards.

One of them stepped forward, looking dubiously at the papers in Wachelm's tightly clenched fist. "We weren't told anything about a prisoner transfer."

Tyreta felt the tension increase. Here they were at the first hurdle, about to trip and land flat on their faces, but Wachelm suddenly seemed to grow in stature, raising his chin defiantly.

"Of course you weren't. This needs to be done discreetly."

The guard took the papers and began to read, squinting in the wan light of those lamps. As he mouthed the words silently, the other one looked Tyreta up and down. She was suddenly conscious of the markings on her face and wondered if her eyes might give them away. Maybe she shouldn't have come, she was standing out like a sore thumb.

"All right," the guard said, when he'd read enough of the docket. "Open up."

The other guard raised his hand. From beyond the high gate came the sound of a metal bar sliding on its runner, and with a squeak of hinges it opened. Tyreta nodded up at Colbert, who flicked the reins of the two horses and they pulled the cart through the open gateway.

She and Wachelm followed the cart into a spacious courtyard. More pyrestone lamps hummed on the walls, and Tyreta felt a strange relief that at least not all the city's artifice had been smashed to nothing. The light revealed more of that grim gaol—a stark grey edifice, dreadful and silent. She had never even known this place existed, but then why would she? It was hardly somewhere her mother would bring her on a sightseeing tour.

A portly man appeared from within the building and shuffled toward them as he tucked his shirt into his waistband. It looked as though he'd been stirred from his slumber, and was none too pleased about it. Most likely he was the duty sergeant. With any luck he'd be as lacking in vigilance as his guards.

"What's going on?" he demanded, smoothing his unruly hair with a chubby hand.

The gate guard handed him the forged papers Wachelm had provided. The sergeant looked them over, then Wachelm, then the papers again.

"This is signed by Lord Rearden himself."

"It is," Wachelm replied, looking more officious than Tyreta had ever seen him. Which was impressive considering how nervous he'd been on the way here.

The sergeant looked incredulous. "I wasn't informed ahead of time. Where are these prisoners bound for?"

The slightest raising of Wachelm's chin. "That's none of your concern."

A narrowing of eyes from the sergeant. "They are *my* prisoners."

Wachelm stepped forward, jabbing a finger at the docket. "As you can see quite clearly in black and white—they are *my* prisoners now."

Tyreta had to quell the urge to pat Wachelm on the back for his performance as the sergeant waggled the docket in front of Wachelm's nose. "These are dangerous men. I will have to double-check—"

"I am on a schedule. We have connections to make. Should I inform the Guildmaster that we are to be delayed? Or perhaps I should wake him, and have him come here to confirm his orders?"

Tyreta could see the sergeant was torn about what to do and she tensed, readying herself for all this to go wrong. Then his shoulders sagged.

"No need to disturb Lord Rearden at this hour, I suppose. Your documentation all appears to be in order."

Lena and Torfin had already climbed down from the back of the wagon, and the four of them followed the duty sergeant, who led them toward the imposing prison. Tyreta allowed herself a glance back as they fell within the shadow of the building, seeing Colbert and Maronne still sitting atop the wagon. Colbert offered the slightest nod of encouragement, before Tyreta crossed the threshold into the gaol.

The silence was oppressive, heavy like an iron weight. Their footfalls echoed along the corridors of steel and stone, clanking as they marched below the ground level and into the dungeons beneath. They passed row upon row of solid oak doors banded in iron, and the only sound was the jangle of the duty sergeant's keys as they dangled from his fist.

The deeper they went the more the stink of decay intensified. Tyreta could only imagine what it must have been like to be incarcerated in a place like this. The dark and isolation were bad enough to endure, but the smell grew more rank with every step.

Once they'd descended to what must have been the lowest level of the dungeons, more guards became visible through the shadows.

The sergeant reached a door more heavily reinforced than any of the others and began to rifle through the bunch of keys. As her eyes adjusted to the gloom, Tyreta could see more doors lining the walls of the endless corridor.

After fishing out the relevant key, the sergeant held it up for one of his guards. "Open them. And be quick about it."

The guard looked confused. "All of them?"

"That's the order," the duty sergeant replied.

"But... they haven't been let out of their cells since—"

Wachelm noisily cleared his throat. "Might I remind you, I am still on a schedule?"

"Yes, yes," the sergeant replied, waving a hand at the guard. "Let's get this underway."

The guard looked unconvinced, but took the key anyway and approached the first door. He fumbled the key into the lock and twisted it before turning the stiff handle and hefting the door open. After taking a step back and placing a hand to the sword at his side, he said, "Out."

A hulking figure made its slow way from the cell, squinting in the torchlight. The prisoner's shoulders were hugely muscled, head a bearded slab. Tyreta had seen these warriors before, bedecked in their armour of artifice and steel, but even without it, and after months of imprisonment, they were still a formidable sight.

The shirt he wore hung off him in rags, and a rank smell assaulted them all as he stepped out. The more she watched, the more saddened Tyreta became. As the guard opened the rest of the reinforced doors, that sadness turned to anger. More doors, more dishevelled Titanguard, until nine of them waited in the corridor.

"Is that all of them?" asked the duty sergeant.

The guard nodded, before Wachelm raised his hand. "Right then, this way."

Torfin led them back up through the corridors. Tyreta stood and watched as the nine prisoners filed past her, eyes blank, following without question as though all the dignity and defiance had been beaten from them. Only the last one offered her a second glance. His dark eyes regarded her with recognition, and she held her breath a moment at the prospect of him giving her away. Instead, he averted his gaze and followed the rest out from the oppressive confines of the dungeon.

She was the last to follow, feeling the breath of the duty sergeant on the back of her neck as they made their way into the relative fresh air of the courtyard. Lena was loading the last of the prisoners into the back of the wagon, with Colbert and Maronne looking anxious atop the drivers' seats, eager to be away.

As Torfin and Lena climbed into the wagon after the prisoners, Wachelm turned to the duty sergeant. "My thanks. I will be sure to pass along how cooperative you were to Lord Rearden, and—"

"What is going on here?"

The voice boomed through the starkness of the courtyard. Everyone turned to see a slender figure marching through the open gate. As he strode into the pyrestone light, Tyreta could see he was well-dressed, but dishevelled, his shirt hanging out to the side, tunic unbuttoned to the nipple.

"Governor," the duty sergeant said, suddenly flustered. "I was just about to finish administering the transportation of these prisoners."

"I was informed of no such transfer," the governor replied, looking the wagon up and down with suspicion.

Tyreta felt their carefully laid plan begin to tumble around her ears, but Wachelm quickly snatched the docket from the sergeant's hand, thrusting it toward the governor.

"I can assure you, all is in order," he said, sounding more confident than ever. "Rearden Corwen authorised the transfer himself."

The governor took the docket between finger and thumb before unfurling it. He held it up to one of the buzzing lamps as he read. It seemed to take him an age.

"Yes," he said eventually. "This does indeed appear to be in order, as you say." Tyreta did her best to avoid sighing in relief. "However, I have just had a very long and very informative dinner with the Guildmaster..." He looked directly at Wachelm, eyes narrowing. "...and Rearden mentioned none of this to me."

Tyreta didn't wait for the governor to scream an order to his guards. The whole thing was fucked, and there was nothing left to do but run for it.

She slammed the rear doors to the wagon, sliding the bolt shut before banging on the back with her palm. "Go!"

Colbert needed no further encouragement, whipping the reins and yelling from the bottom of his lungs. As the horses bolted and the wagon lurched, the guards surrounding them were already drawing their swords. Only Wachelm and Tyreta remained, surrounded by a bunch of angry-looking gaolers.

"I can explain everything," Wachelm said, holding up his hands.

The wagon was trundling its way through the open gate and away into the night as the governor stepped forward, lips curled back in fury.

"You can explain it to Rearden."

Wachelm chewed over the words for a second, before his eyes narrowed behind those thick eyeglasses. "Fuck that!"

He balled a fist before smashing it into the governor's face. The man went down, as shouts of alarm echoed around them, and not for the first time tonight Tyreta found herself dazzled by Wachelm's mettle.

"Seize them!" barked the duty sergeant, stepping back from any threat of violence.

As the guards closed in, Wachelm regarded her with a mournful expression. "I'm sorry."

"Don't apologise," she replied, already clenching her fists, already tapping the web, already feeling that familiar sense of overwhelming power. "Just close your eyes and get ready to run."

The buzz of the pyrestone lamps intensified, their light becoming blinding. The guards were forced to shield their eyes as the noise rose to a whine, then a high-pitched wail before the first of them burst into shards. One after the other they exploded, showering the guards in glass and plunging the courtyard into darkness.

Tyreta grabbed hold of Wachelm's robe, dragging him toward the open gate. As the guards lurched around blindly, her eyes adjusted in an instant and she easily avoided them as they swung their swords wildly. Wachelm stumbled along as she dragged him through the gate and out onto the street. Behind them the angry shouts of the prison guards echoed.

They ran into the welcome dark, Wachelm struggling to stay on his feet as she all but dragged him along the cobbles. Tyreta allowed herself a glance back, but there was no one coming after them. The guards at the gate were too stunned or too slow to offer any kind of pursuit.

When they'd put enough distance between themselves and prison, she allowed Wachelm to stop running. He leaned against a wall, wheezing in air, looking like he might retch at any moment.

"Are you all right?" she asked, seeing him tremble on unsteady legs.

"I... will be... when I can breathe again."

She patted him on the back. "You did great back there. And that punch—who knew you had that in you."

He managed to look up at her, his eyeglasses misted over. "Not me."

She looked down the street. Still no signs of anyone chasing them, but news of what had happened would soon spread. "We have to keep moving."

Wachelm nodded his agreement. "Follow me."

He led her on through the streets, and Tyreta found herself more and more impressed with the way he quickly recovered. Wachelm was an actuary, used to a life of ledgers and scrolls, but here he was adapting to life as a rebel like he was born to it.

Eventually, he delved along a side street into almost pitch darkness, before leading them down to a cellar. Quietly he rapped on the door with his bony knuckles, and they waited in silence until the door opened a crack. Once whoever was inside recognised them, the door was thrust wide, and Wachelm led her in.

Torfin, Lena, Colbert and Maronne were already waiting, still in their dull grey uniforms. No sooner had they entered than Lena rose from her chair and patted Wachelm on the shoulder with her meaty hand.

"You made it," she said, beaming, offering him the tankard she'd been holding.

"I wouldn't have, not without Tyreta," he replied, taking the tankard and swigging down whatever was in it.

"Where are the Titanguard?" Tyreta asked.

Lena gestured to a dimly lit passageway that led further into the underground complex. Tyreta wasted no time, eager to greet the men they'd taken such pains to rescue.

At the end of the passage was a small room, made to look even smaller by the hulking men who waited within it. They'd already been given food and drink, and were gobbling down the last of the bread and meat as though they hadn't eaten in a year.

She regarded the men she had freed, wondering what to say. None of them even acknowledged her, but then she supposed they had more important things to do right now, like fill their empty bellies.

"Is anybody hurt?" she asked.

One of them looked up at her, and she saw it was the one who'd offered her a lingering glance at the gaol. He shook his head in answer to her question.

"I am—"

"Tyreta Hawkspur," the Titanguard finished. "We know who you are. Though you look a little different to the last time we saw you."

For a moment she considered explaining what had happened, before realising these men probably didn't care. "My mother has an army massed to the east of the city. Their attack is imminent, but they'll need help from the inside if we're to guarantee victory. I know you've all been through a lot, but I'm hoping you'll be able to help."

Slowly the Titanguard rose to his feet. Within the prison she had thought these men big, but hadn't appreciated just how towering they truly were. He glared down, still looking stern and grim despite being locked away in a pit for months.

"Point us at the Archlegate, Hawkspur, and we will tear down everything in our path to slay him."

She suppressed a smile of relief. "I was kind of hoping you'd say that."

He bowed his head. "I am Cullum Kairns."

"It's good to—"

A door opened at the far end of the chamber, putting the

Titanguard immediately on edge. Olstrum walked in, as though he were hosting a cocktail party for the great and good of Torwyn.

"Ah," he said, gesturing at his new guests. "I see your plan worked."

One of the other Titanguard surged to his feet and stepped toward Olstrum. "Traitorous dog. I should kill you now."

"Wait," Tyreta replied, trying to get between them before the man throttled Olstrum where he stood. "He's on our side."

"Lies," the Titanguard spat. "He dies now."

"Peace, Dagamir," Cullum said, grasping the man's thick arm and holding him back, as Olstrum cowered. "At least give him a chance to explain first."

"Hawkspur speaks the truth," Olstrum said quickly. "I am only here to help. And I'm the reason you're all free. Believe me, we will need one another if we're to bring down Sanctan."

The Titanguard stared at the diminutive figure of Olstrum. The man who had betrayed their emperor and been instrumental in his death. Tyreta could well understand what they must be feeling.

Cullum turned to her. "Do you trust him, Hawkspur?"

How quickly things changed. Now she realised she held Olstrum's life in her palm.

"I believe he will help us," she replied. "And he's the only chance we have."

Cullum looked back to Olstrum, his stern glare softening slightly. "All right then. You will have the Titanguard. But it will serve you better if it has its armour back."

"Already taken care of," Olstrum replied. "And as soon as I receive word from Lady Rosomon, you shall have everything you need to take your vengeance on the Ministry. In the meantime, I suggest you get some rest and eat your fill."

With that, he offered Tyreta a nod and took his leave. She watched him go, sure she recognised something new in that narrow gaze of his. Gratitude perhaps? Respect? Whatever it was, he could keep it. If Olstrum wanted to show his appreciation, he would take her right to Sanctan, and let her loose.

# ANSELL

They returned to the camp at dawn. Kassian led his horse by the reins, Olstrum's wife sitting atop it. Behind him, her two children shared the saddle of Ansell's steed. Finally came Keara, who had not seen fit to forego her saddle for anyone, but she could be forgiven for her selfishness since the wound in her leg had left her with a slight limp.

The sentries on duty had clearly anticipated their return, allowing them through unmolested. Someone ran ahead to notify the Guildmasters, and by the time their little procession reached the centre of the encampment, Rosomon Hawkspur and the other leaders of the Guilds were already waiting.

"My lady," Kassian said, helping Olstrum's wife down from the saddle. "This is Ulia Garner."

Rosomon stepped forward, taking the woman's hands in a warm greeting. "It is a pleasure. Please, you and your children should rest in my quarters. There is much we need to speak of."

Ansell had already lifted the two children gently to the ground and they rushed to their mother's skirts. Rosomon's bodyguard guided the family away, as she stepped toward Ansell.

"I see you held to your oath," she said.

"I did." He looked out across the camp, toward the Anvil. Toward where Grace was waiting for him. "And now I would only ask that you let me go."

Little emotion in her eyes as she considered the words. "That wasn't part of the deal. When this is all finished, then we may speak of your fate."

"No. I have to leave. Now." As much as he tried to keep the anger and desperation from his voice, he was sure he failed.

Rosomon was unmoved, even taking a step closer to him, which disconcerted her guardians. "You think I don't remember you? Think I don't know you were the one who almost killed my son? Who murdered my brother? Be thankful your reward isn't a gallows tree."

Ansell could see hands slowly moving to weapons in his periphery. The only one who didn't move was Kassian, but he could draw his blade in the blink of an eye. If Ansell tried to escape now there was no way he would survive.

"He helped us," Keara said suddenly, doing little to defuse the tension. "He saved my life. Kassian will tell you."

Again, Rosomon chewed over the words with little emotion. "And for that, I am sure you're grateful. Take him back to his cage."

There was no point trying to resist as the Armiger troopers surrounded him, wrangling him across the camp to where the cages still stood. Lugard was waiting, kneeling in prayer, as Ansell was shoved into his prison.

For most of the day his brother remained on his knees, eyes closed. Ansell was given food and water as afternoon wore on to evening, and it wasn't until he had finished his prayers that Lugard even noticed he was back.

"Did you find what you were looking for?" Lugard asked, taking up his bowl of congealed gruel that had lain untouched for hours.

"I did as I promised."

Lugard shrugged those broad shoulders. "And the Archlegate will damn you for it."

There was a time when the prospect of that ignominy might have worried Ansell. When he might have feared it. Not so now.

"Sanctan damned me the first day he ordered that I do his bidding. And I damned myself by obeying him."

Lugard swallowed down a lump of porridge. "Perhaps not."

Ansell moved a little closer. He would have expected Lugard to be the least compromising where such matters were concerned. His brother had always been such a slavish adherent of the Draconate.

"What do you mean?"

Lugard laid down his bowl. "I surrendered. I threw down my arms and allowed myself to be imprisoned because deep in my heart I knew I was serving a man unworthy of his position. You were not the only one to be seduced by his lying tongue."

"It was not just his tongue I should have been wary of," Ansell spat, the shame of his stupidity turning to sudden anger. "I witnessed his deeds and did nothing to stop him. I was party to them. Complicit in his sins."

A look of sympathy crossed Lugard's stern features. "Because you are a man of duty, Beckenrike. As are we all. That is why we were so easy to fool. We made the mistake of believing the tenets we follow are embodied within one man. And that man could never be questioned. It was the dedication to our oaths that made us vulnerable to his iniquities."

Ansell shook his head, refusing to be absolved so readily. "I should have seen it. Made a different choice. I should have stopped him when I had the chance."

"We all should. Do not take all this on your own shoulders. I bear some of that burden too, as do the rest of our brothers."

"I am knight commander, Lugard. If not my shoulders, then whose? I was the closest to him from the beginning. I bear the greatest guilt, and I must atone for the lion's share of his sins. But how, now that I am trapped in here?"

The cage that surrounded him looked a more formidable prison than ever. It was all Ansell could do not to give in to despair.

"We yet live, Ansell," Lugard said, gripping the bars in his granite fists. "And while we do, there is still a chance for us to atone for our misdeeds."

"Not from within this cage."

"No, you are right on that. But perhaps there is still time. The Hawkspur woman cannot keep us imprisoned forever. Our future depends on what her intentions are. Do you think she will kill us?"

"The Hawkspur woman? Doubtful. I think she just wants a return to the way things were. She has been wronged, and it has unleashed the warrior within her. But that is not her nature. I do not think her so wicked as to seek our execution."

"Tell that to the Ursus," Lugard replied, with a wry edge to his voice.

Ansell had heard the story. How Rosomon Hawkspur had wreaked her vengeance at Oakhelm. But was that not simply righteous justice? Would Undometh not have approved?

"If she wanted us dead, I am sure she would have ordered it by now. Not let us linger here in this cage."

"I think you are perhaps a little naive, Ansell. We live as long as we are useful. And I doubt very much she will be the only one who has a say in our fate. Her fellow Guildmasters may well want blood when all this is over."

"Then best we do not consider the worst of all outcomes."

"Agreed," said Lugard, sounding more determined than ever, despite being trapped. "I would still make my own fate. Perhaps I was too rash to give over my sword. It might have been better if I'd fought and died at the hand of Maugar Ironfall. That would have been a worthy end."

Ansell remembered his own battle with the swordwright. Remembered how supreme an opponent Maugar had been. Lugard was right—to die at the hand of such a warrior would have been a noble end indeed.

"It serves us ill to dwell on what could have been."

Lugard shrugged. "Maybe. Maybe not. Have you not already admitted how differently you would have acted were you given your time again?"

Indeed he would. For a start he would never have left Grace behind, not that Lugard needed to know it. "You are right, but still, dwelling on the past is folly. All I know now is that I must return to the Anvil the first chance I get."

"For what? Duty? You seek to right those wrongs you think you committed? To kill Sanctan? Because that will be a dark and difficult road."

"Yes, for duty. But perhaps not in the way you think. I must right a mistake, a poor decision I made, and it does not require the death of the Archlegate."

"But it will help you atone?"

Ansell wasn't sure it would, but neither did he care. He would have told Lugard that much, but before he could answer someone approached their cages through the dark. Keara glanced to left and right as she moved closer, still limping awkwardly on her wounded leg, and clearly none too keen to be seen here.

"You boys comfortable?" she asked.

Lugard didn't bother to hide his look of disdain, as he stepped back into the shadow of his cage. Ansell leaned closer, curious to know why she had come.

"About as comfortable as we look."

She regarded the bars, the bare ground on which they slept, and for a moment Ansell was sure he saw sorrow in her eyes. "You don't deserve this."

Keara was making all the right noises, but he knew she could not be trusted. "How would you know what I deserve?"

She stepped closer, placing her hand close to his own where it rested on the bars. An act of intimacy perhaps. One that Ansell found strangely disquieting.

"I know you're a good person at heart. I know you saved my life. Saved that woman and her children."

"I was bound by an oath."

"Yeah sure. Me too, but I still see you, Ansell. I see past all this...." She gestured at him as though pointing out he was more than a statue without feeling or weakness.

"And tell me—did you see past Sanctan?"

His quip had its intended effect, and her false confidence waned for a second. Suddenly she looked serious, moving close enough to whisper.

"No, I didn't. But I see him now. I see everything clearly. Maybe that's why I've come."

"What do you mean?"

"I mean one way or the other we're both fucked." Her casual

profanity might have moved Ansell before all this began, but he had grown used to her outbursts in recent days. "If Sanctan wins there's no place for either of us in the future he will build. If the Guilds win, we still lose. But maybe there's a third option."

Ansell couldn't begin to pretend he knew what she was talking about. This all seemed like riddles within riddles, but then he had never been the most artful.

"Speak plainly, Keara. What do you want?"

"I'll tell you what I don't want. To go back to the way things were. The way things were for my Guild. If we win this, the Hawkspurs and Ironfalls and Marrlocks will just use the Hallowhills like they've always been used. I want better than that. I want more."

"And I can help you with that?" It seemed unlikely from within his cage.

"You both can." She nodded toward Lugard, still watching from within the shadows. "With the Drakes and the webwainers united we could rise up against whoever wins this. Sanctan is finished. You don't trust him any more than I do. But an alliance between the Hallowhills and a Ministry with the Drakes in charge... think about what we could build. A new order. The Great Wyrms and the power of artifice, united as one."

Ansell could barely parse the thought. Such a union seemed alien to him. Artifice was anathema to the Draconate, like oil and water.

"The Ministry will never stand with the sorcerers of the Hallowhills. It goes against everything we—"

"I'm offering you a way to win here," she hissed, frustration getting the better of her.

Now it was Ansell's turn to lean in closer. "You are offering us damnation."

Keara slapped her palm against the bars. "Are you such a damned fanatic that you'll let this opportunity just sail on by? I could give you more power than the Guilds ever will."

"You think power is all we covet?"

"I don't give a shit what you covet. This is about not being put in chains by the Hawkspur bitch after she burns down the Anvil."

"I thought she was your ally."

His simple statement cooled her ire slightly, and her hand moved toward the three scars that marred the flesh of her cheek before she lowered it again. "She is... for now. But as soon as she gets what she wants who knows what's next. For me *and* you."

"She is right," Lugard said from the dark. "We are relying on the goodwill of our captors. We have to trust they will show mercy, and as we have already discussed, brother, it was trust that led us to this. A cage."

Lugard was right. His blind faith had brought him here. It was time to walk his own path. Something he had almost done weeks earlier. A plan he still regretted abandoning.

"So you would free us?" he asked her.

Keara nodded. "Right now. I owe you that much at least for saving my arse back at that chapel. Once you're out, lay low, then gather the rest of your Drakes. When the Anvil has fallen, I'll meet you with my wainers and we'll take down whoever remains. We could rule together. The Draconate will still have the people's faith. The Hallowhills will see that artifice keeps them fed. It's the best outcome for everyone."

It seemed so simple a plan, but Ansell knew better than anyone how plans were subject to change. Nevertheless, what choice did he have?

"Very well."

Keara's mouth creased into a smile. "Now you're talking."

She drew one of her knives, imbuing it with her webwainer's sorcery. The yellow pyrestone glowed for a moment, the steel of the blade turning white before she slashed at the lock of the cage. It fell away with a hiss, and she moved to the cage holding Lugard and did the same. They both stepped out to freedom, though perhaps not quite free yet.

"Head east," Keara said. "You can hide in the Alderwood—"

"I will go to the Anvil," Ansell replied.

She cocked an ear as though she hadn't quite heard him right. "You'll what? Are you fucking crazy? That city is about to become a war zone."

"There is something I must do."

Keara slammed the knife back into the scabbard at her side. "This is like talking to a brick wall. I said, lay low until—"

"And I said, very well."

She clenched her teeth in frustration. "We have an agreement, Ansell. If you can't even stick to the first part of the plan, how can I trust you to stick to the second? If you can't do as you're told the deal is off. I only have to open my mouth and shout for—"

Lugard struck her with an open hand to the neck. The strength of the blow was enough to knock her to the ground, where she lay still. Ansell could only hope it wasn't fatal, but there was little he could do if it was.

"I thought she would never fall silent," Lugard said. "Come, we must be swift before the guards come. If we strike east we can leave this conflict behind until—"

"As I said, brother, I am bound for the Anvil."

Lugard considered his words for a moment. He opened his mouth, perhaps to argue that it was madness, but thought better of it. "Whatever awaits there clearly means much to you. If it is atonement you seek then I will not stand in your way."

"If we don't get out of here now, there will be no atonement for either of us."

Lugard nodded, leading the way from the cages. The camp was dark, the guards at the cages grown complacent over the last few days, stopping anyone from approaching but giving little consideration to anyone escaping. Neither Lugard nor Ansell were adept at stealth, but they managed to hold to the shadows as they crept toward the edge of the camp.

Ansell could almost see their way to freedom ahead. Then the boy blundered into their path...

He stepped out of the shadows carrying a pan he had used to collect water from a stream, his Mantid Battalion uniform just discernible in the dark. His mouth gaped open when he saw them both, eyes widening. Only five yards away, but still far enough to yell before they could stop him.

The pan of water fell from his hand, spilling on the ground as he went for the sword at his side. Both Drakes moved as one, but the trooper shouted his warning before they could reach him. Lugard's fist caught his jaw, silencing him and driving him to the ground. He grabbed the boy's hair, pulling it back, exposing the neck, ready to drive his stiffened fingers into the throat, but Ansell grabbed his wrist.

"We have to run."

Lugard abandoned the fallen trooper, rising to his feet as Ansell dragged him toward the tree line ahead. Other voices were raised in alarm now. So much for a stealthy escape.

The voices grew louder as they ran to the relative safety of the wood. Lugard pushed Ansell forward, stopping and turning to face their pursuers.

"Run, brother!" he shouted, dashing back toward the light.

Ansell stopped. He could not allow Lugard to sacrifice himself in such a manner, but... Grace. He had to reach the Anvil. Had to ensure she was safe from the coming storm. From Sanctan.

As he turned back toward the woodland, he heard Lugard's bellow behind him attracting any and all who could hear it. "Come face me! Come taste the might of Ammenodus!"

It stirred him. Shamed him. But he knew it was too late. If he ran back to help his brother, they were both finished. Ansell allowed the trees to envelop him as he fled, hoping Lugard's sacrifice would not be in vain.

# FULREN

He could tell the encampment was busy. From where he sat he could sense movement in the distance, as though they were mobilising for something. Fulren had no idea what for—there hadn't been any kind of action for days, until the prisoners broke out the other night.

Maybe he should have helped. Gone after those fugitives as they fled and proven his worth. But in the last days Fulren had found himself less and less interested in other people's expectations. Only his own desires.

He knew envoys from Nyrakkis were here. A black ark hidden somewhere in the woods not half a mile from his own camp. He almost yearned to find out who they were, but the prospect of that excited and frightened him in equal measure. The fact that they might be able to explain what was going on with his body, with his mind, made him both insanely curious and terrified. It was reason enough to leave that ark well alone. That, and the memories it might bring back of her...

Fulren would have asked his mother about it, but they hadn't spoken since his first meeting. As much as he wanted to be by her side, to reassure her, he also understood she had a lot to deal with, and he had little desire to add to her woes.

"Are you all right?" Verlyn asked from where she sat nearby.

She hadn't spoken to him much either in the past few days. He must have looked particularly sullen for her to comment on it now.

"I'm just sick of sitting around doing nothing."

And it was true, the monotony was crippling. Especially now that he'd had a taste of what he was capable of. The exquisite thrill of the hunt, of the kill. As much as he had tried to push it down, it plagued his mind, taunting him with such promise. He couldn't wait until the moment he could indulge that need once more, but knew he had to push the feeling down.

"Is that all?" Verlyn continued. "Only I see you looking into the woods. Toward that ark. I guess it brings back bad memories for you."

He hadn't even realised he was doing it. She was right of course; it did bring back memories—horrific ones he would sooner forget. But along with those were memories he took pleasure in. The smell of her, the taste of her when she kissed him...

"I was a prisoner in Nyrakkis and it almost destroyed me. But it also helped make me..." He held up his hands, one of flesh and one of steel.

"They cursed you, Fulren. What they did to you was not a gift."

"Without the power they gave me I would never have survived the Bridge of Saints. Would never have lived long enough for you and Ashe to find me."

"You don't know that."

He almost laughed at her. "Of course I do. And you know it too. But it's not just that."

Fulren gazed through the trees once more, his glyphsight focusing through the murk, seeing the distinctive black outline of the ark beyond the woodland. It formed a void of dark magic his vision could not penetrate.

"What is it?" she asked.

How to explain that there was a demon through those woods, lurking within the bowels of that ship? That along with it might be the woman he thought he had lost on top of a mountain. Despite seeing her fall, only to be claimed by that eagle, he still had the pressing feeling she was here.

"When I was in Nyrakkis I grew close to someone. She helped me..."

"And you think she is here? Brought by that airship?"

Another glance back though the woodland. He couldn't see her, nor sense any arcanist aura, but the feeling she was here just wouldn't go away.

"I can't be sure," he said, all the unease building up. Making him feel tense, feel small, despite what he knew he was capable of.

"There's only one way to find out, I guess," Verlyn said casually, as though it wasn't such a big deal. "There's nothing to stop you wandering over there to find out."

He shook his head. "No. That's all in the past anyway. Even if it is her—"

"What are you so afraid of?"

"Nothing," he replied, too quickly. It was a lie. He was afraid of the reaction he might get if he was right and she was waiting for him on that airship. Emony had proven what a monster he'd become, she had almost told him as much. He couldn't go through that again. "But just...look at me."

"You are still Fulren Hawkspur. Still the man you were."

"Am I?" Right now he genuinely didn't know.

"We all change. But deep down, we all stay the same too. If there was something between you and this woman, it can't have just been snuffed out in a few short months. Things like that don't just go away."

He wasn't so sure of the truth in that. If Emony's reaction had taught him anything it was that he had changed beyond measure. Fulren had always been close to Emony growing up and there was an expectation that perhaps they would eventually be wed, not only for the good of their Guilds but due to the affection they bore one another. He had been wrong about that and could well be wrong again.

"Face it," Verlyn continued, "you don't have a clue what will happen until you go and see."

"Some things are best left buried," he replied, feeling the fear more than ever.

Verlyn stood, and he saw her familiar red aura spark, that anger catching fire.

"And some things aren't. I'd burn the world just to spend another minute with Ashe. To have the chance to rush into that fire till it burned me to cinders. But if you're too much of a coward to take a chance, Fulren, then you just sit there and wonder what could have been."

He could see her roiling, seething, even as she walked away and left him alone. It should have stirred him to action but still he sat, wallowing in his own fear and apprehension. He had stoked her ire, and for that he was sorry. A sorrow made worse by the fact that she was right.

Fulren stood, grabbing the cloak he now kept like a second skin and wrapping it around his shoulders. His helm lay nearby—the one that would mask him from the world. For a moment he considered leaving it behind, but it was as much a part of him as the artifice that augmented his flesh.

As soon as he placed it over his head the world coalesced in vivid colours, woodland coming to life in stark contrast to the shadows of his glyphsight. With every step across the leafy ground he felt dread rising.

Almost a half mile through those trees something wicked awaited. When he had first been taken away in that ark, what seemed a lifetime ago, he had felt the presence of its demon engine like a dark cloud hanging over him. Now, the closer he got, the more it felt like an infection—a plague upon the very land he walked.

He glanced around for reassurance, perhaps looking for crows in the trees, his familiars to offer some comfort, but they were not here. Even his ever-present companions were too afraid to accompany him on this journey. With every step he fought the urge to flee, until finally the trees thinned out and revealed a clearing. In its midst sat that black ark, squatting like an iron gargoyle. Fulren could sense its demon lying in repose, and it sensed him in return, mewling at his presence, teasing him. It took all his will to block out its fiendish call.

As he paused at the threshold to the clearing he saw the ark was not the only thing he had to be wary of. Nine guardians stood vigil, and he realised he had encountered their like before in the frigid cold of the Huntan Reach, when one of them had almost killed Jagdor. They stood like statues, golems in ebon armour, but they were still very much human. As Fulren watched he could feel the power of the necroglyphs they bore beneath that black plate, and sensed their vigilance, despite none of them making a move to challenge him.

"Who is in charge here?" he asked, sounding more confident than he felt.

There was no answer but the echo of his own words. He may as well have been standing in a clearing of ancient statues.

"I have come to—"

The nine moved as one, clearing a path to the gaping mouth of the ark, and Fulren felt every nerve tense as someone walked down the gangway from within its bowels. He recognised her almost immediately, that lithe figure, her gainly tread like a panther on the prowl.

Wenis was smiling, that familiar look he had hated at first, but soon came to cherish. Fulren stood and waited as she made her way closer, not taking her eyes off him as she came to stand a couple of feet away.

"Fuck," he breathed.

"Mmm, tempting," she crooned, raising a suggestive eyebrow. "But can we not at least say hello first?"

All those old memories flooded back, along with the regrets he harboured, the chances not taken, the things unsaid. And now, when he had a chance to say them, he was all but tongue-tied.

"It's me... it's Fulren."

Wenis shook her head, looking up at him as though he were a child who'd disappointed her. "I know that, Fulren Hawkspur. I would know you anywhere."

"I... I would have come sooner, but..."

She pressed a slender hand to her chest as though flattered. "Aww, were you nervous to see me again? I am touched."

"No... I mean, it was just... My mother has made it clear that no one is to come here. I was just—"

"Ah, Lady Rosomon." She looked at him sideways, as though the name alone conjured bad memories. "Yes, we have spoken. She was most insulting. And that mouth of hers—was she raised by sailors?"

Fulren was struck by the sudden urge to defend her. "I mean... I can't imagine you're her favourite person. You took me away from her. And then with this..." He gestured with his good arm, the human one, toward what was hidden beneath his cloak.

"This?" she asked.

He would have to reveal his true self sooner or later. May as well be sooner.

With his normal hand he unclasped his cloak, letting it fall. Fulren rose on those articulated legs, which offered a gentle sigh as the hydraulics kicked in. He raised his metal arm, showing her his body in all its terrifying glory.

"I know, it's hideous. But—"

"Take off that helmet," she demanded, showing no fear or revulsion at his appearance.

"What?"

"Are you deaf now? That helmet, take it off."

She'd seen his face before, his scars and milk-washed eyes, but not like this. Wenis had not witnessed the golem that he had become.

Still, he raised his hands and lifted the helm from his head, the clarity of his vision immediately replaced by the dark mist of glyph-sight. Wenis took a step closer, reaching up a hand to touch his face. At the feel of her fingertips Fulren held his breath, and she moved her hand down, caressing the metal of his arm. He could feel it prickle as though it were flesh, and when he could take no more he stepped away from her.

"I shouldn't have come. You don't need to see me like this."

"Like what?" Wenis asked.

He wanted to say it. To express how bereft he was at what he had lost, at what he had become, but he could not. Suddenly he was having to fight back tears in front of the last person he would ever want to see them.

He wouldn't have blamed her if she'd fled like Emony, but instead Wenis placed a hand to his chest. "You are more beautiful now than the first day I laid eyes on you."

Fulren shook his head, refusing to believe it. "I am a monster."

Was that a giggle? It sounded so carefree, so out of place. "We are all monsters in our own way."

She placed a hand to the back of his neck, pulling him down as she stretched up on tiptoes. Her kiss was as cool and sweet as he remembered it. A kiss that sent him light-headed, as though he'd been drugged.

"You still taste the same," she breathed, once she'd had her fill of him.

"Well, that's one thing at least."

Another laugh, like a sigh of summer breeze in the leaves. "I would have made the journey from Nyrakkis just for that."

"Why have you come?"

Her smile wavered. "I was sent here to meet with your mother. To present an offer of alliance in return for our help."

"And she accepted?"

"In a way." She turned, gesturing to the ark sitting there impotently. "But as you can see, we are still waiting for our orders, like the faithful little pets we are."

"Yeah, me too," Fulren replied, sympathising with her frustration.

Wenis turned back to him, a familiar mischievous look about her. "Then perhaps we should not wait for permission. We should act."

Fulren felt a sudden pull of excitement. The thought of defying his mother was something he had never considered before, but now its allure was almost irresistible. Almost.

"But... my mother—"

"Do you ask her approval for everything? You are a man now, Fulren. A warrior. Look at you." She gestured to the artifice that augmented his body as though it were the most resplendent armour. "You are exalted. Blessed above all others. You need no approval."

As she spoke he could feel his confidence rising. The realisation that he was beholden to no one filling him with excitement. "Yes. Maybe you're right."

"You know I am." She beamed. "Together, you and I... we could end this war in a single stroke."

"You mean, kill Sanctan?"

A sly nod of her head as she relished the prospect. "Your dragon priest is the key to all this. If we were to cut the head from that snake the body would die without so much as a twitch."

The more he thought on it, the more sense it made. He had already proven he could cut through any bodyguard Sanctan might have. All he had to do was get close enough.

"You could get me to him?" Fulren regarded that brooding airship, fighting his fear of what it harboured in its tomb of an engine room.

"Your wish is my command," Wenis replied.

He did his best to ignore the suggestive tone in her voice. "Then we'll do it. But not in secret. I will have to tell my mother what the plan is. She'll see the sense in it." He looked back at Wenis. "One thing I don't understand is why you're here with an offer of alliance. Your queen tried that before and it didn't work out so well. Why have you returned?"

A grave look crossed her face. One he'd seen rarely on those delicate features. "There is a greater threat to us. One that could consume all of Hyreme. Queen Meresankh has sent me to aid your mother as a demonstration of... goodwill. That we might later unite to face what is coming."

If Wenis had returned at the behest of her queen it must have been grave indeed. "What threat?"

"The Scions of Iperion Magna have formed a union, and they are even now mustering for war. For domination of our lands and yours. We need one another, Fulren. Or both our nations are doomed."

It was hard to believe. Impossible even. But Fulren had long since learned to accept the impossible.

"Then I guess we have to win this."

"And we will," Wenis said, moving closer to him again. "Together."

# CONALL

As the land flashed by beneath him, so too those chaotic thoughts assailing his mind. Memories roiled among fantasies as he soared upon the back of that eagle. Even the harsh winds blowing in his face could not sweep away the plague of his thoughts, no matter how high or how fast he flew.

Donan. Poor, loyal, stupid Donan. Curse him for his fucking persistence. Conall was a murderer now. A traitor. All the good he had done to help his mother, the Guilds, to try to end this war, was swept away in a torrent of piss because he thought he could control whatever was lurking deep in his soul. And as usual, he had been so very wrong.

They would be after him, the Viper Battalion, moving north in his wake. They could never catch him though. He was free of them, for a while at least. But they were coming, and with them would come word of what he had done. Not yet though. Not yet.

When he saw the great white walls of the Anvil below, thoughts of what lay behind him faded. Not a mile to the east of the city, the Guild encampment stood out starkly against the green of the countryside. His mother had certainly gathered a formidable army about her. From his lofty vantage point, he could see they had flocked in their thousands, but then she'd always had a knack of bringing people round to her side. And now her long-lost son had returned.

If he had any sense, Conall would have flown away. Steered the eagle in some random direction and left all this far behind. But he couldn't, he had to land, had to join the Guild army. And as much as he told himself it was to aid his mother in her fight, he knew it wasn't. He needed help. Needed someone to take away this curse. There was no way he could do it alone, and so the only option was for him to land, to find his mother and hope that somehow he could rid himself of the demon inside, before it took control of him, root and branch.

Gritting his teeth, he tugged the rein, urging the war eagle to wheel about and head for the centre of that great encampment. No point trying to hide his arrival, they'd be able to see him approach from ten miles away.

As he swooped closer he could already see activity, as the troopers on the ground scrambled to meet him. Once the eagle glided in to land, he was quickly surrounded by a dozen armoured soldiers, all aiming splintbows.

Conall climbed down from the beast's back, keeping a grip on the leash as the troopers closed in. Bloodwolf Battalion by their uniforms—nasty by reputation but disciplined at least. Still, he would have to talk fast before one of them decided to shoot first and ask questions later.

"Identify yourself!" a trooper shouted, before he had the chance.

Conall raised his hands, feeling the tension, anticipating that voice creeping into his mind, urging him to reach for the blade in the shadows.

"I'm Conall... Conall Hawkspur."

Silence, along with looks of confusion, before one of them said, "He's dead. You can't be—"

"No," another one interrupted. "That's him. I've seen him before. It's... it's really him."

Someone pushed their way through the troopers, carrying a heavy torso on rangy legs. His weathered face regarded Conall in disbelief, pipe dangling precariously from his mouth. From what Conall knew, Oleksig Marrlock wasn't a man who was easily shocked, but here he was, looking on with slack-jawed amazement.

"Yep," Conall said, feeling an unfamiliar discomfort on being the centre of attention. "It's me."

"See to the bird," Oleksig commanded, suddenly shaken from his malaise. "You'd best follow me, lad."

As the troopers warily approached the eagle, Conall followed Oleksig. His stomach was roiling, made no better by the stench of the pipe smoke that hung in the air.

"Is my mother here?" Conall asked. "Is she safe?"

"She is," Oleksig replied, as Conall struggled to keep pace with his lengthy stride. "And she'll be eager to see you. Despite the fact you look like warmed-up shite."

Conall was keenly aware of how unkempt he was. He'd spent more days than he could count sleeping in the wilds, and there'd been little time to tend to his appearance. He adjusted the patch over his eye, vainly thinking it might improve the way he looked, before abandoning the idea as a bad job.

As they made their way through the camp, he was mindful of everyone watching. Most of them looked little better than he did, a ragtag collection of miners and Armigers driven to the edge of endurance by this conflict. Mantid and Bloodwolf banners hung at the edges of the camp, and he recognised the staunch figures of Blackshield warriors standing guard. Even a couple of stormhulks loomed in the distance.

"The Hallowhills are here?"

Oleksig nodded. "They are. Joined us weeks ago. And a good job they did. We'd most likely have been slaughtered on the road here without their help."

Conall recalled a distant memory of the Karna. Of Keara, and the night they spent together. Perhaps she was here too, though perhaps best not to think on that reunion right now.

"My mother thinks we can trust them?"

Oleksig took the pipe from his mouth and grinned. "Of course not. But while they're more scared of us than the Ministry, I think we'll be just fine."

"What about my mother? How has she been?"

"A tower of strength, for us all. Which is remarkable after all she's sacrificed. Wyke destroyed. Jagdor dead."

Conall had known about Wyke, but never let the notion of all those lost lives enter his mind. But... "Lancelin Jagdor is dead?"

It gave Oleksig pause. "Yes... I'm sorry. I didn't think. Your father was..."

Was killed by that man, and Conall had always suspected his mother had conspired to make it happen. If Jagdor had joined her so readily and died at Wyke then perhaps the rumours about them were true after all. But Conall had to quash that notion down. Now wasn't the time to open up old wounds.

They walked on in silence as the ground rose up toward a hilltop. The throng of people thinned out as Conall passed a group of swordwrights he barely recognised. Was that Borys Marrlock? Thalleus Brisco? Maugar and his daughter nodded a welcome at him, though he could see the disbelief in their eyes. News of his untimely demise had clearly preceded him.

A row of warriors stood barring his way at the top of the hill. Huge shields, huge spears, beaten leather armour bearing a combination of Archwind and Hawkspur Guild symbols. And standing among this grim bodyguard, his mother.

She looked regal, despite the humble blue garb she was wearing. Still, he could see the fragility there, her hands clasped, jaw set as she watched him approach. It seemed so long since he'd last seen her. So much had happened since they had stood together in the Anvil, she so proud of him, he so proud of his longbarrel. It had been everything to him, that weapon, a mark of respect from his uncle, but now he realised how insignificant it was. Now, as he stood looking into his mother's eyes, he knew what a fool he had been to put such store by material things. None of it mattered anymore.

"What have you been through?" she said, her voice strong despite the anguish in her eyes.

It was such a long story, with so much pain, but his mother wanted to know and who was he to keep it from her?

"I was shipwrecked. Picked up by pirates. Traded in the Magna."

There it was, boiled down to a few words. He should have told her at length of Arcturius. Of Senmonthis. Of the sorcery he had seen, and that still lurked within him. Instead, he only told her what he had to.

"I escaped. Crossed the Drift. And here I am."

He held his arms out as though presenting himself as a gift. Some fucking prize he was—a broken waif chewed up and spat out by the wasteland.

His mother stared into him like she used to when he told her bad news, usually about some trouble he'd got himself in. There was pain in that look too, as though she knew this time there was nothing she could do to get him out of it.

"It is good to have you home."

She stepped forward, kissing him lightly on the cheek. All the while he didn't move. Couldn't move.

"I was with the Viper Battalion to the south," he said, trying to fill that awkward silence. "They're making their way north but I..." *Killed my friend and fled.* "...made my way here in advance of them. I thought you could use the help."

"And I am grateful for it," she said, looking anything but. "We are about to end this, Conall. I would have you by my side when we finally bring down the Ministry."

"Do you know where Tyreta is?" Conall asked suddenly, remembering what Sonnheld had told him. Hoping she was not a prisoner in Castleteig, or worse.

Again his mother looked as though she were holding everything in, that behind her mask, she was on the verge of breaking. "She is...in the Anvil."

"What? Is she a prisoner? What's happened."

"She is on a mission of her own."

"In the Anvil? The very place you're about to attack?"

"We needed someone inside the walls of the city. Someone to drum up support. Tyreta is our ace in the pack."

"And you allowed this?" He could feel his anger growing, head spinning as he gritted his teeth, but within the maelstrom his mother's face stared back, calm and still.

"Are you all right?" she said, voice booming all of a sudden. "Do you need to rest?"

He stepped back, stumbling on nothing, as one of her guards grabbed him and held him up.

"No," he replied, too loud and too harsh, wrenching his arm free. "No, I'm fine. I'm just... tired."

"Then you should rest," she said, coddling him. Always giving him what he wanted so he'd just shut up. "But first you should—"

"I should what?" Too harsh the reply, but he was sick of this already, of the facade she always put on.

"You should see your brother."

Clarity hit him all too hard. The whirling stopped, along with his heart. "Fulren is here? But he..."

"It seems you're not the only son I have capable of escaping Malador."

"Where... where is he?"

Rosomon nodded to one of her hulking bodyguards. "Ianto. Please show Conall where his brother is."

That was it—being dismissed already. Appeased. Distracted. But as ever, he just accepted it.

Conall turned like he'd been banished to his bed with no supper and followed Ianto without offering his mother a second glance. It was stupid of him. He should have told her straight what was ailing him, been honest, asked for help.

No. He didn't need any help. He was Conall fucking Hawkspur. He could beat this on his own.

"We will talk later, Conall," his mother said, as he followed her bodyguard like a lost dog.

"Sure," he replied, dreading the prospect already.

His head was spinning, and all he could think was that the next time they did speak she would want to know everything, and by rights he should tell her. All this time he had hoped she could help him, and perhaps she was the only one... but no. There was no one who could help him.

The bodyguard led them on toward the woodland and into the trees. The noise of the camp faded behind him, but he couldn't shake the feeling that he was being watched. The trees seemed to loom over him in judgement, and even when he saw a clearing ahead it still felt as though he was shrouded in accusation.

A woman was the first person he saw. Perhaps the same age as his mother, dark hair, and a steely set to her eyes as she watched him approach. Nearby was a wagon, and horses grazing close to it. No sooner had he made his way into the clearing than his mother's bodyguard turned to go.

"Where is he?" Conall asked.

The man offered no answer before leaving him alone with the woman. Conall turned his attention to her, unable to shake the feeling that there was something familiar about that face.

"Hello," he said, trying to sound as friendly as he could when he saw the wariness in her expression. "I'm looking for Fulren."

Those steely eyes narrowed, as though he'd asked her for a kiss and she was in no mind to give him one.

"Fulren Hawkspur?" he said, just so they were in absolutely no doubt.

"Who are you?" she asked.

This was turning out to be much trickier than he'd anticipated. "I'm Conall. His brother."

Before she could answer there was movement through the trees. A boy, no... a man stepped into the clearing. Conall nearly smiled, nearly rushed forward to embrace him, before he realised this was not the same brother he had left at the Anvil.

Fulren wore a dark cloak covering him from shoulder to foot, leaving only his head visible. Scar tissue stretched in a band across his eyes and he stared blindly, though still made his way sure-footed from the trees. It was all Conall could do to hold himself back. To stop himself rushing forward to embrace his little brother and hold him close, like he should have done all those months ago at the aerie.

"Conall?" Fulren said, as he stopped but a few feet away. "I thought I could hear your voice."

Conall would have answered, told him he was here and that he would take care of him now, but the words wouldn't come. He could barely take care of himself. Besides, despite his lack of sight, there was something about Fulren, standing tall and confident, that suggested he needed no help.

"I guess I should give you two some privacy," the woman said, standing and making her way from the clearing.

Conall realised he had to get a grip on himself. This was Fulren, his baby brother. He stepped forward, reaching out to embrace him, but Fulren pulled away, raising an arm. Only it wasn't an arm.

The cloak slipped off his shoulder, revealing more of Fulren's body, his legs moving with animal grace, their metal sheen catching the afternoon sun.

"What's happened to you?" Conall gasped.

"I've..." Fulren tried to pull his cloak back over his shoulder before thinking better of it and leaving himself exposed. "I've changed since I last saw you."

"No shit," Conall breathed. "But I guess we both have."

He wanted to open up, to tell his brother all he had been through, what he still suffered, but he doubted even Fulren would understand, despite the thing he had become.

"I bet your changes weren't as drastic as this?" Fulren said, flashing a trace of his easy smile, though even that had changed. Less carefree. Almost bitter on that scarred face of his.

"Let's just say I'm only half blind."

Fulren reached out a hand, the one that was still flesh, and gently touched Conall's face. As soon as his fingers brushed the patch over his eye, Conall flinched, reluctant to let his brother's touch linger on that old wound.

"How did you manage to escape from Nyrakkis?" Conall asked, keen to move on.

"I was rescued. By Jagdor."

Just the mention of that man's name made Conall bristle. "But... why would he?"

"Because he loved our mother."

Of course he did. Conall had always known it, but the fact still did little to curb his disdain, for Jagdor and her. The knowledge she had conspired with him, even to rescue Fulren, made his anger burn even brighter. Not that he would let Fulren know it.

"I guess that doesn't matter anymore. I heard he...perished at Wyke. What does matter is that we're here. And we're alive."

"We are," Fulren agreed. "But we still have a fight on our hands to put things back the way they were."

Conall's gaze drifted to the fire burning in the centre of the clearing. In those flames he saw only portents of doom. Nothing would ever be the way it was.

"Did they tell you about Tyreta?" he asked, keen to change the subject yet again.

"Volunteered for a dangerous mission in the Anvil. I know—little Ratface. Who would have thought?"

Just the way he spoke about her brought a smile to Conall's face. Suddenly all notion of change and doom were gone, and it was back the way it should be. A feeling that was all too fleeting, quickly consumed by the dark shadow hanging over him.

He would have loved to confess his fears, to tell Fulren everything, and it was hard to stop himself. He could not burden his brother with this though. Especially after all he had suffered.

"What did they do to you in Nyrakkis?" he asked, once again regarding those steel limbs that moved with such ease, like a natural extension of his brother's body.

Fulren flexed the metal hand that looked like a steel talon. "They gave me...a gift."

Conall found that hard to swallow. He had heard that said before, when he had been a prisoner in Arcturius. The red gem was a gift, the demon, its power. He had wanted none of it. It had been no gift. It was a curse, and nothing else.

"But...look what they've done to you."

"I only lost my sight in Nyrakkis. This..." He held up that metal arm as though it were some kind of trophy. "...this happened here, in Torwyn. And I wanted it. I accepted it as the boon it was, after my old body was broken."

Fulren spoke with some relish, and there was no doubting his conviction. For a moment, Conall wondered if he should do the same—simply accept what he had become—before dismissing that temptation.

"So who's your new friend?" Conall gestured toward the trees where the woman had disappeared.

"Verlyn? She is my saviour. Though in return, I've only brought her pain."

That one was easy to relate to, as he was reminded of sudden foul thoughts. Of Donan. Of Nylia. Both left dead in his destructive wake.

"She looks familiar."

"Does she? I doubt you've ever met her before. She's just a webwainer who left the Guild. Someone whose path I crossed by chance."

"Yeah, it's funny the friends you make when you're desperate." Conall thought once again of Nylia. Of how they had established a bond that could only have been forged in Arcturius.

"So what do you think will happen when all this is over? Will we ever really be able to go back to how it was before?"

There was a stricken tone in Fulren's voice, as though he knew that things could never be the same. Conall didn't have the heart to tell him he agreed.

"We'll try to rebuild, I guess. That's all we can do."

This time when his brother smiled it was just like the Fulren of old. "It's nice that you're finally talking like a Guildmaster."

"Yeah. And it only took a revolution for me to do it."

"Sometimes we just need a little push."

Conall grinned back. "Right. Just a little push."

Movement in the trees behind. Conall turned to see the big Titanguard was back. "Your mother has requested you follow me," he said. "Both of you."

Conall looked back to Fulren. "Best not keep her waiting."

Slowly Fulren's smile faded. "No. I think this might be the first step toward putting things back together."

# ROSOMON

A meeting of all her generals, yet she barely noticed any of them. All she could see were her two sons—Fulren and Conall returned from the dead, now standing beside her ready to fight. She felt her pride swell at that. All they had been through, and yet they still stood stalwart, ready to defend her nation, her Guild. It was all she could have ever asked for.

But she could not think on that now. On how the family she had thought lost was almost reunited once more. She could not allow herself that luxury. There would be no triumphant reunion until she ended this war.

They were gathered around her, crammed into the cloying confines of that familiar tent. Kassian and Ianto stood the closest, as ever, but that did little to settle her nerves. Falko and Rawlin were at the opposite side of that wooden table—the one they had brought with them all the way from Oakhelm. Oleksig was to her right, filling the tent with that pungent miasma as he puffed away on his pipe. Keara was near to him, looking unsure of herself. How much she had changed since Rosomon first met her. Back then she had been so brimming with arrogance. Now she looked like a little lost girl, no matter how much she tried to hide it behind a scowl.

Maugar and Xorya were shoulder to shoulder, as were Thalleus and Borys. Even the witch-woman from Nyrakkis was here, standing all too close to Rosomon's youngest son. Lurking like a spider, as though she might steal him away again at any moment and drag him off to her web.

"We go in two days," she said, breaking the uncomfortable silence.

"About damn time," Rawlin grunted immediately, as though it was exactly the news he had been waiting for.

Not to be outdone, Falko slapped a steel-clad hand to the wooden table. "I will ready my troopers for the assault."

"No," Rosomon said, reminding everyone that she was in charge. That these men were here at her behest, not the other way around. "We don't have the numbers for an all-out assault on the city. Even with two Armiger Battalions. Even with Oleksig's miners and the Blackshields. Even with the Hallowhills. A frontal attack on the walls of the Anvil will only lead to a slaughter."

It took Oleksig to stop puffing on that pipe and break the stunned silence that followed. "So what's the plan?"

"We will attack, but it will only act as a demonstration of intent. The people of the Anvil must be shown what we are capable of, but I will not launch a full-scale attack and put the lives of innocent people in jeopardy. The assault will be limited to a small unit, the gates breached, but the city will remain untouched."

Falko looked to Rawlin in confusion, then back at Rosomon. "So you'd launch a suicide mission instead? Rosomon, that is madness. Anything less than an all-out attack will be crushed immediately. It will simply be a waste of our troops."

She pressed her fist to the polished wood of the tabletop, biting back her frustration. "I am trying to end this with as few casualties as possible. Once the people within the city know what they face, they will reconsider keeping us out."

Oleksig chuckled. "Ah. I think I know what you're doing." He glanced over toward Wenis. "You intend to send her knights."

"I do," she replied, glad someone had cottoned on to her intentions.

Wenis shrugged. "They are at your disposal. But I would like to point out that they are not immortal. Your general is right, it may be a waste. A glorious and violent one. But a waste, nonetheless."

For a moment Rosomon wondered if Wenis actually gave a damn about those silent, black-armoured warriors. "It will be enough. Trust me. If they are as good as you say they are, then they'll cause enough damage to give the city's defenders pause. A shock attack is all we require."

"But what then?" Falko asked, not bothering to hide the frustration in his voice. "We sit back and hope Sanctan loses his nerve? That man will oppose us no matter how powerful he thinks we are. He will sacrifice every man, woman and child in the city."

"Perhaps he will," she replied. "But he is not the only man defending the Anvil. He is only as powerful as his followers allow. If the people within those walls think they are facing an insurmountable force they will beg us for terms."

"Nine men?" Maugar said, as much to himself as anyone. "You hope to assault the city gates with nine men?"

Rosomon shook her head, thinking back to Alumford. To that little town on the river, that held such significance now. "Not just nine men. An army."

Maugar creased his brow. "What are you talking about, Rosomon?"

"I am talking about using everything at our disposal to make the people of the Anvil think we have an army from Nyrakkis come to raze the city. We have dyes from Alumford. Artificers and smiths to forge enough armour, or an approximation of it, to make it look as though the Talon, the Armigers, the miners, are a horde come across the Drift."

Maugar's wrinkled brow rose as he finally understood. "A horde. Yes, I see it."

Falko shook his head, in no mood to agree. "That's a mighty risk you're taking. All on a ruse that might be exposed at the first turn."

"This is all a risk," Rosomon replied.

"And there's more." Fulren stepped forward, his mechanical legs whispering as he moved. "More that we can do. Wenis and I will help with that."

He had made no mention of this before, and Rosomon felt a rising dread. "What have you got planned?"

Fulren glanced to Wenis, who stepped forward by his side as though they were joined together in some conspiracy. "Under cover of night, Wenis can get me into the city aboard her vessel. If I can enter the Mount. Find Sanctan—"

"No," she said, not wanting him to finish, even though she knew what he was about to say. "No, it's too—"

"Risky?" Fulren replied. "You said yourself, this is all a risk."

She looked at those blind eyes so filled with determination. Saw what he had become. A man... no... more than a man.

"Very well," she answered before she could change her mind. "If you manage to find him, kill him. But until that happens we stick to the plan, send the nine to the gates of the Anvil and show them who we are."

"Ten."

A single voice from the back of the tent, filling Rosomon with yet more dread. Conall stepped forward, as all eyes fell on him. He looked as though he might brook no argument, and despite all her instincts screaming at her, Rosomon knew that she could not refuse another of her children as they volunteered to challenge their enemy.

"I will go with the knights of Nyrakkis," Conall said. "Someone has to lead them."

Wenis suddenly snorted a laugh. "And you think that someone is you, my prince?"

She looked him up and down, as though mocking the vagabond he resembled. As Conall glared back at her with his one eye, Rosomon was sure she noticed her arrogant facade waver slightly.

"I do," he replied. "If you can think of someone better, let's hear it."

Wenis had no suggestions. Rosomon looked to her generals and her fellow Guildmasters. Maugar did not offer himself. Neither did Borys or Thalleus. Only Kassian was brave enough to step forward.

"My lady, I will—"

She held up her hand, and he fell silent. She had once thought all her children lost. Now her eldest, so soon returned from death, wanted to throw himself to the wolves, and yet she could not deny him. He was not just her son anymore, he was a man. A warrior. He had grown so much, and would one day lead their Guild. She could not protect him any longer.

"Conall will go with them. He will lead the assault on the gate."

He was staring right back at her, a look of surprise on his face, before he nodded his gratitude. Rosomon took a cleansing breath, gently laying her palms flat on the table.

"There is no guarantee this will work. And if it fails then Falko, Rawlin, you will get your wish. A full assault will be the only option left open to us. We have to hope that the turmoil within the city will be enough to break its spirit. That the defenders of the Anvil will lose their appetite for war and surrender."

She turned and nodded toward Ianto, who obediently marched from the tent.

"You all have your jobs to do. Let us hope we have fortune on our side."

There were no lively cries of assent, only a muted silence as one by one they all filed from the enclosed confines of the tent. Rosomon was the last to step outside, breathing slightly easier as she was met by the cool night air.

Down the slope to the grassy plains, Ianto was already talking to her artificers. In response, they began to tinker with the iron mortar at their feet, loading a missile and priming the firing mechanism.

Olstrum's wife had been very specific during Rosomon's conversation with her. She could only hope that the metallurgist had mixed the right salts for the appropriate colour.

A dull boom, and fire shot into the night sky before it burst into crackling light, blasting an azure hue across the heavens.

This plan would only come to fruition if the ordinary folk of the Anvil were on her side. Now it was down to Tyreta and Olstrum.

# KEARA

Not quite the rousing speech she'd been expecting, but at least they'd formulated their plan. And not a particularly good one either, but she was in no mood to start picking holes in it. Her head hurt too much. At least the Drake who'd struck her was dead, and with Ansell gone no one would ever know it was her who'd let them out.

She winced again at the pounding headache. One of the healers had told her it was a side effect of the concussion, that it would go away on its own in a day or two. Right now it felt like her skull was about to split. Not much help to her when she had an imminent attack to prepare for.

The camp was abuzz, all around were people preparing for the big charade. Hundreds of miners were sitting by the firelight, painting their clothes, along with the metal plates they'd been given to simulate armour and helms. By the light of a dozen forge fires, smiths were still hammering away. Someone walked by carrying two buckets of pitch, and from the look on his face he had no clue where he was going.

"Do you know where these need to be?" he asked, innocently enough.

Keara stared back at him through the dark. "Does it look like I'm in fucking charge?"

He timidly walked away, all browbeaten and still none the wiser. Perhaps she'd been a little harsh, but she was almost at her limit with all of this. It was a dumb frigging plan, and of course, just to add a little spice to the ruse, the Hallowhills would be at the vanguard ready and waiting for it all to go wrong.

Keara stopped, her legs starting to shake. It was suddenly hard to breathe. Her head throbbed, the wound in her thigh ached, and the prospect of another battle seemed all too much. Maybe she should just run away and wait for it to blow over.

No. That wasn't an option. Not now when the end was so close. She just had to hold it together for a little longer and everything would slip into place. Damn she could use some drop right now, just to take the edge off. She'd have settled for a decent bottle of wine, or even a shit bottle, but all she could do was close her eyes and concentrate on one breath after the other.

Just as she started to feel a little calmer, she spied him, sitting alone at the edge of the camp. Conall was painting his own armour, sitting in the moonlight with a paintbrush in hand. He looked like a little lost dog, just like when she'd seen him for the first time in Agavere. A dog she couldn't resist taking home.

What was he thinking, throwing himself into the fray like that? Did he have some kind of death wish? He'd certainly been carefree enough in the Karna when they'd spent the night together.

The sudden memory of that encounter brought a smile to her face. That brief time they'd spent together hadn't been the best, but he was far from the worst she'd ever had. But then it hadn't been about pleasure. He was a trophy. The heir to the Hawkspurs, conquered before she took down the whole Guild. Still, he'd managed to leave an impression on her. His tenderness, maybe. His vulnerability underneath all that arrogance. Showing in his most private moment that he was just a little boy in a man's body.

Now look at him—ready to march into the jaws of the dragon to save them all. There was a definite quality there she'd not noticed before. Potential for greatness that began to tug at her ambition.

With Conall Hawkspur on Keara's side Rosomon would have been forced to show her more respect. And an alliance between

Guilds wasn't unheard of. A union of convenience that might have other perks.

Keara almost laughed at the prospect. He was handsome enough, but from what she'd experienced, he was pretty mid-witted. And that eyepatch. It did make him look a damn sight more manly, but still...

"It's been a while," she said, finding herself standing over him as he dabbed at the helmet with his brush.

Conall looked up, as though he'd been deep in thought and not just concentrating on his task. At first he looked confused, then realisation dawned, just a little.

"Don't say you've forgotten all about me after our night in Agavere. That could hurt a girl's feelings."

"Keara?"

"Yes, Keara. Still the same woman you fell asleep on all those months ago. Although I guess I've changed some. This is a little gift your sister gave me."

She ran a finger down her cheek, showing him the trio of scars that would be there forever. Conall barely registered the gesture, looking right through her as though she were a ghost.

Keara moved closer, noting how drawn and gaunt he was. How the one eye she could see was ringed with shadow. "Although to be fair, you look like you've been in the wars yourself."

He touched the patch over his eye in a self-conscious gesture. This was not the man she had met in Agavere. For all his bluster at least he'd been confident, full of life. Keara had no idea who this was.

"May I?" she asked, gesturing to space on the wooden stump beside him.

"Be my guest," he replied, shuffling up and giving her room.

She sat down, struggling to make herself comfortable on the cold hard surface. "Sorry I left you hanging back in the Karna. I'm sure you appreciate I had a lot of things on my mind."

"Like rebellion?" he replied. "Like murder?"

Perhaps she deserved that. "Like doing the best for my Guild. Just like you would have done."

"And how did that turn out for you?"

She offered a smirk. "I don't know yet. Still working on it."

He absently picked at the dried paint on his fingers, and she noticed his nails were bitten down to nubs. It reminded her of the time she'd been alone with Olstrum and seen how the stress of his position had left him a wreck of a man.

"It was a brave thing you did," she continued. "Volunteering to assault the gates. You didn't have to. Why would you join that vanguard? It's a suicide mission."

The slightest shrug of his shoulders. "Just trying to make myself useful."

No answer at all, and it almost moved her to anger for reasons she couldn't quite work out. "Bollocks. You're risking your life needlessly. This isn't bravado, Conall, you're too old for that shit. It's like you're trying to get killed."

Gently he placed down the helmet he'd been painting and put the brush in its bucket of pitch. His one eye scanned the dark as though searching for an answer through the night.

"We're none of us safe until someone puts an end to this. I need to make a stand." He turned to her, as though seeing her for the first time. "Just doing what's best for my Guild."

"Wow, you have changed. When I first met you in that shithouse bar, I got the impression you couldn't give a damn about the Hawkspur name. Now here you are, willing to die for it."

"A lot's happened since that shithouse bar."

"So I see." She gestured at him, all slump-shouldered and drab. "Want to tell me about it?"

This time when he looked at her it was like he could see into her soul. Like every one of her dirty secrets was laid bare to him.

"Like you give a fuck?"

Keara tried to shake of the unnerving feeling he was giving her. "Maybe I don't. Or maybe I do and you're not the only one who's changed."

He carried on staring, for just a little too long, as though reading her like a book.

"No. I don't think you have."

Definitely not the answer she was looking for. Maybe because it was truer than she'd like to admit.

"Look, one way or the other we're gonna have to work together, Conall. I know you might still be a little hurt about the way things happened in Agavere, but—"

"I couldn't give a fuck about Agavere. I just choose my friends with better care than you do."

As soon as he said it, she could see a little vulnerability behind the facade he was putting on. His jaw tightened, like he was stifling a sob, but his eye still glared defiantly. He was hurting, and trying to hold it all in.

"And you've lost people, I get it. I understand what you're going through." She reached out a hand to take his. "I've lost people too. People I cared about."

Before she could touch him, he grasped her wrist, squeezing it so tight she almost cried out in pain.

"Have you?" he said through gritted teeth, almost a snarl. "I doubt that. I doubt you've ever really cared about anyone but yourself."

He said it so harshly there was spittle on his chin, and all the while that grip grew ever tighter until she could stand it no more.

Keara wrenched her hand free. "Looks like we don't know each other at all." She stood, all sympathy drained from her as she saw the vicious little whelp he truly was. "Good luck throwing yourself to the wolves. I hope you don't die."

She would have stormed off, but instead waited, giving him a chance to think again. To perhaps redeem himself a little with an apology. Instead, Conall reached down and picked up the half-painted helmet, plucking the brush from the pitch bucket and carrying on with his work.

She wanted to shout, to rage, but instead all she could do was turn away and leave him to his misery. He was another dead end. One more potential ally spitting in her face. Even her own people hated her, and for the first time in her life she realised she was surrounded by strangers.

With nowhere else to turn, she made her way back to the Hallowhill part of the camp. When she got there, they were hard at work, which was something, she supposed. Hallowhill artificers were checking over the stormhulks, webwainers by their side testing out the limits of the pyrestone in their conversion chambers. It made Keara realise there were more important things to think on right now than one sulking ex-lover. The whole camp was mobilising for war, and here she was moping like a spoiled child.

No one offered her so much as a hello, but that was no surprise. All she'd done was lay a brick wall between herself and her people. There was still a chance to change that though.

Galirena and Vikmar were in deep conversation as she made her way toward them. Vikmar offered her the slightest nod of acknowledgment, but Galirena looked in no mood for pleasantries.

"Come to see us off before the battle?" she asked.

Keara felt her anger suddenly burn, but doused it out as soon as it came. She wanted respect, but respect wasn't something you demanded. It had to be earned.

"Fuck that," she replied, looking Galirena right in the eye. "I'll be coming with you."

She took some pleasure from the woman's look of surprise.

Vikmar just looked confused. "What?"

"Like I said before—I'll shed blood with you. Every last drop if I have to."

Vikmar looked even more surprised, but also a little impressed.

Galirena not so much. "The great Lady Rosomon not give you any other choice?"

Keara was starting to wonder what the fuck she had to do to win these people over.

"Enough of this shit." She leaned in so close Galirena had to lean backwards. "Listen up, and listen fucking good. There's a fight coming, and we're all gonna be a part of it. And no matter how that ends, we'll have another battle straight after. Because when this is over, Rosomon or Sanctan, or whoever is left standing, will give us nothing that we don't take with our own hands. And don't doubt that I intend to claim what we're owed, no matter who I have to burn to get it."

Galirena shook her head. "But Hawkspur agreed to an alliance with us. She promised—"

"Her promises are for shit. We'll help her take the Anvil. Then *we* take the Guilds. Only question is, are you with me? Or are you both happy to stay as the loyal little serfs you are?"

They looked at one another, Vikmar still with that bewildered expression, but gradually Galirena developed steel in those eyes of hers.

"How do we know you mean it this time?"

"Because I'm the fucking Guildmaster," she said, louder than she wanted, but not caring who heard. "I carry the Hallowhill name. This Guild is all I have, and I'm not going to let the Hawkspurs, or any of those Guild arseholes, keep pressing our faces in the dirt. But I can't do this on my own. I need you. I need all of you to trust me as much as I'll trust you. I'm relying on the both of you to spread the word. Every webwainer in our Guild needs to be ready. When I give the call, they need to answer, or we're all finished."

More steel behind Galirena's eyes, but Vikmar was starting to smile, as though he only just understood. They looked at one another, nodding in unison, and it filled Keara with more hope than she'd felt in months.

Now it was Galirena's turn to smile. "So when does this happen?"

"When we've sealed our victory over the Ministry, and the other Guildmasters are picking over the spoils of the city, that's when we strike. We'll be more than strong enough, as long as we stick together."

Keara held out her fist. Vikmar was first to plant his hand on top of it in a gesture of solidarity, with Galirena quick to follow. As they all smiled at one another, Keara realised that the throne she had coveted so many weeks ago had just moved that step closer.

# PART TWO

# AWAKENING

# TYRETA

From the rooftop she looked out across a shrouded cityscape. The Anvil was quiet, as though it knew what was coming. It couldn't know, though. Nobody else could know what that signal had meant, that flash of blue light exploding on the horizon.

Olstrum stood with her. She had seen a change in him since her mother sent the signal. A light in his eyes that hadn't been there before. Still, he offered not so much as a word on what might be coming.

"Where are they?" Tyreta asked, her voice hushed as she watched for any sign of movement among the dark streets.

Olstrum allowed himself a smile. "Patience, Hawkspur."

Then she saw it, starting as a distant flicker, a light across the city between twin towers. Then another began to wink through the night. And another.

More and more came, uncountable as they illuminated the city like fireflies all springing to light at once. And with them a distant incoherent shout, echoing across the Anvil like a call to arms. It was soon joined by more, rising up in a chorus. And among those shouts of freedom came calls for alarm, until they were answering one another like a battling choir.

What a beginning.

Now for the end.

The Mount stood prominently in front of her. Olstrum had picked this lonely building to watch from because of how close it was to the seat of the Ministry. The vast monolith of stone and marble was eerily silent amid the burgeoning fires sprouting up around it. Close by, there was little sign of rebellion in the streets. No rioting citizenry to bring down the might of their oppressors, and Tyreta began to think something had gone wrong.

"Nothing's happening," she said, unable to take her eyes off the Mount, at any moment expecting the Archlegate to ride forth at the head of his Drakes and quell any dissent.

"Patience, Hawkspur," Olstrum replied for the second time.

Despite his assurance she wasn't convinced. This hadn't been the plan. There was supposed to be an uprising, but despite those fires and that distant shouting, this was most definitely not it.

"You'd better not still be playing both sides," she said, this time louder.

The wry expression on Olstrum's face never wavered. "My side was never in question. Now I know they are safe, I will keep to my word. Have no fear on that."

He sounded convincing enough. But then he always did, and still nothing was happening.

"Are you sure you told them—"

This time Olstrum raised a hand to silence her. "Patience, I said."

Tyreta felt her jaw begin to ache as she ground her back teeth. She could taste saliva filling her mouth in anticipation of the hunt. Patience had never been one of her virtues. Neither had trust, but she would just have to get used to it. What other choice—

A bell, all too near, pealing out a monotonous chime.

Another quickly answering it with a different timbre.

One more, to serenade the city with its reprise.

She glanced toward Olstrum, and this time his wry grin was gone. Now he was beaming with delight like a child at the fest. Damn that sly dog.

A glint from above. A distant spark catching her gaze and forcing her to look up. Light spread in the night sky, a channel of flame growing to an inferno in the shape of a giant halo as the skyway ignited above their heads, encircling the city in fire.

"Damn it," she breathed. "That is..."

"Just the start," Olstrum finished, his face lit up by the conflagration.

The shouting grew louder, getting closer. Screams joined with that noise, as more fires burned. Light and sound spreading through the city in a storm of hope and despair.

"How many people do you have?" she gasped, as more and more fires took, and the faint voices rose to a bellow, a chorus, a whole orchestra.

"I told you, I have contacted my entire network. Now we'll see how effective those years of work truly were, and if all that planning is enough to bring down the Ministry."

She turned away from the parapet, making her way toward the stairwell down into the building. "Then what are we waiting for?"

He followed her down the worn stairs and through the guts of the old building. On the bottom floor they were waiting, eyes keen, seething like lions in a cage. Tyreta had seen the Titanguard up close before in their armour of office, and they were truly a sight to behold. But she had never seen them ready for war before. Never seen them resemble such mighty statues of steel and iron, with their hydraulics whirring, pyrestones humming, gripping shield and lance in readiness for battle.

Cullum was the only one without his helm, his eyes greeting her with keen anticipation. He looked like a giant, capable of smashing down a mountain if he had to.

"It's started," she told him, as if he hadn't already heard.

"Then let us finish it," he replied, donning his great helm, its red plume catching the lantern light.

Olstrum was already unbolting the door, swinging it wide before leading them out onto the street. It was a brave gesture for such a little man, as though he suddenly had something to prove, but Tyreta guessed he had much to make amends for.

The clank of steel-shod boots echoed off the paving slabs as she followed the Titanguard out. So much for a stealthy approach, but then the Titanguard were not built for subterfuge. They were defenders of the Archwind throne, and the emperor's hand of doom. They would smash their way to vengeance, not creep after it through the shadows.

Smoke was already filling the street, as shouts echoed from every alleyway. The Mount was only a hundred yards away, and as they approached Tyreta expected its vast doors to open at any moment, for Drakes to pour out and offer them some resistance. Instead, the way was clear, and with every step Tyreta felt the excitement grow, the anticipation making every hair on her body stand rigid.

She could hold herself back no longer, striking ahead and lunging for the ornate door. Gripping the iron rings, she pulled, almost desperate to tear it open, to take on anyone in her way, but it was locked fast.

"Stand aside," ordered Cullum, voice resounding within his helm as he strode forward, raising his iron lance and flicking the trigger that activated its pyrestone mechanism. The blade hummed in response...

"Wait." Olstrum barred his path as blue light flared from the weapon.

He looked so tiny beside Cullum's towering frame, but the Titanguard halted in his tracks before slowly lowering his lance, the static dancing along its blade winking to nothing.

Olstrum fished in his waistcoat pocket, plucking out a ring with three keys upon it. There were three tiny keyholes, set within the door's intricately gilded centrepiece, that Tyreta hadn't even noticed. With nimble fingers, Olstrum placed the keys within the locks, turning them one after the other to the clicking sound of consecutive bolts. Then, with the slightest push, the door swung inward.

He stood back, allowing them to enter, and Cullum shoved his way through, the door swinging wider as he was followed by the rest of the heavily armoured warriors. Before she could follow them, Olstrum offered her a solemn nod. He wasn't coming with them, but then what use would he have been anyway? Tyreta nodded back, quelling the strange feeling that this was the last time she would ever see him, before following the others inside.

Holding her breath, she expected to be greeted by rank upon rank of dragon knights. There was no one inside. Altars stood forgotten, strewn with extinguished candles, strands of wax running down to pool on the unpolished floor. Religious trinkets lay scattered and abandoned by their celebrant owners, as the ancient statues of dragon gods leered down at them.

Tyreta strained her senses, trying to discern if anyone was waiting for them in the dark, but there was nothing. Not even the faintest buzz of a pyrestone. For all intents, this huge temple to the Great Wyrms had been left to the looters.

Unperturbed, Cullum led them deeper. As she followed, in the shadow of those ferocious effigies of marble and granite, her unease grew. Tyreta had come here as a child—for her grandfather's funeral, her uncle's investiture as emperor—and she had thought it an imposing place then. She had always been irreligious, even as a child, but her fear of those dragons had been very real, and it made her hate this place even more.

"Where is everyone?" one of the Titanguard asked, his voice muffled within his helm.

"The upper chambers," Tyreta replied. "Sanctan has to be there. He will have seen the fires. Heard the riot. He will know someone is coming for him."

"He won't know who though," Cullum said, increasing his stride across the smooth floor.

There was a vast curving staircase at the other side of the main chapel, and they hurried toward it. All the while Tyreta felt on edge, peering into the shadows, ears pricked for any sound, but there was still nothing. No legates scurrying in the dark. No Drakes lying in wait to pounce. This all stunk of a trap, and the farther they ventured into this dragon's lair, the worse that smell got.

"Something's not right," she said, stopping when they reached the top of the stairs. "This is too easy. We're walking into danger, I can feel it."

Cullum turned his helmed head toward her. "No. We are not the ones who should be afraid. Sanctan is here somewhere. I know it."

He led his men on, none of them offering her a second glance as they filed past. She should have turned back, should have fled this evil place, but there was no running away now.

The Titanguard led her onward, across a hallway that funnelled into a long expanse of corridor. Tapestries lined the walls, torches illuminating them for fifty yards or more, but Tyreta barely noticed the decoration. Her eyes focused immediately on the little girl sitting in the middle of that hallway, with her back to the wall.

"What is this?" one of the Titanguard growled, stopping in his tracks. Even Cullum seemed unsure of what to do.

The girl was reading by the light of a candle, the book she held almost too big to balance on her lap. Tyreta made her way closer before kneeling by the girl's side.

"Hello," she said, trying to sound as kind as she could manage, despite her instincts screaming at her that this was some kind of ruse.

"Hello," the little girl replied, eyes still fixed on the pages of that book.

"Are you alone? Do you know where everyone's gone?"

She shrugged her slight shoulders. "Father just told me to wait here."

Father? She had to be talking about Sanctan. Tyreta had heard the rumours; Maronne had mentioned talk of him siring a bastard. That the girl had been kidnapped. That the Archlegate had set his dogs on the Burrows to get her back and they'd left half a dozen corpses in their wake.

"Your...father?" The little girl nodded, and Tyreta recognised something familiar to those eyes of hers. "What's your name?"

She looked up from her book, pale face lit up by the candlelight. "Grace."

"Leave her," Cullum said. "We have a job to do. We don't have time—"

"We can't just leave her here," Tyreta said, eyes fixed on that pale little girl. "What if the mob comes to ransack the Mount. What then?" She reached her arms out to the girl. "You should come with me."

Tyreta lifted her off the floor before she could argue, the huge book sliding off her lap. The girl weighed almost nothing as she sat on Tyreta's hip.

"My book," Grace said, as though it were the only toy she had ever owned and she was bereft at the thought of leaving it behind.

Tyreta glanced down. The book was lying face up, and she recognised the arcane script across the cover—the Draconate Prophesies.

"You can leave that thing," she said, turning her back on that cursed tome. "It's not worth reading anyway."

Cullum was already leading the rest of the Titanguard further along the corridor, just as Tyreta sensed someone behind her. Before she could turn a voice called out, "Grace?"

A tall figure lurked in the shadows of the corridor. Tyreta couldn't quite see his features, but she recognised that voice. It froze her to the spot, made her almost tremble with the urge to attack. Here she was, holding a child, and all she wanted to do was fling herself along the corridor and rip that man's throat out.

Lorens was smiling as he stepped into the torchlight. The first thing Tyreta noticed was the stump of his right hand, the one her mother had hacked off. It did little to quell the fire within her. How could she feel sorry for this bastard, the man who had sunk so low as to betray his own father? To turn his back on his family in favour of his misplaced faith.

"You!" Cullum barked on seeing the man who had betrayed his master. The boy who had brought down an empire, and his emperor with it.

"Wait!" Tyreta cried, but the Titanguard were already moving, already charging at what must have been bait for a trap.

Pistons hissed as their armour responded, powering them forward. Pyrestones ignited, lances coming alive with blue flame, smoke belching from outlet vents. The corridor trembled beneath their tread as they sprinted at the object of their ire, but Lorens showed no fear. He simply stood, waiting for them to fall upon him.

Tyreta gripped the child tighter, bracing herself for the inevitable violence, but instead there came an ominous grating sound, a clanking of chains, a clicking of cogs. Before the Titanguard could reach Lorens, a solid iron grate slammed down to bar their way forward.

Cullum halted in his tracks, as did the rest. Before they could think to retreat, another iron grille slammed down behind, caging them in that granite corridor like animals in a pen. Cullum snarled in rage as he struck at the bars with his lance. Sparks flew but the grille held. Beyond them, Tyreta could see Lorens had already disappeared.

"Get us out," one of the Titanguard demanded of her, from the other side of his cage. "There must be a counter-lever. Some mechanism that opens this." He slammed a fist on the bars.

She nodded, still holding tight to Grace as she made her way back down the corridor, seeing an adjoining chamber. As she passed beneath the arch and into that room, she was overwhelmed by a sense of dread, but it was too late. Tyreta knew she was already surrounded.

Moonlight lit the huge chamber through a vast glass ceiling. At its centre, Sanctan Egelrath was flanked by his Drakes, each one with sword in hand, silent as stone. At the edge of the chamber, shrouded in shadow, she could also see there was a single insignificant legate, cowering in the dark, not even trying to hide the fact that he was terrified.

"Greetings, cousin." Sanctan beamed, as though she'd just arrived for dinner. "I see you've met Grace."

Yes, now she saw him next to that girl the resemblance was unmistakable. She was his daughter beyond any doubt.

"Don't come near me," Tyreta spat, gripping Grace tighter. "I mean it."

Sanctan's smile faded as he looked suddenly disappointed. "Come now, Tyreta. Do you honestly think I'd believe you capable of hurting a child? That is really not your style."

Of course he was right, and damn him for knowing it. "I guess that's the difference between us."

A look of hurt, feigned no doubt, as he gestured to his cowering legate. "Willet, if you would."

Despite his obvious fear, the legate moved closer, holding out his arms to take the girl. It would have been so easy for Tyreta to strike. To kill that legate and hold on to her only bargaining chip, but what then? She'd have killed a harmless priest, and Sanctan would still have her trapped like a rabbit in a snare.

Willet took Grace in his arms and retreated a safe distance, as the Drakes moved to surround her. In the distance she could still hear the Titanguard raging, slamming their weapons against the iron bars that caged them.

"Are you impressed with my new contingencies?" Sanctan asked. "I had those gates fitted after the storming of Archwind Palace. Just on the off chance something similar happened here. I guessed that the Mount would become the target of rebels should things go wrong. Still, I didn't anticipate you would manage to gain entry so easily. I'm guessing you had help. Olstrum, by any chance?'

Tyreta said nothing, but she felt some kind of relief knowing that Olstrum hadn't been a part of this trap.

"Yes," Sanctan continued. "I knew he would turn his back on me eventually."

"You took his wife," she snarled, unable to control herself any longer, feeling that animal coming to the fore. "His children. Did you think that would make him loyal to you?"

Another shit-eating smile on that shit-eating face of his. "Of course not. I thought it would make him obedient. But every cur will turn on you in the end. Especially if you spare the lash once too often."

"So you've finished using him, do you expect to use me now? Think my mother will surrender to you because you've got her daughter? I have news—someone tried that before and it didn't work out so well. And if you think you can take me alive, think again."

Sanctan looked disappointed in her. "Oh, I think we're past all that. Can you hear it?" He gestured toward the open archway behind him that looked out onto the city, the sounds of burgeoning violence drifting in on the night air. "The people have risen. Only chaos reigns now. All we have left is to fight to the last."

"Don't make me laugh, Sanctan. You think I believe you'll sacrifice yourself for anything?"

His smile faded, eyes becoming two hollow pits of scorn. "You have no idea what I'm willing to sacrifice. What I'm willing to burn down to see the Draconate reborn." He spoke the last word with relish as his eyes flitted to the little girl in that legate's arms.

Before Tyreta could think more on the implications of that, the Drakes took a step closer, that armoured wall closing in around her. There was no way out. No amount of talking that would see her freed of this. Only violence.

Her instincts were already taking over, vision sharpening along with the claws at her fingertips. Saliva filled her mouth, but she pushed down the animal within, waiting for her moment.

"You're mad," she snarled.

Sanctan shrugged as though it was obvious. "Mad? Despite appearances, Tyreta, I am practically incensed. But not as incensed as your mother will be when I launch your severed head from the walls of the Anvil."

This was it. No more time for pointless barbs. It was time to fight, and her body knew it—every muscle tensing, claws itching to rend and tear.

Before she could decide which armoured knight to strike first, she heard a howl from beyond the chamber, as though the sky itself were raging. Then the sound of fluttering wings, all too close. One of the Drakes turned his helmed head toward the open archway in time to a shrill squawk.

Sitting on the sill of that open window was a little black bird.

# FULREN

The ark cruised above the burning city, above the fires and the screams, but all he could focus on was the power emanating from belowdecks. That demon groaned in protest, held fast by the arcanist thralls standing just a few feet away from Fulren. He remembered the first time he had experienced this, remembered how appalled he had been at the treatment of those condemned prisoners. Now that his necroglyph allowed him to sense the creature they controlled, it was even more horrifying, but he could not let it unman him. There was a job at hand, and he could not be swayed from his purpose.

The airship dropped down toward the rooftops, through the burning halo of the skyway, and he felt the sudden intensity of the heat. Through the flames he focused on the Mount, squatting amid the streets of the Anvil, looking like the only place that wasn't on fire.

"What a sight to see!" Wenis bellowed above the howl of the wind and the crackle of flames. She was staring down with a joyous expression, loving every second.

"There." Fulren pointed toward the Mount, desperate for her to focus on the task at hand. "Get us closer."

"All right, all right. Must you ruin my enjoyment of everything?'

Before he could chide her further, she stood stock still, arms by her side, and began to concentrate. The green glow of her necroglyphs stood out stark against the dark night as her eyes rolled back, turning black as jet.

The airship began to bank, listing in the sky as that demon within growled its protest. The Mount loomed larger below, its five dragon spires leering at them, as though they might spring to life and defend the place with rending claw and fiery breath.

Through the glyphsight of his helm, Fulren could see every facet of the building stand out starkly, and he quickly scanned it for signs of life. Through a huge upper window set between the spires he could see perhaps a dozen figures appearing like yellow silhouettes within the vast chamber. Perhaps Sanctan and his Drakes, perhaps not. There was only one way to find out.

As the ark came to a stop twenty feet above it, Fulren climbed up onto the gunwale, gripping his sword tight. "Don't go anywhere."

The black film faded from Wenis's eyes. "I'll be waiting, don't worry."

She looked unusually concerned, but he tried not to think on that as he concentrated, filling the air around him with the dark power he had so recently learned to harness. Instantly the sky began to fill with noise as a host of crows fluttered from the surrounding rooftops, wheeling and cawing their approval like fiendish heralds.

As they filled the sky in a black cloud, he leapt from the airship, those birds surrounding him in a flock, swooping down with him as his metal legs smashed into the glass rooftop. The window shattered beneath him, the sound like a knell as he dropped into the chamber below. Despite the disorientation, he landed deftly, his legs adjusting automatically to cushion his fall, his sword flashing to life with a hum and a spark of flame.

The men within staggered back as he landed among them, Drakes, fully armoured but stunned by his sudden arrival. They paused for a moment, unsure what to do and giving Fulren time to scan the room. Before any of them could move to stop him, he recognised the target of his ire, Sanctan, cowering at the far side of the chamber.

And at the other side... Tyreta?

Through his glyphsight he could see her aura was furious; a red flurry of rage surrounded by twisting spinning motes of blue and green.

"Kill the beast," a voice resounded from nearby.

Fulren fuelled his blade, its song rising from hum to howl and igniting with fire. He swung it in a blazing arc, the first Drake's sword deflected with ease, but there was already another swinging at him. Ducking the blow, he knew this fight would be harder than before. These were no mere Armiger troopers, they were warriors born.

Another strike of a sword he anticipated easily. Time seemed to slow as Fulren ducked the blade, his legs moving with grace as he slipped beneath its sweeping arc. But too fast.

A shield, solid as a stone wall, smashed into his shoulder, the clank deafening as it struck the metal of his arm. He stumbled away, scuttling across the hardwood floor, legs gripping tight to a stone pillar before another sword swung at him. Pushing off against the stone, he hurtled through the air, spinning as he went, his own fiery blade slashing angrily and clanging off a shield, sending the Drake staggering back.

His steel arm rose on instinct to parry another sword, the jolt of it barely registering. The pyrestone blade swept about him in a flurry and he surrounded himself with roaring flame and sparking light, forcing the Drakes to back away. At the same time Fulren scanned the chamber, searching out his target. Before he could spot Sanctan, the Drakes rallied.

In they came again, ruthless, fearless despite his appearance and the ferocity of his attacks. Their rage bore down on him, those knights unrelenting in their zeal to defend their Archlegate.

"Get him to safety!" one of them roared, before charging in with abandon.

Desperation roiled up in Fulren's gut as he realised Sanctan was about to escape. His necroglyph seared as he fuelled the pyrestones in his limbs and blade and he swept the weapon left to right, sword smashing against both shield and amour. His leg shot up, talon foot slamming into a breastplate and sending the Drake flying like a rag doll across the room.

No time to think as one more Drake charged, sword raised high. Fulren caught the steel in his clawed hand and wrenched it free of the knight's grip. Then he snatched the lip of the Drake's shield, bending the metal, flinging that aside before plunging his flaming blade deep through the man's breastplate.

The Drake fell as Fulren's ire rose. He was enrapt in the slaughter now, fuelled by righteous vengeance, and he spun, ready to face the next armoured behemoth. But he was met by no enemy.

It was just a girl, eyes staring at him in terror as she was held tight in the arms of a skittish priest.

Fulren forced himself to stop. Feeling his urge to kill overwhelming his senses, but he would not do it. He was in control, not the beast inside.

His helm was struck a heavy blow—noise resounding in his skull as his teeth gnashed. In that instant he lost all connection to his metal limbs, to the necroglyph that powered them, that gave him succour, and he went sprawling. Instantly he was scrabbling to his feet, but his glyphsight was fractured, the world around him no longer visible with any clarity.

His enemies were running, he could see that much. Rushing through a distant arch as he staggered after them, but it was no good. His legs felt alien to him now. Left arm so heavy, hanging limp from his shoulder. Sword extinguished in his hand.

Sanctan was gone. Even the frightened priest had followed those Drakes with the girl in his arms.

"Wait!" a voice called after them.

A voice he recognised, though it sounded dull through the heavy helm on his head. Lorens, his cousin. But what was he doing here?

Fulren shook his head, desperate to restore his wits. Everything around him appeared cracked and broken, as though he were looking through a shattered lens. His legs responded to his will, but only sluggishly. And through his impaired vision he realised with dread that one Drake remained.

The knight advanced, gripping his sword in both hands, determined to defend the way as his Archlegate fled. Fulren desperately tried to tap the necroglyph, to ignite his blade once more, but that fire had been extinguished. He was all but defenceless as the Drake bore down.

A snarl of feral rage before an inhuman beast leapt from the shadow. It fell upon the Drake, who grunted, struggling as this animal began to attack with all the ferocity of a wounded lion. Claws tore at his armour, lashing great rents in the steel. He tried to swing his sword, but the beast grabbed his arm in a clawed hand, and Fulren winced at the sound of snapping bone.

Fulren realised he was watching Tyreta take on that mighty warrior, but within her burned a power brighter than any Fulren had ever seen. One that filled him with a dread he had never felt, not even in the arena of Nyrakkis, nor the demonic dreamscape of his mind.

She drove a fist into the Drake's helm, the dull thud sickening as steel dented and blood splashed from the visor. He fell back, toppling like a statue to hit the wooden floor with a resounding clang.

Tyreta stood over the body, heaving in breath. She turned to regard Fulren, those eyes glaring like a jungle beast that had seen a man for the first time, unsure of who was hunter and hunted.

Then she forgot him, head turning to glare across the chamber. To where Lorens had fled through an archway. Fulren opened his mouth to call her name, but she was already loping away in pursuit of new prey.

He was left alone, shaking, confused. The sword began to feel lighter in his grip as he slowly regained his senses, but nausea infested him to his core, and it was all he could do to quell the vomit rising from his gut. Fulren had come to kill Sanctan, but he was gone. Now all he felt was weak. All he had left was escape.

Looking up through the smashed window, he was unable to see the ark against the night sky. Rather than panic, instinct took over and as his senses gradually cleared, his metal limbs clawing at a nearby pillar. The granite crunched beneath the talons of his feet and he crawled up with the agility of a spider, toward the open air above. Gripping tight to his sword, he reached over the lip of the broken window frame and clambered onto the roof.

The sky was ablaze. Thick smoke filled the air as the burning halo of the skyway roared in flame. He glanced toward the edge of the rooftop, scanning the cityscape for any sign of the airship, but it was gone.

Fulren cursed, wondering what he might do, when suddenly he heard it—that inhuman wail, heralding the black ark as it rose into view beyond the lip of the Mount's rooftop. Wenis leaned across the gunwale, beckoning him toward her.

"Come on!" she screamed, but he could hardly hear above the din of the streets, the tolling of bells, the crackle of fire, all assaulting his senses.

Still in a daze, he loped across the roof, hearing the panes of glass crack beneath the steel of his feet. His pace increased, legs propelling him faster, as he ran like a beast toward the roof's edge.

He leapt, claw reaching out and barely managing to grasp the gunwale of the airship as it continued its rise. Wenis grabbed him, dragging him over the edge where he landed in a heap on the deck.

"Are you all right?" she shouted as she helped him up. "Is the deed done?"

Fulren pulled off his helm, heaving in a breath of cloying smoky air, before shaking his head. "Sanctan is gone. He escaped. Just... let's get out of here."

In that moment he remembered Tyreta, still within the Mount. The urge to stay and rescue her was overwhelming, until he remembered what she had become right in front of his eyes. His sister was no longer a feckless girl. She was fearsome, a beast of the night. And perhaps his sister no longer. Still, she was his kin and he had to do...

The ark lurched as something thudded against the hull. Before he could even wonder what had struck them, an explosion tore through the deck, sending shards of wood and iron into the sky. The airship listed dangerously, and Fulren braced himself on steel legs, grasping Wenis before she fell.

Half the forecastle had been blown away by some artificer's device launched at them from the ground. As he watched, another lump of winking metal zipped by before exploding, sending light and heat fizzing into the night.

"We have to go!" Wenis cried.

Even as she said it, the ark was swerving toward the east, headed toward the relative safety of the city wall. Fulren's eyes were drawn to the arcanists who remained standing on the deck, already shivering and convulsing from the effort of keeping them airborne.

The ark continued to cruise above the rooftops, but they were losing altitude, that explosion hampering the ship's performance. Before Fulren could wonder what to do, another missile arced over them, and he ducked before it detonated all too close. When he turned his head he could see figures, indistinct upon a nearby rooftop. Armigers, desperately defending their city from the Maladoran demons sent to plague them. Between them they frantically loaded a mortar, preparing to lob another volley in the ark's direction.

But they weren't alone. Through the noise and smoke Fulren heard the distant clack of splintbows being primed, saw the outline of half a dozen troopers aiming their way.

"Get down!" he shouted.

A volley of bolts ripped across the deck. Fulren watched helplessly as they tore into the half dozen arcanists, who fell one after the other, until only a single one remained. He was tall, black eyes staring at the sky. In his side was a splintbolt, blood seeping out in rivulets, but somehow he remained standing.

"Can you still get us out of here?" Fulren asked.

Wenis stared at the corpses of those condemned thralls. "With no more arcanists I cannot control the demon within the vessel's engine."

They were losing altitude fast now, that lone arcanist trembling more violently with each passing second.

"Maybe... maybe I can," Fulren said, not waiting for Wenis to offer an opinion.

He rushed to the open stairwell that led into the bowels of the ship and clambered down to the bottom deck and the claustrophobic chamber that held that groaning sarcophagus. It was so hot, so oppressive that he paused, his determination almost giving out. But he could not hesitate now, there wasn't time.

Reaching out with his metal claw, he laid it upon the surface of that demon tomb. Immediately his necroglyph seared, pain coursing down his spine, into his skull, into his brain. His teeth gnashed as he resisted the agony, and when he forced open his eyes, he was no longer below the deck of the ark...

The temple was bleak. Ancient. One side of it had rotted away entirely, opened to the blasted landscape outside. Within was a stone altar intended for the most wicked purpose, its surface stained red. A grim place for grim deeds.

Its single inhabitant, the grimmest thing of all.

It leered at him from atop that altar. Teeth razor sharp, yellow maw of a head from which peered the tiniest black eyes. Horns drooped down past its prominent jaw as it crouched, long arms dangling almost to the ground, ending in chipped and broken claws.

*I wondered if you might come*, it said, mouth dripping with ichor, voice a mound of grit churning in a mill. *I could taste you.*

"Enough," Fulren said, striding closer to it on legs that were all too human. "You have to get us—"

*I spit on your demands, half-man. Release me and I will give you your life. That is the only deal. Your only bargain.*

Somehow the creature's grin widened, but Fulren felt nothing. No fear, no disgust. Only urgency.

"I told you, I don't have time."

He strode closer, moving faster on those human legs, and the demon's tiny eyes changed—the surety in them draining as Fulren raced toward the altar.

The demon reared, jaws wide, talons splayed as it prepared to rend him apart, but Fulren was the faster, the stronger. A fist to that creature's jaw and it fell. Another to smash its teeth. It slashed at his face, raking those nails across his flesh, but Fulren was impervious now. Supreme in his dominance of this creature in this place.

He grasped it by the throat, raising it high, hearing it croak in panic. Fulren's body was growing, swelling as his dominance swelled. This plane was nothing—a playground for him to hold sway over, along with everything that dwelled within.

"This is not your realm," Fulren growled, his voice inhuman. "I rule here."

The demon was mewling now, realising it was powerless against this interloper.

*Yes*, it managed to beg.

"Yes? Yes? Say it again. Say it like you mean it."

The thing let out a gurgle in its throat. A cowardly murmur as it wept in terror.

*Yes...my master...*

Fulren came to, reeling back from the sarcophagus, no longer feeling the intense heat. He could not resist a smile as he looked down on that dormant tomb. At the demon slaved to his will.

His stomach suddenly churned, reminding him that the ark was still losing altitude. He raced out of the engine room, back up the stairs and out onto the deck. Buildings loomed over them on both sides as they plummeted toward the street below. Wenis was standing at the centre of the iron sigil on deck, fists clenched, the glyphs on her arms raging bright. The last of the arcanists was lying prone at her feet, having succumbed to his wound.

She stared at him in panic. "I cannot do this alone."

"You can," he replied, already feeling that demon in his head. Knowing it would obey him in all things from now on.

Even as he spoke the ark juddered, prow rising. Fires raged about them, more bolts striking the hull, but it would not stop them.

He saw the sudden delight in Wenis's eyes as the airship responded to her will and gained altitude, rising ever higher to leave the rooftops far below them. As the fires continued to rage, the streets consumed by chaos, the airship soared over the city wall, leaving the clangour behind.

"I...I don't understand," Wenis said, grinning in relief. "We should be in a thousand pieces. What did you do?"

Fulren shrugged. "I don't really know."

But he did know. He had slaved a demon to his will. Made no bargain, no foul pact. Merely seized the thing and made it his tool. He just didn't want to admit it.

# CONALL

The main gate of the Anvil was less than fifty yards away. Atop it he could see the defenders watching, as though they had no idea what to do next. They weren't the only ones.

Conall was flanked on both sides by silent warriors, armour black as ebon, swords held straight before them, as though they stood in vigil for a dead king. For his part, Conall stood with his sword drawn by his side, trying to catch his breath in the cloying confines of the helm.

Not one of these knights had spoken a word to him so far, and yet here he was, ready to lead them. His mother had wanted this to be a shock attack, and he had volunteered to take command, but how was he to do that if they couldn't even communicate? Too late to ask now.

Noise bellowed from within the city. Shouts of panic and alarm and anger. Smoke billowed, and above it all the skyway burned in a bright ring. It looked magnificent. At least if he died it would be on an auspicious night. After so long thinking he would perish lost and alone in the Drift, he supposed this was at least a glorious way to die.

The nearby whirr and stomp of stormhulks rose above the din. No more time to ponder. Time to fight.

He vainly tried to catch his breath again, as he watched the stormhulks march past, advancing on the gates. In response, the defenders made a half-hearted attempt at repelling them and he could hear bolts tamping off those iron carapaces. It was followed by the blast of a longbarrel, its shot bouncing harmlessly off armour plate. Once the stormhulks were within range they unleashed their devastation.

Fire and hail assaulted the city, the iron of those huge gates bowing under the onslaught. It took less than a minute to reduce them to molten slag as a dozen war machines rained all their fury.

Conall hefted his sword as the gates began to collapse. When the first one had fallen he took a step forward, and in response the rest of the knights moved, their tread uniform, as mechanical as those stormhulks. Once the second gate fell, Conall ran.

The stormhulks lumbered aside as the ten dark-armoured knights charged at the breach they had made. The gap was on fire, their path into the city hidden behind smoke and flame, but still they ran. Conall tried to bite down the terror, the prospect of death all-consuming, as he sprinted toward the fray. All too late, he saw what awaited them.

Just beyond the threshold a rank of Armiger troopers stood, every one of them aiming a splintbow. He was only twenty yards from the gate, but he would never make it across that killing ground before he was spitted by a score of bolts.

Damn, he should have brought a shield!

His pace slowed, but it was too late to turn back now. Beside him, the knights of Malador slowed too, but they didn't halt, instead raising their left hands in unison, just as the shout went up for the troopers to loose.

A wave of nausea overwhelmed Conall as green miasma manifested in front of them. The volley soared from within the opening, bolts flitting through the air swift and deadly. As soon as they hit that green cloud all impetus was halted, and a hundred bolts fell to the ground, littering their path.

The knights advanced relentlessly toward the opening, and Conall marched with them despite the madness of it. He bit down the urge to charge, matching the pace of the dread knights, that green miasma still lingering in front of them. The defenders were firing at will now, the odd stray bolt puncturing the ground in front of them.

Beyond the flames burning at the breach, he could see the defenders still arrayed in a line. Conall gripped his sword tighter, as though it might help against the overwhelming odds, against the fire they were marching right into.

Still the knights did not stop, and as they reached the threshold those fires winnowed before them. More fell sorcery Conall could only be thankful for, but it wouldn't help against the army that was waiting for them. He held his breath as they strode through the fire, and he saw they were within ten yards of the enemy now—a phalanx of shields barring their path to the city. All that was left now was to get slaughtered.

"Charge!" he bellowed, but the knights ignored him.

Conall could barely catch his breath as they continued their slow march into the enemy's maw. Spears jutted from behind the wall of shields. Swords and axes by the dozen waiting to hack them down.

He could make out details now. Pennants held aloft with bear and griffin and crow. The dragon helm of a Drake towering over the rest. Revocater hauberks of red and yellow. They all melded into one, just as the nine knights struck.

It was a chorus as black swords smote those shields. Conall would have joined them, but he was too riven with fear. Too stunned by this madness to join in the fray.

It took the first blow to shock him from his daze as his pauldron rang to the sound of striking steel. His sword came up on instinct, batting a spear aside. That mix of faces and uniforms blurred into a mess as he swung his sword in response, feeling the hard impact in his hand as he struck steel plate. He was snarling—the only one making a noise, as the other knights fought in utter silence.

A roar of defiance came up from the defenders as they realised they were facing only ten men, but it didn't last. One of the Caste called upon his powers, bare hand held out to launch a gout of alchemical sorcery. A scream in reply as someone's face melted.

Conall tried to ignore the horror of it, but he could barely hold down the vomit rising in his throat. He yelled again, trying to instil as much courage as he could manage before launching himself at the line. One of the defenders, wearing a uniform he didn't recognise, screamed in panic, retreating back through the massed ranks.

Before he could feel any satisfaction at inflicting such terror, his helm clanged, struck by a stray missile. As he staggered, an armoured figure lurched at him from the defensive line, bear helm terrifyingly close as he raised an axe. Conall managed to parry, but the impetus knocked him back a step. Another swing of the axe, and he was forced to duck.

This was madness. All of it. He should never have volunteered for this. He was just trying to prove himself, when there was nothing to fucking prove. He'd die here and all because of his pride and—

*I am here.*

Conall parried that axe again, desperate to ignore the whisper. He could not give in so easily. And not so soon.

*You are not alone, Conall.*

Beside him a black knight hacked down a Revocater, opening him from chest to guts. Another took a splintbolt to the pauldron, but ignored it, fighting on regardless.

*Do not be afraid.*

That axe scythed toward Conall again. This time when he brought his sword up to parry, the blow was so solid the weapon flew from his grip. He staggered back from another swing, glancing around for his fallen blade, but it was lost amid the insanity.

*Reach out. You are mighty, Conall, but I will make you mightier.*

He scrambled for a fallen shield, raising it up in time to catch yet another axe blow. It drove him back to his knee, and he braced himself as the shield was battered again and again.

*You will die here, Conall Hawkspur. Reach for me.*

"No!" he screamed.

But he knew it was the only way...

*The sky went black. Surrounding him was a tumult—an endless war as far as the eye could see. Gnashing teeth. Snarling faces, magnificent in their savagery. A sea of clamouring violence as winged leather flapped, sinew and muscle straining, claws rending and tearing, and he amid the fury.*

*It was terrifying to behold. But he was not terrified.*

*There was nothing for him to fear in this place.*

*He was the one to fear.*

*The shadow sword was in his hand, mist rising from it, wisps of vapour contorting with the faces of the slain. Yearning for the next soul to take.*

*Across the battlefield he could see the battle raging within the shadow of four vast ziggurats. Temples to living gods. And from atop each of those towering monoliths they watched. Witnessing the carnage they had wrought with their eternal feuding.*

*One of them he recognised immediately—Senmonthis—that elongated jaw, that towering frame, those horns, wings... an eyeless face witnessing everything with glee.*

*She inspired such hate within him. Now would be his time for vengeance.*

*The sword growled as he swung, hacking through demon flesh, cutting a swath. They fled before him, scrambling aside to offer a path to that ziggurat as the violence escalated around him. Blades rang off ebon armour. Fire belched, bathing him in its light and scorching heat, but he could barely feel it.*

*His sword scythed in every direction, thirsting, claiming, feeding, and with every demon whose soul he took, its blackened flesh turned molten and filled the sky with cloying smoke.*

*The stair to the summit of the tower was guarded by hulking brutes, but they offered little resistance. He stalked ever upward, sword singing a tune to which he danced and wheeled. It claimed the spirit of every leering beast that stood in his path, and he was all the more joyous for their suffering.*

*When he reached the summit, she was waiting for him. Senmonthis was bedecked in chains, that grinning horned head made all the more hideous with its lack of eyes.*

*"Do you see me?" he asked, in no mood for this moment to be wasted. He wanted her to know it was him. To know fear in this final moment.*

*The grin widened on that monster's face. "I see you, Knight of the Dusk. Death Caller. Seeker of Souls."*

*He revelled in every name. "Then you know why I have come."*

*"You have come to devour." Senmonthis relished every word, taking as much pleasure in the saying of it as he did in the hearing.*

*Before he could advance, she stretched out her upper limbs, arms elongating, bone cracking as barbed whips extruded from those wrists. They lashed out, sparking off the stone at her feet. Before he could react, one of them slashed at his arm, leaving a rent in his armour.*

*Pain. For the first time in an age. Exquisite and maddening at the same time.*

*The whips lashed again, this time grasping his free arm and yanking him closer. Her breath was fetid, horned head so close, but he did not balk. The shadow sword swung, and he lopped off that writhing appendage, which fell to the ground, spilling ichor that fizzed and bubbled on the stone.*

*Before Senmonthis could cry out in agony, the sword struck again, sliding deep into the monster's gut, seeking, probing as it sheared through black organs. The Scion fell to her knees, one tentacle of an arm hanging limp, face no longer grinning but mournful.*

*"See me," he spat, reaching up to remove his dark helm. That maw hung open as she recognised his face. "See what you wrought. See who I have become."*

*"No," Senmonthis mewled. "Not you. It cannot..."*

*"Yes," he replied, his eye glowing, casting the world in a red hue.*

*Then that maw twisted, a sneer of contempt. "You may have bested me, demon hunter, but you will never vanquish us all. You will die as surely as the night consumes the day."*

*He leaned closer. "A day you will never see."*

*The shadow sword sang as he pulled it free, then he swung with abandon to sever that bestial head. The body slumped, pumping more corrosive juices as he knelt and picked up the horned skull. Walking to the edge of the ziggurat, he raised it for all to see.*

*Far below, the battle subsided. Those warring demons paused in their violence to look upon him, victorious at the tower's summit.*

*He let out a howl, echoing across the field toward those three other towers and the beasts that waited atop them. A howl of triumph. A howl of challenge...*

Conall came back screaming.

The world solidified into gruesome clarity, as the stark haze of his dream faded in the daylight.

Silence, as his heart thundered.

Corpses were piled high beneath his feet, a space surrounding him as though none dared to challenge his might. From within his helm he could see the remaining defenders watching in shock. Some had already dropped their weapons in surrender. Others stumbled away in their eagerness to escape.

Had he done this?

Looking down, he saw the smoking blade in his grip. The blank-eyed bodies at his feet, armour slashed, flesh splayed open. A red river running.

That blood sparked a yearning. A need within him for more. The shadow blade wanted to strike, to claim more souls for its pile, and Conall could not resist its urging, no matter how much he tried to wrest control.

His mouth opened wide, issuing a bellow of feral rage. A challenge, just like the one in his dream.

In the distance he heard a horn sound. Remembering it was a signal he had been told to listen for, but he could not remember the reason.

No matter.

*Feed.*

A whisper, but deafening. Compelling. Commanding.

He took a step forward, searching out the next enemy, his next victim, but someone grasped him in an iron grip before he could hunt them down.

Conall tried to resist, to shake off that steely embrace, but before he could, another arm grasped him and he realised they were knights of the Caste. His allies. They dragged him back, away from the shadow of the gate, and as sunlight struck the sword in his hand it faded away like the dawn.

Still he screamed, still he raged in those terrified faces. Challenging the next enemy, demanding the next soul. Howling his defiance as the knights dragged him away from the devastation he had wrought, and back through the gate.

# FALL OF THE ANVIL

He stood amid the carnage, staring along with the rest of the stunned crowd. Sholto could barely believe what had just happened, but the evidence of it was lying there for all to see. Bodies, torn and bloody, scattered all about the gateway.

Someone was moaning for help. Another screaming. There had only been ten of them. Ten black-armoured devils from Nyrakkis. And now they were gone it was all he could do not to weep.

"What do we do now?" someone shouted.

It took him a moment to realise they were talking to him. But who else? He was the one in charge, after all.

Sholto looked about him, seeing the faces of other defenders glaring back. They were in as much shock as he was. He couldn't be the only one with authority here, could he? Where in the Lairs was the Corvus Battalion? Surely Marshal Tarjan should have been in command, he was the ranking officer.

"I don't know," was all Sholto could manage.

Through the collapsed gates he could see the knights retreating, still dragging that frenzied demon with them. Beyond them, a horde awaited. An army of dark knights, identically clad in their ebon armour. If only ten of them had managed to do this, what might a legion do?

"Where did they come from?" someone whispered.

Sholto turned, seeing an adjutant beside him. He hadn't had the opportunity to learn his name. Or anyone's name for that matter. He wasn't even supposed to be in command, but the battle at Alumford had seen him elevated quickly through the ranks. The storm of fire they had faced at the battle on Mordant River had whittled away his superiors until he found himself in this lofty, and altogether undeserved, position.

He tried to avoid looking out of that gate again, toward what waited for them. It would only have unmanned him yet further. How had the Guilds managed to strike a bargain with Malador? How had the Hawkspur woman gained such favour with those monsters?

"Your orders, Captain?" the adjutant said, this time with more urgency.

"I don't know," Sholto said, turning his attention to the task at hand. "Maybe...maybe help the wounded? Clear the breach of bodies?"

That was it. Focus on what he could control. Try to ignore what he couldn't.

The adjutant nodded, moving to help someone lying nearby. Sholto stumbled among the pile of corpses. He could hear someone whimpering for help from among the bodies, but could see no one left alive.

Just ten of them. Ten knights wielding dark sorcery to cut down a hundred. One of them with a demon weapon in his hand, howling as it cut them apart...

"Where...where do we take them?"

Sholto looked up to see two troopers carrying what looked like a corpse, before the wounded man they held writhed in pain.

"Get the casualties back beyond the second perimeter." They looked at him blankly and he gestured beyond the barricade. "That way, damn it."

His raised voice instilled some urgency. Around him the stunned defenders started to move at his order, but it didn't take long for him to realise this was a pointless escapade. They didn't need to clear the way, they needed a stronger barricade.

"Where are the militia? And the bloody Revocaters?" he demanded.

A trooper he barely recognised shook his head. "The militia have run, Captain."

Sholto saw a group of torn bodies wearing yellow. A red-plumed helmet lay abandoned nearby. That answered where the Revocaters were.

"We need more troopers. Someone needs to send word to Marshal Tarjan."

The adjutant looked at him wearily. "I've already sent someone."

"The Drakes then. We need them here. And find something to shore up that bastard gate."

The adjutant pointed weakly toward the blazing breach. "There's... nothing left to shore up."

Sholto squeezed his fists tight in frustration. "The Archlegate, for fuck's sake. Someone needs to tell him what is happening here. We need to parley with the Guilds before we're overrun."

"I sent a messenger when the stormhulks were advancing, Captain. He returned to say the Archlegate is not to be found."

"What do you mean, not to be found? Where has he gone?"

"No... I mean, he's at the Mount, but the doors are barred."

"But we need help!" Sholto screamed. "Someone to tell us what to do."

The adjutant's reserve abandoned him, and he grabbed Sholto by the arms. "There is no one."

A flash of inspiration hit Sholto like a bolt. "Rearden. Guildmaster Rearden is the next senior figure. He must be somewhere nearby."

The adjutant screwed up his face in confusion. "That paper shuffler? What in the Lairs will he—"

"Just send fucking word!" Sholto screamed in the man's face.

The adjutant took a step back, realising finally who was in command. With an obedient nod he turned on his heel and rushed to find Rearden.

More groans as the wounded were gradually shifted away from the gate. Sholto turned his back on the misery, trying to subdue the sick feeling rising from his gut. The flames still licked at the iron frame of the great gates, and he could see the waiting army beyond.

Looking up forlornly, he noticed that at least the fire consuming the halo of the skyway had gone out, leaving a black ring across the morning sky. Other fires still burned across the rooftops though. If he'd had any sense, Sholto would have run. His officers had gone. His troopers perished. All was lost.

Sholto swallowed down the bile, taking hold of his sword for all the strength it gave him. No, he would stay. After all, he was in command now, and should behave in a manner befitting an officer. But he shouldn't have been in charge. It shouldn't have been left up to him to inspire confidence in the face of such horror. That was the job of their Archlegate, but where was he now?

Willet struggled down the worn stone stairs in their wake. The tunnels beneath the Mount were a mystery to him, but he was quickly becoming acquainted with them as they twisted every which way.

The Drakes strode on ceaselessly, lighting his path with their torches as he struggled to keep up, the task made all the more difficult with that little girl in his arms. Grace was mercifully silent, holding on to him as though he might protect her from what lurked in the darkness. At least one of them had some faith in him.

When they eventually came out into the predawn air, he blinked against the sudden breeze, feeling relief wash over him. They were to the north of the city, and he could see smoke rising from beyond the wall. As his eyes adjusted to the gloom, he saw that a tiny landship terminal awaited them, an engine idling on its track.

"Is it ready?" Sanctan demanded as he strode toward it.

The driver stepped down from the engine, wringing his cap nervously. "Yes, Archlegate. All is prepared."

"Then let's be on our way, man."

The driver bowed, climbing back into the engine. Willet immediately heard the hum of pyrestone energy, the clack and grind and whirr of artifice as the machine began to idle. He had never liked these infernal engines, and had thought the last of them dismantled. Clearly Sanctan had saved one for his own use, to hasten his escape.

One of the Drakes opened the door to the single carriage coupled to that engine. Sanctan made his way toward it as though he were an honoured passenger on some pleasure trip.

"Where are we going?" Willet asked, gripping Grace tighter.

It was an impertinent question. Who was he to ask such a thing rather than blindly obey? But there was something about this that unnerved him even more than riots in the city. More than demons in the Drift.

"Ah, Legate Kinloth," Sanctan said, pausing at the step to the carriage. "I had quite forgotten you were here." He turned, stepping closer, that false smile making Willet's stomach churn. "Hand Grace over to me. Your work here is done."

Everything he had ever learned, ever seen, had taught him to obey his Archlegate without question. Not anymore. Now Willet found himself instilled with an odd sense of courage he had never known existed, and despite being surrounded by Knights of the Draconate, he chose this moment to defy his master.

"I asked where we are going." He stepped away, holding Grace protectively.

Every eye was on him, but he dug deep for his courage. This was an innocent child and somehow Willet knew she was in danger. His own life didn't matter any longer.

"Since you're so insistent, we are heading north." Sanctan gestured along the landship line as though it were obvious.

"To where?" Willet asked, shocked at his own stubbornness. "Wyrmhead? The Guilds will know that is where—"

"To Kalur's Fist, Legate Kinloth, since you are so determined to know. Grace is about to become part of something magnificent. She will become the key to our new beginning. Our apotheosis."

"In the mountains?" Willet asked. The notion seemed ridiculous.

As he spoke, Grace suddenly took an interest. "The mountains? We're going to the mountains?"

Sanctan smiled that benevolent smile. The one he had offered from the pulpit a thousand times when presenting himself as a father to all. "Yes, dear heart. We are going to the mountains."

"Why?" Willet asked, more forcefully than he could ever have imagined himself capable of.

A dark shadow crossed Sanctan's brow, the mask slipping. "You are trying my patience, Kinloth."

Behind him the keening sound of the engine increased, creating a sense of urgency and reminding them all what little time they had left. Willet would have run, but he was surrounded by a wall of steel.

"What is at Kalur's Fist?" he persisted.

Sanctan sighed. "You know very well what secret Kalur's Fist holds. You are familiar with the Draconate—"

"Prophesies, yes of course I am." It took only a moment's thought to remember the significance of the place. "The Fist is the final lair of the Great Wyrm Undometh."

Sanctan nodded as though Kinloth were a neophyte and he was pleased with his observance of scripture. "His resting place, yes. But the Great Wyrm of Vengeance will rise once more. The Anvil may be lost to us, but the Ministry is far from defeated."

Willet began to panic. Not for himself but for the innocent child in his arms. "But you can't—"

"Oh, I can," Sanctan spat, eyes suddenly aflame. "And I will."

Willet looked into that little girl's eyes, realising what Sanctan intended. Remembering the scripts and all they entailed—*Only with the greatest of sacrifices...*

"No," Willet said, wondering where he might go, what he might do. "I won't let you."

Sanctan sucked down his frustration. "You cannot stop me, Legate Kinloth."

A heavy hand clamped down on Willet's shoulder. It gripped him tight, and he almost cried out from the pain of it. Before he could move, another knight stepped forward, taking hold of Grace and wrenching her from his arms. He almost sobbed at how powerless he was to stop them, how worthless he truly was as her defender.

As the knights glared down at him, Grace was conveyed to the waiting arms of the Archlegate. The driver poked his head out of the engine, his impatience plain for all to see.

"We're ready to go."

Sanctan nodded to him, then turned back to Willet. "Such a shame you won't be joining us."

Strength had always eluded Willet. Courage and steel were far from his purview, but there was a first time for everything.

He wrenched his shoulder from the grip of the knight holding him, hearing the cloth of his cassock tear. Another knight placed a hand to the hilt of his blade, but Willet was already running, already fleeing for his life.

The shadows enveloped him as he stumbled toward the secret tunnel that led back to the Mount. He ran, even faster than he had that day in the Drift, leaving the little girl to her fate. Leaving himself with nothing but shame.

Running. It seemed that was all they'd done tonight. Set fires. Run. More fires. More running. At least Maronne wasn't alone in this madness.

There was a mob...no...a horde of them, torches held high as though hunting witches of old. Only now it was the priests who should fear, and the whole city was united in its defiance of them.

At her side was Colbert, his handsome face framed in the yellow light of the flames. Big Lena and bigger Torfin right behind, sweating from the exertion, but grinning all the same. Maronne had no idea where they were going, but it wouldn't be long before they found something else to burn. Another statue to topple. Another Ministry bastard to hang.

Torfin's pace increased, as though he could feel it too. His meaty fist gripped his torch as he took the lead, and Maronne struggled to keep up. She almost shouted at him to slow down, to leave something for the rest of them. When they turned the next corner she wished she had.

The first clap she recognised all too well. That chorus of noise as splintbolts whipped past her, riffling her hair as she stumbled to a stop. In front of her, Torfin fell, riddled with bolts, torch spilling from his grip.

A barricade blocked the road, behind it the telltale yellow of Revocater uniforms. More bodies fell, and the crowd around her faltered. A scream tore the air as the mob came to a stop. Suddenly all their zeal drained away. Just silence as they regarded dead friends, who seconds before had been filled with the vigour of life. The crowd were ready to retreat, to run away from these bastards who would happily see them crushed underfoot.

Maronne was having none of that.

"Stand your ground!" she howled, trying not to look at Torfin lying dead in the road. "This is where we show them who owns the streets."

The Revocaters were already reloading, and she could hear the clack as they slipped in fresh clips and cocked those weapons.

Maronne pulled her knife, raising it high, so the light of their torches glinted off the blade. "Follow me! Death to the Ministry!"

And she was running, not knowing if anyone would follow, gripping that knife tight for reassurance. She'd always had it—thirty years or more she'd wielded that blade in hands calloused by a thousand miles of yarn threaded on her loom. Now those hands would be used for murder.

Howls of fury assaulted her ears as she ran toward that barricade. The mob was with her and it made her heart soar, but only for a moment as she saw those Revocaters aiming again. Twenty feet, fifteen, ten—they wouldn't make it before…

The first splintbow fired, but the Revocater's aim was off. Seeing the crowd bearing down on their defences must have struck fear into those cowards, and a stream of bolts flew overhead as Maronne and her fellow rebels hit the barricade. The sound of it was deafening; the clash of boots against wood, the clatter of furniture and beams being torn down.

Another clap of fire, another whoosh of bolts past her head, and Maronne was again lucky not to die. Clambering over the wall, she saw a face staring at her. Young. Terrified. Her knife jabbed into his chest and he howled in pain, screeching like he'd stubbed a toe rather than been stabbed. It was the last thing she'd expected as he stumbled back, dropping his splintbow and reaching for the sword at his side.

It was bigger than her knife, all right. He would run her through before she could get close, but before he could, someone from the crowd bowled into him, knocking him to the ground.

They were swarming all over the barricade now. A chair smashed into the head of one Revocater. Someone shoved a burning torch into another's face, and this one howled like he meant it.

Maronne staggered down the other side of the defensive wall, looking for someone else to stab, but before she could find anyone her foot slipped on the loose planks. She went down as the crowd continued to swarm, stomping all over her. In the confusion she lost grip on her knife, on her torch, and covered her head as she was trampled into the dirt.

Someone else slipped nearby, falling right on top of her, and all of a sudden it was impossible to breathe. She was gonna suffocate here, killed by her own damned people after avoiding death at the hands of the Ministry for so long. Fuck her luck.

A hand grasped her shirt, dragging her clear, and she gasped, like she'd been plucked from a river by some divine hand. Big Lena looked down, blood spattering her face, shouting something Maronne couldn't quite hear.

As she slowly came to, taking in the scene around her, she realised they'd already won. Most of the Revocaters had fled, some still running away down the main promenade. Others were being kicked to snot, dragged along the ground pleading and wailing as they were beaten.

A rope had already been thrown over one of the torchposts and a man in a yellow uniform was being hauled up by his neck. The mob cheered at his misery, watching him dance till he could kick his legs no longer.

On top of the barricade a thin man in rags was dancing a jig with a Revocator helmet on, red plume swishing this way and that, as someone else held up a severed head like a trophy.

Maronne bent over, hands on her knees as she tried to gather her wits and her breath along with it. When she managed to suck in enough air to stop her head spinning she looked back at that barricade, even now being torn down. What had the Revocaters even been defending on this stretch of shitty road?

One glance south and she saw it. Towering over them, scroll sigil carved onto the side of the crumbling facade... the Corwen embassy.

"There could be more inside!" a man shouted, pointing at the building as though he'd just noticed it at the same time as Maronne. "Let's loot the place!"

"Wait!" she shouted.

The man's face screwed up in confusion. "What?"

She bent over, picking up a fallen torch before hefting it and flinging it through a lower window.

"Fucking burn it."

The man yelled his approval, and he was joined by more voices. Torches, burning planks, anything they could set aflame was hurled through the windows of that embassy, the place that had come to encapsulate their misery over the past months. Immediately the fires took, all those parchments and scrolls the Corwen Guild had spent so much time writing catching fire in no time. Flames began to flicker from the lower windows, licking up the white walls to turn them black, consuming that tower like a serpent eating its prey.

Everybody howled gleefully as they watched, but Maronne had to stifle her joy. There was something bitter to this. As though it was no longer about Ministry and Guild. This was about the people and their oppressors, no matter what form they took. It was about wresting back control for every person in Torwyn who'd ever been crushed under the heel of either of those bastard institutions.

The burning papers started to flutter free, raining cinders and ash on them like snow.

"Where now?" Colbert asked, his square-jawed face blackened by soot.

Maronne had no idea. Maybe the Mount? Maybe the Guildhall?

Before she could decide, the crowd was already moving. That mass of angry, joyous, violent city folk making their way down the street like a tidal wave.

Maronne let herself be swept along.

The whole place was burning. Cloying air threatening to seal his throat shut. Rearden had almost screamed himself hoarse commanding his actuaries to rescue what they could, but they would never save it all. This building had been so packed with ledgers and dockets the flames had taken quickly, and now he stood amid an inferno, listening to the distant screams, wondering how in the Lairs it had all come to this.

A timber cracked above his head, snapping him from his daze. Smoke surrounded him and he knew he had to run, but where? The stairs down to the entrance hall were ablaze. He could still hear the screams from below, but there was silence above. It was the only way.

Rearden clawed his way up the winding staircase, dragging his old bones along as quick as his creaky legs would allow. As he reached the top he heard a mournful wail calling out his name, begging for help.

"You'll have to help your damned self," he growled, cursing the nasal sound he now made after that bastard Drake had snapped his nose.

There was a single window in the upper chamber, and he surprised himself with his quick decisiveness—picking up a nearby chair to throw through the glass. Damn, it was heavy, and he let out an involuntary croak as he lifted it, putting all his strength into muscles too long left to atrophy.

A satisfying crash as the chair flew through the pane, heat blossoming as air rushed out of the opening, but he was already clambering through, ignoring the shards that cut his arms and legs, the blood smearing his hands as he gasped for air.

He almost collapsed onto the rooftiles but managed to stay standing on unsteady feet. Peering over the edge, he could see a crowd gathered below. That mob who had come with only murder in mind.

Rearden was suddenly conscious of the yellow robe that adorned him. It was tattered now, smoke-smudged and bloody, torn at hem and cuff, but it still marked him for who he was.

With surprising vigour, he ripped it off, casting it aside and standing half naked in nothing but his white undergarments. Then he gingerly made his way down the sloping roof and grasped the clay drainpipe. He held on with a clawlike grip as he slid down it, almost losing control, almost crying out in panic as he descended. As he passed a broken window, flame suddenly billowed out. He could feel the intense heat, hear someone shouting for help inside. Too late for them, but perhaps not for—

He lost his grip, hand slipping on the pipe, arms flailing, legs kicking as he plummeted. His stomach lurched before he hit the ground, and he yelped as he landed on his back.

Winded, he thought about trying to rise but reconsidered, fearing he had broken his back. There he lay in the backyard of the embassy amid a bed of flowers, a soft landing if ever there was one to be had. Surely it couldn't all end here.

As he began to move, realising he was more or less unhurt, it was all he could do not to laugh. Dragging himself to his feet, he looked down at himself, at his wrinkled flesh filthy from the grime and mud. He must have been a bloody sight, but at least he was alive.

Not for long if he didn't get a move on.

Rearden bolted for the back gate before pausing and listening for a moment. When he could hear no angry mob at the other side, he gently slid the bolt back, opening the gate a crack. There was no one to be seen in the back alley, and he slowly crept out of the yard as the embassy burned behind him.

Smoke marred his vision as he slunk along the alley, holding on to the wall for purchase. The end of the alleyway lay ahead, and he could see rioters rushing back and forth beyond. When he heard the sound of tramping feet he froze.

They were here. They had come for him. To drag him through the streets and lynch him in front of a baying mob.

Those footsteps drew closer, and Rearden could hear a huff of fevered breath, bracing himself before the inevitable blow to the back of his head...

A man rushed past. Pausing only for a moment to look Rearden up and down before bursting into laughter at his dishevelled appearance. Then, not giving him a second thought, the man ran on.

Rearden allowed himself a snigger at his good fortune. Perhaps he would get out of this in one piece after all.

Staggering on, he reached the end of the alleyway. The street beyond was in chaos, a barricade burning bright, and were those... corpses hanging from the torchposts?

He looked away, trying to ignore the carnage as he struck out, stumbling down the street, ignoring the rioters as they ran along beside him. If he could keep his head down, not make a fuss, not draw attention then he might just—

"You!" a voice called, all too close.

Rearden didn't wait, hoping beyond hope he was not the focus of that demand.

"I said, you. Stop!"

The voice was closer now. No doubt who they were talking to.

Rearden stumbled to a stop, holding his hands up in surrender. This was it... this was how it would end.

"I'm just a man," he croaked. "Just an innocent man."

"Rearden Corwen?"

Of course they knew who he was. Rearden was Guildmaster, after all. One of the most revered in all of Torwyn.

Slowly he looked up, unable to stop his hands shaking. Half a dozen Armiger troopers in dark Corvus uniforms were glaring at him through the smoke.

"Oh thank the fucking Wyrms," Rearden breathed. "Where in the Five Lairs is Marshal—"

As though he had conjured the man with fell sorcery, Tarjan appeared from the smog, marching with purpose. When he saw Rearden he stopped, but he looked far from pleased to see him. In fact there was a desperate edge to his expression.

"Rearden?" Tarjan looked him up and down. "What are you doing running around the city half-dressed. Are you trying to get killed?"

"Never mind what I look like," Rearden snapped. "What is going on here? Why haven't you ordered your men to quell this damned riot?"

Tarjan's shoulders slumped. "You haven't heard? The Anvil is lost, man. The Hawkspur woman has formed an alliance with Maladoran sorcerers. There's an army of the bastards at our gates."

Rearden could not believe his ears. Sanctan had assured him all would be well, but now he realised how stupid he'd been to trust that fanatic.

"But we—"

"Fuck *we*," Tarjan snarled, suddenly finding his mettle. "There is no *we*. I'm getting my battalion out of the city before the whole place is turned to ash." He took a step closer, almost threateningly. "I suggest you find somewhere safe to hide."

He turned, but Rearden snatched at his sleeve. "Wait. Take me with you."

Tarjan wrenched his arm free. "You're finished, Corwen. You started all this, remember? I doubt the Hawkspurs will look mercifully upon you when this is done. Or anyone with you." He turned to his troopers. "Move out."

Rearden watched helplessly as they hustled along the street and disappeared into the smoky haze. Until now he hadn't realised how truly powerless he was. How weak.

Nevertheless, he couldn't stand around all night waiting for the mob to string him up alongside those hapless Revocaters. So he began to move, at first slowly, directionless as though lost in a maze. Perhaps surrender was his best option. Find Rosomon Hawkspur and fall upon her mercy.

No, that was out of the question. Even if his pride could suffer that wound, it was doubtful she would offer clemency after all he had done. He had to escape the city. He just had to find a way to—

A hand grabbed his vest, tugging him through the cloying smoke. He panicked, holding up his hands, squeezing shut his eyes, thinking this time he was surely doomed.

"No, no, no," he sobbed.

"Guildmaster?"

Rearden opened one eye. A trooper of the Griffin Battalion stared back with a bewildered expression.

"Rearden Corwen?" the man asked. "I've been sent by Sergeant...Lieutenant...I mean Captain Sholto. You're needed at the southern gate."

Rearden shook his head in confusion. "What for?"

The trooper's look of confusion deepened. "To...take command."

The street was still filled with dark choking smog. Screams could be heard in the distance, fires licking the sky.

"Take command of what?" Rearden demanded.

The trooper shook his head in frustration. "Just come on."

He grabbed Rearden's arm tightly, dragging him away through the streets.

"We can't hold them much longer!" someone screamed.

Emblyn thought she recognised the voice, but wasn't quite sure of the man's name. Whoever it was, they were right. Their barricade stood firm for now, but all around them it looked as though the city was on fire. She could see all the way across those rooftops, every one of them smouldering or ablaze. It wouldn't be long before they were all consumed in the flames.

Even if the barricade in front of them held and they weren't burned alive, their position was vulnerable with so many other points if ingress, so many alleyways and passages for the rioters to come down. Emblyn was no Armiger marshal, only a senior celebrant of the Draconate Militia, but even she could tell that if the mob attacked from any direction but north they were finished.

Something smashed against the barricade. A clatter of wood and stone as missiles rained down around them.

"We have to retreat," another voice pleaded.

To her left, Constanz popped his head over the barricade, firing wildly with his splintbow. She'd told them to reserve their ammunition, but it looked like panic had taken over.

In reply to his wild volley, Constanz was hit in the head by something solid. It made a dull clank as it smashed into his skull, and he fell back screaming. Blood covered his face, but Emblyn just stared, as though she were watching everything through a distant lens.

Kristen raced forward, kneeling beside Constanz but not knowing what to do. Then he looked at her with terror in those doleful eyes. "We have to get out of—"

"We hold!" Emblyn bellowed, before he could finish. Before his desperation made her think twice about staying. Before it put enough fear in her to agree.

She suddenly remembered what she'd been told when ordained by the Archlegate himself. The newly formed militia would be the

Shield of the Wyrms. They would defend the Anvil and Torwyn to the last. Emblyn remembered how proud she had been. How eager to carry out that duty.

Glass shattered near her head, spattering her with foul-smelling spirit. No... oil.

One of her militiamen stared at her for a moment, his face dripping with it, before another crash, a spit of fire, and he went up in flames.

Screams, loud and shrill, and she could only watch as he ran, fell, floundered on the ground. One of the others tore off his cloak, wrapping it around the burning man, vainly trying to extinguish the fire, but it looked like it was already too late.

Emblyn turned back to the barricade, steeling herself with a brief prayer to Ammenodus before moving closer and daring a glance over the top. Through the haze she could see them not fifty feet away. That crowd of heretics just waiting to charge. They were building themselves up, growling and spitting, ready to attack again. This was it.

"Load up!" she shouted, scrambling back down from the barricade, and fumbling a clip into the stock of her splintbow with numb fingers.

The rest did as she ordered, all the zeal stripped from them, but at least they remained loyal. Obeying her orders... for now.

"On my signal. One volley."

Nods. Desperate eyes. Fear.

She paused, just as long as she dared, listening to the sound of tramping feet drawing nearer...

"Now!"

They all stood, aiming over the makeshift parapet, less than a dozen of them against the horde. The clack of their splintbows was deafening, sounding like a monotone chorus as she felt her weapon buck in her grip. The volley of bolts soared into the smog. Screams went up. Jeers. Shouts of hate. But the charge was halted.

Gradually the noise subsided as that choking cloud grew thicker. She squinted into the murk, expecting the mob to rally. As the grey haze was blown aside for a second by the breeze, she saw they had fled. At least for now.

Someone came running from the south. Emblyn's heart almost stopped, and she fumbled for another clip of bolts, before she recognised the black and grey uniform of the approaching militiaman.

"Message from the gate," the lad said, eyes wide, face filthy. He looked more urchin than soldier. "The Ministry has surrendered. It's over."

"What?" Emblyn spat.

"The Archlegate is gone," the boy said, and she couldn't tell if he was happy about it or just desperate. "The Guilds have breached the main gates. And they've brought a... Maladoran army. All is lost."

Yep, that was definitely desperation.

Emblyn cast an eye over the rest of her unit. They had looked fearful before, but now it seemed they were on the edge of panic. The prospect of a siege had filled them all with dread, but sorcerers? But surely not even the Guilds would side with those demon worshippers.

"We need confirmation," she said, trying hard not to believe it was true.

"We need to run," snapped Kristen, still kneeling over Constanz, who was lying still on the ground in a pool of blood. "We need to get out of the city before—"

"All right," Emblyn snapped, so tired of trying to hold everything together. Surely if the Archlegate was gone then all was lost. "Then maybe we can retreat to—"

"No."

That single word cut through the panic and tension in the air. All eyes turned toward the road behind them, and Emblyn saw an impossibly tall figure approaching through the fug—a woman in a slate grey cloak, steel plate beneath, blade in hand. Karina, a High Legate of Ammenodus Rex, come to save them all. Emblyn had met the woman once before, she had been present when the militia were first ordained. She had said the rites of conferment for them all, and here she was in their hour of need like a Wyrm-blessed saint to save the day.

"We will defend this channel," Karina continued. "The Archlegate is still with us. The Great Wyrms are watching."

The young lad who'd brought the message from the gate shook his head. "Fuck that. We can't stay here. We'll all be killed. I'm gone."

He turned, feet slipping on the greasy cobbles as he made to run. Casually, Karina plucked the splintbow from Emblyn's hand, raised it, fired. Three bolts struck the young lad in the back and he fell silently.

The rest of them looked on in horror as Karina handed the splintbow back.

"Now, on your feet. There is still much work to be done."

Emblyn looked down at the splintbow in her hands, the one that had just killed that boy. Then she saw the look on Karina's face—filled with confidence. Filled with faith.

"You heard the High Legate. On your feet. Check your clips. We're here for the duration."

As they responded to her command, Emblyn glanced back out across the barricade. There was movement through the wispy smoke once more. That crowd was gathering for another attack.

He fled through the mist. It stank, the acrid taste infesting his throat, his nostrils. Hard to breathe. Impossible to see.

There were other people within the murk, but he couldn't tell if they were friend or foe. It didn't matter. All Lorens could think about was escape, and there was no one to help him.

He couldn't see her. Couldn't hear a thing, but he knew she was coming. Whatever Tyreta had become, it was no longer human. She was a demon. The kind of creature the Archlegate had warned them about all along. One that was determined to claim his soul...

There, through the smoke, he saw something that looked like... salvation?

The river. Barges at the dock. Someone moving in the dark, loading those vessels with crates and barrels. As he staggered closer, he could barely quell his delight on seeing the welcome sight of Corvus troopers. Surely one of them would remember him from his time at Ravenscrag. Surely they would be able to stop her, or at the very least take him to safety.

"Help!" he called out as he stumbled toward them on trembling legs.

They stopped what they were doing, turning to see his pathetic figure through the haze. Silence as they looked upon him with curious eyes. Lorens recognised at least two of them, but damn him for his memory—he could recall no names.

"Lorens?" one of them said eventually.

"Yes," he replied, almost laughing in delight. "Yes, it's me. You remember, brother?"

The trooper looked at him sideways. "Yeah, I remember you. But do you remember me?"

Now there was a question. The face might have rung a bell, but then most of these troopers had the same grim look to them. Curse him for not taking the time to learn some names at Ravenscrag.

"No idea, have you?" the trooper said eventually.

"I do," Lorens said, a little too quickly. A little too desperately. "We drank together. We played cards, you and I, as we looked out over the edge of the world. Out onto the endless Drift."

Another of them slammed his crate down on the deck of the barge. "You haven't got a fucking clue who we are. We're nothing to you, Archwind, and we never were. So don't try and pretend we're friends now."

Something echoed in the distance. It might have been a cry of woe. Or it could have been a howl.

"Please... help me."

"Fuck off, Lorens," came the reply.

Anger welled within him. These damned troopers should know their place. The city might have fallen to shit, but he was still the favoured of the Archlegate.

"Where is the marshal? Where is Tarjan. I demand to speak with him. He will—"

Someone shoved him from behind. His legs were like jelly, betraying him on that dockside, and he went sprawling. To add insult he heard a couple of troopers laugh at his misery.

"I said fuck off, you clumsy bastard."

More laughing. More impotent rage. Another noise in the distance. This time a definite howl. And so much closer.

He scrambled to his feet, ignoring the jeering as he made his way back up from the riverside, squinting in the half light, willing his legs to keep moving.

The place was anarchy, mobs of people moving with little purpose. Every window smashed. Roads scattered with debris and bodies. At the end of one street he could just make out a crowd gathering with something akin to purpose. But were they loyal to the Ministry or the Guilds? Could he risk approaching? Asking for aid?

No, he just had to escape, find somewhere safe. But there was nowhere. All he could do was wander aimlessly until she found him. Until...

Lorens fell again. His knee hit the cobbles hard, scuffing his flesh and provoking a sob of pain. So desperate was he to protect the stump of his right hand that he landed heavily on the left. His palm slammed down on shattered glass and he whimpered as he was cut.

*No. Don't cry. Don't show weakness, for the first time in your miserable life. It's time to get up. Time to escape, to live, to prove you can do one damned thing right.*

He raised his hand, seeing a shard of glass sticking out of his flesh. Lorens grasped it in his teeth and pulled it from his palm, tasting blood on his lips. This was no good. He wouldn't last another hour if he didn't pull himself together. But where to go...?

The breeze blew a gap in the smoke, and he spied an alleyway. Somewhere to hide at least. Dragging himself up, he stumbled into the dark confines, half blind and maddened with fear. His fingers brushed the greasy walls as he tried to run, stumbling all the way until finally he all but fell from the other end of the alley.

Lorens came to a stop behind a barricade. A dozen or so militia were defending it, splintbows gripped tight. He realised these were his people, loyal to the Archlegate, and for the first time since he fled the Mount he thought he might live through the night after all.

At his approach, a couple of the militia looked over their shoulders, brows furrowing as they caught sight of his wretched form. A one-handed beggar wandering in the gloom.

As the rest shot their bows sporadically over the defences, Lorens saw a tall, cloaked figure standing in their midst. Her blonde hair cascaded over her grey-cloaked shoulders, and the steel armour beneath marked her as a High Legate of Ammenodus Rex.

He was truly saved.

"High Legate?" Lorens said, almost too meekly to be heard above the din.

She turned, looking him up and down with disdain.

"I am Lorens," he added quickly, desperate to be recognised. "Lorens Archwind."

That look of disdain did not waver. "I know who you are."

Despite her scornful expression, he let himself breathe a little easier. "I need help. There is a—"

She gestured toward the barricade. "Can't you see we have important business here?"

"You don't understand." He stepped forward, fighting the urge to kneel and grasp at the hem of her cloak. "You have to help me. Tyreta Hawkspur, my cousin. She is coming for me. She is—"

The High Legate slapped him across the cheek with her gauntleted hand. His ear rang, and he tasted blood in his mouth.

"Don't be such a coward. Only by grasping courage like a brand can we hope to defy the dark. Only then will the light of Ammenodus be cast upon us."

Lorens shook his head, trying to clear it. "But...you...don't understand. She has become an abomination."

A glimmer of doubt in the High Legate's stern gaze. She leaned closer. "Has she indeed? And what might she have done to make you think such a thing?" She leaned even closer. "Has she been treacherous? Committed an act of such monstrosity that she was turned away from the grace of the Wyrms? Perhaps she betrayed her sire?"

"What? What do you mean?"

But he knew what she meant. No, Tyreta had not betrayed her sire, but Lorens had. Lorens had abandoned his own father in favour of his faith, and it was clear this High Legate found it a monstrous act, despite his pious reasons.

Realising he would receive no help from her, Lorens took a stumbling step backwards as the High Legate turned her attention back to the barricade. The militia were still firing their splintbows across it, one of them doing his best to shove a rioting man back over the meagre defences with what looked like a broom.

Lorens turned, staggering on again, desperate to leave this

madness behind him. He kept running, terror rising with every step, until he heard the sound of the Whitespin rushing from up ahead.

The Bridge of Saints came into view, newly repaired, lined with freshly hewn statues of the Great Wyrms. And beyond it, bearing the symbols of the Draconate in place of the Guilds, stood Archwind Palace. His grandfather had built that edifice. It was where he had been raised as a child. Surely it would protect him now, as it had then.

Gripping his stump of a wrist close to his chest, Lorens ran across the bridge, desperate to make it home.

Rosomon sat atop her horse a quarter mile from the city. It was almost dawn, but the sky was lit up like a summer day by the fires that licked the air. Through the breach in the wall all she could see was yellow flame, all she could hear was the sound of a city dying.

"What do you think is happening in there?" Oleksig asked, eyes fixed dead ahead.

"Chaos," she replied.

"And was that your intention all along?"

She didn't have an answer for that. Her intention had been to take back the city. To try to do it with as little loss of innocent life as possible. It seemed she had failed in one of those.

Glancing to her left, through the gloom she could see those knights of the Caste standing silently. Amid them, Conall knelt, helm discarded, head bowed.

How she would have loved to climb down from her saddle and offer him some comfort. To tell him he had done well. That he was a hero. But Rosomon could never embarrass him in such a manner. When all this was over there'd be time enough for plaudits. For now, she still had a war to win.

A shout from somewhere among the ranks of warriors surrounding her. Movement at the gate. A contingent of Armiger troopers was marching from the city and toward them along that road. Among their ranks a pennant was held aloft, and as she squinted Rosomon could see it marked them as Griffin Battalion.

Ianto strode forward raising his arm and signalling for the front rank of the Guild army to be on guard. In response the stormhulks strode forward, weapon turrets aiming at the approaching troopers.

"Looks like they have an envoy with them," said Falko, craning his thick neck as he peered through the waxing dawn light.

Kassian shook his head. "Looks more like Rearden Corwen."

The contingent stopped fifty yards down the road. A lone figure struck out from their midst, and Rosomon could just see he was half-naked.

"Where are his clothes?" Oleksig wondered, as the sorry figure of Rearden Corwen approached.

He really was in his undergarments. Spindly legs carrying him toward them and gradually revealing more of his pathetic, filthy form with every step. Rosomon gritted her teeth, quelling her rising fury as he drew closer.

Rearden stopped ten yards away, looking up at her sheepishly.

"Rosomon," he croaked.

She thought about answering, but instead slid from her saddle and walked closer, gripping the Hawkspur sword for reassurance. She could smell the smoke stink of his flesh and stained underclothes. See how desperate he was about the eyes. It was all she could do not to spit in his face.

"Rearden," she replied.

He appeared lost for more words, and she wasn't inclined to help him. His eyes darted to left and right, seeing only enemies where a year before had been friends.

"I...I just—"

"Where is Sanctan?" she demanded.

Rearden shook his head. "I don't know. I swear. Rumour has it he has fled the city already. We...we..."

He looked back, seeing the troopers of the Griffin Battalion far behind him. If Rosomon ordered Rearden killed right here, right now, there was nothing they could do to stop it.

"We would like..."

He faltered, but she knew what he wanted. A truce. Surrender. However he wanted to put it. But his pride wouldn't let him.

"Say it," she demanded.

Rearden sighed. "Not going to make this easy on me are you, Rosomon?"

She most certainly was not. No need to tell him that though. No need to say anything at all now she was in the ascendent.

He looked like he was trying to swallow, but didn't have enough spit in his mouth to get the deed done. "Very well. In light of the fact the Anvil is in flames, and you have allied yourself with demon worshippers from across the Drift, I have no other choice but to offer terms of surrender on behalf of—"

"Very good," she said, having heard more than enough of his prating. "I accept your unconditional surrender."

Ignoring him completely, Rosomon gestured to her allies.

Falko nodded, and Rawlin was already signalling to his troops. Horns blew as the Bloodwolf and Mantis began to advance. The Blackshields were next, forming rank as they approached the gates.

Rosomon watched from a distance as they marched upon the city. The defenders began to pour out, throwing down their weapons and raising their arms in surrender. The pennant of the Griffin Battalion was flung down too. No sign of any others, but she was sure they would follow soon enough.

"Why would you ever trust them?"

She turned at the words, seeing Rearden still standing nearby, his gaze locked on the ranks of that black-armoured horde lining the road, their spears held aloft, shields bearing the strange sigils of Malador.

He turned to her, eyes blazing. "The Maladorans will betray you in the end. You have won a victory here, but it will be for nothing when they stab you in the back."

"Will it?" she asked. "Do you really think me so foolish? Look closer, Rearden."

His brow furrowed as he turned back to the mass of warriors. In the dawning light, the paintwork on that armour was becoming clearer. The hastily stitched surcoats. The daubed sigils.

"No. No you can't have. They're just...no!"

Rosomon nodded to Kassian, who grasped Rearden by the neck and drove him to his knees. The Guildmaster of Corwen looked up at her, his anger fled, fear evident on his hawkish features.

"No more words from you," she said, as though scolding a child. "Or your head will end up alongside Jarlath's."

Oleksig approached from further up the road, as a scout he had been conversing with quickly turned and headed back toward the gates.

"It's still chaos inside," he said. "What should we do?"

She gazed along that long road. To that city she had always hated. Part of her wanted to watch it burn to the ground, but they had not come this far to see their capital in ashes.

"We end it," she said, turning to Keara.

The Hallowhill nodded back in acknowledgment, looking to her stormhulks and raising an arm. Like a well-drilled unit on the parade ground, the vast machines began to stomp toward the gate.

Rosomon turned to Maugar. "Your Blackshields will follow them in. Marshals, it will be your job to bring order." Rawlin and Falko nodded their acknowledgment.

As they began to advance on the gate, Kassian leaned closer. "It won't be easy quelling two sides of a riot. Not without bloodshed anyway. You could end up just as reviled as Sanctan if things go south."

"No doubt," she replied, having calculated that risk. "But someone has to take charge. Someone has to make the hard decision and bring this to an end. And I want Sanctan found, Kassian."

He nodded obediently, heading off with the rest as they advanced on the city.

She was left with her Titanguard, watching from a distance with Ianto and the rest as the city continued to roil. Looking down, she regarded Rearden on his knees, a single tear tracking down his cheek as he watched the Anvil burn.

One enemy crushed.

It was a good start, but she would not be satisfied until Sanctan was on his knees right beside him.

# TYRETA

It was carnage on the streets. Wild as the jungle. Danger at every turn.

She relished each moment as she stalked her prey, searching for sign, tasting his scent, knowing she was closer with every step.

Her senses were alive, nerves and muscles tensed, with only one focus—to track down Lorens. He could not be far. The bastard had evaded her in the Mount, lost her among the tightly packed streets, but she was gaining. She could smell his fear. It left an easy trail to follow. Not long now before she sank her teeth into his throat.

Sudden violence nearby. Her attention was focused ahead, but she could still see danger in her periphery, still hear the sickening noise as someone was being beaten, and if it didn't stop they'd be dead before long. Perhaps she should have stopped it, but Tyreta could not stop. Could not quell the beast inside urging her ever onward.

For the first time since the jungles of the Sundered Isles, Tyreta had given in, allowing the animal within to take over completely. The rush was exquisite and the city came to life with frightening clarity. Noises she had filtered out came to her in a rush, and she could discern every one—the mad laugh of a frolicking rioter, the pained squeal of a beaten militiaman, the panicked keening of a child crying for its mother.

Streets and alleyways rushed by to left and right, but Tyreta felt no fatigue. The closer she got to her prey the more resolute she felt. The more her hunger grew, her thirst. The path ahead stank of him and it would not be long before she could sink her fangs.

The trail led her down an alley, dark and dank. She raced along it, eyes focused on the light at the end, until she rushed out onto the main thoroughfare, bounding on all fours.

Her eyes darted left and right. The street was shrouded with cloying smoke, the stench of cinders filling the air. To one side stood a barricade, as grey-clad militia did their best to hold back the clamouring masses. Among them stood a grey-cloaked High Legate, barking orders and litanies both.

"What the fuck is that?" one of the defenders shouted, spotting Tyreta standing but a few feet away.

She should have run, continued her hunt, but instead her lip curled up in a contemptuous sneer.

The High Legate turned, revealing dull armour, as she looked upon Tyreta with hate. "What kind of creature is this?"

"It's a demon," one of the militia whimpered. "It's something from the Drift brought by those damned Maladorans."

"Kill it." The High Legate snarled her command.

Ignoring the barricade, almost all those militia turned toward Tyreta, aiming their splintbows or raising their blades.

Around her, the world slowed as Tyreta focused in on fresh prey. She heard the snap of splintbows, but was already bounding forward. As the first bolt shot toward her she darted to one side, feeling it whip the air as it flew by. Another she ducked, letting it soar past harmlessly. A third sailed well wide of her...

Pain, biting in its clarity as a fourth bolt cut a slice from her arm. Tyreta howled in fury at the insult. Then she was upon them.

Her claws raked the first of the militia across the eyes. He staggered away, crying out in alarm as he dropped his weapon and reached for the tattered mess of his face. She turned to a second, and he stumbled back from her sweeping claws before she could reach him. A third was raising his splintbow, and she snatched it from his hands, snapping it in two, before snarling hot breath in his face. Seeing his fear. Savouring it—

A gauntleted fist smashed into her jaw.

Tyreta fell to the hard cobbles, spitting blood.

When she looked up, that armoured priest was bearing down, her sword raised, face full of fury. "You will be consumed in the breath of the Wyrms, fiend."

Tyreta rolled aside as the blade swept down, cracking the paving stone. Her teeth bared as she leapt to her feet, and before that sword could swing again, she had pounced, jaws clamping to the legate's throat. The taste was like honey as she tore at the flesh, blood running down her chin, spattering her cheeks.

The High Legate fell, steel-clad hand clamped to her neck to staunch the flow, but it was too late. She convulsed for a moment in her death throes, as the world clarified around Tyreta. Strands of the web snaked in every direction, bright and vivid, as though by consuming that lifeblood she had garnered a stronger connection than ever before.

She spun, looking for more prey, but at the sight of their leader bested so gruesomely the rest of the militia had fled. All but one.

The man cowered at the foot of the barricade and Tyreta could see as well as sense his terror—his heart beating within his chest, eyes transfixed. As the urge to leap forward, to taste yet more blood, almost took over, Tyreta wrested control.

This was only a waste of her precious time. Lorens could not escape.

She was running again, following his trail toward the river. The Bridge of Saints spanned that rushing torrent and she increased her pace, gasping not from fatigue but from hunger as she bounded across the bridge.

The palace loomed ahead, and as she ascended the stairs to the vast entrance she remembered the last time she had walked this path. Back then she had been greeted by her uncle's embrace, like being crushed by a bear, but that was just a memory now, replaced only by fury.

Taking the stairs four at a time, she finally reached the summit, seeing the stained-glass frontage and five stone dragons leering down above the entrance—vast doors of oak and banded iron. The hinges to those great doors bowed and snapped as she threw herself against them, and she came to a stop in the entrance hall, sniffing the air, sensing him close.

"Lorens!" she screamed, more of a howl than a word.

He was here. She knew it.

Wasting no time she raced to the wide twisting staircase, rushing ever upward, past the draconic emblems that now besmirched every square foot of the place. The Ministry had destroyed everything her family stood for, drowned that legacy in filth, and soon they would be punished for it.

The taste of blood on her lips was fading, and she yearned for more. Up she ran, out onto a huge open hallway, marble columns rising high to the vaulted ceiling.

There, in the distance, she could see him staggering, hear him gasping. Lorens fell, exhausted, sobbing in his desperation. He knew she was here, but there was nowhere left for him to run.

Tyreta quashed the urge to sprint, to pounce on him and end this. She would take her time. Savour it.

Every nerve tingled as she strode after him. His sobs grew louder and he dragged himself to his feet, stumbling away as he gripped tight to the stump of his wrist. She watched him reach the open archway that spanned the length of the hall, stepping out onto the long balcony that overlooked the city.

Warm air hit her as she followed him out. The sun was rising in the distance, casting light over the smouldering rooftops of the Anvil, the sound of rioting dying with the coming of dawn.

Tyreta focused on Lorens as he fell toward the balcony, and she suddenly realised where she was. This long jetty was where the ark from Nyrakkis had landed so long ago. The one that had taken her brother away.

Lorens had stopped his sobbing, but he must have realised death was near as he crawled to his feet and turned to her. There was no fear in his eyes. Only resignation.

The closer she got, the more the beast within her waned. Tyreta was instead flooded by memories of when they had both lived different lives. Of when Lorens and Conall had talked and laughed at the Hollow. How she would watch them with envy, wanting to join in but never feeling a part of their kinship. Lorens had always been kind to her though. Always as much a brother as Conall and Fulren. The real brothers she had lost because of all he had caused.

She stopped some feet away, looking down at the sorry man Lorens had become. Whatever he had hoped to achieve with all his poor decisions was lost to him now.

"Do it," he whispered. "Just end all this."

Her attention flitted to the scene below. The fires still burning. The crowds running rampant through the streets.

"End this? Isn't this what you wanted, Lorens? Anarchy? Fire? The breath of your Wyrms?"

He shook his head regretfully. "This was never what I wanted. He told me... told me it would be so different. Promised me a new world. A better one."

"And you believed him?" she bellowed, the sudden thought of Sanctan filling her with such a fury she almost lost herself to the beast once more.

"Yes," Lorens barked defiantly. "Yes, I believed him. Every damned word. And despite all this, how things have ended, part of me still does."

Tyreta couldn't find it in herself to feel anger anymore. Lorens was like a child, believing in fanciful tales all his childhood, only to learn they weren't true after all.

"You burned everything down. So many lives lost. And for what?" She gestured to the chaos below. "How can this be any better than what we had before?"

Lorens smiled, as though she'd told some wry joke. For the first time she realised how much he and Wyllow looked alike. But inside, they were nothing alike.

"You just said it, Tyreta. What *we* had. Haven't you thought about anyone else? What about the men and women scratching a living in the mines and manufactories? Living and dying in misery, so that we can sit in our estates. *He* offered a better way. A way for everyone to prosper."

She remembered the Sundered Isles, and what misery the Guilds had wrought with their profiteering. It was impossible to argue he was wrong.

"You know it," Lorens continued. "You see it too. We had too much. We were driven by avarice, not altruism. My father, our grandfather, they didn't see it. We lost sight of what really mattered. We were blinded by greed."

Suddenly she was finding it hard to catch her breath. Lorens was making so much sense, Tyreta could hardly tell right from wrong anymore.

"But... we can still change it," she said, desperate to salvage something from all this turmoil. "Still do the right thing."

The grin on his face grew wider. "Now that we have burned it all to the ground. Yes, perhaps we can."

Again her gaze was drawn to the carnage below. The ashes from which they would have to rebuild a city. A nation. So much suffering. So much misery.

"There had to be a better way than this."

"Did there? Even if we could have shown my father, your mother, what they were doing, do you think they would have listened? Do you think they would have given up all they had gained, just to alleviate the pain of these people?"

Another scream from below. Toward the south there was movement. Armigers in the streets pushing westward. Stormhulks advancing, ready to quell the masses.

Lorens was right. Her mother and uncle would never have given up all they had built. Even now Lady Rosomon was seizing back control, crushing all in her path, quashing dissent with ruthless efficiency.

Tyreta stepped away from Lorens, all thoughts of murder drifting from her mind. Suddenly she was so very tired.

"We can make all this better," he whispered, taking a step closer to her. "We can fix this, Tyreta. Just you and I. Hawkspur and Archwind united once again."

As he spoke his left hand moved down to his side. The sun began to crest the eastern horizon, his blade flashing in its light.

Lorens slashed at her with the knife, slicing her arm, but she was faster, her reaction instinctive as her claws raked his jaw. He yelped, staggering back and dropping the blade as his hand came up to staunch the wound. His leg caught on the lip of the jetty and he lost his balance, toppling over the side.

Instinct took over again, and she dashed forward to catch him. Lorens reached out with his right arm...but there was no hand there to grasp as she snatched at nothing. He slipped away from her, screaming as he plummeted toward the ground below, the sound lost amid the violence now gripping the city.

Tyreta raised her hand, seeing her claws shining red in the dawn light. Only now did the pain of the knife wound begin to sear, blood running down her arm. Tearing off a strip of cloth from her shirt, she tied it around the cut, just as she had done in the jungle of the Sundered Isles in what seemed a lifetime ago.

Back then she had been desperate, running for her life, pursued by predators. Now she was the hunter.

But far below, more hunters were abroad. Hunters sent by her mother to quell the very people she thought they had come to liberate.

# ANSELL

He had been shown secret ways beneath the city when only a neophyte. Tunnels, ancient and winding, known only to those faithful to the Draconate. In all the years the Guilds had been dominant in Torwyn they had never found them, and Ansell could only be grateful for that as he neared the Mount.

It stank down here, and several times he'd had to stop and retch. The river flowed above the tunnels and leaked fetid water through the brickwork. At every turn he had expected to find his way blocked by collapsed debris, but so far his route had been without obstacle.

Eventually, he reached a section of passageway lit from above. Looking up he saw an iron grille rusted with age through which he could hear the riot and see the indistinct forms of people rushing by. It only served to remind him that time was running out.

He continued to slosh ankle deep through the sludge, the tunnel rising and falling ahead of him. Just as he began to think he might never reach his goal, a ladder stood at the end of the tunnel, time-worn and rusted. Each rung was bent with age, and he had no idea if it would take his weight. Nevertheless, Ansell grasped it, pulling himself ever upward until he reached the iron cover. With some difficulty he pushed it aside, squeezing himself through the gap, gasping in relief as he found himself in a back alley close to the Mount.

Immediately he was assailed by the stench of smoke. Panicked voices echoed along the alleyway as he forced himself on, ignoring the sounds of violence all around. As he came out into a ransacked street he saw a shop being looted, its windows smashed. Someone was hanging by his neck from a post nearby, and corpses lay scattered in Ansell's path. He heard laughter, alongside the sound of gentle weeping, but it stirred no sorrow in him. Only a keen sense of urgency.

Sanctan was responsible for all this, with his mindless ambition, and Ansell had more than played his part in kindling those flames. It might be too late for him to make amends to the thousands who now suffered, but he could at least put one thing right. He could find Grace and take her somewhere safe, far from her father's poisonous grip.

The Mount came into view up ahead. Ansell had half expected to see it in flames, but there it stood, as indomitable as ever. One of its huge stained-glass windows had been smashed, its great doors standing wide, but it was otherwise unmolested. He paused for a moment, wondering what he might find within the beckoning darkness, but there was no use wasting his time with apprehension. Gritting his teeth, he strode across the threshold.

Inside he could hear distant voices, muffled and indistinct. The first thing he saw was the prone body of a dead legate, but Ansell felt nothing. The dead man could well have been yet another innocent casualty of the war he had started, or someone just as complicit in these events as Ansell was.

Mounting the stairs to the upper level he saw a group daubing paint on the walls as one of their number casually smashed idols with a hammer. Short months ago, Ansell would have been enraged at such desecration. Now he was unmoved. It seemed his faith had truly left him, but what would the Great Wyrms do to chide him for it? Were they even watching? If such heresy was allowed to go unpunished within the very walls of their temple, then it appeared not.

The deeper he wandered through the corridors, the more evidence he saw that his notion was right. The place had truly been defiled; paint daubed everywhere, tapestries and portraits slashed, the fragile trinkets and idols that had stood in pride of place now reduced to shards.

Every chapel was abandoned, and there was no sign of any legates or his brother knights. Turning a corner he was faced with iron gates barring his way along the passage. Drawing closer he saw that those iron bars were now bent and warped, as though whatever had been caged within had smashed its way to freedom. Ansell dismissed the mystery, growing ever more desperate to find Grace among this now unfamiliar place.

At the end of the corridor was the entrance to the librarium. His boots crunched on broken glass as he entered, and a smoky breeze blew in where the glass ceiling had been smashed. Through the dawning light he saw a body lying prone in the centre of the chamber.

Ansell knelt, noting the armour was dented and punctured in places. He recognised Hurden's face, but instead of his usual stern visage he looked almost serene in death. There was still some severity to his dark brow though, even in his final peace.

At least one of them had found it at last.

Ansell closed his eyes, trying to recall the relevant litany for a fallen brother and finding it strange that he could not remember it. Dismissing the idea, he opened his eyes and laid a hand on Hurden's breastplate.

"Rest easy, my brother," he whispered, before rising to his feet and looking about the chamber, seeing only carnage.

Moving to the northern wall, he felt for the lever situated behind the mounted stone head of a dragon. Pulling it, he heard the familiar click before one of the bookshelves revolved to reveal a dark tunnel.

Torches lined the narrow passage, and Ansell delved inside. He didn't have to go far before he saw another armour-clad figure in his path. This one was kneeling, as though he had been in prayer, but then slumped against the side of the tunnel wall as he succumbed to his wounds.

Ansell paused, crouching down to check if this one was still alive. The knight's helm had already been discarded, and in the flickering light he saw the face of his brother, Everis. Blood was congealed in his ears and nose, his eyes half-closed in death. His abandoned helm had a huge dent in it, most likely the blow that had ended him.

He had been left here to die with no one to tend him. Everything about that went against their code of brotherhood, but it was not wholly unexpected. Sanctan had forced them all to break so many oaths on his journey to power.

Ansell would have said another prayer, but his sense of urgency only grew. Leaving Everis kneeling to his gods, he plunged down the passage, deeper into the guts of the Mount, hoping he was not already too late.

The torches lit a path all the way down through the great temple, and beneath its very foundations. He knew eventually it would come out north of the city, and he found himself racing along, heedless of any danger that might be waiting. As he rushed through a vestibule, just a few yards short of the exit, he almost didn't see a figure cowering in the shadows.

Ansell stopped, squinting in the gloom at the legate, who was hugging his knees, lips moving in silent prayer. Was that... Kinloth?

The pair regarded one another for a moment, before Kinloth said, "I'm sorry."

Ansell had ordered this boy to take care of Grace in his absence. It appeared he had failed in that duty.

"Kinloth, where—"

"You asked me to protect her, but I couldn't."

As he sobbed, Ansell felt an unexpected note of pity. He had given the boy an impossible task. Of course he had failed. "Where has he taken her?"

"North. They are heading to the Fist. He means to... to bring back Undometh. He will let nothing stand in the way of his vengeance."

Ansell knew the Prophesies well. Knew what sacrifice would be needed were Sanctan to bring back one of the Great Wyrms. *Only with the greatest of sacrifices can Undometh truly be raised.*

"Grace," he breathed.

"You'll never catch them," Kinloth said mournfully. "They took a landship at the north terminal. They'll be miles away by now."

It seemed he was too late. Still, no reason for him to give in.

"Stay here. And stay hidden." He turned to leave before pausing. "And pray that the Guilds show you mercy when this is all over."

He raced on through the passage. There were no torches here, just his memories to light his way. Surely he was not too late.

The passage ended at a crossroads. The northern route would take him to that secret terminal, but they were already long gone. Instead, Ansell headed east, along a passage that would bring him out onto the Parade of Builders. He stumbled along it in the dark, hearing the sound of tumult on the streets above. Eventually he reached a door, his hand feeling for the bolts that secured it shut. Numb fingers slid those rusted bolts aside and he shoved the door with his shoulder. It burst open out onto a nondescript alleyway and he was dazzled by the morning light, the air stifling, noise intense as he was assailed by distant shouts and the whirr of engines from those infernal machines.

Ansell staggered onto a street packed with people fleeing every which way. Stormhulks strode along the thoroughfare, burning all in their path with each fiery plume.

The drumming sound of hoofbeats, the panicked whinny of a horse, and he turned to see a Revocater captain riding wildly toward him. He pulled up a few short yards away, turning to half dozen yellow-clad men fleeing the onslaught.

"Rally to me," the captain said, his red plume dancing erratically as he tried to keep his horse under control in the chaos.

His men seemed less enthusiastic, some of them already abandoning their duty and fleeing in the other direction. Ansell stole upon the opportunity, rushing forward and grasping the captain's yellow tunic before dragging him from the saddle. He landed heavily, sword clattering along the paved street.

Before the captain could recover, Ansell climbed into the saddle, expecting the Revocaters to at least fire a volley, but the rest were already fleeing now that their leader had been laid low.

A stormhulk loomed through the grey cloud, the staccato report of its heavy splintbow deafening, but Ansell had already put heels to flanks. The horse galloped along the Parade of Builders and toward gates that were open to the north, both horse and rider heedless of the chaos surrounding them. As he crossed the boundary of the gates and left the Anvil behind, Ansell kicked his steed harder along the road. His quarry was miles ahead, but he was not beaten yet. Not while he still breathed.

# KEARA

They progressed steadily along the Parade, a painfully slow advance, but she guessed they were never going to do this quickly. The rioters were dug in like rats, and clearing them out was a painstaking job. One that would have been more fun if she'd been piloting a stormhulk, but she guessed she had to look the part—striding ahead for all to see, directing her followers like some hero of legend. If they hadn't respected her before, they'd damn well better now.

She felt the buzz of the web keenly as those stormhulks ploughed ahead. Their power was awe-inspiring, and it brought a smile to her face watching the rioters flee in panic at the mere sight of them. Beside her, two webwainers carried volt guns, bringing the air to life with static as they mowed down any stragglers. One more wainer had a shoulder-mounted cannon with its deafening report, blasting holes in anything that moved. The fire from its muzzle flashed, lighting up the woman's goggles, and for a moment Keara got a memory of Hesse. She would have loved striding through this carnage, not a care in the world. Probably best not to think of her right now though. That might ruin the jubilant mood.

They'd managed to reach the end of the parade and the stormhulks had come to a stop. Immediately they came under fire from behind a barricade to the east, and Keara could just see grey-uniformed militia manning its defences. Dumb of them to still be here, but dumb wouldn't see them spared.

"Concentrate fire!" she shouted, leaping atop the shattered base of a fallen statue and pointing down the street like she was brave or something.

The volley of fire from the stormhulks was devastating, blasting the barricade apart, sending bodies flying. Even more glorious was the crackle of static energy that made her hair stand on end before a bolt of bright lightning streaked down the street, catching one of the fleeing defenders and tearing him to bloody strips.

Keara followed as the stormhulks continued their advance, targeting everything in their path and burning the remains. When they reached the end of the road, the stormhulks came to a standstill and Keara trotted closer to see why.

A clack of internal bolts and the hood of one stormhulk flipped open. Galirena peered down from her lofty position.

"The way ahead is blocked," she said, pointing toward the central hub of the city. "We can't reach the Cogwheel unless we go past that."

Keara strained her eyes through the smoke, seeing a massive barricade in their path. Huge chunks of masonry had been shifted to block the street. It was impossible to tell if it was held by those loyal to Guild or Ministry.

"Keep moving," Keara said, trying to sound as determined as she could. "We have to take the Cogwheel. Once we hold the centre of the city we hold everything."

Galirena looked uncertain. "Those people could be—"

"We have no choice." Keara set her jaw, glaring up at the webwainer.

Galirena nodded, albeit reluctantly, and slammed down the hatch. As one, the stormhulks continued their march, and the air buzzed with energy once more. They unleashed their infernal weapons on the barricade, other webwainers mopping up any unlucky stragglers, but resistance was thinning the closer they got to the Cogwheel.

This was ruthless naked madness, but Keara was determined to salvage something from it in the end. All she had to do was bring order to these streets any way she could. Then they'd have their moment.

As the stormhulks smashed through the boulders ahead, Keara spotted Armigers advancing along the street to the east, Mantid pennants flying proudly and Marshal Falko marching at the head of his troopers.

"The Burrows are subdued!" she shouted above the noise.

He nodded, wincing at the din. "And we've taken the northern district surrounding the palace."

"The Cogwheel will be ours soon. What about the Mount?"

"Rawlin has led his battalion there, but I don't know if it's secured yet."

"We almost have this area locked down," she shouted. "I suggest you make sure we'll get no surprises from the east, and I'll meet you at the Mount."

He nodded his response, and she was impressed with her own sense of authority. A few days ago she doubted Falko would have treated her as an equal, but here he was, listening to her tactical advice and heeding it.

As the Mantid troopers tramped away toward the east, she followed her webwainers as they advanced on the Cogwheel. Resistance was thinning out, but before the might of her stormhulks it would have been insane to offer any further defiance.

The Cogwheel was visible now, towering over the surrounding streets. She could see another barricade had been erected, this one even larger than the first, and her stormhulks were struggling to bring it down, despite the intensity of their barrage.

One of her wainers approached, a young man of barely twenty summers. Delion, that was his name, and Keara impressed herself that she'd remembered it.

"They're dug in!" he shouted. "We'll have to bring the whole barricade down to get through."

"So? What are you waiting for?"

Delion shook his head. "But they're just civilians. Lady Rosomon told us—"

"Fuck Lady Rosomon. We need to end this. Now. We won't get a better chance."

"Look!" someone shouted, before Delion could reply.

She saw another of her wainers pointing at the barricade—a girl called Parise—damn she was getting good at this. From amid the barricade a white flag was flying. Surrender.

It was obvious the stormhulks hadn't seen it yet, as they continued to rain bolts and superheated shot on the defences. Keara strode forward, hands raised to attract their attention, shouting for Vikmar and Galirena to stop their assault. One by one the stormhulks ceased the attack, the air gradually going quiet.

As the dust settled she could still hear distant sounds of violence from elsewhere in the city, but a strange sense of peace settled over the Cogwheel. For a while there was no sign of life from behind that barricade, until eventually someone stepped out into the morning sunlight.

The tattered green robes she wore marked her for a High Legate of Saphenodon. Her hands were trembling as she stepped forward tentatively, grey hair hanging lank, face covered in dust. She moved toward Keara with as much dignity as she could manage, but there was no hiding the fearful look in her eyes. Only natural considering this was just a scholar of the Ministry, not a warrior-priest.

"Well?" Keara asked as the woman drew nearer. "Ready to surrender?"

The priestess looked back over her shoulder. There were others peering from behind the defences now; legates, Revocaters, civilian militia.

"Perhaps," the High Legate replied. "As long as Lady Rosomon is ready to offer mercy."

Keara felt her back teeth gnash. Why the fuck did everyone insist on asking about that woman?

"It's me you have to worry about right now. Forget the Hawkspurs."

The woman nodded her understanding. "There are ordinary people behind that barricade. Scared people. Terrified of the Maladoran demons you have brought with you from across the Drift. We need guarantees—"

"If you don't surrender to me, here and now, the Maladorans will be the least of your worries."

Keara saw the woman swallow hard. There was fear there, but also defiance. Perhaps not just a cowardly scholar after all.

Before either of them could continue, there was a commotion behind. Keara turned to see the imposing sight of Titanguard striding past her followers. In their full armour they were a sight to behold, but she remembered how easily she and her fellow wainers had brought them down in the palace those months ago. That confidence faltered, though, when she saw Rosomon Hawkspur approaching with them. Of course she was bloody here, ready to snatch any glory Keara might salvage from this whole mess.

Rosomon came closer, calmly stepping through the carnage to stand before that barricade as though she was impervious.

"High Legate," she said, ignoring Keara completely.

The priestess bowed low. "Lady Rosomon. I...I beseech you for mercy. I do not beg it for myself, but I would ask these people are not sacrificed needlessly. I am more than willing to face any retribution on their behalf as a senior representative of the Draconate."

"They will not be harmed." The finality in Lady Rosomon's statement was palpable.

"I have your guarantee?" Still, not quite good enough for the Ministry.

"I guarantee there will be fair treatment for all. Including you."

With every word, Keara's anger burned brighter. This should have been her moment. An opportunity to accept the enemy's surrender. These were all words that could have been coming from her mouth, but not now. The Hawkspurs had arrived to ruin it all yet again.

"Very well," the High Legate said before offering another bow, this one lower than the first.

She walked back to the barricade to deliver her message. As Keara watched her go, she was conscious of how close Rosomon was standing. Keara's fingers twitched, as the temptation to draw her knife and seize what power she could felt almost impossible to subdue. She was surrounded by her webwainers after all. It would be nothing for them to render the Titanguard useless, and with a dozen stormhulks at her disposal she could end all this right here and now. The throne would be hers for the taking.

A clack as something was thrown from behind the stone defences, and she was shaken from her daydream. Splintbows, swords, axes, even sticks and garden tools were being flung over the barricade. Then, one by one, the defenders appeared, looking sorry and beaten, crowding together, militia and Revocaters, all glancing at one another as though they had no idea what to do.

Rosomon stepped forward, climbing atop one of those boulders so they could all see her. Elevating herself above the masses, of course.

"Hear me!" she called out, voice echoing across the Cogwheel. "I offer an amnesty to all those who surrender to the Guilds. Spread the word. Let everyone know so we can end this worthless violence and start to rebuild. We know you were all drawn in by the Archlegate's empty promises. Do not feel bad, you weren't the only ones. Sanctan Egelrath's venomous lies have spread far across our nation. But he is gone now. The Guilds remain. And we offer mercy to all those who throw down their arms. This conflict is over. There is no longer anything to fear."

"What about the Maladoran devils you brought to our gates?" someone was brave enough to shout from the crowd.

Keara noticed a twitch at the corner of Rosomon's mouth. No doubt she was pleased with her ruse.

"You have nothing to fear from them. They are already gone. All that remains now is Torwyn and its people. One nation once again."

By all that was fucking holy this woman could talk all right. But even as she did, Keara found her hands moving away from the knives at her side. If there'd been a chance for a coup, it was most certainly gone now.

"Bless you, Lady Rosomon!" someone cried. "You've offered us more mercy than Sanctan ever would."

Keara had to stop herself rolling her eyes as the call of *Hawkspur*,

*Hawkspur* rose up from the sorry-looking rebels. It was almost more than she could stomach.

As Rosomon Hawkspur lapped up her newfound adoration, Keara turned away from the Cogwheel she'd just taken such pains to capture. It should have been the name of *Hallowhill* that was rising up in the midst of the city. But it wasn't.

It was just another chance gone begging.

# CONALL

It was strange seeing such jubilance after everything that had happened. The screams and the fires had been replaced by music, laughter, even a few harmless fireworks. The Anvil had gone from battlefield to festival in less than a day.

Conall left the streets behind him, entering the palace to the nods of the guards on duty. Of course he wasn't challenged, but then he was easily recognisable—the one-eyed Hawkspur who had assaulted the city gates single-handed. Well, not quite single-handed, but ten men against a thousand had still been a brave move.

As he walked up the vast staircase they were already taking down those Draconate idols and people were even celebrating in here—a couple of troopers laughing as they exchanged an open flask, two palace servants sharing a passionate kiss down a gloomy corridor. Conall would have felt envious, or even thought about joining in, but his mood was far from celebratory.

But celebrate he must.

As he reached the summit of the palace, walking into the vibrant hall, he remembered the last time he had been here. They'd welcomed the emissary from Nyrakkis that day. Celebrated her arrival in a whirlwind of sycophantic greetings and false smiles. Conall had hated the place then. He hated it now.

Everyone had come to honour their victory. All those Guild dignitaries, patting one another on the back, patting Conall on the back as he tried a smile in return here, offered a nod there, the faces washing by in a vaguely familiar wave. Oleksig, Maugar, Borys, Falko, this marshal of that battalion, this adjutant of another.

"Well done, Hawkspur. You should be proud of yourself."

Nod of appreciation.

"It must be a relief that all this is over and the Guilds are back in charge."

Another nod of appreciation, palm greased. No idea who that was.

"Things should start to get back to normal around here. You have a bright future ahead."

A false smile of acknowledgment, though he was beginning to wonder if things would ever get back to normal.

Before any more awkward approaches, Conall dragged himself away from the huddle of minor luminaries, looking for a quiet corner so he could gather his thoughts. The more he looked for one, the more he realised there were no quiet corners here as someone breezed by pressing a full glass of something into his hand. Another laughing face he didn't recognise, among a host of others.

He was lost at sea all over again. Trapped amid the tempest. Surely he wouldn't be missed if he slipped away. Or perhaps he needed a little lubrication. Just enough to loosen him up so he could enjoy the storm.

The glass was still in his hand and he thought about throwing back that drink. As he looked at it, the very notion made him feel ill, nausea coming for him in a wave.

There was nothing else for it—he had to get out.

He tried his best not to stagger as he shouldered past a gaggle of Armiger officers. All he had to do was find the damned archway he'd walked in through, but he couldn't see it past the ocean of faces.

Then he managed to focus on one he recognised. An island in the storm.

Tyreta.

They regarded one another for a moment, so close, but perhaps so far away. They'd not spoken a word since he'd left her at Goodhope before all this started. Before the old Conall had died. There'd been no opportunity for them to speak since the city had been retaken, and now that she was finally right in front of him he just didn't know what to say.

"All right?" she asked, so simply. But he guessed it didn't have to be so hard.

"All right?" he asked right back.

"I thought you were dead."

Almost. Closer than she could have possibly imagined. "No. I'm very much alive."

"So I see. And so typical of you to come back from the dead just in time for the booze to start flowing."

He could see from the uneasy look on her face how she felt about this whole zoo of a gathering. A face much leaner than the last time he'd seen it, faded marks swirling up from her neck, hair shorn at the sides and cropped short on top. It was like staring at a stranger.

"You not feeling in a party mood either?" he asked, still not sure of what to say.

She looked about the place, not bothering to hide the sneer on her lips. "Look at them all congratulating themselves on a job well done. As though we've won something."

He glanced around the hall, knowing exactly what she meant. "Let them have their victory. They've earned it. The hard work to rebuild will begin soon."

"Yeah, and we'll all have our part to play." She sounded distant. More serious than he'd ever known. It hurt to think that the playful, mischievous girl he'd left behind was gone now.

"You don't sound too enthused about that prospect."

Her jaw clenched. It was strange, but she looked more like a caged animal than the heir of a Guild.

Conall placed his hand on her shoulder. "You don't have to be here, you know. You could just—"

"What?" she said, looking deep in his eyes. "Run away?"

For a moment he didn't consider that such a bad idea. "Where's Fulren?"

Tyreta nodded toward the huge arch that led out onto the jetty of the palace. "On the airship. With that woman from Nyrakkis."

Conall followed her gaze, looking out into the night where that ark would be sitting.

"He never did like these events."

"He's not the only one."

Conall looked back at her, seeing her watching proceedings with barely tamed disdain. "No. I guess he isn't."

For a moment he thought that maybe he should gather all three of them together and they could leave. Run as far away from here for as long as they could. Maybe forever. Surely that would be best for all three of them, to run from the Guilds, their mother. Torwyn. Find a quiet spot in a foreign place and start again.

"Chin up," he said instead. "This will all be over soon."

At last, a smile on his sister's face, and for that fleeting moment he had her back again.

"I guess so."

He placed his drink down on a table, the nausea starting to subside. "Maybe I'll go and see him. Say hello. I never really got a chance to talk to him before."

"Sounds like a good idea. I imagine I'll see you later."

"You bet."

He offered her a wink, before pushing his way through the crowd toward that archway. The closer he got, the more he began to realise this was the best idea. He was in danger, and so was everyone around him. If there was anyone who could help him it was Fulren. After all, his brother had harnessed the sorceries of Nyrakkis. Maybe he could help with whatever Conall had been cursed with. And that arcanist he was so fond of, surely she would know how he could rid himself of it. Maybe they'd both take him away in their airship. Get him far from here.

Yes... that was it. Just escape. Go somewhere they might understand what was happening—

*No. You cannot run.*

Conall staggered to a stop, teeth clenching tight at that voice loud as thunder in his skull.

He felt the nausea return in a turbulent wave. His head spinning. Every face surrounding him roiling in a bilious sea, melding together, roaring with laughter at his malaise.

Then he saw her among the crowd. His mother's features becoming distinct within that cauldron of faces. Standing there so self-assured. Drinking in the attention, the adoration.

Conall took a step toward her. He held no weapon, but that didn't matter. He could summon a blade with but a thought. *His* blade.

No.

He stopped, fists clenched, but still staring. This was not the way. He had to get a grip on himself. Stay in control. He was not a puppet. He was not...

*Do it. Now. Before it is too late.*

Sickness welled up inside as his head throbbed. He raised a hand, touching his top lip, looking down to see blood on his fingertips. As he did so, his other hand reached into the shadows, feeling the hilt of that sword tease his palm. It was there, just waiting for him. All he had to do was take it...

A cheer from across the hall.

Conall shook his head, clearing the haze, before he looked over at what had caused the ruckus. From the crowd gathering around the entrance, it was obvious someone popular had arrived. He squinted past the mass of bodies as someone pushed their way through... Sonnheld, adorned in his full plate, Viper Battalion troopers at his shoulder. And... Sted.

As eager as the gathering was to greet the returning heroes, Sonnheld retained his grim visage as he spoke with urgency. Gradually, Conall could see expressions changing. Sonnheld had brought news, dire news, that could only relate to one thing.

He watched helplessly as Sted broke from the gathering, rushing toward his mother. Keen to bring her the grim tidings of her son and what he had done. What he had become.

Conall took a step back, hoping to lose himself in the crowd. Ducking his head, he did his best to look as inconspicuous as he could, ignoring every face, every pat on the back, every gracious word aimed his way.

There was a door nearby. A side exit out of here. His only way to escape unseen.

Conall ran for it, knocking into someone and spilling a drink. The glass fell to the tiled floor, smashing into a thousand pieces as he barged past. No time for apologies as he wrenched the door open and dived through.

Stairs disappeared into the dark, and he all but fell down them in his haste to flee. When the door slammed shut behind him he was cast in shadows, and Conall let them consume him as he ran for his life.

# ROSOMON

A clatter of trays and the smash of a glass brought her back to stark clarity. She'd been staring through the window, lost in her labyrinth of thoughts, but now the world came back in a rush.

Serfs were still clearing away the detritus from the gathering they had held the previous night. A gathering that had come to such a sudden and disturbing end. Rosomon had been advised to retire to her chamber and rest after such trying news, but there was no way she could rest now.

Conall had murdered a man. Betrayed the Viper Battalion and fled. There had to be some kind of explanation, and she would not believe him a traitor until she heard the real story from his own lips.

He had helped them take the city, damn it. How could he betray them? There must have been some reason for his actions, but he had disappeared before she had a chance to find out the truth.

Rosomon shook her head, turning her attention back to the matter at hand. Falko had been about to speak before being interrupted by those serfs, and he cleared his throat to continue.

"Most of the Corvus Battalion were rounded up before they could flee the city aboard their barges."

Rosomon thought that ironic. She had fled the city aboard a barge herself when all this began.

"And Tarjan?" asked Oleksig, looking a little worse for wear after his excesses the night before.

"He is in our custody."

Progress at least, but still no word of the one man she wanted the most. Her nephew was nowhere to be found, but Rosomon would not stop until there was a reckoning.

"So the city is secure?" Oleksig continued.

"It is," Falko confirmed. "Maugar and his Blackshields, along with the Mantid and Bloodwolf, patrol every district. So far there has been no dissent. The militia, and those civilians who supported the Ministry, have been good to their word. Now the cleanup begins."

Teams had already been dispatched to see that the carnage wrought during the siege was cleared away, that everyone was fed and sheltered, the rebuilding begun. Tyreta herself was among them. After what had happened to Conall, Rosomon might have thought her daughter would be inconsolable, but Tyreta had thrown herself into her duties as a Guild heir should.

"What about beyond the Anvil?" Oleksig asked, continuing to steer the conversation, but with so much plaguing her thoughts Rosomon was happy to allow it.

Falko stiffened. "The Auroch and Tigris Battalions have offered their surrender in exchange for clemency. I don't think it will be too long before the Phoenix and Raptor do the same."

Oleksig turned to Rosomon, his eyebrow raised. "Clemency? Do we think that's the right thing? After everything they've done?"

"No," she said immediately, the fire stoked within her. "There will be no clemency. None."

Rosomon regarded the men surrounding her, as though waiting for them to disagree. Sonnheld stood with his hands on his twin swords, a man who had been through much and stayed loyal to the Guilds throughout this conflict. He offered no opinion.

In turn she glanced to Ianto and Kassian. They didn't disagree, but Falko looked pained by the notion.

"So we just annihilate them?" he asked. "Is that how we want to be seen? As murdering tyrants? Was that not the regime we have just quashed?"

Oleksig shrugged. "They could be stripped of their Armiger status. Cast down. Forbidden from raising arms."

Falko nodded. "That's one option, I suppose."

"No," Rosomon said. All eyes turned to her once more. "That just sends trained warriors into the fields and streets of Torwyn. Men and women who tried to destroy this nation. That is no justice. There has to be a reckoning. Punishment."

"You mean executions," Sonnheld said.

"That's exactly what I mean," she replied, surprising herself. But there was no other option. They had been betrayed. Thousands had died. The Armiger marshals could not simply slip away with impunity.

"It sets a tricky precedent," Falko said. "The Armigers have rules. And just because they backed the wrong side doesn't mean they should be killed for it."

"Backed the wrong side?" Rosomon said. "They committed treason. Abetted the murder of the emperor."

"You can't hold the Armigers responsible for that," Sonnheld said. "It could have been any one of us who followed the Ministry instead of the Guilds."

"Then why didn't you?" Rosomon said, almost spitting the words.

Sonnheld had no answer. Neither did the others. She knew her anger was getting the better of her, and for good reason. She couldn't rid herself of thoughts of Conall—why he had turned against them, how it must have been something to do with his capture by those bastards in Iperion Magna. His betrayal had to be some sorcerous plot, but despite that it all led back to one man. If not for Sanctan, her son would never have been shipwrecked. Never forced into slavery. He would never have suffered at the hands of those demons.

"Any word of Sanctan?" she asked, keen to change the subject.

Again, she was met with awkward silence, until Falko said, "Nothing yet."

Rosomon tried to control her breathing, before looking to Ianto. "Very well. Bring them in."

Ianto nodded, before marching through the arch. Rosomon once again found herself gazing out of the window that looked down upon a city that was so quiet now. As she watched the teeming streets, Oleksig came closer, gripping his pipe between his teeth.

"I know you've been through a lot," he said quietly. "We all have. But we may have to make compromises if we're to hold everything together."

She didn't look at him, still taking in the sight below. "Do you think I am losing control? That my need for vengeance is clouding my judgement?"

"No...I just..."

"It isn't. I see more clearly than I ever have, Oleksig. Don't ever doubt that."

He sighed, taking a step back. Perhaps her response had been a little harsh. Then again, perhaps not harsh enough. Before she could decide which, she heard Ianto returning.

Her imperator marched at the head of a group of Armiger troopers, Rawlin among them. In their midst were four grey-robed legates and two others in red and green, High Legates of the Draconate. The priests looked suitably subdued, just the way she wanted them.

Ianto had them stand in a row and Rosomon let them wait in silence. As they stood, she could see them squirming in their raiment of office. While the Ministry was in control they would have worn those robes like armour. Now they were like metal plate on drowning men.

"Where is he?" she said eventually.

A couple of the legates looked at one another dumbly. The priest in green kept his eyes on the ground. The one in red had his chin raised in defiance.

Rosomon took a step closer, making sure they could all see her. "We have turned this city upside down. Searched every shadowy nook of the Mount. We have found no trace. So I will ask you again, where is he?"

More silence. More nervous shuffling from those grey-clad legates. Only the High Legate of Undometh dared look her in the eye.

Rosomon glared back. "Do you think yourselves immune to retribution? Do you think yourselves armoured in faith? That your Wyrms will grant you salvation from me?"

The one in red robes offered a sneer. "You dare? You think you can hector us? Threaten us? We stand with the strength of the Five Great Wyrms. We will never betray—"

Rawlin stepped forward swiftly, punching the priest in the gut. He doubled over, falling to his hands and knees, retching as he tried to fill his lungs.

"I won't ask again," Rosomon said, ignoring the man's wheezing. "Where is Sanctan Egelrath?"

"Kalur's Fist," said a quiet voice from among that smattering of grey robes.

Her eyes fell on a young man with blond hair and a worried look about him. A face she thought she recognised.

"I know you."

He nodded, but she could tell he didn't know if it was a good thing or bad that she did. "My name is Willet, my lady. Willet Kinloth. We spoke once before... before all this began. I was posted to—"

"Why Kalur's Fist?" she asked, before Willet decided to relate his entire life story. "Why somewhere so remote, with no prospect of help from his followers?"

Willet glanced around at the other priests, as though one of them might answer for him. None of them offered him so much as a glimmer of hope in that regard.

"He seeks to bring back Undometh. To offer a sacrifice, as it is written within the Prophesies."

A guffaw, as Oleksig found the notion preposterous. "He hopes to raise a bloody dragon?"

Willet nodded, as though there was nothing preposterous about it at all. "That is his plan, yes."

Oleksig shook his head. "The man is clearly mad."

He was right in that regard, but Sanctan's plan was still not beyond the realm of possibility. Rosomon had already heard tell of magics far fouler than dragons. If the Scions of the Magna could summon demons, then what difference Sanctan conjuring a Wyrm from its slumber? Not that it would stop her pursuing him. Her only issue now was finding him alive.

"How far ahead of us is he?"

"He left the night you breached the city gates," Willet replied.

"Two days' start?"

Willet nodded. "He took a landship north. The last one still functioning."

Oleksig sighed in frustration. "So more like five days' start. We'll never catch him before he reaches the mountain. Once he realises there is no dragon to raise he will most likely disappear. We'll never see him again."

"Or perhaps he'll succeed," Falko said. "Perhaps the Prophesies are real. Perhaps Undometh will rise again, and then we have a bigger problem than just Sanctan."

That silenced them all. Even Oleksig.

"It doesn't matter," Rosomon said, ignoring Falko's warning. "Whether we believe he has the power to bring back one of the Great Wyrms or not, there may still be a way to catch him before he reaches the Fist."

She turned, making her way through the vast archway that led out onto the jetty beyond. The wind whipped at her as she walked toward the far end, closely followed by her entourage. Up ahead, the ark sat waiting for her like a black gargoyle. It felt like it was watching her as she drew closer, grumbling in anticipation of her arrival.

Nine dark knights stood vigil. Day and night they had been there, taking no sustenance nor rest. They unnerved her more than she would ever admit, but she approached them anyway.

Before they could move to bar Rosomon's path, Wenis walked down from within ark's yawning maw, every step taken with balletic grace. Damn, that woman loved to make an entrance.

"Ah, Lady of Hawkspur." She smiled widely, as though they were old friends. "I assume you have come to see your son? He is very well by the way. I have been—"

"I came to speak with you."

Wenis looked surprised, then abashed by such a compliment. "Me?"

"I need your airship, one more time. I must reach a mountain peak far to the north. And I must reach it quickly."

Wenis turned, gesturing to the damaged hull and the bent iron of the ark's gunwales. "As you can see, it has received quite a beating. It took every ounce of puff to fly it up here to this lofty peak. But your son is tinkering away somewhere. He assures me it may fly again soon."

"It is important we leave with all haste."

"It is? And what could be so pressing that—"

"Sanctan. The one you call the Dragon Priest. He has fled north to summon one of his Great Wyrms. He is the one I must stop."

Wenis raised her slender eyebrows and puckered her lips. "How very daring."

Rosomon ignored how this woman made light of everything. "Do you believe it can be done? That he could call forth this beast? I am less inclined to believe in such superstition, but I know your people—"

She stopped as Wenis grinned at her. "Whether we believe in superstition is not the important part. Superstition believes in us, Lady of Hawkspur. That is all that matters."

Noise from within the ark, the clanking sound of metal feet on iron steps, as Fulren appeared. Wenis held out her hand as though presenting him.

"Ah, here is the wounded soldier."

Fulren nodded in acknowledgment of her joke, but Rosomon could see the discomfort he was in.

"Mother," he said.

"Fulren, I was just—"

"Yes, I heard. You need the airship. But it's still in a bad way."

"Can it be repaired?"

He looked unsure. "Maybe. I think. But this thing is not powered by any artifice or sorcery we are familiar with. However..." He looked back at it, as though it were a living creature demanding respect. "I think I can circumvent the current control system. Use pyrestone to power the engine rather than..."

He left that last part hanging in the air. Rosomon didn't even want to consider what it might be that gave this infernal contraption the capability to fly.

"Good. How long do you think before we can leave?"

"Not too long, if my theory works. But I'll need help."

"And you will have it. Anything you want."

Wenis clapped with joy. "How wonderful that we are all working together. Like one big happy family."

Rosomon didn't rise to the bait, keeping her focus on Fulren. "So tell me, how do we get this thing working?"

Her son smiled. "Well…"

# ANSELL

It had been a day since he had passed the abandoned landship, along with the corpse of its driver. The man had been dead when Ansell found him, his body already cold. No telling how far ahead they were, but the discovery had instilled a greater sense of urgency in Ansell, one that was not shared by the weary horse beneath him.

Nevertheless, he pushed the steed to its limit, ignoring the shaking in its legs, the shortness of its breath. Only when he finally saw Wyrmhead, rising like a sentinel across the rolling plain, did he allow it to slow its pace.

The tower was as majestic as he remembered, the last surviving bastion of the Draconate Ministry, now the Guilds had wreaked their revenge. In the past, the fortress had always filled him with awe, but also an overwhelming sense of belonging. A home in which he could find solace, no matter what he had endured or what might weigh on his mind. Now, with every yard closer, it only prompted a sense of foreboding.

When finally he reached it, Ansell climbed down from his horse and hobbled the beast with the rein. The huge oaken door barred his way, still standing despite what the tower had clearly suffered. There had been a siege here, at this holy site, but Wyrmhead had managed to endure.

The surrounding curtain wall was nought but rubble, the masonry and statues that had peered proudly from the veneer of the tower now smashed to pieces. Scorch marks marred every surface, but those doors still stood. Doors that he noticed lay open to him.

He reached out and pushed them wider with a creak, a breath of cold air greeting him from within. As he stepped inside, he remembered how this place had once felt alive, with legate and serf going about their business of worship. It had been a serene sanctum to their gods. Now it was like a tomb.

Ansell listened for a moment, trying to discern if anyone was here. When he heard nothing, he thought perhaps Sanctan and his entourage had already left, that he should leave this place, filled with its old ghosts, and continue his pursuit to the Fist. He quelled that notion. Despite the urgency of his mission, Ansell felt compelled to search further, and took the huge winding stair upward into the dark, ears pricked for any sign that Sanctan, and more importantly Grace, was still here.

Flight after flight, he peered down the corridors and into the vestibules, but saw no sign of anyone. The higher he went, the more he considered what he might do if he did find them. His brothers would be armed and armoured, and here he was, in the rags of a beggar. He did not even have his faith to shield him any longer. It would be so easy for them to cut him down, and all this would have been for nothing.

Dismissing the thought, he arrived at the uppermost level. It was the sanctum of the Archlegate. A humble place with a simple chair beside the hearth. Glass doors opened out onto the surrounding balcony and Ansell paused at the threshold. The wind was harsher here, blowing in his face as though admonishing him. But then admonishment was no less than he deserved. This was the very spot where he had murdered Gylbard. Slid that sword into his back to steal the last breath of a pious old man. The memory of it was like a blade in his own gut. All this could have been avoided if he had chosen to strike the heart of the traitor, Sanctan, rather than his former master.

A sudden mewl stirred Ansell from his reflection. He turned in time to hear a meow, low and needy, as along the precarious balcony strutted a cat.

Tapfoot.

Just the memory of that name raised a rare smile, one that tugged at the necrotic flesh of his mouth. Among all the names he had forgotten over the years, those of all the men he had killed, this was the one he remembered. And it belonged to a cat, of all things.

Ansell reached out a hand to offer the animal a fuss, but it recoiled from him. Only natural. He had, after all, slaughtered its master. Best to leave it alone.

He turned away from the balcony and the frigid wind. No sooner had he done so than an errant gust blew through the vestibule, agitating the long-dead ashes in the hearth. The pages of a book flapped in the breeze, and Ansell moved closer to the table on which it lay. The Draconate Prophesies, but then what other book would it be? A strip of leather had been left to hold open those pages, the passage that was marked filling him with dread, reminding him of the urgency with which he had travelled.

*The Wyrms will rise once more. Within their lairs they slumber, but with the greatest of sacrifices shall they return to walk the plains, cross the seas and soar above the mountains.*

Ansell knew those words well. Part of the story of Aigos the Penitent, first written in the ancient tongue of the Vardals. He sacrificed his own child to bring back Undometh, who would go on to face the might of the Archmages, along with the other Great Wyrms. That sacrifice had been made at Kalur's Fist, exactly where Sanctan intended to make his.

"You are too late."

The voice cut the cold air. Ansell turned, seeing an old woman in the doorway, her grey robes marking her as a lowly legate. She must have turned to the faith late in life to be so burdened by years and yet not reach the rank of High Legate.

"How do you know I am late? You have no idea what I seek."

She took a step into the room. "Why else would you have come to this place? You follow the Archlegate, but he is already gone. He told me what happened at the Anvil. What happened to his great plans and what he intends to do about it."

"Sanctan told you?"

"Of course. The Archlegate shares everything with his faithful brood."

If only she knew. If only she were wise enough to see through him, but then no one else had been, so why would a lowly legate?

"How long ago was he here?"

"They rested for only one night before carrying on their journey north."

"And how many are they?"

"The Archlegate and four of your brothers."

"And the girl?"

The mention of her seemed to fill the woman with a little levity, a smile creeping up the side of her wizened mouth. "Yes, Grace. Such a sweet little thing she is. Though quiet. Not like most children her age."

"And you know what he intends to do with her?"

She looked at that book, pages still fluttering in the wind. "I have surmised it." Then she looked back at him, more determined than before. "But it is not our place to question—"

"Maybe not *your* place."

She nodded knowingly. "You seek to stop him."

"I do. And that surprises you?"

She smirked, shaking her grey-haired head. "I am old. Very little surprises me anymore. Even when the Ironfalls came to raze this place to the ground I was not surprised by it. Nor was I fearful. The Great Wyrms—"

"Spare me," Ansell spat. "I have spent a lifetime listening to prating priests spouting litanies about the gods. I will listen to them no more."

He made his way toward the stairs, and she moved from his path.

"It will be a difficult journey," she offered as he strode by.

He paused, feeling tired all of a sudden, and so very hungry. "I know."

"It's cold in those mountains. Perhaps I can find you a coat. And some food for the road north."

He looked her up and down, confused by the contradiction in her. "I thought you were one of his faithful. Yet you would help me stop him?"

"Oh, I am faithful. Obedient to the last, but I am not altogether without compassion. I have not yet had that driven from me."

"So you will help me defy an edict of the Archlegate? Despite that faith?"

She raised her hands, showing her palms. "I would merely offer warmth and sustenance to a man in need of it. The rest lies with the will of the Wyrms."

Ansell felt his burden lift, ever so slightly. "Thank you."

"Come," she said, heading down the stairs. "We must be swift. They have a head start."

# FULREN

He struggled to get comfortable in the tight confines of the engine room. Steel piping and an array of tools surrounded him. Oil soaked his hands and smeared his face. Normally Fulren would have liked to work in a much tidier environment, but that was a luxury time would not allow.

Carefully he connected the conduit that would funnel a cooling agent directly into the engine core. As he was about to install the compression ring it slipped from his greasy hand and clattered to the floor.

"This won't work," Wenis said.

She had told him that already. More than once. It was starting to grate on his nerves even more than the filthy conditions.

"Have a little faith."

"The creature in that sarcophagus is not some pet for you to command. It seeks any way to defy you and free itself from its prison. Now you think it will obey you because you have encased it in wires and attached your stones to it?"

Fulren wasn't certain, but the arcanist magic of Nyrakkis channeled the demon's power by sorcerous means. Surely he could do the same with artifice.

He glanced around the chamber, noticing for the first time how much it had changed since he'd started working on it. Wires connected scores of conversion chambers full of pyrestones—blue and red—that would run circuits of energy to the central core they had rigged on the deck. It had taken him a full day and night without sleep, but the work had given him something else to think about other than the news about Conall. One blessing at least.

"Can you just trust that I know what I'm doing. As I said... faith."

Wenis leaned closer. "If faith is what you are hoping for, then I fear we are doomed to stay here until the end of time."

He picked up the compression ring again, gripping the conduit tighter and managing to secure it without dropping the thing. A quick tug and he was satisfied it would hold. At the same time, he was sure he heard a distant clang of metal, as though there were something physical within the sarcophagus of the engine room trying to get out.

That demon was raging against him. Roaring at the desecration of its earthly tomb. It knew its time was almost at an end. Fulren could only hope it was right.

"Let's find out if I'm right, shall we?" he said, squirming from the mess of cables and piping.

He led Wenis up onto the deck, where a group of artificers were still making final touches to the mechanical rig they had secured within that arcane symbol. As Fulren appeared they stopped their tinkering and stepped back. He could see they looked nervous, and with good reason. It was bad enough that they had to be aboard this infernal ark, let alone tampering with sorcery they could barely understand. Not one of them had volunteered to help him in the engine room, and he could hardly blame them.

"Is it ready?" he asked.

One of the artificers stepped forward, Philbert, the most senior of their number. He pulled the skullcap from his head and wrung it in his bony hands.

"Yes," he said, nodding that balding head. "Yes, I think so, my lord."

Fulren tried to smile back at the old artificer, to reassure him there was nothing to fear. "How many times, Philbert, there's no need to call me that."

Wenis giggled. "I quite like it... Lord Fulren."

He looked down at her, his glyphsight picking out the motes of light that made up her face. "So do you want to try it out?"

She curtsied as though at court in bygone days. "Yes, my lord."

The gaggle of artificers moved clear of the iron symbol and the ugly device squatting in its centre. It was a solid engine of iron, an altar of artifice in the midst of that unholy arcanist symbol. Beneath it were strands upon strands of wire and piping connected to the tomb belowdecks. Within, a mess of manifolds, gaskets, cylinders and valves, all connecting pyrestones to a central core. It looked horrendous, but Fulren was confident it would work. He had to be.

Wenis stepped close to the machine. She looked tiny beside it as she held out her hands, static filling the air as she summoned her Maladoran sorceries. She closed her eyes, lifting her head and raising arms already glowing green with the magic of her necroglyphs.

Fulren sensed the air around him grow heavy as the engine began to grumble and moan, the pyrestones within bursting to life. Below them, he could hear the demon whine in its tomb as the ark's engines coughed and sputtered to life.

There was a hum, and with it a feeling of weightlessness. The ark rose a few inches from the ground, the wood of the deck and iron of the bulwarks groaning at the effort.

Fulren heard a dull explosion. Then another, as a pyrestone within the engine shattered, flinging red glass across the deck. The ark slammed to the ground, and a couple of artificers wailed as they lost their footing.

"Damn it," Wenis snarled. "The demon resists. I told you we could never control it with your mechanical abomination."

Fulren clenched his steel fist tight in frustration, looking to Philbert, who was gripping the gunwale for purchase. "Any clue how to fix this?"

Fearfully, Philbert looked to his fellow artificers, but none of them had any ideas, or if they did lacked the courage to speak them.

Philbert looked back helplessly. "Perhaps supplementary conversion chambers at the cardinal points of egress might funnel more power through the conductors?"

"Worth a try I suppose," Fulren replied, all out of ideas himself.

Reluctantly, the artificers approached the engine once again, taking up their tools. Before Fulren could begin to help them, Wenis gestured across the deck and out along the jetty.

"You have a visitor."

Fulren looked over the gunwale, seeing Verlyn approaching the ark. She had the hood of her cloak pulled close over her head, despite the bright sun shining down.

"Carry on," Fulren ordered the artificers, before heading through the airship.

He stepped out of the hatch and past the knights who stood in perpetual vigil. Verlyn had stopped some yards away, and he greeted her with a smile.

"Verlyn."

"Fulren," she replied, not offering a smile of her own. "I just came to..."

"You're leaving, aren't you?" It was all he could assume.

Verlyn nodded. "It's time. There's no more to be done."

Fulren guessed she was right. The Ministry had been beaten and Ashe avenged. Other than tracking down Sanctan and seeing him punished, Verlyn had done everything she'd set out to.

"Where will you go?"

She took in a long breath. "I need to find some old friends. Get reacquainted. I've left it long enough."

"You can always stay, you know." Fulren felt a sudden tug of loss. They had never grown close despite their time together, but he had come to rely on her. "There's no need for you to go anywhere. I'm sure my mother could find a place for you here."

"I'm sure she could." A hint of disdain in her voice. "But no. The Anvil isn't for me." She looked him up and down. "And perhaps it isn't for you either."

"What does that mean?"

She took a step closer, as though she might embrace him, but stopped short. "Can you really see yourself staying here? Being accepted, after what you've become?"

He hadn't even considered it. "My mother will—"

"Gods, Fulren, don't you see it? Your mother doesn't need you any more than you need her. You have power now. Real power. And it's not born of this place. If you have any sense, you'll get as far from this city as you can. This country. There is a cancer at its heart, and it will eat away at you if you let it."

Something in her had changed. He had seen Verlyn mad before, enraged, but this time there was a venom he had never witnessed before.

"What... what are you talking about?"

"This war is over, but the division, the hate... that will never end. The Guilds are just as malevolent a machine as the Ministry, only all its parts work against one another as often as they work in union. They need to be held together by a stronger will than your mother is capable of. If left to her, it will eventually fall apart."

He shook his head. "No. A year ago maybe you might have been right, but my mother has changed. She's been tempered by the war, like we all have. She's stronger now than I've ever known her."

"Is she? Or is it all for show, Fulren? A mask she's wearing to stop Torwyn breaking apart. One that might slip at any time."

He resisted the urge to walk away, to turn his back on her and not listen. "Why do you even care? You're leaving all this behind anyway, Ministry and Guild."

That seemed to curb her ire slightly, but there was still an intensity to her eyes Fulren could see even with his glyphsight.

"I guess when I was with Ashe I didn't care about any of it. Now though..." She shook her head, as though ridding it of old memories. "Anyway, I just wanted to say goodbye."

Her final words sounded regretful, as though she knew this was the end. That they would never speak again.

"All right then. But please, take care." He reached out to touch her, but she had already pulled away.

"And you, Fulren."

As he watched her leave he could only wonder what might become of her. There was so much bitterness still there. After all she had done to avenge Ashe it had done nothing to heal the wounds. It hurt him to think that she had been through all this for nothing.

Hurt even more that perhaps what she'd said about him not belonging here was right.

He raised his metal hand, flexing clawlike fingers. He could feel them, as though they had nerves, despite there being no flesh, bones or tendons. Only steel and wire. Half machine, half man, held together by sorcery he could barely understand.

A deep belch behind him, and Fulren turned to see a gout of smoke rising from the rear of the ark. It was followed by a thrumming sound as the engine within revved, louder and louder. No longer the screeching protestations of the demon within. Now it sounded just like any pyrestone engine.

The artificers up on the deck gave a chorus of cheers, and Philbert was just visible throwing his skullcap into the air in celebration.

They'd done it. The airship was working.

When Fulren looked back over his shoulder to see if Verlyn had seen their success, she was already gone.

# KEARA

The streets were eerily calm, considering what had happened only two days previously. That chaos was now replaced by a kind of tranquil mundanity. Right now, she couldn't say which she preferred.

Her attention was taken by a low buzz far above the Anvil. A black dot like a beetle in the sky, that airship travelling north, making a very different sound to when it had arrived. No longer the howling dread of Nyrakkis. Now the low hum of artifice as Lady Rosomon made her way to the Dolur Peaks to exact her vengeance on Sanctan. Keara couldn't find it in her heart to wish her good luck. Maybe it would be better if she failed. Or at least better for the Hallowhills. Truth was, Keara had no idea if she was better off with Egelrath or Hawkspur. Looked like either way she'd be a slave.

She shook her head, vainly trying to clear the prospect of thraldom from her mind. Best not to think on what might happen when Rosomon got back. Best keep her eyes and ears open to the here and now.

People were watching her as she made her way through the city. Not for the first time she regretted walking these streets alone. Keara wanted to make a point by showing how unafraid she was, showing that there was peace in the Anvil now, and she'd helped make it happen. Looked like not everyone shared her belief from the evil looks she was getting, but she couldn't blame them for being angry with her methods.

Her fingers never strayed too far from the knives at her hips, not that she expected to use them. Despite the looks she was getting it was obvious the fight was gone out of these people. There'd be no appetite for reprisals. At least not from these nobodies.

It was the Guilds she had to be wary of. The smell of retribution was on the air, vengeance against those who'd brought about the uprising, and Keara didn't know yet whether she'd be in their sights. Which meant it was exactly the right time for her to make a move. Swift and decisive, while everyone was still licking their wounds. That throne wouldn't stay vacant forever, and the longer Keara waited, the less chance it would be her arse warming it.

Up ahead she could see Armigers marshalling the clearing up of rubble, and with them, one of her own stormhulks. They worked together with such harmony that she couldn't help but consider if this was the way it was always meant to be—each part of Guild, Armiger and citizenry in symbiosis, uniting for the good of Torwyn.

All thoughts of striking up more rebellions and seizing thrones faded as she watched them work in unison. The mere notion of yet more violence suddenly made her stomach churn. It was enough to give her pause, and she turned away from the scene before her nerve gave out altogether.

The Whitespin flowed away to her left and she paused at the riverside for a moment. Traffic was moving along it once again, the gentle putt-putt-putting of barges filling the air like a distant melody. Damn, as much as she hated this river, she couldn't help but find that noise reassuring. Made her glad to be alive.

Now all this shit was over she should have been glad. Should have clutched on to this peace and held it tight. Taken her win. Shown her gratitude, rather than thinking of her own blind ambition. The farther she walked into the city, the more she was reminded of what she had to be grateful for. Just the call of a market trader selling their wares felt like soft music. But no, not selling...giving that food away. Helping the struggling city folk, despite the fact that they had hardly anything to give.

It was all so admirable. So inspiring.

Keara caught herself. Where just a year before she'd have considered a thing like that pathetic, now she found herself moved by such an altruistic gesture. It kind of made her want to be a better person, and she found herself smiling for the first time in...

"Apple?" someone asked.

She looked around, seeing an old man with a basket full of them, holding one out to her. It shone in the sunlight, all juicy and tempting, and sparking a memory of when she'd arrived here months ago. Ulger had helped himself to a stallholder's apple back then, like some playground bully. Now this old man was handing them out like treats.

"Thank you," she said, taking the apple from his hand, wondering if this was some kind of trick, but the man just smiled and nodded his acknowledgment, before moving on to someone else.

She watched him go before taking a bite. It was sour—not quite as juicy and sweet as it looked—but then nothing ever was. Everything in her life turned bitter eventually. Sanctan's betrayal. The deal she'd had to make with the Hawkspurs, but at least there still was a deal. She should be thankful for the second chance, and looking around at the state of the city, Keara knew her webwainers and stormhulks would be needed for some time to come. And as long as she was useful, she was safe.

She left the marketplace behind and headed up to the Cogwheel, starting to feel a little safer on the streets. Maybe it had all been in her head. Maybe no one was out to get her after all. The city folk certainly looked more preoccupied with cleaning up this place than seeking retribution.

Groups were clearing away rubble, hammering down collapsing walls, collecting anything valuable and stacking it neatly. There were no uniforms here, no officers barking orders. Just everyone working for the good of their city. A few short days ago these people had been lobbing rocks at one another and chasing down dissenters with flaming torches. Now they were helping one another rebuild. Surely there was a lesson in there somewhere.

"We need more carts." A voice she recognised from among the throng.

Squinting in the sunlight, Keara spotted the lean form of Tyreta bloody Hawkspur... but of course it was. Who else would be here, mucking in with the throng?

"See if you can get someone from the manufactories to loan us more," Tyreta said to a couple of young lads. They nodded and ran off obediently.

How typical of a Hawkspur. Ingratiating herself with the commoners. Pitching in like she cared. Keara knew it was all for show.

She thought about walking on by. Leaving Tyreta to her virtue, but she just couldn't leave well enough alone. As Tyreta moved further into one of the derelict buildings, Keara followed.

"Impressive, Hawkspur," she said, before Tyreta could load up more fallen masonry into a cart. Tyreta stopped what she was doing but didn't look around. "Doing your bit for the city? It's kind of admirable really."

"It's my duty," Tyreta said, turning slowly. "Maybe you should think about doing the same. Or have you just come to watch other people clear up the mess you made?"

Haughty as always, the arrogant bitch. "I played my part. Did what I needed to and put things right. Just ask your mother if you don't—"

"Put things right?" Tyreta took a threatening step forward.

Those eyes looked more like an animal's than ever, but Keara refused to be intimidated. "Yes, I have. The Guilds would never have won this without me."

"So what? Do you want a reward?"

Now it was Keara's turn to step closer. "Maybe I do. Maybe I should get the respect I deserve for starters."

Tyreta's face screwed up into a disdainful sneer. It made her pretty features ugly, feral even. "You get to live. That should be reward enough after what you did."

The truth of that took all the fire out of Keara's belly. Tyreta was right. Maybe she should just take her win and leave things be. There were so many times she thought she'd never make it out of this alive, but here she was, still standing. Besides, she had wronged this girl with her betrayal. Literally slid her knife into one of Tyreta's friends. It wasn't like she deserved any forgiveness.

"Look, we've both done things. Bad things. Both lost people. But the Guilds are back in their rightful place. We need to start looking forward."

"Just forgive and forget?" Tyreta didn't sound too convinced by the idea.

"Just be pragmatic, that's all. The Hawkspurs and Hallowhills are going to need one another to rebuild Torwyn."

Tyreta gestured at the rubble surrounding her. "I'm already doing my part in that." She looked Keara up and down. "So what are you doing?"

She certainly wasn't going to make this easy. Keara moved that little bit closer, talking that little bit quieter, trying to sound just a touch more reasonable.

"All I'm saying is that we've worked together before to bring this thing to an end. We'll be working together from now on. We don't need to be friends, but..."

Tyreta turned her back, focusing on her rocks. Keara felt a flash of annoyance at the rebuttal. She couldn't just leave it like this.

"I'm trying my best here. All I'm saying is..." Keara almost couldn't form the words. "...I'm just...I'm sorry. For everything. All that's happened. And I'm sorry for what you've had to go through, especially with your brothers. I know Conall was—"

Tyreta moved like lightning, spinning, face twisted in rage. This time there was no questioning the animal within her, as she reached out and grasped Keara's throat.

Her breath was cut off as she was raised into the air and slammed against the crumbling wall. Tyreta's claws dug into the flesh of her neck, but all Keara could focus on were those eyes, sickly yellow, pupils two slits as they glared with hate.

Keara kicked out with her legs but couldn't find purchase. Already her vision was clouding, her fingers fumbling at the hilt of those daggers.

"Go on," snarled Tyreta, voice only half-human. "Draw them, if you can."

Keara gave out a pitiful choking sound, realising she'd never be able to unsheathe them and imbue any power before her head was ripped off. Instead, she raised her hands in surrender.

Tyreta growled in frustration, flinging Keara aside. She landed amid the rubble, body crumpling as she huffed in air, ignoring the cuts and bruises. The humiliation hurt far more.

Slowly she rose, doing her best to quell the anger, and turned to face Tyreta. The bitch was glaring, though the feral aspect to her had all but drained away. A tingle in Keara's fingers as they hovered close to her daggers. She could draw them now. Fuel them with all her power and light this whole place up.

Instead she raised a hand to her neck, dabbing at the flesh and seeing the blood on her fingertips. "You've made your position clear, Hawkspur."

With as much dignity as she could muster, she turned and left Tyreta amid the rubble. Walked past those diligent civilians as they carried on with their labours. Ignored the vendors giving away their wares. For some reason they suddenly didn't look so charitable.

This time as she passed, she realised these people weren't just ignoring her. They were laughing at her. Taunting her behind her back. Spitting and cursing her name.

They wouldn't disrespect her for much longer.

Eventually she found a team of webwainers working on the main throughfare. Among them was Galirena, marshalling a couple of stormhulks as they shifted boulders too large for the cleanup teams to handle. She smiled as Keara approached, likely glad the fighting was over. How could she know that for the Hallowhills, this was far from over?

"We need to talk," Keara said.

The contented expression on Galirena's face faltered. "About what?"

Keara leaned in close, teeth almost gnashing. "About the future of our fucking Guild."

"Sounds serious."

"It is. Remember when I told you to spread the word? To get our people ready? Well, now is the time."

Galirena frowned. "You mean—"

"I mean we're done wallowing in the shit with the rest of these fuckers. The Guilds have just fought a long hard war. They're weak. The Armigers are in disarray. Now is as good a time as any to make our move. We're seizing control."

Galirena's look of confusion gradually faded as Keara spoke, until eventually she nodded. "All right. We're with you."

For the second time in a day Keara allowed herself a smile. "I was hoping that's what you'd say."

She turned and made her way back toward their barracks. It was fortunate Galirena had said that...it would have been a shame if Keara had been forced to kill her on such a sunny day.

# TYRETA

She picked up a boulder in one hand, most likely too heavy for a man twice her size to lift. The cart juddered as she slammed it down. Damn that bitch, Tyreta should have killed her. Ripped her head off and drank from the stump. She tried to breathe, hoping it would calm her. No good. Maybe if she exhausted herself with all this work it would make her feel better.

Another rock. This time it took two hands, but she hefted it with a growl in her throat. A clatter as she slammed that rock into the cart alongside the first.

No, that wasn't going to work either. Damn Keara Hallowhill and damn this whole fucking place.

Another rock lay at her feet. A lonely little thing just staring at her. Taunting her. Tyreta stooped and grasped it, holding it out in front of her as she squeezed. Her teeth ground together as she tightened her grip, desperate to crush it in her fist, but not even she was strong enough to break rocks in her hand. Instead she yelped in frustration, turning, flinging the thing against the wall. It smashed, shattering into a hundred pieces... right next to Sted's head.

"Easy there!" Sted shouted, ducking instinctively. "There's safer ways to clear away all this shit than lobbing it at folk."

"Sorry," Tyreta said immediately, feeling even stupider.

Sted walked closer, an unusually sympathetic look in her eye. "You okay? Or is that a stupid fucking question?"

Tyreta nodded, though she was far from okay. "Yeah, I'm fine. I just saw someone I'd rather not..."

"Have to kill?"

Tyreta smiled. Sted always had a habit of putting things in plain language. "So you saw her?"

A nod. "I did. And I can only imagine how you feel about that twat. But there's an armistice. Even though retribution tastes damn good, we've got to swallow it down no matter how strongly we feel."

If even Sted could get her head around the truce, then Tyreta should definitely have made the effort. Maybe changing the subject would help.

"Have you heard anything about Conall?"

"No," Sted said with a sigh. "But we've got the whole of the Talon out looking. There's no sign that he left the city, but then who knows? He could be anywhere."

"I just don't understand it. What could be wrong with him? He wouldn't just kill Donan for no reason. He was such a gentle soul."

"No, he wouldn't. But I saw him that night. There was something different about him. A devil inside. One he must have brought back from the Drift."

Maybe it hadn't been such a good idea changing the subject after all. Now all Tyreta wanted to do was bury herself in this work even more, but she doubted that would take her mind off her brother.

"You here for the day?" Sted asked.

As useless as Tyreta felt, she could only nod. "I have to do something."

Sted began to roll up her sleeves. "Best we get on with it then."

She wanted to tell Sted her help wasn't necessary, that she had more than done her duty to the Hawkspurs and the people of Torwyn, but she could hardly turn down such a gesture. So the two of them carried on clearing up the mess as best they could as the afternoon wore onto evening, but it seemed an endless and thankless task. No matter how hard Tyreta worked she couldn't rid herself of the pain and anger. So much suffering and all for nothing. So much lost by so many. She should have been joyous at their victory, that the Guilds had managed to defeat the tyrants of the Ministry, but the longer she toiled the more pointless all that strife seemed.

As night drew in, she could see that Sted was starting to struggle. Tyreta could have carried on until the morning, and she doubted Sted would give in before she dropped. It wasn't her style to lose face, so best Tyreta give in for the both of them.

"I think we've done enough for one day," she said, watching as the other workers began to filter away into the dusk.

"Oh, thank fuck," Sted said, dropping a particularly large boulder on the ground. "I thought you were never gonna stop."

Tyreta clapped a hand to her shoulder. "Let's get some rest. I think we've earned it."

Sted screwed up her nose. "Fuck that. It's been a long day—we deserve a drink."

"I don't think—"

"Then don't think, Hawkspur. There's an alehouse not too far from here, and it's open all night long."

Tyreta thought about arguing, but she'd already learned that there was no point trying to change Sted's mind when it was made up. With renewed vigour, Sted led them away from the devastation and along a labyrinthine path of alleyways. Armiger troopers stood watch at every corner, and Tyreta remembered how she'd felt walking these streets so recently. Then it had been militia and Revocaters she'd been wary of. Now the Armigers held sway, along with the Blackshields. She had to admit, it didn't feel any less menacing.

Sted eventually raised her arms at a lopsided sign hanging from the wall of one particularly seedy looking back alley. "Here we are."

Tyreta squinted through the gloom. *The Dripping Bucket* was scrawled in crumbling black paint, and someone had made a cursory effort to draw an appropriate rendition of one below it. They probably shouldn't have bothered.

"You bring me to all the best places. Who comes up with these stupid names for taverns anyway?"

Sted shrugged. "Whoever it is, they're probably fucking shitfaced.

Which is exactly how we'll be in about an hour, if I have anything to do with it."

She led the way, swinging the door wide before striding in with all the urgency of someone desperate for a drink. Inside, the atmosphere was subdued. No raucous welcome here, just furtive glances from assorted booths as the patrons nursed their tankards and smoked their pipes.

"I'm not sure this was such a good idea," Tyreta whispered, wary of the looks they were getting.

"Relax," Sted said, slapping her on the arm. "What's the worst that could happen?"

Tyreta followed her further into the room, remembering when she'd heard those words before. Wyllow had said that very same thing before they'd entered the tavern in New Flaym. It was a bittersweet memory.

Before Sted could find a table, Tyreta saw a group she recognised. Handsome Colbert was sitting with big Lena and a brooding Maronne. They looked filthy, their clothes bedraggled, and it appeared that Tyreta hadn't been the only one doing her best to shift the city's rubble.

"Maybe we should sit over here," Tyreta said, leading Sted toward the table.

At her approach, Colbert smiled. "Tyreta?"

She offered him a smile back, wondering how he always managed to keep his teeth so white. "It's good to see you."

"And you," he said, rising to his feet and gesturing to the empty chairs at their table. "Please, join us."

As she sat down, she noticed that Maronne looked far from pleased at her arrival, but Lena shifted a chair so Sted could sit down beside her.

"So, who are your friends?" Sted asked, offering Lena a warm grin.

"This is Colbert." The handsome one, but that didn't need saying. "Lena and Maronne. They helped me break out the Titanguard."

"How very brave," Sted replied, still looking into big Lena's eyes. "My name is Lieutenant Stediana Walden of the Hawkspur Talon."

She held out her hand for Lena to shake, seemingly oblivious to the rest of them.

"Nice to meet you," Lena replied, shaking the proffered hand in a meaty fist.

Sted grinned. "Pleasure is most definitely mine."

Colbert signalled the barman for more drinks, before turning his attention back to Tyreta. "So how are you? Things got pretty rough, good to see you made it."

She nodded. "Things got pretty rough for everyone."

"Rougher still for some," Maronne said, staring into her drink.

It was only then that Tyreta realised one of their number was missing. "Where... where's Torfin?"

Maronne raised a thumb and jabbed it toward the door. "Most likely in one of those holes they've dug west of the city."

"I'm sorry," she replied, unable to think of anything better to say at the news that he was dead.

"Are you?" Maronne looked up from her drink, obviously unconvinced.

"Of course I am. Torfin was a good man. And I understand how much everyone has lost to beat the Ministry."

Maronne's eyes narrowed. "You do? Really?"

Before Tyreta could answer, Sted placed a hand between them on the table. "No one has sacrificed as much as Tyreta and the Hawkspurs to end this whole thing."

"That a fucking fact?" Maronne almost spat the words in Sted's face.

The scrape of a chair as Sted rose to her feet. Tyreta put a hand on her wrist to calm her, but it didn't look like it would do any good. Luckily Colbert stood too, placing himself between the women.

"Hey," he said, voice stark in the quiet barroom. "We're all on the same side here."

Slowly Sted and Maronne sat back in their seats. Tyreta leaned in closer to Maronne, who didn't seem too keen to look her in the eye anymore.

"I am sorry. Truly. But it's over now. And things will get better from here. I promise—"

"Will they?" Maronne gazed over, looking suddenly drunk and very tired. "Better for who?"

"For everyone," she replied, without really thinking about what that meant.

Maronne glanced around the room at the sorry gathering of patrons. "Apart from there being a few less of us now, and half the city is reduced to rubble, looks to me like everything is pretty much the same. The little people are rewarded by everything going back to the way it was. The only ones claiming the spoils are the Guilds."

She accentuated her last word with a jab of her finger in Tyreta's direction.

There was silence then. A sullen mood hanging over them as Tyreta tried to think of how to explain. But there was no explaining. Everything Tyreta had seen and heard since the Sundered Isles told her that Maronne was right.

There was a clank of tankards as the serving lad brought their drinks over. He placed them down with a clunk and a slosh of ale before retreating into the dark.

Tyreta took a tankard and raised it. "To Torfin."

Maronne made no move to touch her own drink, but Colbert, Lena and Sted all raised theirs and toasted the big man.

"I mean it," Tyreta whispered. "The Guilds will change. There'll be more for everyone. I'll make sure of it." It was as much for her own benefit. As though by making the promise it might help it come true.

Maronne took a long draft of her beer before looking right at her. "I'm sure you will."

She slammed the empty tankard back down on the table and stood. Without another word she walked out into the night.

"She's not very friendly," Sted muttered, taking another drink.

Tyreta stared in Maronne's wake. That woman had been right all along. Right with her suspicion. Right with her disdain. Things would never change, no matter how much Tyreta wanted them to.

Suddenly the ale was a little too bitter for her taste, and she pushed the tankard across the table. "I'm going to go."

Sted looked at her with an awkward wince. "Will you be okay?

Only I might hang around for a while." She nodded her head toward Lena.

"Have yourself a good night."

Tyreta stood, suddenly feeling a little light-headed, despite the small amount of ale she'd drunk. As she stepped out into the cool night air, nausea hit her in a rush and she staggered, leaning against a wall to vomit in the gutter.

Pushing herself upright, she stumbled down the road away from the tavern. A cat in the shadows raised its hackles at her before hissing and disappearing into the shadows.

A hundred voices seemed to be talking in her ears, but one was louder than the rest...Lorens, his face mournful as he spoke to her atop the palace.

*What about the men and women scratching a living in the mines and manufactories? Living and dying in misery, so that we can sit in our estates.*

*We had too much. We were driven by avarice, not altruism. We lost sight of what really mattered. We were blinded by greed.*

*Even if we could have shown my father, your mother, what they were doing, do you think they would have listened? Do you think they would have given up all they had gained, just to alleviate the pain of these people?*

He had been right all along, and it made her suddenly wonder if she'd been on the right side through all of this. Tyreta had always been loyal to her mother, to the Guilds, even if she hadn't known how to show it, but now it felt as though she didn't belong with them anymore.

Didn't belong anywhere.

Holding down the nausea as best she could, she let the dark city streets take her.

# ANSELL

He stumbled, sliding in the drift, hands digging into the snow as he tried to avoid landing flat on his face. The wind howled at him again, laughing at him, taunting him. He would ignore it, as he had ignored all else on this journey. Ansell was close now. He could only hope he wasn't too late.

The horse had died a day before. He had lost sign of their trail the day before that, but the pass up into the mountains to Kalur's Fist was a single track. Only one way in. Only one way out. As long as he met no one coming back this way, he knew there was still a chance.

A drop in the wind, a gap in the snowfall, and he spied it up ahead. That peak jutting up defiantly against the sky, a sign he had almost reached that fabled resting place. The tomb of a god, where Undometh was said to slumber. And as he squinted, eyes still streaming from the cold, he was sure he could see them for the first time; figures labouring through the snow toward the summit.

He pushed himself on, scrambling harder across the rocks. His feet and hands were numb, and it felt as though he were walking on blocks of stone, but it would not stop him. The knowledge that there was still time instilled more urgency within him. It fuelled his aching legs, made his blood pump faster in his frozen veins. If there was a chance he might save her then he could not tarry. Not while his heart still beat.

Gradually the ground flattened out as sheer cliffs rose around him. Sheltered from the squall, he realised he stood on a flat plateau surrounded by five standing stones. Spiralling designs were carved into the bare rock beneath his feet and on the faces of those dolmen. A shrine to the Great Wyrms, so far from any worshippers.

*Almost there. Just keep on moving.*

Ansell pushed himself on, leaving the shrine behind him. The path sloped up steeply and he all but crawled toward the summit. It led him to a sheltered rock shelf, and when Ansell raised his head he saw the entrance to a cave yawning wide. Before it, his brothers stood barring his way; four of them, fully armoured, swords drawn.

He refused to be daunted, here at the final obstacle, and he staggered to a stop before them. Breath misted from within those dragon helms, frost covering the steel of their armour, heavy cloaks adorning their shoulders, ruffling in the breeze.

"It is over," Ansell said, desperate to hide the chattering of his teeth. "There is no sense to this. Not now."

They remained silent, but the one on the far left turned his head ever so slightly, as though to see what his brothers might do. None of the others gave him any sign they were even listening.

"You have been lied to," Ansell continued. "You follow a man unworthy of your deference. Surely you can see that?"

Now the one on the far right turned his head. The knight next to him sighed, mist huffing from that helm.

Slowly he reached up, taking off the helmet and showing his face. The grim visage of Regenwulf looked upon Ansell, and for a moment he felt a stab of hope. When he saw how accusingly his brother regarded him, Ansell felt that hope flutter away on the frigid wind.

"We follow as we have always followed, brother," Regenwulf said, not an ounce of doubt in his voice. "You know that."

Ansell suddenly felt as though he might collapse from exhaustion, but somehow he managed to stay on his feet. "I understand. But for what purpose do you follow now? To sacrifice an innocent child in a vain attempt to bring back the gods?"

A twitch of Regenwulf's mouth beneath his thick moustache,

as though he struggled to understand. "The Wyrms must rise. It is written. This is the only way for us to win back what was lost."

"And you would murder a child to accomplish it? Has not enough blood been spilled already?"

Regenwulf shook his head, dismissing the notion. "Sanctan says—"

"Sanctan lies!" Ansell bellowed into the wind. "He can no more raise the Wyrms than I can halt this storm."

A shadow of doubt now crossed Regenwulf's brow. He glanced to left and right, as though expecting his brothers to help him in this. They offered him nothing.

Ansell stepped closer, holding out his empty hands in a pleading gesture. "We have bled and killed for this man, and it has all been for nothing. No more, Regenwulf. It is time for this to end."

Regenwulf shook his broad head in disbelief. "We bled for Torwyn, brother. And we reclaimed it for the Draconate. This..." He gestured to the yawning entrance to the mountain. "This is the only way we can hold on to—"

"Torwyn was never ours to claim. We are not tyrants. We are Torwyn's protectors. We always were. But not Sanctan. He would seize it for himself, and he has used you all to do it."

A hiss, as the knight on the far left slowly sheathed his sword. As though in silent agreement with Ansell, he took a step away from the entrance. For a moment, Regenwulf looked as though he might do the same, but he held fast.

"You know I speak the truth," Ansell pleaded. "Let me enter. I have to stop him. Let no more blood be shed for that man."

Regenwulf's eyes searched the frosty ground and he shook his head as though it ached. "But he is the Archlegate. Ordained by the High Legates. Chosen of the Wyrms."

"He was chosen of himself."

Regenwulf gritted his teeth as though the very idea of it pained him. "No. It was prophesied. Written for all to see. Gylbard passed so that Sanctan could rise and bring about our salvation."

Ansell felt his heart sink. There was no other way now. He had to tell Regenwulf the truth of it.

"Gylbard passed because... I slew him. On Sanctan's order."

The confusion left Regenwulf in an instant, to be replaced by anger. A dark shadow fell across his brow that spoke only murder.

"You?"

Ansell's shoulders slumped. He had gambled. He had lost. "Yes. Me, to my eternal shame. And it has left a stain on my soul that can never be cleansed. But let me try, brother. Let me save her."

Regenwulf tightened his grip on his sword. "I should have left you in that derelict storehouse. I should have let that monster cut you to pieces."

"Yes, you should." Ansell stepped forward, offering himself willingly. "And had I more time I would kneel and let you put right your mistake. But now I must enter that cave."

Tears were welling in Regenwulf's eyes. "It was all a lie."

"Brother, I have to—"

Fury ignited Regenwulf's face as he raised his blade. The sword crashed down, but the swing was sluggish, and Ansell managed to duck it despite his fatigue. As Regenwulf drew back for another strike, Ansell leapt forward to grab his wrists.

Regenwulf had always been strong as a bear, the advancing of his years never marring his might, and Ansell was forced to grab the naked blade, feeling the sharpened steel slice his palm as he did so. They struggled for supremacy, watched by their brothers, spitting and snarling as they fought. Their feet slipped on the icy ground, both men grunting in desperation as they tried to wrest control of the sword. Then Ansell saw a change in Regenwulf's furious eyes, and it looked for a moment as though something broke inside him.

The blade twisted in Ansell's hand, sword pivoting to pierce Regenwulf's gut beneath the breastplate. Before Ansell could stop himself, the impetus of his struggle forced the blade deeper.

Regenwulf froze, staring straight into Ansell's eyes, before all the strength left his body and he collapsed to the ice. Ansell grasped him, holding him close as warm blood spilled down his legs and across Ansell's hands.

"You have to finish it, boy," Regenwulf spat through gritted teeth. "You can't leave it like this. Time to clean up your mess. Time to make amends for all of us."

Ansell opened his mouth to speak a final word to his brother knight. The man who had trained him. Raised him. The man who had let him win this final fight. But there were no words left to speak.

Choking back a bellow of grief, Ansell plunged the blade deeper beneath that breastplate and into Regenwulf's rib cage. The light went from his brother's eyes instantly.

Had he more time, Ansell would have knelt and prayed for Regenwulf's soul, but time was a commodity he no longer possessed. Instead he rose to unsteady feet, facing the three remaining knights who still barred his path, as the wind howled its lament.

Above the sound of the storm came a noise. It was a low hum, as though a host of voices were raised in chorus. Turning, Ansell could see a black spot in the distance—the infernal airship from across the Drift.

"No more time, brothers," Ansell said.

The knight in the centre stepped aside. As soon as he moved, the others did the same, offering Ansell a way into the Fist. A glance back to see the approaching ark was making its way toward the flat shrine before Ansell stumbled inside.

It was little warmer within the cave, but the noise of the storm relented as soon as he entered, the howl of the wind replaced by the steady echo of his own footsteps. There were torches lit within ancient sconces carved into the walls, but it was still difficult to see any distance. Ansell staggered on, the granite path occasionally falling away to one side or the other into oblivion below. His route twisted within the mountain, taking him deeper as he listened intently for any sound. It wasn't until he heard that crooning voice echoing along the tunnel that he was spurred into further haste.

His legs burned as he began to run, loping across a bridge, his every muscle aching, crying for him to stop, but Ansell would not stop, not when he was so close.

At the far side of the bridge he saw them; Sanctan standing atop another shrine as old as time, beyond it a drop into the void, and with him at the edge of that precipice was Grace. They were holding hands, looking out over the edge as though admiring some spectacular vista. Ansell slowed, terrified he might spook Sanctan, make him act rashly.

When he was within but a few feet he stopped, huffing in air, blood dripping from his hand. He flexed his fingers, relieved that the tendons were not severed.

"Sanctan," he said.

The Archlegate turned, tightening his grip on Grace's hand. Ansell had no idea what kind of greeting to expect, but it was not the benevolent smile he received.

"Ansell," Sanctan replied. "Brother Ansell, I did not think I would ever see you again." He sounded genuinely pleased that they were reunited.

"Don't do this," Ansell pleaded. "Just... let her go."

Sanctan looked down, as though seeing Grace for the first time. When she looked back up at him his smile grew even wider.

"I thought I knew the way. I read the Prophesies a thousand times, and it was all so clear."

"Just give her to me," Ansell said, this time with more vehemence, holding out his hand.

Sanctan ignored him. "Sacrifice that which is most precious and the Wyrms will rise."

Ansell moved that bit closer. If Sanctan was to pitch the girl over the edge, perhaps he would be quick enough to save her.

"This is not the way."

Sanctan looked up, the mask gone, revealing the madman he had always been. "Oh, but it is. Only I was wrong about one thing. About what it was I had to sacrifice."

He knelt down beside Grace, looking into her eyes. The look only a father could give his daughter. "Run to Ansell, little one."

Sanctan released Grace's hand. Without another look back she ran the short distance to Ansell, and he gathered her up in his arms.

"You see, I know what I am now," Sanctan continued. "What I was and what I have become. And perhaps you were right about me all along, brother. I thought that the thing most precious to me was my trueborn kin. I was wrong. My greatest sin has always been my pride. My vanity. And you, Ansell, were always a willing victim of it." He looked back over the precipice into the long dark below. "But the Wyrms *will* rise. I shall see to it... with the greatest sacrifice a man like me could make."

He stared at Ansell, stretching out his arms as though offering beneficence to his brood. Then he leaned back, allowing oblivion to take him.

Ansell turned Grace's face away as Sanctan pitched over the side and disappeared. For untold moments he waited, perhaps expecting the mountain to quake or for a roar to echo from its depths. All he heard was the distant sound of the storm outside.

"Can we go now?" Grace asked.

He almost laughed, smiling so wide his taut skin ached. "Yes, we can."

Ansell carried Grace back across the bridge, past the ancient sconces and through that winding tunnel until the yawning entrance to the cave spread welcome light in their path.

"Now I've seen the mountains," Grace said matter-of-factly, "I don't think I like them very much. It's cold here."

"It is," he replied gently. "Perhaps you will like the sea better."

She nodded. "Perhaps."

The wind whipped them as they stepped outside. Regenwulf's corpse and his brother knights were gone, but other warriors were approaching in their place. Titanguard clanking their way up the snow-rimed slope. And at their head was the Hawkspur woman.

Ansell held Grace close, knowing this might be his last chance. Soon she would be taken from him, but she would be safe at least. For all this woman was his enemy, he was certain she would never harm a child.

When she reached him, Rosomon gestured to her Titanguard, and four of them marched swiftly past Ansell and into the Fist, though there would be nothing for them to find. The rest surrounded him as he shivered in the cold.

"Is he alive?" she asked.

Ansell shook his head. "No. You have won."

Rosomon glanced at the girl, then back at Ansell. If he had not been holding Grace there was little doubt she would have ordered him slain. Still, this was the end of it. No reason to delay. Not anymore.

"You should take her," he said. "She is your kin."

Again Rosomon regarded Grace. Her severe expression faltered, as though she recognised something of Sanctan in the girl's eyes and realised the truth of his words.

She turned to one of her leather-clad scouts, nodding her head briefly. As the scout stepped forward to take Grace, the girl gripped tighter to Ansell's shoulder.

"No. I want to stay with you."

The scout paused, unsure of how to proceed. Ansell looked deep into Grace's eyes, smiling as best he could. Something he had learned to do only recently. Something only Grace could have taught him.

"I have to go away."

She shook her head. "I don't care. I want to come with you."

There was a sudden swelling in his throat as he fought to speak. "Where I am going you cannot follow, Grace."

"I can," she snapped, growing angry, squirming in his grip. "I *can* come."

He tried to loosen his grip on her, but she held on tighter. Ansell gestured to Rosomon.

"This woman is your aunt. She will take care of you now."

"No!" she shouted defiantly, but the scout had already taken hold of her.

Grace grasped his coat for as long as she could before the scout pulled her clear. Ansell listened to her wail, a sound that cut deep into his chest, piercing the chill of his heart.

Rosomon regarded him with a deep and curious look he could not quite parse. She continued to stare as one of her Titanguard bound his wrists, and two others clamped gauntleted hands to his shoulders and led him down the mountainside.

Not the swift death he had expected. Not the mercy he had hoped for.

As he walked, the wind began to calm. The storm was finally over at least.

# ROSOMON

If they had expected to witness the Archlegate driven to his knees before them they would be as disappointed as she was. Sanctan Egelrath had escaped them all. Taken his own life in one final act of defiance. Spitting in the face of the Guilds and robbing them one last time.

As much as she thought it might be the best of all results, she knew that without a corpse, proof he was truly dead, there would be some who did not believe it. A little part inside her didn't quite believe it herself, but then why would the Drake lie? Why would that little girl... what was her name, Grace?

Rosomon's kin. Sanctan's bastard, now her responsibility, but there would be time to deal with that later. First she had to give her fellow Guildmasters the ill tidings.

The path to the Guildhall was a swift one, and when she reached that auspicious building she found it hard to ignore what the Ministry had done to it. Their desecration of the Guild symbols in favour of religious icons was almost too much to bear. Even now they were painting over the depictions of Great Wyrms, hammering down stone dragon heads, but which Guild insignia would replace them in these new times was a mystery even to Rosomon.

Ahead of her she could hear voices speaking in hushed tones. Once she and her Titanguard entered the great hall, those voices fell to silence. Kassian and Ianto took their places by the door as Rosomon became the focus of attention. They were all here—Oleksig, Maugar, Sonnheld, Rawlin, Falko, Emony, Xorya, Borys, Thalleus. Everyone who had helped her win this, now come to hear news of her final victory. And of course, claim the spoils.

The stone seats were positioned in their familiar places around the huge circular chamber, but Guild banners no longer adorned them. At least the symbols of dragons had been torn down here, as the shattered marble and alabaster on the ground attested.

"Well?" Maugar uttered, breaking the silence.

Rosomon took a breath before she announced, "Sanctan Egelrath is dead."

A ripple of approval; smiles, sighs of relief, a slap of the hand on the arm of a seat.

"Do we have proof?" Maugar asked. "Can we parade his corpse for all to see?"

"Alas, it lies at the bottom of a chasm in Kalur's Fist. You are free to try and retrieve it, Maugar, but it may be more hassle than it's worth."

He tugged at his dark beard in frustration, but voiced no desire to go chasing cadavers in the mountains.

"It's for the best, anyway," she continued. "Parading the corpse of an Archlegate would only make a martyr of him. A beacon around which his faithful brood would gather. This way he is gone for good. Wiped from the face of the world, with nothing to mark his passing."

"This is good news." Oleksig beamed, pipe secured between his teeth. "So now, with that grim business done, we must decide what to do with the rest."

Of course. Rosomon had almost forgotten about the other conspirators in all this. Now that she had been reminded, her retribution would be swift.

"Trials would be most appropriate. Carried out under the statutes of Torwyn and performed publicly."

"Aye," Maugar agreed. "Perhaps this is a job for the Justiciers, since we have a Guildmaster involved."

"No," Rosomon said. "This will be judged by the people of

Torwyn. They have suffered most through this civil war. It is only right that they be offered the chance to decide the fate of those who were responsible."

Oleksig furrowed his brow. "But that way it's doubtful any prisoners will be offered clemency. It will be a death sentence."

Rosomon knew well that it would. It was exactly the fate she had planned for them. "If that is what the people decide, Oleksig, then that is the justice that shall be meted out."

"Hold on." Maugar raised a meaty finger. "I want justice as much as anyone. The Ironfalls have suffered, and their Guildmaster was murdered. But we didn't just overthrow a tyrant to become tyrants ourselves."

Rosomon wasn't quite sure she was hearing right, especially not from Maugar.

"He's right," Oleksig agreed, before she could answer. "And Rearden is a Guildmaster after all. He should only be judged by his peers. Not by the citizenry."

"What is wrong with you?" she snapped, clenching both fists, wresting control from her anger. "It's like you want mercy for him. After all he has done." Maugar and Oleksig glanced at one another as though they had decided on this already.

Oleksig leaned forward in his seat. "Rosomon, if we execute all those who followed the Ministry it may only rouse support for their cause. There are still many within Torwyn who thought what they did was right. If things had gone differently, it could just as easily be us on trial."

This stank of conspiracy. Plans formulated while she was absent.

"And what of the Armiger marshals who took up arms against us? Will they see justice at the hands of the people whose lives they have destroyed?"

Rawlin glanced to Falko, who looked toward Sonnheld. He raised his chin, clearly the one they had chosen to deliver the news.

"They will not, Lady Rosomon. They will be judged under the laws of the Armigers." He lowered his mismatched eyes, as though ashamed at his betrayal, before offering her a look of conciliation. "It was war. Enemy leaders cannot just be executed at the whim of the masses."

Perhaps a reference to her actions at Oakhelm. Perhaps a suggestion that the marshals were now beyond her retribution. It seemed much had been decided while she was hunting down their most dangerous enemy.

"And you are all agreed?" She watched as Falko, Rawlin and Sonnheld nodded solemnly. "So what punishment does the law of the Armigers decree?"

"Sarona and Tarjan will be stripped of their rank," Rawlin replied. "They, along with key officers, will be imprisoned aboard the *Sternhaul* for a term yet to be decided."

Her hands were shaking now, those balled fists yearning for something to strike. "And what of the other battalion leaders?"

"The remaining four battalions who sided with the Ministry have been offered amnesty in return for their surrender. So far the Phoenix, Auroch and Tigris. There is no word from the Raptor Battalion as yet."

"And what if they decide to refuse your offer? Will you at least try and bring them to heel?"

Rawlin seemed reluctant to answer, but Oleksig leaned forward, tapping his pipe on the arm of his great granite chair. "Come now, Rosomon. Surely your thirst for blood is sated now the war is done. The Archlegate is gone. There is nothing more for the Armigers to fight over. They will come to an accord eventually; we don't have to hunt them down like errant dogs."

"And what of the dog we have in a cage, Oleksig? What have you and Maugar decided we should do with Rearden? Because you have already made that decision, haven't you?"

He drew in a long breath as Maugar stroked at his dark beard. None of the others seemed ready to speak, and it was left to Emony—young, innocent, naive Emony—to do it for them.

"If we execute Rearden while offering amnesty to the Armiger Battalions it could make us look unjust. Tyrannical. Cruel."

"I disagree," Rosomon replied. "I think it makes us look strong. Decisive. But it is clear you all made up your minds while I was pursuing the very man who put us in this situation. You have all cooked up this solution in my absence because you knew I would object. This endgame that satisfies none of us, and offers no justice for the people of Torwyn."

"Come now, Ros," Maugar said. "It's the only way. The Guilds must show mercy. Must demonstrate that they are different to the Ministry in all things."

"And what about demonstrating strength, Maugar?" She was raising her voice, but this was getting away from her. Damn them for making her do this. "Your brother was murdered, along with thousands of your people. I don't know what deal you've made to forget that, but it can't be worth this. We have to do what is right. We have to show Torwyn what happens when you defy..."

She stopped, realising who she reminded herself of.

Sanctan.

"It has been decided," Oleksig said. "A vote taken, in your absence, yes, and for that we apologise. But there is one more point which we could not come to a decision on. That falls to you alone. What do we do about Darina Egelrath? Her part in this is uncertain, but she was still a key figure among the conspirators. We understand she is your sister-in-law. We also know there's no love lost."

Rosomon felt sick. The last thing she wanted was to consider that harpy. Darina was wicked, that was certain, but there was no way to prove she had anything to do with her son's crimes. She had even said as much to Rosomon at the Cogwheel the day Sullivar was murdered.

"Have her sent to Wyke," she said without thinking too hard on it. "She can have the Hollow. It's what she's always wanted. She can rot there for all I care."

Rosomon almost surprised herself with how merciful she had been. But then she was already beaten. She would get no justice here, so what benefit would there be to killing Darina with no other conspirators to join her?

"Very well," Oleksig said. "The Drakes have been disavowed. Most of them fought to the last during the siege anyway. With Rearden's current incarceration, we also took the liberty of disbanding the Revocaters. I'm sure that meets with your approval."

"And the legates?" she asked, hardly caring anymore.

Silence, as though they had no idea, before Maugar said, "We cannot very well dismantle our nation's priesthood. Perhaps their High Legates can be persuaded that Guild rule is now best for Torwyn.

I'm sure they'll be easy enough to persuade without the Drakes to back them."

"Very well," Rosomon said, glad this was almost over. "It looks like you've thought of everything."

"Not quite," Maugar said, in an uncharacteristically subdued voice.

The chamber went quiet, as though they knew what he was about to say. No one else wanted to speak further. Not even brave little Emony.

"Out with it then," Rosomon snapped.

"Olstrum," said Maugar. "He was key to all this. Instrumental in bringing down the emperor. He betrayed you. He betrayed all of us. If there needs to be an execution, it should be him. He's a commoner after all. Not a marshal or Guildmaster. It would be a good way of showing—"

"No. I bear no love for Olstrum, but he was as much a victim as the rest of us. Manipulated by Sanctan. Blackmailed."

"He was your brother's consul," Oleksig said, as though she didn't already know that. "A trusted member of his palace staff. And he betrayed him to his death."

"His family was held hostage."

"The people will not accept—"

"The people will understand if we explain it to them," she spat.

"Thousands have died," Maugar said. "As you pointed out, my brother among them. Olstrum could have stopped all this before it began. He chose not to. He chose his own family before untold numbers of innocents. Think about Wyke, Rosomon. Think about your brother. There needs to be a symbol of reckoning for all those dead."

"Are you not listening? His wife, his children were threatened. He had no choice. Who among you would have done any different?"

"I'm sorry," Oleksig said, sounding anything but sorry. "It's been decided."

"So I see. You intend to let Olstrum take the fall because he is no Guildmaster or Armiger marshal. He is an ordinary man, so he is expendable. And the rest of you are agreed?"

Rawlin nodded but could not meet her gaze. "Olstrum is as much to blame as anyone. Maugar and Oleksig are right, he has to be punished. We have to be seen to act, and swiftly."

Falko and Sonnheld also nodded their agreement as Rosomon felt this all slipping away from her. These men had followed her loyally through the war, but now it was over they didn't need her anymore. They had already decided Torwyn's fate, and more importantly, Olstrum's, without need of her opinion.

"He...he could disappear. We could send him somewhere with his family. Give him a new life. He could be just another name on a casualty list."

"He dies," Maugar said, a determined set to his face. "And in public."

"You are still a swordwright, Maugar," she snapped, biting back desperately. "Not a Guildmaster."

He reclined in his stone seat. "I am now. And my Blackshields are key to holding this peace together."

"So now you threaten me? Our alliance? Over this?"

He let out a frustrated sigh. "Rosomon, I would happily follow you into the Lairs themselves, but on this I will not be swayed."

Invoking the Lairs already. How quickly they slipped into old ways. How quickly the old enemy was forgotten when it suited.

"Neither will I," Oleksig confirmed.

Rosomon's eyes scanned the gathering. Those who did not avert their gaze looked defiant. There was no one else to speak for Olstrum, and she was but one voice. She could have railed, could have threatened, but then this tenuous union would have been put in jeopardy. Rosomon could not risk that for one man.

"Very well," she said, biting back a rising nausea. "Is our business concluded?"

"For now," Maugar said.

For the first time she noted how close he was sitting to her brother's vacant throne. The one Sullivar had ruled from. The one that would soon need to be filled.

Rosomon turned, walking from the Guildhall, feeling a heavy weight upon her shoulders. One she thought she had shrugged free of when Sanctan plunged from that chasm.

But she was not free. It was clear, now more than ever, that there were still battles to fight.

# KEARA

She marched through those quiet city streets shrouded in darkness. Apt really, considering how she'd been kept completely in the dark by her so called allies since the day they'd brought this city to heel.

The victors had held their meeting in the Guildhall. A meeting she had not been privy to. Confirmation, if ever she needed it, that the Hallowhills were going to be treated as they always had. That Hawkspur promises meant nothing. That what she had planned was the right thing... the only thing she had left to her.

The manufactory stood out stark and black against the skyline. She had no idea what it had been used for during times of peace, but now it was a garrison from which she would strike at the heart of the Guilds. The birthplace of her revolution.

Vikmar was standing outside, waiting for her as she stepped up the ramp to the entrance. He looked nervous, but that was only natural. They were about to declare yet another war—stage a coup against the might of the Guilds and the Armigers. Strike at the heart of their enemy while they slept, glutted on a victory that wasn't theirs to claim.

"Are they ready?" she asked.

He nodded. "Waiting for you inside."

Vikmar grasped the handle to the door and opened it. She stepped into the manufactory, to be greeted by a vast chamber. Rusted machinery filled every corner, dimly lit by a few pyrestone lamps. This place seemed haunted by the ghosts of its workers, but soon it would be resurrected. Reborn in the light of the Hallowhills' ascendancy.

Galirena and Rodita both waited for her, leaning against one of the big machines. Of her other webwainers there was no sign.

"Where is everyone?" she asked.

Galirena gestured to an adjoining door. "Preparing the stormhulks in the warehouse next door."

Keara felt relief wash over her. For a moment she had thought perhaps the rest of her followers had lost their nerve. It was reassuring to know they were as eager for this as she was.

"How many hulks do we have?"

"Around twenty-five," Galirena replied. "All polished, refurbed and ready to go."

"And webwainers?"

"Over a hundred."

A hundred. It would be enough to take a city. And when the Anvil fell, Torwyn would surely follow. The people would flock to the Hallowhills once they realised that neither Ministry nor Guilds could give them what they needed. That only the Hallowhills could provide for them, keep them safe, allow them to prosper.

"Does everyone know their job?" she asked.

Galirena nodded casually, as though Keara were a fussy washerwoman. "Just like you planned. We secure the palace and lock it down first. Take out the Titanguard. Then the stormhulks will split into five units and take control of the main thoroughfares in all major districts. Our wainers will split into units and take out the Guild and Armiger leaders. Hawkspurs first."

"Excellent," she replied, after listening to Galirena parrot her plan almost word for word. "Sounds like we're ready."

Excitement was welling up inside her, quashing down the apprehension. There was no choice in this now. All doubt had to be expelled. No point going into this half-arsed. After all, you couldn't spark just half a rebellion.

"I'd best check on the troops before we begin," she said, almost relishing the sound on her tongue. The words of a war leader. An empress. Maybe she'd give them an inspiring speech. One that would be recorded in the annals.

Or maybe don't get too carried away.

"They're all waiting for you," Galirena said, gesturing to the adjoining door. "Through there in the warehouse."

Keara felt her excitement almost reach a crescendo as she turned the handle and walked through. There was an adjoining room—an administrative chamber filled with abandoned papers and schematics. They all lay forgotten, but not for long. Once she had staged this takeover, the city would thrum to the tune of industry once more. The Hallowhills would spur a new age of innovation. A resurgence of invention.

As she approached the door on the far side of the room, she was surprised there was no sound beyond it. No excited and nervous chatter. No noise of artificers making last-minute adjustments to stormhulks and weapons.

Maybe everyone was just apprehensive. Understandable before the final battle, but Keara would be sure to put them at ease.

She opened the door, striding through, ready to proclaim herself ready and lead her followers to victory. Instead she was greeted by blackness, the only light streaming into the warehouse through the open door she had entered by. Not a soul to greet her.

Steel claws of panic ran down her spine. Reaching out with her senses, she probed for the nearest source of pyrestone energy... there, a lamp on the wall.

Stretching her power along the web, she touched that source of light, fuelling the pyrestone so it would illuminate the room.

Nothing.

The bulb was unresponsive, as though something were blocking her from stimulating its conversion chamber and the source of energy within.

When the door slammed shut behind, plunging her into pitch black, her hands went instinctively to the knives at her side. Drawing those blades, she felt them suddenly hum—one sparking, the other burning in response to her will. A halo of blue and yellow light surrounded her, but it was not strong enough to penetrate far into the dark.

Movement in the black as something loomed ahead of her, rising up, huge and nightmarish. A blank-faced helm appeared, light dancing off its metal surface, and she could hear heavy breath from within.

Keara lashed out, blue light flashing in an electric arc, but before she could strike the giant gripped her wrist, steel claw clamping it tight. In her panic, the dagger flashed bright, and she screamed as the vice-like claw tightened. The dagger fell from her hand to clatter on the ground.

She struck with the second weapon, fuelling it with her fear, and it burned white-hot. The blade lashed down at that helm, leaving a molten line across the steel. It was the last thing she saw before she was flung across the chamber.

The second dagger fell from her hand as she hit the ground. The wind was knocked from her, head clattering against the hard floor, all light extinguished. Keara gasped, trying to stand, but the thing was on her before she could rise to her hands and knees.

Its weight was heavy on her chest, that steel claw grasping her throat and pressing her down. It drew closer, an emotionless steel mask, huffing in air with that deep inhuman throat. Keara tried to scream, but no sound would come...

With a flashing wink of light, pyrestone lamps ignited all around the warehouse. It was almost blinding, but she managed to focus on the demon holding her helpless. In the stark light she saw it was a hideous thing; a melding of man and engine—steel legs, metal arm, that elongated mask with no eyes.

Then it released her.

She scuttled back along the polished floor, gasping for air, hand reaching to her throat. Her eyes were fixed on that creature, squatting there, a golem of metal and man.

"Give me one reason not to kill you."

Keara dragged her eyes from the beast, to see who had spoken. Rosomon Hawkspur walked slowly into the light, gazing with contempt. But of course. Who else would it fucking be?

"Shit," Keara breathed.

The Hawkspurs knew what she had planned. She had been betrayed, here at the end, when she was just about to seize her glory.

"You got to them," she said, spittle flecking from her lips. "You threatened my people."

"Did I?" Rosomon answered. "Or did I simply explain to them they'd be better served by demonstrating loyalty to Guilds, rather than their errant Guildmaster?"

"You lied to them," Keara snarled in fury. "Like the Guilds have always lied. You're no better than Sanctan Egelrath."

Rosomon considered those words for a moment. She seemed to find them more amusing than insulting. "I didn't have to lie. Your people know a good deal when they hear it. But that doesn't matter right now. You still haven't given me a reason not to kill you."

Because she didn't have one, but there was no need to take these last moments lying down. Keara struggled to her feet, dusting herself off. May as well look presentable at the end. She had no daggers anymore. No way to fight this thing. She had only one weapon left... defiance... useless as it was.

"Fuck you."

It was a worthless barb. Rosomon didn't even feel it, as she looked at that metal demon she had conjured with the help of her Maladoran allies.

There was a sword in its hand now, blade impossibly thick, adorned with pyrestones. With a spark, the blade came to life, thrumming with power, the steel turning white as it was fuelled with scorching heat.

Her first instinct was to grit her teeth and resist. To reach out and dampen the pyrestone energy in that sword and give herself a fighting chance. The slightest probe of her senses told her that was impossible. The sword was powered by no webwainer gift she had ever known. Darkness shrouded it. Sorcery from beyond the Drift she could not hope to combat.

The clank of a metal foot as the beast stepped closer, stalking toward her like the shadow of death itself. Keara was shaking now; no amount of defiance could stop it. She'd always hoped to face her end with courage, but it looked like she'd be trembling like a coward.

A flash, as the pyrestone lamps on the walls flickered on and off. A whirr as a nearby bank of machinery began to operate all on its own. At first she thought it was a consequence of the monster's arcanism, but it stopped in its tracks, the helmet turning as it regarded the machinery that had come alive of its own accord.

Rosomon's brow was creased in confusion as she focused on Keara. "That you?"

"No. Me," said another voice, before Keara could answer.

Damn it, just how many people had decided to join this bloody execution?

A woman was watching from the edge of a bank of machines. Her body was cloaked but her head unhooded. She watched on with a curiously arrogant look to her face... a face Keara thought she recognised from her distant past.

The monster lowered its sword, powering down the pyrestones within it, until the arcane energy in the blade fizzled out. Slowly it raised an arm and took off the blank helm, revealing a handsome face beneath, blind eyes scanning the room. He had the look of Rosomon to him. Her son Fulren, returned from the dead.

"Verlyn?" he said.

But that was not the woman's name.

"Mother?" Keara asked, feeling her legs about to betray her.

Fulren's scarred brow screwed up in confusion. "What's going on? Verlyn, why are you here?"

Rosomon stepped forward, her confident air vanished. "I don't know who you think this is, Fulren, but her real name is Lucasta Hallowhill. Rumoured to have been murdered by her husband. But it's quite clear she is very much—"

"Alive," said Lucasta. "And returned to take back my Guild. And my daughter." She looked at Keara, who still couldn't stop the trembling in her limbs.

"I admire the sentiment," Rosomon said. "But Keara was stirring yet more rebellion. I cannot allow that. She has to be dealt with."

Lucasta shook her head. "Come now, Rosomon. We have lost

too many daughters. Too many sons. Let us have peace, before the greater war begins."

Rosomon looked as surprised as her stern features would allow. "You know?"

"I know enough."

"And you will help? You and your Guild?"

"I will," Lucasta replied, gesturing at Keara. "And she is my price."

"Fuck this!" Keara bellowed, doing her best to stop shaking and understand what was going on. "What greater war are you talking about? What is happening... and where in the Lairs have you fucking been?"

A smile on her mother's face, as though she suddenly admired the fire in her daughter's belly. "All in good time. For now, we must return home." She turned, regarding Rosomon as though it were a done deal.

Lady Rosomon looked none too happy about it, but she also looked so very tired. "As you wish. But expect a visit from me before you leave. There is much for us to talk about before you go back to the Web."

Lucasta bowed low, but managed to make it look as though it were just for show. Then she looked to Keara.

"Come."

Just like that. Like a dog summoned to its master's knee. Keara Hallowhill was nobody's bitch and yet she walked, obediently, to her mother's side.

"Verlyn..." Fulren didn't seem to know what to say. It was clear this was as much a surprise to him as to anyone.

Lucasta shot him an emotionless glance. Whatever they'd shared up until now clearly meant nothing to Keara's mother.

"Verlyn is dead. She died on a farm, far to the south of here."

Without giving him a second glance, Lucasta Hallowhill marched from the warehouse. Keara followed her mother to freedom, before anyone could change their mind about it.

# CONALL

He was cold, shivering and so bloody hungry, but it wasn't a new experience. In fact he'd grown pretty familiar with it over the past year. Nowhere safe to hide. No one to turn to. For once he might even have welcomed the voice in his head, but even that was silent.

Only one thing was certain—he had to get away from here, as far and as fast as he could. Up to now he'd failed at that. Every time he'd tried to flee there had been some Armiger trooper, some city militia, some Blackshield in his path.

His only option had been to scuttle away into the dark like a rat. There was no way he would conjure his shadow blade and cut a path through them. That would just prove to the world that he was the monster they all believed him to be. So he'd stayed hidden, keeping to the back alleys and sewers. Avoiding anyone who might get in his way. Only now desperation had stirred him from the pit. The belief that there was one person who might be able to help him. Might be able to understand.

He looked up at the vast palace, and framed in the night sky was that jetty, jutting out across the city. Perched on the end of it was his last means of salvation.

Fulren would help him. Maybe take him away in that airship to a new place where they would know what was happening inside Conall's mind. Perhaps even make him normal again.

A hope too far perhaps, but one thing was for sure; he couldn't stay here another night.

The way to the palace was shrouded in darkness, the pyrestone lights that had been smashed during the riots, not yet repaired. There were guards at the doors, but with no emperor sitting within those hallowed confines security was only cursory, and easy enough for him to slip by.

The palace itself seemed deserted as he made his way up the vast staircase. No patrols watching for intruders, but it still did nothing to calm the beating of Conall's heart.

He eventually found himself on the uppermost level, within the glass-roofed hall he had fled from a few short days ago. It was abandoned now, but a small fire still winnowed in its pit at the room's centre.

Conall stole across it, a thief in the dark with nothing to steal but his own sanity. The wind hit him hard as he stepped out onto that jetty, howling across it like a demon. And through the night ahead, he could see the hulking airship squatting in the dark, just waiting for him.

He marched as fast as he could. Below, the city was calm as its lights twinkled like stars. It was a beautiful thing to see from such a height. He could only hope the lights in Nyrakkis were so pretty. Or the lights anywhere, as long as they were a long way from here.

"Conall?"

That voice he had dreaded hearing, even more than the one in his head.

He turned slowly, cursing under his breath. His mother stood but a few feet away, her jaw set, but he could see the torture behind her eyes.

"Mother," was all he could think to say.

She was on her own. No Titanguard, no swordwright. Just the two of them, alone at last.

Shit.

"Conall, are you hurt?" she asked.

"No, I'm not," he said, taking a step back, trying to put as much distance between them as he could.

She stepped after him, holding out her hand. "I don't know what's wrong, but I can help you. Sonnheld told me what happened, what you did, but I know there must have been a good reason. Whatever they did to you in the Drift, or in Iperion Magna, whatever you've suffered, we can get over it. We'll get through this together."

All the right words. But then his mother had always been good at that.

"You can't help me with this. Not now."

Another step closer, and he matched it with another step back.

"Whatever you say, Conall. But just know that I will always—"

"You have to get back, Mother. You have to stay away from me."

She shook her head, confused. "Please, we have all lost so much. I can't lose you too."

A sudden sob in his chest. All he wanted to do was fall to his knees and give in. Have her hold him and stroke his hair. Soothe away the nightmare just like when he was a boy. He should have told her everything, but he just couldn't. She would never understand.

He could see in her eyes that she was in as much pain as he was. If she did truly love Jagdor, losing him must have been more than she could bear...

"What do you mean, *can't lose me too*? Do you mean lose me as well as that bastard Hawkslayer?"

No. That wasn't what he wanted to say. He could see that hurt her as her eyes searched the ground. Looking for old memories of a man who would never come back.

"It wasn't what you think, Conall."

And he knew she was speaking the truth. He knew how hard it must have been for her when she was young. Taken away from all she knew. Thrust into a world she did not want, with a man who never loved her. It was only natural she would seek solace in the arms of someone who did. Conall the boy had never understood the pain she suffered, but Conall the man...

"Did you ever really love my father?"

Spiteful words from his lips again. Not *his* words. Not *his* thoughts.

His mother gritted her teeth, grasping her side as though he had shoved a knife in, just like he had with Donan.

"Conall, your father and I were forced together. The decision wasn't ours, but we always loved you. Always—"

"You're lying," he spat. No idea why he'd said it. It was cruel and unnecessary, but there was no way he could stop himself. "You never gave a second thought to what I wanted. Always pushing. Always lecturing about duty and responsibility and the importance of our fucking Guild."

She shook her head, tears coming fast. "No. That's not how it was. I only wanted—"

This time it was his turn to take a step forward, and for her to take one back. He could see she was scared of him now, but that was only natural. He was acting cruel and spoiled and threatening, even if he didn't mean it...

*Now. Do it now.*

That voice stabbed at his mind like a rapier, sharp and bloody. He winced at the sound, feeling the dread in his guts.

"No...I can't."

"Can't what?" his mother asked. "Conall, what's wrong? Just tell me. I can help. We can make this all right."

*Do it now. Reach for me. Strike, and you will be reborn. A new dawn...*

He screamed, fingers pulling at his hair as though he might tear off his scalp. Words formed on his lips, a begging plea that manifested as a pained shriek.

A hand touched him. His mother trying to ease his pain, and it was all he could do to push her away, shoving her as far from him as he could.

Conall stumbled as fire ignited behind his eye, and he could barely quell his scream of agony. "Don't come near me. I can't stop—"

Another stab of pain, a white-hot lance through his eye socket. Conall grasped the patch on his face and tore it free. He bellowed but it did no good, his skull feeling as though it would crack in two.

"Con!" He heard his mother's shout above his own.

Gasping for air, he stumbled back, falling against the edge of the jetty. Through the twisting burning pain he focused, seeing someone else racing toward them from within the palace. Sted and Tyreta, rushing to help his mother... or help him?

Fuck, he had no idea. He was so confused, so tormented.

"Stay back," he barked, when they were within a few feet.

Tyreta stopped, holding out a hand for Sted to halt her advance.

"Conall," his mother said, her face a mask of torment. "You have to calm down. You have to let us help you."

He gritted his teeth, but instead of another scream of pain a bitter laugh issued from his mouth. All those memories, all that old hatred, came back in a flood. The life he might have had with the father he barely knew. The happiness stolen from him.

"Help me?" He was focused on her now, seeing her face in a red haze. "You can't help me. No one can help me now."

She reached for him, but he may as well have been across an ocean. "I don't know what those devils did to you across the Drift, but I know I can help. I'm here for you like I've—"

"You've never been there for me," he spat. "No one has. No one other than..."

*Yesss. You are right, I am here. Just reach out and take me.*

There was a familiar feeling against his palm. The reassuring weight. It needed to be wielded, and only by him. They were part of the same being, and he hungered as it hungered.

Conall stepped away from the edge of the jetty, standing upright as the pain in his head relented. The world had turned red as he focused on his mother. The shadow sword whispered, and it made his lip curl upward in delight.

"No, Conall!"

His sister's shout, offering a warning in the moment before she leapt at him. He swung, but she dodged the blade, so swift she was almost invisible. Another swing intended to take his sister's head, but there was no guilt, no apprehension.

Again she dodged that hissing sword, reacting like lightning, and her claw slashed him across the shoulder. He grunted, drawing back the blade again, lunging at her. Tyreta skipped aside, the blade nowhere near close enough, but Sted was right behind, the tip of that sword spearing toward her throat.

Conall froze. Sted had her arms up, eyes wide, staring at him. She was his friend. He could never—

*Kill her.*

"No," he snarled.

*Kill her.*

"I won't do it!"

A feral growl of rage. He turned in time to see his sister leap again, claw slashing at his face. Now it was his turn to dodge, to lash out in response. He felt the blade cutting flesh, followed by her howl of pain.

She fell at his feet, but Sted was quick to grab her, pulling her out of range of his death strike. Tyreta grasped the wound on her arm, eyes no longer feral. There was only pain there—his little sister, wounded and bleeding.

Conall dragged his eyes from her. His mother still stood a few feet away, refusing to run. Refusing to beg. She looked at her son as though she was resigned to this. As though she knew the fate that awaited her.

His eye still burned, but there was no pleasure in the pain anymore. It grew in intensity, that red light casting a deathly hue on his mother's face.

There was no other way. He knew that now.

Conall raised the sword, and it sighed, as though it were about to drink for the first time in an age. As though his mother's blood would slake a thousand-year thirst.

It swept down, ringing as it struck another blade. This one thrummed with energy, pyrestones fuelling electric light that danced along its length. Smoke and lightning coiled as the swords struck one another.

Fulren's blank-faced helm leered at him. His claw of an arm raised, those steel legs braced in a fighting stance. Conall backed away as his brother stood between him and his quarry. Defending their mother...

Their mother...

He could not do this. He had to wrest control from...

No... he *did* have to do this. It was his only purpose.

Conall gritted his teeth, feeling saliva drip down his chin. There was no fell voice compelling him now. This was his fate, as surely as any he might have planned for himself. This was what he had been born for.

The shadow blade lashed out, forcing Fulren back apace on those metal legs. He was quick to counter, fuelling his pyrestone weapon, making it sing as it swept back at Conall. Their swords clashed, light sparking as they tested one another. Again and again, blades of shadow and fire ringing in the night.

Conall knew this was no longer his brother. Fulren had become a demon. He had to be defeated.

A growl as he called upon all his strength, pushing his body beyond limit. The pyrestone sword parried again, pain jolting up Conall's arm. Like a striking snake, Fulren's metal claw struck, tearing at Conall's chest and raking his flesh.

He staggered back, grunting, feeding on the pain. Warmth anointed his body as blood gushed from the wound. It fuelled him with the certainty that he had to kill his brother.

The shadow blade moved of its own accord, smashing into that steel arm again and again, driving Fulren back. His brother raised his blade, the pyrestone energy waning in the face of such an onslaught, but Conall was not done. Another sweep of his sword, and the weapon was sent spinning from Fulren's grip. One last effort and he sliced at his brother's gut, tearing him open.

Fulren grunted as he collapsed, the helm falling from his head and rolling across the jetty. Conall advanced, ready to claim victory as his brother looked up at him, those blind eyes staring in pain.

*You must slay this demon.*

"No," Conall whispered, clinging on to one last vestige of humanity. That last thread of his free will, frayed so thin it might break in an instant.

*Do it*, the sword demanded. A command he could never resist, but...

Fulren's face. That little boy he had watched grow to manhood. This was no demon.

Conall lowered his arm, the shadow blade hissing in protest. He looked over at his sister, lying wounded on the ground. Then at the horror in his mother's eyes.

He had caused this. But these were not the actions of Conall Hawkspur. This was the creature in his head, and he would resist it to his death.

"No," he said again, this time louder, this time more determined.

Pain flared once more, stabbing into his skull, drilling as that thing had drilled and probed when it had torn the eye from his head.

He staggered, hand clamping to his face, but the pain only intensified, along with his defiance.

"No!" he screamed. "I won't!"

It felt as though his head might explode. His ears rang with the intensity of it as he was driven to his knees.

*Obey.*

His scream was agony in his throat. "Never."

Conall stabbed the ground with the shadow blade, driving it into the stone. Hot wind billowed around him, the agony in his head unbearable, but he would bear it.

*You are damned.*

A laugh, bitter from his lips. "I am Conall Hawkspur. I am no demon's puppet."

The wind whipped up to a hurricane, a vortex holding the jetty in its grip. Conall clenched his teeth, sensing something behind him... a gateway opening up to consume him. From within it, dark winds howled, myriad voices snarling and baying for his soul. A door to the Lairs themselves.

He forced himself to look one last time to his family. To Fulren and Tyreta. To his mother. The pull of that demon gate was irresistible, but he knew this must happen. It was the only way he could save them.

It grasped him, its tendrils hauling his essence through the gate into a nightmare.

One last defiant scream. A scream of victory.

Then he was gone.

# FULREN

Wenis dabbed at his stomach wound. For all her talents, she was certainly no healer, but she'd tried her best. The wound had been stitched, ointment slathered. If there had been any poison within that demonic sword of Conall's, it had left no taint. Some good fortune at least.

Fulren tried to wrest the image of his brother's last moments from his mind, but it was futile. That last defiant scream. That gate manifesting before their eyes, roiling in a vortex that led to somewhere foul and forbidden. Watching helplessly as Conall was dragged into it, ripped from the world, before the gate closed, winking from existence, leaving only silence behind. It haunted Fulren. It most likely always would.

"So what can you tell me?" he asked.

She stopped dabbing at the laceration. It came as something of a relief.

"I am not sure what you want to hear."

"Where is he?"

Wenis shook her head. "I do not know for sure. The magic of the Scions is a potent brew."

"I know that, but—" He stopped as she dabbed at the wound again.

"In Nyrakkis we bargain with our patrons. And in return we are offered gifts through a conduit between worlds. The necroglyphs make that transition possible. But in Iperion Magna... those conduits are sometimes much more powerful. More tangible."

"Like a gate between this world and theirs?"

She shrugged.

"So he might be alive?" Fulren asked, grasping at any hope he could.

She regarded him gravely. That rare look she got when she was serious. "If he is, Conall is in a place you can never follow."

That answer only made him more determined. "Can never? Or should never?"

"Pick whichever one makes you feel better, Fulren. Either way, your brother is lost."

Fear in her voice. If that place was enough to strike fear in Wenis of Jubara, it must be terrible indeed. Still, Fulren was undaunted.

"If I come with you, back to Nyrakkis. If I help you with your fight against the Scions, perhaps there might be someone there who could help me find him."

She shook her head, standing up and discarding the ointment-covered rag. "It is more important that you come to form an alliance. Conall is gone. As we all will be if we do not fight against what is coming. It is more important now than ever that your mother help us. I know she is grieving, but—"

"Then we must go and persuade her," Fulren said.

"Now?"

Fulren rose gingerly, feeling the pull of those stitches, relieved that they held. "When would be a better time?"

"She has just lost her son," Wenis replied, with uncharacteristic sympathy.

"I know that. And we are all in pain. But there are other sons and daughters who will suffer if we do not form this alliance."

Her look of surprise faded, and she nodded, offering him a cloak to put about his shoulders.

Wenis led them from the confines of the ark and out onto the jetty. The sun shone, offering a bright new day. Hope now, where only the night before this had been a place of horror. Fulren followed her past the spot where Conall had disappeared. Nothing remained to signify that anything had happened, but for a single chip in the stone flagging.

At the arch to the upper vestibule, Ianto stood vigil. He stepped aside as Fulren and Wenis walked in, where waited his mother.

A fire pit burned in the centre of the room. She sat staring into the flames, silent. Fulren could almost feel her sorrow. Evidence enough of her pain that she had stayed here all night, close to the spot where Conall had disappeared. It felt almost sacrilegious that he would disturb her grief, but this could wait no longer.

"Mother, we must talk."

At first no answer. Then, slowly, she looked up. There were no tear tracks on her cheeks, but still she looked haunted by what had happened. Just when she had secured her great victory, it had been snatched from her in the cruellest of ways.

"You know I sat in this very spot the night you were taken from me," she said, voice so lost. So weak. Then her eyes turned to Wenis. "The night she took you from me." Then she faced the flames again. "I had hoped to find a solution in the fire, but it did not come. In the end sending Lancelin had been the only way. All I could think of."

"My father would never have refused," Fulren said.

She looked suddenly ashamed, as though her darkest secret had been revealed. She opened her mouth as though she might explain why she had chosen to abandon her marriage vows and seek comfort in the arms of Jagdor, but struggled to find the words.

"You do not need to justify yourself, Mother. I understand."

"I *do* need to justify myself. It was never what it seemed. Not what Conall thought—"

"None of that matters now." Fulren laid his hand on her shoulder. "All that matters is that we prepare for what is coming."

Slowly she looked at Wenis once more. "Our deal?"

Suddenly Wenis didn't look so comfortable now that she was the focus of attention. "I don't like it any more than you do."

"You have no idea how little I like this," Rosomon fired back. "How do I even know any of this is true?"

"Why would I lie about it? What would Queen Meresankh have to gain?"

It was enough to placate Rosomon, and she turned back to the fire. "So what would you want from us?"

"We would have your support. Your armies. Your machines. Everything. We would have you unite Torwyn in this one purpose—to defeat the Scions and defend your people."

"I will need to send envoys to ascertain the dangers. To learn exactly what it is you know. Although an exchange of emissaries didn't work out too well last time."

"That's why I will go," Fulren said.

His mother's silence told him all he needed to know about her opinion on that. She shook her head almost imperceptibly, hands balling into fists.

"You would go back to Malador? Willingly this time? For all you know you could meet the same fate as your brother."

"I will be safe. I trust Wenis."

His mother's mouth twisted in a bitter grin. "You once told me not to trust anyone."

"I did. But we are past that now. This is more important than our fear of what lies over the Drift in Nyrakkis."

"You don't belong there, Fulren. You belong here, by my side."

He knelt, leaning closer, doing all he could to reassure her. She had just lost a son, so recently returned to her. Now she was to lose another.

"Look at me, Mother. I do not belong here anymore. I am a monster to the people of Torwyn. But in Nyrakkis, I could be a bridge between our nations."

He could sense her weakening. Still no tears, but now she grasped his arm as though she might never let go.

"I cannot stop you, Fulren. I know that much."

"I will come back. This time I go freely, not as a prisoner."

Lady Rosomon rose to her feet, and a little strength seemed to return to her. She looked at Wenis gravely. "Do I even need to say it?"

Wenis raised her arms, as though it was obvious. "If anything happens to Fulren there will be nowhere in all of Hyreme I can hide from you?"

"Then we understand one another."

Fulren grasped his mother's hand, feeling how tightly she held him. "I will see you again. Sooner than you think."

Rosomon raised a hand, fingers caressing his face and the scar that marred his eyes. "I will hold you to it."

With that he turned, before he saw any more of his mother's pain.

# ANSELL

The dank stone walls of the cell wept moisture, each block slick and grimy. Surrounding him was an odour of damp and sweat and decay he could not get used to. Dull light lanced in through a tiny window, granting scant relief, but perhaps he would have been better in the blackness of a dungeon. At least there he would not have been able to see the filth that surrounded him. What he had been reduced to.

He shifted his bulk on the rotting pallet that served as his bed, pain lancing through his joints with every movement. The heavy iron shackles chafed his wrists, but he suffered it, almost welcomed it. At least it meant he was alive, but how long he would benefit from that privilege was anyone's guess.

A rusted metal tray sat untouched in front of him, bearing a stale crust of bread crawling with weevils, and a wooden bowl filled with some thin grey slop that might have been gruel before it congealed into sludge. The rancid smell turned his stomach and he'd resolved not to eat it. And not just because of how it disgusted him. What would have been the point of prolonging his miserable existence? If starvation did not get him, he doubted the Guilds would allow him to live much longer anyway. Better to fade away than allow them that final victory. To string him up before a baying crowd and leave him hanging as a symbol of their dominance.

He winced again at the knife-sharp ache in his ribs. Beneath the rags they'd given him to wear, bandages wrapped his various wounds. He had been tended with brusque, uncaring efficiency, the Guild healers stopping the bleeding and stitching him back together so he wouldn't inconveniently perish before they decreed it was his time. So here he languished, the frigid chill that had afflicted him in the Dolur Peaks now replaced by a constant, throbbing cold deep in his bones, that no amount of warmth could banish.

A sudden angry itch, and he scratched at his face, nails digging into the ruined flesh and puckered scar tissue. The necrotic skin around his mouth irritated him incessantly now, a maddening sensation he could never escape, like ants skittering across his face. A final curse. One he was condemned to bear until he was laid to rot in his grave. At least it was a curse he would soon be free of, along with all his others.

His teeth ground as he forced himself not to think on that despair. He would not succumb to it, not now, but what else was there...?

Idly he ran his fingers across the string of beads encircling his wrist. The ones that clumsily spelled out his name. His sole remaining comfort in this festering hole, the memory of a girl he would have sacrificed everything to save.

But had he truly saved her?

That question haunted him. She might be free of Sanctan's poison now, but was she really safe in the hands of the Hawkspur woman? What sort of life awaited the daughter of the Archlegate, who had been a mortal enemy to the Guilds and caused such strife? He could only hope it was a better fate than the one that awaited him. There would be no escape from this cell. No last-minute reprieve or rescue. He'd known that the moment the rusted manacles snapped shut around his wrists. All that remained was to endure the pain, embrace the hopelessness and pray that when his end came, it would be swift.

A distant clang as the reinforced door to the corridor outside was opened. Perhaps his end was approaching more swiftly than he thought. When heavy footsteps echoed to a stop outside his cell and keys jangled in the lock, that notion became a stone-hard certainty.

The door screeched open on rusted hinges. It was followed by a pneumatic hiss as two Titanguard stomped in, heads ducking beneath the low ceiling. They stopped, two bronze statues regarding him from behind their full helms. Ansell could almost feel their disdain. Their barely leashed urge to stamp him to offal.

Rosomon Hawkspur strode in after them, stopping a few feet before him. A flickering pyrestone lamp from the corridor beyond threw distorted shadows across her stern features, turning her eyes to pits of darkness and her mouth to a cruel slash.

There she stood for untold moments, just staring. Anyone else and he would have thought her gloating over him, but no. Not the Hawkspur woman. She was not given to the petty vindictiveness of others, Ansell knew that much. He could only hope she was genuinely pondering his fate. At least then he had a chance, but a chance at what?

"Do you know why I've come?" she asked finally.

In truth, he had no idea. "To look upon your brother's killer one last time before he dies?"

It seemed as good a reason as any.

She took a step closer. So close Ansell could have reached out to touch her despite his chains.

"In truth... I don't really know. Don't really know why I'm here or... what I will do with you."

"It seems that, under the circumstances, you have very little choice in the matter."

Something flashed in her eyes. Some kindling of agreement. "That's truer than you know. I have found that recently my options have become... limited. I'm sure that's as much a surprise to you as it was to me. But never fear, I have set about rectifying that particular quandary."

"How is Grace?" he asked, without thought. The only thing he really wanted to know.

"Safe, of course. But if I were you, I'd be more concerned about what's in store for Ansell Beckenrike."

"It doesn't matter what happens to me. As long as she is cared for."

That look of steel in her eyes softened. "She's with her family now. And they will see that no harm comes to her."

A breath escaped him. One of relief. For so many days all he had thought about was seeing Grace liberated from the clutches of Sanctan Egelrath and taken somewhere far from anyone who might hurt her. He had failed at the second part, and had to trust that Rosomon might do that job much better than he.

"She asks for you," Rosomon added. "She wept for a whole night, insisting that I bring you to her. She was very demanding for such a small child, but that could just be testament to her Hawkspur blood. Nevertheless, it vexed me. I am confused by why this innocent child would show such attachment to a monster like you. But then, you and your ilk can be persuasive when you want to be."

Ansell raised his chained hands. "Do I look persuasive now?"

The faint ghost of a smile on her lips. "No. You don't. And I don't think there was ever anything artful to you at all. But there are others among the Draconate who were."

*Were.*

That word was crushing in its finality. It told him, as if he was in any doubt, that all this was over. That his brotherhood was no more. All he had ever believed since Regenwulf had found him in that abandoned warehouse was now burned to nothing.

The sudden thought of Regenwulf brought a lump to his throat. Not just for the way Ansell had been forced to kill him, but the way his brother had seemed to want it. In the end, Regenwulf realised all he had fought for was a lie. That knowledge had brought him such despair that only death would free him.

"Tell me then, what is to become of my brothers? Now all this is over, and their Archlegate is dead, there is no need for them to fight. Will you show them any mercy?"

"No. They will be hunted to the last." She let that hover between them for a moment, cold and stark in that dank cell. "Did you expect a different answer?"

"I hoped there might be no need—"

"No need? The Drakes are rabid dogs. You think the death of your Archlegate will curb them?"

"Yes. Their figurehead is no more. And I knew many who already harboured doubts about the Ministry's course. We are the defenders of our brood. Guardians of Torwyn, of its people. It was never meant to come to this."

"And yet it did. Thousands dead for a foolish ideal. What does that tell you?"

"That wasn't us. Sanctan betrayed everything we believed in."

"And still you served him until the bitter end. Obeyed his every whim, even though it went against your instinct to protect." She cocked her head, studying him like an insect. "Tell me, how long before you questioned the atrocities you committed in his name? How many years did you blindly follow, content in your righteousness?"

It was a difficult question, and the answer shamed him to his core.

"I questioned it too late. But when I did, I acted. Tried to rectify those wrongs. Why do you think I am here?"

"And what of your brothers? Would they also show the same remorse?"

He thought back, to the doubt he had not only felt but seen in others. "Some of them..."

"Some of them. But not all. And that is why I must hunt them down, root them out and destroy them."

"You're right. We were loyal to a fault. I see that now. But do you think butchering good men will right any of those wrongs?"

"I'm not looking for redress, Ansell. Nor revenge. I am protecting my people. The Drakes aren't mindless brutes. They're far more insidious. Intelligent, devout, principled men who've been twisted to commit atrocities, all while remaining certain of their own righteousness. That's what makes them the perfect weapons for a tyrant. Why they're so dangerous if left alive."

Her words bit deep, because he could not refute them. How many times had he suppressed his doubts and convinced himself he was doing the work of the Great Wyrms? It had made it so easy to slide his blade into Gylbard's back. To murder the emissary from Nyrakkis. To slay the emperor. To start a war. Even when innocent blood dripped from his fingers and the screams of the dying echoed in his ears, he'd never wavered. Not until Grace. Not until it was too late.

Sanctan had exploited their righteous zeal and rigid discipline, moulding them into instruments of conquest and oppression, while letting them believe they were doing the Wyrms' sacred work. And they had followed, obeying with such blind conviction, never questioning the horrors inflicted at their hands.

"So I am to die with them."

It was not a question. He knew the certainty of it without doubt. After all she had said there could be no other way.

"You will. But it will not be alongside your brothers. It will be far from here. I will not martyr you in front of your faithful. Your death will not be mourned."

Another pause while she looked at him, taking in his piteous state, as though she wanted it stamped on her mind so she could recall it in the future. Remember him defeated.

"Then you have come to a decision after all," he said.

"Yes, it seems that I have," Rosomon replied. "Now if you'll excuse me, there are other matters to which I must attend."

Then she turned and swept from the cell, followed closely by her Titanguard.

The door slammed closed. The lock clicked again. He was left alone with only the dripping walls and half-light for company.

Ansell reclined on the uncomfortable pallet and stared blankly at the tray of congealed gruel once more. Her ruthless judgement traced echoes in his mind, drowning out all other thoughts.

His brothers condemned. The Draconate shattered. His faith in the Wyrms and their purpose eroded to dust. What was left for him now but a traitor's ignoble death in some far-flung corner of the realm? At least Regenwulf had received the honour of a death in combat. Not so for the mighty Ansell Beckenrike.

Grim laughter bubbled up in his chest, the twist of his lips stinging the flesh about his mouth. All those years of righteous conviction, of certainty in his holy cause, only to end like this—chained in a filthy hole, disgraced and reviled, with nothing but the cold comfort of the death that awaited him.

*Embrace it.*

That was all he could do. Even if he could escape the clutches of the Guilds once more, what could Torwyn offer him now?

Persecution, most likely. He would be hunted like a dog until his dying day. And where would he hide when the witch from Nyrakkis had marked him so distinctively?

His stomach cramped violently, reminding him how long it had been since he'd last eaten. The mouldy bread and dubious sludge looked even less appealing than before, but the insistent pangs in his gut were becoming harder to ignore.

Ansell rolled onto his back with a groan and stared up at the mildewed ceiling.

Grace. His chest constricted at the memory of her tear-stained face. That girl had been all he'd lived for since losing his faith. And nothing had changed since then, not really.

Jaw clenched against the pain, Ansell levered himself upright and reached for the tray.

# ROSOMON

There was a crowd gathered just outside the gates of the city gaol. She had expected them to be baying for blood, screaming at the bars, flinging stones. They were silent, as though holding a vigil for a dying saint.

Ianto stood waiting at the main doors, impressive in his full regalia. Beside him were his fellow Titanguard, all equally splendid, clad in the might of the Guilds and the battle armour it had built for them. Not a few short days ago many of them had been imprisoned within these walls. How fortune changed so fast.

Kassian walked from within the dark corridor of the gaol, looking his usual solemn self. But then it was most appropriate now on such a solemn day.

"Is he ready?" she asked.

"Yes, my lady," Kassian replied. "Should we proceed?"

She glanced back at the crowd, wondering if they even wanted this. If perhaps she should have done more to stop it. But she had been powerless. There was nothing she could have done to defy them all. Those Guildmasters and marshals.

Still, here at the end, she began to wish she had.

"Yes."

A single word. So easy to say, but with it she knew there would be no chance of reprieve. No longer an opportunity to save him, no matter her feelings.

Kassian walked back into the gaol. She heard his muffled voice, the stomping tread of armoured feet. Then Olstrum appeared, squinting in the sunlight, flanked by two more Titanguard. He looked scared, she could see it in his eyes, but he handled it with a stoic resolve.

It seemed so ridiculous that this insignificant man posed enough of a threat to warrant such monstrous guardians. But he wasn't insignificant, she had to keep telling herself that. He had been instrumental in so much misery and death. This was the only way it could end.

Olstrum fixed Rosomon with as imperious a look as he could. "Are my family...?"

"Safe," she reassured him. "And far away from here. I will make sure they are well taken care of. Have no fear on that."

A smile of relief on his face. "I know you will. Despite how much recent events have changed us all, I know you are still a decent woman, Rosomon."

As much of a compliment as she could have hoped for, but then compliments mattered little now.

"You should know this is not what I wanted. You don't deserve—"

"Don't I? My family has been spared, but how many others have been torn asunder, murdered, because I was too cowardly to make that sacrifice? No. I think this is exactly what I deserve. So let's get on with it, shall we?"

She moved from his path, allowing the Titanguard to lead him across the cobbled courtyard. Again, as she watched him being led to the huge iron gates, she regretted giving in to her fellow Guildmasters. When they stopped at those gates, Kassian standing by them as the crowd waited beyond, she wondered if even now it was too late to stop this.

"Shall we?" Kassian asked, as though offering her that chance.

Rosomon nodded, knowing that chance was long gone. Even if she'd wanted to, the whole of the Anvil was waiting for this execution. This symbol that the war was over. That the main instigator of their misery was to meet his fate.

With a creak, the iron gates were pulled open. Lining the road from the gaol were troopers of the Bloodwolf, Viper and Mantid Battalions. They had cleared the way, holding back the gathered crowd, who seemed in no mind to surge forward and seek their own justice. This was ceremony, pure and simple, and they were happy to see it performed.

Rosomon stuck close to the procession as Olstrum was marched through the streets to his fate. With every turn of a corner, she expected to be met by a baying mob, but was surprised each time when greeted by silent onlookers.

She observed the crowd as she walked by, realising that no one dared catch her eye. Not one of these people who she had liberated from Sanctan's tyranny was willing to look at her. Not one nod of acknowledgment or word of gratitude, as though she were the tyrant now. Perhaps they were right. What more proof was needed than the fact she was about to execute one of her enemies right before their eyes?

They turned the last corner, seeing the Cogwheel ahead, raised above the level of the streets. Surrounding it, the whole of the Anvil looked to have come to witness this final act.

Now there was noise. Starting as a lulled hiss, but soon growing to vociferous boos. A shout from afar, indiscernible but clearly hostile. Still Olstrum walked with all the dignity he could muster, despite the fear he must have felt inside.

As they mounted the platform, Rosomon nodded at Oriel, who was waiting patiently. She regarded Olstrum as he walked past, and Rosomon expected her to spit in his eye at any moment, but she retained her dignity. Oriel would have her justice soon enough.

Oleksig and Maugar were here too. Solemn. Emotionless, despite how vehemently they had insisted this happen. Rosomon had no time to wonder how they might regard the proceedings before the crowd's antipathy turned to violence.

The first missile was thrown wide, hitting the flagstones and bouncing well clear of its intended target. The next, a piece of rotten fruit, spattered on the armour of one of the Titanguard. Before long the patter of stones rang a tune in time to Olstrum mounting the scaffold. A single rope dangled from the gallows, and still he looked on impassively, making no sound, protesting no innocence, despite the fact it was he alone to be slain before the mob, rather than with his fellow conspirators. And conspirators who bore more guilt than him.

One of the gaol's functionaries awaited, mask across his mouth, cap pulled down tight to cover his eyes. The man secured the noose around Olstrum's neck and took a step back toward the lever that would drop the condemned man through a trapdoor.

Rosomon could only watch, teeth grinding together as she stopped herself from bringing this whole circus to an end. Resisted letting this man go back to the family he had fought so hard to keep alive.

As she watched, a missile flew straight and true to hit Olstrum on his forehead. The crowd cheered as he stumbled, and Rosomon could see it had opened up a gash in his scalp. Blood poured down his eye, the sight of it emboldening the crowd yet further, and more stones were flung.

"Ianto," she said, gesturing toward Olstrum.

Her Imperator nodded a reply, signalling for one of his fellow Titanguard to join him. Together they mounted the scaffold, the whole structure shaking under their weight as they marched to Olstrum's side. Together they raised their shields, deflecting any further missiles flung by the crowd.

Seeing their sport scuppered, the mob rose in uproar. They screamed at the functionary to hang him, the noise resounding about the Cogwheel so loud Rosomon felt sick to her stomach. After all these people had suffered, all they had lost, they still thirsted for yet more blood.

The masked gaoler leaned forward, whispering something in Olstrum's ear, perhaps asking him if he had any last words. Whatever he said, Olstrum shook his head, resigned to his fate. Perhaps even eager for this to be over with.

As the gaoler stepped back toward that lever, Rosomon realised that this was her last chance. If she wanted this to stop this, it would have to be now.

A glance across at Maugar and Oleksig, and she saw no remorse. There was even a little spark of zeal in Maugar's eye. The crowd cheered on, almost hysterical. If she tried to stop this there would be another riot, and she remembered well what had happened the day her brother died.

The hangman gripped the lever, and the crowd hushed. Rosomon closed her eyes before the clack of the door swinging, the thud as the rope went taut. The crowd roared its approval.

When she opened them again Olstrum was gone, his body hidden beneath the scaffold. A small mercy at least, but the rope was still taut. The crowd still cheered. It made her sick to her stomach.

She turned from the scene, pushing past her Titanguard, ignoring Kassian's concerned words. Past Rawlin and Falko and Sonnheld watching from the edge of the Cogwheel, as one of them asked if she was all right.

Rosomon entered the crowd, shoving her way through, hearing them jeer, too enrapt in what they were witnessing to notice it was even her. Once out the other side, she delved deeper into the maze of city streets, heedless of what danger might lurk, desperate to get away, even from her own guardians.

The city was all but abandoned with everyone at the Cogwheel to see justice done. Rosomon was alone here, and could have been in much danger. But danger no longer held any fear for her. Conall was gone. Fulren about to leave her. Lancelin lost. All she had left was Tyreta, the daughter who couldn't wait to get as far from her mother's side as she could. There was nothing left, so what matter her life?

On she wandered, her mind roiling with thoughts of injustice. Of how helpless she had become, despite what she had achieved. She did not stop until she saw the palace looming up ahead.

It was like a beacon. The monument her grandfather had built. A bastion for the Archwinds, of which she was still one, regardless of her name. It looked bare now, and the closer she got the more empty a place it seemed.

Perhaps she should have been the one to restore it. To take that vacant throne for her own. It had been her father's and her brother's after him, but she had never wanted it. All she had desired was Lancelin and her children, and now they had been taken from her.

As Rosomon entered the huge lobby, she felt the stark legacy of that building in all its historic glory. The weight of that heritage felt as though it hung about her neck, pulling her down. Before it could drown her under its burden, she saw someone was approaching along that long hallway.

Talon scouts walked in procession toward her, leading an old woman in their midst. Darina Egelrath had aged since this war began. No longer did she look so assured, so magnificent in her expensive gown. Now she looked weary, aged, made to look all the more dowdy beside the Talon in their ceremonial armour. It was one small honour Rosomon had granted her before her exile back to Wyke.

She stopped not five feet away. Darina might not have had her jewels to augment her appearance, but she still carried that look of spite she'd worn since the day Rosomon had married her brother.

"Don't get comfortable on your throne," Darina said.

Rosomon knew she didn't have to justify anything to this woman, but she couldn't hold her tongue. Not now. "I never wanted a damned throne. I never asked for any of this. It was your son—"

"My son is dead. My brother is dead. You have seen to that."

Neither act was any of Rosomon's doing, but there was no point trying to explain. Not to Darina. She was so tangled in her own hatred it made her deaf to the truth.

"Go back to Wyke, Darina. Take the Hollow, or what remains of it, and be thankful for the time you have left."

Darina lurched forward before the Talon could stop her, face only inches away. "Your children have become monsters." She whispered the words with such venom Rosomon could almost taste it. "And so have you."

Rosomon raised a hand, gesturing for the Talon to proceed. Two of them grabbed Darina by the arms and ushered her from the palace.

Perhaps she was right. This war had changed everything, and Rosomon had been forced to become someone else entirely. Something else. But if there were monsters coming from Iperion Magna, she would need to become equally monstrous to challenge them.

Maybe sooner than anyone might think.

# TYRETA

She couldn't work out whether this was a formal send-off as they waited atop the palace jetty. There weren't many people here, but those that were present had dressed in their finest. It didn't matter either way. Tyreta had never given much store to formality, and she wasn't about to start now.

The airship hummed in anticipation, and she could feel the buzz of pyrestone energy through the flagstones at her feet. Where once that machine had groaned and howled, now it sang. She wondered how it had been so transformed, but that would have meant a long boring conversation with Fulren. In the past she would have avoided one of those like the plague. Now, just as he was leaving, Tyreta would have happily listened to her brother all day.

She glanced across at her mother, who stood stern as ever. Alongside her was the equally stern Kassian and the even sterner Ianto. Sted was there too in her dress uniform, which she still managed to make look unkempt.

Tyreta's eye wandered across the city. It was quiet now after the din of its celebrations. And execution. In the centre of the metropolis, she could just see the Cogwheel standing out stark against the surrounding buildings. The site of the war's last atrocity.

She knew she shouldn't have gone. Perhaps she had thought there was something she could do, but against that baying mob they were all helpless. The wheels of Olstrum's end had been set in motion, and once they started rolling no one could stop them. Even her mother hadn't been able to do anything... if she had even tried.

Tyreta didn't want to think the worst, but it gnawed at her. The fact that Olstrum's corpse was still hanging there for all to see, so the city would know they had not been cheated of his death, made her feel sick. People walked by like it was the most normal thing in the world, and yet still had the brass nuts to call themselves civilised. It was barbarism, and Tyreta knew she was complicit in it. She couldn't help but hate them all for that.

The clanking sound of her brother's feet, and she looked toward that ark. He was coming closer, stalking them like some mechanical beast. Tyreta doubted she'd ever get used to seeing him like that, but now she wouldn't have to. He was leaving her. Leaving them all.

Fulren walked to their mother first. They spoke words that were lost in the wind, but Tyreta could tell they were both just holding it together. Her mother looked about ready to crack, to fall on her knees and weep, but she didn't. She offered her son one final embrace and took a step back.

Then Fulren moved toward Tyreta. For so long she'd thought him dead. That she had lost two brothers. Now, after the fleeting elation of getting them both back, she was to lose them all over again.

"Look after Mother, Ratface," he said with a smile. As though none of this mattered, like he was just going for a stroll and he'd be back for dinner.

Tyreta forced a smile. "I will, Tinhead. But I can't help but think maybe I'm the wrong person for that job."

That brought a knowing grin to her brother's face. "Trust me, you're the right choice. More than me, more than Conall, you were always the one." He hugged her before she could suggest he was talking shit. "I'll see you when I get back," was all he added, before turning on his metal heel and striding toward the airship.

Tyreta couldn't help but doubt his words. She had a haunting feeling that she'd never see him again. That she would be left alone with all the obligations of the Hawkspur Guild hanging over her.

The wind whipped up as she watched him enter the airship and the yawning mouth close behind him. Its engine ignited with life as the buzzing intensified, and there was a rumble beneath her feet before it took off. The air filled with static as pyrestone energy bloomed around them and the airship took to the sky.

Tyreta saw her mother drag her eyes away as it began to cruise into the distance. Then she took a step closer.

"We have to talk," her mother said.

As ever, it sounded more like a command than a request. One that Tyreta knew she could not refuse.

They walked away from the palace, and her ever-present guardians, toward the end of the jetty. The airship was still visible, but her mother never gave it a second glance. It felt as though she had forgotten about Fulren already. Back to business.

As Tyreta gazed down, she began to realise just how quickly things were returning to a semblance of normality. The city looked just as it had when they'd last come to visit her uncle. The skyway, which had been turned black by fire, was now operational once more. A landship was even disembarking from the distant southern terminal.

"We have much work ahead, you and I," her mother said, looking out on that same vista. Perhaps seeing a very different thing. "You've grown into a capable woman, and I'll need you now more than ever."

As she listened to the words, Tyreta wanted to feel heartened. Her mother needed her. Valued her. How that would have filled her with joy but a few short years ago. Now though, there was something else that called to Tyreta. Something wild, within and without.

"Will you?" she asked, hoping that perhaps there was some kind of caveat. Some way she might be freed from the burden of her mother's expectations.

"Of course I will. There is a darkness beyond the Drift. One we must all stand against. The Guilds are united once more, but I will still need people I can trust."

Tyreta glanced back along the jetty, toward where Kassian and the Titanguard stood. "Looks to me like you've got more than enough capable followers, Mother."

"I need *you*." Her mother moved a step closer, taking her by the arms and looking deep into her eyes. It was an earnest look. One that might be shared among equals. "I need our family."

How many years had she waited to be treated this way? How many times had she wanted her mother to accept her for who she was? And now...

"Our family is broken," Tyreta said, unable to stifle the words despite knowing the harm they would cause. "Maybe it always was."

A brief flash of confusion on Lady Rosomon's face. "Tyreta, the Guilds will—"

"Guilds, Ministry, what's the difference? Remember what I've seen, Mother. I've witnessed the atrocities of the Ministry and the Guilds. I've seen what we do on the Isles."

"That will change. I promise—"

"You fought so hard. You won, Mother, but you're still just a cog in a machine. You say things will change, but how much power do you think you really have? You just let them...let them kill Olstrum. After everything he did to help us."

"I had no choice in that."

"Of course you did. But you compromised. You bargained, just like you'll have to do every day for the rest of your life. Why would I want to be a part of that?"

"This is important, Tyreta. This is bigger than either of us."

Tyreta couldn't hold back her laugh of disbelief. "Not bigger than you, Mother."

Lady Rosomon's hold on her tightened, as though Tyreta might slip away at any moment and be cast adrift on the tide. "You have to stay. You have to help me."

"No."

There was more finality to that last word than she'd intended. More steel. More defiance. She saw the look of hurt on her mother's face. The realisation that this plan was not going her way, and Tyreta felt a sudden guilt. After all her mother had been through, all she had lost, now it was Tyreta who had thrust the final blade.

"You're right," Tyreta said. "I am different, and I have grown. But I've grown beyond all of this." She gestured out across the city.

Over the hubbub and mundanity. "I never wanted it anyway, you always knew that."

"You have to step up, Tyreta. You have to accept who you were born to be."

As stirring as her words were, they lacked conviction, as though she knew this battle was lost.

"That's what I'm doing." Tyreta took her mother by the hand. "This was never what I had in mind for me. It wasn't part of my plan, it was yours. Even if I hadn't gone to the Sundered Isles, even if I hadn't been changed in the jungle, this was never my future. It was yours."

"I can't do this without you," her mother said, voice almost cracking.

"Yes you can." Tyreta turned on a smile, hoping it might help. It didn't seem to do the trick.

"Where will you go?" Lady Rosomon asked with resignation.

Tyreta hadn't even thought about it. "Maybe back home to Wyke. There's plenty to do there rebuilding the city. Who knows what I'll do after that, but it needs to be my decision. I have to decide my own fate."

She looked into her mother's eyes, expecting her to refuse. Instead, Rosomon grasped her tight, squeezing her as though she might never let go. Then she released her, turning back to the end of the jetty to watch that distant airship disappear beyond the mountains.

Tyreta was finally free. But it felt as though she had just lost everything to achieve it.

# KEARA

It was nothing but a shell now. A relic, blackened and burned. She'd grown up in this old manse. Knew every nook and cranny. Now, as the rain poured down around her, drowning this dead corpse of a house, she didn't miss it at all.

She felt no sorrow for this old place. The only sorrow was for herself. Alone. Again.

This weary old building had always been symbolic of her Guild. Now that it was nothing but ashes, it felt even more apt. The Hallowhills were done, and Keara had helped make it happen. Despite all her plans, all her efforts, she was back in the Web without a pot to piss in and not a friend in the world.

Fucking great job.

Her foot struck something on the ground. Something metal. It shifted among the black sludge and she recognised it as the grammahorn that had been playing the night she'd set this place aflame. It had issued such a dolorous tune, but now it was the only thing in this whole place still intact. Maybe it even worked.

Keara pressed with her senses, feeling for the pyrestones within, and realising they were still active. A little nudge further and she stimulated the cores, sensing the energy pass along those wiry conduits.

A whine, discordant and harsh, followed by a scratchy monotone repeated over and over, mocking the tune the grammahorn had played when this house had burned to death. Now it sounded like a dirge.

Keara kicked the metal box across the debris, watching it bounce, feeling the pain in her foot. Nothing worked in this fucking city anymore.

"I never liked this place."

The voice made Keara flinch, and she turned, hands reaching to the blades that were no longer at her side. Her mother was standing so close, like a silent shadow, hair drenched, face stern. Was this the same Lucasta Hallowhill who had abandoned her all those years ago? Keara could barely remember.

"Then I guess I did you a favour burning it to the ground," Keara replied, wondering if her mother also appreciated her cremating the old bastard who still lived here.

Lucasta nodded, picking her way closer through the detritus. "I suppose you did. But we will build another. Just as we will rebuild the Hallowhills."

It sounded a fanciful notion, especially with them both standing among the wet sludge of their home. "I thought you made a deal with the Hawkspur."

"Did I?"

Now it was just getting confusing, and Keara had never been tolerant of cryptic nonsense. "Yes, you fucking did. I was standing right there, remember?"

That brought a wry smile to her mother's face. "Do you think I would so readily throw everything away? My birthright? My legacy?"

Her words stirred a long-suppressed anger in Keara. "You did once. Left it all behind and ran away, remember? I thought—"

"You thought wrong." The wry smile was gone from Lucasta's face in an instant, to be replaced with hard eyes and a set jaw. "I have returned. And this Guild is ours now. Nothing will change that."

Keara was encouraged by the fact that her mother had said *ours*. "So what about the Hawkspurs? You were friends with one of them... Fulren? You'd so easily go against them now?"

"You're making assumptions. That boy was a means to an end. A way for me to get what I needed at the time. And it worked. We were never friends."

"So you'd betray him so easily? Betray Lady Rosomon?"

"Is it betrayal if you're simply reclaiming what is yours by right?"

Keara knew damn well it wasn't, but still none of this added up. Especially not now when they were starting from such a position of weakness.

"Even if we wanted to reclaim what was taken from us, how do you know the other webwainers will even follow you? They turned their backs on me in the end."

Lucasta's eyes narrowed. "They will show faith in their Guild and their Guildmaster, or we will cast them out. Besides, there's more to the Hallowhills than just webwainers."

"What does that mean?"

Lucasta raised her face to the drizzle, letting it bathe her for a moment. "Young Fulren was no webwainer, and yet he harnessed artifice like none of us could dream. You saw it yourself."

Indeed she had. The thing behind that helm had possessed more power than any webwainer she'd ever known, and the terror of it still haunted her. "You're talking about sorcery. Magic we might not be able to control."

Lucasta closed her eyes, letting that rain anoint her. "You're right. But what is the alternative? To serve the Hawkspurs until the end of time?"

No, that would never stand. "So what do we do? Rosomon will be watching every step we take."

"For now she might. But I have offered her help with one final task. A show of faith. One last thing that will see a permanent end to the conflict we have just survived. It will demonstrate my loyalty and show some much-needed goodwill."

"What task?" Keara knew nothing of it, and it only frustrated her that she'd been left out of her mother's plans.

Lucasta shook her head, gazing at her daughter like the child she had abandoned. "Nothing you need worry about."

Keara tried to let it wash over her. Difficult, but as her mother stepped closer, placing a gentle hand on her shoulder, she only felt more at ease.

"So," Lucasta said gently, "are you with me?"

Keara looked out over the ruined manse, sitting in the midst of a ruined city. It seemed impossible that they would wrest any kind of salvation from this. A mountain to climb.

"Yes, Mother. I am with you."

# REQUITAL

Wyke had been her childhood home. The sheer beauty of it brought back so many memories. Darina had yearned to return here after being sent away to marry her simpleton of a husband, but now she had reclaimed her ancestral right and was back in the Hollow. Ironic, for it felt a hollow kind of victory. One given to her by that cunt Rosomon. A stinging wound that might never heal, but at least Darina had been granted her life.

Looking out from the balcony she could see how the city was being restored, the dam rebuilt. There had been devastation here. A heavy price paid by these people, but the folk of the Hawkspur Guildlands were a resilient breed. She knew that better than anyone.

Her eye was drawn to the tallest structure below—a solid black obelisk standing where the bell tower had been. A monument to the dead. A constant reminder of what they had lost.

Darina needed no monument to remind her of what she had lost. Her son was dead. Her brother. The only men she had ever really cared for, and now she had to live without them for the rest of her days. Live with the knowledge that the woman responsible for their deaths had deigned to grant her a reprieve.

How she had always loathed that Archwind bitch. Curse the day she had ever snaked her way into their family. She had never loved

Darina's little brother, but then Melrone had always been led by foolishness and blind ambition. Lured in by what the Archwinds could give him, and it had been his downfall.

A noise from within the library behind—the subtlest clearing of a throat. Darina turned to see Emeria standing inside, waiting patiently. The girl was young for a lady's maid, but from what Darina had seen so far she was competent enough.

"The candidates have arrived for the position of new steward," the girl said, as Darina made her way in from the balcony.

With everything that had happened recently, Darina had almost forgotten that the old one had died. She vaguely remembered him from her childhood, though she couldn't quite recall his name. Little surprise he was dead. He must have been ancient, and well overdue to be replaced.

"Very well then, let's go and see them."

Emeria curtsied before leading her on through the vast wooden corridors of the Hollow. It had been a long time since she'd been here, but these panelled walls and polished floors were so familiar to her. Not so much their barrenness though. When Melrone had lived here these corridors had been adorned with hunting trophies and heirlooms of the Hawkspurs. Rosomon had had them all removed after having her husband murdered, but Darina would see that insult put right soon enough.

When finally they reached the main feast hall, she saw that at least some antique weapons still remained hanging in pride of place above the hearth. Glaziers were hard at work replacing broken panes within the tall stained-glass windows. Someone was even retouching the wooden floorboards.

Emeria crossed the hall to stand beside three men who waited in silence, hands clasped in front of them, eyes averted to the floor. Darina couldn't help but be pleased at their deference. This was a good sign.

"Here they are, ma'am," Emeria said, gesturing to the trio.

Darina walked closer, regarding the one on the left. He was old, perhaps as old as their previous steward. He glanced up with rheumy eyes, before lowering his gaze. It was doubtful that one would last out the winter.

The next candidate was shorter than Darina, thick about the middle, bald, unkempt, like a scruffy egg. No, he would not do at all.

When she regarded the one on the right, it was all she could do to quell a sigh of relief. Broad about the shoulders, square about the jaw. Young. Thick head of hair. What more could she ask for?

Emeria gestured toward the old man. "This is—"

"That won't be necessary," Darina said, unable to take her eyes off the tall specimen in front of her as she patted him on the shoulder. "This one. You two may leave."

Emeria nodded at the others, and they shuffled from the hall as fast as they could manage.

"A good choice, ma'am," Emeria said.

"Of course it is," Darina replied, accepting her sycophancy with grace. She had always been a woman of taste. Apart from when choosing a husband.

"The evening draws in, ma'am. Dinner will be served just before nightfall, and as requested, I have taken the liberty of drawing you a bath."

How efficient. Perhaps her time at the Hollow wasn't going to be too insufferable after all. Emeria was certainly a good find.

"Then let's not leave it to cool." She signalled for the girl to lead on.

Offering her new steward one last lingering look, she followed up the carved wooden staircase to her chambers at the summit of the Hollow. Everything was prepared—mirror and powder on the dresser, fresh sheets on a huge comfortable bed. Furs draped across every surface should she feel the need to stave off the cold. Her thoughts immediately went to her new steward, and other ways she might keep herself warm when the chill winds blew in off the coast.

Emeria helped her disrobe. There was a full-length mirror, surrounded by an oak frame, and Darina couldn't help but catch herself in it. Seeing that naked old body of hers reminded her once more of what she had lost. Of all that wasted time. Of what remained.

As Darina donned a towel, Emeria opened the door to the bath chamber, as though anticipating every need of her mistress. She was to be commended, but perhaps not just yet. It wouldn't do to laud her with too much praise too soon. That might set the wrong precedent.

"Everything is ready, ma'am," Emeria said as Darina stepped into the room.

It was comfortably warm. A fire in the hearth, steam rising from the bathtub. The girl took the towel as Darina stepped into water heated to the perfect temperature. It was as though Emeria's skills were preternatural.

She reclined with a sigh, and Emeria picked up a jug, dipping it in the water. Gently she poured it across Darina's hair, smoothing the thin strands with her fingers.

"Shall I apply the oils, ma'am?"

For a moment Darina thought that would be an excellent idea, until she was suddenly struck by a better one.

"Perhaps... our new steward might do the honours? What do you think?"

Emeria smiled knowingly. "An excellent idea, ma'am. In fact, I have already taken the liberty."

She placed the jug back down on the table and opened the adjoining door. The new steward of the Hollow stood waiting, his shirt now discarded, the muscles of his chest seeming to ripple in the firelight.

By the Lairs, that girl really did think of everything.

"Very well, Emeria, you may leave."

The girl bowed briskly, before walking past the steward and closing the door behind her. He looked a little awkward, still unable to meet Darina's gaze, but he'd soon get over his shyness.

"You may proceed," Darina said, gesturing to the jug and oils on the table.

He walked forward obediently, pouring a little oil onto his hands and rubbing them together. Darina closed her eyes as he began to massage her wrinkled flesh, and she gave a little moan as he paid particular attention to her neck and shoulders. His hands were soft yet firm, and it was certainly not his first time at this. She began to feel those old forgotten stirrings as his attentions grew firmer.

"What's your name, boy?" she asked. It was only appropriate she know it before things went further.

"Amalric, ma'am."

That name chimed in her memory, but at first she couldn't quite place where she'd heard it before. The heady mix of warm water and firm fingers made her head swim, until it came to her in a flash of inspiration.

"Wasn't that the name of the previous steward?"

"Yes, ma'am," the boy replied. "He was my grandfather."

The water suddenly felt chill around her. Those gentle fingers now gripping like iron. Darina opened her mouth to speak, to protest, as Amalric grabbed a fistful of her hair and shoved her under the surface.

She clawed at him, but his other hand grasped her wrist tight, squeezing like a steel manacle. From below the water she could see his face, emotionless as he plunged her further under.

Legs thrashed in her panic, but a second figure was at the bathtub now—Emeria—looking down with what? Concern? No. Hate.

The girl grabbed both her legs, holding her tight as Amalric held her beneath the surface. Her throat strained as she screamed her last under the water. A scream that was lost, replaced by only fluid in her lungs.

Energy was sapping from her limbs, but still that boy and that girl held on tight. Held her fast as the water filled her. As the life left her. As it all faded...

He had been riding for an age, or at least that was how it felt. Rearden had never been a horseman, in fact he couldn't remember the last time he'd sat upon one of these sweating, huffing beasts, but he was determined to endure it. The promise of what lay at the end of this journey would be worth the suffering. Or so he was led to believe.

A glance over his shoulder, through the wood, and they were still there. The Talon scouts hadn't said a word since they'd left the Anvil—not that he was keen to engage them in conversation—but he could still sense their hatred of him. Could imagine what they really wanted to do to him, but he was still a Guildmaster, damn it. He deserved their tolerance if not their respect. No such luck. They had pushed him ever onward, despite his complaints.

Before he could yet again ask for a rest, and some relief from this damned nag and the incessant flies that buzzed around its stinking hide, the path led them out of the woodland. Flat open ground rolled away to the bottom of a hilly rise, a river flowing through it, and in its centre sat a tiny cottage. It was all alone by that river. A peaceful, white-painted retreat, looking like the object of some landscape painter. Not quite where Rearden had envisioned spending his final years, but not bad. Not bad at all.

They plodded on, hooves clacking over a little bridge and up to that little house. Rearden wasted no time in climbing down from the infernal beast, his legs shaking, almost abandoning him altogether, but he managed to hang on to the saddle for a moment and steady himself.

One of the scouts nudged his horse forward, unstrapping a pack from the saddle and letting it fall to the ground with a thud. All Rearden's worldly possessions in a single bundle.

Before he could ask them what he was supposed to do now, they reined their horses around and trotted away, back over that bridge and toward the wood. He would have cursed them, snarled his disdain at their backs, but he couldn't help but feel a little grateful. He had been spared, after all. Had not had to share Olstrum's fate on the gallows, which he had thought a certainty at one point.

Limping toward the bundle, he untied the cord that bound it, picking up one of the bags, before having to stretch out his back. Damn that horse and damn this journey. At least he was here now. Best see what kind of accommodations his fellow Guildmasters had deemed fit for him.

On trembling legs, he approached the cottage. The door had a single keyhole, but he'd been given no key. Tentatively he reached out, turning the handle, feeling the flush of relief as the door opened. But then he was in the middle of nowhere. Why would he even need to lock the door? Then again, perhaps it would be best if he found a locksmith at the nearest village and had him secure the place. Better safe than sorry.

With one last glance about the front garden, appreciating how well tended it was, he pushed the door and entered. It smelled musty inside and had clearly been empty for some time. Nevertheless, it looked homely enough; the wooden floor clear of debris, a chair near the hearth, and a shelf full of books.

Rearden allowed himself the slightest of smiles as he closed the door behind him, laying his bag down on the rug that sat in the centre of the room. The walls were adorned with paintings, all depicting pastoral scenes. In all his years he'd never been one for art, preferring the spartan look of white walls and the neatness of ledgers. But then, this was his life now. Best he grow used to it.

A low arch led deeper into the house, and Rearden began to explore further. A large window shone light into a second lounge. It was bright and airy, like a reading room, with a single armchair at the centre. Rearden stopped when he saw someone already sitting in that chair, a large book shielding their face.

His blood ran cold. He was supposed to be the only one here... wasn't he? Was this a servant perhaps, left for him out of respect for his rank?

"Hello?"

The book was slowly lowered, revealing a face he recognised. One he was at first relieved to see, until he remembered what he had done to this boy.

"Wachelm?" Rearden said. "What... what are you doing here?"

A smile on Wachelm's lips as he put the book aside, then peered at Rearden through his spectacles. "Is that any way to greet an old friend?"

Rearden had never considered them friends. Wachelm had always been his subordinate, and a treacherous one at that. A subservient, who had taken sides with the upstart Hawkspur woman.

Nevertheless, he quelled his anger. All that was finished with, and he supposed they were now equals in a strange kind of way.

"I mean... welcome. It is good to see you."

"Is it?" Wachelm asked, tilting his head curiously. "You don't look that pleased."

Rearden tried to affect as welcoming a smile as he could, but it was difficult under the circumstances. "I am just surprised, that's all. I was led to believe I would be the only one here. Have you been sent to watch over me?"

"After a fashion."

Rather vague of him. In another life, Rearden might have chastised Wachelm for being so cryptic, but now it didn't feel appropriate.

"Well... I do hope we can put past differences aside. The war is over after all."

Wachelm looked as though he found that answer perplexing. "Past differences? You mean when you had me flogged?"

Rearden had wondered when that might come up. Clearly Wachelm wasn't as eager to leave things in the past.

"I know now that was a mistake. It was just... unfortunate—"

"It certainly was for me, Rearden."

Wachelm spoke his words with steel. He had always seemed so unassertive, but now there was a darkness to him. Then again, Rearden supposed that being whipped might do that to a man.

Before he could think to apologise further, he heard the creak of a floorboard. Someone else in the house.

"Look." Rearden held up his hands in a placatory gesture. "I have come to an agreement with the Guildmasters. Lady Rosomon herself has offered me clemency. Forgiveness for all past transgressions in exchange for my future compliance. I was allowed—"

Wachelm shushed him. It was a long deliberate noise he accentuated by putting his finger to his lips as you might with a noisy child.

"Lady Rosomon has changed her mind on that," he said, still reclining in that chair. "It has been decided that unfortunately you cannot be allowed to live."

"Wait." Someone entered from the next room—a burly woman, arms thick with corded muscle. "There's no need for this." A man came in, a handsome one, with nothing in his eyes but murder. "Wachelm, you can't." One more woman, this one lean, with a face of beaten leather. "Please..."

"Please?" said Wachelm. "How many times must you have heard that over the course of the war? And how many times did you listen?"

Rearden's eyes were welling with tears, his hands clasped tight in front of him. He had always thought begging might be beneath him, but right now it seemed the most appropriate thing under the circumstances.

"Please don't kill me, Wachelm. You can't do this. Please."

"Perhaps I can't," the young actuary said. "You might be right about that. I don't think I could watch you die, in all honesty." Rearden sighed in relief as Wachelm took the spectacles from his face and produced a rag from his pocket. "So I guess I won't watch."

Wachelm turned away as he began to clean those lenses. The big woman lurched forward, grasping Rearden about the neck. He barely had time to gasp before the handsome man lunged, plunging a blade into his gut all the way to the hilt.

As he drew it out it seemed to drag all the air from Rearden's lungs. He barely had a chance to try for another breath before the lean-limbed woman stabbed him too.

She leaned in close, nose almost touching his, teeth gritted tight. "This is from Olstrum."

Then they both went at it, knives plunging, as the world faded, and the last thing Rearden saw was Wachelm cleaning his eyeglasses...

"Don't look so fucking glum," Sarona said as they trundled along in the back of the wagon. "Five years isn't such a long time in the great scheme of things."

Tarjan's sour look didn't shift. His usually slick hair was a tousled mess. Pristine uniform replaced by prison rags. His eyes met hers, as though his only thought was to strangle her.

"A week aboard the *Sternhaul* will feel like a year. How long do you think five years will feel?"

"Listen." She leaned closer. "I'm not looking forward to this any more than you are. But I'll do the time. It's better than being dead. And besides, do you really think we'll serve the full sentence? Remember we have support all across Torwyn. As soon as word gets out what's happened to us there'll be an outcry. That Hawkspur slut can't keep us in the brig forever."

His sour look only deepened. "I wish I shared your optimism."

Sarona leaned back with a sigh. There was just no helping some people.

The wagon trundled on a little longer before rumbling to a stop. They'd been able to smell the stink of the sea and hear the screech of gulls for some time, so it was obvious they weren't far from their new home.

A snap of bolts, the creak of a door, and the back of the wagon was bathed in light. Sarona was the first to move, only too eager to be free of the wagon's confines, and as she squinted in the daylight, Tarjan struggled down behind her. She had expected to see Blackshields, or maybe Talon. What greeted her brought a rare smile to her lips.

Troopers of the Tigris, Auroch and Raptor stood in neat rows. Their pennants held high as though they were the honour guard in a victory parade, rather than lining the dock to the *Sternhaul*.

"What's this?" Tarjan asked.

Three officers were approaching. Marching side by side like a welcoming committee. Marshal Mermaduc, wearing his ridiculously large helmet forged in the shape of a tiger's head. Beside him the moustachioed face of Walgan, marshal of the Auroch. Then came Ancretta, cradling her raptor helm in the crook of her arm.

Walgan was the first to greet them, slamming a gauntleted fist to his breastplate and grinning wide.

Sarona was starting to feel a little underdressed. "What are you all doing here?"

Walgan gestured with a thick arm, as though presenting those Armiger Battalions for inspection. "We agreed to come as requested. It was part of the amnesty that we arranged for the Armigers. We are to walk with you as guard of honour to the *Sternhaul*. A show of respect from Lady Rosomon."

Sarona regarded the three marshals, then the ranks of troopers lining their path. "More likely it's to find out if you will obey her every word. Test your loyalty."

Ancretta grinned, slapping a hand to Sarona's shoulder. "Come now. We know this is all for show. Just a symbol of our commitment to the treaty we were all forced to sign. Don't look so miserable. You won't be kept prisoners for long."

"Damn right we won't," Tarjan snapped. "In fact, why wait at all? Why not just free us now? We could all five of us unite our battalions. Then who would stop us?"

Mermaduc shook his head, that vast helm swaying from side to side. "Really, Tarjan? You know it's not the right time. The Guilds are in full control, but once things have settled down a little, we will hold a moot of the Armigers. Then we will see just how loyal Rawlin, Falko and Sonnheld are. They are wise men. They know where their bread is buttered, and it's not with the Guilds anymore."

As much as Sarona wanted to agree with Tarjan that now was as good a time as any, she knew Mermaduc was right. They had to wait for things to settle, and for the Guilds to grow complacent. There would be time enough for another coup later.

"Come," Walgan said. "See the honour guard we have amassed for you."

He led them down the slope toward huge gates at the end of the throughfare. Sarona couldn't quite see the grim form of the *Sternhaul* beyond them, the prison ship that would be her home for the next five years. Still, the closer she got the more apprehensive she felt.

As they passed abandoned shacks and storehouses, that uneasy feeling only grew worse. There were troopers lining every yard of their route, but no other guards. No representatives of the Guilds. Not even a civilian administrator or two.

"So all three of you signed the peace treaty?" Sarona asked, perhaps needing to reassure herself that they were safe.

"What choice was there?" Walgan replied.

"And what of your old contracts with the Guilds? What of your forts and assets in the Karna or the Drift?"

Walgan shrugged those broad armoured shoulders. "I assume there will be a renegotiation of terms. Nothing too punitive, I'm sure. Oleksig and Maugar have been most reasonable up till now."

They were getting nearer to those wooden gates, vast and ominous.

"So it was those two who allowed this?"

Walgan furrowed his brow. "As I said, we were offered a chance to show willing and act as your honour guard. Lady Rosomon was the one who arranged it all."

They had come to a stop, and Ancretta gestured for two of her men to unbar the gate ahead.

Sarona was suddenly finding it difficult to breathe, as though there were something cloying in the air. "And doesn't that make any of you suspicious?"

"Why would it?" Walgan said.

A clatter of wood, as the guards moved aside the huge beams sealing the doors shut. Then a creak of hinges.

"Because for the first time since the uprising began, we are all in the same place."

Something huge pushed its way through the doors. No time to shout any warnings as it stomped forward, looming over them all.

A howl as a heavy volt gun charged, static heavy in the air. Sarona staggered back at the subsequent blast of lightning, seeing Ancretta from the corner of her eye as she was blasted to ribbons in a blinding flash of light.

The stormhulk advanced relentlessly and Sarona was already stumbling away, too late to shout any orders. That volt gun whined again, charging up another blast, but she was already turning, already running.

From a warehouse beside her, another stormhulk smashed through the wooden doors, unleashing a staccato clap of heavy splintbow fire.

Sarona turned to see if anyone was with her, just in time to witness Tarjan's chest explode as superheated shot smashed through his rib cage. Walgan was running right behind her, but a ball of fire consumed him, the infernus cannon not relenting as he howled, falling to the ground, rolling in vain to try to extinguish the flames.

The troopers who had lined their way tried to bring weapons to bear, but they were shot down in the neat rows in which they were stood. It was like someone knocking down pins at a fair as they were blasted apart.

Bolts whipped past Sarona's head, and she dashed on. Mermaduc had managed to get just ahead of her, but no farther before mortar fire took him out. He was flung twenty feet into the air, bits of him scattered in every direction. His ridiculous helm bounced in front of her and she almost tripped over it in her haste to flee.

The sharp sting of a missile impaled her thigh. Sarona's leg gave way, and she fell to the dirt in a heap. Breath came feverishly as she tried to rise, but her leg felt as though it had been severed. She clawed at the earth, dragging herself along as fleeing troopers fell all around her.

A motorised whine behind, ominously close. She turned, seeing the stormhulk in pursuit, that relentless machine lumbering toward her. There was no time to scream as it raised its massive steel foot and slammed it down...

He was trembling as he walked the main corridor toward the chancel. Swimming in apprehension, but so far from the shore. Willet was no stranger to such feelings, but this time he was determined to show that he was the one in command.

Damn his nerves. Damn his cowardice, now wasn't the bloody time. This was the Mount, after all. And he had two armoured knights at his shoulders. Surely there was nothing left for him to fear.

Those two Drakes marched alongside him as though taking him to his execution. At least that's what it felt like. Ridiculous, he knew they were for his own protection, but still Willet couldn't shake off the feeling he was done for.

A swift glance at one of them offered him no clue who it was. He had seen these knights without their helms in the Sanctum more than once, but when their armour was donned they all looked the same. More curious was the fact these two had been allowed to retain their honoured positions where other Knights of the Draconate had been cast down or killed. Not the time to think on that now. He had more pressing matters to worry over.

The archway to the chancel loomed ahead, and his stomach lurched, as though his nerves couldn't fray any further. He gripped tight to the medallions about his neck, wondering if it was worth a quick prayer.

No. He would do this without aid from the Wyrms. This was a task ordained by Guildmaster Rosomon, and it would be Willet Kinloth who performed it, without help from his dragon gods.

His feet padded softly on the marble floor of the enormous chancel, drowned out by the steel tread of the Drakes. A single table sat at its centre, and they were all waiting for his arrival. Evidently in no mood for it either.

As each of the High Legates in their differing robes of office glared at him accusingly, his two guardians did nothing to assuage his fears. Willet's legs trembled for a moment, but he forced them on, unable to take his eyes off the luminaries who were expecting him.

High Legate Rassekin sat in his grey cloak and steel armour. He was the newly selected representative of Ammenodus Rex, after Karina had been killed during the siege, but no less a grim example of his creed. Beside him was Marsilia in the black of Ravenothrax, then Barnier in the green of Saphenodon. Halinard reclined in his red robes of Undometh, eyes watching intently as Willet approached, and finally Amiranda in the blue of Vermitrix, her eyes closed and hands clasped in prayer.

Their conspiratorial chatter ended as Willet and the Drakes came to the table. A single vacant seat awaited him, but Rosomon had advised him to stand throughout the proceedings. It would give him more authority, she had said, and who was he to argue?

"I..." All eyes were on him, hanging on his every word. "I... would like to thank you all for attending. As you know, we are convened for the selection of a new Archlegate—"

"We know that," Halinard snapped, leaning across the table, unable or unwilling to hide his sneer of disdain. "Question is, why are you the one doing the convening? Is there no one more senior who could have accomplished the job?"

Amiranda patted a gentle hand on the tabletop, opening her eyes and regarding Willet with kindness. "Now, now, Brother Halinard. Let the boy speak."

"A pertinent question," Willet answered, his hands gripping the inside of his sleeves, so they wouldn't fidget and make it even plainer that he was out of his depth. "I have been sent on the express orders of Guildmaster Rosomon Hawkspur—"

A grumble of discontent from Rassekin, who balled his gauntleted hands into fists. "So she is in charge now. This is a travesty."

Barnier laid a withered old hand on Rassekin's armoured one. "Yes, she is in charge. And I understand how that must grate, but we should all be thankful we are allowed to sit here at all."

It did little to pacify Rassekin, who stared in fury, but Halinard was the one to slam his hand down first. "She murdered Egelrath. Our Archlegate. The divine representative of the Wyrms. Are we supposed to be thankful for that?"

"Peace, brother," Barnier said in his croaky old voice. "We find ourselves in this situation because of unwise decisions in the past. Let us not compound them by resorting to anger."

"Unwise decisions?" spat Rassekin. "You forget yourself, Barnier. We all made our decision based on the threats to Torwyn. To our brood. Just because it ended in defeat did not make it unwise. Those threats still exist."

"High Legates," Willet said, raising his voice over their quarrelling, desperate to be heard. He unrolled the parchment in his hand, ready to read the screed. "If we may continue. The selection of a new Archlegate—"

"Is one for the High Legates alone," Halinard snapped. "Not for the Guilds, and certainly not for some neophyte." His last word was positively dripping with contempt.

"These are the orders of Lady—"

The scrape of a chair as Rassekin rose to his feet. "This is preposterous. Not in a thousand years has the Ministry been so cowed. You all need to grow a spine. We may have lost the battle, but not the war. By the tenets of Ammenodus Rex, we will rise again."

Silence, as his words echoed through the chancel, before Amiranda sighed gently. "Please sit, Brother Rassekin."

His face twisted in fury and he balled those armoured fists again as though he might smash the table to kindling. "And who will make me? Any of you cowards?"

A ring of steel, the swing of a blade, and Rassekin's head was parted from his armoured shoulders. It bounced on the table, as arterial spray shot up from his body and it crumpled in a clanking heap.

Halinard shot to his feet, shock marring his face, before a blade burst through the red robes covering his chest. More blood spattered on the polished surface of the table and the bright blue robes of Amiranda. As the sword was wrenched free, Halinard collapsed forward, head bouncing off the table before his red-robed corpse collapsed to the floor.

The chancel was silent. No screams of alarm, no panic. Willet heard the faintest rustle and realised it was the parchment he still held in his trembling fingers. It seemed a little superfluous now, considering what had just happened.

One of the Drakes took a rag from his belt and wiped the crimson from his blade, as the other one removed his helmet, revealing a mature face framed by grey hair. For the first time, Willet realised they did not carry Draconate swords, but swordwright blades. With all his fearfulness he hadn't spotted that these were not Drakes at all.

Footsteps echoed, breaking the silence. Lady Rosomon stepped into the light that illuminated the table, looking down at the murdered men, lit up in the flickering flames of the torches. Barnier looked on, his toothless mouth agape. Marsilia bore an equally shocked expression. Only Amiranda maintained some modicum of reserve, though she could do little about the blood that spattered the blue of her raiment and flecked her pale cheek.

Rosomon sat herself in the empty seat, ignoring the corpses that marred this hallowed place. "To the business."

Barnier closed his mouth, turning to Marsilia, who offered him the slightest shake of her head in return.

"The business?" Amiranda whispered.

Rosomon gazed back at her. "Of who will become the new Archlegate. I propose Legate Kinloth here." She casually gestured toward him. "I will assume two abstentions, so are there any objections from the three of you?"

Barnier swallowed audibly. Marsilia offered the slightest shake of her head. Amiranda whispered, "No."

"Well, that was easier than I expected." Rosomon rose to her feet, offering Willet a curt pat on the shoulder. "Congratulations, Archlegate."

With the curtest of bows, she strode from the chancel, followed by her two swordwrights in their Drake armour.

Willet glanced at the three remaining High Legates, who gazed back with equal bewilderment.

Holy shit.

# ANSELL

On and on and on the cart rattled. Wheels trundled. Horses snorted. Hooves clopped. The road was endless, but he did not lament. It was far too late for that.

The confines of the wagon were oppressive, and despite the cold he had been sweating ever since they had departed the Anvil. Perhaps one of his many wounds had grown infected. Perhaps he would die before he even reached the site of his execution.

Perhaps, perhaps, perhaps.

His hands were bound tight, ropes digging into his wrists. There would be sores for sure when they took them off, but he'd be dead by then, so it didn't really matter. Despite the hood over his head, he could still tell he was surrounded by soldiers in here. They didn't speak a word, but he could feel their nervousness. Understandable. Ansell was a dangerous man, despite the fact that he was weak, bound, blind.

They were taking him somewhere remote to be executed, which most likely meant there'd be no baying crowd. He had that to be thankful for, at least. He'd heard Olstrum hadn't received the same privilege. That was unfortunate. It was doubtful he deserved such a fate, but then *deserve* had very little to do with it.

Ansell had tried not to think on Grace too much as they trundled on, but his thoughts were all he had in this tiny box. He would never see her again, he knew that. It was his only regret in all this. He could only hope she would get to live a normal life now. That there would be someone to watch over her. Someone better than Sanctan at least. Someone better than their gods.

The Wyrms had abandoned him, but it was only to be expected, as he had after all turned his back on them. He should have done it sooner. Should have throttled Sanctan the moment he learned of his seditious plans, and presented his head to Gylbard.

Should have, should have, should have.

The wagon rocked, the droning sound of its wheels changing as it veered off the road. It clattered across a bridge, then rumbled over stone, before coming to a halt.

Around him the men moved as he heard the creak of doors opening, followed by a cool breeze.

"Out," ordered a stern voice.

Ansell rose, ducking his head below the roof of the wagon as someone grabbed his arm. He was guided down a metal step and onto solid ground, almost losing his balance, but managing to stay upright.

The hood was wrenched from his head, and he squinted in the sun. He was standing in the courtyard of a fortress. An Armiger one, on the edge of the Drift, the pennants of the Bloodwolf Battalion flapping in the wind. This was Fort Uthan, two hundred miles from the Anvil. They really had taken great pains to execute him far from prying eyes. As he scanned the courtyard and caught sight of the gallows already erected and waiting, he finally knew how.

Troopers were glaring at him from every corner of the fort— from the garrison block, to the bastion, to the parapets. All of them had weapons at the ready, as though they might cut him down at the slightest provocation. Not that he could blame them; he was a Drake after all. A symbol of the Draconate Ministry. The cause of all their trouble. Let them hate him. It was their due.

A tall man stepped closer, dark hair shorn close to his scalp, chevrons on his arm marking him as some kind of officer.

"Did he give you any trouble?" the man asked, still staring at Ansell.

One of the troopers who had accompanied him in the wagon shook his head. "None." He fished in a bag at his side before producing a rolled-up parchment, sealed with wax, and offered it to the officer.

"From the lady?" the officer asked as he took it.

"Aye."

The officer nodded knowingly, breaking the seal and unfurling the parchment. As he read, he squinted. Then his brow furrowed. Then his eyes widened. He looked at Ansell. Then back at the letter.

"So do we hang the ugly fucker now?" one of the troopers asked impatiently.

One of the others laughed. "Should give this bastard a kicking first."

The officer finished reading, then carefully folded the parchment in half, then in half again. His gaze slowly rose till he was looking Ansell in the eye. Then he reached to his side and drew his knife, a long glistening blade with a slight curve to the edge.

So not even the mercy of the gallows. He was to be gutted slowly.

When the officer took a step closer, Ansell thought about fighting. Perhaps offering one last sliver of defiance. It would have done no good, and so instead he stood, and he waited.

The officer took his bound wrists, and Ansell winced as he grasped the bandaged hand wounded by Regenwulf's blade. With a twist of his knife, he neatly sliced through the ropes and allowed them to drop to the ground. Immediately his men looked all the more nervous, some offering one another confused glances.

Ansell rubbed at those sore wrists, feeling the string of beads still tied to them. Grateful he had them here, at the end. The only gift that had ever mattered to him.

"Open it," the officer said, gesturing at the gate, as though he were annoyed at his own order.

"What?" came the startled reply.

"I said, open it," the officer snarled, his patience run to nothing.

Ansell heard the clank of metal, the strained noise of the winch as the troopers obeyed. This was not the way things were supposed to go. He was to be executed. Quietly and out of the way.

His eyes fell to the piece of parchment still in the officer's hand. One that could only have come from the Hawkspur woman. Mercy, when she had every reason, every right, to slay him.

"We're just letting him go?" a forlorn voice cried.

The officer was still watching Ansell like a hawk. "Aye, into the Drift. A day that side of the gate and he'll wish we'd swung him by a rope."

He pointed toward the yawning arch, moving closer to it, and Ansell followed. They stopped at the threshold. At the gate to oblivion beyond. A strip of dead earth where the condemned were sent to die.

A gesture of his hand and one of the troopers placed a sheathed blade in the officer's grip. One look at Ansell and he flung the sword through the open gate, where it clanked onto the ramp leading down to endless waste.

"Go on then," he said.

It was all the invitation Ansell needed, and he walked through the gate and down the ramp. A warm wind stroked his face. Bitter air teasing his nose.

Behind him he heard the clicking of the windlass as the portcullis was lowered, before the ominous thud of it hitting the ground. The blade was at his feet, and Ansell stooped to pick it up. It was heavy, a burden he would have to carry into the wastes, but one that might keep him alive. At least for a while.

The wooden gate slammed closed behind him.

No going back now.

Ansell walked into the Drift.

# FULREN

He leaned out as far as he could from the deck, letting the warm wind tousle his hair. The sensation of being so high, so free, made him feel as though he were flying like the hawk he was named for.

Fulren remembered how daunted he had been cruising in that airship the first time. Not knowing what was in store once he reached Nyrakkis. Now though, the lands beyond the Drift held no fear for him. They would surely welcome him, now they had common cause. War was coming. One in which he would surely be key. But as much as he knew he had value to the Queen of Nyrakkis, he also knew he had to tread carefully.

He turned from the gunwale to face the deck. The arcanist sigil was no longer there, replaced by the ugly engine he had constructed to augment the airship's power. Pyrestone converters now meant there was no need for arcanists to be sacrificed, and for that alone he could be proud. The whole ship buzzed with energy, he could feel it to his core. But that engine wasn't the only thing that kept this vessel aloft.

The demon in its sarcophagus still moaned and raged now it was fuelled by pyrestone, and not by the sorcery of damned souls. Eventually Fulren would develop the artifice so it needed no demon at all. He had even left his schematics with Philbert and his artificers back at the Anvil, so they might build on the theoretics themselves. With luck, they would create a whole fleet of ships before the storm rose from Iperion Magna.

As he saw Wenis come from the lower deck, all thoughts of innovation vanished from his head. She walked slowly toward him, a cat on the prowl. When she reached the gunwale she leaned back, letting the wind catch her hair.

Fulren just watched her. He had adapted so well to the vision his necroglyph gave him, it was better than his real eyes, allowing him to see so much more beauty in the world. Or maybe it was just her.

"Sleep well?" he asked.

She smiled and rolled her shoulders. "Like a baby. Only I howl less when I wake. You know I was never able to sleep aboard these vessels before. Your alterations are most definitely for the better."

"The first of many," he replied, unable to take his eyes off her.

"Yes. If we are to challenge what is coming we will most certainly need to embrace change. But it will not be easy to persuade the Houses that they must accept your artifice. Let alone Queen Meresankh."

"The queen sent you for a reason. To instigate an alliance. And you succeeded. She knew you would persuade us to help you, and if we are to do that we'll need to develop new ways of working together. New ways to combine our strengths. A price will have to be paid if we are to defeat the Scions. Compromises made."

"And yet you have already paid such a high price." She absently caressed the metal of his arm. He could feel it, as though she were stroking flesh and not alloy. "Do you ever regret it?"

He thought on that for a moment, but as he gazed at her, all thought of his sacrifice fled. With his arcanist sight he could see every contour of her face, every facet in her eyes.

"None," he said.

She smiled in response. "That is the right answer, Prince of Torwyn."

Wenis craned her neck, stretching up to kiss him softly on the lips. Fulren remembered the first time she had done that in Jubara.

How it had made his head spin. How confused he had been. Even now it sent a tingle down his spine stronger than any sensation his necroglyph had given him.

"What was that for?" he asked, looking about the deck self-consciously.

She teased his cheek with her fingertips. "Merely a statement of intent. And don't be bothered about them." A casual gesture toward the Caste warriors standing like statues. "They don't care."

Fulren glanced toward those armoured knights. His glyphsight showing him nothing but black silhouettes where there should have been dancing motes of light. Before he could ponder on that, the shrill peal of a bell rang out from the forecastle.

Wenis turned toward the noise. "What the fuck is that?"

Fulren was already scanning the skies around the airship, focusing on the larward horizon. Dark shapes were making their way nearer, borne on leathern wings.

Bandits preparing to attack. Just like the first time he had travelled across the Drift.

"Some old friends come to welcome you home, by the looks of things."

Wenis growled in her throat. "Am I cursed never to find any peace? Not even a thousand feet above the ground?"

Fulren raised himself on steel legs, stalking across the deck to where his sword lay. He picked up the blade, feeling that extension of his body, looking forward to putting it to use. In his steel claw he raised his helm, placing it over his head. The world came into focus with stark clarity.

The necroglyph on his back began to burn in response to his will, and he welcomed the pain. In his hand the sword whispered a murmuring tune, pyrestones flaring to life, light dancing along the blade.

Across the skies those cloaked riders came once more.

This time, they held no fear for him.

# TYRETA

She could feel the energy from the engine coursing through every metal panel of the landship. It hummed a tune to her, filling her with a strange kind of nostalgia. Not an unpleasant sensation, but one she'd gladly have foregone.

Gazing out of the carriage window, she watched the forest fly past. Before the war, before the betrayal and murder and endless loss, she'd travelled on a landship to the Anvil. It had all seemed so simple then. So easy. Everything had been mapped out for her, despite how much she'd railed against it. Now as she made her way home, she realised nothing had changed.

And at the same time, everything had.

The trees of the Alderwood, once so familiar, now looked different. They were more alive to her eyes, and she felt somehow connected to them, as though they were calling to her. Inviting her...

"You glad to be on your way home?"

Sted's voice made Tyreta start. She looked across at her friend, sitting cross-legged on the seat, redstalk dangling from the side of her mouth. In all honesty, Tyreta had no idea if she was glad or not.

"Sure."

Sted nodded, as though that had been the only answer to give. Then she gazed through the window at the forest flashing past.

Tyreta wondered if she was seeing the same thing. Somehow, she doubted it.

"I can't wait to get back," Sted said, the redstalk bouncing with every word. "Back to my old village north of Wyke. That's if it's still standing after..." Sted dismissed the thought with a tiny shake of her head. "There's this tavern I used to go in. Everybody knows everybody. Right friendly place. You'd like it there."

Tyreta was sure she was supposed to agree, but she just couldn't bring herself to answer. She was pretty sure she'd hate it there. Right now, the thought of a crowd, of people chugging down ale in a smoky tavern, made her want to be sick.

"So what's the first thing you'll do when you get back?" Sted persisted.

Through the window, Tyreta caught sight of a deer bounding through the undergrowth. She felt a strange urge to rush from the carriage, leap from the train and pursue it. Her flesh tingled at the prospect, but she quickly fought it down.

"I have no idea."

Sted sighed in frustration. "Well, fuck. I'm really glad I decided to join you on this trip. Talking to you is really making the journey fly by."

She looked at Sted, seeing her annoyance, feeling guilty she wasn't a better travelling companion. "I'm sorry. I was just—"

Sted shook her head. "No, I'm sorry. I know you've been through a lot, and with everything that's happened with Conall. Last thing you want is me prattling on."

Tyreta nodded, but she knew it wasn't just that. It was all the other things that went along with it. The world was returning to normal for everyone around her, but for Tyreta everything had changed. She was seeing things differently now. As though watching through someone else's eyes. Or something else's.

Sted leaned forward. "He came back from the dead once, you know. There's no reason he won't do it again."

Tyreta affected a smile. It was the gracious thing to do, considering Sted was trying her best. But her best would never be enough to put Tyreta's fears aside. To allay the discomfort she felt in her own skin.

"I'm just gonna get some air," she said, before rising to her feet. Sted made to stand too. "Want me to come?"

"No. You just relax. I think I need to be alone for a bit."

"Sure," Sted replied, reclining in her seat.

She looked a little awkward, as though she should have been doing something to help. It only made Tyreta feel guilty. There was nothing Sted could do for her now. Nothing anyone could do.

Tyreta made her way through the carriage, desperate to escape its stifling confines. It was so hard to breathe it felt as though she'd been sewn into a sack and thrown in a lake. From the way people were furtively looking at her, her discomfort must have been obvious. All those eyes on her, and it was all she could do not to scream.

At the end of the carriage she clawed her way up the winding metal stair that led to the observation platform. Immediately the wind took her breath away, but it was a blessed relief, as though it were blowing away all her ills. The earthen smell of the Alderwood, a flock of birds in flight above, and she felt a sudden release.

Tyreta had left her mother behind in the Anvil, left her alone to fix the mess the war had caused, but she still felt ensnared. Trapped by expectation. Responsibility. As she gripped the rail of the deck, she knew now that no matter how far she went she would never be able to escape completely.

Wyke would hold no cure to what afflicted her. Civilisation and the shadow of the Guilds would always hang over her, always watching, always expecting. There was nowhere that Tyreta Hawkspur could call home. Nowhere she might belong.

She gripped the rail so tight it began to hurt her hands. Teeth grinding until her jaw ached. As she cast her gaze across the front of the landship, she knew what she had to do. There was no other way.

As she moved forward, closer to the engine, she once more recalled that fateful journey she had made so long ago to the Anvil. Remembered how she had teased the engine's core and sped up the landship. Caused so much panic. Ignited her mother's rage.

Tyreta closed her eyes, raising her hands, convening with the web. She reached out with her power, sending it coursing along ephemeral strands to the engine, feeling the throbbing of that machine and the burgeoning energy of the pyrestones within. A little more effort and she began to reduce that power, nullifying the stones so they no longer burned but winnowed down to nothing.

The landship jolted, its speed reducing until it came to a shuddering stop. Voices within the carriage rose in confusion, and she could hear the pilots in the engine shouting at one another in a panic.

With a single bound, she leapt from the observation deck, landing on the ground deftly. There was silence now, but for the sound of the forest. It was alive, her every sense triggered by the smell and taste and noise.

Quickly she unbuttoned her tunic, casting it aside as she strode toward the tree line. Before she could reach it, she heard a shout behind her.

Sted was at the carriage door, face a mask of concern. "Where the fuck are you going?"

It raised a smile from Tyreta. The first in so long.

"Tell my mother..." What? How could she ever explain? "Oh, you'll think of something."

Without waiting for Sted's reply, Tyreta turned and ran into the forest.

# ROSOMON

It was an upper chamber of the palace, one with a window large enough to see most of the Anvil from. She hadn't thought it appropriate that she conduct business in her brother's throne room. At least not yet.

This might have been a quiet haven of sanctity, so high above the bustle of the city, but there was no chance of that with the seething air of rage that hung over it.

"Fuck sake, Ros, what were you thinking?"

Oleksig glared from across the room, gripping his pipe tight in his hand as though he might crush it.

"Careful with the language," she replied.

That took some of the fire from his eyes, and he glanced to one corner where Grace sat quietly. She hadn't even acknowledged his outburst, carrying on scribbling on that parchment with her charcoal.

Oleksig stepped closer, more conspiratorially so the girl might not hear him if he swore again. "Five Armiger marshals. Two High Legates. A Guildmaster. And your own sister-in-law. Murdered, Rosomon. Slaughtered in cold blood."

*Murdered* seemed a curious word for him to use under the circumstances. She was finding it difficult nowadays to distinguish between that and execution. Certainly, the latter was justified in some eyes. And to Rosomon, those nine killings were more than justified.

"I really don't know what to tell you. It was all an unfortunate misunderstanding really."

"A misunderstanding?" He caught himself before he yelled any louder. "The remaining marshals are incensed. There is talk of them tearing up their treaties. And you know as well as I do how hard it was to get them to sign in the first place. This is a delicate peace we have arranged, Rosomon. You've risked it all."

"Hold your nerve," she said dismissively. "The marshals know any further action against us would destabilise Torwyn once again. And we have come to very generous contractual terms with them. They won't risk that."

"And what about Maugar? He's threatening to take his Blackshields and leave for the Forge immediately, never to return. We need him right now, to keep order in the city."

Most likely Maugar was annoyed he hadn't had the nerve to kill those traitors himself.

"Maugar will come around. Leave him to me."

"Don't you realise what a dangerous precedent you set in murdering Rearden? If one Guildmaster can be slaughtered without repercussion, then we all can."

Rosomon found it rather hypocritical he hadn't had the same reservations when they'd killed Jarlath. Even so, he may have had a point, but they were all at risk anyway. Less so, now Rearden was out of the frame.

She turned toward the wide-open window, listening to the distant clank of the manufactories operating once again. "They're not coming for us with pitchforks, Oleksig. In case you hadn't noticed."

"But you've made martyrs of them."

She almost laughed at that notion. The thought of anyone worshipping Rearden Corwen's memory was preposterous.

"I've made corpses of our enemies."

Oleksig moved even closer, his jaw working as he prepared for another tirade. He stopped when there was a knock at the door.

"Enter," she said, keen for something to distract them from this pointless argument.

The door opened. Wachelm was the first to walk through it, wearing the neatly cut yellow robe of Corwen. Then came Willet in his stark white Archlegate raiment. Finally, Philbert Kerrick walked in, his tunic the deep red of Archwind.

"What's this?" Oleksig asked, gesturing at the new arrivals, as though they were on their way to a gala he hadn't been invited to.

"I thought introductions were necessary," Rosomon replied. "Just so we know where we all stand. There is much to prepare for in the months ahead. The threat from Iperion Magna has been made clear to me, and I have taken certain steps to reestablish order throughout Torwyn."

"*You* have taken steps?" Oleksig said incredulously. "Without consulting the other Guildmasters? This should have been talked over in the Guildhall. We should all have—"

"This is Wachelm," Rosomon interrupted, before Oleksig could rile himself up further. "The new Guildmaster of Corwen. Philbert here, who you already know, has been appointed standing Guildmaster of Archwind, since there is no hereditary heir left to take that position. And of course, you are aware of the recent ordination of our new Archlegate."

Oleksig regarded each of them in turn, before his gaze lingered on poor Willet. "You've been busy, Ros."

"We all have," she replied. "As will you be."

She nodded to Wachelm, who sheepishly handed Oleksig a small ledger. Oleksig took it, regarding the leatherbound book as though it were covered in something nasty.

"Guildmaster Wachelm has taken the liberty of calculating ore requirements for the next five years, and arranging quotas for each of the mines in all territories."

Oleksig glanced to Wachelm with a disdainful look, then at the ledger, then her. "But I have always been in charge of—"

"From now on the Guilds will work as a singular entity, Oleksig. I have seen enough of what chaos brings. That time is at an end."

His nostrils flared and he nodded, realising what all this was. "So you're handing me quotas? And what might happen if I fail to meet them? Will you have a bath waiting to drown me in?"

"Don't be so dramatic, Oleksig."

"Dramatic?" His eyes began to twitch, his jaw working more frenetically than ever. "Dramatic?" He flung his pipe across the room. It sailed over Rosomon's head and through the open window.

Their eyes locked, and she wondered if he had anything else to say. For a moment she regretted not having Kassian or Ianto present, but she hadn't thought that necessary. Now it seemed like Oleksig might go too far.

Instead, he gripped his ledger tighter and spun on his heel. Philbert shuffled from his path as he stalked to the door and wrenched it open. The sound of it slamming behind him echoed through the chamber.

"That didn't go too well," Wachelm said, pushing his spectacles up his nose.

"Actually, it went much better than I anticipated," Rosomon replied. "At least it was his pipe he flung through the window and not the ledger."

She regarded that window, the skyline, the birds flying past. She wondered if Oleksig's fears were indeed founded. If there would be pitchforks. If the martyrs she had made would really inspire yet another uprising. All that was possible, but she could only focus on one crisis at a time.

"Philbert, have you had a chance to review the schematics my son provided you with?"

Instinctively the old artificer reached for the skullcap he usually wore atop his head. On finding it missing, he simply scratched his bald scalp.

"We have. And we are still trying to decipher some of the diagrammatical instruction, but it looks promising."

One good piece of news at least. "I want all your resources put into this. A fleet must be established within the next nine months."

Philbert fumbled with the sleeve of his new red uniform. "That's...erm...that's a tight schedule."

"It is."

She let that hang there, giving Philbert the opportunity to argue, to say he could never meet such a deadline. Instead he remained silent, and eventually Wachelm cleared his throat.

"As well as quotas for the mines, I took the liberty of drawing up schedules for the smithies of Ironfall. I have taken account of the fact the Forge has considerable rebuilding to do."

Rosomon looked forward to delivering that news to Maugar. She could only imagine how he would spit his anger. "And the other thing?"

"A new administrative committee has been established to replace the Radwinter Guild, just as you ordered. And its duties have been disseminated among the smaller agricultural Guilds. I've crunched the numbers, and it will be more efficient in the long run."

More efficient and much less of a threat. With the head literally cut from one of the major Guilds it meant resistance to her current position was limited to the Marrlocks and Ironfalls. And she would ensure they were far too busy to stage any kind of interference in her plans.

"And the Hallowhills?"

Wachelm raised his brow. "Lucasta has been surprisingly compliant. Her webwainers have been dispatched to every corner of the Guildlands and are even now aiding with the reconstruction effort."

"How very helpful of her. But do make sure you keep a close eye on their movements. We wouldn't want anyone going rogue."

Wachelm nodded his assent. "Yes...Lady Rosomon."

His pause made her wonder what he was really going to call her. Empress perhaps? But she had made no move to adopt that title. Made no attempt to sit on the throne. But there may well come a time...

"And Archlegate. Tell me, how is your brood?"

Despite his robes of office, and the authority they gave him, Willet still looked like a little boy who'd just been caught in a lie. "Erm... the appointment of High Legates in the two vacant positions is still ongoing. There has also been some concern over the Mount's security since the Knights of the Draconate are no longer—"

"I mean the people, Willet. What is the general mood? Are Oleksig's fears of martyrs founded in any way?"

A shade of doubt across his face, as he tried to work out exactly what she meant. "I...I don't think so."

"Then I expect you to find out. For sure. And soon."

He nodded his blond head anxiously. "Yes, Lady Rosomon."

She regarded them all. Her closest counsel. The men she would need to control a nation.

"We all know our tasks. Until we convene again, gentlemen."

They all bowed as one, as though they'd rehearsed it that way, and turned to leave. It was somewhat reassuring that they were so loyal, but she'd learned that loyalties could shift in times of upheaval. And it was doubtless such times were on the way.

The sound of charcoal breaking, and a little voice saying, "Fuck sake."

Grace stared forlornly at the parchment in front of her. Then at the broken chalk in her black-stained fingers. Rosomon stepped closer, seeing the smudge streaked across the paper. Then she noticed what the girl had been drawing.

It was a crude likeness, but it was definitely Rosomon. Even drawn by a child's hand, she looked imperious. Stern. Made all the more commanding by the crown Grace had drawn upon her head.

"That's enough of that," Rosomon said, holding out her hand.

Obediently, Grace set down the paper and chalk, and scrambled to her feet. She flattened down her little blue tunic, leaving a smudge on the material, but Rosomon did her best to ignore it. There'd be time enough later to teach the girl about decorum and deportment.

Grace took Rosomon's hand, and together they walked to the window to take in the sight. The steam rising from those forges and manufactories. The rumble of the skyway. The chugging sound of the barges. A landship cruising into the terminal.

"What are we looking at?" Grace asked eventually.

"We are looking at home," Rosomon answered, wondering how long it would stay like this. Wanting to take in this moment and remember it for as long as she could. This peace. This normality. Before it was all thrown into chaos once more. "Now come. We have much to prepare for, you and I."

# EPILOGUE

It stood a hundred leagues west of Goltha Skar. Qyarthenon, that hallowed zikkurat in the desert. A black finger of stone jutting from sun-baked sands, its onyx flank cracked and weathered by the merciless breath of the searing winds that had harried it for over a millennium. The bones of countless sacrifices littered its base like a jagged necklace, picked clean by circling carrion birds. The horrors this place had witnessed belied imagining, but today there would be no bloodletting. Or at least Maelor hoped.

At the flat summit of Qyarthenon, four portals stood at the cardinal points, each archway supported by towering ebon pillars engraved with eldritch script that pained the eyes to read. The ancient stone shimmered in the heat, yet exuded the chill of death. And in the midst of those portals, Maelor Kytheris paced, his pale hands clasped behind his back, skeletal fingers twitching in agitation. The Scions were late. Of course. The self-important wretches each wishing to make an entrance, to be the last to arrive so they might become the focus of attention. A subtle game of dominance. But Maelor had no patience for their conceits today.

Their carefully laid plans had been upended by that venomous thorn Rosomon Hawkspur. She had proven herself formidable, striking down the Draconate Ministry to unite all under an iron fist.

Maelor cursed under his breath for the hundredth time. Their plans had veered off course, and so soon. Now he had been left with no other choice than to gather the Scions once more, but as High Steward of the Obsidian Ward and Herald of the Tetrarchy, such was his privilege.

Still, the decision had given him pause. He had summoned the four here to discuss this disastrous turn of events and formulate a new strategy, but it was a dangerous gambit. For a thousand years the Scions had been at one another's throats, and gathering them all together was always a dangerous prospect. If they ever deigned to show.

Sweat trickled down Maelor's gaunt cheeks as the pitiless sun climbed higher. How much longer would he be forced to wait, with the fate of Iperion Magna hanging in the balance?

A stiff desert breeze tugged at his robes, fluttering the black fabric around his emaciated frame as he caught sight of himself in the mirror surface of an ebon pillar. Wispy white hair clung to his skull in lank strands that stirred fitfully. His skin bore a pallid sheen, as though he were half a corpse already, a sepulchral figure in the stark brilliance of day. He could barely remember ever being young, or a time when he had not served these immortal mages. Those long years had seen him withered with age, and now it seemed they were determined to see him wither to nothing before they honoured his summons...

The southern portal rippled. Its void-black surface transformed to shimmering quicksilver, and Maelor held his breath. Which Scion would deign to arrive first? In what guise would they cloak themselves—a human form or some terrifying demonic aspect?

To his relief, a wizened crone tottered through the portal, leaning on a gnarled stick. White hair straggled about a face latticed with wrinkles, watery eyes clouded by cataracts as bony hands clutched a tattered shawl about stooped shoulders.

Maelor was not fooled by this frail facade. He could feel the aura of malice radiating from the creature, cold and ancient. It grew even more malevolent as Senmonthis smiled her greeting.

"Maelor," she croaked.

The herald swept into a bow, long sleeves trailing. "Welcome, Scion Senmonthis. My gratitude for your timely attendance."

"Ever do I strive for punctuality," she replied, not even attempting to hide the sarcasm in her tone.

As Maelor straightened, feeling the subtle crack in his vertebrae, the western portal flared to swirling life. Shadows gathered, congealing into humanoid forms that marched through with jolting, mechanical steps. Each towering figure was sheathed in lacquered armour, eyes blank white pits in expressionless helms. The reek of embalming spices mingled with the tang of oil, the stink of artifice. These were undying bodyguards. Animated warriors, crafted with dark science to protect their master.

And there he was, ducking his horned head as he emerged. Ten feet tall, corded with black sinuous muscle, crimson eyes alight with malefic power. Bagdemagus, warlord-arcanist of Goltha Skar. Sorcerous energies crackled from his crimson glaive as he surveyed the summit with a sneer of disdain, not even sparing a glance for Maelor.

The herald bowed again nonetheless, fighting to keep the tremor from his voice. "Hail, Scion Bagdemagus."

The hulking archmage offered him the barest glance. "Spare me your fawning, Maelor. Where are the others?"

As if in answer, the eastern portal flashed pale blue, disgorging four lissom figures. Women clad in segmented cerulean armour, their almond eyes cold and cruel above azure veils, each with one hand resting on the wire-wrapped hilt of a curving sabre. Sword mages, Sisters of the Sibilant Word, who could slay with a whisper.

The guards took up positions to either side as another figure glided through—Celebrai, striding like an empress. She wore a towering headdress wrought from beaten silver in the form of a cowled serpent, slitted amber eyes glowing beneath. Her flawless ebony skin was sheathed in a gown of liquid shadow that writhed about her lithe frame. Full lips were painted the purple of bruised flesh, and they quirked in a subtle smile as she surveyed the assembly.

Maelor felt his shrivelled heart stutter in his sunken chest. Celebrai was hauntingly beautiful, with a cold, imperious majesty that made his knees want to buckle. But the herald knew what malice lurked beneath that darkly perfect mask. He bent at the waist, breath caught in his throat.

"I bid you welcome, Scion Celebrai."

"Rise, Maelor." Her voice was warm honey. "Such obeisance ill suits you."

Maelor straightened, trying to compose himself, as the north portal began to judder and hum. A sickly green miasma seeped through, reeking of rotting vegetation. All eyes turned as two hulking durrga warriors stomped out, goat-like faces scowling from beneath great helms, downy skin crisscrossed with scars. Unusually, both bore identical armour of bright plate, unlike the scavenged leather and bone worn in their natural habitat of the Karna, their spears wrought by the most skilled smiths.

Behind them marched a dozen more, but these bore their master aloft on a palanquin of carved ivory. Ekediah the Betrayer, Arch Contemptor of Tallus Rann, was a grotesquely corpulent figure sheathed in flaking scales, the stench of decay and narcotic mist preceding him. His lipless mouth hung agape, rheumy eyes rolling in a bloated toad-skull. Stubby fingers gripped the mouthpiece of a waterpipe, rings of lapis and malachite flashing. Balanced on one meaty thigh was an obsidian bowl heaped with squirming, bioluminescent things, mewling and nipping at each other. As Maelor watched in revulsion, Ekediah plucked one of the wriggling morsels and popped it into his gaping maw. Yellowed teeth crunched before iridescent ichor spilled down his warty chin.

The herald bowed low one final time, bile burning his throat, praying none of his disgust showed. "You honour us with your presence, Scion Eke—"

A burbling chuckle from the Arch Contemptor cut him off. "Yes. You may begin, Herald. Swiftly, if you please. I have a bacchanal to attend when this tedious business is done."

Maelor straightened, feeling the tension crackling between the Scions like static. These beings loathed one another with a passion harboured over centuries of feuding. Only their mutual hatred of their neighbours, and an inhuman lust for power, allowed them to hold this fragile alliance together. But after their recent defeats, even that might not be enough. Maelor had to conduct matters swiftly, before things got out of hand.

He raised his wizened hands for attention. "Mighty Scions, I thank you all for assembling here on such short notice. I know our plans have gone...awry of late. The Hawkspur has proven more tenacious than anticipated. But I assure you, our compact still stands. If we reaffirm our—"

"Spare us the pontification, High Steward." Bagdemagus's guttural snarl cut through the arid air like an axe. Then he stabbed one thick finger at Senmonthis. "This is *her* fault. She was the one tasked with destabilising Torwyn. Instead that simpering hag played her games too poorly, and now look. The rebellion quelled. The Guilds united under a single banner, stronger than ever."

Maelor suppressed his irritation. They could ill afford to descend into puerile sniping. Not now.

"Please, this accomplishes nothing. We are not here to trade recrim—"

"I said we should just have sent my assassins," Bagdemagus bulled on, ignoring him completely, crimson eyes boring into Senmonthis with pure venom. "I have plenty to spare. But no. Senmonthis knew best. Her sorcery would prevail and she would have her puppet on the throne of Torwyn. And now look where we are."

Senmonthis said nothing, cracked lips pursed, cataracted eyes unreadable as she returned Bagdemagus's baleful glare. The air between them thrummed with malice.

"Nevertheless," Maelor continued. "We have to—"

"Have to?" Celebrai said, amber eyes flashed as she levelled an imperious stare at Maelor. "Have to what? Accept where we are? The Hawkspur woman has seized her advantage. Consolidated power. Soon she will ally with that jackal queen in Nyrakkis, despite our efforts to sow discord." Her lip curled in an exquisite sneer. "The cattle grow bold. United, they may prove...unassailable. So I ask you, what now, Maelor? What is our next move?"

"No next move," burbled Ekediah around a mouthful of writhing things before he gulped, then grinned, showing needle fangs inscribed with profane runes. "Plans failed. Torwyn holds. We go home now, yes? Back to fighting and feuding. The old ways were always more interesting."

Bagdemagus smashed a fist into his breastplate with a clang. "Good. I've missed hearing the screams of your devotees as I flay them alive, you bloated maggot."

This was spiralling out of control. Maelor knew he had to act decisively, or see all their schemes crumble to dust, and he steeled himself to deliver the dangerous suggestion he'd been nursing.

"Enough!" Maelor's normally reedy voice cracked out with resonance, echoing between the crumbling stones. Four sets of inhuman eyes regarded him, and he drew himself up before his advantage faltered. "If the alliance between Torwyn and Nyrakkis now looks inevitable, then perhaps we must form one of our own."

Silence, as the suggestion percolated among the Scions. A warm breeze cut across the top of the zikkurat, and for a moment Maelor wondered if it was the last sensation he might ever feel before one of them destroyed him for his impertinence.

Then Ekediah gestured at his durrga. "Some of us have already formed alliances, Herald."

Maelor shook his head. "No. I'm not talking about slaves. About mortals. This will require reaching out to beings infinitely more dangerous. And infinitely more powerful."

Celebrai fixed him with a lethal stare. "Are you suggesting that we reach out across the Dominions?"

"That's exactly what I'm suggesting," Maelor replied. "For centuries the archmages have channelled magics through the Veil. Now I would see us open a gateway, and allow in—"

"You cannot be serious." Bagdemagus's basso rumble made him sound more furious than usual. "Treat with those... creatures? Have you taken leave of your meagre senses, High Steward?"

Maelor fought down his fear of the Scion's wrath and held his ground. "I assure you, I am quite serious. For what other choice remains open to us? Failure? And besides... one among our number is already pursuing such a path."

In the deafening silence, Maelor took his gamble, and fixed his gaze upon Celebrai. In turn her amber eyes almost scorched holes in him, but he didn't flinch. Yes, he was taking an awful risk exposing her secret dealings. But if something had to shock the Scions into action...

"Is this true, Celebrai?" croaked Senmonthis, eyes narrowing to slits. "You have been treating without us? That's a dangerous game to play."

Celebrai inclined her head just a fraction. "I do not deny it. There are bargains to be struck, for those with the courage and cunning to do so. The realms across Dominions offer great power for those bold enough to seize it."

"Bold? Or reckless?" spat Bagdemagus. "Those things are as likely to devour us as deal with us."

"And that is why Celebrai cannot treat with them alone." Maelor's gaze swept the assembled Scions. "None of us can. But together, with a united front, we may stand a chance of harnessing their power and recruiting from their number. Of paying the price that must be paid, and living to celebrate the victory it will bring."

Ekediah took a long draw from his waterpipe before exhaling a stream of green smoke. "Risky. Dangerous. Like sticking your tongue in a beehive, yes? Maybe get honey, maybe get stung."

Senmonthis stepped forward, voice creaking from her withered lips. "I have peered beyond the Veil. Seen portents and omens in the entrails of the world. And I tell you now... death stalks us. No matter what path we tread. A warrior comes, born from the very flesh we seek to dominate. Human-born, but he cannot be stopped by any power, in this realm or beyond."

Bagdemagus sneered. "Riddles and ravings, you old bitch. You expect us to cower from your prophecies?"

Senmonthis gave a fatalistic shrug. "Do as you wish. I merely speak what I have seen. It makes no difference what we do. Our fate is splayed out in the guts of the future."

"Is it splayed out as clearly as you predicted your triumph over the Hawkspur woman? Because that didn't turn out quite the way you foresaw."

"All is for a reason."

Bagdemagus barked a laugh across the flat summit. "Is it? And what reason is there to embark on any further crusade against Torwyn? Against Nyrakkis? If such a crusade is already doomed?"

"I did not say it was doomed," Senmonthis replied, a wry smile on her toothless mouth. "Just that a dark warrior is coming and he intends to lay us all low. Whether we rise victorious from the fires he will kindle still hangs in the balance."

Maelor raised his hands again. "Then I put it to you all, here and now, that we follow the path across Dominions and entreat for aid. Are we agreed? Will you take this fell road? Bargain with the powers beyond, and accept their price? Or will you retreat to your cities and wait for our enemies to grow strong enough to challenge us outright?"

A weighted pause, as Bagdemagus glowered, Ekediah puffed thoughtfully on his waterpipe, and Senmonthis watched from beneath hooded lids. But Celebrai's smile glittered like a poisoned blade. Maelor waited with bated breath, feeling the future balanced on that knife's edge.

"I am committed to this path already," Celebrai said at last. "But I cannot walk it alone. At least, not yet. If the rest of you are with me though..."

She let the sentence hang, heavy with dark promise.

Ekediah gurgled contemplatively, then shrugged, sending a ripple through his corpulent flesh. "Sounds more interesting than the same old feuds we have entertained for a thousand years. Why not?"

Maelor turned to Senmonthis, and the old woman simply acknowledged with the faintest of nods. Finally, all eyes turned to Bagdemagus, who glowered from beneath his helm, gauntleted hands flexing at his sides. For a long moment, only the arid wind spoke, then slowly he nodded.

"I do not like this. The things beyond are fickle and ravenous. Dealing with them brings peril. But better that than to watch helpless as our foes grow stronger. Very well. I too will treat with them."

Maelor nodded, feeling a wave of relief wash through him. He had done it. Herded these ancient, stubborn beings onto the same benighted path. Now he just prayed it would be enough.

"Then we are agreed. I shall visit each of you in your own domains to negotiate the terms and plan a way forward. A way forward that will be long and dangerous, but united we cannot fail."

With that, he bowed low, signalling the meeting over. One by one, the Scions took their leave. Ekediah was borne through his portal on the back of the durrga, leaving a green miasma in his wake. Bagdemagus stalked away, muttering darkly, his undying guards clanking beside him. Celebrai offered not so much as a nod of acknowledgment as she all but glided back through her gate, Sisters of the Sibilant Word slinking behind her like serpents.

Only Senmonthis lingered, fixing Maelor with her glass-eyed stare. For a moment, she almost looked concerned, but then she shook her head, smile widening.

"Maelor Kytheris, you may yet damn us all. And perhaps that is all we deserve."

With that she turned, leaning heavily on her staff as she struggled back through her portal. An affectation for sure, but one Maelor would never presume to question.

When the eldritch light had waned from the final portal, he stood alone atop the Qyarthenon, listening to the moaning wind. Perhaps Senmonthis was right. Perhaps his desperation to salvage their schemes would only seal their ruin. But what other choice remained?

Torwyn had rallied behind a new empress, an alliance with Nyrakkis imminent. No, he could not let their enemies rise so high. Even if it meant dancing with the darkest of powers. The Scions of the Magna had to prevail, or perish in the attempt.

And yet... that prophecy haunted him. A dark warrior destined to be their downfall? Could there exist but a single foe strong enough to throw down the Tetrarchy itself? Especially one born to mortals.

Maelor shook off the insidious thought. Surely it was a mistake. A misreading of the augurs. The Great Wyrms were dead. Mankind had no gods left, no divine protectors, let alone mortals powerful enough to challenge the Scions. Once their pacts were sealed nothing could stop them. And then Torwyn, Nyrakkis, Hyreme itself would tremble before the assembled might of Iperion Magna.

This Maelor vowed, atop that wind-scoured zikkurat, as the sun sank, and shadow claimed the dunes once more.

And so it would be.

# ONE YEAR LATER

Eldon's knees protested with each laboured step, joints popping like corn kernels in a fire. The steep trail snaked endlessly ahead, taunting him, but Finch bounded along a few paces in front, spry as a month-old lamb, voice raised in song.

> "Oh the wicked Egelrath,
> His plots did all go stale,
> The Guilds broke down his temple gate,
> And made his face turn pale."

Eldon grimaced. Trust his nephew to make light of it all with his fool singing. Those memories were still raw for many, but then Eldon guessed everyone dealt with it in their own way.

> "His Drakes all fought with blade and fist,
> But fell like wheat in rows,
> Their armour rent by rebel's kiss,
> Their corpses left for crows."

Blinking sweat from his eyes, Eldon squinted at the craggy summit of Ayan Tarn looming above. Their little boat would be waiting up there on the lake, just as it always was, and then he could get his breath back. This trek never seemed to get any easier though.

> *"The Hawkspurs soared on wings of might,*
> *Their talons sharp and keen,*
> *They tore the tyrant from his height,*
> *And claimed the victor's sheen."*

Eldon was of half a mind to tell the lad to shut his yap, but he held his tongue. No use spoiling Finch's good cheer. Let him make a joke of it if he wanted. Maybe that was the only way to stomach the horror of it all, what had befallen them in that pointless war.

> *"They found his body broken,*
> *At the bottom of a hole,*
> *No more lies were spoken,*
> *The wyrms devoured his soul."*

And what had it changed? They still had fields to plough. Still had machines to build. The circle of the year kept turning, the seasons never stopped coming. And after all that strife, the Guilds were still in charge. Only now they had an empress instead of an emperor. Not that she called herself that, but they all knew what she was.

> *"Now Rosomon, the Guildess fair,*
> *Holds Torwyn's fate in hand,*
> *With justice firm and wisdom rare,*
> *She'll heal the wounded land."*

The steep path finally levelled out onto a stretch of relatively flat ground. Eldon paused to catch his breath, one weathered hand braced against the rough bark of a gnarled yew. Finch halted and turned back, flashing a grin.

"Getting slow in your old age, eh?"

"Watch it, boy," Eldon growled. "I could still tan your hide if you lip off too much."

Finch raised his hands in mock surrender, and they resumed walking, Eldon lagging a few steps behind. The intermittent shade of the odd tree was a blessed relief from the sweltering sun, a fragrant breeze stirring the leaves overhead and cooling the sweat on his brow.

"You hear about that rogue Drake they caught down in Millfield?" Finch said. "Took six of 'em to bring him down, if the rumour's true."

Eldon grunted. "Aye. What of it?"

"Hanged him in the village square, they did. Sheriff didn't lift a finger to stop 'em neither."

Eldon was silent a long moment. "Can't say as I blame 'em. After everything that lot did to..."

His words trailed off as the memories threatened to surge up like bile. Fields and villages put to the torch at the merest suggestion of sedition. Artifice smashed to pieces and livelihoods destroyed. Children going so hungry they cried all the night through. Eldon shook his head to banish the ghosts.

"Still don't make it right," Finch said quietly.

Eldon had no reply to that. The wounds were still too fresh, the grief too raw. He wasn't sure he had it in him to feel sympathy for any of Sanctan's brood. Not after all they'd wrought.

With a sigh, he trudged on, following Finch up the winding trail as it rose toward the summit and the dark waters that awaited them there, cradled in the mountain's stony heart. The tarn spread before them, looking like a sheet of polished obsidian, reflecting the odd cloud in the sky. Their little rowboat bobbed gently against the shore, oars shipped and waiting. Finch hopped in and took his place on the forward bench while Eldon eased himself down with a grunt, old joints creaking.

With a concerted shove, Finch pushed off from the muddy bank and they glided out into open water. Ripples fractured the surface in their wake as Finch set to the oars, lean muscles bunching as he pulled in long, smooth strokes. Eldon busied himself readying their gear—checking the rods and lines, making sure the hooks were sharp and clean.

When he was satisfied, he upended the bait pouch into his palm. Worms squirmed and writhed, pale pink against the calloused brown of his skin, and he grimaced. Nasty buggers. He much preferred a lumber fly, but the unseasonably hot weather meant pickings had been slim of late.

Satisfied as he could be with the bait, Eldon reached next for the anchor rope, a heavy coil with a lead weight at one end. As soon as he picked it up, he swore under his breath. The damn thing was a mess of knots and tangles. He shot Finch an exasperated look.

"Thought I told you to stow this proper last time."

Finch just shrugged, not breaking the rhythm of his strokes. "Musta slipped my mind."

Eldon swallowed another curse and set to work picking at the knots with blunt nails. Finch rowed on, steering them toward the centre of the lake where the depths were murkiest and the largest fish lurked. When he judged they'd gone far enough, he let the oars trail and reached for his rod.

"What I don't get," Finch said as he baited his hook, "is where these little fishy bastards come from. I mean, it's a lake on top of a bloody mountain. Not like they can swim up from the river."

Eldon hardly glanced up from his painstaking work on the rope. "There'll be tunnels, won't there? Leading down to the aquifers and streams in the Marches."

"Huh?" Finch flicked his line out with a practiced snap of the wrist. It hit the water with a delicate splash. "Speakin' of tunnels, you hear what they're up to at the Forge these days?"

Eldon raised a brow. "Do I want to know?"

"Ships. Bloody great metal ships that can fly, if you can believe it. Artificers found a way to make 'em float, using pyrestone."

Eldon just snorted and shook his head. Nonsense. Or maybe not. By all accounts a huge black airship had come over the Dolur Peaks just over a year before. If those sorcerers in Nyrakkis could build one, then why not the Archwind Guild? It made him wonder what they might dream up next.

Without warning, Finch's rod bent nearly double. The line pinged taut, vibrating like a plucked lute string.

"Whoa!" Finch yelped, rising to his feet and hauling back on the rod, eyes wide. "I've hooked us a monster."

Eldon dropped his tangled rope and lunged forward to help. Too slow. Finch lurched as the surface of the water surged, flailing for balance. His elbow cracked into Eldon's jaw...

Pain exploded in his skull. Eldon toppled backwards, arms pinwheeling. The boat's edge caught him right behind the knees, and he had a split second to glimpse Finch's horrified face, mouth agape, before the cold water engulfed him and he sank like a stone.

The anchor rope with its heavy lead weight was snarled around his foot, pulling him down with frightful speed. Eldon tried to kick free but only succeeded in tangling himself further. Frigid water stabbed into his eyes, his nose, his lungs. He thrashed in pure animal panic, fighting the inexorable drag into the quiet depths to no avail.

Deeper and deeper he sank, the weight of the rope and his sodden clothes pulling him down till his lungs burned and he desperately held on to his last gulp of precious air, but it was a losing battle. He could feel his strength fading, his struggle growing weaker.

Silvery bubbles streamed from his nostrils as he finally exhaled, unable to hold it any longer. Water rushed in to fill the void, frigid and merciless. It was almost a relief to let go, to surrender to the inevitable. A strange lassitude crept over him and his body went slack as he drifted in the icy dark, feeling the lethargy of drowning take hold. This was it. This was how it would end...

Vague movement in his periphery.

Something vast shifted in the depths below him. Weak shafts of sunlight filtering down from above glinted on a sinuous flank armoured in massive scales the colour of corroded copper. Then a great slitted eye opened, easily as tall as a man, and rolled ponderously to fix him with a stare that spoke of aeons.

Terror jolted through Eldon like lightning. The paralysis that had claimed him shattered and he was abruptly aware of the burning in his lungs, the leaden weight of his limbs, the rope still tangled around his foot. With a wordless yell that burst from him in a torrent of bubbles, he wrenched his foot from the snarled line.

Unencumbered, he kicked for the surface with every last shred of strength left in him. That eye watched him go, unblinking, unfathomable, fading from view like a nightmare dismissed by the first rays of dawn.

Eldon erupted from the surface with a great whooping gasp, sucking in blessed air. He flailed weakly, barely able to keep his head above water. Strong hands seized him under the arms and hauled him up and over the side of the boat to land in a sopping heap on the bottom.

"By the Five!" Finch babbled, ashen-faced. "I thought... I thought for sure you were..."

"Shut up and row," Eldon wheezed in a panic. "Get us to shore. Now, lad!"

Finch fell to it like a man possessed, fairly hauling on the oars. The boat surged forward, driven by his desperate strokes. Eldon huddled into himself, shaking uncontrollably. His mind shied from the memory of what he'd seen down there in the gelid blackness, but all the while he could not take his eyes from the lake, any moment expecting that beast to burst from beneath the surface and roar its coming to the world.

It seemed to take an age for them to reach the shore, and Finch scrambled out and helped Eldon onto the grassy bank. They both collapsed there, chests heaving.

"What in the Lairs happened?" Finch asked when he'd caught his breath. "What did you see down there?"

Eldon just shook his head, still shivering. How could he possibly put it into words?

"We need to leave," he said hoarsely. "Gather the gear. We're not coming back here."

Finch looked ready to argue, but something in Eldon's haunted expression made him swallow his protests. He just nodded and hastened to collect their scattered tackle.

Eldon turned to look back at the lake, deceptively placid under the clear sky. He shuddered, feeling the phantom sensation of seeing that thing undulating in the abyssal deep. Waiting. Watching.

He'd never liked this bloody place.

Now he knew why.

# ACKNOWLEDGMENTS

And so it ends...at least for now.

The Age of Uprising trilogy has been a real labour of love, and there are a few people I definitely have to thank for helping to make it happen.

First and foremost, huge thanks to Bradley Englert, my editor, for seeing the potential in the pitch and allowing me to bring the series to life. Thanks to agent John Jarrold for organising the deal with his trademark aplomb. Thanks to Lauren Panepinto for commissioning such classy covers. And thanks to audio producer Thomas Mis, and all the voice talent, for making the audio version of the books so special. Also, thank you to anyone and everyone at Orbit US who has been involved in the production of the trilogy in any way, large or small.

Finally, thanks to the Hawkspurs for living in my head rent-free for the past five or six years, and sorry for everything I put you through.

It was nothing personal.

Richard Ford
2024

# extras

# meet the author

R. S. FORD is a writer of fantasy from Leeds in the heartland of Yorkshire. He also writes historical fiction as Richard Cullen, and his novel *Oath Bound* was longlisted for the Wilbur Smith Adventure Writing Prize in 2022. If you'd like to learn more about his books, you can visit his website at wordhog.co.uk, follow him on Twitter at @rich4ord, or join him on Instagram at @thewordhog.

Find out more about R. S. Ford and other Orbit authors by registering for the free monthly newsletter at orbitbooks.net.

# if you enjoyed
## ENGINES OF WAR
### look out for
# THE LAST VIGILANT
## Kingdom of Oak and Steel: Book 1
### by
# Mark A. Latham

*The last member of an ancient order is forced out of hiding to defeat a great evil, in this thrilling epic fantasy debut perfect for fans of Richard Swan and Anthony Ryan.*

*Shunned by the soldiers he commands, haunted by past tragedies, Sargent Holt Hawley is a broken man. But the child of a powerful ally has gone missing, and war between once-peaceful nations is on the horizon. So he and his squad have been sent to find a myth: a Vigilant. They are a rumored last survivor of an ancient order capable of performing acts of magic and finding the lost. But the Vigilants disappeared decades ago. No one truly expects Hawley to succeed.*

*Then, in a fabled forest, he stumbles upon a woman who claims to be the last Vigilant. Enelda Drake is wizened and out of practice, and she seems a far cry from the heroes of legend. But they will need her powers, and each other, to survive. For nothing in their kingdom is as it seems. Corrupt soldiers and calculating politicians thwart their efforts at every turn.*

*And there are dark whispers on the wind, threatening the arrival of a primordial and powerful enemy. The last Vigilant is not the only myth returning from the dead.*

# PART ONE

# BEFORE THE DAWN

*I am the seeker after the truth.*
*I am the voice of the meek.*
*I am the sword of justice.*
*I am the healer of the cursed.*
*I am the watcher against the darkness.*
*I am everywhere and nowhere.*
*I am everyone and no one.*
*The gods made me, the gods protect me,*
*and the gods will one day take me.*

—Taken from the Vigilant Oath

# extras

# Chapter 1

*Lithadaeg, 23rd Day of Sollomand*
*187th Year of Redemption*

Holt Hawley hunched over the reins, the wagon jolting slowly down the track. Sleet stung his face, settling oily and cold on his dark lashes and patchy beard.

The whistling wind had at least drowned out the grumbling of his men, who sat shivering in the back of the wagon. Their glares still burrowed into the back of his head.

It mattered not that Hawley was their sargent. The men blamed him for all their ills, and by the gods they'd had more than their fair share on this expedition. Twice the wagon had mired in thick mud. On the mountain road, three days' rations had spoiled inexplicably. Now their best horse had thrown a shoe, and limped behind the wagon, slowing their progress to a crawl. They couldn't afford to leave the beast behind, but risked laming it by pressing on. Whatever solution Sargent Hawley came up with was met with complaint. He was damned if he did and damned if he didn't.

Tarbert rode back up the track, cutting a scarecrow silhouette against the deluge. He reined in close to the driver's board, face glum, still mooning over the hobbling horse that was his favourite of the team.

"V-village ahead, Sarge," Tarbert said, buckteeth chattering. "Godsrest, I th-think."

"You see the blacksmith?" Hawley asked.

"Didn't s-see nobody, Sarge."

"Did you ask for him?"

"Not a soul about."

"What about a tavern?" That was Nedley. It was only just dawn and already he was thinking of drink.

"No tavern, neither."

"Shit on it!" Nedley grumbled.

"That's enough," Hawley warned. He pulled the reins to slow the horses as the wagon began to descend a steeper slope.

"Typical," Beacher complained.

Hawley turned on the three men in the back. Beacher was glaring right at Hawley, face red from the cold, beady eyes full of reproach.

"What is?" Hawley said.

"Three days with neither hide nor hair of a living soul, then we find a deserted village. Typical of our luck, isn't it, *Sargent*?"

Ianto sniggered. He was an odd fish, the new recruit. A stringy man, barely out of youth, yet his gristly arms were covered in faded tattoos, symbols of his faith. His hair showed signs of once being tonsured like that of a monk, the top and rear of his scalp stubbled, fringe snipped straight just above the brow. He'd proved able enough on the training ground, but would speak little of his past, save that he'd once served as a militiaman in Maserfelth, poorest of the seven *mearcas* of Aelderland. He'd bear watching; as would they all.

Hawley turned back to the road, lest he say something he would regret.

"*Awearg*," someone muttered.

Hawley felt his colour rise at the familiar slight. Again he held his tongue.

The men mistrusted Hawley. Hated him, even. Bad enough he was not one of "the Blood" like most of them, but even Ianto was treated better than Hawley, and he was a raw recruit. For Hawley, the resentment went deeper than blood lineage. For his great "transgression" a year ago, most men of the Third agreed it would've been better if Hawley had died that day. They rarely passed up an opportunity to remind him of it.

## extras

These four ne'er-do-wells would call themselves soldiers should any common man be present, but to Hawley they were the scrapings from the swill bucket. Hawley's days of fighting in the elite battalions were over. Now his assignments were the most trivial, menial, and demeaning, like most men not of the Blood. Beacher, Nedley, and Tarbert served under Hawley in the reserves only temporarily—it was akin to punishment duty for their many failings as soldiers, but their family names ensured they'd be restored to the roll of honour once they'd paid their dues. For those three, this was the worst they could expect. For Hawley and Ianto, it was the best they could hope for. Command of these dregs was another in a long list of insults heaped on Hawley of late. But command them he would, if for no other reason than a promise made to an old man.

The words of old Commander Morgard sprung into Hawley's mind, as though they'd blown down from the distant mountains.

*What you must do, Hawley, is set an example; show those men how to behave. Show them what duty truly means. But most of all, show them what* compassion *means. When I'm gone, I need you to lead. Not as an officer, but as a man of principle. Can you do that?*

Hawley had not thought of Morgard for some time. He reminded himself that the old man had rarely said a word in anger to the soldiers under his command. He had trusted Hawley to continue that tradition when he'd passed.

He'd expected too much.

From the corner of his eye, Hawley saw Tarbert cast an idiotic grin towards Beacher. Then Tarbert spurred his horse and trotted off down the slope.

The dull glow of lamps pierced the grey deluge ahead. Not deserted, then.

They'd travelled two weeks on their fool's errand, as Beacher liked to call it. And at last they'd found the village they searched for.

Godsrest.

\* \* \*

"Godsrest" sounded like a name to conjure with, but in reality was a cheerless hamlet of eight humble dwellings, a few tumbledown huts, and one large barn that lay down a sloping path towards a grey river. The houses balanced unsteadily on their cobbled tofts, ill protected by poorly repaired thatch.

Two women summoned their children to them and hurried indoors. That much was normal at least. As Hawley knew from bitter experience on both sides of the shield, soldiers brought trouble to rural communities more often than not. There was no one else to be seen, but though the sun had barely found its way to the village square, it was still morning, and most of the men would be out in the fields. There was no planting to be done at this time of year, especially not in this weather. But it was good country for sheep and goats, for those hardy enough to traipse the hilly trails after the flock. In many ways, Hawley thought soldiering offered an easier life than toiling in the fields. A serf's lot was not a comfortable one, not out here. Here, they would work, or they would starve.

Hawley cracked the thin layer of ice from a water trough so the horses might drink. Tarbert unhitched the hobbling gelding from the back of the wagon and led it to the trough first.

Beacher spat over the side of the wagon. "I can smell a brewhouse." He looked to Nedley, hopefully, who only snored.

The yeasty scent of fermenting grain carried on the wind. A late batch of ale, using the last of the barley, Hawley guessed. It'd be sure to pique Nedley's interest if the man woke up long enough to smell it.

"We're not here to drink," Hawley said.

"Why *are* we here? There's nothing worth piss in this wretched land. You know as well as I there's no Vigilant in those woods. Not the kind we need."

"If they've got his ring, stands to reason he exists."

"Pah! Dead and gone, long before any of us were born. More likely the merchant found an old ring and was planning to sell it, but when he lost his consignment, he invented this fairy story to save his neck. Face it, he had no business being this far north.

The only people who use the old roads are outlaws and smugglers. Mark my words, we're chasing shadows. There's no True Vigilant anywhere."

Hawley had been ready for this since they'd left the fort, but it made him no less angry.

"So what if there isn't?" Hawley snarled. "You reckon that frees you from your duty?"

"My *duty* is to protect the good people of Aelderland, not travel half the country looking for faeries."

Ianto leaned against the wagon, watching the argument grow. Nedley stirred at last, peering at them from the back of the wagon through half-closed eyes.

Maybe Beacher had a point, but this wasn't the time to admit it. Hawley took a confident stride forward, summoning his blackest look. Beacher shuffled away from his advance.

"If there's a True Vigilant, he'll be able to find them bairns. It's them you should be thinking about."

"There's only one child Lord Scarsdale cares about—that Sylven whelp—and only then because his bitch mother wants to start a war over him. That's what you get, putting a woman in charge of an army."

Hawley waved the protest away tiredly. He'd heard it all before.

"Besides," Beacher went on, growing into his tirade, "even you can't believe they still live."

*Even you.* Beacher's lack of respect was astounding. He'd barely known Hawley at the time of the sargent's great transgression. His animosity was secondhand, but seething nonetheless. Men like Beacher needed something to hate, and in times of peace, that something might as well be one of their own. Sargent Holt Hawley, the Butcher of Herigsburg, bringer of misfortune: "awearg."

"Then we'll find the bodies, and take 'em home," Hawley snapped. "If you can't follow orders, Beacher, you're no use to me. Leave if you like. Explain to Commander Hobb why you abandoned your mission."

Beacher looked like he might explode. His face turned a shade of crimson to match his uniform. His hand tensed, hovering over the pommel of his regulation shortsword.

*Do it, you bastard*, Hawley thought. The sargent had taken plenty of abuse this last year, maybe too much. Some of the men mistook his tolerance for cowardice instead of what it really was: penance. It made them think he would shy from a fight. It made them overreach themselves.

"They say a True Vigilant can commune with the gods." The voice was Ianto's, and it was so unexpected, the tone so bright, that it robbed the moment of tension.

Hawley and Beacher both turned to look at the recruit, who still leaned nonchalantly against the wagon, arms folded across his chest.

"Commune with the dead, too. And read minds, they say. That's how they know if you're guilty of a crime as soon as they look at you. Such a man is a rarity in these times. Such a man would be… valuable."

"Speak plain," Beacher spat.

Ianto pushed himself from the wagon. His fingers rubbed at a little carved bone reliquary that hung about his neck, some trapping of his former calling. "Just that the archduke sent us, as the sargent said. The Archduke Leoric, Lord Scarsdale, High Lord of Wulfshael. Man with that many titles has plenty of money. Plenty of trouble, too—we all know it. The Sylvens could cross the river any time now, right into the Marches. Might even attack the First, then it's war for sure."

"The First can handle a bunch of Sylvens," Beacher said.

"Maybe." Ianto smiled. "But maybe there's a handsome reward waiting for the men who find the True Vigilant and avert such a war. I don't know about you, brother, but I think it would be not unpleasant to have a noble lord in my debt."

"And what say you, *Sargent*?"

Hawley almost did not want to persuade Beacher to his cause at all. Part of him thought it would be better to throw the rotten apple from the barrel now, and be done with it. There was a saying among the soldiers "of the Blood"—something about cutting a diseased limb from a tree. But for all his faults, Beacher was liked by the others. Hawley was not. That would make harsh discipline difficult to enforce.

"I say if by some miracle we turn up a true, honest-to-gods Vigilant after all this time," Hawley said at last, "they'll be singing our names in every tavern from here to bloody Helmspire. But if you don't follow your orders, we'll never know, *will we*?" Hawley added the last part with menace.

"And if... *when*... we don't find the Vigilant?" Beacher narrowed his eyes.

"Then we return to the fort, and be thankful we've missed a week of Hobb's drills." Hawley held Beacher's contemptuous glare again.

In the silence, there came the ringing of steel on steel, drifting up the hill from the barn.

Hawley and Beacher looked at Tarbert as one.

"No blacksmith?" Hawley said.

Tarbert laughed nervously.

"There you go," Ianto said. He came to Beacher's side and patted the big man on the shoulder. "Our luck's changing already."

Beacher finally allowed himself to be led away, still grumbling.

The sargent stretched out his knotted back, feeling muscles pop and joints crack as he straightened fully. Only Tarbert matched Hawley for height, but he was an arid strip of land who barely filled his uniform, with a jaw so slack he was like to catch flies in his mouth while riding vanguard. By contrast, Hawley was six feet of sinewy muscle, forged by hard labour and tempered in battle. He shook rain from his dark hair, and only then did he remember he was not alone.

Nedley was still on the wagon, watching. For once, he didn't look drunk. Indeed, there was something unnerving in the look he gave Hawley.

Hawley shouldered his knapsack, and hefted up Godspeaker—a large, impractical Felder bastard sword. Non-regulation: an affection, a prize—a symbol of authority. The men hated that about him, but Hawley could barely care to add it to the tally.

"Make yourself useful, Nedley," Hawley said, strapping the sword to his back. "Find some supplies. And bloody *pay* for them. Show the locals that we mean well."

Hawley snatched the reins from Tarbert, who still looked forlorn. He cared more for the gelding than for most people. Baelsine, named for the blaze of silver grey that zigzagged up its black muzzle. He talked to it like a brother soldier.

"Help Nedley. I'll go see the smith."

# if you enjoyed
## ENGINES OF WAR
### look out for
# GRAVE EMPIRE
## Book One of the Great Silence
### by
## Richard Swan

*Blood once turned the wheels of empire. Now it is money.*

*A new age of exploration and innovation has dawned, and the Empire of the Wolf stands to take its place as the foremost power in the known world. Glory and riches await.*

*But dark days are coming. A mysterious plague has broken out in the pagan kingdoms to the north, while in the south, the Empire's proxy war in the lands of the wolfmen is weeks away from total collapse.*

*Worse still is the message brought to the Empress by two heretic monks who claim to have lost contact with the spirits of the afterlife. The monks believe this is the start of an ancient prophecy heralding the end of days—the Great Silence.*

**extras**

*It falls to Renata Rainer, a low-ranking ambassador to an enigmatic and vicious race of mermen, to seek answers from those who still practice the arcane arts. But with the road south beset by war and the Empire on the brink of supernatural catastrophe, soon there may not be a world left to save....*

## PROLOGUE

# THE FORT AT THE END OF THE WORLD

*"Watch for when the leaves grow, when the trees blossom into life and birdsong returns to the air. The sound you hear on the horizon is not the thunder of late spring: 'tis cannon! 'Tis drumming, and shot! As with the sowing and the harvest, so we have made seasons of warfare. ''Tis the fighting season', it will be announced, and the men march off to be reaped."*

FROM CHUN PARSIFAL'S
*THE INFINITE STATE*

**Sovan Territory**

ALDA RIVER VALLEY

## extras

*Dear Father,*

 *Well. I am a long way from home.*

 *I have spent some time calculating it; the crossing over the Stygion Sea will take the better part of a week. This letter is my attempt to focus my mind on something except seasickness.*

 *It was five hundred miles to get out of Sova herself, and the abutting Prinzpatriate of Mirja (there is little of note there except the cathedral at Balodiskirch, which is rather magnificent). It was another five hundred to get halfway through the Margraviate of Grenzegard. The locals refer to it simply as "The Interior", and it is a much benighted land, filled with mines, earthworks, smelters, the air thick with the poisonous fog of industry.*

 *We kept well clear of Saekaland for our own safety, for the pagans there have taken to testing the Sigismund Line weekly; then we clipped the northernmost foothills of the Great Southern Dividing Range. I had hoped to see some of the rainforest greenery of the Reenwound, but it is all coal and iron ore mines and logging stations there, and the earth is turned and compacted and being excavated for the new canal system. I did, however, see the thaumaturgic wind generators being installed by teams of engineers, though they were not yet working. They are a modern marvel, though it seems there is no part of the Empire now untouched by the fires of industry, and much of the natural beauty of the world – to say nothing of the native peoples within it – is being excised at an alarming rate.*

 *We detoured at the last moment to Kalegosfort, and I had thought we might see some pagan Saekas there, but we remained unmolested. A mercenary company was added to our caravan, and then we tracked across the (hot!) countryside to that easternmost spur of land of the contiguous Sovan Empire to Port Gero. A journey of a thousand miles – and that is only halfway. One wonders how the Empress hopes to govern such an enormous and increasingly disparate nation; even leaving aside* the discontent of the subjugated, the distances alone make an incredible challenge for Imperial logisticians.

We spent three days in Port Gero before I caught sight of the vessel we were to take across the Stygion Sea. It was a rather remarkable ship, a forty-two-gun frigate called the **Lord Ansobert**, *though the fellows with me thought it very shabby indeed. We embarked on the 1st of the month, an apparently auspicious date, though to me it seemed like any other. As I sit here in the hold, we are five days into an anticipated seven and neither hair nor hide of a mer-man, though they are known to be in these waters. My candle is almost burned to the nub, so I shall return to this letter once the picture for the rest of my journey becomes clearer.*

{Two days later – the 8th}

*Well, Father, some ~~drama~~ excitement on the journey. The planned debarkation point had been the colonial town of Tajanastadt, at the southernmost tip of the peninsula where the Long River meets the Stygion Sea. Instead, a storm put us well off course and nearly dis-masted the ship. Instead we have travelled north through the Haraldan Strait, which sits between Maretsburg – our new destination – and Vitaney Island. The latter I have been examining through the first mate's spyglass, which I troubled him to lend me, for many hours. So many whaling stations and ships you never did see, nor so many gulls. The latter are vermin, covering the island with their guano. They pluck at the offcuts of whale-meat, though it seems to me that very little of the corpses are wasted. A fascinating industry, though with so many of the wretches pulled from the ocean it is a wonder there are any left. One can see readily why it exercises the mer-men so (still not one sighting! The first mate tells me they are a reclusive mob).*

*We are due in Maretsburg at first light. Then it is another several hundred miles of travel west across the peninsula to*

## extras

Slavomire, the largest Imperial town in the ~~fiercely contested~~ Alda River Valley. I know you wished a safe posting for me, and I shall endeavour to remain in Slavomire if I can, perhaps in some sort of supply role. I do not think the town itself has been under any sort of attack for several years now.

I shall write again soon.

{Five days later – the 13th}

Dear Father,

A little more on this letter before I seal it. I have been recommended to do so before I leave Slavomire on account of the irregular postal collection further west.

We moved across the countryside by mule. For most of the journey I was more or less alone save the company of my guide, a mountain tribesman who spoke good Saxan. The New East is a gloomy place, there can be no question of that. I had been told many times that the most dangerous part of my journey was the crossing of the Stygion Sea, though now I am in and amongst the pine forests and hills and mountains here, I am thoroughly unsettled. Our Great Enemy, the armies of Casimir and their allies in Sanque, are supposed to have no claim to these lands east of the Line of Demarcation, but there are a great many confederations of mountain tribesmen whose loyalties are unclear at the very best of times. ~~Even though we saw no one or thing, I felt many pairs of eyes watching me.~~

I had hoped to remain in Slavomire – no such luck. The colonel there ordered me immediately on to Fort Romauld, though even that is not my final destination. That misfortune belongs to Fort Ingomar, the so-called "fort at the end of the world". It sits on Aldaney Island, a little piece of land which bifurcates the River Alda for which the valley is named. This is the closest fort to the enemy and almost the centrepiece of the entire disputed country. ~~I confess, Father, that I am frightened at such a prospect.~~

> *I fear such a long journey has given me much too much time to think. It had seemed to me so much more exciting in the regimental headquarters in Badenburg. But after several days in the New East, I feel very much under the yoke of homesickness. I have heard so many rumours of spirits and ghosts and witches and drudes in these forests. They were easy to dismiss in Sova, but it is not so easy to dismiss now. I fear I have acted in haste in*

I have no doubt I shall remain safe. Major Haak, who runs Fort Ingomar, commands a fine reputation and is not known for squandering his forces. I shall endeavour to "keep my head on my shoulders" per your injunction and write whenever my time permits me. Kiss Mother for me and wish Osbeorn and Aldhard luck with all their endeavours. Tell Leonie I shall write to her separately and assure her of my affections.

Yours in unanticipated haste,

Peter

---

Too much time to think – and still more of it now. That had been, and remained, the problem.

It was difficult to know who had first floated the idea of Peter joining the Sovan Army. It had been a couple of years ago now. He had never been especially enthused about it, but when his father had purchased him a commission, and laid out a feast in his honour, and forced his elder and younger brothers to endure it – young men who were both more interesting and talented than Peter had ever been – he'd been swept up in the excitement of it all.

His father might have purchased him the commission, but had it been his *idea*? He cared for Peter dearly. It seemed unlikely he would be pleased with the prospect of him fighting Casimirs and Sanques in the New East.

Where, then, had the idea germinated? His beau, Leonie? Her interest in him had been steadily drying up to the point where her affection was almost exhausted. But seeing him in the uniform of the 166th Badenburg Regiment had turned her around somewhat. He had been much too pleased with the resumption of their courtship to appreciate just how skin-deep her affections were. His mother, too – a cold woman who seemed to much prefer his brothers – had wept tears of pride in seeing him so turned out. Perhaps the blame lay with one, or both, of them?

His friends, a collection of clerks and novice bankers and market speculators, had affected jealousy. He was going to the land of the wolfmen, he was going to sail across the Stygion Sea – perhaps he'd see a mer-man! – he was going to *see* the New East and Sova's holdings there and give the Casimirs and Sanques and their pagan allies a good thrashing. They slapped him on the shoulder, red-faced and perspiring in the city taverns around the Imperial Bank of Sova and the South Seas Trading Company. It was *exciting*, daring, bold and brave, and after several glasses of wine and several more of brandy, he too had given in to these seductive ideas.

Now he remembered those drinking sessions with contempt. His friends' enthusiasm had been nothing but a hollow salve, designed to soothe his nerves. Oh, they were happy enough to bet on the price of furs from Valerija, or whale oil from Vitaney Island; but the idea of travelling to the colonies and traipsing through hundreds of miles of empty mountain forest to trap furs, or bludgeon a mer-man to death with the butt of a musket to wrench the whalebone from his hands so that a pampered Sovan woman could have her stay firmly braced – well, suddenly it didn't seem so glorious or exciting. They would never taste the reality of it.

But Peter would.

Too much time to think, and too many rumours about this place. The fighting here was not like the civilised land wars up and down the length of the River Kova, which separated the Sovan Empire from Casimir. The war in this rugged terrain was one of traps and ambushes, dirty tricks and terror tactics. And if the colonists in Slavomire were to be believed, it was a place in which men simply vanished, never to be seen or heard from again.

He could well believe it. As he moved through the Alda River

Valley, he could not take his eyes off the gloomy forest around him. It was filled with foetid pools and dark nooks and tangled outcrops of rock throttled with grasping vines. Ahead of him, his guide, a man of middling age with milk-pale skin and faded blue geometric tattoos running down the sides of his neck, led him and their mule down a path that was indistinguishable from the surrounding earth. Above, the trees were so thick that the sun hardly penetrated the canopy.

He swore as his right boot disappeared into a bog. Nema Victoria, what was he *doing* here? How had he accepted the tub-thumping bombast of his fellow officers back in Badenburg so readily? The closer he got to Fort Ingomar, the more he wanted to turn back. It was miserable enough without the enemy. The air was filled with constant drizzle, whilst the rattle of woodpeckers' beaks and the thrashing of rabbits through the carpet of leaves set him on edge. Every defile and outcrop and log looked as though it concealed interlopers. The feeling of being observed was so acute it was tangible—

He came up short. The guide had stopped, and he had almost walked into the back of the mule. The mule's ass – there was a pun fit for the officers' mess.

"What's the matter?" he asked. He sounded testy, in a way that only haughty Sovan officers could sound, but it was born of tension. He was deeply anxious.

The guide, a gregarious man, looked suddenly nervous.

"*Mi preĝas, ke temas ne pri kathomo,*" the man muttered.

"What?" Peter hissed.

"Please, Mister Kleist," the guide said, motioning for him to be quiet.

Peter fell silent. They waited for a long, excruciating minute. "Death," the man said. He took a large sniff, and scooped the air up under his nose in an exaggerated manner. "Smell."

Peter could smell nothing except the petrichor of the pine forest. Nonetheless, he pulled his pistol out of its sash.

The guide noticed this and seemed uneasy. "No, no," he said, holding out a hand. "Put away. Make angry. Yes?"

## extras

Peter had no idea what he meant, and shook his head. He felt his palm begin to sweat around the pistol's grip.

The guide sucked his teeth, scanning the foliage with a practised eye. "Come," he said. "Quick."

"The mule—" Peter started, but the guide simply grabbed him by the wrist and pulled him along.

Peter's heart raced as they dived into the brush. The forest was thick with low-hanging branches and carpeted with ferns, roots and leaf litter. Somewhere to the north he heard a noise, an animal cry, but not one he was familiar with.

"Low, here." The guide pointed to the floor, and Peter dropped. The guide removed Peter's tricorn. "Lower," he said urgently. "Hide."

Peter felt sick. The two of them crouched in the gloom, waiting. Ahead, the forest air thickened with mist. There was ... *something* out there. For the first time Peter smelt the death the guide had mentioned. It was not unlike decaying fruit and vegetables left out in the sun, a sickly, cloying scent.

They waited there for a very long time, an hour at least. Every time Peter moved to shift his weight, the guide gripped his shoulder and quietly shushed him. Every time he tried to ask what was happening, the man simply shook his head and would not be drawn. Peter wondered whether he should assert himself more and insist the man give him answers, in keeping with what his superiors would expect. But the guide was terrified, and so Peter was too.

Eventually the danger passed, and they pressed themselves up. Peter was soaking from the damp earth. He kept his pistol in his hand, though the damp was likely to have fouled the powder by now.

The guide said nothing, but rather motioned for him to follow. His gestures were not frantic, but there was an expression of ... it was difficult to tell. Concern? Possibly even excitement. Peter felt wary again. He turned around, but there was nothing behind him. Just tens of miles of pristine forest wilderness clothed in veils of mist. The Great Northern Barrier Range rose gigantically in the distance, snow-capped grey peaks gutting the low cloud layer like knives in a belly. That was a place so infamously impassable – its terrain so treacherous, the storms so violent – that no modern Sovan argonauts had made it across.

The guide did not wait, and Peter swore as he moved after him. He chased him down a rocky slope tangled with ferns, twice nearly turning his ankle on a moss-covered rock. "Slow down, damn you," he called after him, though the man did not.

Peter felt very conscious that they were leaving the putative trail and the mule even further behind, and was increasingly concerned that the guide was in fact an enemy agent who was going to lead him off and cut his throat. But then a dreadful smell hit him, and he heard the buzzing of flies, and knew immediately that the man had led him to a body.

"Nema Victoria," he breathed, trying to get the rotten vegetable stink out of his nose. The guide had led him to a small clearing which abutted a brisk, fast-running stream, and he stood at the edge of it, pointing to the centre. There lay three bodies, twisted and broken, their necks and chests laid open and now the preserve of hundreds of flies. All three men had been violently decapitated, and one of those heads had been skewered on a pole which itself had been thrust into the earth upright. Bits of torn uniform and viscera lay strewn about the clearing, and Peter saw the unmistakable black fabric, silver frogging and polished pewter buttons of Sovan soldiers.

"What happened?!" he demanded of the guide, his nerves thrumming like plucked harp strings. The man was what the Sovans called a "mountain tribesman", a native of this part of the world. Some of the tribes had allied with the Sovans; some had allied with the Casimirs and the Sanques. Some had allied with neither, and killed indiscriminately. At first blush this grisly tableau looked to be the work of savage pagans – but the claw marks suggested otherwise.

The guide shrugged warily. He clearly had *some* idea, though he would not say it out loud. He pulled a small blade from a pouch mounted on the back of his belt, and with a deftness which belied his age clambered up the trunk of a nearby tree. There he cut down the body of a fourth man that Peter had not even noticed. It squelched grossly into the undergrowth.

## extras

"Where are their heads?" Peter asked, swallowing down his rising gorge. His heart was pounding, and his legs felt weak. He wanted desperately to sit down. "This is Sovan territory! This is supposed to be pacified land!"

The guide winced at him. "Come," he said in Saxan. "No path. Walk now."

"Who did this?!" Peter snapped. Or perhaps more to the point, *what* had done it? He might have thought it the work of canister given the bodies' ferocious disassembly, though there was no sign of shot anywhere. And besides, the corpses had clearly been rent and mauled.

"You tell the major," the guide said. He scanned the forest again, listening, searching, smelling. "Time to go now."

"Wait," Peter said, letting out a long, shaky breath. "Just . . . hold on a minute, damn you."

He went up to the corpses of the four men. With hands trembling and bile in his gullet, he rummaged through the blood-soaked clothes and took a few things — letters, a monogrammed pocket watch — and stuffed them in his haversack, bloodying the contents as he did so. Then, pleased with this thinking in spite of the circumstances, he rejoined the guide.

"What about the mule?" he asked, looking back up the slope.

The man shook his head. "It wait here." Then he turned and picked out a route amongst the undergrowth.

Peter swore under his breath. A very large part of him was tempted to desert. To turn back. To resign his commission, to sell it, and return to his family home in Imastadt. It would be in disgrace — but at least he'd be alive. But fear of embarrassment, of being judged by his friends and family and peers, meant that he could not.

And so with his heart and belly full of fear, he cast one last forlorn look at the corpses, now certain that a similar fate awaited him; and then he followed the guide to the fort at the end of the world.

## Follow us:

**f** /orbitbooksUS

**X** /orbitbooks

▶ /orbitbooks

Join our mailing list to receive alerts on our latest releases and deals.

## orbitbooks.net

Enter our monthly giveaway for the chance to win some epic prizes.

## orbitloot.com